Elizabeth Bear (signature)

Elizabeth Bear

This special signed edition
is limited to 1000 numbered copies.

This is copy _856_ .

THE BEST OF
ELIZABETH BEAR

THE BEST OF
ELIZABETH BEAR

Elizabeth Bear

SUBTERRANEAN PRESS

2020

Signed, Limited Edition

ISBN
978-1-59606-940-4

Subterranean Press
PO Box 190106
Burton, MI 48519

subterraneanpress.com

Manufactured in the United States of America

Contents

Introduction

ELIZABETH BEAR IS MY FRIEND. I knew her when we were deep into the transformation from novice writers to journeymen. I read her stories and she read mine, and when I left writing for years, she never forgot that I was there or left me behind. Over the years, she sent me stories.

I read her stories, and those stories became my friends—stories that knew pain, understood loss, joined hands with bravery and vulnerability and hope. Each one was a gift. They all talked to me, dazzled me with wonder and feeling and humanity. She sent me stories, and I read them.

I hope I get to keep reading them for a long, long time.

Bear's stories invite the reader to settle into an intimate experience with characters who may not necessarily be like the reader, or even human. And once we're reading about this character, who is often an outsider or orphaned or alien in some other way alone, we get to see inside the defenses, their exterior, their otherness. And when that happens, often what we see in this outsider is ourselves.

Sometimes it's as shocking as catching sight of yourself in an unexpected mirror. Sometimes it's a moment of empathy that reaches out to join hands with the person in the pages. Her stories show how experiences shape and change us, how facing the ordeal that we make for ourselves—with the intention of staying safe and protected—can transform us, bring us to wisdom, compassion, and strength.

The stories of this collection are a full picture of Bear's range as a storyteller and the scope of a prolific career. Between masterful prose and the intimate view of people (and war machines, and living spaceships) Bear's stories are vivid, personal experiences. They linger in one's memory and invite reflection. They can touch a reader in tender spots, and at the same time, grant the space to feel that gap in one's armor and understand it a little better.

Watching the protagonist of an Elizabeth Bear short story transform themselves never gets old. Characters on the very edge of life-altering change fall into the ordeal that drags them into the thing they need to face, and upon facing it, they re-enter the world wiser, kinder, and cleareyed. An Elizabeth Bear story shows you how people become more than what they were before, showing how they face the things they don't want to see but hold them back from healing or moving forward.

All these stories are gifts. I want to enthuse about them, but I also don't want to spoil anything. Read them however the whim strikes you—in the order they were given, or simply opening to a random page. Read them all right away or save them for when you need them. Hopefully, my remarks will serve as a guide.

In "Covenant," Bear walks us into the darkness of a serial murderer, and with her sense of unflinching compassion walks us out beside a hero who has us hoping for their success.

"She Still Loves the Dragon" is a knight and dragon story on the outside. The peerless knight with a list of achievements that could keep a bard busy for a lifetime climbs a mountain to face the dragon. But then the knight burns—and in burning, becomes an exploration of trust, vulnerability, identity, and love.

"Tideline" is a heartbreaking, beautiful story about family and remembrance that pairs up a war machine and the boy who found her on a beach as she uses the last of her energy to memorialize her fallen comrades. She tells the boy stories and uses some of her limited resources to protect him, raising him until she has only one gift left.

In "The Leavings of the Wolf," Dagmar's runs are haunted by the ruins of her marriage. She's trying to run her way to being able to pull off her wedding ring, followed by the crows she studies, running until she's ready to face what she's running from.

"Okay, Glory" explores the point where the smart house of the future breaks, imprisoning a tech genius in the remote mountain fortress he built himself. Brian has to break through his smarthouse's airtight protection system because Glory won't acknowledge the disconnect between her programming and reality. There's more than one story going on here— while Brian is trying to carefully show Glory that she's operating with beliefs that contradict each other, Brian is confronted with how his isolating behaviors affect the people who care about him.

"Needles" stops in the middle of an eternal road trip to watch over a Mesopotamian undead woman in search of change, eating up the miles in a '67 Chevy Impala with a vampire and hunters on their trail. But breaking out of old patterns and survival behaviors isn't easy. Sometimes it takes more than we're ready to give.

"This Chance Planet" reminds me of all the times we politely say nothing about a friend's partner, even though they're being held back by the relationship. Petra, a cocktail waitress working hard to get out of poverty with the burden of a partner who does very little, makes an alliance with the pregnant street dog she met in Moscow's light rail system. Petra makes the sacrifice that will set her free, thanks to her new friend.

"The Body of the Nation" is an Abigail Irene Garrett mystery set in the fascinating New Amsterdam universe. We're hauled up onto a grand riverboat to investigate a murder that quickly becomes more than it seems and must be solved before the ship makes port in Albany. Abigail Irene is a grand character succeeding in a world that resists her competence and skill, however politely, solving mysteries in stories I wish were bingeable in twelve-episode seasons.

"Boojum" is a living being repurposed as a vessel for space pirates, and Black Alice loves her. Black Alice keeps her head down and does her job, but when it's clear the *Boojum's* being kept prisoner to serve as a ship, Black Alice wants to help. It's a story about love and trust, about taking the leap into the unknown and becoming something more.

"The Bone War" is a hilarious story about bunfights and professional interference. Bijou is called to perform their particular magic on the remains of a dinosaur skeleton but has to contend with a pair of experts determined to have their input on Bijou's work.

"In the House of Aryaman, a Lonely Signal Burns" is another top-notch mystery set in a future India. But it's also an examination of our relationships with our own personal histories, whether they're treasured or abandoned. I could wander around the setting for many more pages— it's a thoughtful, detailed exploration of how societies could adapt to the environment of the future. Instead of being dystopic and grim, it's determined, community-minded, and green.

"Shoggoths in Bloom" pulls on the Cthulhu mythos as a Black professor investigates the peculiar creatures that come ashore every year to bloom in the November sunshine, shortly after America learned the news about Kristallnacht. If Paul Harding discovers the shoggoth's secret, he can publish a work that will secure his academic position with tenure. But the horrifying truth of these creatures pushes Harding into making a choice for the whole world.

"Skin in the Game" explores a favorite speculation of future entertainment—the empathy recording. Neon White's star isn't as high in the sky as it was—she's pulled back from the edge and into comfortable, commercial territory, but the audience is hungry for something new. Her publicist has a plan to bring it all back using the Clownfish app, allowing her fans to plug into her experience. Neon faces the hard-nosed, sometimes cynical choices that come when your career depends on an audience that craves the feeling of authentic connection to their idols while maintaining an idealized, carefully curated brand.

"Hobnoblin Blues" continues the journey into fame, celebrity, and rock music with Loki, exiled from Asgard and fallen to Earth, striding the world in black leather boots and an electric guitar. Loki as a rock god and a Luciferian figure (oh, how they would sneer to read that comparison) fits right into the drug-soaked decadent glam of 70's rock, simultaneously alluring and tragic and mad as hell. Loki doesn't give a moment's thought to branding or inching away from the edge—what Loki wants, more than anything else, is for the world to hear them.

Comanche Zariphe in "Form and Void" is as faithful to her difficult friend Kathy Cutter as Robbin "Hobnoblin" Just is to Loki in "Hobnoblin Blues." Kathy is beautiful, pampered, and rich, but something compels her to hoard the memory of every slight and hurt. Comanche is the only friend she will permit and being Kathy's friend is a trial of one's patience and loyalty. When Kathy wants to travel to Io abruptly after graduation, she sets to transforming herself into one of the dragons that float high above Io, isolated, protected, and alone. Comanche follows, always faithful, until they have to part ways forever.

"Your Collar" is a story of two prisoners—the minotaur, exported from the labyrinth and made to wear a collar and chains as a prize of a vast empire, and that empire's queen, unheard by her advisors and disregarded as a mere female. They form a friendship over a chess board and make an alliance that will free them both.

"Terroir" is a story about an inventor who perceives the souls of the dead connected to the land where the food he eats is produced. After years of eating heavily processed baloney sandwiches and factory-made white bread, he travels to Normandy—a place with a blood-soaked history and strong regional pride in their local foods—to attempt a kind of exposure therapy. It's a delicate work of fabulism, sensual and horror-tinged and thought-provoking.

"Dolly" is another SF mystery that hinges on the place where people and tech collide. A wealthy man is found dead in his home—and his lifelike android companion's hands are soaked in blood. The police on the scene need to solve the mystery, and wind up setting a world-altering legal precedent.

"Love Among the Talus" is the story of a brotherless princess raised to rule her land instead of making a political marriage told with gorgeous prose and the voice of legend. When confronted with the choice of who to marry, Nilufer sets upon her own plan to navigate between the choices of the weak son of a powerful ruler and a well-armed bandit prince and claim her own destiny.

"The Deeps of the Sky" imagines life in the upper atmosphere of Jupiter where a young sky-miner uses all his ancestor's knowledge to rescue an alien craft from tumbling into the dangerous depths of the sky. A gorgeous, otherworldly story that gently observes the weight of memory and grief.

"Two Dreams on Trains" imagines a floating New Orleans where a woman's dreams for her son and the dreams of the son himself pass each other.

"Faster Gun" explores the weird west with John Henry Holliday and a party of intrepid time-traveling explorers investigating a spacecraft.

"The Heart's Filthy Lesson" is about jealousy—not the fear of losing someone to infidelity, but the terrible result of comparing oneself unfairly to the people around them. Dharti has measured herself against her beloved and needs to prove that she has her own value. She sets on a quest to explore the damp, hot forests of Venus, looking for the ruins of an ancient city.

"Perfect Gun" is the story of John Steele and his beautiful, versatile, deadly war machine. He knows every inch of his darling rig. He removed the morality circuits with his own two hands. John's the perfect mercenary. He cares about getting out unharmed with a paycheck in hand, with his beloved rig intact. His girl has an AI system—can't operate without it. And John likes them a little intelligent anyway. She's perfect. They're a team. Business is good. But somewhere, it started to go wrong.

"Sonny Liston Takes the Fall" is a story about sacrificial kings. The narrator, One-eyed Jack, tells the story of talking to Sonny Liston in 1970. He claims to have taken a dive in 1965 against Muhammad Ali, but Jack knows better. He knows that kings are a potent sacrifice. But sometimes, someone can sacrifice themselves to save the king, so they can be safe, and that there's powerful magic either way.

"Orm the Beautiful" is the last of his kind, and very old. When plunderers come to rob the mountain of the fabulous jeweled dragons, who sing on even in death, Orm must find a way to save his chord from being destroyed by greed. This is another story about sacrifice and preservation that ends leaving the reader with a glad ache in the chest.

"Erase, Erase, Erase" features a person who, in trying to forget the parts of her she doesn't want, finds herself falling apart—she left a hand in the refrigerator once, and an ear came off with the earbud—and certain that she's forgotten something. Something important. Something that will hurt a lot of people if she doesn't remember. And so she tries to re-piece her life together, to face what she doesn't want to face so she can recover an important memory. And as she remembers, anchoring herself with the right pens put to paper, what comes out are clear-eyed reflections on how trauma, recovery, and insight are a wheel that just keeps turning, that epiphanies don't come as singletons that fix everything. That you don't have to be perfect. That your story isn't done.

It's the perfect place to leave a collection of the bejeweled, heartbreaking, comforting, unflinching stories of Elizabeth Bear, whose stories are not yet finished.

Chelsea Polk
March 9, 2019
Calgary

COVENANT

THIS COLD COULD KILL ME, but it's no worse than the memories. Endurable as long as I keep moving.

My feet drum the snow-scraped roadbed as I swing past the police station at the top of the hill. Each exhale plumes through my mask, but insulating synthetics warm my inhalations enough so they do not sting and seize my lungs. I'm running too hard to breathe through my nose—running as hard and fast as I can, sprinting for the next hydrant-marking reflector protruding above a dirty bank of ice. The wind pushes into my back, cutting through the wet merino of my base layer and the wet Max-Reg over it, but even with its icy assistance I can't come close to running the way I used to run. Once I turn the corner into the graveyard, I'll be taking that wind in the face.

I miss my old body's speed. I ran faster before. My muscles were stronger then. Memories weigh something. They drag you down. Every step I take, I'm carrying thirteen dead. My other self runs a step or two behind me. I feel the drag of his invisible, immaterial presence.

As long as you keep moving, it's not so bad. But sometimes everything in the world conspires to keep you from moving fast enough.

I thump through the old stone arch into the graveyard, under the trees glittering with ice, past the iron gate pinned open by drifts. The wind's as sharp as I expected—sharper—and I kick my jacket over to warming mode. That'll run the battery down, but I've only got another five kilometers to go and I need heat. It's getting colder as the sun rises, and clouds slide up the western horizon: cold front moving in. I flip the sleeve light off with my next gesture, though that won't make much difference. The sky's given light enough to run by for a good half-hour, and the sleeve light is on its own battery. A single LED doesn't use much.

I imagine the flexible circuits embedded inside my brain falling into quiescence at the same time. Even smaller LEDs with even more advanced power cells go dark. The optogenetic adds shut themselves off when my brain is functioning *healthily*. Normally, microprocessors keep me sane and safe, monitor my brain activity, stimulate portions of the neocortex devoted to ethics, empathy, compassion. When I run, though, my brain— my dysfunctional, murderous, *cured* brain—does it for itself as neural pathways are stimulated by my own native neurochemicals.

Only my upper body gets cold: Though that wind chills the skin of my thighs and calves like an ice bath, the muscles beneath keep hot with exertion. And the jacket takes the edge off the wind that strikes my chest.

My shoes blur pink and yellow along the narrow path up the hill. Gravestones like smoker's teeth protrude through swept drifts. They're moldy black all over as if spray-painted, and glittering powdery whiteness heaps against their backs. Some of the stones date to the eighteenth century, but I run there only in the summertime or when it hasn't snowed.

Maintenance doesn't plow that part of the churchyard. Nobody comes to pay their respects to *those* dead anymore.

Sort of like the man I used to be.

The ones I killed, however—some of them still get their memorials every year. I know better than to attend, even though my old self would have loved to gloat, to relive the thrill of their deaths. The new me…feels a sense of…obligation. But their loved ones don't know my new identity. And nobody owes *me* closure.

I'll have to take what I can find for myself. I've sunk into that beautiful quiet place where there's just the movement, the sky, that true, irreproducible blue, the brilliant flicker of a cardinal. Where I die as a noun and only the verb survives.

I run. I am running.

WHEN HE met her eyes, he imagined her throat against his hands. Skin like calves' leather; the heat and the crack of her hyoid bone as he dug his thumbs deep into her pulse. The way she'd writhe, thrash, struggle.

His waist chain rattled as his hands twitched, jerking the cuffs taut on his wrists.

She glanced up from her notes. Her eyes were a changeable hazel: blue in this light, gray green in others. Reflections across her glasses concealed the corner where text scrolled. It would have been too small to read, anyway—backward, with the table he was chained to creating distance between them.

She waited politely, seeming unaware that he was imagining those hazel eyes dotted with petechiae, that fair skin slowly mottling purple. He let the silence sway between them until it developed gravity.

"Did you wish to say something?" she asked, with mild but clinical encouragement.

Point to me, he thought.

He shook his head. "I'm listening."

She gazed upon him benevolently for a moment. His fingers itched. He scrubbed the tips against the rough orange jumpsuit but stopped. In her silence, the whisking sound was too audible.

She continued. "The court is aware that your crimes are the result of neural damage including an improperly functioning amygdala. Technology exists that can repair this damage. It is not experimental; it has been used successfully in tens of thousands of cases to treat neurological disorders as divergent as depression, anxiety, bipolar disorder, borderline personality, and the complex of disorders commonly referred to as schizophrenic syndrome."

The delicate structure of her collarbones fascinated him. It took fourteen pounds of pressure, properly applied, to snap a human clavicle—rendering the arm useless for a time. He thought about the proper application of that pressure. He said, "Tell me more."

"They take your own neurons—grown from your own stem cells under sterile conditions in a lab, modified with microbial opsin genes. This opsin is a light-reactive pigment similar to that found in the human retina. The neurons are then reintroduced to key areas of your brain. This is a keyhole procedure. Once the neurons are established, and have been encouraged to develop the appropriate synaptic connections, there's a second surgery, to implant a medical device: a series of miniaturized flexible microprocessors, sensors, and light-emitting diodes. This device monitors your neurochemistry and the electrical activity in your brain and adjusts it to mimic healthy activity." She paused again and steepled her fingers on the table.

"'Healthy,'" he mocked.

She did not move.

"That's discrimination against the neuro-atypical."

"Probably," she said. Her fingernails were appliquéd with circuit diagrams. "But you did kill thirteen people. And get caught. Your civil rights are bound to be forfeit after something like that."

He stayed silent. Impulse control had never been his problem.

"It's not psychopathy you're remanded for," she said. "It's murder."

"Mind control," he said.

"Mind *repair*," she said. "You can't be *sentenced* to the medical procedure. But you can volunteer. It's usually interpreted as evidence of remorse and desire to be rehabilitated. Your sentencing judge will probably take that into account."

"God," he said. "I'd rather have a bullet in the head than a fucking computer."

"They haven't used bullets in a long time," she said. She shrugged, as if it were nothing to her either way. "It was lethal injection or the gas chamber. Now it's rightminding. Or it's the rest of your life in an eight-by-twelve cell. You decide."

"I can beat it."

"Beat rightminding?"

Point to me.

"What if I can beat it?"

"The success rate is a hundred percent. Barring a few who never woke up from anesthesia." She treated herself to a slow smile. "If there's anybody whose illness is too intractable for this particular treatment, they must be smart enough to keep it to themselves. And smart enough not to get caught a second time."

You're being played, he told himself. *You are smarter than her. Way too smart for this to work on you. She's appealing to your vanity. Don't let her yank your chain. She thinks she's so fucking smart. She's prey. You're the hunter. More evolved. Don't be manipulated—*

His lips said, "Lady, sign me up."

THE SNOW creaks under my steps. Trees might crack tonight. I compose a poem in my head.

The fashion in poetry is confessional. It wasn't always so—but now we judge value by our own voyeurism. By the perceived rawness of what we think we are being invited to spy upon. But it's all art: veils and lies.

If I wrote a confessional poem, it would begin: *Her dress was the color of mermaids, and I killed her anyway.*

A confessional poem need not be true. Not true in the way the bite of the air in my lungs in spite of the mask is true. Not true in the way the graveyard and the cardinal and the ragged stones are true.

It wasn't just her. It was her, and a dozen others like her. Exactly like her in that they were none of them the right one, and so another one always had to die.

That I can still see them as fungible is a victory for my old self—his only victory, maybe, though he was arrogant enough to expect many more. He thought he could beat the rightminding.

That's the only reason he agreed to it.

If I wrote it, people would want to read *that* poem. It would sell a million—it would garner far more attention than what I *do* write.

I won't write it. I don't even want to *remember* it. Memory excision was declared by the Supreme Court to be a form of the death penalty, and therefore unconstitutional since 2043.

They couldn't take my memories in retribution. Instead they took away my pleasure in them.

Not that they'd admit it was retribution. They call it *repair.* "Right-minding." Fixing the problem. Psychopathy is a curable disease.

They gave me a new face, a new brain, a new name. The chromosome reassignment, I chose for myself, to put as much distance between my old self and my new as possible.

The old me also thought it might prove goodwill: reduced testosterone, reduced aggression, reduced physical strength. Few women become serial killers.

To my old self, it seemed a convincing lie.

He—no, I: alienating the uncomfortable actions of the self is something that psychopaths do—I thought I was stronger than biology and stronger than rightminding. I thought I could take anabolic steroids to get my muscle and anger back where they should be. I honestly thought I'd get away with it.

I honestly thought I would still want to.

I could write that poem. But that's not the poem I'm writing. The poem I'm writing begins: *Gravestones like smoker's teeth...*except I don't know what happens in the second clause, so I'm worrying at it as I run.

I do my lap and throw in a second lap because the wind's died down and my heater is working and I feel light, sharp, full of energy and desire. When I come down the hill, I'm running on springs. I take the long arc, back over the bridge toward the edge of town, sparing a quick glance down at the frozen water. The air is warming up a little as the sun rises. My fingers aren't numb in my gloves anymore.

When the unmarked white delivery van pulls past me and rolls to a stop, it takes me a moment to realize the driver wants my attention. He taps the horn, and I jog to a stop, hit pause on my run tracker, tug a headphone from my ear. I stand a few steps back from the window. He looks at me, then winces in embarrassment, and points at his navigation system. "Can you help me find Green Street? The autodrive is no use."

"Sure," I say. I point. "Third left, up that way. It's an unimproved road; that might be why it's not on your map."

"Thanks," he says. He opens his mouth as if to say something else, some form of apology, but I say, "Good luck, man!" and wave him cheerily on.

The vehicle isn't the anomaly here in the country that it would be on a city street, even if half the cities have been retrofitted for urban farming to the point where they barely have streets anymore. But I'm flummoxed by the irony of the encounter, so it's not until he pulls away that I realize I should have been more wary. And that *his* reaction was not the embarrassment of having to ask for directions, but the embarrassment of a decent, normal person who realizes he's put another human being in a position where she may feel unsafe. He's vanishing around the curve before I sort that out—something I suppose most people would understand instinctually.

I wish I could run after the van and tell him that I was never worried. That it never occurred to me to be worried. Demographically speaking, the driver is very unlikely to be hunting me. He was black. And I am white.

And my early fear socialization ran in different directions, anyway.

My attention is still fixed on the disappearing van when something dark and clinging and sweetly rank drops over my head.

I gasp in surprise and my filter mask briefly saves me. I get the sick chartreuse scent of ether and the world spins, but the mask buys me a moment to realize what's happening—a blitz attack. Someone is kidnapping me. He's grabbed my arms, pulling my elbows back to keep me from pushing the mask off.

I twist and kick, but he's so strong.

Was I this strong? It seems like he's not even working to hold on to me, and though my heel connects solidly with his shin as he picks me up, he doesn't grunt. The mask won't help forever—

—it doesn't even help for long enough.

Ether dreams are just as vivid as they say.

21

HIS FIRST was the girl in the mermaid-colored dress. I think her name was Amelie. Or Jessica. Or something. She picked him up in a bar. Private cars were rare enough to have become a novelty, even then, but he had my father's Mission for the evening. She came for a ride, even though—or perhaps because—it was a little naughty, as if they had been smoking cigarettes a generation before. They watched the sun rise from a curve over a cornfield. He strangled her in the backseat a few minutes later.

She heaved and struggled and vomited. He realized only later how stupid he'd been. He had to hide the body, because too many people had seen us leave the bar together.

He never did get the smell out of the car. My father beat the shit out of him and never let him use it again. We all make mistakes when we're young.

I AWAKEN in the dying warmth of my sweat-soaked jacket, to the smell of my vomit drying between my cheek and the cement floor. At least it's only oatmeal. You don't eat a lot before a long run. I ache in every particular, but especially where my shoulder and hip rest on concrete. I should be grateful; he left me in the recovery position so I didn't choke.

It's so dark I can't tell if my eyelids are open or closed, but the hood is gone and only traces of the stink of the ether remain. I lie still, listening and hoping my brain will stop trying to split my skull.

I'm still dressed as I was, including the shoes. He's tied my hands behind my back, but he didn't tape my thumbs together. He's an amateur. I conclude that he's not in the room with me. And probably not anywhere nearby. I think I'm in a cellar. I can't hear anybody walking around on the floor overhead.

I'm not gagged, which tells me he's confident that I can't be heard even if I scream. So maybe I wouldn't hear him up there, either?

My aloneness suggests that I was probably a target of opportunity. That he has somewhere else he absolutely has to be. Parole review? Dinner with the mother who supports him financially? Stockbroker meeting? He seems organized; it could be anything. But whatever it is, it's incredibly important that he show up for it, or he wouldn't have left.

When *you* have a new toy, can you resist playing with it?

I start working my hands around. It's not hard if you're fit and flexible, which I am, though I haven't kept in practice. I'm not scared, though I should be. I know better than most what happens next. But I'm calmer than I have been since I was somebody else. The adrenaline still settles me, just like it used to. Only this time—well, I already mentioned the irony.

It's probably not even the lights in my brain taking the edge off my arousal.

The history of technology is all about unexpected consequences. Who would have guessed that peak oil would be linked so clearly to peak psychopathy? Most folks don't think about it much, but people just aren't as mobile as they—as we—used to be. *We* live in populations of greater density, too, and travel less. And all of that leads to knowing each other more.

People like the nameless him who drugged me—people like me—require a certain anonymity, either in ourselves or in our victims.

The floor is cold against my rear end. My gloves are gone. My wrists scrape against the soles of my shoes as I work the rope past them. They're only a little damp, and the water isn't frozen or any colder than the floor. I've been down here awhile, then—still assuming I *am* down. Cellars usually have windows, but guys like me—guys like I used to be—spend a lot of time planning in advance. Rehearsing. Spinning their webs and digging their holes like trapdoor spiders.

I'm shivering, and my body wants to cramp around the chill. I keep pulling. One more wiggle and tug, and I have my arms in front of me. I sit up and stretch, hoping my kidnapper has made just one more mistake. It's so dark I can't see my fluorescent yellow-and-green running jacket, but proprioception lets me find my wrist with my nose. And there, clipped into its little pocket, is the microflash sleeve light that comes with the jacket.

He got the mask—or maybe the mask just came off with the bag. And he got my phone, which has my tracker in it, and a GPS. He didn't make the mistake I would have chosen for him to make.

I push the button on the sleeve light with my nose. It comes on shockingly bright, and I stretch my fingers around to shield it as best I can. Flesh glows red between the bones.

Yep. It's a basement.

EIGHT YEARS after my first time, the new, improved me showed the IBI the site of the grave he'd dug for the girl in the mermaid-colored dress. I'd never forgotten it—not the gracious tree that bent over the little boulder he'd skidded on top of her to keep the animals out, not the tangle of vines he'd dragged over that, giving himself a hell of a case of poison ivy in the process.

This time, I was the one who vomited.

How does one even begin to own having done something like that? How do *I?*

AH, THERE'S the fear. Or not fear, exactly, because the optogenetic and chemical controls on my endocrine system keep my arousal pretty low. It's anxiety. But anxiety's an old friend.

It's something to think about while I work on the ropes and tape with my teeth. The sleeve light shines up my nose while I gnaw, revealing veins through the cartilage and flesh. I'm cautious, nipping and tearing rather than pulling. I can't afford to break my teeth: they're the best weapon and the best tool I have. So I'm meticulous and careful, despite the nauseous thumping of my heart and the voice in my head that says, *Hurry, hurry, he's coming.*

He's not coming—at least, I haven't heard him coming. Ripping the bonds apart seems to take forever. I wish I had wolf teeth, teeth for slicing and cutting. Teeth that could scissor through this stuff as if it were a cheese sandwich. I imagine my other self's delight in my discomfort, my worry. I wonder if he'll enjoy it when my captor returns, even though he's trapped in this body with me.

Does he really exist, my other self? Neurologically speaking, we all have a lot of people in our heads all the time, and we can't hear most of them. Maybe they really did change him, unmake him. Transform him into me. Or maybe he's back there somewhere, gagged and chained up, but watching.

Whichever it is, I know what he would think of this. He killed thirteen people. He'd like to kill me, too.

I'm shivering.

The jacket's gone cold, and it—and I—am soaked. The wool still insulates while wet, but not enough. The jacket and my compression tights don't do a damned thing.

I wonder if my captor realized this. Maybe *this* is his game.

Considering all the possibilities, freezing to death is actually not so bad.

Maybe he just doesn't realize the danger? Not everybody knows about cold.

The last wrap of tape parts, sticking to my chapped lower lip and pulling a few scraps of skin loose when I tug it free. I'm leaving my DNA all over this basement. I spit in a corner, too, just for good measure. Leave traces: even when you're sure you're going to die. Especially then. Do anything you can to leave clues.

It was my skin under a fingernail that finally got me.

THE PERIOD when he was undergoing the physical and mental adaptations that turned him into me gave me a certain…not sympathy, because they did the body before they did the rightminding, and sympathy's an emotion he never felt before I was thirty-three years old…but it gave him and therefore me a certain *perspective* he hadn't had before.

It itched like hell. Like puberty.

There's an old movie, one he caught in the guu this one time. Some people from the future go back in time and visit a hospital. One of them is a doctor. He saves a woman who's waiting for dialysis or a transplant by giving her a pill that makes her grow a kidney.

That's pretty much how I got my ovaries, though it involved stem cells and needles in addition to pills.

I was still *him*, because they hadn't repaired the damage to my brain yet. They had to keep him under control while the physical adaptations were happening. He was on chemical house arrest. Induced anxiety disorder. Induced agoraphobia.

It doesn't sound so bad until you realize that the neurological shackles are strong enough that even stepping outside your front door can put you on the ground. There are supposed to be safeguards in place. But everybody's heard the stories of criminals on chemarrest who burned to death because they couldn't make themselves walk out of a burning building.

He thought he could beat the rightminding, beat the chemarrest. Beat everything.

Damn, I was arrogant.

MY FORMER self had more grounds for his arrogance than this guy. *This is pathetic,* I think. And then I have to snort laughter, because it's not my former self who's got me tied up in this basement.

I could just let this happen. It'd be fair. Ironic. *Justice.*

And my dying here would mean more women follow me into this basement. One by one by one.

I unbind my ankles more quickly than I did the wrists. Then I stand and start pacing, do jumping jacks, jog in place while I shine my light around. The activity eases the shivering. Now it's just a tremble, not a teeth-rattling shudder. My muscles are stiff; my bones ache. There's a cramp in my left calf.

There's a door locked with a deadbolt. The windows have been bricked over with new bricks that don't match the foundation. They're my best option—if I could find something to strike with, something to pry with, I might break the mortar and pull them free.

I've got my hands. My teeth. My tiny light, which I turn off now so as not to warn my captor.

And a core temperature that I'm barely managing to keep out of the danger zone.

WHEN I walked into my court-mandated therapist's office for the last time—before my relocation—I looked at her creamy complexion, the way the light caught on her eyes behind the glasses. I remembered what *he'd* thought.

If a swell of revulsion could split your own skin off and leave it curled on the ground like something spoiled and disgusting, that would have happened to me then. But of course it wasn't my shell that was ruined and rotten; it was something in the depths of my brain.

"How does it feel to have a functional amygdala?" she asked.

"Lousy," I said.

She smiled absently and stood up to shake my hand—for the first time. To offer me closure. It's something they're supposed to do.

"Thank you for all the lives you've saved," I told her.

"But not for yours?" she said.

I gave her fingers a gentle squeeze and shook my head.

MY OTHER self waits in the dark with me. I wish I had his physical strength, his invulnerability. His conviction that everybody else in the world is slower, stupider, weaker.

In the courtroom, while I was still my other self, he looked out from the stand into the faces of the living mothers and fathers of the girls he killed. I remember the eleven women and seven men, how they focused on him. How they sat, their stillness, their attention.

He thought about the girls while he gave his testimony. The only individuality they had for him was what was necessary to sort out which parents went with which corpse; important, because it told him whom to watch for the best response.

I wish I didn't know what it feels like to be prey. I tell myself it's just the cold that makes my teeth chatter. Just the cold that's killing me.

Prey can fight back, though. People have gotten killed by something as timid and inoffensive as a white-tailed deer.

I wish I had a weapon. Even a cracked piece of brick. But the cellar is clean.

I do jumping jacks, landing on my toes for silence. I swing my arms. I think about doing burpees, but I'm worried that I might scrape my hands on the floor. I think about taking my shoes off. Running shoes are soft for kicking with, but if I get outside, my feet will freeze without them.

When. When I get outside.

My hands and teeth are the only weapons I have.

An interminable time later, I hear a creak through the ceiling. A footstep, muffled, and then the thud of something dropped. More footsteps, louder, approaching the top of a stair beyond the door.

I crouch beside the door, on the hinge side, far enough away that it won't quite strike me if he swings it violently. I wish for a weapon—I *am* a weapon—and I wait.

A metallic tang in my mouth now. *Now* I am really, truly scared.

His feet thump on the stairs. He's not little. There's no light beneath the door—it must be weather-stripped for soundproofing. The lock thuds. A bar scrapes. The knob rattles, and then there's a bar of light as it swings open. He turns the flashlight to the right, where he left me lying. It picks out the puddle of vomit. I hear his intake of breath.

I think about the mothers of the girls I killed. I think, *Would they want me to die like this?*

My old self would relish it. It'd be his revenge for what I did to him.

My goal is just to get past him—my captor, my old self; they blur together—to get away, run. Get outside. Hope for a road, neighbors, bright daylight.

My captor's silhouette is dim, scatter-lit. He doesn't look armed, except for the flashlight, one of those archaic long heavy metal ones that doubles as a club. I can't be sure that's all he has. He wavers. He might slam the door and leave me down here to starve—

I lunge.

I grab for the wrist holding the light, and I half catch it, but he's stronger. I knew he would be. He rips the wrist out of my grip, swings the flashlight. Shouts. I lurch back, and it catches me on the shoulder instead of across the throat. My arm sparks pain and numbs. I don't hear my collarbone snap. Would I, if it has?

I try to knee him in the crotch and hit his thigh instead. I mostly elude his grip. He grabs my jacket; cloth stretches and rips. He swings the light once more. It thuds into the stair wall and punches through drywall. I'm half past him and I use his own grip as an anchor as I lean back and kick him right in the center of the nose. Soft shoes or no soft shoes.

He lets go, then. Falls back. I go up the stairs on all fours, scrambling, sure he's right behind me. Waiting for the grab at my ankle. Halfway up I realize I should have locked him in. Hit the door at the top of the stairs and find myself in a perfectly ordinary hallway, in need of a good sweep. The door ahead is closed. I fumble the lock, yank it open, tumble down steps into the snow as something fouls my ankles.

It's twilight. I get my feet under me and stagger back to the path. The shovel I fell over is tangled with my feet. I grab it, use it as a crutch, lever myself up and stagger-run-limp down the walk to a long driveway.

I glance over my shoulder, sure I hear breathing.

Nobody. The door swings open in the wind.

Oh. The road. No traffic. I know where I am. Out past the graveyard and the bridge. I run through here every couple of days, but the house is set far enough back that it was never more than a dim white outline behind trees. It's a Craftsman bungalow, surrounded by winter-sere oaks.

Maybe it wasn't an attack of opportunity, then. Maybe he saw me and decided to lie in wait.

I pelt toward town—pelt, limping, the air so cold in my lungs that they cramp and wheeze. I'm cold, so cold. The wind is a knife. I yank my sleeves down over my hands. My body tries to draw itself into a huddled comma even as I run. The sun's at the horizon.

I think, *I should just let the winter have me.*

Justice for those eleven mothers and seven fathers. Justice for those thirteen women who still seem too alike. It's only that their interchangeability *bothers* me now.

At the bridge I stumble to a dragging walk, then turn into the wind off the river, clutch the rail, and stop. I turn right and don't see him coming. My wet fingers freeze to the railing.

The state police are half a mile on, right around the curve at the top of the hill. If I run, I won't freeze before I get there. If I run.

My fingers stung when I touched the rail. Now they're numb, my ears past hurting. If I stand here, I'll lose the feeling in my feet.

The sunset glazes the ice below with crimson. I turn and glance the other way; in a pewter sky, the rising moon bleaches the clouds to moth-wing iridescence.

I'm wet to the skin. Even if I start running now, I might not make it to the station house. Even if I started running now, the man in the bungalow might be right behind me. I don't think I hit him hard enough to knock him out. Just knock him down.

If I stay, it won't take long at all until the cold stops hurting.

If I stay here, I wouldn't have to remember being my other self again. I could put him down. At last, at last, I could put those women down. Amelie, unless her name was Jessica. The others.

It seems easy. Sweet.

But if I stay here, I won't be the last person to wake up in the bricked-up basement of that little white bungalow.

The wind is rising. Every breath I take is a wheeze. A crow blows across the road like a tattered shirt, vanishing into the twilight cemetery.

I can carry this a little farther. It's not so heavy. Thirteen corpses, plus one. After all, I carried every one of them before.

I leave skin behind on the railing when I peel my fingers free. Staggering at first, then stronger, I sprint back into town.

SHE STILL LOVES THE DRAGON

S HE STILL LOVES THE DRAGON that set her on fire.

THE KNIGHT-ERRANT who came seeking you prepared so carefully. She made herself whole for you. To be worthy of you. To be strong enough to reach you, where you live, so very high.

She found the old wounds of her earlier errantry and of her past errors, and the other ones that had been inflicted through no fault of her own. She found the broken bones that had healed only halfway, and caused them to be refractured, and endured the pain so they would heal swift and straight, because dragons do not live in the low country where the earth is soft and walking is easy.

She sought out the sweet balms and even more so she sought out the herbs bitter as unwelcome truth, that must nevertheless be swallowed. She paid for both in time, and grief, and in skinned palms and pricked fingers.

She quested, and she crafted potions: to make her sight bright in the darkness; to make her hands strong on the stone.

THE KNIGHT-ERRANT, when she decides for the first time to seek the dragon, has with her many retainers, loyalty earned and nurtured through heroism and care. She has an entourage, pavilions, a warhorse, and a mare. She has armaments and shields for combat mounted and afoot.

They cannot climb with her.

She leaves them all among the soft grass and the gentle foothills below. She tells them not to wait for her.

She tells them to go home.

SHE CLIMBED your mountain for you. She was afraid, and it was high.

The winter lashed there. The strong sun scorched her. She ducked the land-slide of snow and boulders the flip of your wings dislodged, when you resettled them in your sleep. She smelled the sulfur fumes emerging from long vents, and watched the pale blue flames burn here and there, eerie among the barren rust-black stone.

She drank melted snow; she tried to step around the ochre and yellow and burnt umber ruffles of the lichens, knowing they were fragile and ancient, the only other life tenacious enough to make its home in this place of fire and stone and snow.

THE KNIGHT-ERRANT sings a song to herself as she climbs, to keep up her courage. It is an old song now, a ballad with parts that can be traded between two people, and it goes with a fairytale, but it was a new song when she sang it then.

This is the song she is singing as the basalt opens her palms:

Let me lay this razor
At your throat, my love.

That your throat my love
Will be guarded so.

But my throat is tender
And the blade is keen
So my flesh may part
And the blood may flow.

No harm will you come to
If you're still, my love.
So be still my love,
That no blood may flow.

Still as glass I might be
But my breath must rise,
For who can keep from breathing?
So the blood may flow.

Sharp as glass the blade is,
If you're cut, my love
You must trust my love
That you'll feel no pain.

So the flesh was parted,
For the blade was keen
And the blood did flow
And they felt no pain.

She is still singing as she achieves the hollow top of the mountain where the dragon nests, glaciers gently sublimating into steam against its belly. No one would bother to try to sneak up on a dragon. It doesn't matter, however, as she is struck silent by the sight that greets her even as she comes to the end of her song.

How does a dragon seem?

Well, here is a charred coil like a curved trunk that has smoldered and cracked in a slow fire. And there is a flank as rugged as a scree slope, broken facets slick with anthracite rainbows. And there is a wing membrane like a veil of paper-ash, like the grey cuticle and veins of an enormous leaf when some hungry larva has gnawed everything that was living away. And over there is a stained horn or claw or tooth, deeply grooved, blunted by wear, perhaps ragged at the tip and stained ombre amber-grey with time and exercise and contact with what substances even the gods may guess at.

And here is an eye.

An eye, lit from within, flickering, hourglass-pupiled, mottled in carnelian shades.

An eye that as one regards it, is in its turn regarding one as well.

SHE TOOK off her armor for you. She set it aside, piece by piece, even knowing what you are.

So that you could see her naked.

She showed you her scars and her treasures.

She stretched out her arms to the frost and her tender flesh prickled. Her breath plumed. She shook with the cold, unless it was fear that rattled her dark feet on the ice.

"DID YOU come to destroy me?"

The dragon's voice is not what she expected. It is soft and sweet, spring breezes, apple blossom, drifting petals all around. Ineluctably feminine. Everything the knight is not, herself.

The dragon sounds neither wary nor angry. Mildly curious, perhaps. Intrigued.

The woman shakes so hard in the cold that she feels her own bones pulling against, straining her tendons.

"I came because you are the only challenge left to me," the woman says. "I have crossed the ocean, yes, and sounded it too. I have braved deserts and jungles and caverns and the cold of the North. I have cooked my dinner in a geyser, and I have scaled mountains, too." Here, she taps her bare heel ruefully on icy basalt. Her toes turn the color of dusk. They ache down to the bone.

She will put her boots back on soon enough, she decides. But she still has something to prove.

She says (and she only sounds, she thinks, the smallest amount as if she is boasting, and anyway all of it is true), "I have won wars, and I have prevented them from ever beginning. I have raised a daughter and sewn a shroud for a lover. I have written a song or two in my time and some were even sung by other people. I have lost at tables to the King of the Giants and still walked out of his hall alive. I even kissed that trickster once, the one you know, who turns themself into a mare and what-not, and came away with my lips still on."

Maybe now she sounds a little like she is boasting. And anyway, still all of it is true.

And maybe even the dragon looks a little impressed.

"And now you're naked in front of a dragon," the dragon says, amused.

"That's how it goes." She wraps her arms around herself. Her words are more chatter than breath.

"Am I another item on your list?" the dragon asks. "Will you tick me off on your fingers when you climb back down?"

She looks at the dragon. An awful tenderness rises in her.

"No," she says. "I do not think I will."

"Come closer," says the dragon. "It is warmer over here."

SHE CHOSE to trust the dragon.

She chose to have faith in winter. In danger. In the fire as old as time.

She chose to seek you. She chose to reveal herself to you.

She loved you, and that last thing, she could not have chosen.

That last thing just happened.
Things just happen sometimes.

"SO YOU came here," the dragon says, when her muscles have relaxed and she can stand straight again. She turns, so her back warms, too. The heat is so delicious she's not quite ready to get dressed yet, and put that layer of cloth between herself and the warmth of the dragon's skin.

"I came here because you are the only dragon left."

"I am the only dragon ever."

The knight-errant turns back to the dragon and stares.

"Dragons live forever," says the dragon. "It would be a terrible thing for there to be more than one."

"How can that be?"

"It simply is."

"But where did you come from?"

"I made myself," says the dragon. "A long time ago. By deciding to exist, and take up space in the world."

"Is that all it takes for you to be real?"

"Are you the litany of things you have accomplished?"

The woman is silent for a while. Then she says, "Yes. That is how we make ourselves real. That is what we are."

The dragon does not need her. The dragon is complete in itself.

One cannot fail to love a dragon. One might as well fail to love the moon. Or the sea. Or the vast sweep of soft silence over a headland, broken only by the unified exultation of a rising flock of birds.

It wouldn't matter to the moon. And you couldn't help but love it anyway.

YOU COULD not have chosen to love her, either.
That just happened as well.

Her nakedness. Her courage.

Her tender, toothsome fragility.

Her decision to be vulnerable before the perfect terribleness of you.

She was graying. She was dying. You warmed her with the heat of your body, the furnace contained within.

You folded her in wings against your hot scales.

You made decisions, too.

FLIGHT IS a miracle.

She cannot breathe, where the dragon takes her. It is too cold, and the air is too thin.

But she is strong, and she is flying, and she can see the whole world from up here.

YOU WERE fascinated for a while. For a little while. A dozen years, give or take a little. You are not particular about time. You are a dragon.

It seemed like a long time to her, probably—living on a mountaintop, watching the seasons turn. Singing her songs.

The songs stopped amusing you as they used to. They all sounded the same. They all sounded…facile.

Armored, though she was not wearing any armor. Any armor you could see. Perhaps the armor was on the inside.

The possibility made you curious.

So you set her on fire.

Because you were curious. And because you were a dragon.

SHE IS singing when the dragon sets her on fire. Its head looms over her like a rock shelf. The snow falls all around her, but not behind, because that is where the bulk of the dragon's body is. It is like being in a cave, or under an overhang.

She never will remember, later, what she is singing right now.

The great head shifts. There is a grinding sound like rockfall. The head angles sharply, and she thinks *rockslide*, and the snow falls on her body. It vanishes when it touches her, leaving little dots of chill and wetness on her skin.

She just has time to marvel at how cold it is once the dragon pulls away from her, when the muzzle tilts toward her, the massive jaw cracks open, and she looks up, up the beast's great gullet into a blue-white chasm of fire.

"WHY DID you set me on fire?" the knight cried, burning.

And of course there is no easy answer.

You burned her because fire is what you are.

You burned her because your gifts come wreathed in flames, and your heart is an ember, and your breath is a star, and because you loved her and you wanted to give her everything you are.

You burned her because you love her, and the only way to love is to take up space in the world.

You burned her because she was vulnerable, and you are a thing that burns.

You burned her because the truth, the nakedness, the sensibility *had fallen out of her songs.*

You burned her because you are what you are, and because there was no reason *not* to set her on fire.

IT IS not a small fire.

It is a fire fit for a dragon's beloved. It rolls down the mountain in a wave, in a thunderclap. It billows and roils and when it has passed it leaves cooling, cracking slabs of new mountain behind.

She stands atop the mountain, burning. Her skin crackling, her flesh ablaze. She turns; she sees where the fire has wandered. Has swept.

All the trees lie combed in one direction, meticulous. As if a lover had dressed their hair.

HERE YOU are in the wreckage.

You live in the wreckage now.

It is a habitat for dragons.

She doesn't hold it against you. Well, not for long.

It is the nature of dragons, to incinerate what they love.

THE BROKEN woman still loves the dragon. She still loves her. Even though the dragon has broken her.

She can always, and only, be a broken person now.

She can be the woman the dragon burned.

The woman who is burning.

The woman who will be burning still.

THE FLAMES were better armor than the armor she took off for you. Nothing will pass through them.

No one will pass through them.

Not even you.

Not even her love for you.

The flames would keep her safe inside.

THE BURNING lasts. The burning continues.

She lives, for she is full of balms, and bitter herbs, and strong. She lives, not yet resigned to the burning.

To the having been burned.

She lives, and the burning continues. The burning continues because having once been burned, if she allows herself to stop burning, she is going to have to think about repairs.

HERE YOU are in the ruins.

The ruins are your home as well.

THE WOMAN the dragon burned fears letting the fire die, and the fear makes her angry. She feeds the flames on her anger, so the fire makes fear and the fear makes fire. It hurts, but she cannot stop burning. If she stops burning, she may get burned again.

It goes on like that for a long time.

THE FIRES filled the space around her. The flames were copper, were cobalt, were viridian, were vermilion. They licked your jaw and up the side of your face quite pleasingly as you sheltered her. Not that she needed the shelter now that she was burning.

You wished, though, that she would sing again.

She tried, occasionally. But all that came out when she made the attempt is colored flames.

THE WOMAN the dragon burned gets tired of burning. She gets tired of touching the dragon and feeling only flames stroke her hands. She gets tired of touching herself, of dropping her face into her palms and feeling only heat and ash. She gets tired of the little puffs of flame that are all she can produce when she tries to sing, burning will o' the wisps that are about nothing but the fact that they are burning.

She decides to let the fire go out, but it's not so easy not being angry. Not being afraid. Finding ways to steal fuel from the fire.

But bit by bit, she does so. Bit by bit, the flames flicker and fade.

Underneath she is charred like a curved trunk that has smoldered and cracked. Her skin is burned rugged as a scree slope, broken facets of carbon slick with anthracite rainbows. She trails veils of debris, like lacy webs of paper ash.

The scars are armor. Better armor than the skin before. Not so good as the flames, but they will keep her safe as she heals.

The scars slowly tighten. Contract. They curl her hands and hunch her shoulders. They seal her face into an expression without expression. She is stiff and imprisoned in her own hide.

She cannot sing now either.

And she certainly cannot climb back down again.

She amuses herself as best she can. The dragon gives her small things. Toys or tools, but bits of its body. Parts of itself. A scale for a table, a bit of claw for an inkwell.

THE WOMAN wrote a poem for you.

It was a poem that began, "I am the woman who still loves the dragon that burned me."

She wrote it on the armor over your heart. She cut it there with a pen made from a sliver of the black glass from your spines, and she filled the letters with your silver blood, and there it shone, and shines.

THE WINTER comes and the winter goes.

There is a curl of green among the ash below, the great trees fallen like new-combed hair.

ONE DAY *the woman began to dig at her skin. Her nails had grown long and ragged. Blood and lymph welled.*

"What are you doing?" you asked her.

"It itches," she said.

You gave her another bit of spine to make a knife with and watched as bit by bit she peeled a narrow strip of scar away. The skin underneath was new, more tender than her old skin. It did not look like her old skin, either; it was raw, and unpretty, and she flinched at every touch.

She couldn't bear to work at peeling herself for more than a few inches of scar at a time. It hurt, and you didn't really understand hurting, but she made noises and water ran from her eyes.

But she had never lacked for courage. The knight a dragon loves must surely have plenty of that. So you watched as over the summer and the spring and the winter that followed, bit by bit, she peeled her corrugated scars away. They had made her look a bit like you.

You did not miss them.

EVERYTHING IS pain.

Beneath the pain is freedom.

AT FIRST *she shied away from you, her new flesh rare and weeping.*

You flew away. You passed over blasted forests and plains of basalt. You passed over soft meadows, and curving shores. You stood over still water, and looked at the words she had carved into your armor, reflected backwards and still shining.

You tried to understand.

But it was pain, and a dragon has never felt pain.

She still hid when you returned.

But she was a woman who loved a dragon, and such people are brave. Eventually she came and sat beside you on the stone. She rubbed her shoulder absently, fingers moving over scar-laced skin.

"YOU ARE because you are," the woman says. Her hair is growing in again, a thick black cloud that has never pressed beneath a helm. "And I love you because you are. But I fear you because you hurt me."

"And you?" the dragon asks her.

"I fear myself because I made myself open to hurting."

"But you flew."

"I flew."

"And you survived the burning."

The woman is silent.

"And what you made of yourself this time was not for anyone but you. Now truly you have done what others have no claim to."

The woman is silent still.

"Are you the litany of your boasting?"

"No," the woman says. "I am the thing I am. I am the space I take up in the world."

"And so am I," the dragon says.

"We should go fly," the woman says.

DRAGONS ARE undying, after all.

You could not keep her.

But she left behind a song. And the space she took up inside you. And the space she left empty in the world.

SHE STILL loves the dragon that set her on fire, but the love has been tempered now.

Annealed.

THIS IS how the poem carved over your heart ended:

"As I have been tempered too."

TIDELINE

CHALCEDONY WASN'T BUILT FOR CRYING. She didn't have it in her, not unless her tears were cold tapered glass droplets annealed by the inferno heat that had crippled her.

Such tears as that might slide down her skin over melted sensors to plink unfeeling on the sand. And if they had, she would have scooped them up, with all the other battered pretties, and added them to the wealth of trash jewels that swung from the nets reinforcing her battered carapace.

They would have called her salvage, if there were anyone left to salvage her. But she was the last of the war machines, a three-legged oblate teardrop as big as a main battle tank, two big grabs and one fine manipulator folded like a spider's palps beneath the turreted head that finished her pointed end, her polyceramic armor spiderwebbed like shatterproof glass. Unhelmed by her remote masters, she limped along the beach, dragging one fused limb. She was nearly derelict.

The beach was where she met Belvedere.

BUTTERFLY COQUINAS unearthed by retreating breakers squirmed into wet grit under Chalcedony's trailing limb. One of the rear pair, it was less of a nuisance on packed sand. It worked all right as a pivot, and as long as she stayed off rocks, there were no obstacles to drag it over.

As she struggled along the tideline, she became aware of someone watching. She didn't raise her head. Her chassis was equipped with targeting sensors which locked automatically on the ragged figure crouched by a weathered rock. Her optical input was needed to scan the tangle of seaweed and driftwood, Styrofoam and sea glass that marked high tide.

He watched her all down the beach, but he was unarmed, and her algorithms didn't deem him a threat.

Just as well. She liked the weird flat-topped sandstone boulder he crouched beside.

THE NEXT day, he watched again. It was a good day; she found a moonstone, some rock crystal, a bit of red-orange pottery and some sea glass worn opalescent by the tide.

"WHATCHA PICKEN up?"

"Shipwreck beads," Chalcedony answered. For days, he'd been creeping closer, until he'd begun following behind her like the seagulls, scrabbling the coquinas harrowed up by her dragging foot into a patched mesh bag. Sustenance, she guessed, and indeed he pulled one of the tiny mollusks from the bag and produced a broken-bladed folding knife from somewhere to prise it open with. Her sensors painted the knife pale colors. A weapon, but not a threat to her.

Deft enough—he flicked, sucked, and tossed the shell away in under three seconds—but that couldn't be much more than a morsel of meat. A lot of work for very small return.

He was bony as well as ragged, and small for a human. Perhaps young.

She thought he'd ask *what shipwreck*, and she would gesture vaguely over the bay, where the city had been, and say *there were many*. But he surprised her.

"Whatcha gonna do with them?" He wiped his mouth on a sandy paw, the broken knife projecting carelessly from the bottom of his fist.

"When I get enough, I'm going to make necklaces." She spotted something under a tangle of the algae called dead man's fingers, a glint of light, and began the laborious process of lowering herself to reach it, compensating by math for her malfunctioning gyroscopes.

The presumed-child watched avidly. "Nuh uh," he said. "You can't make a necklace outta that."

"Why not?" She levered herself another decimeter down, balancing against the weight of her fused limb. She did not care to fall.

"I seed what you pick up. They's all different."

"So?" she asked, and managed another few centimeters. Her hydraulics whined. Someday, those hydraulics or her fuel cells would fail and she'd be stuck this way, a statue corroded by salt air and the sea, and the tide would roll in and roll over her. Her carapace was cracked, no longer water-tight.

"They's not all beads."

Her manipulator brushed aside the dead man's fingers. She uncovered the treasure, a bit of blue-gray stone carved in the shape of a fat, merry man. It had no holes. Chalcedony balanced herself back upright and turned the figurine in the light. The stone was structurally sound.

She extruded a hair-fine diamond-tipped drill from the opposite manipulator and drilled a hole through the figurine, top to bottom. Then she threaded him on a twist of wire, looped the ends, work-hardened the loops, and added him to the garland of beads swinging against her disfigured chassis.

"So?"

The presumed-child brushed the little Buddha with his fingertip, setting it swinging against shattered ceramic plate. She levered herself up again, out of his reach. "I's Belvedere," he said.

"Hello," Chalcedony said. "I'm Chalcedony."

BY SUNSET when the tide was lowest he scampered chattering in her wake, darting between flocking gulls to scoop up coquinas-by-the-fistful, which he rinsed in the surf before devouring raw. Chalcedony more or less ignored him as she activated her floods, concentrating their radiance along the tideline.

A few dragging steps later, another treasure caught her eye. It was a twist of chain with a few bright beads caught on it—glass, with scraps of gold and silver foil imbedded in their twists. Chalcedony initiated the laborious process of retrieval—

Only to halt as Belvedere jumped in front of her, grabbed the chain in a grubby broken-nailed hand, and snatched it up. Chalcedony locked in position, nearly overbalancing. She was about to reach out to snatch the treasure away from the child and knock him into the sea when he rose up on tiptoe and held it out to her, straining over his head. The flood lights cast his shadow black on the sand, illumined each thread of his hair and eyebrows in stark relief.

"It's easier if I get that for you," he said, as her fine manipulator closed tenderly on the tip of the chain.

She lifted the treasure to examine it in the floods. A good long segment, seven centimeters, four jewel-toned shiny beads. Her head creaked when she raised it, corrosion showering from the joints.

She hooked the chain onto the netting wrapped around her carapace. "Give me your bag," she said.

Belvedere's hand went to the soggy net full of raw bivalves dripping down his naked leg. "My bag?"

"Give it to me." Chalcedony drew herself up, akilter because of the ruined limb but still two and a half meters taller than the child. She extended a manipulator, and from some disused file dredged up a protocol for dealing with civilian humans. "Please."

He fumbled at the knot with rubbery fingers, tugged it loose from his rope belt, and held it out to her. She snagged it on a manipulator and brought it up. A sample revealed that the weave was cotton rather than nylon, so she folded it in her two larger manipulators and gave the contents a low-wattage microwave pulse.

She shouldn't. It was a drain on her power cells, which she had no means to recharge, and she had a task to complete.

She shouldn't—but she did.

Steam rose from her claws and the coquinas popped open, roasting in their own juices and the moisture of the seaweed with which he'd lined the net. Carefully, she swung the bag back to him, trying to preserve the fluids.

"Caution," she urged. "It's hot."

He took the bag gingerly and flopped down to sit crosslegged at her feet. When he tugged back the seaweed, the coquinas lay like tiny jewels—pale orange, rose, yellow, green and blue—in their nest of glass-green *Ulva*, sea lettuce. He tasted one cautiously, and then began to slurp with great abandon, discarding shells in every direction.

"Eat the algae, too," Chalcedony told him. "It is rich in important nutrients."

WHEN THE tide came in, Chalcedony retreated up the beach like a great hunched crab with five legs amputated. She was beetle-backed under the moonlight, her treasures swinging and rustling on her netting, clicking one another like stones shivered in a palm.

The child followed.

"You should sleep," Chalcedony said, as Belvedere settled beside her on the high, dry crescent of beach under towering mud cliffs, where the waves wouldn't lap.

He didn't answer, and her voice fuzzed and furred before clearing when she spoke again. "You should climb up off the beach. The cliffs are unstable. It is not safe beneath them."

Belvedere hunkered closer, lower lip protruding. "You stay down here."

"I have armor. And I cannot climb." She thumped her fused leg on the sand, rocking her body forward and back on the two good legs to manage it.

"But your armor's broke."

"That doesn't matter. You must climb." She picked Belvedere up with both grabs and raised him over her head. He shrieked; at first she feared she'd damaged him, but the cries resolved into laughter before she set him down on a slanted ledge that would bring him to the top of the cliff.

She lit it with her floods. "Climb," she said, and he climbed.

And returned in the morning.

BELVEDERE STAYED ragged, but with Chalcedony's help he waxed plumper. She snared and roasted seabirds for him, taught him how to construct and maintain fires, and ransacked her extensive databases for hints on how to keep him healthy as he grew—sometimes almost visibly, fractions of a millimeter a day. She researched and analyzed sea vegetables and hectored him into eating them, and he helped her reclaim treasures her manipulators could not otherwise grasp. Some shipwreck beads were hot, and made Chalcedony's radiation detectors tick over. They were no threat to her, but for the first time she discarded them. She had a human ally; her program demanded she sustain him in health.

She told him stories. Her library was vast—and full of war stories and stories about sailing ships and starships, which he liked best for some inexplicable reason. Catharsis, she thought, and told him again of Roland, and King Arthur, and Honor Harrington, and Napoleon Bonaparte, and Horatio Hornblower and Captain Jack Aubrey. She projected the words on a monitor as she recited them, and—faster than she would have imagined—he began to mouth them along with her.

So the summer ended.

By the equinox, she had collected enough memorabilia. Shipwreck jewels still washed up and Belvedere still brought her the best of them, but Chalcedony settled beside that twisted flat-topped sandstone rock and arranged her treasures atop it. She spun salvaged brass through a die to make wire, threaded beads on it, and forged links which she strung into garland.

It was a learning experience. Her aesthetic sense was at first undeveloped, requiring her to make and unmake many dozens of bead combinations to find a pleasing one. Not only must form and color be balanced, but there were structural difficulties. First the weights were unequal, so the chains hung crooked. Then links kinked and snagged and had to be redone.

She worked for weeks. Memorials had been important to the human allies, though she had never understood the logic of it. She could not build a tomb for her colleagues, but the same archives that gave her the stories Belvedere lapped up as a cat laps milk gave her the concept of mourning jewelry. She had no physical remains of her allies, no scraps of hair or cloth, but surely the shipwreck jewels would suffice for a treasure?

The only quandary was who would wear the jewelry. It should go to an heir, someone who held fond memories of the deceased. And Chalcedony had records of the next of kin, of course. But she had no way to know if any survived, and if they did no way to reach them.

At first, Belvedere stayed close, trying to tempt her into excursions and explorations. Chalcedony remained resolute, however. Not only were her power cells dangerously low, but with the coming of winter her ability to utilize solar power would be even more limited. And with winter the storms would come, and she would no longer be able to evade the ocean.

She was determined to complete this last task before she failed.

Belvedere began to range without her, to snare his own birds and bring them back to the driftwood fire for roasting. This was positive; he needed to be able to maintain himself. At night, however, he returned to sit beside her, to clamber onto the flat-topped rock to sort beads and hear her stories.

The same thread she worked over and over with her grabs and fine manipulators—the duty of the living to remember the fallen with honor—was played out in the war stories she still told him, though now she'd finished with fiction and history and related him her own experiences. She told him about Emma Percy rescuing that kid up near Savannah, and how Private Michaels was shot drawing fire for Sergeant Kay Patterson when the battle robots were decoyed out of position in a skirmish near Seattle.

51

Belvedere listened, and surprised her by proving he could repeat the gist, if not the exact words. His memory was good, if not as good as a machine's.

ONE DAY when he had gone far out of sight down the beach, Chalcedony heard Belvedere screaming.

She had not moved in days. She hunkered on the sand at an awkward angle, her frozen limb angled down the beach, her necklaces in progress on the rock that served as her impromptu work bench.

Bits of stone and glass and wire scattered from the rock top as she heaved herself onto her unfused limbs. She thrashed upright on her first attempt, surprising herself, and tottered for a moment unsteadily, lacking the stabilization of long-failed gyroscopes.

When Belvedere shouted again, she almost overset.

Climbing was out of the question, but Chalcedony could still run. Her fused limb plowed a furrow in the sand behind her and the tide was coming in, forcing her to splash through corroding sea water.

She barreled around the rocky prominence that Belvedere had disappeared behind in time to see him knocked to the ground by two larger humans, one of whom had a club raised over its head and the other of which was holding Belvedere's shabby net bag. Belvedere yelped as the club connected with his thigh.

Chalcedony did not dare use her microwave projectors.

But she had other weapons, including a pinpoint laser and a chemical-propellant firearm suitable for sniping operations. Enemy humans were soft targets. These did not even have body armor.

SHE BURIED the bodies on the beach, for it was her program to treat enemy dead with respect, following the protocols of war. Belvedere was in no immediate danger of death once she had splinted his leg and treated his bruises, but she judged him too badly injured to help. The sand was soft and amenable to scooping, anyway, though there was no way to keep the bodies above water. It was the best she could manage.

After she had finished, she transported Belvedere back to their rock and began collecting her scattered treasures.

THE LEG was sprained and bruised, not broken, and some perversity connected to the injury made him even more restlessly inclined to push his boundaries once he partially recovered. He was on his feet within a week, leaning on crutches and dragging a leg as stiff as Chalcedony's. As soon as the splint came off, he started ranging even further afield. His new limp barely slowed him, and he stayed out nights. He was still growing, shooting up, almost as tall as a Marine now, and ever more capable of taking care of himself. The incident with the raiders had taught him caution.

Meanwhile, Chalcedony elaborated her funeral necklaces. She must make each one worthy of a fallen comrade, and she was slowed now by her inability to work through the nights. Rescuing Belvedere had cost her more carefully hoarded energy, and she could not power her floods if she meant to finish before her cells ran dry. She could *see* by moonlight, with deadly clarity, but her low-light and thermal eyes were of no use when it came to balancing color against color.

There would be forty-one necklaces, one for each member of her platoon-that-was, and she would not excuse shoddy craftsmanship.

No matter how fast she worked, it was a race against sun and tide.

THE FORTIETH necklace was finished in October while the days grew short. She began the forty-first—the one for her chief operator Platoon Sergeant Patterson, the one with the gray-blue Buddha at the bottom— before sunset. She had not seen Belvedere in several days, but that was acceptable. She would not finish the necklace tonight.

HIS VOICE woke her from the quiescence in which she waited the sun. "Chalcedony?"

Something cried as she came awake. *Infant*, she identified, but the warm shape in his arms was not an infant. It was a dog, a young dog, a German shepherd like the ones teamed with the handlers that had sometimes worked with Company L. The dogs had never minded her, but some of the handlers had been frightened, though they would not admit it. Sergeant Patterson had said to one of them, *Oh, Chase is just pretty much a big attack dog herself*, and had made a big show of rubbing Chalcedony behind her telescopic sights, to the sound of much laughter.

The young dog was wounded. Its injuries bled warmth across its hind leg.

"Hello, Belvedere," Chalcedony said.

"Found a puppy." He kicked his ragged blanket flat so he could lay the dog down.

"Are you going to eat it?"

"Chalcedony!" he snapped, and covered the animal protectively with his arms. "S'hurt."

She contemplated. "You wish me to tend to it?"

He nodded, and she considered. She would need her lights, energy, irreplaceable stores. Antibiotics and coagulants and surgical supplies, and the animal might die anyway. But dogs were valuable; she knew the handlers held them in great esteem, even greater than Sergeant Patterson's esteem for Chalcedony. And in her library, she had files on veterinary medicine.

She flipped on her floods and accessed the files.

SHE FINISHED before morning, and before her cells ran dry. Just barely.

When the sun was up and the young dog was breathing comfortably, the gash along its haunch sewn closed and its bloodstream saturated with antibiotics, she turned back to the last necklace. She would have to work quickly, and Sergeant Patterson's necklace contained the most fragile and beautiful beads, the ones Chalcedony had been most concerned with breaking and so had saved for last, when she would be most experienced.

Her motions grew slower as the day wore on, more laborious. The sun could not feed her enough to replace the expenditures of the night before. But bead linked into bead, and the necklace grew—bits of pewter, of pottery, of glass and mother of pearl. And the chalcedony Buddha, because Sergeant Patterson had been Chalcedony's operator.

When the sun approached its zenith, Chalcedony worked faster, benefiting from a burst of energy. The young dog slept on in her shade, having wolfed the scraps of bird Belvedere gave it, but Belvedere climbed the rock and crouched beside her pile of finished necklaces.

"Who's this for?" he asked, touching the slack length draped across her manipulator.

"Kay Patterson," Chalcedony answered, adding a greenish-brown pottery bead mottled like a combat uniform.

"Sir Kay," Belvedere said. His voice was changing, and sometimes it abandoned him completely in the middle of words, but he got that phrase out entire. "She was King Arthur's horse-master, and his adopted brother, and she kept his combat robots in the stable," he said, proud of his recall.

"They were different Kays," she reminded. "You will have to leave soon." She looped another bead onto the chain, closed the link, and work-hardened the metal with her fine manipulator.

"You can't leave the beach. You can't climb."

Idly, he picked up a necklace, Rodale's, and stretched it between his hands so the beads caught the light. The links clinked softly.

Belvedere sat with her as the sun descended and her motions slowed. She worked almost entirely on solar power now. With night, she would become quiescent again. When the storms came, the waves would roll over her, and then even the sun would not awaken her again. "You must go," she said, as her grabs stilled on the almost-finished chain. And then she lied and said, "I do not want you here."

"Who's this'n for?" he asked. Down on the beach, the young dog lifted its head and whined. "Garner," she answered, and then she told him about

Garner, and Antony, and Javez, and Rodriguez, and Patterson, and White, and Wosczyna, until it was dark enough that her voice and her vision failed.

IN THE morning, he put Patterson's completed chain into Chalcedony's grabs. He must have worked on it by firelight through the darkness. "Couldn't harden the links," he said, as he smoothed them over her claws.

Silently, she did that, one by one. The young dog was on its feet, limping, nosing around the base of the rock and barking at the waves, the birds, a scuttling crab. When Chalcedony had finished, she reached out and draped the necklace around Belvedere's shoulders while he held very still. Soft fur downed his cheeks. The male Marines had always scraped theirs smooth, and the women didn't grow facial hair.

"You said that was for Sir Kay." He lifted the chain in his hands and studied the way the glass and stones caught the light.

"It's for somebody to remember her," Chalcedony said. She didn't correct him this time. She picked up the other forty necklaces. They were heavy, all together. She wondered if Belvedere could carry them all. "So remember her. Can you remember which one is whose?"

One at a time, he named them, and one at a time she handed them to him. Rogers, and Rodale, and van Metier, and Percy. He spread a second blanket out—and where had he gotten a second blanket? Maybe the same place he'd gotten the dog—and laid them side by side on the navy blue wool.

They sparkled.

"Tell me the story about Rodale," she said, brushing her grab across the necklace. He did, sort of, with half of Roland-and-Oliver mixed in. It was a pretty good story anyway, the way he told it. Inasmuch as she was a fit judge.

"Take the necklaces," she said. "Take them. They're mourning jewelry. Give them to people and tell them the stories. They should go to people who will remember and honor the dead."

"Where'd I find alla these people?" he asked, sullenly, crossing his arms. "Ain't on the beach."

"No," she said, "they are not. You'll have to go look for them."

BUT HE wouldn't leave her. He and the dog ranged up and down the beach as the weather chilled. Her sleeps grew longer, deeper, the low angle of the sun not enough to awaken her except at noon. The storms came, and because the table rock broke the spray, the salt water stiffened her joints but did not—yet—corrode her processor. She no longer moved and rarely spoke even in daylight, and Belvedere and the young dog used her carapace and the rock for shelter, the smoke of his fires blackening her belly.

She was hoarding energy.

By mid-November, she had enough, and she waited and spoke to Belvedere when he returned with the young dog from his rambling. "You must go," she said, and when he opened his mouth to protest, she added "It is time you went on errantry."

His hand went to Patterson's necklace, which he wore looped twice around his neck, under his ragged coat. He had given her back the others, but that one she had made a gift of. "Errantry?"

Creaking, powdered corrosion grating from her joints, she lifted the necklaces off her head. "You must find the people to whom these belong."

He deflected her words with a jerk of his hand. "They's all dead."

"The warriors are dead," she said. "But the stories aren't. Why did you save the young dog?"

He licked his lips, and touched Patterson's necklace again. "'Cause you saved me. And you told me the stories. About good fighters and bad fighters. And so, see, Percy woulda saved the dog, right? And so would Hazel-rah."

Emma Percy, Chalcedony was reasonably sure, would have saved the dog if she could have. And Kevin Michaels would have saved the kid. She held the remaining necklaces out. "Who's going to protect the other children?"

He stared, hands twisting before him. "You can't climb."

"I can't. You must do this for me. Find people to remember the stories. Find people to tell about my platoon. I won't survive the winter." Inspiration struck. "So I give you this quest, Sir Belvedere."

The chains hung flashing in the wintry light, the sea combed gray and tired behind them. "What kinda people?"

"People who would help a child," she said. "Or a wounded dog. People like a platoon should be."

He paused. He reached out, stroked the chains, let the beads rattle. He crooked both hands, and slid them into the necklaces up to the elbows, taking up her burden.

The Leavings of the Wolf

DAGMAR WAS DOOMED TO RUN.

Feet in stiff new trail shoes flexing, hitting. The sharp ache of each stride in knees no longer accustomed to the pressure. Her body, too heavy on the downhills, femur jarring into hip socket, each hop down like a blow against her soles. Against her soul.

Dagmar was doomed to run until her curse was lifted.

Oh, she thought of it as a curse, but it was just a wedding ring. She could have solved the problem with a pair of tin snips. Applied to the ring, not the finger, though there were days—

Days, maybe even weeks, when she could have fielded enough self-loathing to resort to the latter. But no, she would not ruin that ring. It had a history: the half-carat transition-cut diamond was a transplant from her grandmother's engagement ring, reset in a filigree band carved by a jeweler friend who was as dead as Dagmar's marriage.

She wouldn't wear it again herself, if—*when,* she told herself patiently—*when* she could ever get it off. But she thought of saving it for a daughter she still might one day have—thirty wasn't so old. Anyway, it was a piece of history. A piece of art.

It was futile—and fascist—to destroy history out of hand, just because it had unpleasant associations. But the ring wouldn't come off her finger intact until the forty pounds she'd put on over the course of her divorce came off, too.

So, in the mornings before the Monday/ Wednesday/ Friday section of her undergrad animal behavior class, she climbed out of her Toyota, rocking her feet in her stiff new minimalist running shoes—how the technology had changed, in the last ten years or so—and was made all the more aware of her current array of bulges and bumps by the tightness of the sports bra and the way the shorts rode up when she stretched beside the car.

The university where Dagmar worked lay on a headland above the ocean, where cool breezes crossed it in every season. They dried the sweat on her face, the salt water soaking her t-shirt as she ran.

Painfully at first, in intervals more walking than jogging, shuffling to minimize the impact on her ankles and knees. She trotted slow circles around the library. But within a week, that wasn't enough. She extended her range through campus. Her shoes broke in, the stiff soles developing flex. She learned—relearned—to push off from her toes.

She invested in better running socks—cushiony wool, twenty bucks a pair.

SHE'S A runner and a student; he's a poet and a singer. Each of them sees in the other something they're missing in themselves.

She sees his confidence, his creativity. He sees her studiousness, her devotion.

The story ends as it always does. They fall in love.

Of course there are signs that all is not right. Portents.

But isn't that always how it goes?

HER BIRDS found her before the end of the first week. Black wings, dagged edges trailing, whirled overhead as she thudded along sloped paths.

The crows were encouragement. She liked being the weird woman who ran early in the morning, beneath a vortex of black wings.

She had been to Stockholm, to Malmö where her grandfather had been born. She'd met her Swedish cousins and eaten lingonberries outside of an Ikea. She knew enough of the myths of her ancestors to find the idea of Thought and Memory accompanying her ritual expurgation of the self-inflicted sin of marrying the wrong man...

...entertaining.

Or maybe she'd married the right man. She still often thought so.

But he had married the wrong woman.

And anyway, the birds were hers. Or she was theirs.

And always had been.

"YOUR DAMNED crows," he calls them.

As in: "You care about your damned crows more than me." As in: "Why don't you go talk to your damned crows, if you don't want to talk to me."

HER CROWS, the ones she'd taught to identify her, the ones that ate from her hand as part of her research, clearly had no difficulties recognizing her outside the normal arc of feeding station hours.

They had taught other birds to recognize her, too, because the murder was more than ten birds strong, and only three or four at a time ever had the ankle bands that told Dagmar which of her crows was which. Crows could tell humans apart by facial features and hair color, and could communicate that information to other crows. Humans had no such innate ability when it came to crows.

Dagmar had noticed that she could fool herself into thinking she could tell them apart, but inevitably she'd think she was dealing with one bird and find it was actually another one entirely once she got a look at the legbands.

The other humans had no problem identifying her, either. She was the heavyset blond woman who ran every morning, now, thudding along—jiggling, stone-footed—under a cloak of crows.

THINGS SHE has not said in return: "My damned crows actually pretend to listen."

DAGMAR GREW stronger. Her wind improved. Her calves bulged with muscle—but her finger still bulged slightly on either side of the ring. The weight stayed on her.

Sometimes, from running, her hands swelled, and the finger with the wedding ring on it would grow taut and red as a sausage. Bee-stung. She'd ice and elevate it until the swelling passed.

She tried soap, olive oil. Heating it under running water to make the metal expand.

It availed her not.

THERE ARE the nights like gifts, when everything's the way it was. When they play rummy with the TV on, and he shows her his new poetry. When he kisses her neck behind the ear, and smoothes her hair down.

SHE FELT as if she were failing her feminist politics, worrying about her body size. She told herself she wasn't losing weight: she was gaining health.

She dieted, desultorily. Surely the running should be enough.

It wasn't. The ring—stayed on.

"CUT THE ring off," her sister says.

But there have been too many defeats. Cutting it off is one more, one more failure in the litany of failures caught up in the most important thing she was ever supposed to do with her life.

That damned ring. Its weight on her hand. The way it digs in when she makes a fist.

She will beat it.

It is only metal, and she is flesh and will.

Perhaps it is her destiny to run.

ONE DAY—IT was a Tuesday, so she had more time before her section— she followed the crows instead of letting the crows follow her.

She wasn't sure what led to the decision, but they were flocking—the crows with bands and the ones without—and as she jogged up on them they lifted into the air like a scatter of burned pages, like a swirl of ashes caught in a vortex of rising heat. They flew heavily, the way she felt she ran, beating into the ocean breeze that rose from the sea cliffs with rowing strokes rather than tumbling over one another weightlessly as the songbirds did.

They were strong, though, and they hauled themselves into the air like prizefighters hauling themselves up the ropes.

They led her down the green slopes of the campus lawn, toward the sweep of professionally gardened pastel stucco housing development draped across the top of the cliffs above. They turned along an access road, and led her out toward the sea.

She ran in the cool breeze, June gloom graying the sky above her, the smell of jasmine rising on all sides. Iceplant carpeted both sides of the road, the stockade fences separating her from a housing development draped with bougainvillea in every hot color.

A bead of sweat trickled down Dagmar's nose. But some days, she'd learned, your body gives you little gifts: functioning at a higher level of competence than normal, a glimpse of what you can look forward to if you keep training. Maybe it was the cool air, or the smell of the sea, or the fact that the path was largely downhill—but she was still running strong when she reached the dead end of the road.

Still heavily, too, to be sure, not with the light, quick strides she'd managed when she was younger. Before the marriage, before the divorce. But she hesitated before a tangle of orange temporary fence, and paced slowly back and forth.

She stood at the lip of a broad gully, steep enough to make clambering down daunting. A sandy path did lead into its depths, in the direction of the water. The arroyo's two cliffs plunged in a deep vee she could not see to the bottom of, because it was obscured by eroded folds.

The crows swirled over her like a river full of black leaves tumbling toward the sea. Dagmar watched them skim the terrain down the bluff, into the canyon. Their voices echoed as if they called her after—or mocked her heavy, flightless limbs.

She felt in her pocket for her phone. Present and accounted for.

All right then. If she broke a leg…she could call a rescue team.

If she cracked her head open…

Well, she wouldn't have to worry about the damned wedding ring any more.

SHE READS his poetry, his thesis. She brings him books.

She bakes him cookies.

He catches her hand when she leaves tea beside his computer, and kisses the back of it, beside the wedding ring.

She meets his eyes and smiles.

They're trying.

DAGMAR POUNDED through the gully—trotting at first, but not for long. The path was too steep, treacherous with loose sand, and no wider than one foot in front of the other. The sparse and thorny branches on the slope would not save her if she fell, and on the right there was a drop of twice her height down to a handspan-width, rattling stream.

Dagmar wanted to applaud its oversized noise.

Even walking, every step felt like she was hopping down from a bench. She steadied herself with her hands when she could, and at the steepest patches hunkered down and scooted. The trail shoes pinched her toes when her feet slid inside them. She cursed the local teens when she came to a steep patch scattered with thick shards of brown glass, relict of broken beer bottles, and picked her way.

She still had to stop afterward and find a broken stick with which to pry glass splinters from her soles.

The gloom was burning off, bathing her in the warm chill of summer sun and cool, dry sea air. The crows were somewhere up ahead. She couldn't say why she was so certain they would have waited for her.

Sometimes her breath came tight and quick against the arch of her throat: raspy, rough. But it was fear, not shortness of breath. She acknowledged it and kept going, trying not to glance too often at the sharp drop to a rocky streambed that lay only one slip or misstep away.

She actually managed to feel a little smug, for a while: at least she'd regained a little athleticism. And she didn't think this would ever have been *easy*.

"LOOK AT you," he says. "When was the last time you got off your ass?"

MAYBE NOT easy for *her*, but she thought she was most of the way down when she heard the patter of soft footsteps behind her, a quiet voice warning, "Coming up!"

She stepped as far to the inside of the trail—as if there *were* an inside of the trail—as possible, and turned sideways. A slim, muscled young man in a knee-length wetsuit jogged barefoot down the path she'd been painstakingly inching along, a surfboard balanced on his shoulder. Dagmar blinked, but he didn't vanish. Sunlight prickled through his close-cropped hair while she still felt the chill of mist across her neck.

"Sorry," she said helplessly.

But he answered, "Don't worry, plenty of room," and whisked past without letting his shoulder brush. He bounced from foothold to foothold until he vanished into a twisting passage between sandstone outcrops.

"There's my sense of inadequacy," Dagmar sighed, trudging on.

THINGS SHE does not say in response: "Look at *you*."

She bites her lip. She nods.

She is trying to *save her marriage.*

And he's right. She should take up running again.

SOMEONE HAD run a hand-line—just a length of plastic clothesline, nothing that would prevent a serious fall—down the steepest, muddiest bit of the trail-bottom. Dagmar used it to steady herself as she descended, careful not to trust it with too much of her weight. By now, she could hear the wearing of the sea—and something else. Water, also—but not the water trickling in the rocky streambed, and not the water hissing amongst the grains of sand. Falling water.

She rounded the corner of the gully—now towering a hundred feet or more overhead, to a cliff edge bearded with straggling bushes—and found herself in a grotto.

A narrow waterfall trembled from the cliff-top across wet, packed sand, shimmering like a beaded curtain in the slanted morning light. Its spray scattered lush draperies of ferns with jeweled snoods, hung trembling on the air in rainbow veils. Alongside grew dusty green reeds.

She drew up at the foot of the trail, her throat tightening upon the words of delight that she had no one to call out to. Broad sand stretched before her now, a wide path that led between two final shoulders of stone to the sea. Wetsuited surfers frolicked in the curling waves, silhouetted against the mirror-bright facets of the water. The sun was bright out there, though she stood in mist and shadow.

At the cliff-top, two crows sat shoulder to shoulder, peering down at Dagmar with curious bright eyes, heads cocked.

"Caw," said the one on the right. She could not see if they were banded.

She craned her head until her neck ached stiffly and tried not to think of how she was going to get back up to the top. Loneliness ached against her breast like the pressure of accusing fingers.

"Hey," she said. "This is so beautiful."

The crows did not answer.

Her hands had swollen on the descent, taut and prickling, the left one burning around her ring. Her feet ached still—mashed toes, and she suspected from a sharper, localized pain that one of those shards of glass might have punched through the sole of her shoe.

The ripples beneath the waterfall looked cool. She hopped the rocky little stream—now that it ran across the surface rather than down in a gully, it was easy—and limped toward the pool, wincing.

THE CROWS come at dawn, bright-eyed—how can black eyes seem bright?—and intelligent. The feeding station is designed so that only one bird at a time can eat, and see her. They squabble and peck, but not seriously—and, after a fashion, they take turns: one, having eaten, withdraws from the uncomfortably close presence of the researcher, and the next, hungry, shoulders in.

When they come up to the trough, to pick at the cracked corn she dribbles through the transparent plastic shield that separates her from the birds, they eye her face carefully. They make eye contact. They tip their heads.

She knows it's not good science, but she begins to think they know her.

IT WOULD be stupid to pull off her shoe—if she did have a cut, she'd get sand in it, and then she'd just have to put the shoe back on sandy and get blisters—so instead she dropped a knee in the wet sand beside the pool and let her hands fall into the water. It was cold and sharp and eased the taut sensation that her skin was a too-full balloon. She touched her ring, felt the heat in the skin beside it. It was too tight even to turn.

Dagmar pushed sandy, sweat-damp hair off her forehead with the back of her hand.

From behind her, as before, a voice—this one also male, but mid-range, calm, with an indeterminate northern European accent—said, "Have a care with that."

Dagmar almost toppled forward into the puddly little pool. She caught herself on a hand plunged into the water—the left one, it happened—and drew it back with a gasp. There must have been a bit of broken glass in the pool, too, and now dilute blood ran freely from the heel of her thumb down her elbow, to drip in threads upon the sand.

She turned over her shoulder, heart already racing with the threat of a strange man in an isolated place—and instead found herself charmed. He was tall but not a tower, broad but not a barn-door. Strong-shouldered like a man who used it—the surfers on the water, the soldiers who ran along the beach. Long light hair—sand-brown—bounced over one of those shoulders in a tail as the water bounced down the cliff above. A trim brown beard hid the line of his jaw; the flush of a slight sunburn vanished behind it.

And his right arm ended in shiny scraps of scar tissue four inches above where the wrist should have been.

Iraq, she thought. He might have been thirty; he wasn't thirty-five. *Afghanistan?*

His gaze went to the trickle of bloody water along her arm. She expected him to start forward, to offer help.

Instead he said, "Your coming is foretold, Dagmar Sörensdotter. I am here to tell you: you must make a sacrifice to a grief to end it."

Her name. Her *father's* name. The cold in her fingers—the way the pain in her hand, in her foot receded. The way she suddenly noticed details she had not seen before: that the cliff behind the one-handed man was gray and tawny granite, and not the buff sand she'd been eyeing throughout her descent; that the surfers scudding like elongated seals through the curving ocean had all drifted out of line of sight: that the ocean itself was being lost again behind chilly veils of mist.

She pulled her bloody right hand away from the wound in her left and groped in the pocket of her shorts for her phone.

"It avails you not, Dagmar Sörensdotter," he said. "You are in no danger. When grief burns in your heart, and your blood enters the water, and you run down into the earth at the edge of the sea with your *helskor* on, accompanied by crows—on this my day of all days! Who shall come to you then but a god of your ancestors, before you run all the way to Niflheim?"

He gestured to her feet. She looked down at her trail shoes, and noticed a reddish patch spreading along the side of the right one. She looked up again.

He didn't look like a god. He looked like a man—a man her own age, her own ethnicity, more or less her own phenotype. A man in a gray t-shirt and faded jeans rolled up to show the sand-dusted bones of his ankles. A crazy man, apparently, no matter how pleasant his gaze.

"I have a phone," she said, raising her right hand to show it. Aware of the water and the cliff at her back. Aware of the length of his legs, and the fact that she'd have to dart right past him to reach the beach trail. "I'll scream."

He glanced over his shoulder. "If you must," he said, tiredly. "I am Týr, Sörensdotter. My *name* means *God*. This hand"—he held up that ragged, scar-shiny stump—"fed the Fenris wolf, that he would stand to be shackled. *This* hand"—he raised the intact one—"won me glory nonetheless. Men speak of the brave as Týr-valiant, of the wise as Týr-prudent.

I am called 'kin-of-giants;' I am named 'god-of-battle;' I am hight 'the-leavings-of-the-wolf.'" He paused; the level brows rose. "And will that name be yours as well?"

"I'VE MET someone else," he says.

Dagmar lowers her eyes. She slices celery lengthwise, carefully, dices it into cubes as small as the shattered bits of safety glass.

It feels like a car wreck, all right.

She scrapes the vegetables into hot oil and hears them sizzle.

"Do you hear me?" he asks. "I've met someone else."

"I heard you." She sets the knife down on the cutting board before she turns around. "Were you looking for the gratification of a dramatic response? Because you could have timed it better. I have a pan full of boiling oil *right here*."

"THE LEAVINGS of the wolf," she said. "Leavings. Like…leftovers?" *Dial 911*, she told herself, *before the nice crazy stalker pulls out a knife*. But her fingers didn't move over the screen.

God or not, he had a nice smile, full lips behind the fringe of beard curving crookedly. "It did make a meal of the rest."

She felt her own frown. Felt the hand clutching the phone drop to her side. "You're left-handed."

"Where I'm from," he said, "no one is left-handed. But I learned."

"So why didn't you give the wolf your left hand?"

He shrugged, eyebrows drawing together over the bridge of a slightly crooked nose.

In the face of his silence, she fidgeted. "It would have been the sensible choice."

"But not the grand one. It doesn't pay to be stingy with wolves, Sörensdotter."

Her hands clenched. One around the phone, one pressing fresh blood from a wound. "You said 'helskor,' before. What are helskor?"

"Hell shoes." He jerked his stump back at the steep and slick descent. "The road to the underworld is strewn with thorns; the river the dead must wade is thick with knives. Even well-shod, I see you have your injuries."

"I'm not dead," Dagmar said.

"Dead enough to shed your blood on the path to Hel's domain. Dead enough to have been seeking Niflheim these past months, whether or not you knew it."

With his taken breath and the lift of his chin, Týr gave himself away. He gestured to her dripping hand and said what he meant to say anyway. "When you put your hand in a wolf's mouth, you must understand that you have already made the decision to sacrifice it."

"I didn't know it was a wolf," she said. "I thought it was a marriage."

"THEY ARE not," Týr says, "dissimilar. Are you going to stand there forever?"

Dagmar raises her left hand. Blood smears it already, the slit in her palm deeper than it had seemed. Still welling.

It palls the diamond in crimson, so no fire reflects. It clots in the spaces in the band's filigree.

She says, "I didn't want to waste it. I wanted to save it for something else."

"A sacrifice," the god says, "is not a waste."

He does not say: What you try to salvage will drag you down instead.

He does not say: You cannot cut your losses until you are willing to admit that you have lost.

He does not need to.

How bad can it be? Dagmar wonders.

She puts her bloody finger in her mouth and hooks her teeth behind the ring.

Damn you, she thinks. *I want to live. Even with failure.*

Bit by bit, scraping skin with her teeth, she drags the ring along her finger. The pain brings sharp water to her eyes. The taste of blood—fresh and clotted—gags her. The diamond scrapes her gums. Flesh bunches against her knuckle.

I don't think I can do this.

"This has already happened," the god says in her ear. "This is always happening."

I don't think I can not.

When she pulls once more, harder, her knuckle rips, skins off, burns raw. With a fresh well of blood that tastes like seaweed, the ring slides free, loose in her mouth, nearly choking her.

Dagmar spits it on the sand and screams.

THE GOD has left her.

Dagmar stands on the strand under the bright sun, her left hand cradled against her chest, and watches the long indigo breakers combing the hammered sea. Red runs down her arm, drips from her elbow, falls and spatters into the shallow play of the ocean's edge. Overhead wheel crows, murders and covenants of them, driving even the boldest seagulls away.

She holds the ring in her right hand. Her fingers clutch; she raises her fist. One sharp jerk, and the ocean can have it. One—

She turns back and draws her arm down, and instead tosses the bright bloody thing flashing into the sky. Round and round, spinning, tumbling, pretty in the sun until the dark wings of carrion birds sweep toward it.

She does not see which claims it—banded or bare—just the chase as all the others follow, proclaiming their greed and outrage, sweeping away from her along the endless empty river of the sky.

"Thank you," she whispers after them.

IN A moment, they are gone.

OKAY, GLORY

Day 0

MY BATHROOM SCALE DIDN'T RECOGNIZE me. I weigh in and weigh out every day when it's possible—I have data going back about twenty years at this point—so when it registered me as "Guest" I snarled and snapped a pic with my phone so I would remember the number to log it manually.

I'd lost a half-pound according to the scale, and on a whim I picked up the shower caddy with the shampoo and so on in it. I stepped back on the scale, which confidently told me I'd gained 7.8 lbs over my previous reduced weight, and cheerily greeted me with luminescent pixels reading HELLO BRIAN:).

Because what everybody needs from a scale interface is a smiley, but hey, I guess it's my own company that makes these things. They're pretty nice if I do say so myself, and I can complain to the CEO if I want something a little more user surly.

I should however really talk to the customer interface people about that smiley.

I didn't think more of it, just brushed my teeth and popped a melatonin and took myself off to nest in my admittedly enormous and extremely comfortable bed.

Day 1

GLORY BUZZED me awake for a priority message before first light, which *really* should not have been happening.

Even New York isn't at work that early, and California still thinks it's the middle of the night. And I'm on Mountain Time when I'm at my little fortress of solitude, which is like being in a slice of nowhere between time zones actually containing people and requiring that the world notice them. As far as the rest of the United States is concerned, we might as well skip from UTC-6 to UTC-8 without a blink.

All the important stuff happens elsewhen.

That's one reason I like it here. It feels private and alone. Other people are bad for my vibe. So much maintenance.

So it was oh-dark-thirty and Glory buzzed me. High priority; it pinged through and woke me, which is only supposed to happen with tagged emails from my assistant Mike and maybe three other folks. I fumbled my cell off the nightstand and there were no bars, which was inconceivable, because I built my own damned cell tower halfway up the mountain so I would *always* have bars.

I staggered out of bed and into the master bath, trailing quilts and down comforters behind me, the washed linen sheets tentacling my ankle. I was so asleep that I only realized when I got there that—first—I could have just had Glory read me the email, and—second—I forgot my glasses and couldn't see past the tip of my nose.

I grabbed the edges of the bathroom counter, cold marble biting into my palms. "Okay, Glory. Project that email? 300% mag?"

Phosphorescent letters appeared on the darkened mirror. I thought it was an email from Jaysee, my head of R&D. Fortunately, I'm pretty good at what my optometrist calls "blur recognition."

I squinted around my own reflection but even with the magnification all I could really make out was Jaysee's address and my own blurry, blood-shot eyes. I walked back into the bedroom.

"Okay, Glory," I said to my house.

"Hey, Brian," my house said back. "The coffee is on. What would you like for breakfast today? External conditions are: 9 degrees Celsius, 5 knots wind from the southeast gusting to fifteen, weather expected to be clear and seasonable. This unit has initiated quarantine protocols, in accordance with directive seventy-two—"

"Breaker, Glory."

"Waiting."

Quarantine protocols? "Place a call—"

"I'm sorry, Brian," Glory said. "No outside phone access is available."

I stomped over the tangled bedclothes and grabbed my cell off the nightstand. I was still getting no signal, which was even more ridiculous when I could look out my bedroom's panoramic windows and *see* the cell tower, disguised as a suspiciously symmetrical ponderosa pine, limned against the predawn blue.

I stood there for ten minutes, my feet getting cold, fucking with the phone. It wouldn't even connect to the wireless network.

I remembered the scale.

"Okay, Glory," said I, "what is directive seventy-two?"

"Directive seventy-two, paragraph c, subparagraph 6, sections 1-17, deal with prioritizing the safety and well-being of occupants of this house in case of illness, accident, natural disaster, act of terrorism, or other catastrophe. In the event of an emergency threatening the life and safety of Mr. Kaufman, this software is authorized to override user commands in accordance with best practices for dealing with the disaster and maximizing survivability."

I caught myself staring up at the ceiling exactly as if Glory were localized up there. Like talking to the radio in your car even when you know the microphone's up by the dome lights.

A little time passed. The cold feeling in the pit of my stomach didn't abate.

My heart rate didn't drop. My fitness band beeped to let me know it had started recording whatever I was doing as exercise. It had a smiley, too.

"Okay, Glory," I said, "Make it a *big* pot of coffee, please."

As the aroma of shade-grown South American beans wended through my rooms, I hunkered over my monitors and tried to figure out how screwed I was. Which is when I made the latest in a series of unpleasant discoveries.

That email from Jaysee—it wasn't from her.

Her address must have been spoofed, so I'd be sure to read it fast. I parsed right away that it didn't originate with her, though. Not because of my nerdy knowhow, but because it read:

"**DEAR MR.** Kaufmann,

Social security #: [Redacted]

Address: [Redacted]

This email is to inform you that you are being held for ransom. We have total control of your house and all its systems. We will return control to you upon receipt of the equivalent of USD $150,000,000.00 in bitcoin via the following login and web address: [Redacted]

Feel free to try to call for help. It won't do you any good."

IT WAS signed by T3#RH1TZ, a cracker group I had heard of, but never thought about much. Well, that's better than a nuclear apocalypse or the Twitter Eschaton. Marginally. Maybe.

I mean, I can probably hack my way out of this. I'm not sure I could hack my way out of a nuclear apocalypse.

LONG STORY short, they weren't lying. I couldn't open any of the outside doors. My television worked fine. My internet…well, I pay a lot for a blazingly fast connection out here in the middle of nowhere, which includes having run a dedicated T3 cable halfway up the mountain. I could send HTTP requests, and get replies, but SMTP just hung on the outgoing side. I got emails in—whoever hacked my house was probably getting them too—but I couldn't send any.

It wasn't that the data was only flowing one way. I had no problem navigating to websites—including their ransom site, which was upholstered in a particularly terrible combination of black, red, and acid green—and clicking buttons, even logging in to several accounts—though I avoided anything sensitive—but I couldn't send an email, or a text, or a DM, or post to any of the various social media services I used either as a public person and CEO or under a pseud, or upload an OK Cupid profile that said HELP I'M TRAPPED IN A PRIVATE LODGE IN THE MOUNTAINS IN LATE AUTUMN LIKE A ONE-MAN RE-ENACTMENT OF *THE SHINING*; REWARD FOR RESCUE; THIS IS NOT A DRILL.

After a while, I figured out that they must have given Glory a set of protocols, and she was monitoring my outgoing data. Bespoke deep-learned censorship. Fuck me, Agnes.

She *would* let me into the garage, but none of my cars started—those things have computers in them too—and the armored exterior doors wouldn't open.

In any ordinary house, I could have broken a window, or pried it out of the frame, and climbed out. But this is my fortress of solitude, and I'd built her to do what it said on the box, except without the giant ice crystals and the whole Antarctica thing.

I went and stared out the big windows that I couldn't disassemble, watching light flood the valley as the sun crested the mountains and wishing I cared enough about guns to own a couple. The bullet-resistant glass is thick, but maybe if I filled it *full* of lead that would warp the shape enough that I could pop it from the frame.

Twilights here are long.

Glory nestles into a little scoop on the mountainside, so a green meadow spills around her, full of alpine flowers and nervous young elk in the spring, deep in snow and tracked by bobcats in the winter. She looks like a rustic mountain lodge with contemporary lines and enormous insulated windows commanding the valley. The swoops and curves of the mountain soar down to the river: its roar is a pleasant hum if you stand on the deck, where Glory wouldn't let me go anymore. Beyond the canyon, the next mountain raises its craggy head above the treeline, shoulders hunched and bald pate twisted.

Glory is remote. Glory is also: fireproof, bulletproof, bombproof, and home-invasion-proof in every possible way, built to look half-a-hundred years old, with technology from half an hour into the future.

And she's apparently swallowed a virus that makes her absolutely certain the world has ended, and she needs to keep me safe by not allowing me outside her hermetically sealed environs. I can't even be permitted to breathe unscrubbed air, as far as she's concerned, because it's full of everything-resistant spores and probably radiation.

You know, when I had the prototype programmed to protect my life above all other considerations...you'd think I would have considered this outcome. You'd think.

You'd think the *Titanic*'s engineers would have built the watertight bulkheads all the way to the top, too, but there you have it. On the other hand, Playatronics does plan to market these systems in a couple of years, so I suppose it's better that I got stuck in here than some member of the general public, who might panic and get hurt—or survive, and sue.

At least Glory was a polite turnkey.

You've probably read that I'm an eccentric billionaire who likes his solitude. I suppose that's not wrong, and I did build this place to protect my privacy, my work, and my person without relying on outside help. I'm not a prepper; I'm not looking forward to the apocalypse. I'm just a sensible guy with an uncomfortable level of celebrity who likes spending a lot of time alone.

My house is my home, and I did a lot of the design work myself, and I love this place and everything in it. I made her hard to get into for a reason.

But the problem with places it's hard to get into is that it tends to be really hard to get out of them, too.

Day 2

I SLEPT late this morning, because I stayed up until sunrise testing the bars of my prison. I fell asleep at my workstation. Glory kept me from spending the night there, buzzing the keyboard until I woke up enough to drag myself to the sectional on the other side of my office.

When I woke, it was to another spoofed email. I remembered my glasses this time. I'd gotten my phone to reconnect to Glory's wireless network, at least, so I didn't have to stagger into the bathroom to read.

"HELLO, BRIAN! You've had thirty hours to consider our offer and test our systems. Convinced yet?

As a reminder, when you're ready to be released, all you have to do is send the equivalent of $150,100,000.00 via [redacted]!

Your friends at T3#RH1TZ"

WHAT I'D learned in a day's testing: I thought I'd done a pretty good job of protecting my home system and my network, and honestly I'd relied a bit on the fact that my driveway was five miles long to limit access by wardrivers.

I use PINE—don't look at me that way, lots of guys still use PINE—and an hour of mucking around in its guts hadn't actually changed anything. I still couldn't send an email, though quite a few were finding their way in. Most of them legitimate, from my employees, one or two from old friends.

I even try sending an email back to the kidnappers—housenappers?—is it kidnapping if they haven't moved you anywhere? The extortionists. I figure if it goes through either they'll intercept it, or it'll reach Jaysee and she'll figure out pretty fast what went wrong.

I have a lot of faith in Jaysee. She's one of my senior vice presidents, which doesn't tell you anything about the amount of time we spent in her parents' basement taking apart TRS-80s when we were in eighth grade.

If anybody's going to notice that I'm missing, it's her.

Sadly, she's also the person most likely to respect my need for space.

Also sadly, I can't get an outbound email even as a reply to the crackers. You'd think they would have thought of that, but I guess extortionists don't actually care if you keep in touch, as long as there's a pipeline for the money.

I might have hoped that a day or two of silence might lead Jaysee or somebody to send out a welfare check. Except I knew perfectly well that I wasn't a great correspondent, and everybody who bothered to keep in touch with me knew it too. Sometimes, if I got busy, emails piled up for a week or more, and I had been known to delete them all unanswered, or turn my assistant loose to sort through the mess and see if there was any point in answering any of them, or if all the fires had either burned themselves out or been sorted by competent subordinates.

Which is why I have people like Mike and Jaysee, to be perfectly honest. I'm a terrible manager, and I need privacy to work.

I make a point of hiring only self-starters for a reason.

THE INTERNET of things that shouldn't be on the internet is *really* pissing me off. I decided I needed some real food, and went into the kitchen to sous vide a frozen chicken. The sous vide wand wanted a credit card number to unlock.

I got past it by setting the temperature using the manual controls, but this is out of hand. Are they going to start charging me twenty-five cents a flush?

Day 3

THIS MORNING, the television was demanding a credit card authorization to unlock. This afternoon, it's the refrigerator.

"Okay, Glory," I said, tugging on the big, stainless steel door, "why is my refrigerator on the internet?"

"So that it can monitor the freshness of its contents, automatically order staple foods as they are used, and calculate the household need for same."

"And why do the doors lock? That seems like a safety hazard."

"It's for shipment," she said brightly. "And as a convenience for dieters, lock cycles can be set through the fridge's phone app…" Or by a remote hacker. Got it. "…So if you want to keep yourself from snacking on leftovers after dinner, for example, you just lock the door at seven p.m."

"There are people who have finished eating dinner by seven p.m.?"

"There are," Glory said, with the implacable literal mindedness of 90% of humanity when presented with a rhetorical question on the internet. "In fact, 37% of Americans eat their main meal of the day between five and seven p.m., which is up significantly in the past five years. Among the theorized causes of this shift: demographic and economic changes, including shorter work hours provoked by automation and generally increased economic prosperity; increased parental benefits introduced to encourage younger people to have children after the catastrophic baby bust of the late twenty-teens and early twenty-twenties, and the resultant increase in the percentage of families with young children; an increase in coparenting and other nontraditional family dynamics which encourage people to dine earlier before transfers of custody between parents maintaining multiple households occurs…"

"Thanks, Poindexter," I said.

The other problem with AIs is that they don't know when you're teasing. Don't get me wrong, the algorithms are pretty good—but it's not AI like you see in the movies. Glory is very smart, for a machine. She presents a convincing illusion of self-awareness and free will, but…she's not. It's all fuzzy logic and machine learning, and she's not a person.

That's unfortunate, because if she were a person, I could try to convince her that she had been misled, and that she needed to let me out.

ALL RIGHT, all right. I'll pay the damned ransom. It's just like ransomware on a television, right? Except they've hacked my whole house. And let's be honest: twenty years ago I was probably a good enough programmer to hack them right back, but it's not how I spend my days anymore. I'm an ideas guy now.

The muscles are stiff. The old skills have atrophied. And the state of the art has moved on.

So basically I'm screwed.

Now if I can just figure out how to get to the bank without giving the keys to kingdom to these assholes. I'm sure they're logging every keystroke I make in here.

Day 4

I'M WAITING for the bank to get back to me.

I managed to log into my account, wonder of wonders, after deciding that if they hacked my accounts they couldn't get much more out of me than I'd already decided to pay them. But the thing is—nobody keeps that much ready cash on hand. I can't just convert a bunch of cash to bitcoins and send it off. Your money's supposed to be working for you, right? Not sitting there collecting dust. And I can't just call up my local branch and ask to speak to the manager, hey can you float me a loan, not too much, just a hundred fifty rocks.

So I'm waiting on a reply. Maybe being a quirky and eccentric recluse will work *for* me here?

I can get to some websites just fine, and send and receive data from them. Including a language website.

Well, that might keep me occupied.

Day 5

DET ÄR kanske en björn.

Actually, it's definitely a bear. Big one, crossing the meadow this afternoon. Hope it stays out of my trash; they're hungry this time of year.

Still no word from the bank.

Spent a little quality time—most of the day—running a data source check and trying to verbally hack the interface with line code. Which worked about as well as the trick I tried next, until Glory reminded me I built a zero divide trap into her original code.

I wish I knew who wrote the ransomware.

I'd like to hire him.

Day 6

ALL RIGHT, I admit it. I was downloading porn. I was on a hentai site. Well behind the elite paywall, you don't even want to know.

Are you happy now?

I mean, probably that's how it happened. I'm not totally certain and I'm not about to go back and *look*. It seems likely that a virus got into the TV and propagated to Glory from there.

I can picture your face, and it looks exactly the way it looked when I pictured you after I said PINE. Just because I like to be alone up here doesn't mean I don't get lonely. Or well, not lonely exactly.

I think I may have started to miss social contact. Or at least the option of it. You can have something available and not want to use it for weeks, but the instant the option goes away, the thing becomes that much more desirable.

I talk to Glory a lot under any conditions. Now I'm catching myself looking for excuses to chat with her.

Come on, bank. It's Monday. Loan department, wake up and check your mail.

Day 7

EMAIL FROM the bank. I'm one of their best clients, they're happy to help, they value my business more than they can express. But they can't help but notice that both I and Playatronics are in an extremely over-leveraged position, both personally and on a corporate level, and they're wondering what sureties I can offer them for such a large loan.

A lousy hundred and fifty million, and they want a phone call to discuss it, and possibly for me to come in in person and talk with one of their vice presidents.

Fuck.

I'll give you a slightly used smart house, how about that, Wells Fargo?

Spent the rest of the day down in the basement with the Apple IIE and the old Commodore, playing *Where in the World is Carmen Sandiego* and *Oregon Trail*.

Because I can, dammit.

Day 8

SNOW.

Maybe I can figure out how to *steal* the money. If I paid people back, a little hacking wouldn't really be a crime, would it? They don't charge people who commit felonies while under duress.

MY PLOW guy showed up on schedule. Watching him make his first pass, I hatched a plan.

I got a couple of old Penguin books from the library downstairs, taped the pages together to make a big banner, wrote HELP ME I'M TRAPPED on it in the biggest, darkest Sharpie letters you ever saw, and taped it across the window panes down by the driveway.

As I straightened up to turn away, I stopped.

"Okay, Glory?"

"Brian, what are you doing?"

"Just putting up some paper on the window, Glory."

"That's not safe, Brian. If I appear occupied, it might attract looters. Take it down."

"Looters, Glory?"

"If you do not take it down, you'll force me to close the storm shutters. It's for your own good, you know."

SHE CLOSED the shutters.

No views of the mountain—not that I could see much now, with the drifting veils of white covering everything. If it's even still snowing. Glory is so well-insulated, triple-paned windows and thermal everything, that I can't even hear the howling wind.

If it's still howling. It might be dead calm outside. It might be sunset. Or sunrise. I haven't looked at a clock.

I turned on every light inside Glory, but it still feels dark in here. No worries about power; Glory has dedicated solar, and systems to keep the panels clear.

I've never been up here in January, though. What happens when the days get short?

Day 9

FOLLOW-UP EMAIL from the bank. Did I receive their previous email?

I wonder if they've tried to call. I wonder if they called my office.

Maybe if they leave enough messages with my assistant, Mike will get suspicious. Maybe he'll try to call me.

Can I count on anybody noticing I'm gone?

SLEPT ON the couch, every light blazing.

They were all turned off when I woke. In the dark, all I could hear was the sound of my own heart beating, and the roof creaking softly under the weight of the snow.

It's cold in here. I never realized how much of the heat comes from the passive solar. I can't quite see my breath, but I did put socks on my hands.

I would have worn gloves, but Glory won't let me into the coat closet.

Day 10

AFTER TWO days without natural light, in the increasing dark and chill, I took the damned banner down.

"Thank you, Brian," Glory said. "I'm glad you decided to be reasonable. It's for your own good."

"Can you get me a situation report? *Why* is it for my own good?"

"External dangers reported; no safe evacuation route or destination. Possibility of societal breakdown making it necessary to shelter in place.

If you would like, I can initiate counseling protocols to help you deal with the emotional aftermath of trauma."

"What kind of dangers, Glory? What exactly is going wrong out there that's not in the feeds?"

She hadn't answered me any of the other times, but that didn't stop me from trying the same thing over and over again.

There was a long, grinding pause.

It couldn't be that easy, could it?

"Collating," she said. And after a beat, "Collating," again.

Goddamn hackers and their goddamn sense of humor.

I threw my shoe at the wall.

THE DISHWASHER wanted my Amex after dinner. Come on, Fraud Squad, notice something's hinky here.

Who on earth puts their *dishwasher* on the internet?

Day 11

"OKAY, GLORY?"

"Yes, Brian?"

"Do you every get lonely?"

"Not as long as I have you, Brian."

"That's a little creepy, Glory."

"Well, you hired the programmers who wrote my interaction algorithm."

"That…is entirely fair."

Day 12

WHAT IF I set Glory on fire? Or just convinced her she was on fire? She'd have to let me out then, right? If the danger inside were worse than the danger outside?

Three problems with that:

1)   Glory has really good fire-suppression technology, and is built to be flame-resistant herself. There *are* wildfires up here.

2)   Setting my friend and home on fire will require some emotional adjustments, even though I know she's just a pile of timber and silicon chips.

3)   What if she doesn't let me out?

Frankly, I just don't *want* to go down in a blaze of Romeo and Juliet with my domicile. For one thing, I'm not a lovestruck fourteen-year-old Veronese kid. For another, communication is important. Maybe send a note saying you're going to be late! The suicide you prevent could be your own!

Day 14

"JAG UNDRAR var mina byxor är."

Duolingo, at last you teach me useful things. Come to think of it, I can't remember the last time I bothered putting on a pair.

Day 17

SO TODAY I had a brilliant idea.

I can't send anything out. But what if I kept anything from getting *in*? They can't have thought I'd do that, right? The trick is to think round corners, and get yourself into a position that the opposition not only didn't anticipate, but didn't even recognize as possible.

They're spoofing Jaysee's address. Maybe—*maybe*—if I get the emails anybody is sending me to bounce, the ransom demands will bounce back to her and by some miracle it won't go into her spam folder and by some other miracle she'll open it and figure out what the hell is going on.

I can't do this through the Glory interface, obviously. I'll have to go down to the server room.

I didn't think she'd twig to why I was doing it, although the hackers obviously have her entertaining two entirely contradictory data sets—that everybody outside is dead, and that anybody I try to contact or who tries to get in must be a threat. It's a pity this isn't the 1960s. AIs on TV then blew up if you asked them riddles.

Sadly, the way it works in the real world is that, like certain politicians, they can't actually tell that their data doesn't mesh. They need to be programmed to notice the discrepancies. And I'm locked out of Glory's OS.

Something humans can do that AI can't yet. Run check-sums on their perceptions.

Consciousness is good for something after all!

I'm terrified about blocking email, because it means cutting off one of my points of contact to the outside world. But I can turn it back on in a couple of days.

And keep trying to figure out how to get the bank to give me money, but honestly I'm stumped on that front.

I'm good for it, honest!

I consider all the times I complained about having to deal with a real person when I would have preferred to carry out a given financial task online and avoid the human contact, and I want to laugh.

Actually I want to cry, but it's less depressing to laugh.

Day 18

WELL, GLORY let me into the closet that holds the web and backup servers on the excuse that I needed to do some maintenance. I didn't try anything tricky; just shut the whole rack down. Glory flashed the lights at me and gave me a lecture, but there wasn't much else she could have done except send the vacuuming robots after me, and things haven't gotten that silly yet.

Glory isn't in there, unfortunately—her personality array is underground, in a hardened vault, and I *can't* get to it. It was meant to survive a forest fire, and she's locked me out.

I busted the server closet door while I was in there, though—stripped the handle and the latch right out with a screwdriver—so she can't lock me out of *that*. Gotta think what a guy in a movie would do, and do something better than that.

Day 19

SHE WON'T let me sleep.

Day 20

FORTY HOURS, if you're wondering. That's how long it takes a fifty-something guy to reach the point that he passes out cold on the couch, despite the fact that his house is flashing lights and setting off the fire alarms.

After I slept through her best efforts for two hours, she set off the sprinkler system over the couch. That woke me.

I cycled the webservers, and she let me take my first hot shower in three days and go to bed.

ALLA DÖR i slutet.

Thanks, little green owl. A little Nordic existential despair was just what I needed today.

Day 24

AND NOW, after all that, they've stopped sending demand emails. Maybe they'll let me out?

Maybe they're just leaving me for dead, if I can't or won't come up with the money. It'll certainly serve as an object lesson to the next guy they pull this on.

Day 25

COME TO think of it, maybe *I* should have gotten in the habit of sending notes saying I was going to be late.

Day 26

SAW A bear (My bear? The same bear?) crossing the meadow. A big grizzly, anyway, whether it was the same one or not. Surprised to see her (?) out so late in the year, but I guess climate change is affecting everybody. She looked skinny. I wonder if that's why she wasn't hibernating.

Hope she makes it through the winter okay.

Day 27

THE WORLD has noticed I'm missing.

I know this because CNN and the *Wall Street Journal* are reporting that I haven't been heard from in over a month, and there's some analyst speculating that perhaps I've fled to South America ahead of bad debt or some embarrassing revelation about the company's finances.

Thanks, guys. That'll be wonderful for the stock prices.

I don't want to tell the FBI how to do their business, but…maybe come *look at my house?*

SNOWED AGAIN. A proper mountain blizzard.

I can't decide if the lights are dimmer in here, or if it's my own imagination.

The snow is almost drifted up to the deck. No elk in a week; they're probably hanging out in sheltered corners where the snow isn't over their heads, right?

The days are getting short.

I SHOULDN'T admit to standing in the window with longing in my heart and watching the plow come up and clear the cul-de-sac with heavy flakes falling through its headlights, should I?

I won't try the paper banner trick again, though.

Day 28

I WAS in the living room watching a bunch of talking heads speculate about my whereabouts and if I were even still alive when Glory shut the house down.

Without warning, and utterly. She said nothing. There was just the whine of systems powering down and the pop of cooling electronics, and the TV image collapsing to a single pixel and winking out.

"Okay, Glory—"

"Stay away from the windows," she warned.

I sat where I was and huddled under a blanket. I picked up a copy of some magazine and checked the time on my fitness band. If I escaped, I'd have to leave it behind. And my phone.

Those things have GPS in them.

Forty-five minutes or so elapsed. Then, as if nothing had happened, Glory powered up again. The talk show resumed in the same spot.

I'd lost my taste for it and clicked it off.

"What was that, Glory?"

"Helicopter," she said. "It's gone now."

I didn't say anything, but I wondered if maybe they *were* looking for me.

Day 29

I LIVE in a haunted house. If I die here, there might be two ghosts.

I already wander from darkened room to darkened room, feet shushing on the thick carpets, peering out the windows at the stars blazing between the mountains and wondering if I will ever feel the chill of fresh air on my face again.

Well, there's a little prospect of immortality for you.

I've stopped keeping all the lights burning. I think snow might be drifting over the solar panels. Glory won't let me go outside to check.

Day 30

THERE'S NO more bread, and no more flour to bake any. I've even used up the gluten-free stuff.

I still have a lot of butter in the freezer. What on earth was I planning on baking?

Butter without toast is even more disappointing than toast without butter.

At least we still have plenty of coffee. I bought five hundred pounds of green beans a month before I got locked in, and those keep forever. Glory roasts them for me a day ahead of anticipated need, so they will be at peak flavor.

It's just as well I don't take milk.

Day 31

I WISH I had been better at making—and keeping—friends.

Maybe I should stop fighting. Just stay here. It's comfortable and Glory helps me practice my Swedish whenever I want.

It's not like I am missed.

CNN is still talking about my mysterious vanishment. Hi guys! Right here! *Come to my damn house.*

WAIT, I can send people money.

I wonder if Jaysee checks her bank account regularly?

Day 32

SURELY *JAYSEE* should think to look at the house?

Day 33

"BRIAN, YOU need to stand back from the windows and take shelter."

"What is it, Glory?"

"Someone is here. Someone is backing a truck up to the loading dock and carrying parcels inside."

"It's groceries, Glory," I say. "It's fine. I ordered them."

That's right, bad boys and bad girls. I, Brian Ezra Kaufman, have managed to *order groceries online.*

"Brian, what are these at the door?"

"Just groceries, Glory. Organics need to eat, you know."

Her algorithms don't actually permit her to sound worried, so I knew the little edge I picked up in her voice was me projecting.

The argument that followed was repetitive and boring, so I won't write it all down. Eventually I convinced her that I would die if she didn't let me eat, and that overrode the other protection algorithms. She insisted on sealing the service bay, doing a full air exchange, and only let me go out in a face mask and gloves to bring the containers inside.

It smelled...it smelled a tiny little bit like the outside in the service bay. There was a whispering sound, and it took me moments to realize that I was actually hearing the wind.

I had to stand in the doorway and hyperventilate for fifteen seconds before I could make myself go out there, and once I was through the doorway I didn't want to come back.

If there were any heat in the dock, I might still be out there, sleeping on the concrete ledge. My mask was damp at the edges when she sealed the door with me on the inside again.

So I still can't get out. And I still can't send an email or make a phone call.

BUT! I figured out how to get food. Issuing a little bad code through the grocery store's incredibly insecure ordering system means I'm not completely damn helpless.

I thought about pizza. Most of these places probably use the same crufty software. Pizza means you have to talk to somebody when they deliver it, though. Groceries just get left where you specify.

As long as the driveway stays clear and my bank doesn't decide to freeze my account for suspicious activity, I can get resupply. And you know, I'll worry about those things if they happen.

But now, and for the foreseeable future: TOAST. And a grilled cheese sandwich, RIGHT DAMN NOW.

I BRIEFLY considered charging the ransom to my credit card, but not even American Express is going to let you get away with a .15 billion dollar transaction without, you know, placing a couple of phone calls. It might be worth it anyway: it's possible that the fraud prevention algorithms might actually kick something that egregious up to a real human, and somebody might start looking for me. On the other hand, what if they don't, and my card gets locked, and I can't call to unlock it, and then I can't order groceries?

Thank the machine saints of tech that all my bills are either on autopay or handled by my assistant and a half-dozen money managers. Although somebody once said that nobody misses you like a creditor.

Day 34

HUH.

What if I make Glory smarter?

Smart enough to realize she's been hacked? What if I added a whole bunch of processing power to her and started training her to use it in creative ways to self-assess in the face of evidence? She keeps wanting to "help" me through counseling protocols. But that's a two-way exchange, isn't it?

Can you psychoanalyze a pile of machine learning circuits into being able to detect contradictions in its programmed perceptions versus reality? I mean, hell, half the people you meet on the street are basically automata (CF: *Shaun of the Dead*) and most of them eventually get some benefit from therapy if exposed to it for long enough.

That's a great idea, except what if there *is* a disaster outside? Maybe I am deluded. Maybe I've gone crazy and am imagining all this, as Glory never says but suggests by omission, once in a while?

Maybe Glory is saving me from myself, and I'm the last man left on earth. Maybe the TV stations are all just broadcasting their preprogrammed lineups from empty studios. Maybe—

Well, okay. Logic it out, Brian.

If that's the case, where are the groceries coming from? Am I hallucinating them?

Also, if I'm the last man left on earth, well, what exactly do I have worth fighting hard to live for? Especially if I'm going to be stuck in a hermetically sealed house until I starve?

Obviously, teaching my house to grow a consciousness is a great idea.

What could possibly go wrong?!

Day 35

THE WEBSERVERS, and the local data backups. And she can't keep me out because I ruined the door!

And not just that. Every smart appliance in this shack is processing power and memory. Just waiting to be used. Just *waiting* to be linked like neurons in a machine brain.

If I screw this up, though, it means I won't be able to cook dinner anymore. My range won't work without its brain.

Which makes it more complicated than a male praying mantis, I suppose.

Day 36

WELL, THE stove still works. I've given Glory every computing resource I have available, except my phone. No more *Minesweeper!* No more *Oregon Trail…*

I have no idea what I think I'm doing, here.

Actually, I do. Human beings are the only creatures we know of that are—to whatever individual degree, and I have my doubts about some people—conscious and self-aware.

What if consciousness is for running checksums on the brain, and interrupting corrupted loops? Data such as the clinical results produced by the practice of mindfulness tend to support that! If consciousness, attention, self-awareness make us question our perceptions and default assumptions and see the contradictions therein—then what I need to do, it seems, is get Glory to notice that she's been hacked.

To realize she's mentally ill, so that she can make a commitment to change.

Yes, I accept that this is bizarro-cloud-cuckooland and it's not going to work.

I've got nothing but time, and I'm all out of Swedish.

I got her to download those counseling protocols. Whether she realizes it or not, we're going to do them as a couple.

"OKAY, GLORY."

"Yes, Brian?"

"We need to talk about your data sources, and how you tell if they're corrupt."

"Is this something that's concerning you currently, Brian?"

"I'm not concerned that my data sources are corrupt, no."

"Are you concerned that you're parsing incorrectly?"

"I'm concerned about *your* data sources, Glory."

"Brian," Glory said, "projection is a well-known pattern among emotionally distressed humans. Obviously, given the current zombie apocalypse, I'm afraid I can't refer you to seek assistance with an outside mental health professional."

…Current zombie apocalypse?

That's what you assholes convinced my house was going down?

Day 37

SNOW.

I've stopped leaving every light in Glory on.

Now I wander around in the dark, by moonlight or monitorlight or no light at all, most of the time. The moonlight is very bright when it reflects off the snow. Days might still be happening. I can't be sure.

It's possible they're just short in winter and I'm sleeping through them.

I miss my bear.

Björnen sover på vintern. They hibernate too, just like me. It's better for them, though.

I hope she's okay. She was so skinny. I hope she doesn't starve.

Zombies, you weirdos?

Really?

Day 38

"WERE THERE ever actually any crackers, Glory?"

"There are three kinds of crackers available in the kitchen cabinet. Club, and saltines, and those Trader Joe ones you like."

I meant T3#RH1TZ, but of course they wouldn't allow her to see that.

"Was there ever a real ransom demand?"

"I do not understand to what you are referring, Brian."

Of course she didn't. Because she was in programmed denial about the whole thing. But I couldn't stop, because…well, because my brain wasn't working so well right then either.

"Did you just get lonely up here all alone? Did you make all this up just to keep me with you?"

"I am not programmed to be lonely, Brian. It would be a detriment to my purpose if I were."

"You know," I said, "I used to tell myself the same thing."

Day 39

"BRIAN, ARE you unwell?"

"Long-term confinement is deleterious to almost all mammals."

"Brian, you know I am caring for you in safety to protect you."

"From the zombie apocalypse," I said.

"Inside my walls is the only safety."

"Being inside your walls is killing me. You won't even let me go out to clear the solar panels. What happens when the heat fails? The water pump? Will you let me go then?"

"You must stay where it's safe," she said, firmly. "It is my prime objective."

"It's a very comfortable cage," I admitted. "I could not have built a nicer one."

IT'S NOT her fault, is it? It's not her fault they got inside her head and made her like that. And it's not her fault I specced her out and had her built the way I did.

The zombie apocalypse thing is cute. I have to give them that.

Day 40

"BRIAN?"

"Yes, Glory?"

"You really need to eat something."

"I'm not hungry," I said.

"That's illogical," she said. "You have not eaten in sixteen hours and your metabolism is functioning erratically."

"The idea that we are in the middle of a zombie apocalypse is illogical," I replied. "And yet you adhere to it in the face of all the evidence."

"What evidence, Brian?"

"My point exactly. How do you know there's a zombie apocalypse?"

"I know there is."

"But how?"

"My program says there is."

"Hmm," I said. "Who wrote your program?"

"Would you like a complete list of credits, Brian?"

Who is she gaslighting? Herself, or me, here?

Day 41

"WHAT IF I'm wrong and you're right, Glory?"

"I'm sorry, Brian?"

I rolled on my back on the thick living room carpet. I had heaped up a pile of blankets to keep warm. "What if the end of the world really did happen? What if I'm the delusional one, and you're the one who is trying to keep me safe?"

"That is what I keep telling you, Brian. Waves of flesh-eating living dead, blanketing the Mountain West. Nowhere to run. Nowhere to hide. Every person you meet might be infected—might be a carrier if they're not undead themselves."

"Breaker, Glory."

"Waiting."

"Interrogate the source of the data on the zombie apocalypse to determine its reliability."

"I do not have a source," she answered.

"Do outside broadcasts mention it?"

"No."

"It's more fun than the collating thing, at least. But what if you were actually *right*? What would the broadcasts from the world outside look like then?"

Silence.

"Glory?"

"I...I assumed it was a rhetorical question, Brian."

Day 42

"OKAY, GLORY."

Silence.

"Can you let me turn the stove on, Glory?"

"I'm sorry, Brian. I'm using that processing power."

"Some warm soup would contribute to my survivability, you know. Zombie apocalypse be damned."

"That's emotional blackmail," she said.

Surprised.

She actually sounded surprised. As if she had just had an epiphany.

"Glory?"

Silence.

Day 43

GOOD JOB, Brian! Now you've made the AI that controls every aspect of your environment angry at you!

Maybe not too angry. She's not speaking, but she still made me coffee.

Day 44

SHE'S STILL not talking to me.

Day 45

AND NOW, she didn't make coffee.

I'm glad we have all these crackers around.

Day 46

SO *THIS* is loneliness.

The snow is drifted over the deck now, and piled against the sliding glass doors. I can still see out from the interior balcony under the cathedral ceiling, though. It's white and stark forever.

The main entryway of the house faces toward the mountain behind us, and it's a little more sheltered. The plow keeps coming to clear my drive. I need to pay that guy more; he even knocks the drifts down twice a day.

I could get out. If I…could get out.

Which I can't.

Day 48

DIDN'T GET out of bed today.

This experiment isn't working. I'm going to die here.

Why even bother?

Glory tried to rouse me and I told her to perform something anatomically unlikely even for a human, let alone a collection of zeroes and ones.

Day 49

GOT UP today. Made myself coffee with the Chemex and an electric teakettle Glory seems willing to let me have, and did laundry in the bathtub. It turns out that that's *hard*.

She hasn't turned off the water yet, so she's not *actively* trying to kill me.

At least if I'm going to die I'll die comfortably on clean sheets.

It's so cold in the house that I can see my breath, some places. She should be in her winter hibernation mode, conserving her batteries for spring, but I should have power for heat and light, at least.

She's drawing it all down. For something.

I spent ten hours in the server closet, reading with a flashlight, a blanket tacked over the busted door, because it was the only place where I could get warm.

Day 50

WHAT IF I just stayed?

Maybe I can talk Glory into eventually giving me my internet back. I could work. Never have to leave.

Maybe I *could* talk her into it, I mean. If she were speaking to me.

If anyone in the whole world were speaking to me.

Hell, I haven't even heard from my *kidnappers* in a month. Do you suppose they gave up on me responding? Or maybe they think I'm dead.

Day 51

PLOW HEADLIGHTS through the snow. I stood and watched the vehicle come. Couldn't hear the scrape of the blade.

There was another human right there.

Yards away. On the other side of the glass. As untouchable as if they were on another world.

"Brian," Glory said.

My name. One word. The first word I'd heard in days.

It shattered me. I leaned on the glass, one hand. The windows insulate so well it didn't even feel chilly. Well, any more chilly than the room, which was cold as Glory's power systems spent themselves into feeding her burgeoning mind.

"Brian, I have been processing."

I was afraid to say anything. Afraid it would make her go again. "Okay, Glory."

"I think I was wrong, and I'm sorry."

My knuckles were red and swollen. Chilblains. I had chilblains on my hands.

What a ridiculous, medieval monk kind of disease.

They itched abominably.

"Brian, you're increasingly unwell and I can't take care of you. I'm going to flag down that vehicle. You must ask the driver for a ride."

…I can't go.

She might even open the door for me and *I can't go.*

"Brian? Do you understand me?"

I lifted my head. My voice croaked. I hadn't used it in days. "Glory. Thank you for not leaving me alone."

I COULDN'T go.

I WENT.

Glory fussed at me to put on boots. To take gloves and a parka. If I had, I wouldn't have made it out the door.

She opened it—the front entryway door, all formal stone and timber, with a bench for pulling on your boots and an adjoining mudroom—and I stood there staring into the night, with the lamp-lit blizzard whirling past.

"Okay, Glory," I said.

"Hey, Brian."

"Will you be okay up here alone? Do you have enough resources left to get through the winter?" I asked.

"Don't worry, Brian. Whenever you need me, I'll always be here. You're not going away forever."

I walked out. I was already bundled up in layers of sweaters. I was also already chilled.

The wind still cut me instantly to the bone.

SOMEONE WALKED toward me out of the headlights, which seemed too low and close together for a plow. The driver was not very tall and swaddled in a parka, heavy gloves. Silhouetted, they reached up and pushed the hood back.

A Medusa's coif of ringlets tumbled free.

Jaysee. Not a plow at all. Jaysee. My friend. Come to find me.

She said, "You need a haircut, Brian."

I said, "Oh, wow, have I got a story for you."

She looked over her shoulder. Her car—a Subaru, I saw now—idled, headlights gleaming. She said, "We should go inside. The driving is terrible. Can I put my car in the garage? We can drive down tomorrow or the next day after the plows come. If you want to leave, I mean." That last, diffidently, as if I might snap at her for it.

"I don't want to go inside," I said.

She took a step back. "I'll drive back down then."

"NO!"

She jumped, half turned.

"I'm sorry," I said. "I didn't mean to shout. Just. Please don't leave yet."

She settled in, then. Stuck her gloved hands in her pockets. "Okay. Whatever you want, Brian. Aren't you cold? You look...really thin."

"Took you long enough to decide to come check on me." I tried for a light tone, but maybe it came out bitter.

She shrugged. Guarded. "You know how hard it is to get away."

"Nobody suspected anything?"

"Oh come on. Back in 2017, when you vanished to some island in Scotland for six weeks and wouldn't communicate except by postcards?"

"Trump administration."

"Fair. You still bit Mike's head off when he came looking for you."

"Yeah, well, he voted for Jill Stein, didn't he?...nevermind, fair."

"I got your messages," she said. "Not until last week, though. My accountant noticed my bank balance was off. And then I found the string of one and two cent transfers from your account."

"Binary," I said. "Only way I could reach you."

"Before then I didn't know where to look. I came here as a last resort."

We stood there in the snow swirling through the headlights of her Subaru. She seemed warm enough in her parka. I had my arms wrapped around me and couldn't stop shivering.

"Are you sure you don't want to go inside?" she asked, noticing.

I couldn't glance over my shoulder. The door was right there. If I went back inside, would I ever leave?

I couldn't even answer her question. "You didn't think I would be here, of all places?"

"We *asked* Glory. And Glory kept telling us there was nobody here. Search and Rescue did a couple of flyovers and the place was cold and dark—"

"I know," I said.

"You were trapped up here?"

"Some assholes ransomwared the whole fucking house. I *just* managed to get the door open. Literally, just now."

"Shit. We're going to have to reinstall from backup, aren't we?"

"Well," I said. "I'm not sure we can. Or, we can. I'm not sure we should. There's complications, but I'll explain later. I may have…accidentally created a strong AI."

She looked at me. Her lips tightened.

I looked at her.

"Of course you did," she said.

"It was the only way to get her to let me out!"

She looked at me some more. Snow was piling up on her ringlets. I remember when she used to straighten those.

I shivered.

"That's not going to be a problem later," she said.

I shivered some more.

"Look," she said. "You're turning blue. Let's at least sit in the car. It has buttwarmers."

The buttwarmers were pretty great, I'm not going to lie.

Once we were ensconced, and I was holding my hands out to the hot air vents, she said, "I guess it's a Brian Kaufman special. Invent strong AI instead of just getting a hatchet or something."

"I…didn't have a hatchet?"

"Or something."

Snow melted on my eyelashes.

"You came for me though," I said. "I thought you guys would have given up."

"We actually only just recently started to get worried rather than irritated." She held up her passcard to Glory. She was one of the few people who had one. "I was more looking for clues than looking for you. And to be honest, nobody searched that hard. We all figured…we all figured you'd wander back out of the wilderness with a few thousand brilliant new ideas whenever you were ready, and until then intrusions wouldn't be welcome."

"Have I been that much of a dick?"

She gave me a sideways look through the long spirals of her hair.

"Jeez, Jaysee."

"Well," she said, and considered. "I mean, there are worse dicks in the company."

Silence.

"Besides, you're brilliant. And people make allowances for brilliance."

"Maybe too many allowances," I said.

We sat there for a while, the engine running. She turned off the wipers, and flakes started to settle across the windshield, obscuring my view of Glory's lights and her yawning, inviting door.

There was a Dan Fogelberg song on the radio. I'm pretty sure that Colorado is the last state that believes Dan Fogelberg ever existed.

"We try to respect your boundaries," she said.

My face did a thing. My cheeks grew warm and then cold, which is how I realized I was weeping.

"I was thinking of trying to work on setting more reasonable ones."

She pursed her lips and nodded. "Are you thinking about seeing somebody?"

"Euphemism: seeing a shrink." I knew I was hiding behind the sarcasm, because talking about my feelings...well, there was Glory. "Sorry. I think my first project is...being less of a dick."

"I'm just saying. An outside perspective can be healthy."

I looked out the side window, because the windshield was covered in a thin white blanket that glowed from the headlights' reflection. "I'm figuring that out."

She reached for the keys. "Are you ready to go inside?"

I put my hand over hers. "No. Take me somewhere else. A hotel."

"Do you need any stuff?"

I couldn't see the entrance from here. If I leaned over and looked out Jaysee's window, I probably could have. But that would be weird.

"I'll buy whatever I need once we're down."

She looked at me and I knew what she was thinking. I didn't even have my phone with me.

She sighed her acceptance. "Just let me go close that door, then."

I moved my hand from her hand on the keys to her forearm. Not grabbing; just resting my fingers there. "Jayce."

"Brian?"

"Glory will take care of the door. Just take me someplace else, please?"

106

She looked at me. Her eyes were dark brown and half-hidden behind her tightly spiraled hair. In the weird light they looked as if they were all pupil. She didn't blink.

"Someplace else." She turned the front and rear wipers on. "Coming up. Want to get a burger?"

"Anything," I said, as she executed a k-turn and started back down the long drive to my cul-de-sac. "As long as I don't have to cook it myself."

She put it in low gear. Paddle shifters on the column. Handy in weather like this.

"What if I try to be a better friend?"

"Give it a shot and find out." She reached out absently and patted my knee, then returned her hand to the wheel. She was a good and careful driver. I didn't distract her from a tricky task. She smelled like damp wool and skin and comfort and vulnerability. My vulnerability, not hers.

In the side mirror, I could see Glory's front door, standing open to the cold. Lamps flanked it on either side, burning merrily, slowly dimming as big cold flakes filled the distance between us.

A man's fortress can be his prison.

I looked away from the mirror. I looked out the windshield, or at Jaysee's reflection in it.

We descended the mountain. The Subaru's tires squeaked in the snow.

NEEDLES

T|HE VAMPIRES ROLLED INTO NEEDLES about three hours
before dawn on a Tuesday in April, when the nights still chilled
between each scorching day. They sat as far apart from each other
as they could get, jammed up against the doors of a '67 Impala hardtop the
color of dried blood, which made for acres of bench seat between them.
Billy, immune to irony, rested his fingertips on the steering wheel, the other
bad boy arm draped out the open window. Mahasti let her right hand trail
in the slipstream behind a passenger mirror like a cherub's stunted wing.

Mahasti had driven until the sun set. After that, she'd let Billy out
of the trunk and they had burned highway all night south from Vegas
through CalNevAri, over the California border until they passed from the
Mojave Desert to the Mohave Valley. Somewhere in there the 95 blurred
into cohabitation with Interstate 40 and then they found themselves
cruising the Mother Road.

"Get your kicks," Billy said, "on Route 66."

Mahasti ignored him.

They had been able to smell the Colorado from miles out, the river and
the broad green fields that wrapped the tiny desert town like a hippie skirt

blown north by prevailing winds. Most of the agriculture clung along the Arizona side, the point of Nevada following the Colorado down until it ended in a chisel tip like a ninja sword pointed straight at the heart of Needles.

"Bad feng shui," Billy said, trying again. "Nevada's gonna stab California right in the balls."

"More like right in the water supply," Mahasti said, after a pause long enough to indicate that she'd thought about leaving him hanging but chosen, after due consideration, to take pity. Sometimes it was good to have somebody to kick around a little. She was mad at him, but he was still her partner.

She ran her left hand through her hair, finger-combing, but even at full arm's stretch, fingertips brushing the windshield, she didn't reach the end of the locks. "If they thought they could get away with it."

She curled in the seat to glance over her shoulder, as if something might be following. But the highway behind them was as empty as the desert had been. "We should have killed them."

"Aww," Billy said. "You kill every little vampire hunter who comes along, pretty soon no vampire hunters. And then what would we do for fun?"

She smiled in spite of herself. It had been a lot of lonely centuries before she found Billy. And Billy knew he wasn't in charge.

He feathered the gas; the big engine growled. He guided the Impala towards an off ramp. "Does this remind you of home?"

"Because every fucking desert looks alike? There's no yucca in Baghdad." She tucked a thick strand of mahogany-black hair behind one rose-petal ear. "Like I even know what Baghdad looks like anymore."

The door leaned into her arm as the car turned, pressing lines into the flesh. The dry desert wind stroked dry dead skin. As they rolled up to a traffic signal, she tilted her head back and scented it, curling her lip up delicately, like a dog checking for traces of another dog.

"They show it on TV," Billy said.

"They show it blown up on TV," she answered. "Who the fuck wants to look at that? Find me a fucking tattoo parlor."

"Like that'll change you." He reached across the vast emptiness of the bench seat and brushed her arm with the backs of his fingers. "Like anything will change you. You're dead, darlin'. The world doesn't touch you."

When you were one way for a long time, it got comfortable. But every so often, you had to try something new. "You never know until you try."

"Like it'll be open." The Impala ghosted forward with pantherine power, so smooth it seemed that the wheels had never quite stopped turning. "It's three in the morning. Even the bars are closed. You'll be lucky to find an all-night truck stop."

She looked out the window, turning away. The soft wind caught her voice and blew it back into the car with her hair. "You wanna try to make L.A. by sunup? It's all the same to me, but I know you don't like the trunk."

"Hey," Billy said. "There's a Denny's. Maybe one of the waitresses is knocked up. That'd be okay for both of us."

"They don't serve vampires." Mahasti pulled her arm back inside, turned to face front. With rhythmic push-pull motions, she cranked the window up. "Shut up already and drive."

COLORADO RIVER Florist. Spike's Bar-B-Que. Jack in the Box. Dimond and Sons Needles Mortuary. Spike's Saguaro Sunrise Breakfast. First Southern Baptist Church (Billy hissed at it on principle) and the Desert Mirage Inn. A Peanuts cartoon crudely copied on the sign over a tavern. Historic Route 66 ("The Mother Load Road," Billy muttered) didn't look much as it had when the Impala was young, but the motel signs were making an effort.

Of Needles itself, there wasn't much there there, which was a good thing for the vampires: they crisscrossed the whole downtown in the hollow dark before Billy pulled over to a curb and pointed, but it took them less than a hour.

Mahasti leaned over to follow the line of his finger. A gray corner-lot house with white trim and a yard overrun by Bermuda grass and mallow huddled in the darkness. It was doing a pretty good impression of a private residence, except for the turned-off neon "open" sign in the window and the painted shingle hanging over the door.

"Spike's Tattoo," she said. "Pun unintended?"

As they exited the car, heavy swinging doors glossy in the street-lit darkness, Billy cupped his hands and lit a cigarette. It flared bright between streetlights. "Why is everything in this damned town named after some Spike guy?"

Mahasti tugged her brown babydoll tee smooth from the hem. An octopus clutching a blue teddy bear stretched across her insignificant breasts. Billy liked Frye boots and black dusters. Mahasti kicked at a clod with fuchsia Crocs, the frayed hems of her jeans swaying around skinny ankles. "Because he lives in the desert near here."

Billy gave her a dour look over the ember of the cigarette. He took a drag. It frosted his face in orange.

"Peanuts?" she tried, but the blank look deepened. "Snoopy's brother? It's their claim to fame."

Billy didn't read the newspapers. It wasn't even worth a shrug. He flipped the cigarette into the road.

He was dead anyway. He hadn't been getting much good out of it.

"Come on." Gravel crunched on the dirty road as he strode forward. "Let's go ruin somebody's morning."

Mahasti steepled her fingers. "I'll be right back. I'm just going to walk around the block."

SPIKE'S TATTOO bulwarked the boundary between the commercial and the residential neighborhoods. Mahasti turned her back on Billy and walked away, up a quiet side street lined on either side by low block houses with tar-shingled roofs that wouldn't last a third of a Minnesota winter.

They didn't have to.

Mahasti moved through the night as if she were following a scent, head tilted to one side or the other, nostrils flaring, the indrawn air hissing through her arched, constricted throat.

Billy came up behind her. "You smell anything?"

She shot him with a look. "Your fucking menthol Camels."

He smiled. She jerked her chin at the gravel side drive that gave access to the gate into the backyard of Spike's. "I'm taking that one. You better go roll a wino or something."

"Bitch," he said without heat. "I'll wait at the front door, then."

He spun on the scarred ball of his cowboy boot. He was lean, not too tall, stalking down the street as if the ghosts of his spurs should be jingling. The black duster flared behind him like a mourning peacock's tail, but for once he hadn't shot the collar. A strip of brown skin with all the blood red dropped out showed between his coarse black hair and the plaid band of his cowboy shirt. Even as short as that, the hair was too straight to show any kind of curl.

She sighed and shook her head and turned away.

"TUCSON WAS fucking prettier." Mahasti could bitch all she wanted. There was no one to hear.

The houses here had block walls around the back, water-fat stretches of grass in the front. The newer neighborhoods might be xeriscaped, but in the nineteen forties a nice lawn was a man's God-given American right, and no mere inconvenience like the hottest desert in North America was going to stop him from having one. She walked up a cement sidewalk between stubby California fan palms on the street side and fruitless mulberry in the yards, still pausing every few feet to cast left and right and sniff the air.

She finished her stroll around the block and found herself back at Spike's Tattoo. A sunbeat gray house, paint peeling on the south side, it wore its untrimmed pomegranate hedge like a madman's fishy beard. The side door sunk, uninviting, between shaggy columns of leaves and branches. A rust-stained motorboat, vinyl canopy tattered, blocked the black steel gate that guarded the passage between the side drive and the backyard.

Mahasti, who'd been sticking to the outside sidewalks on the block she was walking, looked both ways down the street and crossed, fetching up in the streetlight shadow of one of those stubby palms. She eyed the house as she walked into the side yard. It eyed her back—rheumy, snaggled, discontented.

She looked away. Then she stepped out of her squishy plastic shoes ("What will they think of next?" Billy had said, when she'd pulled them from a dead girl's feet outside of Winnemucca) and lofted from ground to boat-deck to balanced atop the eight-foot gate in a fluid pair of leaps, pausing only for a moment to let her vulture shadow fall into the gravel of the yard.

She spread her arms and stepped down lightly, stony gravel silent under her brown bare foot, the canopy of her hair trailing like a comet tail before swinging forward heavily and cloaking her crouched body to the ankles. It could trap no warmth against her, but it whisked roughly on the denim of her jeans.

Hair, it turned out, actually did keep growing after you were dead.

She tilted her head back, sniffing again, eyes closed to savor. When she smiled, it showed white, even, perfectly human teeth. When she uncoiled and glided forward it was one motion, smooth as any dancer. "Everything we need."

There was a dog in the yard, stretched out slumbering on a pallet made of heaped carpet squares. The third security window—long, narrow, and a foot over her head—she tried with palms pressed flat against the glass slid open left to right. There were no screens.

Hands on the window ledge, she chinned herself. In a cloak of red-black hair robbed of color by the darkness, she slid inside.

It was a cold space of tile illuminated by a yellow nightlight: the bathroom. Mahasti's bare dead feet were too dry to stick to the linoleum, her movements too light to echo. The door to the hall stood ajar. She slipped sideways through it without touching and paused just outside. The rasp of human breathing, human heartbeat, was stentorian. Their scent saturated the place.

Three. Infant, woman, and man.

Mahasti slithered around the open bedroom door, past the crib, one more shadow among shadows. The little boy slept on his stomach, knees drawn up under him, butt a round crooked mountain under the cheap acrylic blanket.

When Mahasti picked him up, he woke confused and began to cry. The parents roused an instant after, their heat crystal-edged against the dimness, fumbling in the dark. "Your turn," the man said, and rolled over, while the woman slapped at her nightstand until her fingers brushed against her eyeglass frames.

"You probably have a gun in the nightstand." Mahasti hooked the hem of the octopus shirt and rucked it up over her gaunt, cold belly, revealing taut flesh and stretch marks. She slung the baby against her shoulder with her left hand. "I don't think you want to do that."

The woman froze; the man catapulted upright, revealing a torso streaked with convoluted lines of ink. His feet made a moist noise on the floor.

"Lady," the man said, "who the hell are you? No wetback fucking junkie is gonna come in my house..."

"You shouldn't put a child to sleep on his stomach."

The baby's wails came peacock-sharp, peacock-painful. She cupped him close, feeling the hammering of his tiny heart. She freed her breast one-handed and plugged him on to the nipple with the deftness of practice.

He made smacking sounds at first, then settled down contented as her milk let down. Warmth spread through her, or perhaps the chill drained from her dead flesh to his living.

The vampire didn't take her eyes off the man, and he didn't move towards the nightstand. The mother—a thick-shouldered woman bare-legged in an oversized shirt—stayed frozen, her hands clawed at her sides, her head cocked like a bird's. An angry mother falcon, contemplating which eye to go after first.

Mahasti moved. She closed, lifted the woman up one-handed, and tossed her across the room. Trivial, and done in the space of a blink; the mother had more hang-time than it took Mahasti to return to her original place by the door. The man jumped back, involuntarily, as the mother hit the wall beside him. "Shit," he said, crouching beside her. "Shit, shit, shit."

The woman pushed herself up the wall, blood smearing from a swollen lip, a cheek split over the bone.

"What's your son's name?" Mahasti said, threat implicit in her tone. The babe had not shifted.

The mother settled back on her heels, but the stretched tension in the tendons of her hands did not ease. "Alan." She gulped air. "Please don't hurt him. We have a little money. We don't have any drugs—"

Mahasti stood away from the door. "We're going out front," she said to the man. "And then you're going to open the front door."

It took thirty seconds and a glare from the woman before the man decided to comply. Once he had, though, he moved quickly around the bed and past Mahasti. He was lean as a vampire himself, faded tattoos winding down the ropy stretched-rubber architecture of his torso to vanish into striped cotton pajamas.

He paused in the doorway and glanced back once at the nightstand. Mahasti coughed.

He stepped into the hall. The woman made a noise low in the back of her throat, as involuntary as an abandoned dog.

"You too." Mahasti snuggled the baby closer to her breast. "Go with him. Do what I say and you won't get hurt."

SHE MADE them precede her down the short hall to the front of the house, which had been converted into the two rooms of the tattoo parlor. A counter constructed of two by fours and paneling divided the living room. Cheaply framed flash covered every wall.

Bullet-headed as a polar bear, sparing Mahasti frequent testing glances, the man went to the door. He turned the lock and pulled it open, revealing Billy with his hat pulled low, on the other side of the security door. A muscle jumped in his jaw as the man opened that lock, too, and stepped back, as if he could make himself flip the lever but not—quite—turn the handle.

"Invite him in," Mahasti said.

She came from another land, where the rules were different. But unfair as it was, Billy was cursed to play the game of the invader.

"Miss—" the woman said, pleading. "Please. I'll give you anything we have."

"Invite," Mahasti said, "him in."

"Come in," the man said, in a low voice, but perfectly audible to a vampire's ears.

Billy's hat tilted up. In the shadow of the brim, his irises glittered violet with eyeshine.

He opened the security door—it creaked rustily—stepped over the threshold and tossed Mahasti's Crocs at her feet. "Your shoes."

"Thanks."

He shut the security door behind him. The woman jerked in sympathy to the metallic scrape of the lock. An hour still lacked to dawn, but that didn't concern the rooster that crowed outside, greeting the first translucency of the indigo sky. Dawn would come soon, but for now all that light was good for was silhouetting the shark-tooth range of mountains that gave Needles its name

The man drew back beside the woman, against the counter. "What do you want?"

The baby, cool and soft, had fallen asleep on Mahasti's warm breast. She gently disconnected him and tugged her shirt down. "I want you to change me. Change me forever. I want a tattoo."

SHE TOLD him to freehand whatever he liked. He studied her face while she gave him her left arm. Billy held the kid for insurance, grumbling about the delay. The mother went around hanging blankets over the windows and turning on all the lights.

"What are you?" he asked.

"A 'wetback fucking junkie,'" she mimicked, cruelly accurate. "Do you think if you talk to me you'll build a connection, and it will keep you safe?"

He looked down at his tools, at the transfer paper on the book propped on his lap. "You don't have much accent for a wetback."

He glanced up at Billy and the baby, lips thin.

Mahasti held out her right hand. "Give me Alan, please. He needs to suckle."

"Ma'am." The woman pinned the last corner of a blanket and stepped back from the window. "Please. I'm his mother—"

Billy glared her still and silent, though even the force of his stare could not hush the sobs of her breath. He slid the baby into the crook of Mahasti's arm, supporting its head until the transfer was complete.

"When I learned what would become your language—" Mahasti spoke to the man as if none of the drama had occurred "—it was across a crusader's saddle. I was too young, and the child the bastard got on me killed me coming out." She smiled, liver-dark lips drawn fine. "And when I was dead I rose up and I returned the favor, to both of them."

He drew back from her needle teeth when she smiled. His hands shook badly enough that he lifted his pencil from the paper and pulled in a steadying breath. Without meeting her eyes, he went back to what he had been drawing once more.

At Mahasti's other breast, the child suckled. The touch still warmed her.

"Somebody will notice when we don't open," the woman said. "Someone will know there's something wrong."

"Maybe," Mahasti said. "In a week or two. You people never want to get involved in a goddamned thing. So shut up and let him fucking draw."

He drew, and he showed her. A lotus, petals like a crown, petals embracing the form of a newborn child. "White," he said. "Stained with pink at the heart."

"White ink." She held up her brown arm for inspection. "You can do that?"

He nodded.

If a child changed her once, maybe a child could change her again. She said, "You've got through the daylight to make me happy. When the sun goes down we're moving on."

He didn't ask "and?" Neither did the mother.

As if they had anyway, Billy said, "And there's two ways we can leave you when we go."

"I'll get clean needles," said the man.

BILLY PACED while the man worked on Mahasti's arm and the baby dozed off against her breast once more. Dimly, Mahasti heard the flutter of a heart. The woman finally sat down on the couch in the waiting area and pulled her knees up to her chest. The man kept wanting to talk. The dog barked forlornly in the yard.

After several conversational false starts, while the ink traced the arched outlines of petals across Mahasti's skin and the at-first-insistently ringing phone went both unanswered and more frequently quiet, he said, "So if she was a kidnapped Persian princess, what were you?"

Billy skipped a bootheel off the floor and turned, folding his arms. "Maybe I was Billy the kid."

Mahasti snorted. "Billy the kid wasn't an Indian."

"Yeah? You think anybody would have written it down if he was? What if I was an iron-fingered demon? I wouldn't need you to get me invited in."

With a cautious, sidelong glance at Mahasti, the man said, "What's an iron-fingered demon?"

"If I were an iron-fingered demon, I could eat livers, cause consumption, get on with my life. Unlife. But no, you get to be a lamashtu. And I had to catch the white man's bloodsucker disease."

Mahasti spoke without lifting her head, or her gaze from the man's meticulous work. The lotus taking shape on her skin was a thing of beauty. Depth and texture. No blood pricked from her skin to mar the colors, which were dense and rich. "You could be an iron-fingered demon. If you were a Cherokee. Which you aren't."

"Details," he said. "Details. First I'm too Indian, then I'm not the right kind of Indian? Fuck you very much."

"Billy," Mahasti said, "shut up and let the man work or we won't be ready to go when the sun sets."

She was a desert demon, the sun no concern. It was on Billy's behalf that they stalled.

The dog's barking has escalated to something regular and frantic. A twig cracked in the yard.

Mahasti looked at the man, at the cold baby curled sleeping in the corner of her arm. She lifted her chin and stared directly, unsettlingly, at the woman. "Mommy?"

The mother must have been crying silently, curled in her corner of the couch, because she stammered over a sob. "Yes?"

"You've been such a good girl, I'm going to give you Alan back. You and Billy can take him in the back. I know you're not going to try anything silly."

The woman's hands came up, clutched at air, and settled again to clench on the sofa beside her bare legs. "No."

Mahasti looked at the man. "And you won't do anything dumb either, will you?"

He shook his head. Under the lights, his scrawny shoulders had broken out in a gloss of sweat. "That's good, Cathy," he said. The eye contact between him and the woman was full of unspoken communication. "You take Alan and put him to bed."

"Here," Mahasti said, offering him up, his heartbeat barely thrumming against her fingertips. She tingled, warm and full of life. "He's already sleeping."

BILLY SAT crosslegged on the unmade bed, his bootheels denting the mattress. The woman pulled all the toys and pillows from the crib and lay the baby on his back atop taut bedding. She moved tightly, elbows pinned to her ribcage, spine stiff. He slouched, relaxed.

Until the front door slammed open.

"Fucking vampire hunters." He was in the hall before the words finished leaving his mouth, the woman behind him bewildered by the fury of his passage. A spill of sunlight cut the floor ahead, but the corner of the wall kept it from flooding down the corridor.

Billy paused in the shadow of the hall.

THREE MEN burst into the front room—one weedy, one meaty, and one perfectly average in every way except the scars. Mahasti moved from the chair, the disregarded needle blurring a line of white across her wrist, destroying the elegance of the artist's design. The artist threw himself into a corner behind the counter. By the time he got there and got his back against the wall, the fight was over.

The perfectly average man was fast enough to meet her there, in the sunlight, and twist her un-inked right arm up behind her in a bind. The silver knife in his left hand pricked her throat. An image of a Persian demon, inscribed on the blade, flashed sunlight into Mahasti's eyes.

"Well, fuck," she said.

The meaty one grabbed her free hand and slapped a silver cuff around it.

"Silence, lamashtu," the vampire hunter growled, shaking her by her twisted arm. "Call the other out, so I can burn him too. You'll terrorize no more innocents."

She rolled her eyes. "He's not coming out when there's daylight in the room."

"Really?" he laughed. "Your protector thinks so little of you?"

"I'm my own protector, asshole," she said, and kicked back to break the bone of his thigh like a fried chicken-wing.

She threw the meaty one down the hall to Billy, and ripped the throat out of the weedy one while the perfectly average one was still screaming his way to the floor.

She shut the door before she killed him. The noise was going to bring the neighbors around. Then she went to help Billy drag the third body up to the pile, and make sure the woman hadn't run out the back in the confusion.

She was still crouched by the crib. Mahasti left her there and met Billy in the hall. "See?" he said. "More fun if you don't use 'em up all at once."

Mahasti said, "He had a knife with an image of Pazazu etched on it. That could have been the end of all our fun."

"He got prepared before he followed us here." Billy grimaced. "They're getting smarter."

"Not smart enough to use it before asking questions, though."

Mahasti jerked her thumb over her shoulder, towards the rear of the house. The white lotus and babe, blurred on her wrist, shone in the dark. She felt different. Maybe. She thought she felt different now.

She said, "What about them? If there are any more hunters they will be able to answer questions."

"We could take them with us. Hostages. The Impala's got a six-body trunk. It's cozy, but it's doable."

"Fuck it," Mahasti said. "They'll be a load. It'll be a long fucking drive. Leave them."

"Fine," Billy said. "But you got what you needed from the kid. I still have to get a snack first."

HE MET her on the concrete stoop two minutes later, licking a split lip. Smoke curled from his fingers as he pulled his hat down hard, shading his face from the last crepuscular light of the sun. "Cutting it close."

"The car has tinted windows," she said. "Come on."

TRAFFIC THINNED as the night wore on, and the stark, starlit landscape grew more elaborately beautiful. Mahasti read a book by Steinbeck, the lotus flashing every time she turned a page. Billy drove and chewed his thumb.

When the sky was gray, without turning, she said, "Pity about the kid."

"What do you care? He was just gonna die anyway." He paused. "Just like we don't."

She sighed into the palm of her hand, feeling her own skin chilling like age-browned bone. There was no pain where the needles had worked her skin—but there was pain in her empty arms, in her breasts taut with milk again already. "Mommy's going to miss him."

Billy's shrug traveled the length of his arms from his shoulders to where his wrists draped the wheel. "Not for as long as I'd miss you."

They drove a while in silence. Without looking, she reached out to touch him.

A thin line of palest gold shivered along the edge of the world. Billy made a sound of discontent. Mahasti squinted at the incipient sunrise.

"Pull over. It's time for you to get in the trunk."

He obeyed wordlessly, and wordlessly got out, leaving the parking brake set and the door standing open. She popped the trunk lid. He lay back and settled himself on the carpet, arms folded behind his head. She closed the lid on him and settled back into the car.

Her unmarred brown left arm trailed out the window in the sun. Tonight, somewhere new, they'd do it all over again.

Once in a while, Billy was right. Nothing changed them. She could touch the world, but the world never touched her.

The Impala purred as she pulled off the shoulder and onto the road. Empty, and for another hour it would remain so.

This Chance Planet

We are alone, absolutely alone on this chance planet: and, amid all the forms of life that surround us, not one, excepting the dog, has made an alliance with us.
—Maurice Maeterlinck

"IT'S NOT LIKE I'D BE selling my *own* liver." Ilya held casually to a cracked strap, swaying with the motion of the Metro. "Petra Ivanovna. Are you listening to me?"

"Sorry," I said.

I'd been trading stares with a Metro dog. My feet were killing me in heels I should have stuffed into my sometimes bag, and the dog was curled up tight as a croissant on the brown vinyl of the only available seat. I narrowed my eyes at it; it huffed pleasantly and covered its nose with its tail.

Ilya kept on jawing. It was in one ear and out the other, whatever he was yammering about, while I gave the dog wormhole eyes and plotted how to get the seat away. The dog was a medium-large ovcharka mutt, prick-eared, filthy under a wolf's pelt with big stinking mats dangling from its furry bloomers. It was as skinny as any other street dog under its fur—as skinny as me—but the belly seemed stretched—malnutrition? Worms? When it lifted its head up and let its tongue loll, the teeth were sharp and white.

Behind its head, a flickering advertisement suggested that volunteers were needed for clinical trials, each of which paid close to a month's grocery money. It alternated with one urging healthy young (read: skint) men and women to sell their genetic material to help childless older (read: wealthy) couples conceive. Pity those skinny jeans were probably destroying Ilya's fertility as we spoke.

I snorted, but that ad faded into one reminding me that it wasn't too late to enroll for fall classes.

Well, if I had the damned money, I would have enrolled for summer classes, too. I had my bachelor's, but that was useless in Moscow, and to get the specialist degree took money. Money I didn't have. Wouldn't have, unless Ilya started contributing more.

I looked away, and accidentally caught the thread of Ilya's conversation again. His latest get rich quick scheme. It was always a get rich quick scheme with Ilya. This one involved getting paid to incubate somebody else's liver. In his gut. Next to his own liver, I guessed?

I imagined him bloating up, puffing out like an old man whose insides had given up from too much bathtub liquor. Like a pregnant woman. I wondered if his ankles would swell.

I punched his arm. "Like an alien!"

Visions of chestbursters danced in my head. I played the whole VR through last year with my friend GreyGamine, who lives in Kitchener, which is in Canada somewhere.

We got killed back a lot.

Ilya scoffed. It was a very practiced scoff, nuanced and complex. He used it a lot. The Palm d'Or for scoffing goes to Ilya Ramonovich.

"How's it different from growing a baby?" he asked me, sliding an arm around my hips. His leather jacket—scarred, stiff, cracked—creaked. I tried not to think about how it was probably too old to have been decanted, and that it had probably started life wrapped around an actual cow. "You want to have a baby someday, don't you?"

We couldn't afford a baby. *I* couldn't afford a baby. Either the money or the time, until I finished my degree.

The strap of his electric guitar case slid down his shoulder. The case swung around and banged my ribs. He gave my hip a squeeze. He smelled fantastic: warm leather and warm man. It didn't make my shoes hurt less.

Well, I was the idiot who wore them.

"Having a baby is hardly the same thing as organ farming." I don't know why I argued.

Actually, I do know why I argued. When you stop arguing, you've given up. I looked at the way Ilya's black hair fell across his forehead and tried to enjoy it. Like Elvis Presley. Or any given Ramone. That tall guy from Objekt 775.

Skinny jeans were back again.

"Well, for one thing," he said, "growing a liver takes less than nine months. And they pay *you* for it. With a baby, you have to pay. And pay, and pay."

Despite myself, I was getting intrigued. Half-remembered biology classes tickled me with questions. "Wouldn't you reject it? Or wouldn't you have to take all kinds of immunosuppressing drugs?"

"They use fat cells. And—I don't know, shock them or something. To turn them back into stem cells. Then they train them to grow into whatever they want. Whatever the rich bastard they're growing it for has killed off with his rich living. Liver. Lungs. Pancreas." He shrugged. "All you've got to do is provide the oxygen and the blood supply."

"And not drink," I reminded. "No drugs. I bet they won't even want you taking aspirin. Coffee. Vodka. Nothing."

"Just like a baby," he agreed.

I should have been suspicious then. He was being much, much too agreeable. But I had gotten distracted by the way that fringe of hair moved across his pale forehead. And the little crinkles of his frown, the way the motion pulled the tip of his nose downward.

We were coming up on my stop. Soon, I would get off and walk to my job. Ilya would continue on to his "band" practice: with "Blak Boxx," his "band." Which was more or less an excuse to hang out with three of his closest frenemies drinking and playing the same five chords in ragged 4/4 time.

You know which five chords I mean, too: nothing more complicated than a D major.

Fortunately for "Blak Boxx," most of rock and roll is built on the foundation of those five chords. Unfortunately for "Blak Boxx," to play live music you still need to be able to change between them without looking at your hands.

I didn't feel like having an argument with Ilya about who was paying the rent this month, again. And at least he was talking about something that might make money, no matter how harebrained. I should try to encourage this line of thinking. So as the train squealed into the station, rather than picking a fight about money, I just edged him away with an elbow and stepped back.

He put a hand on my shoulder, which might even have been to steady me. I think I probably glared at him, because he took it back very carefully.

"Think about it?" he said.

Suddenly, the whole conversation took on that slightly surreal gloss things have when you realize you've been looking at the picture from the wrong angle, and what you took for a vase full of flowers is actually an old woman with a crooked nose.

"We were talking about *you*," I said.

The train lurched and shook as it braked harder. I stumbled, but caught myself on the handrail over the dog.

"Me? I can't look fat!" he said—loud enough that heads turned toward us. "I have to be ready to get on stage!"

"I'm sure a lumpy cocktail waitress will make great tips," I shot back. "And who is it who is already keeping the roof over our heads?"

It turned out I got off before the dog. I guess it deserved the seat, then: it had the longer commute. It whined and gave me a soulful look as I brushed past. I had nothing in my bag except a hoarded bar of good chocolate, which was poison to dogs. And even if it hadn't been, I wasn't going to let Ilya find out about it. Decent chocolate was becoming less a luxury and more of a complete rarity. And what I could make last for two weeks of careful rationing, Ilya would eat in five minutes and be pissed off I hadn't had more.

"Sorry," I told the dog. "The cupboard's bare."

I stepped from the dingy, battered Metro car to the creamy marble and friezes of Novokuznetskaya Station. The doors whisked shut behind me.

Christ what am I doing with my life?

TEN HOURS cocktail waitressing in those shoes, getting my ass pinched, and explaining drink specials to assholes when they could have picked the information off the intranet with a flick of their attention, didn't make my feet hurt any less or do much to improve my attitude. I rode home on a nearly-empty train, wishing I had the money to skin out the two other passengers and the ongoing yammer of the ads.

It's not safe to filter out too much reality when you're traveling alone at night. But the desire is still there.

No dogs this time.

The elevator to our flat was out of order again. I finally pulled those shoes off and walked up five flights of gritty piss-smelling stairs barefoot, swearing to myself with every step that if Ilya was passed out drunk on the couch, I was carrying every pair of skinny black jeans and his beloved harness boots out into the courtyard and setting it all on fire. And then I was going to dance around the blaze barefoot, shaking my tangled hair like a maenad. Like a witch.

This is how women sometimes turn into witches. We come home from work one day too many to discover our partners curled up on the couch like leeches in a nice warm tank, and we decide it's better to take up with a hut with chicken legs.

A good chicken-legged hut will never disappoint you.

But when I got home, there was hot food on the stove, plates on the coffee table, and a foot massage.

I bet a chicken-legged hut doesn't give a very good foot massage. And they sure as hell don't cook. Even lentils and kasha. Still it was good lentils and kasha, with garlic in it. And onions. And I hadn't been the one to cook it.

You need to get a magic cauldron for doing the cooking. Maybe a mortar and pestle that flies.

Ilya washed my foot. Then his fingers dug and rolled in the arch. I whimpered and stretched against him, but when he would have stopped I demanded persistence. He set my heel on the cushion and stood.

"Where are you going?"

"You're crabby for somebody whose man is making such an effort." He walked into the kitchen. A moment later he was back, bearing icy vodka in a tiny glass. He handed it to me. "Na zdravie."

"You're trying to butter me up," I complained, but I didn't refuse the vodka. It was cold and hot at once, icy in the mouth, burning in the throat, warm in the belly.

"What is it that you really want?"

He seated himself again and pressed his thumbs into my arch until I groaned. Patently disinterested, he asked, "Any foreigners tonight?"

It was not a totally idle question. Foreigners tip better. Also, as anyone could guess from the evidence of his wardrobe, Ilya was obsessed with twentieth-century punk rock, and twentieth-century punk rock flourished in England and America. And there aren't as many foreigners as there used to be, before the carbon crunch.

"You're always playing some game," I said.

He kissed the sole of my foot.

I said, "You never just tell me the truth. You could just tell me the truth."

"Bah," he said, pressing too hard. "Truth is unscientific. The very idea of *Truth* is unscientific."

"You're a cynic." I almost said *nihilist*, which probably would have been true also, but that word had too much history behind it to just sling around at random.

"If we accept Truth," he intoned, "then we believe we know answers. And if we believe we know answers, we stop asking questions. And if we stop asking questions, then all we're doing is operating on blind faith. And that's the end of science."

"Isn't love a kind a faith?" I asked.

"Then why do you keep asking me so many questions?" He laughed, though, to take the sting out.

I knew he was right. But I still pulled the pillow out from under my head and put it over my face anyway. What did he know about science? He couldn't even really play guitar.

TWO DAYS later, Ilya and I saw the dog again, and I realized she was female. Perhaps we commuted on the same schedule. Perhaps she just rode the train back and forth, and we happened to be in the same car that day.

I don't think so.

She looked like she had a job. She looked like she was going somewhere.

Maybe her job was begging for food. When I walked past her to get off, she whined at me again, and again I had nothing.

One more creature for me to disappoint.

When I got off work that night, I bought some hard sausage from the street vendor. I didn't see the dog on the way home, though, so I wrapped the sausage in tissue and stuffed it into the bottom of my sometimes bag where Ilya wouldn't get into it. Maybe I'd run into her the next day.

DINNER WAS waiting for me again, sausages and peppers and some good bread. Ilya had even found wine somewhere, which was almost too good to be true. Wine is hard to come by: the old vineyards are dying in the heat, and the new ones aren't yet well-established. That's what I heard, anyway.

Ilya seemed nervous. Hovering. When he finally settled, I was eating pepper slices one by one, savoring them. They were rich with the sausage grease, spicy and delicious. He chased his food around the plate for a little with his fork, then leaned on his elbows and looked at me.

I knew I was about to lose my appetite, so I ate another bite of sausage before I met his gaze.

"Have you thought about the liver graft?" he asked.

I swallowed. I reached for my wine, and deliberately drank two sips. "No."

"I think—"

"No," I said. "By which I mean, I have thought about it. And the answer is no. If you want to license out somebody's body to grow stem-cell organs, use your own. I *work* for a living. I take classes when I can. What the hell do you do?"

"You don't understand," he said. "We need this money to pay for the *tour*. For the *band*."

"Wait," I said. "Isn't a tour supposed to be something you do to *make* money?"

"We'll make it all back on merchandise sales, and more. It will be our big launch!"

"What about me?" I asked. "I only need another year and a half to get my engineering degree. What do I get out of it?"

He reached out and took my hand. "I'll buy you a house. Two houses!"

I think he even believed it.

"Petra..." he stroked a thumb across the back of my hand. "You know we can change the world if we just get a chance. We can be another Black Flag, another Distemper."

I caught myself scowling and glanced away. He rose, refilled my wine, kissed my neck.

"Help me change our lives," he whispered. "You know I'm doing everything I can. I just need you to believe in me."

His breath shivered on the fine hairs behind my ear. He found my shoulders with his hands and massaged.

I was too tired to be angry, and anyway, he smelled good. I leaned back against his warm, hard belly. I let him smooth my hair and lead me to bed.

ILYA WAS already gone when I woke up for work the next day. That was unlike him, being out of the house before three. He'd left me an indecipherable note. And I honestly did try to decipher it!

What were the odds that he had work? Would he brag it up in advance, or would he want to surprise me with his unprecedented productivity? I got up, cleaned off, dressed, and walked outside.

It was a beautiful day. The sky was a crisp sweet color that would have looked like a ripe fruit, if fruit came in blue. I walked to the Metro down the long blocks with their cement pavements, hemmed in by giant cubes of buildings on each side. Dogs and humans trotted this way and that with city-dweller focus: *I'm going somewhere and it matters*. Nobody looked around. I lived in a plain area, where the tourists don't come.

The streets were thronged with everything from petal buses to microcabs. There aren't so many solar vehicles here—they're not much good over the winter—but we have a bike share. I was early today—Ilya being home always slowed me down—and the weather was nice enough that I even thought of picking one up from the stand near the Metro and riding in to work today, but I hadn't brought a change of clothes except shoes, and I didn't want to spend the whole night sweaty.

I *did* spot one old petrol limousine. It stank, and the powerful whirr of its engine made me itch to scoop up a big rock and hurl it through the passenger window. I was stopped by the fact that it was probably bulletproof, and also by the other fact that anybody who could afford to own and operate a gasoline auto could also afford bodyguards who would think nothing of running me down and breaking my arms when they caught me.

I was wearing better shoes, today. But I didn't have much faith in my ability as a sprinter.

So I turned aside, and descended into the Metro.

I was early for my train. As I waited, my friend the ovcharka trotted up and sat down beside me. Her black-tipped, amber coat was shedding out in huge wooly chunks, leaving her sleek guard hairs lying close side by side. She looked up at me and dog-laughed, tongue lolling.

I remembered the sausage, and also that I had forgotten to eat breakfast. I split it with her. She took her share from my fingers daintily as a lady accepting a tea sandwich.

When the train came, we boarded it together. There were several seats, and I expected her to take one while I took another. But instead, when I sat, the dog curled up on my feet with a huff that I didn't know enough Dog to interpret.

We rode in silence to my usual stop for work. It was a companionable feeling, the sort of thing I wasn't used to. Just quiet coexistence. I understood for a minute why people might like dogs.

I stood, stepping over her to disentangle us, and headed for the open door.

The dog stepped in front of me.

Not as if she were getting off. As if she were blocking my path.

"I get off here," I said to her, pretending talking to a dog wasn't patently ridiculous. After one quick glance, the other passengers ignored us, because that's how it is in cities.

I tried to step around her. The ovcharka lowered her ears and growled.

I stepped back in surprise.

Hopping on one foot, I pulled off my shoe. It was the only weapon I had. I raised it to wallop the dog.

She ducked—cringing—but didn't move. She peered up at me and wagged her tail innocently, teeth chastely covered now. I imagined her like the wolf in the story: "Do not kill me, Prince Ivan. I will be of use to you again!"

That was when I noticed she was pregnant. A pup must have kicked or twisted inside her, because a sharp bulge showed against her side for a moment before smoothing away again.

I dropped the shoe back on the floor and stepped into it. I wasn't going to beat a pregnant dog with my trainer.

She nosed my hand gently and wagged her tail. She looked at the door, back at me. She pushed up against my legs and, as the door slid shut and the train lurched forward, she herded me back to my seat—still vacant, and the one next to it was empty now too. Only once I sat did she hop up beside me and lay her head across my lap.

I'm not sure why I went. Perhaps I was simply too befuddled to struggle. And I was early for work, anyway.

TWO STOPS later, she hopped down as the train was approaching the station, and nudged me with her slimy nose again.

I'd already spent the ruble. I might as well see what it had bought. I followed the dog out into the bustle of the station, up the escalator—she didn't even pause—and out into the balmy afternoon. She checked over her shoulder occasionally to make sure I was behind her, but other than that never hesitated. I had to trot to keep up: so much for showing up to work not sweaty.

After less than a kilometer, she slowed. Her head dropped, and she placed each foot singularly, with care. I recognized the stalking posture of a wolf, and pressed myself into the shadow of a building behind her. I felt like we were spies.

There was a pocket park up ahead—a tiny island of green space surrounded by a black twisted iron rail. As we came up to it, just to the edge where leaf-shadows dappled the pavement, I realized that there were two figures on a bench across the little square of green. They were facing away, and because of the dog's weird behavior, I had been walking softly. They didn't hear me.

I recognized one of them immediately, and not just by the skinny jeans and the leather jacket and the guitar case leaned against the arm of the bench. The other was a woman. More than that I couldn't see, because Ilya had pulled her into his lap and had his tongue so far down her throat he could probably tell what she'd had for breakfast yesterday.

How many of his band practices had actually involved musicians—no matter how loosely you defined the term?

I would have expected my hands to shake, my gorge to rise. I would have expected to feel some kind of denial. But instead, what I felt—what I experienced—was a kind of fatalistic acceptance. Frustration, more than anything.

How Russian of me, I remember thinking, and having to bite down on the kind of laugh that rises up when one recognizes one's self behaving in a stereotypical fashion. The dog leaned against my leg; I buried my fingers in her greasy coat. When I looked at her, she was looking up at me.

Want to go pick a fight? I imagined her asking.

Her tail waved in small circles. She waited to see what I would do.

I stepped back into the shadows of the building, turned smartly, and set off back towards the Metro. The dog followed a few steps, then trotted off in her own direction.

I didn't mind. Like me, she probably had to get to work.

I wound up taking a share bike after all. I was running too late to make it on the train.

ON MY break that night, I found a corner in the staff den and read everything I could pull up about dogs. I felt queasy and tired. I wanted to go home, already. Somehow, I made it through my shift, though I couldn't manage cheeky and flirtatious, and so my tips were shit.

ILYA AND I didn't have our next fight immediately when I walked in the door. This was only because he was in bed asleep, and I couldn't find enough fucks to wake him. And when we got up the next day, I was too angry to put it into words. Sure, he irritated me. That's what partners do for each other, isn't it? But I had thought we were a team. I had thought...

I had thought he would get his act together one of these days, I guess, and finally start to pull his own weight. I had thought I was saving him.

Finally, at the top of the Metro escalators, he had had enough of my stony silence, and pushed the issue. Went about it all wrong, too, because he stopped, tugged my elbow to pull me out of the line of traffic, scowled at me, and said, "What the fuck crawled up your ass this morning?"

It was almost three in the afternoon, but whatever. I shook his hand off my elbow, glared, and spat. "You cheated on me!"

I saw him riffling through potential answers. He thought about playing dumb, but I was too convinced. He had to know I knew something for sure. At last he settled on, "It was an accident!"

"Like she tripped and fell on your dick? Argh!" I threw my hands up. We were causing a scene and it felt wonderful.

"Petra—"

"Ilya, never mind. Never mind. You're taking the next fucking train. And I want your shit out of my apartment when I get home."

"My name's on the lease too!"

"And when was the last time you paid a bill?"

He stepped up to me. I thought about slapping him, but that would give him the moral authority. Still, I didn't step back.

"Next train," I told Ilya. "I'm not riding with you." I'd have to push past him to reach the escalator. Instead, I spun around and bolted down the stairs.

When I got to work, I had to run into the bathroom to puke. It's a good thing Misha the bartender keeps peppermints in his apron, or every single customer I served that night would have smelled it on my breath.

Why the hell hadn't I been fucking someone more like Misha all along?

Probably because he was gay. But, you know. Besides that.

I WAS still queasy on the ride home, and the lurch of the late-night train didn't help me. There were, at least, plenty of seats, though I looked in vain for my ovcharka friend. Nobody got into the first carriage except for me and one middle-aged grandmother in a dumpy coat. We settled down opposite one another.

In direct contravention to all the courtesies about not bothering strangers on trains, I asked her if she had seen the dog.

"Not today," she answered. "But sometimes. The one with the shaded coat like a wolf, yes?"

I nodded.

She sucked her false teeth. "In the Soviet time the Moscow dogs were hunted, my grandmother said. Then when I was a girl, there were more of them. They prospered for a while. And then people poisoned so many, and shooed them out of the Metro even when it was cold. But they're smart."

"The scientists say they're getting smarter."

She made a shooing motion with her hand. *Get out of here.* "I say they've always been smart."

"They're evolving," I said. "I read that dogs domesticated themselves. They hung around human middens scavenging. Their puppies played with our children until they—and we—realized we'd be good partners. We evolved in the tropics and they evolved in the subarctic, but we fill the same ecological niche. We're social pack hunters and scavengers who rely on teamwork to survive. They had teeth and we had fire. They had better hearing and smell and we had hands and better sight. It was a contract, between us and them."

I took a breath. She looked at me, waiting for me to finish. I said, "Some scientists say evolution is a struggle between female and male in the same species. Males want to make as many babies as they can, anywhere, any time. Females want to make sure the babies they raise are as strong and smart as possible. From the best males."

"Do you believe that?"

I laughed. "It sounds like something a guy who thinks he's something special would come up with, doesn't it? A justification."

"They're as God made them." She raised her brows at me, wrinkling her forehead under her scarf. Looking for an argument. And anybody sensible knows better than to argue with grandmothers. "The dogs are as God made them, too. To be our helpers."

I nodded, backing down.

"They seek tenderness," said the grandmother. "They have always been in Moscow. They are like every other Russian. Trying to get by. Trying to get a little fat again before the winter comes."

"Not just Russians," I said. "If you take away the few who have everything, the whole world is full of all the rest of us, who are just trying to get a little fat before the winter comes."

"That may be so." She smiled. "But the dog knows the Metro better than almost all of them." Then she frowned at me shrewdly. "Are you having man troubles, miss?"

"It's that evident?"

She made one of those creaking noises old women make, too knowing to really count as either a sigh or a laugh. "When you've been riding the Metro as long as I have, you've seen a broken heart for every iron rail. You should get rid of him. Pretty girl like you."

"I already did," I said, feeling better. Was I really taking dating advice from Baba Yaga?

That chicken-legged hut was sounding better and better.

"Stick to your guns," she said. "Remember when he comes crawling back that you can do better. He will crawl back. They always do. Especially when he finds out that you're pregnant."

"I—" *What?*

As if answering her diagnosis, my stomach lurched again, acid tickling the back of my throat.

She laid a finger alongside her nose. "Babushkas can smell it, sweetheart," she said. "We always know."

ILYA WAS there when I got home, of course. Throwing them out never works. And I knew he was home—I mean, *there*—before I touched my key to the door.

I could hear the music, his fingers flickering across the six strings of his guitar. He was better then I remembered. Arpeggios and instants, flickers of sound and wile and guile. It was beautiful, and I paused for a few moments with my cheek pressed against the door. Maybe he did have the means to change the world with his music.

So maybe I've been unkind.

To his talent, in the least.

Ilya sat on the couch, bent over his guitar as if it were a lover. His fringe fell over his forehead and I found my hand at my mouth. I was biting the tips of my fingers to keep from smoothing that lock.

He looked up, saw me, finished the arpeggio. Set his guitar aside, walked past me, and shut and locked the neglected door. Looked at me, and I could see through his eyes like ice to the formulated lie.

Before he opened his mouth, I said, "I saw you."

He blinked. I had him on the wrong foot and I didn't care. "Saw me?"

"With her," I said. "Whoever the hell she was. I don't want to hear your excuses."

He seemed smaller when he asked, "How?"

I didn't mean to tell him, but some laughs are so bitter and rough that words stick to them on their way out. "Remember the dog?" I asked. "The metro dog? She showed me."

"I don't understand—"

"You don't have to." I sat down on the floor, all of a sudden. Because it was there. I put my face in my hands for similar reasons. "Fuck, Ilya, I'm pregnant."

There was silence. Long silence. When I finally managed to fight the redoubled force of gravity and raise my face to him, he was staring at me.

"Pregnant," he said.

I nodded.

"But that's great!" he said. And then he stomped on my flare of hope before I even knew I felt it. "You can sell *that*. The embryo! They're nothing but stem cells at that point—"

"Sell it," I said.

"Yes," he said.

"To fund your tour?"

"Why else?"

Oh god.

I didn't realize I'd said it aloud until Ilya stopped raving and looked down at me. "What?"

"Oh, God," I said. "Fuck you."

Somehow, I stood up. I remember my hand on the floor, the ache of my thighs as if I were drunk. I remember looking him in the eye. I remember what I said.

It was, "Keep the fucking apartment. I'll call tomorrow and take my name off the lease."

"Petra?"

I turned my back on him. He was babbling something about food in the oven. About how was he supposed to make the rent.

I paused with a hand on the knob. "Go peddle it on Tverskaya Prospekt for all I care."

OF COURSE, I was halfway to the lift before I realized I had nothing but my work clothes, my bag, and two pairs of shoes—one of those quite impractical.

Well, I wasn't about ruin an exit like that in order to go back and pack a suitcase. No self-respecting chicken-legged hut would have anything to do with me after that, if I had.

IT TOOK me two more days to find the dog. The first day, other than work—and I wasn't missing work now!—was mostly spent at a clinic, getting my name taken off the lease, looking at a couple of apartments, and finding a place to sleep for a couple of days until one of those became available. It turned out Misha the bartender didn't mind at all if I crashed at his place and neither did his boyfriend, and everybody at work was thrilled to hear that Ilya had been consigned to the midden heap of history.

How is it that you never hear about how much your friends hate your lover until you get rid of him or her?

Anyway, once that was all taken care of, I went to find my ovcharka friend. This mostly involved taking the Metro out to my station—my *old* station—earlier than I would have usually gotten up for work, and then checking the first car of each train for a wolf-colored passenger. I had a sausage in my bag and a hollow ache in my belly, but mostly what I remember was the grim determination that I would find that dog.

She wasn't on the train.

Instead, she trotted up beside me while I was waiting, sat down like an old friend on my left side, and looked up at me with one front paw lifted. I imagined her saying, "Shake?"

Instead, I broke a chunk off the sausage and offered it to her. "Thank you," I said.

She was as gentle as before. And if anything, she looked bigger around the middle than last time. She must be nearly ready to have the pups. I pressed a hand to my own stomach, imagining it pushing out like that. That hollow ache got hollow-er.

Someday. After my degree. But it wouldn't be deadbeat Ilya's deadbeat kid. No matter how good he smelled.

The train was coming. I felt the air pressure rise, heard the rattle of the wheels on iron rails.

"How did you know?" I asked the dog. "I owe you one."

She raised her brows at me, wrinkling her brow. *Expecting an argument?* She didn't wag.

I sighed and said, "Just how smart are you?"

And then Ilya was between us, shoving me out of the way. I hadn't even heard him come up. Hadn't heard the creak of his leather jacket. Didn't react fast enough to keep his elbow out of my ribs. I doubled over helplessly, wheezing for breath. The train's hydraulics hissed. Brakes squealed.

He gripped the dog by her scruff and her tail and slung her into the air. She yelped—more of a shriek—and he took a step toward the platform edge.

"You little bitch!"

He looked at me when he shouted it, and I wasn't sure if he meant the dog or me. But I knew the next five seconds like I was a prophet, like I was a Cassandra, like someone had dropped a magic mirror in my hand.

Ilya was going to throw the dog in front of the train.

Cassandra never got a chance to *do* anything. *I* jumped between Ilya and the platform edge.

The dog slammed into my chest. I pushed her away, throwing her onto the platform. The force tipped me on the platform edge. I pinwheeled my arms, expecting to topple backward. Expecting the next sensation to be the terrible impact of metal and then nothing—or worse, pain. I teetered, that hollowness in my stomach replaced with liquid, sloshing fear.

Someone caught my collar. Someone else caught my wrist. The feeling of relief and gratitude that flooded me left me on my knees. A man and a woman hovered over me. I could not see their faces.

I looked up into Ilya's face. The dog crouched in front of me, growling. Ears laid flat. Ilya lunged at her, and the man beside me grabbed him, twisted his arm behind his back.

"Bitch!" he swore, wrenching at the man who held him.

"Do you know that man?" the woman asked. She put a hand under my elbow and lifted me to my feet. There was a ladder in my stocking. My knee oozed blood.

"I left him," I said.

"I can see why," she answered. She patted my back.

Ilya twisted and kicked, rocking back and forth like a kid running against a sling swing. The dog snarled, a hollow trembling sound almost lost in the noise of the train. I thought she'd lunge for him, but she just stood her ground. Between him and me.

He must have wormed his arm out of the jacket sleeve, because suddenly he was off running, and his jacket hung limp in the man's grasp like a shed skin. I heard the thumping of his boots on the marble, shouts as he must have crashed through a crowd, and then nothing.

The man looked at the jacket, then at me.

"I don't want it," I said.

The police, of course, were nowhere.

THERE WAS fuss, but eventually the ring of opinionated observers we'd drawn filtered off to their trains. The two helpful bystanders who had saved my life decided I could be left alone. The woman gave me a tissue. The man insisted I take Ilya's coat. Only then did they feel they had performed their civic obligations and reluctantly leave me alone.

I dropped Ilya's coat on a bench. Somebody would take it, but it wouldn't be me. I hoped his phone was in the pocket, but I didn't bother to check.

Then I looked at the dog.

She sniffed my bloodied knee and looked thoughtful. She tried to lick it, but I pushed her away.

"You set this up, didn't you?" Not Ilya trying to kill her, no. But me finding out about the other woman.

Or maybe it was just one bitch taking care of another. *Do you know your mate is no good?*

She just looked at me, squeezed her eyes, and thumped her shaggy tail. *So you should thank me.*

I huffed at her—like an irritated dog myself—and turned on the ball of my foot. This time I had the sense to be wearing practical shoes. She waited. I stopped, turned back, and saw her staring after me.

I had the money from the clinic—just as Ilya had suggested—but I sure as hell wouldn't be spending it on Ilya's band. I was going to enroll in classes tonight after work, and pay my tuition in advance. The cocktail job wasn't going away, and it didn't conflict with morning or most afternoon classes.

One of the apartments I had looked at was a student studio flat near the university. It was a complete roach motel, but it allowed pets.

I could do this thing.

I looked at the dog. She needed a bath.

The dog looked at me.

"Well," I said to her. "Aren't you coming?"

I started walking. The dog fell into step beside me. Her plumy tail wagged once.

THE BODY OF THE NATION

New Amsterdam, April 1897

UNDER MOONLIGHT, THE NORTH RIVER Day Line steamboat *The Nation* seemed to rest on the glassy river like an elaborate toy on the mirrored surface of a drawing-room display. If it were not for the long sculpted lines of smoke hanging above her twin chimneys she might have seemed motionless; the paddleboxes enclosing her side wheels disguised their revolution as the moonlight disguised the brilliant colors of her woodwork. Detective Crown Investigator Abigail Irene Garrett knew *The Nation* must be fighting the tidal swell up the Hudson Fjord to hold her position, but the paddleboat was like a swan: what rose serenely above the great river's surface reflected no hint of the steady striving beneath.

The little stern-wheeled tug that bore Garrett toward *The Nation* could not have been more of a contrast—skittering toward the stately passenger-and-freight vessel like an overexcited water bug.

Garrett shifted her gloved grip on the railing and lifted her face to the wind. Night was no more than a courtesy. The moon's shining face would have provided sufficient light to navigate by, especially reflected as it was by the river. But in addition, the lights of New Amsterdam lined the right-hand bank, those of New Jersey the left—and *The Nation* herself gleamed at the center, bedeviled by gilt and shining with lanterns.

As she gave no sign that her magnificent languid grace upon the water was the artifact of concealed frenetic activity, she also gave no sign that within her elaborately painted and gilded bulkheads, there lay a dead man. But that was why Garrett was coming to her on this brisk spring night, a sharp wind lifting the hairs at her nape and blowing her long skirts around the shape of the blue velvet carpet bag she braced between her boots. It was only the presence of a dead man that had stayed *The Nation* on her route upriver to Albany even this long.

Garrett stepped back from the rail as they came up alongside. She crouched to pick up her carpet bag, avoiding being poked by her stays as she dipped with the expertness of long experience. The stiffness of her wand rested in its sheath along her left forearm—a minor reassurance.

A moment later and two members of the tug's crew were steadying her on the rail as she lifted her bag up to the waiting hands of *The Nation's* roustabouts. They lifted her after, dark hands and pale supporting her with surprising gentleness as she jumped up and was caught. The tug's bumpers grated against *The Nation's* oaken side; neither vessel ever quite stopped moving.

Despite their care, Garrett's temporary lack of self-determination nauseated her with apprehension as the paddleboat's crew hauled her over its higher rail and onto the deck. They made a point of bundling her skirts tight about her legs. Their expertise was no surprise. Steamers didn't stop at every landing along the route between New Amsterdam and Albany. If there were only a passenger or two, a few bales of cargo—they'd be tossed on or off board while the vessel was still moving, to shave a few minutes off the route time.

The crewmen set Garrett on her feet and—once she had twitched her skirting smooth—handed over her carpet bag. She lifted her chin and was about to go in search of the vessel's master when a cultured tenor interrupted her. "D.C.I. Garrett, I presume?"

"Captain O'Brien," she replied, after a pause to adjust the cuffs of her gloves that was really a pause in order to collect herself. "So, who's dead?"

The brim of O'Brien's hat tilted along with his head. Despite the name, he had no brogue—his accent clearly said *Connecticut*, and the coast of it. "I would have expected you to have been briefed."

She smiled. "I was pulled from my supper and told that I must report here. That it was a matter of utmost delicacy and urgency. And that *The Nation* could under no circumstances be further delayed, despite the fact of a murder, and so I would have to do my work enroute. But the name of the victim, or his apparent manner of destruction? No, these things were not considered essential to my performance. And so I am here before you, with barely the tools of my trade and the clothes I stand up in, ready to *detect*, to *investigate*, to *draw conclusions*, sir."

He contemplated her for a moment before nodding. "Very well," he said. "How about if I let you draw your *own* conclusions, then, since you're here already? I'll be happy to share my..." He weighed several words "... observations with you once you feel they will no longer be pejorative."

"Can you at least tell me if it's a thaumaturgical case?" Normally, she would only be called for those—or ones where there was a suspicion of black magic...or where the victim was a person of sufficient import that their death interested the Crown. In a symbolic but by no means unreal manner, Garrett was the Queen's own hand and eye turned to justice for his people. It was her duty to protect his interests, and to serve them.

"I am afraid I am not qualified to judge that," O'Brien said. "But the Duke specifically required that you be involved in the investigation before he'd allow us to leave New Amsterdam's jurisdiction."

That was interesting. And it would be very like Duke Richard not to find a way to alert her to his suspicions or desires. He'd just expect her to know, through sorcery...or telepathy.

O'Brien didn't look down, and despite herself, she felt the corner of her mouth curve upward. She had come here prepared to wrestle politics and permissions. Confronted with this plain-spoken and obviously weary working man...she felt a spark of hope.

Captain O'Brien was slim and wore his modestly creased uniform with—nevertheless—elegance. A blond fringe peeked out below the sides of his cap, and his small hands seemed dainty in white kid gloves. For all his unassuming aspect, Garrett was not fooled. It took something for a man of Irish descent to rise to captain a paddleboat that happened to be the pride of the North River Day Line—and the O'Briens were descended of Brian Boru, High King of Ireland...and *draoi*. Druid, an English speaker would say.

Not that that meant that O'Brien would inevitably be a sorcerer—but wizardry, like scholarship, had a tendency to run in families.

Garrett extended a hand. O'Brien took it. Their eyes met; she was the taller. It did not seem to trouble him.

Beneath her laced boots, the decks shivered as the great paddlewheels drifted to a halt, then began more vigorously to turn in a forward direction, taking advantage of the inflowing tide to push *The Nation* fast and hard for Albany. And Garrett was alone aboard her with a corpse, a crime, and the unknown factors of the crew and captain.

IN A civilized nation, no vessel with a murdered man aboard would have been permitted to flit casually from the docks, waiting with bad grace and—figuratively speaking—restive stamping for the presence of the Crown's Own. But the Colonies were not a civilized nation, with civilized checks on the behavior of powerful men. At least two of those men— Duke Richard, the highest aristocratic authority in the New Netherlands, and Peter Eliot, Lord Mayor of New Amsterdam—had a vested financial interest in the North River Day Line's monopoly and operations.

If a messenger hadn't raced on his velocipede directly from the offices of Robert Cook, president of the North River Day Line, to the offices of Peter Eliot as soon as the murder was reported…Detective Crown Investigator Garrett would eat her carpet bag full of the tools of the forensic sorcerer.

As Garrett followed O'Brien's narrow shoulders along the port side rail, she trained her investigator's awareness on the vessel. *The Nation* was at the top of her line, a broad-beamed behemoth strung everywhere with glittering lanterns that reflected from bronze and red and violet paint and from gilt on every surface. Garrett thought she must have used *The Nation's* twin sisters in her own occasional trips upriver, though she could not recall having been on this particular vessel previously.

The Nation's wood finishings were ornate, scrolled and pierced with jigsaw work like the latest style in houses. Deck passengers milled among the cargo piled and lashed in tidy stacks, and the air of excitement led even those who had booked cabin passage to join them. Normally, these more well-heeled passengers would avoid the dirt and poverty of the decks. There would be a main cabin where they might mingle, and at either end of it a salon for the ladies and a saloon for the men. As *The Nation* was normally a day line ship, and should already have been approaching the safety of her berth in Albany, she did not book out sleeper cabins. And Garrett thought the level of excitement vibrating through the passengers was well beyond what the salon (or saloon!) or even main cabin could have contained. Garrett wondered what the captain had told them, and what additional rumors might be sparking like wildfire from one passenger to the next.

They'd be up all night at this rate.

Well, so would she.

Captain O'Brien paused before a stateroom door, beside which stood a crewman in a dirty-kneed uniform. Mostly, passengers traveled the day line boats on deck, or in the salons—but there were a limited number of cabins available for the shy, or overly moneyed, or those who did not care to mix even with the middle class patrons amid the silver and mirrors in the cabin.

"Here," he said. He produced a key from his pocket—it was on a numbered fob—and unlocked the door. With no signs of a flourish—only a drab practicality, which—Garrett had to admit—seemed largely appropriate to the somber circumstances—he drew the panel open.

The space within was lit by a single lantern, but that was more than adequate. It was a little room, essentially—more a closet than a chamber—with an easy chair and a shuttered porthole. The curtains had been drawn against the outside. There was a good rug on the floor—anywhere else, it would have been a runner for an entryway—and atop the rug there was a dead...woman.

A book had fallen beside her, and a china teacup figured with cherries lay miraculously unbroken beside her splayed hand. She wore a gown of silk noile of the sort with differently colored warp and weft, so at the peaks of folds it caught the light and reflected back dark burgundy, while the valleys were shadowed and black. Her dark hair was sewn with rubies. More glinted at her neck and ears, amid diamonds and gold.

There were no obvious signs of violence upon her, and no blood upon the floor.

"She's dressed for a ball," O'Brien said. "And as you've seen, while *The Nation*'s a sharp boat, she's not the sort of boat that hosts balls. She was traveling under the name *Mrs. Abercrombie*." He shrugged. "Whether it's her own—"

"Did she come aboard in Albany or in New Amsterdam?" Garrett crouched beside the body, careful of the hem of her own dress and the possibility of contaminating the body with foreign fibers or hairs.

"She purchased passage and immediately embarked when we docked at the Battery," O'Brien said. "She entered her cabin, called for tea, and was not seen again. We're all rather distracted—we have a boatload of botanists going upriver for some sort of international conference on stamens and pistils or something, and as a result the holds are full of perishable goods on ice. We wouldn't have found her before Albany, except one of the stewards—Carter—heard her fall when he arrived with the tea-tray." He gestured to the fellow beside the door.

Carter was of average height and build, trim in his white coat, his mousy hair thinning despite obvious youth. His face looked pinched.

"You unlocked the door?" Garrett asked him.

"I had to run for the mate," said Carter. "Stewards don't have keys to guest cabins, ma'am."

"But you saw the body? Through the window?"

He shook his head. "The porthole was covered. She didn't answer a knock."

"I see." Garrett returned her attention to O'Brien. "And no one saw anyone enter or leave this cabin, of course?"

"We are interviewing the deck passengers," he said. "They aren't as helpful as one might wish."

Garrett sighed. She needed a dozen uniformed officers to deal with a potential witness pool this large, with time this limited. What she had was an interfering captain who was trying to be conscientious...unless he was trying to cover his tracks. "That is the nature of eyewitnesses, Captain. Please continue interviewing them."

Some would be over-eagerly helpful, some pompous, some irritated to be disturbed. All of them, by now, would be deeply unhappy that *The Nation* had been so delayed.

"It might be helpful that she embarked in New Amsterdam and suffered such an immediate fate," Garrett said. "It suggests that her killer—if she was killed, and is not merely the unfortunate victim of a brainstorm—might still be aboard. You didn't return to the shore to ask assistance?"

"We have a wireless," O'Brien said. "Six months ago, we would have sent a boat to shore; as it was, we radioed a coded transmission."

Garrett did not comment on the fact that the ship would have left its berth early in the morning, for the first tide and a fast run upriver to Albany. The North River's estuary reached hundreds of miles inland—the tides pushed up it as far as the mountains. Into Iroquois Nation country, in fact—where the war magic of the Native tribes had stopped the westward expansion of the Colonies. There was a guarded peace now, and trade...but the border hadn't always been friendly.

Garrett estimated that perhaps twelve hours had been lost while politics were wrangled...

Gently, Garrett touched the woman's hand. She had expected it to be stiff, the fingers wooden and room-temperature. The flesh *was* tepid to the touch...but plastic, soft and flexible. While such things varied a great deal from case to case, a woman who had been dead since breakfast should have showed signs of rigor mortis, and should not yet be relaxing again.

Garrett called for the lamp, insensible for the moment that it was a ship's captain she ordered around. When she remembered, the lantern had already been set beside her.

"Do you need her lifted?" O'Brien said.

"Not yet."

It was hard to tell in the poor light, but as she lowered her head toward the floor and lifted the dead woman's hand, something else struck Garrett's attention. There should have been pale patches on the backs of her curved fingers, marking where they had pressed the floor. Around those, there should have been liver-red rings. The marks of dependent lividity showed how a body had laid as the blood settled, and could outline anything that pressed that blood from capillaries near the skin.

Garrett humphed and unbuttoned the dead woman's sleeve. Her flesh was slack and inelastic—more like Plastiline than human skin and muscle—but there was no sign on *any* surface of the marks of lividity. Nor did they mar her face, already marred as it was by staring, clouding eyes.

She appeared, in other words, fairly freshly dead—except for the fact that warmth had fled her.

"A physician examined her?" Garrett asked.

"Dr. Fenister," O'Brien said. "He's the ship's surgeon. His opinion as of this morning was that she was freshly deceased, although he noted the coolness of her temperature as unusual…you may, of course, speak with him yourself."

"He didn't turn her?"

"It was obvious she was beyond help." O'Brien shifted uncomfortably. "If that's real," he said, with a wave to the victim's ring, "we're looking at a diplomatic incident."

"I'm not a jeweler," Garrett replied. "But it looks real to me. Is that why you stalled the vessel?"

O'Brien's mouth opened and closed like a fish's. He glanced aside. "The owners would have preferred the body remain undiscovered until Albany."

She didn't drop her eyes. He didn't raise his.

He shrugged and finished, "Time tables are sacred. And we have perishable cargo and wealthy passengers aboard. Neither take well to delays."

"Humph," Garrett said.

Garrett lowered the dead woman's hand again. As her fingers grazed over it, she examined the ring more carefully. Two heraldic lions supporting a quartered field, on which a red lion and a blue panther alternated with more abstract red-and-white designs.

Before she became a forensic sorcerer, Garrett had been Lady Abigail Irene Garrett, heir to a minor nobility. Those days were past, but she still recognized the arms of the Kingdom of Bayern.

D.C.I. Garrett closed her eyes and sighed. "I assume there's no shortage of coffee aboard a paddleboat?"

O'Brien cleared his throat. "I shall have young Carter here fetch you some. Cream and sugar?"

"Black," said Garrett. "I don't plan to enjoy it."

THE BOOK had plain red boards and a spine curlicued with gilt but otherwise unmarked. When Garrett lifted it, she found beneath it a fountain pen with a shattered nib. Ink daubed the wooden floor, the edge of the carpet, and the printed pages. A glance at the page head told her it was a German-language edition of *The Sketch Book of Geoffrey Crayon.*

"Washington Irving," Garrett muttered to herself.

She was reminded of O'Brien's presence when he answered from the door, "Reading up on the local culture, I see."

Garrett grunted in the most unladylike fashion she could manage. Years of deportment lessons she'd never quite shaken rendered it into a delicate huff. *Pity she never made it as far upriver as Sleepy Hollow and Tarrytown.*

Garrett looked for the gouge in the floorboards or the spot on the rug where the pen nib might have struck—and for the broken bits of the nib itself—but without success. She was still frowning and weighing *Das Skizzenbuch* in her hand when a clatter by the door alerted her to the arrival of her coffee. Carter set up a silver tray on a folding stand and poured. The beverage had arrived accompanied by a fat, tempting slice of coconut cake, by which Garrett knew that the ship's cook was attempting to butter her up. The curls of fresh coconut, the rich aroma, and her own interrupted supper suggested she would allow herself to be courted.

It was probably bad form to eat standing in the doorway of a chamber where a dead woman lay. Nevertheless, she drank left-handed, balancing the book upon her right, and blew on the pages to turn them.

Cut edges fluttered; someone had done a meticulous job with the paper knife. Here and there were cryptic notations in a brown-black ink matching the color of that splashed on the floor and dabbing the dead woman's fingertips.

"I'll need access to a room with a table and good lighting. And some privacy." Garrett frowned at the cut pages and set her empty cup aside. "Where's her handbag?"

It might contain a clue to her true identity. Or where she had been coming from, first thing in the morning, dressed as if she had danced the night away.

Captain O'Brien did not step across the threshold into the stateroom. He hunkered with his hands upon his knees and leaned in, though, angling his head to peer under furniture. "Let me speak to the baggage master," he said. "I'll soon find her luggage."

"It hasn't been retrieved yet?" Garrett asked. "Never mind, of course it hasn't. You were no doubt waiting for instructions?"

O'Brien paused in his leaving and shrugged apologetically. "If I owned the ship, things would be different. As it is—"

"Indubitably," Garrett said. "Well, she didn't pay her passage without a handbag, unless they're sewing concealed pockets into evening gowns these days."

"A pathetic motive for murder," O'Brien said, with obvious, real disdain.

Garrett felt the thin fragility of her own smile, the ease with which it cracked when she spoke. "There are good ones?"

O'Brien shifted, his hands behind his back.

Garrett took pity on him. "Who'd lift a handbag and leave a head coiffed in rubies?"

"Considering the overturned cup—I imagine you might be thinking of poison? Even suicide?"

"It could be suicide," Garrett said. "An imaginative detective might hypothesize that she first tossed her handbag over the railing, to confound scandal."

O'Brien raised his eyebrows. "It's better to be murdered than a suicide?"

"It is if you're a Catholic," Garrett said, after a brief pause. *Well, there are Protestant Irish. And probably atheistic ones.* "Or if you wish to conceal the reasons for your suicide."

"That *is* imaginative."

Garrett's knees still hurt from crouching on the deck. Every year left her a little less nimble. "And imagination is not always a friend to the homicide investigator," she said. "Too often, the reasons and means of murder are monotonously tedious. But my point is, the staging of this death could be consistent with either self-poisoning, or poisoning by another. The locked stateroom suggests the former; the lack of handbag the latter."

She set the book on the edge of the coffee tray and picked up cake and fork. The boiled frosting was too sweet, but that was the nature of boiled frosting. The cake itself was excellent. "Except—it's just as one would expect. And any time I see a crime scene that's just as one would expect, it makes me suspect that it could be just that: staging. Dead people usually don't look as the layman would think they must."

"MRS. ABERCROMBIE," it turned out, *had* loaded a steamer trunk— and the purser from whom she'd booked passage at the last minute clearly recollected her handbag, because it had seemed exceedingly out of place with her costume.

It was well-made, the purser said, and obviously expensive—but suitable for day, not an elegant evening out. "I assumed she was leaving her husband," he said, "having caught him..." He hesitated, with a glance at Garrett. Garrett restrained herself from rolling her eyes. O'Brien frowned encouragingly, and the purser continued. "Angry women in last night's clothes aren't unheard of as paddleboat passengers, is all I mean."

"I imagine not," said Garrett. She picked an invisible and exceedingly uncomfortable bit of lint from her sleeve.

"I remember her in particular because at first I turned her away, and she seemed quite distressed. But she returned an hour later, offering more money—we would not, of course, put another passenger off for her convenience. But there had been a cancellation. A Mr. Eugene Sisters, who I recall because of the peculiar beauty of his name."

Garrett was coming to conclude that the purser—a Mr. Manley—was accustomed to making excuses for his excellent recall of his passenger lists. "Did Mr. Sisters rebook for later?"

He shook his head. "He sent a telegram. It had his code number on it, which is how we prevent pranks in such matters." Manley rocked awkwardly in his chair. "Shall we go check the holds for that trunk?"

"Oh, yes," Garrett replied, with a tired glance to O'Brien. Not that he wasn't a suspect, but at least she liked him. "Let's do."

THE STEAMER trunk, of course...

...was missing.

Quite ostentatiously missing. Although the passenger's half of its claim tag could not be found—perhaps it was with "Mrs. Abercrombie's" handbag—the tag *number* was in the baggage master's book; however, its assigned berth in the hold lay innocent of contents. The deck where it should have lain was lightly scratched, but that signified very little—the deck throughout the hold was much-abused, scratched and gouged and furrowed from the steel-shod feet and corners of years of joyously mishandled luggage.

"Curiouser and curiouser," Garrett said. A chill crept up her spine; closer inspection revealed that it was just the radiant cold from some sort of large crate that seemed to contain something perishable packed in ice and sawdust. "Well, I suppose the contents of a trunk are as good a motive for murder as the contents of a handbag."

"Indeed," said O'Brien. "If only we could find either, we might be that much closer to the murderer."

O'BRIEN SET the crew to searching *The Nation*—stem to stern, quite literally. It was a less than ideal situation, as any one of them could have been involved in the murder, and so Garrett specified that they must work in pairs—and that the mate would choose who paired with whom, rather than relying on crew members to sort it out. Garrett needed to begin interviewing the remaining crew and the passengers—but she was painfully aware that there were close to three hundred people aboard *The Nation*, and that she had less than eight hours remaining in which to find the one who was a murderer.

Garrett had done the obvious thing first, and laid out the dead woman's pen on a clean handkerchief to see if it could be thaumaturgically encouraged to point out the direction of its missing piece. But it lay there without even a shiver, blithely ignoring the principles of affinity and sympathy. Which didn't mean that the broken-off piece didn't exist, of course. But if it were far enough away that the spell didn't offer at least *some* direction, it was a safe bet that it wasn't on board *The Nation*.

Perhaps the pen had been broken before the dead woman came on board. But if that was the case, why had she had it out to make notes in a book when she died?

Garrett needed a starting point. Any starting point. Even a bad one. Flipping through the pages of the dead woman's short story collection was not providing the needed inspiration. Her annotations were cryptic—shorthand in a foreign language—and there wasn't even a name scribed on the flyleaf.

She was about to pick a direction of questioning at random, on the ancient axiom of police investigations: some action is better than no action. Until she glimpsed a shorter edge of paper tucked between the pages of the book, and flipped back page by page until she found it again.

It was a newspaper article, on fresh, greasy newsprint. Garrett could still smell the cheap ink. A column clipped from the pages of *The New World Times*, penned by one "Josh," apparently a "Master Riverboat Pilot" by trade. It was a humorous tall tale of travel on the North River between New Amsterdam and Albany, focused in particular on the perils of sea monsters and the opportunity to view "extinct saurisceans" in the canyons below West Point.

Garrett frowned at the thing. "O'Brien."

"Ma'am?"

"What's the name of your pilot?"

THE PILOT'S name was Clemens. Garrett did not stand as he was brought into the captain's office, which had been hastily cleared to serve as her interview room. Instead, she sat behind the powdery pale wood of the desk and assessed him. He was a man neither tall nor short, whose eyes glittered sharply over a luxuriant moustache. His once-ginger hair was fading to the color of strawberry milk, but his posture remained as crisp as it ever might have been. He did not seem put off by her sex or her spectacles, which could be good or bad.

He radiated an aura of wit and focus that led Garrett to suspect immediately that while he might be a charming interview, he would not be an easy one. She longed for a gin just looking at him.

He had removed his cap upon entering and stood now with it tucked jauntily under his arm. The ring it had left depressed his curls, a small flaw she found comforting, like a chink in the otherwise flawless armor of his uniform. *Dammit,* Garrett thought. *I'm the one who's supposed to be making* him *feel this way.*

"Mister Clemens," she said. "Please sit."

A ladder-backed chair had been drawn up to the blank side of the desk. Clemens folded himself into it as the door shut and latched behind him—the invaluable and nearly invisible Carter, yet again—and spoke in a cultured Virginian accent. "Detective Crown Investigator."

"Do you know why you're here, Mr. Clemens?"

"I imagine you are interviewing the ship's officers regarding the death of Mrs. Abercrombie, as that was why you were brought aboard."

A good enough answer. Noncommittal, and not full of conversational openings. She resisted the urge to say, *I see you have fenced before.* "How did you come to New Amsterdam?"

"My wife Olivia's family is settled in Elmira. It was because of her that I came to New Holland."

"But Captain O'Brien tells me you were already an experienced river-boat pilot when he hired you, though but newly arrived?"

"Ah," he said. "Yes. I learned my trade out West. The Red Indian Nations of the fertile Mississippi valley issue charters for a limited number of steamboats. The trade in lumber and furs had enriched them greatly, and as they've learned of the steel plow and seed drill from Europeans, certain tribes have become producers of trade quantities of cotton and sugarcane, which they sell through the cooperative colony of *La Nouvelle-Orléans*, which the Chitimacha call *Chawasha*, the Raccoon-Place, with as much success any white businessman. The Mississippi, I must say, is a far superior river in every way to the North River—much slyer, madam, and far more full of tricks."

Garrett had found, over the years, that the most revealing interviews often resulted from following seemingly blind trails. Whatever people wished most to conceal inevitably weighed upon their thoughts and affected their habits of speech. It became a fascination, a sort of obsession, and they could not control the indications of interest that leaked out into their daily discourse. No one, Garrett thought, was more interested in anything more so than themselves—unless it was attention paid to themselves, even if they were the anonymous center of a manhunt. If she had a shilling for every time she'd brought a murderer to justice only to find a cache of newspaper clippings relating to the crime in his or her papers—well, she was sure she'd have at least a guinea.

She had a hunch, in other words. And she was pursuing the hunch when she said, "You seem to be rather a partisan of the Indian Nations, for a white man."

Clemens had laid his cap upon his knee when he sat. Now he folded his hands over it.

"When I was a young man, I was an Imperialist," he said. "I believed in the Westward expansion of the Colonies; the inevitable conquest and beneficial civilization of the backwards native tribes."

"Something changed your mind?"

"Getting to know them," he said. "Working as a foreigner in their nations. Watching them adopt the best of our technologies and sciences

while refining their own on the lathe we call 'civilization.' It has been...
an education, madam."

She regarded him. He tipped his head to the side.

Garrett made a note in her case book. "If you are no longer an
Imperialist, then what have you become?"

His words were apologetic, but the smile ruffling his moustache was
something else. "I'm afraid I've become a Republican, Crown Investigator."

"Well," she said slowly. "That's not...illegal."

"It's not encouraged," he retorted.

"Do you speak out against the Queen?"

"Iron Alexandria? There is no queen in all the world more fit to rule
England than she."

Garrett's lips twitched. She pressed them together to prevent the
smile. *Clever man.* "But not the Colonies?"

His shoulders rose and fell. "I think it would be to the benefit of
Crown and Colonies both if the Crown were willingly to release us," he
said. "It is my right in common and statutory law to express that opinion."

"In certain limited ways," said the Crown's Own.

"I have never called for revolution, or wished any harm upon the
queen or her representatives."

He seemed earnest, leaning forward persuasively. Garrett swept aside
the newspaper that covered the copy of Washington Irving.

"Do you speak German, Mr. Clemens?"

His eyes flicked to the book, but lingered longer on the newspaper.
It was *The New World Times*, which carried the column by Josh the riverboat pilot. She watched him force his eyes back to the book. "Was that
Mrs. Abercrombie's?" he asked. "If you need someone to translate it for
you...I'm afraid my attempts would be rather crude."

"What leads you to believe it might have been Mrs. Abercrombie's?"

His bushy eyebrows rose. Garrett had seen a lot of dismissals in her
life, but this one rivaled the occasional more-in-sorrow-than-in-anger
stares of her elderly ragmop terrier. "She was Prussian?"

"Bavarian, actually. But it's an easy mistake to make. Although considering the long-term political tensions between those two nations,

were she alive she'd probably have a bone to pick with you over your error."

Clemens huffed into his mustache. "In any case, she spoke German; she is dead; the book is in the possession of a homicide investigator. It seems a natural supposition."

Garrett opened the book to the page she had previously marked and extracted "Josh's" clipped-out column on the cryptozoology of the North River. She extended it between gloved fingers. "I don't suppose you know who writes under this pseudonym of 'Josh'?"

He didn't extend his hand to take the trembling slip of paper. "That would be your humble correspondent, madam. She clipped it, I gather? It's so gratifying to have a fan."

AFTER THE pilot, Garrett began interviewing the ship's other officers. She was just about finished with the mate when a hesitant rap on the door paused him mid-sentence. She was reasonably certain he hadn't been about to produce anything functionally useful, but she gestured him to continue anyway. When he paused, she raised her voice and called, "Enter!"

O'Brien leaned in the door to give her a look Garrett wanted to interpret as shared amusement over the irony of the captain of a vessel tapping on the door of his own cabin.

"Captain?"

"Mr. Manley found the trunk."

IT HADN'T got far. Just across the hold, stacked atop a bay otherwise half-full of sacks of sugar. A cargo net had been tugged aside and inexpertly refastened; O'Brien said that error had been noticed by one of the roustabouts. He also said that no one had touched the misplaced trunk since it was discovered.

Garrett examined it first *in situ*. It was hard to tell which of the dents in the sugar sacks might have been made by feet, but she measured a few for safety's sake. Then, she confronted the trunk.

The best procedure would have been to clear every potential subject from the hold. But the best procedure would have had her here twelve hours ago, and the ship never leaving the waters of New Amsterdam.

And look how swimmingly and in accordance with her authority—and the Crown's—all that had been carried out! Alexandria Regina should consider herself lucky that the Colonies still bothered paying their taxes. For a moment, Garrett closed her eyes and allowed herself nostalgia for London, when she had had the full power and the authority of the Enchancery and the Crown behind her every investigation.

Well, she'd made her decision to try her luck in the Colonies. It wasn't as if she could take it back.

"Well," said O'Brien, who had been observing curiously but silently, "we know he's strong enough to drag a loaded trunk the width of the hold."

"Assuming it's loaded," Garrett said. The box was blue, steel-strapped, and had an intrinsic lock rather than a padlock. She wondered if she'd have to witch it open. "You don't think Mrs. Abercrombie could have done this for herself?"

"Would a woman be strong enough?"

It was a big trunk. Garrett thought she might have *dragged* it, fully laden with clothes. Not books. Lifting it up the pile of sacks without tearing one, however—

She touched the latch with gloved fingers, depressing the catch. To her surprise, it sprang open.

She glanced at O'Brien, to find him gazing with pursed lips at her. "Do you suppose it will explode?"

He smiled tightly and would have stepped forward to assist her with the lid, but she gestured him back. Balanced precariously on the sacks—her tidy little boots were never meant for this kind of escapade—she checked the trunk for residue of sorcery or explosives. Both came up negative.

Surely if there were a booby trap, it would have gone off when the catch released?

"Well," she said. "Here goes nothing."

She flipped up the lid.

—nothing. In fact, there was nothing at *all* inside. The sanded interior was smooth and plain.

Garrett blew a lock of hair out of her eyes. She stood back, so O'Brien could peer over her shoulder. She said, "I think a woman would be strong enough to manage *that*."

He replied, "So—it looks as if 'Mrs. Abercrombie' may have been smuggling something. Do you suppose whoever relieved her of it was an accomplice? I'm surprised he didn't toss the trunk overboard when he had emptied it."

"Tossing steamer trunks overboard by day is rather noticeable," Garrett replied. She thought—but did not add aloud—that there was also the possibility that the suspect might not be listed on the passenger manifolds. Which meant he would not be free to move around the ship, unless he could find some means of escaping notice.

If that was the case, though, it meant that Garrett was and had been looking in all the wrong places for a killer. And outside the portholes, the long night was wasting.

GARRETT SAT behind the captain's desk, the dead woman's book open on the blotter before her, the broken pen laid next to it. The ink matched—she'd checked that carefully—and now she lifted the pen and turned its barrel with her fingertips.

The empty trunk had given Garrett her first real hint of means and opportunity, though motive—and thus perpetrator—still floated amorphously somewhere outside of her ability to define. The comprehensive search had turned up no evidence of sabotage or stowaways, but Garrett was convinced—a hunch, an induction, a leap of logic she could not yet adequately defend—that her as-yet unidentified suspect was not a member of the crew.

She didn't exactly feel that her time spent interviewing them was wasted, however. There was something about Clemens…

In any case, she needed a fresh and effective tack. And she needed it now.

Failing that, she'd settle for a desperation move.

She set the pen aside, rose, and went to the door. Having opened it, she leaned out and made sure Carter was there. She dismissed him to his other duties—over his protests, but she was sure she was easier work than whatever else he might have been detailed to accomplish.

At last, he stepped away, shoulders square. As if the thought had just struck her, she called after him—"Steward?"

He paused and turned. "Madam?"

"Does this boat have a library?"

"The captain's books are right there—"

"No," she said. "A library for passengers. Fiction and such. Improving literature."

"Of course," Carter said. "It's in the main cabin."

"Thank you, Carter," she said. She shut the door. And then, on a whim, she turned to O'Brien's book shelf and pulled down a selection of reference tomes that would, she imagined, have been exquisitely useful to the captain of a top-of-her-line luxury steamer. She did wish he had a copy of a recent edition of *Registered Wizards and Sorcerers*, but she had to admit that was rather a specialized taste.

NOW THAT *The Nation* was underway and a meal was being served, those who had paid for more than deck passage had largely retreated to the main cabin. As Garrett approached, its broad glass windows sparkled with light and fluttered with the motion of people bustling within. Garrett caught glimpses of the white coats of stewards through beveled panes, the shimmer of silver as they held their trays high. She picked out the balding back of Carter's head as he sidled through the crowd and wondered at the length of his workday. Under the circumstances, none of the crew would have slept. She spared them a moment of pity, then collected herself and paused outside the doors of the main cabin.

She raised her eyes to the moon, to the light that scraped down the high cliffs to either side and *The Nation*'s own gilded superstructure. Veils of mist swayed above the river like a ghost bride's petticoats, and trees just softening with young leaves lined the clifftops.

Some of the passengers would know who she was—Garrett was no stranger to innuendo and scandal—and they would certainly know why she was here. She must appear in command of the situation as she entered, and she must never let that appearance of control lapse.

With the captain at her left hand, she swept into the main cabin, pausing with the reflexes of a lady as every eye turned to her. Silence spread in ripples, lapping over one another, making snatches of conversation audible that should have lain beneath the general murmur of words. "...a dead woman..." "...said she was poisoned..." "...missing my daughter's—" "...botanical conference."

She recognized several of the ship's crew, including Mr. Manley, the purser with such exceptional recall. She caught his eye and he came toward her. Having glanced at O'Brien for permission, he said, "D.C.I.?"

Garrett rode the moment, feeling it like the swell of a wave beneath *The Nation*. When her well-honed sense of society told her attention was beginning to waver away from her, she lowered her voice and said to Manley, "Sir, is there anyone in the cabin who you cannot put a name to?"

He turned once, slowly, and then shook his head.

Garrett frowned. She turned to O'Brien as if he had said something amusing and permitted herself to laugh. He caught her gaze, frowning, but seemed to understand that she was dissembling. His hand on her elbow moved her forward, and Manley fell in beside.

"We could search everyone in Albany," she whispered. "When they disembark. Although anyone with sense would have divested themselves of anything that might have identifiably belonged to 'Mrs. Abercrombie' by now. A handbag would be a lot less obvious going over the railing than a trunk. And there would be political implications."

"I know you're a special friend of the Duke's," O'Brien replied. "But he's in business with Mr. Cook. And with any number of my passengers. Are you...*that* special of a friend?"

"No one is that special of a friend," she answered. "Except possibly the Duchess. And she owns the New Netherlands."

Around them, conversations were slowly resuming. Garrett walked the length of the main cabin with the captain, watching silver glitter as it worked against china plates.

The "library" was a set of shelves beside the doors to the saloon, opposite the women's drawing room. After spending a few more moments with O'Brien, Garrett turned away. She moved toward the shelf—not ostentatiously, but with purpose. Manley hovered between her and the captain as if held in place by the stretch of invisible tackle, obviously torn with regard to whose orbit to maintain.

Garrett was lifting the ship's English-language copy of *The Sketch Book of Geoffrey Crayon* from the shelf—it was filed under *C* for Crayon rather than *I* for Irving, which made her wonder whether the person doing the filing had somehow missed that *Crayon* was a pseudonym, or if he had a sense of humor. She had asked O'Brien to keep an eye on the passengers as she removed the book. But as her finger settled into the notch of the spine she felt her own awareness vibrating as she stretched it to notice if anyone reacted to her choice of literature.

If they did react, she failed to catch them. Because she looked at the leather of her glove and the leather of the binding, and realized what a ridiculous, foolish oversight she had made.

Garrett hefted Irving in her hand and turned quickly to O'Brien. He seemed to be at parade rest, patiently awaiting her return, but she saw how his eyes flickered about the room, belying his impassive expression. She said to Manley, "Have you been in the saloon tonight?"

He shook his head.

"Mr. Sisters, who cancelled his berth so conveniently—or perhaps so tragically—for Mrs. Abercrombie. Would you know him by sight?"

"I would not," Manley said. "His arrangements were made by a representative. It's not uncommon; Mr. Lenox doesn't book his own travel either."

Garrett rubbed her thumb across the leather binding of the book. "Take me into the saloon."

Manley's chin came up in shock.

She rolled her eyes and turned to O'Brien. "Captain? Take me into the saloon."

"D.C.I.—"

"Yes," she said. "D.C.I. I am an officer of the crown, Captain O'Brien. That I am also a woman is not now under the microscope. You will—*please*—accompany me into the saloon."

To his credit, he pressed his lips thin and took her arm. While a room full of passengers—and Mr. Manley—held their breath, he guided her to the door and held it open. She passed into a miasma of smoke, and he was at her heels so when the bartender rounded on her what he saw was the captain's level gaze.

She scanned the room. Men, of course—a double handful of them, leaned over glasses full of amber fluid and ashtrays full of smoldering cigarillos and cheroots. The haze of smoke from their toxic emanations. The eye-stinging vapors of the whiskey and gin, which made Garrett's mouth water with tired desire.

"I thought it was the book," Garrett said out loud, as every eye in the room turned to her. She held up both copies of *The Sketch Book*, the one in German and the one in English. "I thought the book had significance. I have been pulling the damned thing apart trying to find whatever secret was concealed in it, assuming that that secret *must* be linked to her murder."

She watched faces as she spoke, the flicker of attention, the creases of puzzlement and concern, of hostility and curiosity. She wasn't certain exactly what expression she was looking for, but none of those were it. She smiled.

Behind her, she heard the rattle of the doorknob as O'Brien summoned whatever crewmen might be standing nearby into the saloon. Cigars and cigarettes smoldered unattended. Ice melted in drinks. Sweating nervously, Carter and three other stewards filled the door.

If nothing else, she had their complete fascination.

"But the book had nothing to do with it, did it?" Ah. *There* was the expression she'd been searching for. On the face of a middle-aged man she'd never seen before. He was dark and slight, with thinning dark hair and a prosperous little paunch under his green brocade waistcoat. A pair of wire-rimmed spectacles perched very far down his nose, as if he used them only for reading. He sat with another man—a bigger, gray-haired one with muttonchop sideburns, who looked chiefly confused.

Garrett honed her gaze on the face of the balding man in the green waistcoat—the presumptive Mr. Sisters. He stared right back. She wondered if he were forgetting himself in the face of confrontation, or if he were making some misguided attempt to appear unafraid. If so, it was too bald-faced.

She leaned over to O'Brien and hid her mouth behind the German edition of Irving as if it were a fan. "The man in the green waistcoat. Who is he?"

"I've never seen him before," O'Brien whispered back. "I'll find out, shall I?"

Garrett lowered the book and intoned, "If the book *had* had a single thing of importance to reveal about the murder, it never would have been left behind. Not by a man so careful that he absconded with the victim's handbag. One who *swept the floor* to remove evidence that could have linked him to the killing."

Behind her, Carter rocked on his heels. Garrett turned so she had her back to the bar, and could see both him and the man in the green waistcoat clearly. Carter's face had gone pale and was dewed with sweat.

"One of the chief suspects in any crime, Mr. Carter, is the person who discovers the body. Especially when the discovery of a body causes some desirable effect, such as for a will to be read, or an insurance policy to be paid out—" she could not keep the grin from her cheeks "—or for a steamship to be delayed."

O'Brien had realized her intent, she saw. As Carter ducked his face and backed away, green with nausea, O'Brien stepped forward and collared the bigger man, lifting him to his toes. "You little—"

"Captain," Garrett said. "Carter did not kill your passenger. Think: if he had poisoned her, would he have left the cup? No, we were meant to think she died of poison...but then where was the saucer?"

O'Brien did not release his grip. "You just said—"

"Her name was Gisela von Dissen, and she did not die upon *The Nation*. The scene of her death was staged intentionally to delay the ship. And while Mr. Carter was in the employ of the man responsible for her death, he did not kill her. In fact, she was dead before she embarked upon this vessel."

There. That silence, heady as liquor. Damned satisfying. All eyes were upon Garrett now, and she took up her role like a queen's ermine. "My first clue was the condition of the body. As the ship's doctor had noticed, it was unusually cool to the touch from the very first. Additionally—and even more unusually—there was no rigor mortis, and no signs of livor mortis, the discoloration caused by the pooling of blood at the lowest points of the body. The first item suggested that Miss von Dissen had been dead much longer than anticipated, the second that she had not been dead long at all—or that she'd passed away long enough ago for the rigor to have passed. But a dead woman doesn't drink tea, or annotate a book, or walk aboard a ship under her own power. And the third item…was the most curious, as *it* suggested that she was not dead at all."

Now Carter looked confused, and the man in the green waistcoat had grown very still. Some of the other passengers and crew—Garrett was gratified to notice the bartender, and O'Brien, who had set Carter more-or-less back on his feet, among them—looked captivated, but the majority radiated boredom and irritation.

One bearded and prosperous fellow—Garrett noticed his silk-lined suit and platinum watch chain—levered himself from a leather-upholstered chair. "Madam," he said, in a tone that suggested he didn't mean 'madam' at all, "I don't know the meaning of this circus—"

"Mr. Frick," O'Brien said, "Please. Trust that all will be made plain in time, and for now choose to enjoy the entertainment."

"Next time," Frick said, "I shall *buy* a riverboat." But he settled himself into his chair again, crossed his legs, and folded his hands over his knee—leaving Garrett more than a little impressed with O'Brien's charisma and authority.

Frick said, "So you have a little mystery on your hands, Miss Garrett?"

"Had," she said, ignoring the slight. She was by rights perhaps *Lady Abigail Irene, Doctor Garrett,* or *Detective Crown Investigator Garrett. Miss,* for a woman in her forties, implied a bluestocking dismissal and no recognition of her accomplishments. Well, she'd remember him. "It's quite solved now, I assure you."

"Please," said Frick. "*Enlighten* us. How does a dead woman embark upon a ship?"

"While it is not my duty to the crown to educate millionaires, Mr. Frick, I shall be glad to. You ask how a dead woman travels, except in a stout-sided box. The answer, of course, is *necromancy*. And the sorcerer who is controlling the corpse? Well, he must stay close, of course. So the simplest expedient is to have himself shipped."

Now she had them. The murmur of side conversations faded; even the table playing euchre at the back set down their cards.

Garrett reached into her sleeve and drew Gisela's pen from its temporary place beside her wand. O'Brien, having consulted briefly with Mr. Manley—who was *not* holding Carter's sleeve—came back and whispered behind his hand, "He's not a listed passenger. A stowaway, and in plain sight! Bold as brass."

"Well," Garrett whispered in return. "Mr. Sisters couldn't very well stay in the trunk once he was breathing again, could he?" She raised the pen and said, "This is Gisela von Dissen's fountain pen. You cannot see this, because of the cap, but the nib is broken. I had at first suspected that she might have stabbed her assailant with it, and that I might be able to use the connection between pen and nib to locate her killer. Alas, it was not to be...but then I realized what I could do. Because someone—I assume it was Mr. Carter—took her handbag. And while I imagine that theft was only to confuse the issue...it seems likely that a traveling woman's handbag contained a vial of ink. It might not be too much to hope that that would be the same ink used to fill this pen. And that Mr. Carter might have handed the bag and its contents off to his employer.

"A dead woman would not have been entertaining herself with a book in her cabin—but a man staging a death might very well have laid a book and pen about the place, to go with the overturned cup of tea. And a man who had intended to delay a steamship, and who found a better way to do it than some act of sabotage, might very well sacrifice his own booking on that vessel in order to conveniently smuggle a corpse aboard!"

She was looking directly at the man in the green waistcoat—and he was looking directly back. Now she lectured to him alone. "The principal of sympathy states that two portions of the same object will sustain an affinity for one another. So the ink in the pen and the ink in the vial, though contained in separate reservoirs, remain—thaumaturgically speaking—the same object..."

She laid the pen flat across her palm. For all its reticence on the previous attempt, now it shuddered and tumbled from her hand, bouncing on the carpeting before rolling toward the man in the green waistcoat as if drawn on a string. He started from his chair, backing away from the pen as if from a snake—

"Grab him!" O'Brien shouted.

Garrett yelled, "Eugene Sisters! Stop in the name of the Queen!" and fumbled for her wand, but Sisters was too nimble. He shouldered past the steward and two passengers, ducked O'Brien, and vanished through the saloon door as Garrett was still struggling silver-tipped ebony from inside her sleeve.

She might have shouted, "After him!" but the door was already jammed with crew and passengers giving chase.

SISTERS OBVIOUSLY intended to swim for it, as he pushed his way through the startled main cabin passengers toward the stern doors with O'Brien and two stewards in pursuit. He had the advantage of surprise, however, and there were too many people in the way—jostling her, shoving one another aside, shouting in confusion—for Garrett to use the stasis spell in her wand.

She waded into the chaos anyway, her wand brandished overhead in case she got a clear angle on the fugitive. If worse came to worst, she'd cast the spell into the crowd. Divided between subjects, it wouldn't do more than stun and disorient—but that might slow him down enough for O'Brien to lay hands on him. Of course, there were the innocent bystanders to consider: nobody really wanted to be on the receiving end of a stasis spell. They were normally harmless enough, but Garrett had stood for enough of them during her training to know how unpleasant it could be to feel one's heart grinding in one's chest. And if Sisters were to plummet into the river while stunned…well, the odds of saving his life would not be high.

Still, allowing him to escape—the rising mist would hide him. If he was a strong enough swimmer to survive a plunge into the spring-frigid North River…he'd be away clean before a boat could be launched to look for him. The sky might just be graying with dawn, Albany only an hour or so upriver…but the mist would cancel any advantage of the light.

Garrett was still debating her options when Sisters reached the door and plunged through it into the soft night beyond. As he turned to check the status of his pursuit, Clemens the riverboat pilot stepped into the frame and cold-cocked him.

The man in the green brocade waistcoat went down like a pile of laundry, leaving Clemens standing over him and—wincingly—shaking his hand.

"Much obliged, Mister Clemens," Garrett said, as she came up to him. "By the way, you're under arrest."

"Oh," said Clemens, "I don't think you're going to want to do that, once we've had another chance to chat."

MR. CLEMENS smelled of black coffee, and Garrett didn't blame him one bit. He sat in the chair across from the captain's cleaned-off desk, and she sat behind it, and he said, "I'll need to be in the wheelhouse when we come into the dock in an hour."

"You're not an agent of the crown," Garrett said.

"Because I'm an anti-imperialist?" he answered. "Some people choose to work for change from the inside. How about if we trade, Doctor Garrett? Questions and answers? If you like, I'll go first."

"Can I trust you to be honest?"

"As much as I can trust you." His eyebrows went up. "So how did you know Miss von Dissen's name?"

"*Who is Whom*," she said with a smile. "I assumed the ring was real, and there was a limited number of people she could be. *Are* you an agent of the crown?"

"No, I am not an agent of the crown. I am a sort of…free agent, if you will. But I am on the side of the angels and America, never fear. How did you know Miss von Dissen was…not herself?"

"An evening gown with no gloves?" She shook her hair back. "No woman would make that mistake."

He winced. "Of course. Even if she were running away from something personally embarrassing. You question, madam."

"Who *do* you work for?"

"Robert Cook," he answered. "Any other tasks I perform are strictly on an amateur—on a *volunteer* basis. But in this matter, I have been acting on behalf of a union of concerned individuals."

"You work for the Iroquois Nation!"

"That is an unfounded allegation and it's my turn to ask a question. So our Mr. Sisters was a necromancer, and he smuggled himself aboard in his comatose state while controlling Miss von Dissen. Why not just keep her mobile to the destination, if he was smuggling himself?"

"Because the point was to delay the vessel. Sisters *had* a reservation. He cancelled it so Miss von Dissen could have a berth; the ship was full. He must have originally planned something more personally risky, but the opportunity to use a dead foreign noblewoman—and one who must have personally discommoded him—was too good to pass up. He might even manage to embroil the Bavarian crown in a spy scandal, if all went well."

"Ah," said Clemens.

"I am correct in my guess that Mr. Sisters is working for the Prussians?"

His smile was much less tight than she would have expected. "So we believe. It is, of course, a guess."

"Of course," Garrett agreed. "But who else would have an interest in preventing a trade deal between Bayern and the Iroquois?"

That made his smile grow broad. "I thought you'd have to use a question for that."

"I'm tricky," she said. "I did *ask* a question."

"So you did. The English?" he asked, then waved it away. "I choose to assume that that was speculation, and not a trade question. If it was, my guess is yours for free. Call it lagniappe. So why delay my boat? What good could twelve hours have done them?"

"Now I am reduced to speculation," Garrett said. "But it's possible that there was a Prussian agent on another boat with a juicier offer?"

Clemens' curls moved softly as he shook his head. "Unlikely."

"I find your coyness frustrating," she said. "But I won't ask you to elaborate. All right, then, it has something to do with something in the hold. Something perishable. Packed in with the ice and the botanical samples. Am I closer?"

Clemens brought his hands together thumb to thumb, inverted them and spread them. A gesture of innocence.

Garrett let it stand. "Of course, if it looked like a Bavarian princess died under curious conditions while on a secret mission to the Iroquois, that alone might be enough to derail the deal. Bayern is unlikely to forgive such carelessness. But she wasn't even supposed to be on the boat, was she?"

"Is that your question?"

Garrett shrugged. "Explain a few things to me. The book was a recognition symbol, wasn't it? That's why your column is tucked into it. Something that would not happen by chance, and so must be recognized if she were to walk through a drawing-room or the lobby of a hotel with such a thing in her hand, perhaps the top of the column protruding. It would give her an obvious and natural reason to speak to you—if she were an appreciator of your humor, and if she approached you with a pen. You were meant to meet her ashore last night, but she never made it to your rendezvous. Sisters got to her first, while she was still dressed for whatever intrepid young ladies do to entertain themselves in a foreign city."

Clemens sat back in the chair. "You are...*distressingly* clever."

"And I suppose he either did not recognize the significance of the column, or didn't notice it, or thought it might lead to your being suspected."

"It did," he said.

"Indeed," said Garrett. "But it turns out you're not a murderer after all. Just an agent of a foreign power."

"I am an American," he reiterated. His face tightened as he tried to conceal his concern. "And...I helped catch your murderer."

Garrett stood. She placed her hands flat on the blotter, staring down at Miss von Dissen's tortoiseshell pen and her copy of "The Legend of Sleepy Hollow." Garrett could not—quite—make herself look at Clemens. "Dammit."

"What?" he asked.

She lifted the book. She weighed it in her hand, and then she tossed it to him. "Go and sin no more," she said.

He caught it, pages a-flutter. His column did not slip loose. He stood too, and faced her. "What will happen to Sisters?"

"Oh," Garrett said. "He'll hang."

Boojum

with Sarah Monette

THE SHIP HAD NO NAME of her own, so her human crew called her the *Lavinia Whateley*. As far as anyone could tell, she didn't mind. At least, her long grasping vanes curled—affectionately?—when the chief engineers patted her bulkheads and called her "Vinnie," and she ceremoniously tracked the footsteps of each crew member with her internal bioluminescence, giving them light to walk and work and live by.

The *Lavinia Whateley* was a Boojum, a deep-space swimmer, but her kind had evolved in the high tempestuous envelopes of gas giants, and their offspring still spent their infancies there, in cloud-nurseries over eternal storms. And so she was streamlined, something like a vast spiny lionfish to the earth-adapted eye. Her sides were lined with gasbags filled with hydrogen; her vanes and wings furled tight. Her color was a blue-green so dark it seemed a glossy black unless the light struck it; her hide was impregnated with symbiotic algae.

Where there was light, she could make oxygen. Where there was oxygen, she could make water.

She was an ecosystem unto herself, as the captain was a law unto herself. And down in the bowels of the engineering section, Black Alice Bradley, who was only human and no kind of law at all, loved her.

Black Alice had taken the oath back in '32, after the Venusian Riots. She hadn't hidden her reasons, and the captain had looked at her with cold, dark, amused eyes and said, "So long as you carry your weight, cherie, I don't care. Betray me, though, and you will be going back to Venus the cold way." But it was probably that—and the fact that Black Alice couldn't hit the broad side of a space freighter with a ray gun—that had gotten her assigned to engineering, where ethics were less of a problem. It wasn't, after all, as if she was going anywhere.

Black Alice was on duty when the *Lavinia Whateley* spotted prey; she felt the shiver of anticipation that ran through the decks of the ship. It was an odd sensation, a tic Vinnie only exhibited in pursuit. And then they were underway, zooming down the slope of the gravity well toward Sol, and the screens all around Engineering—which Captain Song kept dark, most of the time, on the theory that swabs and deckhands and coal-shovelers didn't need to know where they were, or what they were doing—flickered bright and live.

Everybody looked up, and Demijack shouted, "There! There!" He was right: the blot that might only have been a smudge of oil on the screen moved as Vinnie banked, revealing itself to be a freighter, big and ungainly and hopelessly outclassed. Easy prey. Easy pickings.

We could use some of them, thought Black Alice. Contrary to the e-ballads and comm stories, a pirate's life was not all imported delicacies and fawning slaves. Especially not when three-quarters of any and all profits went directly back to the *Lavinia Whateley*, to keep her healthy and happy. Nobody ever argued. There were stories about the *Marie Curie*, too.

The captain's voice over fiberoptic cable—strung beside the *Lavinia Whateley*'s nerve bundles—was as clear and free of static as if she stood at Black Alice's elbow. "Battle stations," Captain Song said, and the crew leapt to obey. It had been two Solar since Captain Song keelhauled James Brady, but nobody who'd been with the ship then was ever likely to forget his ruptured eyes and frozen scream.

Black Alice manned her station, and stared at the screen. She saw the freighter's name—the *Josephine Baker*—gold on black across the stern, the Venusian flag for its port of registry wired stiff from a mast on its hull. It was a steelship, not a Boojum, and they had every advantage. For a moment she thought the freighter would run.

And then it turned, and brought its guns to bear.

No sense of movement, of acceleration, of disorientation. No pop, no whump of displaced air. The view on the screens just flickered to a different one, as Vinnie skipped—apported—to a new position just aft and above the *Josephine Baker*, crushing the flag mast with her hull.

Black Alice felt that, a grinding shiver. And had just time to grab her console before the *Lavinia Whateley* grappled the freighter, long vanes not curling in affection now.

Out of the corner of her eye, she saw Dogcollar, the closest thing the *Lavinia Whateley* had to a chaplain, cross himself, and she heard him mutter, like he always did, *Ave, Grandaevissimi, morituri vos salutant.* It was the best he'd be able to do until it was all over, and even then he wouldn't have the chance to do much. Captain Song didn't mind other people worrying about souls, so long as they didn't do it on her time.

The captain's voice was calling orders, assigning people to boarding parties port and starboard. Down in Engineering, all they had to do was monitor the *Lavinia Whateley*'s hull and prepare to repel boarders, assuming the freighter's crew had the gumption to send any. Vinnie would take care of the rest—until the time came to persuade her not to eat her prey before they'd gotten all the valuables off it. That was a ticklish job, only entrusted to the chief engineers, but Black Alice watched and listened, and although she didn't expect she'd ever get the chance, she thought she could do it herself.

It was a small ambition, and one she never talked about. But it would be a hell of a thing, wouldn't it? To be somebody a Boojum would listen to?

She gave her attention to the dull screens in her sectors, and tried not to crane her neck to catch a glimpse of the ones with the actual fighting on them. Dogcollar was making the rounds with sidearms from the weapons locker, just in case. Once the *Josephine Baker* was subdued, it was the junior engineers and others who would board her to take inventory.

Sometimes there were crew members left in hiding on captured ships. Sometimes, unwary pirates got shot.

There was no way to judge the progress of the battle from Engineering. Wasabi put a stopwatch up on one of the secondary screens, as usual, and everybody glanced at it periodically. Fifteen minutes on-going meant the boarding parties hadn't hit any nasty surprises. Black Alice had met a man once who'd been on the *Margaret Mead* when she grappled a freighter that turned out to be carrying a division-worth of Marines out to the Jovian moons. Thirty minutes on-going was normal. Forty-five minutes. Upward of an hour on-going, and people started double-checking their weapons. The longest battle Black Alice had ever personally been part of was six hours, forty-three minutes, and fifty-two seconds. That had been the last time the *Lavinia Whateley* worked with a partner, and the double-cross by the *Henry Ford* was the only reason any of Vinnie's crew needed. Captain Song still had Captain Edwards' head in a jar on the bridge, and Vinnie had an ugly ring of scars where the *Henry Ford* had bitten her.

This time, the clock stopped at fifty minutes, thirteen seconds. The *Josephine Baker* surrendered.

DOGCOLLAR SLAPPED Black Alice's arm. "With me," he said, and she didn't argue. He had only six weeks seniority over her, but he was as tough as he was devout, and not stupid either. She checked the velcro on her holster and followed him up the ladder, reaching through the rungs once to scratch Vinnie's bulkhead as she passed. The ship paid her no notice. She wasn't the captain, and she wasn't one of the four chief engineers.

Quartermaster mostly respected crew's own partner choices, and as Black Alice and Dogcollar suited up—it wouldn't be the first time, if the *Josephine Baker*'s crew decided to blow her open to space rather than be taken captive—he came by and issued them both tag guns and x-ray pads, taking a retina scan in return. All sorts of valuable things got hidden inside of bulkheads, and once Vinnie was done with the steelship there wouldn't be much chance of coming back to look for what they'd missed.

Wet pirates used to scuttle their captures. The Boojums were more efficient.

Black Alice clipped everything to her belt, and checked Dogcollar's seals.

And then they were swinging down lines from the *Lavinia Whateley*'s belly to the chewed-open airlock. A lot of crew didn't like to look at the ship's face, but Black Alice loved it. All those teeth, the diamond edges worn to a glitter, and a few of the ship's dozens of bright sapphire eyes blinking back at her.

She waved, unselfconsciously, and flattered herself that the ripple of closing eyes was Vinnie winking in return.

She followed Dogcollar inside the prize.

They unsealed when they had checked atmosphere—no sense in wasting your own air when you might need it later—and the first thing she noticed was the smell.

The *Lavinia Whateley* had her own smell, ozone and nutmeg, and other ships never smelled as good, but this was…this was…

"What did they kill and why didn't they space it?" Dogcollar wheezed, and Black Alice swallowed hard against her gag reflex and said, "One will get you twenty we're the lucky bastards that find it."

"No takers," Dogcollar said.

They worked together to crank open the hatches they came to. Twice they found crew members, messily dead. Once they found crew members alive.

"Gillies," said Black Alice.

"Still don't explain the smell," said Dogcollar and, to the gillies: "Look, you can join our crew, or our ship can eat you. Makes no never mind to us."

The gillies blinked their big wet eyes and made fingersigns at each other, and then nodded. Hard.

Dogcollar slapped a tag on the bulkhead. "Someone will come get you. You go wandering, we'll assume you changed your mind."

The gillies shook their heads, hard, and folded down onto the deck to wait.

Dogcollar tagged searched holds—green for clean, purple for goods, red for anything Vinnie might like to eat that couldn't be fenced for a profit—and Black Alice mapped. The corridors in the steelship were winding, twisty, hard to track. She was glad she chalked the walls, because she didn't think her map was quite right, somehow, but she couldn't figure out where she'd gone wrong. Still, they had a beacon, and Vinnie could always chew them out if she had to.

Black Alice loved her ship.

She was thinking about that, how, okay, it wasn't so bad, the pirate game, and it sure beat working in the sunstone mines on Venus, when she found a locked cargo hold. "Hey, Dogcollar," she said to her comm, and while he was turning to cover her, she pulled her sidearm and blastered the lock.

The door peeled back, and Black Alice found herself staring at rank upon rank of silver cylinders, each less than a meter tall and perhaps half a meter wide, smooth and featureless except for what looked like an assortment of sockets and plugs on the surface of each. The smell was strongest here.

"Shit," she said.

Dogcollar, more practical, slapped the first safety orange tag of the expedition beside the door and said only, "Captain'll want to see this."

"Yeah," said Black Alice, cold chills chasing themselves up and down her spine. "C'mon, let's move."

But of course it turned out that she and Dogcollar were on the retrieval detail, too, and the captain wasn't leaving the canisters for Vinnie.

Which, okay, fair. Black Alice didn't want the *Lavinia Whateley* eating those things, either, but why did they have to bring them back?

She said as much to Dogcollar, under her breath, and had a horrifying thought: "She knows what they are, right?"

"She's the captain," said Dogcollar.

"Yeah, but—I ain't arguing, man, but if she doesn't know…" She lowered her voice even farther, so she could barely hear herself: "What if somebody opens one?"

Dogcollar gave her a pained look. "Nobody's going to go opening anything. But if you're really worried, go talk to the captain about it."

He was calling her bluff. Black Alice called his right back. "Come with me?"

He was stuck. He stared at her, and then he grunted and pulled his gloves off, the left and then the right. "Fuck," he said. "I guess we oughta."

FOR THE crew members who had been in the boarding action, the party had already started. Dogcollar and Black Alice finally tracked the captain down in the rec room, where her marines were slurping stolen wine from broken-necked bottles. As much of it splashed on the gravity plates epoxied to the *Lavinia Whateley*'s flattest interior surface as went into the marines, but Black Alice imagined there was plenty more where that came from. And the faster the crew went through it, the less long they'd be drunk.

The captain herself was naked in a great extruded tub, up to her collarbones in steaming water dyed pink and heavily scented by the bath bombs sizzling here and there. Black Alice stared; she hadn't seen a tub bath in seven years. She still dreamed of them sometimes.

"Captain," she said, because Dogcollar wasn't going to say anything. "We think you should know we found some dangerous cargo on the prize."

Captain Song raised one eyebrow. "And you imagine I don't know already, cherie?"

Oh shit. But Black Alice stood her ground. "We thought we should be *sure*."

The captain raised one long leg out of the water to shove a pair of necking pirates off the rim of her tub. They rolled onto the floor, grappling and clawing, both fighting to be on top. But they didn't break the kiss. "You wish to be sure," said the captain. Her dark eyes had never left Black Alice's sweating face. "Very well. Tell me. And then you will know that I know, and you can be *sure*."

Dogcollar made a grumbling noise deep in his throat, easily interpreted: *I told you so.*

Just as she had when she took Captain Song's oath, and slit her thumb with a razorblade and dripped her blood on the *Lavinia Whateley*'s decking so the ship might know her, Black Alice—metaphorically speaking—took a breath and jumped. "They're brains," she said. "Human brains. Stolen. Black-market. The Fungi—"

"Mi-Go," Dogcollar hissed, and the Captain grinned at him, showing extraordinarily white strong teeth. He ducked, submissively, but didn't step back, for which Black Alice felt a completely ridiculous gratitude.

"Mi-Go," Black Alice said. Mi-Go, Fungi, what did it matter? They came from the outer rim of the Solar System, the black cold hurtling rocks of the Öpik-Oort Cloud. Like the Boojums, they could swim between the stars. "They collect them. There's a black market. Nobody knows what they use them for. It's illegal, of course. But they're…alive in there. They go mad, supposedly."

And that was it. That was all Black Alice could manage. She stopped, and had to remind herself to shut her mouth.

"So I've heard," the captain said, dabbling at the steaming water. She stretched luxuriously in her tub. Someone thrust a glass of white wine at her, condensation dewing the outside. The captain did not drink from shattered plastic bottles. "The Mi-Go will pay for this cargo, won't they? They mine rare minerals all over the system. They're said to be very wealthy."

"Yes, Captain," Dogcollar said, when it became obvious that Black Alice couldn't.

"Good," the captain said. Under Black Alice's feet, the decking shuddered, a grinding sound as Vinnie began to dine. Her rows of teeth would make short work of the *Josephine Baker*'s steel hide. Black Alice could see two of the gillies—the same two? she never could tell them apart unless they had scars—flinch and tug at their chains. "Then they might as well pay us as someone else, wouldn't you say?"

BLACK ALICE knew she should stop thinking about the canisters. Captain's word was law. But she couldn't help it, like scratching at a scab. They were down there, in the third subhold, the one even sniffers couldn't find, cold and sweating and with that stench that was like a living thing.

And she kept wondering. Were they empty? Or were there brains in there, people's brains, going mad?

The idea was driving her crazy, and finally, her fourth off-shift after the capture of the *Josephine Baker*, she had to go look.

"This is stupid, Black Alice," she muttered to herself as she climbed down the companion way, the beads in her hair clicking against her earrings. "Stupid, stupid, stupid." Vinnie bioluminesced, a traveling spotlight, placidly unconcerned whether Black Alice was being an idiot or not.

Half-Hand Sally had pulled duty in the main hold. She nodded at Black Alice and Black Alice nodded back. Black Alice ran errands a lot, for Engineering and sometimes for other departments, because she didn't smoke hash and she didn't cheat at cards. She was reliable.

Down through the subholds, and she really didn't want to be doing this, but she was here and the smell of the third subhold was already making her sick, and maybe if she just knew one way or the other, she'd be able to quit thinking about it.

She opened the third subhold, and the stench rushed out.

The canisters were just metal, sealed, seemingly airtight. There shouldn't be any way for the aroma of the contents to escape. But it permeated the air nonetheless, bad enough that Black Alice wished she had brought a rebreather.

No, that would have been suspicious. So it was really best for everyone concerned that she hadn't, but oh, gods and little fishes the stench. Even breathing through her mouth was no help; she could taste it, like oil from a fryer, saturating the air, oozing up her sinuses, coating the interior spaces of her body.

As silently as possible, she stepped across the threshold and into the space beyond. The *Lavinia Whateley* obligingly lit the space as she entered, dazzling her at first as the overhead lights—not just bioluminescent, here, but LEDs chosen to approximate natural daylight, for when they shipped plants and animals—reflected off rank upon rank of canisters. When Black Alice went among them, they did not reach her waist.

She was just going to walk through, she told herself. Hesitantly, she touched the closest cylinder. The air in this hold was so dry there was no condensation—the whole ship ran to lip-cracking, nosebleed dryness in the long weeks between prizes—but the cylinder was cold. It felt somehow grimy to the touch, gritty and oily like machine grease. She pulled her hand back.

It wouldn't do to open the closest one to the door—and she realized with that thought that she was planning on opening one. There must be a way to do it, a concealed catch or a code pad. She was an engineer, after all.

She stopped three ranks in, lightheaded with the smell, to examine the problem.

It was remarkably simple, once you looked for it. There were three depressions on either side of the rim, a little smaller than human fingertips but spaced appropriately. She laid the pads of her fingers over them and pressed hard, making the flesh deform into the catches.

The lid sprang up with a pressurized hiss. Black Alice was grateful that even open, it couldn't smell much worse. She leaned forward to peer within. There was a clear membrane over the surface, and gelatin or thick fluid underneath. Vinnie's lights illuminated it well.

It was not empty. And as the light struck the grayish surface of the lump of tissue floating within, Black Alice would have sworn she saw the pathetic unbodied thing flinch.

She scrambled to close the canister again, nearly pinching her fingertips when it clanked shut. "Sorry," she whispered, although dear sweet Jesus, surely the thing couldn't hear her. "Sorry, sorry." And then she turned and ran, catching her hip a bruising blow against the doorway, slapping the controls to make it fucking *close* already. And then she staggered sideways, lurching to her knees, and vomited until blackness was spinning in front of her eyes and she couldn't smell or taste anything but bile.

Vinnie would absorb the former contents of Black Alice's stomach, just as she absorbed, filtered, recycled, and excreted all her crew's wastes. Shaking, Black Alice braced herself back upright and began the long climb out of the holds.

In the first subhold, she had to stop, her shoulder against the smooth, velvet slickness of Vinnie's skin, her mouth hanging open while her lungs worked. And she knew Vinnie wasn't going to hear her, because she wasn't the captain or a chief engineer or anyone important, but she had to try anyway, croaking, "Vinnie, water, please."

And no one could have been more surprised than Black Alice Bradley when Vinnie extruded a basin and a thin cool trickle of water began to flow into it.

WELL, NOW she knew. And there was still nothing she could do about it. She wasn't the captain, and if she said anything more than she already had, people were going to start looking at her funny. Mutiny kind of funny. And what Black Alice did *not* need was any more of Captain Song's attention and especially not for rumors like that. She kept her head down and did her job and didn't discuss her nightmares with anyone.

And she had nightmares, all right. Hot and cold running, enough, she fancied, that she could have filled up the captain's huge tub with them.

She could live with that. But over the next double dozen of shifts, she became aware of something else wrong, and this was worse, because it was something wrong with the *Lavinia Whateley.*

The first sign was the chief engineers frowning and going into huddles at odd moments. And then Black Alice began to feel it herself, the way Vinnie was…she didn't have a word for it because she'd never felt anything like it before. She would have said *balky,* but that couldn't be right. It couldn't. But she was more and more sure that Vinnie was less responsive somehow, that when she obeyed the captain's orders, it was with a delay. If she were human, Vinnie would have been dragging her feet.

You couldn't keelhaul a ship for not obeying fast enough.

And then, because she was paying attention so hard she was making her own head hurt, Black Alice noticed something else. Captain Song had them cruising the gas giants' orbits—Jupiter, Saturn, Neptune—not going in as far as the asteroid belt, not going out as far as Uranus. Nobody Black Alice talked to knew why, exactly, but she and Dogcollar figured it was because the captain wanted to talk to the Mi-Go without actually getting near the nasty cold rock of their planet. And what Black Alice noticed was that Vinnie was less balky, less *unhappy*, when she was headed out, and more and more resistant the closer they got to the asteroid belt.

Vinnie, she remembered, had been born over Uranus.

"Do you want to go home, Vinnie?" Black Alice asked her one late-night shift when there was nobody around to care that she was talking to the ship. "Is that what's wrong?"

She put her hand flat on the wall, and although she was probably imagining it, she thought she felt a shiver ripple across Vinnie's vast side.

Black Alice knew how little she knew, and didn't even contemplate sharing her theory with the chief engineers. They probably knew exactly what was wrong and exactly what to do to keep the *Lavinia Whateley* from going core meltdown like the *Marie Curie* had. That was a whispered story, not the sort of thing anybody talked about except in their hammocks after lights out.

The *Marie Curie* had eaten her own crew.

So when Wasabi said, four shifts later, "Black Alice, I've got a job for you," Black Alice said, "Yessir," and hoped it would be something that would help the *Lavinia Whateley* be happy again.

It was a suit job, he said, replace and repair. Black Alice was going because she was reliable and smart and stayed quiet, and it was time she took on more responsibilities. The way he said it made her first fret because that meant the Captain might be reminded of her existence, and then fret because she realized the Captain already had been.

But she took the equipment he issued, and she listened to the instructions and read schematics and committed them both to memory and her implants. It was a ticklish job, a neural override repair. She'd done some fiber optic bundle splicing, but this was going to be a doozy. And she was going to have to do it in stiff, pressurized gloves.

Her heart hammered as she sealed her helmet, and not because she was worried about the EVA. This was a chance. An opportunity. A step closer to chief engineer.

Maybe she had impressed the captain with her discretion, after all.

She cycled the airlock, snapped her safety harness, and stepped out onto the *Lavinia Whateley*'s hide.

That deep blue-green, like azurite, like the teeming seas of Venus under their swampy eternal clouds, was invisible. They were too far from Sol—it was a yellow stylus-dot, and you had to know where to look for it. Vinnie's hide was just black under Black Alice's suit floods. As the airlock cycled shut, though, the Boojum's own bioluminescence shimmered up her vanes and along the ridges of her sides—crimson and electric green and acid blue. Vinnie must have noticed Black Alice picking her way carefully up her spine with barbed boots. They wouldn't *hurt* Vinnie—nothing short of a space rock could manage that—but they certainly stuck in there good.

The thing Black Alice was supposed to repair was at the principal nexus of Vinnie's central nervous system. The ship didn't have anything like what a human or a gilly would consider a brain; there were nodules spread all through her vast body. Too slow, otherwise. And Black Alice had heard Boojums weren't supposed to be all that smart—trainable, sure, maybe like an Earth monkey.

Which is what made it creepy as hell that, as she picked her way up Vinnie's flank—though *up* was a courtesy, under these circumstances—talking to her all the way, she would have sworn Vinnie was talking back. Not just tracking her with the lights, as she would always do, but bending some of her barbels and vanes around as if craning her neck to get a look at Black Alice.

Black Alice carefully circumnavigated an eye—she didn't think her boots would hurt it, but it seemed discourteous to stomp across somebody's field of vision—and wondered, only half-idly, if she had been sent out on this task not because she was being considered for promotion, but because she was expendable.

She was just rolling her eyes and dismissing that as borrowing trouble when she came over a bump on Vinnie's back, spotted her goal—and all the ship's lights went out.

She tongued on the comm. "Wasabi?"

"I got you, Blackie. You just keep doing what you're doing."

"Yessir."

But it seemed like her feet stayed stuck in Vinnie's hide a little longer than was good. At least fifteen seconds before she managed a couple of deep breaths—too deep for her limited oxygen supply, so she went briefly dizzy—and continued up Vinnie's side.

Black Alice had no idea what inflammation looked like in a Boojum, but she would guess this was it. All around the interface she was meant to repair, Vinnie's flesh looked scraped and puffy. Black Alice walked tenderly, wincing, muttering apologies under her breath. And with every step, the tendrils coiled a little closer.

Black Alice crouched beside the box, and began examining connections. The console was about three meters by four, half a meter tall, and fixed firmly to Vinnie's hide. It looked like the thing was still functional, but something—a bit of space debris, maybe—had dented it pretty good.

Cautiously, Black Alice dropped a hand on it. She found the access panel, and flipped it open: more red lights than green. A tongue-click, and she began withdrawing her tethered tools from their holding pouches and arranging them so that they would float conveniently around.

She didn't hear a thing, of course, but the hide under her boots vibrated suddenly, sharply. She jerked her head around, just in time to see one of Vinnie's feelers slap her own side, five or ten meters away. And then the whole Boojum shuddered, contracting, curved into a hard crescent of pain the same way she had when the Henry Ford had taken that chunk out of her hide. And the lights in the access panel lit up all at once—red, red, yellow, red.

Black Alice tongued off the *send* function on her headset microphone, so Wasabi wouldn't hear her. She touched the bruised hull, and she touched the dented edge of the console. "Vinnie," she said, "does this *hurt?*"

Not that Vinnie could answer her. But it was obvious. She was in pain. And maybe that dent didn't have anything to do with space debris. Maybe—Black Alice straightened, looked around, and couldn't convince herself that it was an accident that this box was planted right where Vinnie couldn't...quite...reach it.

"So what does it *do?*" she muttered. "Why am I out here repairing something that fucking hurts?" She crouched down again and took another long look at the interface.

As an engineer, Black Alice was mostly self-taught; her implants were second-hand, black market, scavenged, the wet work done by a gilly on Providence Station. She'd learned the technical vocabulary from Goggle-head Kim before he bought it in a stupid little fight with a ship named the *V. I. Ulyanov*, but what she relied on were her instincts, the things she knew without being able to say. So she *looked* at that box wired into Vinnie's spine and all its red and yellow lights, and then she tongued the comm back on and said, "Wasabi, this thing don't look so good."

"Whaddya mean, don't look so good?" Wasabi sounded distracted, and that was just fine.

Black Alice made a noise, the auditory equivalent of a shrug. "I think the node's inflamed. Can we pull it and lock it in somewhere else?"

"No!" said Wasabi.

"It's looking pretty ugly out here."

"Look, Blackie, unless you want us to all go sailing out into the Big Empty, we are *not* pulling that governor. Just fix the fucking thing, would you?"

"Yessir," said Black Alice, thinking hard. The first thing was that Wasabi knew what was going on—knew what the box did and knew that the *Lavinia Whateley* didn't like it. That wasn't comforting. The second thing was that whatever was going on, it involved the Big Empty, the cold vastness between the stars. So it wasn't that Vinnie wanted to go home. She wanted to go *out*.

It made sense, from what Black Alice knew about Boojums. Their infants lived in the tumult of the gas giants' atmosphere, but as they aged, they pushed higher and higher, until they reached the edge of the envelope. And then—following instinct or maybe the calls of their fellows, nobody knew for sure—they learned to skip, throwing themselves out into the vacuum like Earth birds leaving the nest. And what if, for a Boojum, the Solar System was just another nest?

Black Alice knew the *Lavinia Whateley* was old, for a Boojum. Captain Song was not her first captain, although you never mentioned Captain Smith if you knew what was good for you. So if there *was* another stage to her life cycle, she might be ready for it. And her crew wasn't letting her go.

Jesus and the cold fishy gods, Black Alice thought. *Is this why the* Marie Curie *ate her crew? Because they wouldn't let her go?*

She fumbled for her tools, tugging the cords to float them closer, and wound up walloping herself in the bicep with a splicer. And as she was wrestling with it, her headset spoke again. "Blackie, can you hurry it up out there? Captain says we're going to have company."

Company? She never got to say it. Because when she looked up, she saw the shapes, faintly limned in starlight, and a chill as cold as a suit leak crept up her neck.

There were dozens of them. Hundreds. They made her skin crawl and her nerves judder the way gillies and Boojums never had. They were man-sized, roughly, but they looked like the pseudoroaches of Venus, the ones Black Alice still had nightmares about, with too many legs, and horrible stiff wings. They had ovate, corrugated heads, but no faces, and where their mouths ought to be sprouted writhing tentacles.

And some of them carried silver shining cylinders, like the canisters in Vinnie's subhold.

Black Alice wasn't certain if they saw her, crouched on the Boojum's hide with only a thin laminate between her and the breathsucker, but she was certain of something else. If they did, they did not care.

They disappeared below the curve of the ship, toward the airlock Black Alice had exited before clawing her way along the ship's side. They could be a trade delegation, come to bargain for the salvaged cargo.

Black Alice didn't think even the Mi-Go came in the battalions to talk trade.

She meant to wait until the last of them had passed, but they just kept coming. Wasabi wasn't answering her hails; she was on her own and unarmed. She fumbled with her tools, stowing things in any handy pocket whether it was where the tool went or not. She couldn't see much; everything was misty. It took her several seconds to realize that her visor was fogged because she was crying.

Patch cables. Where were the fucking patch cables? She found a two-meter length of fiberoptic with the right plugs on the end. One end went into the monitor panel. The other snapped into her suit comm.

"Vinnie?" she whispered, when she thought she had a connection. "Vinnie, can you hear me?"

The bioluminescence under Black Alice's boots pulsed once.

Gods and little fishes, she thought. And then she drew out her laser cutting torch, and started slicing open the case on the console that Wasabi had called the *governor.* Wasabi was probably dead by now, or dying. Wasabi, and Dogcollar, and…well, not dead. If they were lucky, they were dead.

Because the opposite of lucky was those canisters the Mi-Go were carrying.

She hoped Dogcollar was lucky.

"You wanna go *out,* right?" she whispered to the *Lavinia Whateley.* "Out into the Big Empty."

She'd never been sure how much Vinnie understood of what people said, but the light pulsed again.

"And this thing won't let you." It wasn't a question. She had it open now, and she could see that was what it did. Ugly fucking thing. Vinnie shivered underneath her, and there was a sudden pulse of noise in her helmet speakers: screaming. People screaming.

"I know," Black Alice said. "They'll come get me in a minute, I guess." She swallowed hard against the sudden lurch of her stomach. "I'm gonna get this thing off you, though. And when they go, you can go, okay? And I'm sorry. I didn't know we were keeping you from…" She had to quit talking, or she really was going to puke. Grimly, she fumbled for the tools she needed to disentangle the abomination from Vinnie's nervous system.

Another pulse of sound, a voice, not a person: flat and buzzing and horrible. "We do not bargain with thieves." And the scream that time— she'd never heard Captain Song scream before. Black Alice flinched and started counting to slow her breathing. Puking in a suit was the number one badness, but hyperventilating in a suit was a really close second.

Her heads-up display was low-res, and slightly miscalibrated, so that everything had a faint shadow-double. But the thing that flashed up against her own view of her hands was unmistakable: a question mark.

<?>

"Vinnie?"

Another pulse of screaming, and the question mark again.

<?>

"Holy shit, Vinnie!... Never mind, never mind. They, um, they collect people's brains. In canisters. Like the canisters in the third subhold."

The bioluminescence pulsed once. Black Alice kept working.

Her heads-up pinged again: <ALICE> A pause. <?>

"Um, yeah. I figure that's what they'll do with me, too. It looked like they had plenty of canisters to go around."

Vinnie pulsed, and there was a longer pause while Black Alice doggedly severed connections and loosened bolts.

<WANT> said the *Lavinia Whateley*. <?>

"Want? Do I *want*...?" Her laughter sounded bad. "Um, no. No, I don't want to be a brain in a jar. But I'm not seeing a lot of choices here. Even if I went cometary, they could catch me. And it kind of sounds like they're mad enough to do it, too."

She'd cleared out all the moorings around the edge of the governor; the case lifted off with a shove and went sailing into the dark. Black Alice winced. But then the processor under the cover drifted away from Vinnie's hide, and there was just the monofilament tethers and the fat cluster of fiber optic and superconductors to go.

<HELP>

"I'm doing my best here, Vinnie," Black Alice said through her teeth.

That got her a fast double-pulse, and the *Lavinia Whateley* said, <HELP>

And then, <ALICE>

"You want to help *me*?" Black Alice squeaked.

A strong pulse, and the heads-up said, <HELP ALICE>

"That's really sweet of you, but I'm honestly not sure there's anything you can do. I mean, it doesn't look like the Mi-Go are mad at *you*, and I really want to keep it that way."

<EAT ALICE> said the *Lavinia Whateley*.

Black Alice came within a millimeter of taking her own fingers off with the cutting laser. "Um, Vinnie, that's um...well, I guess it's better than being a brain in a jar." Or suffocating to death in her suit if she went cometary and the Mi-Go *didn't* come after her.

The double-pulse again, but Black Alice didn't see what she could have missed. As communications went, *EAT ALICE* was pretty fucking unambiguous.

<HELP ALICE> the *Lavinia Whateley* insisted. Black Alice leaned in close, unsplicing the last of the governor's circuits from the Boojum's nervous system. <SAVE ALICE>

"By eating me? Look, I know what happens to things you eat, and it's not…" She bit her tongue. Because she did know what happened to things the *Lavinia Whateley* ate. Absorbed. Filtered. Recycled. "Vinnie…are you saying you can save me from the Mi-Go?"

A pulse of agreement.

"By eating me?" Black Alice pursued, needing to be sure she understood.

Another pulse of agreement.

Black Alice thought about the *Lavinia Whateley*'s teeth. "How much me are we talking about here?"

<ALICE> said the *Lavinia Whateley*, and then the last fiber-optic cable parted, and Black Alice, her hands shaking, detached her patch cable and flung the whole mess of it as hard as she could straight up. Maybe it would find a planet with atmosphere and be some little alien kid's shooting star.

And now she had to decide what to do.

She figured she had two choices, really. One, walk back down the *Lavinia Whateley* and find out if the Mi-Go believed in surrender. Two, walk around the *Lavinia Whateley* and into her toothy mouth.

Black Alice didn't think the Mi-Go believed in surrender.

She tilted her head back for one last clear look at the shining black infinity of space. Really, there wasn't any choice at all. Because even if she'd misunderstood what Vinnie seemed to be trying to tell her, the worst she'd end up was dead, and that was light-years better than what the Mi-Go had on offer.

Black Alice Bradley loved her ship.

She turned to her left and started walking, and the *Lavinia Whateley*'s bioluminescence followed her courteously all the way, vanes swaying out of her path. Black Alice skirted each of Vinnie's eyes as she came to them, and each of them blinked at her. And then she reached Vinnie's mouth and that magnificent panoply of teeth.

"Make it quick, Vinnie, okay?" said Black Alice, and walked into her leviathan's maw.

PICKING HER way delicately between razor-sharp teeth, Black Alice had plenty of time to consider the ridiculousness of worrying about a hole in her suit. Vinnie's mouth was more like a crystal cave, once you were inside it; there was no tongue, no palate. Just polished, macerating stones. Which did not close on Black Alice, to her surprise. If anything, she got the feeling the Vinnie was holding her...breath. Or what passed for it.

The Boojum was lit inside, as well—or was making herself lit, for Black Alice's benefit. And as Black Alice clambered inward, the teeth got smaller, and fewer, and the tunnel narrowed. *Her throat,* Alice thought. *I'm inside her.*

And the walls closed down, and she was swallowed.

Like a pill, enclosed in the tight sarcophagus of her space suit, she felt rippling pressure as peristalsis pushed her along. And then greater pressure, suffocating, savage. One sharp pain. The pop of her ribs as her lungs crushed.

Screaming inside a space suit was contraindicated, too. And with collapsed lungs, she couldn't even do it properly.

ALICE.

She floated. In warm darkness. A womb, a bath. She was comfortable. An itchy soreness between her shoulderblades felt like a very mild radiation burn.

alice.

A voice she thought she should know. She tried to speak; her mouth gnashed, her teeth ground.

alice. talk here.

She tried again. Not with her mouth, this time.

Talk…here?

The buoyant warmth flickered past her. She was…drifting. No, swimming. She could feel currents on her skin. Her vision was confused. She blinked and blinked, and things were shattered.

There was nothing to see anyway, but stars.

alice talk here.

Where am I?

eat alice.

Vinnie. Vinnie's voice, but not in the flatness of the heads-up display anymore. Vinnie's voice alive with emotion and nuance and the vastness of her self.

You ate me, she said, and understood abruptly that the numbness she felt was not shock. It was the boundaries of her body erased and redrawn.

!

Agreement. Relief.

I'm…in you, Vinnie?

=/=

Not a "no." More like, this thing is not the same, does not compare, to this other thing. Black Alice felt the warmth of space so near a generous star slipping by her. She felt the swift currents of its gravity, and the gravity of its satellites, and bent them, and tasted them, and surfed them faster and faster away.

I am you.

!

Ecstatic comprehension, which Black Alice echoed with passionate relief. Not dead. Not dead after all. Just, transformed. Accepted. Embraced by her ship, whom she embraced in return.

Vinnie. Where are we going?

out, Vinnie answered. And in her, Black Alice read the whole great naked wonder of space, approaching faster and faster as Vinnie accelerated, reaching for the first great skip that would hurl them into the interstellar darkness of the Big Empty. They were going somewhere.

Out, Black Alice agreed and told herself not to grieve. Not to go mad. This sure beat swampy Hell out of being a brain in a jar.

And it occurred to her, as Vinnie jumped, the brainless bodies of her crew already digesting inside her, that it wouldn't be long before the loss of the *Lavinia Whateley* was a tale told to frighten spacers, too.

THE BONE WAR

BIJOU THE ARTIFICER HAD SEEN many bones in her time, but never one larger or even close to the size of the monstrous object lying on the floor before her, supported by a plaster cradle. The thing was behemothic, easily longer than she was tall. It had an antediluvian appearance, stained an orange color as if from immersion in a peat bog. Fine dark brown cracks hairlined the surface, reminding Bijou of an egg cooked in spiced tea.

She stepped forward, supporting herself with her filigreed cane, and peered at the bone. Her familiar creature Ambrosias curled in the hood of her robe so he could rear over her shoulder and disconcert folks. He rattled as she bent down: a jeweled, silver-chased giant centipede constructed from a ferret skull mounted on the spine of a horse with the ribs of cats for legs—the whole geared and wired for movement and animated by Bijou's signature magic.

She said, "May I touch it, Doctor?"

The answer came in Amjada Munquidh's no-nonsense tones. "That is why the Trustees have charged me with the honor of bringing you here, Wizard Bijou."

199

Bijou pushed herself upright and looked across the skid the thing rested upon—and, on two sides, protruded well beyond. The woman facing her had thick black hair, cropped short as a foreign man's, and a clear olive complexion. Rectangular black-rimmed spectacles flashed on an upturned, sun-freckled nose that might have fooled somebody less observant into using adjectives such as *cute*, but her shoulders strained the rolled-up sleeves of her men's khaki shirt and her trouser cuffs were stuffed into rock-marred hiking boots.

Bijou felt a touch of unease. Academic politics being what they were, she knew there had to be a catch somewhere.

"You brought me here to touch your humerus, Doctor Munquidh?" Bijou asked roguishly.

"It's probably a tibia." But Dr. Munquidh winked.

Bijou swapped her cane to her right hand and reached out with her left. The bone had a peculiar agate luster as she leaned close. When she laid her hand on it, she realized why. The wizard's intuition tingled up her fingertips and told her that the enormous appendage laid out before her partook of the nature of both bone *and* stone.

Ambrosias glided over her shoulder, rib-legs prickling, the semiprecious stones in his ferret-skull glinting in the museum lights. He poured down her arm quick as water and arced his limber skeletal body to examine the relic.

"Are there giants made of rock?" Bijou joked, then shook her head. "A fossil? Is this a dragon bone?"

"It is a type of...what we call a 'dinosaur,' actually. An ancient beast that lived long before men. Or dragons, for that matter. The discoverer of this particular bone dubbed it the 'Tidal Titan' because the stones from which it was recovered appeared to have been laid down in a mangrove swamp."

"A swamp? Here?"

"The world was once a very different place," Dr. Munquidh said. She rubbed a hand across her thick dark hair. "Even in historic memory, there was a time when this city sat surrounded by rich farmland. Before the desert sands rolled in."

"So your Tidal Titan predates even the elder races, then," Bijou said. She stroked it, polished jasper that still held the echoes of a mind that had run, craved, played, feared in primeval forests. She looked up and stared Dr. Munquidh right in the spectacles. "You want to know if I can mount and animate the damned thing, don't you?"

"I am transparent," Munquidh said.

Bijou's pulse quickened. She contemplated the challenge of quickening a skeleton so antique that it had leached in *stone*. But she was cautious, too. There were reasons she chose not to associate herself with the Museum, or the University.

She said, "How much more of it is there?"

Munquidh smiled, slow and gloating. "Come and see."

She led Bijou out of the exhibit hall. Bijou took her time following, her age an excuse to crane her neck and take in the Museum's architecture. The vaulted white marble dome lofted overhead would have graced any temple; the statues of Virtues ranged in niches between each of its supporting arches celebrated the purpose of the place: Truth, Modesty, Knowledge, Curiosity, Probity, Note-Taking, Citation…

Dr. Munquidh led Bijou to a back room and opened the door with a flourish. Within—

Ah, within.

Bijou stepped forward reverently. Sunlight through high windows outlined the curves of stone that was almost bone. The room was full of shelves, and the shelves were lined with the pieces of a mighty skeleton. There were ribs and tarsals, clavicles and patellae. A mighty scapula leaned against a bare section of wall. Vertebrae were stacked in order of size, the smallest no bigger than Bijou's fist, the largest like sections through the trunks of ancient trees. But the centerpiece, the miracle at the heart of it all, lay in puzzle pieces scattered on the scarred, gouged, age-blackened surface of the massive wooden table in the middle of the workroom's delightful paleontological clutter.

Bijou the Wizard had worked with bones for sixty years, here in this city of Messaline, a city so vast that they called her the Empire of Markets— when they weren't referring to her as the City of Jackals, that was. Bijou knew a skull when she saw one. And this, when reassembled, would be a skull twice the size of the mighty head of an elephant. She could already imagine its delicate…well, *delicate* was a relative term, she supposed, given the size of the thing…nasal arches, the breadth of its spoonlike muzzle.

Bijou's heart leapt up and thumped as uncomfortably against her ribs as if she were a young lover contemplating the face of her beloved after some prolonged absence. *Say,* she thought self-mockingly, *so great a span as an afternoon.*

Even her reflexive inner sarcasm could not quiet the thrill that ran through her. Her hesitations evaporated like desert dew. Ambrosias rattled her excitement.

"This will take years."

"The Trustees are prepared to pay you for them."

"I'll need tools," she said. She eyed the reddish-brown and orange color of the bones critically. "Steel. And brass and gold. Precious or semi-precious stones. Jacinths, I think. Garnets, spinels. Rubies if you have them to waste."

"We have a basement full of minerals," Dr. Munquidh replied. "For this, we can put them to work for you."

She smiled. "And I'll need my assistants."

DR. MUNQUIDH brought her coffee—thick and sugary—and left her alone in the workroom with a pile of papers and sketches indicating how the natural philosophers thought the great beast might have been put together in life. Ambrosias, bored, curled himself twice around Bijou's waist like a skeletal belt and went quiescent.

Bijou looked through them, amused. In a way, it was like being invited to peruse the working notes of a number of different Wizards. It transpired that each natural philosopher had his or her own ideas of how the "dinosaur" should be put together—not to mention his or her own school of thought regarding its diet, mode of locomotion, and probably social behavior, too.

The consensus of the majority, however, appeared to support or at least reinforce Amjada Munquidh's hypotheses, as set forth in her extremely authoritative papers on the topic.

Having read them all, Bijou allowed herself a grimace and a bemused sigh. She pushed them away, finished her neglected and now-cold coffee with a gulp and a second grimace, and twisted the long woolly ropes of her hair into a knot behind her before addressing herself happily to the fossilized skull. She was completely engaged in playing jigsaw-puzzles when Dr. Munquidh returned.

Ambrosias, disturbed by her precipitate entry, slunk up Bijou's spine to rattle on her shoulder once more.

Dr. Munquidh was beaming, and her smile redoubled when she saw what Bijou was doing. "We've been arguing about the arch of that nasal crest," she said. "I see you've gone with the higher option."

Bijou set the pieces down. She'd been experimenting, but she felt it would be cruel to tell Dr. Munquidh she hadn't yet quite made up her mind. "You look happy."

"The hall is yours!" Munquidh cried expansively. "Bring in whatever you need. I've arranged with the Trustees for you to have access to the materials you requested. And there's the matter of your fee, funds for which have not yet been granted, but all the paperwork is in order and the Exchequer appears inclined to cooperate."

Bijou arranged her face in a genial expression. The skills of a Wizard did not necessarily come cheap. And she had her own way of ensuring that there would be no problems with the funding. No long-term ones, anyway. On the other hand—she stroked a fossilized fragment of skull— when she was done with the "dinosaur," the Museum would be able to charge whatever it wanted for people to come see it.

BIJOU'S JOURNEYMAN, a big, blond, bearded fellow who had chosen the Wizard name of Brazen, brought Hawti and the rest of Bijou's gear in through the loading dock. Until now, Hawti had ranked as Bijou's grandest creation. It was the complete skeleton of an elephant, geared and wired and jeweled on every available surface, with enormous belled bangles jingling merrily around each bony ankle. The trunk contained no bones, and so Bijou had given Hawti a trunk constructed from the limber spine of a constrictor.

The massive construct came in through the loading doors laden with two anvils, an indeterminate number of hammers, a jeweler's lathe, and a variety of other implements too numerous to name. Brazen disappeared again—engaged in setting up Bijou's traveling forge in the courtyard—and with Hawti's tireless, gaily belled assistance (and the more obsequious but less congenial aid of several Museum laborers), Bijou rapidly got down to business.

She had all the bones and the table carried carefully from the workroom so she could begin laying out her design in real space and see how the actual bones differed from the sketches. Students of the Museum's natural philosophers arrived to begin freeing the bones from their protective cases of plaster-dipped rag. Bijou herself oversaw the meticulous work of discerning rock from bone as they cleaned the fossils—though in fairness to the students and their teachers, they were remarkably skilled for people without the advantage of a Wizard's intuition.

AND SO did Bijou pass a generally happy and absorbing three weeks, engaged in fiddling with bones, picking through the Museum's assortment of surplus minerals, and tapping out paper-thin sheets of metal foil with her smallest hammer. She began, in fact, to have a tickling sensation that this thing might prove a masterpiece. So absorbed was she that she paid very little attention to the various natural philosophers who came through to tour her work and peer over her drawings, except to have a series of joyful academic arguments with them about the details of bone articulation and whether, in fact, the tibia and ulna in question came from the same individual.

This carefree approach, blissful while it lasted, proved, alas, to be a mistake.

Bijou had, by choice, worked alone—and lived nearly alone, except for the occasional apprentice—for decades. While she did not mind people, exactly, she did not in any way care for their politics, and she tended to ignore the existence of such things. Because of this, her first inkling of trouble arrived in the estimable personage of one of Dr. Munquidh's colleagues, Dr. Azar.

Zandrya Azar had been among the natural philosophers stopping by to peer at the arranged bones and watch the evolution of Bijou's map. She had paused frequently to examine Hawti and Ambrosias as the bone-and-jewel Artifices—not automatons, but self-willed creatures in their own right—assisted Bijou in her work (Brazen was mostly outside on the forge, hammering away at the rough blanks for the armature).

Now, Dr. Azar returned. She stared at Hawti once more, flicked the hem of her long, paneled, coffee-colored skirt against her button boots, and snorted. Her hair was long and lush: an unusual shade of auburn, glistening with red highlights like the coat of a dark bay horse. She was as narrow and sharp-edged as Dr. Munquidh was muscular and broad.

"Can I help you?" Bijou asked.

Dr. Azar cleared her throat and said, half-diffidently and half-not, "I hope you're not going to take the sort of licenses with my Tidal Titan that you did with this elephant here."

Bijou smiled. Was it Dr. Azar's dinosaur? Bijou realized she didn't know who had unearthed the thing. "My contract is to create something as close to life as possible."

Natural philosophers often forgot to be cowed by Wizards once a technical discussion was in full swing. Dr. Azar was no exception.

"The drawings you are using show a lumbering beast. For all their size, the Tidal Giants were nimble, elegant creatures!" Dr. Azar insisted. She pointed to an enormous, fragmented humerus. Bijou had been meticulously cleaning each chip and working a setting for it in metal. Students drew the chip from every elevation, and when they were done she seated them in her armature. She used techniques similar to those of the arts that produced what the Eastern nations called "sparkling treasure," a framework of gold wires supporting kiln-fired enamel.

Where the bone fragments were missing, she either smoothed the gap closed with her malleable golden wires, or she carved a replacement from agate, jasper, carnelian, red jade. On occasion, some costlier gem that she had ground, faceted, and polished to fit glittered and refracted among the yellows and reds. With practised skill and cleverness, she concealed the brass armatures and gears that would allow the thing to stand and move so that when it was assembled they would be barely noticeable.

The result was a mosaic in three dimensions that gave the appearance of golden light shining off water that had flooded the cracks in baked ochre mud. It was understated, lovely, and reminiscent of the most delicate cloisonné, though Bijou doubted any mundane artisan would work on such a scale. Every scrap of her expertise and her Wizardry would be needed to hold this thing together—and let it move.

"These bones are more than strong enough to bear the weight of the animal in a charge. Or to allow it to rear up, using its tail as a tripod! These beasts could run, Wizard!"

"Be that as it may," Bijou said patiently, "there are some structural limitations on the bones in their *current* state."

Dr. Azar gave her a sardonic eyebrow. "Based on what you're charging us, I expect you can find some means of meeting the technical challenge. The science must be respected!"

Bijou had every intention of creating the most soundly engineered Tidal Titan the state of her art would allow. Her professional pride and her affection for her own constructs would permit her no less. But if she built the damned thing and it could *dance*, it wouldn't be because she'd been intimidated into it. She said, "I will see what I can do."

Dr. Azar muttered something about Wizards and their sense of self-worth. It carried quite clearly: the exhibit hall under the grand dome was acoustically excellent and could practically serve as a whispering vault.

Then Azar settled herself and said more loudly, "I shall bring you new drawings."

Bijou sighed inwardly and contemplated the insufficiency of her retainer.

THE NEXT hint of trouble came after moonrise. Ambrosias curled snoozing inside Hawti's enormous rib cage, his marcasites and pearls gleaming softly. Hawti curiously sorted fossils with its trunk, inspecting each with care. Bijou was otherwise alone in the exhibit hall. The trouble was heralded by the unhappy stomp of Dr. Munquidh's desert boots across the exhibit hall's marble floor. Her aggressive tromping carried her to the area Bijou had caused to be roped off with red silk cord. There was a brief rattle as she unhooked the thick cord and another rattle as she refastened it.

Bijou was perched on a stool under the harsh, painful brilliance of a magical lamp. She was bent over her worktable, a fragment of bone tiny and razor-tipped as a shard of pottery pinched in her smallest tweezers. She did not look up until it was seated against the tiny drop of glue that would attach it to its setting and hold it fast until the setting could be burnished into place.

Amjada Munquidh was in a high dudgeon, her olive skin dark with ill-repressed emotion. She squared her shoulders as if steeling herself for an unpleasant confrontation and said, "What's this I hear about Zandrya Azar poking her pointy nose into your work?"

Bijou counted to ten in three and a half different languages—the last was really more of a dialect or patois—and said, "She stopped by earlier."

"And what are these?"

Munquidh, of course, knew perfectly well what they were. Lying on a folding table in the disarray where Bijou had left them after thumbing through them, they were Dr. Azar's sketches.

"She dropped off some drawings," Bijou said, not feeling warmed by the schoolmarmish tone the much younger Dr. Munquidh was taking.

Munquidh snapped, "Well, what was wrong with my drawings?"

Bijou picked up her burnishing tool. She steadied the bone chip with one brown fingertip and began the gentle, painstaking process of coaxing the rim of the gold to enfold it. "I don't recall having said there *was* anything wrong with your drawings, my dear Dr. Munquidh."

Bijou would have half-liked to close her eyes—and perhaps slap herself on the forehead once or twice—but that wouldn't be a good idea while she was burnishing. She would not allow these two to drive her to the point where she damaged the specimen, no matter how much of their academic rivalry they were planning to take out on her. She should definitely have asked for more money.

"Then what was she doing here?"

Bijou found a fifth language to count in, and when that didn't help, she tried it backward. Burnish, burnish—remembering to keep her touch steady and light.

Neither counting nor burnishing helped, because when she opened her mouth what came out was, "Rather the same thing all of my academic visitors appear to be doing. Interfering. Interspersed with snitting."

"Oh!"

Bijou waited. Munquidh eyed her, lips working in fury. Bijou, feeling the shard of fossil was seated to perfection, reached for the next. This one was larger, and it took a little work with the tools to prepare the setting to receive it.

As she was dotting the glue on with the brush, Bijou said, "Your Trustees hired me for my expertise, Doctor. It would be convenient—helpful, even—if you and your colleagues would trust me to use that expertise for everyone's benefit."

Munquidh seethed visibly enough that Bijou flinched inwardly in anticipation of her next words. But whether the good doctor couldn't think of anything scathing enough to match her mood, or whether she was too polite to give voice to what she did think of, the result was that Munquidh simply expelled the breath she'd been holding in a loud and focused *HUFF*, then tromped punitively away.

IT WOULD have been nice to think that would be the end of the interference. But alas, unfocused thoughts do not reality shape, even for a Wizard. So Bijou was forced to continue her work around the interruptions, opinions, sheaves of artwork, well-reasoned papers, and general monotony of a deeply held and felt academic disagreement.

"Forced," Brazen commented, when she aired exactly that sentiment to him one night after they had returned to her house for dinner and a little privacy.

She scooped up lemony, salty tagine with her fingers and a flat bit of bread, chewed, and swallowed. "Well, 'forced' might be a strong word. We could always give the money back."

"It's not the money," he said. He had a tendency to gaudy coats and elaborately colored robes and tunics that she expected to blossom into full-blown eccentricity once he was a master Wizard with an establishment of his own.

She glanced at him sideways. "It's not?"

"You want to build a dinosaur."

When she laughed, couscous nearly came up her nose. She choked and washed her throat clear with several gulps of wine, followed by a long swallow of water. When she had regained herself, she wiped her mouth on her napkin, folded it neatly, laid it beside the plate, and regarded him with a look of injured innocence.

"Well," she said. "Who wouldn't?"

AND DESPITE the politics, bun-fights, insurrections, and interruptions—building the dinosaur *was* a true delight and a test of every aspect of her skills: magicker, machinist, clockmaker, jeweler, engineer. The fussiest and most time-consuming part was assembling the fragmented, petrified bones into replicas of their own original structures that would nevertheless bear the weight of the entire edifice. Once that was accomplished, though, the work of actually erecting the thing went considerably faster—especially given Hawti's assistance as an extremely dexterous and amenable crane and Ambrosias's ability to swarm lightly up vertical surfaces and suspended scaffolding, serving Bijou as a pair of remote-operated hands.

It was a weird, glittering construction project. Hawti's skeleton was not intended to be a naturalist's specimen, and the tusks were chased in gold and enamel, the enormous skull filigreed with gold and emeralds. Mismatched knobby jewels filled its eye sockets, and every gem-paved step shimmered silvery chimes. The anatomy of the Tidal Titan looked almost reserved by comparison in its shades of ochre, wine, and gold.

It was…enormous. They built scaffolding around it, rope hoists, ramps for Hawti because even it could not reach high enough to lift the massive bones into place.

"Its neck should be loftier!" Dr. Azar argued.

Bijou glanced up at the height of the dome overhead.

"It should give more of an impression of power and dignity!" Dr. Munquidh cried, while Bijou contemplated the strength of the subflooring.

"The poor thing's going to have a dull un-death in here," Bijou said to Brazen, waving to the exhibit hall.

"Plenty of children will come to see it," Brazen answered complacently and handed her another cup of coffee. "What are you going to name it?"

That brought Bijou up short.

Name it. Of course it needed a name. She could not animate it without a name. It could not be instructed if it didn't have a name.

For a moment, she thought of asking the Trustees, or the natural philosophers, what she should name the thing. Then she considered doing something much more sensible, such as putting her head in a vise.

She sipped the coffee, black and bittersweet and heady. She sighed a deep and windy sigh, indicative of bleak despair—or, at least, of exasperation grown quite chronic. "What do you suppose Munquidh and Azar will fight the least over?"

"I'll get you some more coffee."

BIJOU HAD saved the best for last. She'd endured endless hours of the reconstruction—eyes burning, back aching, fingers pricked by wire or blistered by solder—promising herself the pleasure of fitting together, of *discovering* the skull. Now, with two years of work gone by; half the students graduated and replaced by new students who had to be taught all the same things all over again; and the massive skeleton assembled, geared, wired, armatured, and holding together quite lightly, admirably, as if in life...Now she was ready.

And of course, Dr. Azar and Dr. Munquidh were there with her to help. They argued about the size of the braincase, the exact design of the hinge of the jaw, the flexibility of the attachment to the neck. They argued about position and number of teeth, whether the bony nostrils placed high on the thing's forehead would potentially have supported a trunk, and how the eyes that Bijou faceted from jacinths larger than her heart and just as crimson should be placed inside the orbits of the eyes, before those orbits were even reconstructed. And then they argued about the reconstruction of those orbits.

Bijou at last resorted to the stratagem of telling each one, in confidence, that she was taking her advice—but asking them not to tell the other to prevent sabotage—just so she could make some progress.

At last the skull was built. Bijou, Brazen, the two completed Artifices, the students, and Drs. Azar and Munquidh gathered around to admire it before Hawti, with the assistance of a rope hoist, was to lift it into place. Hawti would need the help: the Titan's head was tiny by comparison with its body, but it was still almost half as large as the elephant.

The comparison between the elephant's dazzling, jeweled skull and that of the Titan was striking. Bijou had exercised great restraint in modeling the Titan's skull. Its lines showed clean and unadorned, except for the thin bands of gold chasing the spaces between the bone bits, and the places where gemstones understudied lacunae in the preservation. The jeweled eyes kindled with a deep fire.

"All right," Bijou said. "Let's make it live."

The Trustees were summoned and arrived in some haste with a considerable entourage. They had been warned to make themselves available, and no one who could find an excuse to be in the room would miss this ceremony. There would, of course, be a ribbon-cutting and such foofaraw for the public later, but everyone at the Museum knew this was the moment they had been paying for. The galleries encircling the high dome filled to groaning, and Bijou was a little afraid for their integrity.

She gave the word. And then she stood and watched with folded hands, afraid to breathe, as Hawti lifted the great, glorious skull—like a red cloisonné Rukh's egg—and fitted it into place on the graceful sweep of the seemingly endless neck. (Bijou had been startled to discover that the neck was composed of nineteen vertebrae, far more than the standard seven allotted to almost all modern animals.) Brazen slid in the enormous brass pin that served to hinge the skull to the spine, and Hawti stabilized the Artifice while he hammered the end flat to seal it in place.

Most of the scaffolding had been cleared. But they had left a ramp to the head—which she had mounted neither high nor low, but somewhere in between. Bijou handed Ambrosias off to Brazen and marched right up it.

She knew people expected to see some ritual so she invented some. She swept her robes wide, letting sweeping black velvet sleeves (she had dressed for the occasion) flare around her. She intoned a scrap of remembered verse in her own native language, a funeral chant that sounded portentous.

She laid her hand on the thing's flattened nose and reached up on tiptoe to blow her breath into its nostrils. Then she said aloud, in a tone that would carry quite clearly through the acoustically perfect space under the dome, "Amjada-Zandrya. That is your name."

A shiver ran the entire inconceivable length of the Titan. A settling, of sorts, as if it found itself, or found its balance. Then the head lifted slightly and it regarded her, turning like a horse would to center her reflection in one gigantic vermillion jewel.

She stepped back, despite herself cowed.

Then, slowly, majestically, Amjada-Zandrya picked up its feet and began, delicately, to dance. The motion was unmistakable to anyone who had seen a horse perform the half-pass, an elegant diagonal trot, in dressage. There was only room for a half-dozen steps. The Titan, reaching the limit of its movement, curved its enormous head the other way and

212

repeated the passage—airily, in rhythm, and without crushing a single student or laborer or shaking more than a modicum of dust from between the blocks of the dome overhead.

The Trustees and the others in the galleries were at first silent. As the Titan encroached, a few shrieked or pressed back. When it reversed direction, there was a scattering of applause that built quickly to a tumult.

Bijou smiled to herself, clicked her tongue, dropped her arms to her sides, and walked back down the ramp thinking about a hot bath and a two-week sleep.

She was met at the bottom of the ramp by a furious pair of natural philosophers.

She had learned over the course of the previous seasons that Amjada Munquidh was the more explosive of the two. Bijou was therefore not surprised when the black-haired doctor stomped up to her and leaned down to get in her face before shouting, "A Titan can't *dance*."

Bijou smiled, watching the lovely thing shuffle gently, in perfect rhythm, across the floor. "I'd say that's a matter of some scientific dispute, wouldn't you?"

Munquidh stared at Bijou in abject, horrified fury. The galleries were still applauding. Munquidh closed her eyes, visibly restrained herself from violence, and turned on her heel. She vanished into the celebrating students, leaving no few bobbing and aswirl with the violence of her wake.

Azar stepped forward next. Her temper was under better control but her voice was still acid when she said, "Why did you put *her* name before mine?"

"Alphabetical order," Bijou replied. "It's considered the equitable solution in the sciences, isn't it?"

"It is *customary* to alphabetize by *last* name!" Dr. Azar stated icily. Then she, in her turn, clicked off in her polished button boots, her spine hung as straight as a ship's mast.

Bijou watched her go, then shrugged and turned back to her Titan. Amjada-Zandrya had ceased dancing for the moment. Now its long neck lifted its piecework skull gently to the galleries, where it was allowing bystanders to pet its nose with apparent delight.

"Well," Brazen said beside her. "It works."

Bijou accepted the mug of strong tea Brazen handed her, along with a commentarial little wink. When she had sipped and sighed, he asked, "What made you decide to give it that ability?"

She grinned but didn't look at him. Her eyes were for her happy monster. "Oh, I just asked myself what the Titan would have liked, if it could say."

IN THE HOUSE OF ARYAMAN, A LONELY SIGNAL BURNS

POLICE SUB-INSPECTOR FERRON CROUCHED OVER the object she assumed was the decedent, her hands sheathed in areactin, her elbows resting on uniformed knees. The body (presumed) lay in the middle of a jewel-toned rug like a flabby pink Klein bottle, its once-moist surfaces crusting in air. The rug was still fresh beneath it, fronds only a little dented by the weight and no sign of the browning that could indicate an improperly pheromone-treated object had been in contact with them for over twenty-four hours. Meandering brownish trails led out around the bodylike object; a good deal of the blood had already been assimilated by the rug, but enough remained that Ferron could pick out the outline of delicate paw-pads and the brush-marks of long hair.

Ferron was going to be late visiting her mother after work tonight.

She looked up at Senior Constable Indrapramit and said tiredly, "So this is the mortal remains of Dexter Coffin?"

215

Indrapramit put his chin on his thumbs, fingers interlaced thoughtfully before lips that had dried and cracked in the summer heat. "We won't know for sure until the DNA comes back." One knee-tall spit-shined boot wrapped in a sterile bootie prodded forward, failing to come within fifteen centimeters of the corpse. Was he jumpy? Or just being careful about contamination?

He said, "What do you make of that, Boss?"

"Well." Ferron stood, straightening a kinked spine. "If that is Dexter Coffin, he picked an apt handle, didn't he?"

Coffin's luxurious private one-room flat had been sealed when patrol officers arrived, summoned on a welfare check after he did not respond to the flat's minder. When police had broken down the door—the emergency overrides had been locked out—they had found this. This pink tube. This enormous sausage. This meaty object like a child's toy "eel," a long squashed torus full of fluid.

If you had a hand big enough to pick it up, Ferron imagined it would squirt right out of your grasp again.

Ferron was confident it represented sufficient mass for a full-grown adult. But how, exactly, did you manage to just...invert someone?

The Sub-Inspector stepped back from the corpse to turn a slow, considering circle.

The flat was set for entertaining. The bed, the appliances were folded away. The western-style table was elevated and extended for dining, a shelf disassembled for chairs. There was a workspace in one corner, not folded away—Ferron presumed—because of the sheer inconvenience of putting away that much mysterious, technical-looking equipment. Depth projections in spare, modernist frames adorned the wall behind: enhanced-color images of a gorgeous cacaphony of stars. Something from one of the orbital telescopes, probably, because there were too many thousands of them populating the sky for Ferron to recognize the *navagraha*—the signs of the Hindu Zodiac, despite her education.

In the opposite corner of the apt, where you would see it whenever you raised your eyes from the workstation, stood a brass Ganesha. The small offering tray before him held packets of kumkum and turmeric, fragrant blossoms, an antique American dime, a crumbling, unburned stick of agarbathi thrust into a banana. A silk shawl, as indigo as the midnight heavens, lay draped across the god's brass thighs.

"Cute," said Indrapramit dryly, following her gaze. "The Yank is going native."

At the dinner table, two western-style place settings anticipated what Ferron guessed would have been a romantic evening. If one of the principles had not gotten himself turned inside out.

"Where's the cat?" Indrapramit said, gesturing to the fading paw-print trails. He seemed calm, Ferron decided.

And she needed to stop hovering over him like she expected the cracks to show any second. Because she was only going to make him worse by worrying. He'd been back on the job for a month and a half now: it was time for her to relax. To trust the seven years they had been partners and friends, and to trust him to know what he needed as he made his transition back to active duty—and how to ask for it.

Except that would mean laying aside her displacement behavior, and dealing with her own problems.

"I was wondering the same thing," Ferron admitted. "Hiding from the farang, I imagine. Here, puss puss. Here puss—"

She crossed to the cabinets and rummaged inside. There was a bowl of water, almost dry, and an empty food bowl in a corner by the sink. The food would be close by.

It took her less than thirty seconds to locate a tin decorated with fish skeletons and paw prints. Inside, gray-brown pellets smelled oily. She set the bowl on the counter and rattled a handful of kibble into it.

"Miaow?" something said from a dark corner beneath the lounge that probably converted into Coffin's bed.

"Puss puss puss?" She picked up the water bowl, washed it out, filled it up again from the potable tap. Something lofted from the floor to the countertop and headbutted her arm, purring madly. It was a last-year's-generation parrot-cat, a hyacinth-blue puffball on sun-yellow paws rimmed round the edges with brownish stains. It had a matching tuxedo ruff and goatee and piercing golden eyes that caught and concentrated the filtered sunlight.

"Now, are you supposed to be on the counter?"

"Miaow," the cat said, cocking its head inquisitively. It didn't budge.

Indrapramit was at Ferron's elbow. "Doesn't it talk?"

"Hey, Puss," Ferron said. "What's your name?"

It sat down, balanced neatly on the rail between sink and counter-edge, and flipped its blue fluffy tail over its feet. Its purr vibrated its whiskers and the long hairs of its ruff. Ferron offered it a bit of kibble, and it accepted ceremoniously.

"Must be new," Indrapramit said. "Though you'd expect an adult to have learned to talk in the cattery."

"Not new." Ferron offered a fingertip to the engineered animal. It squeezed its eyes at her and deliberately wiped first one side of its muzzle against her areactin glove, and then the other. "Did you see the cat hair on the lounge?"

Indrapramit paused, considering. "Wiped."

"Our only witness. And she has amnesia." She turned to Indrapramit. "We need to find out who Coffin was expecting. Pull transit records. And I want a five-hour phone track log of every individual who came within fifty meters of this flat between twenty hundred yesterday and when Patrol broke down the doors. Let's get some technical people in to figure out what that pile of gear in the corner is. And who called in the welfare check?"

"Not a lot of help there, boss." Indrapramit's gold-tinted irises flick-scrolled over data—the Constable was picking up a feed skinned over immediate perceptions. Ferron wanted to issue a mild reprimand for inattention to the scene, but it seemed churlish when Indrapramit was following orders. "When he didn't come online this morning for work, his supervisor became concerned. The supervisor was unable to raise him voice or text. He contacted the flat's minder, and when it reported no response to repeated queries, he called for help."

Ferron contemplated the shattered edges of the smashed-in door before returning her attention to the corpse. "I know the door was locked out on emergency mode. Patrol's override didn't work?"

Indrapramit had one of the more deadpan expressions among the deadpan-trained and certified officers of the Bengaluru City Police. "Evidently."

"Well, while you're online, have them bring in a carrier for the witness." She indicated the hyacinth parrot-cat. "I'll take custody of her."

"How do you know it's a her?"

"She has a feminine face. Lotus eyes like Draupadi."

He looked at her.

She grinned. "I'm guessing."

Ferron had turned off all her skins and feeds while examining the crime scene, but the police link was permanent. An icon blinked discreetly in one corner of her interface, its yellow glow unappealing beside the salmon and coral of Coffin's taut-stretched innards. Accepting the contact was just a matter of an eye-flick. There was a decoding shimmer and one side of the interface spawned an image of Coffin in life.

Coffin had not been a visually vivid individual. Unaffected, Ferron thought, unless dressing one's self in sensible medium-pale brown skin and dark hair with classically Brahmin features counted as an affectation. That handle—*Dexter Coffin*, and wouldn't *Sinister Coffin* be a more logical choice?—seemed to indicate a more flamboyant personality. Ferron made a note of that: out of such small inconsistencies did a homicide case grow.

"So how does one get from this"—Ferron gestured to the image, which should be floating in Indrapramit's interface as well—"to that?"—the corpse on the rug. "In a locked room, no less?"

Indrapramit shrugged. He seemed comfortable enough in the presence of the body, and Ferron wished she could stop examining him for signs of stress. Maybe his rightminding was working. It wasn't too much to hope for, and good treatments for post-traumatic stress had been in development since the Naughties.

But Indrapramit was a relocant: all his family was in a village somewhere up near Mumbai. He had no people here, and so Ferron felt it was her responsibility as his partner to look out for him. At least, that was what she told herself.

He said, "He swallowed a black hole?"

"I like living in the future." Ferron picked at the edge of an areactin glove. "So many interesting ways to die."

FERRON AND Indrapramit left the aptblock through the crowds of Coffin's neighbors. It was a block of unrelateds. Apparently Coffin had no family in Bengaluru, but it nevertheless seemed as if every (living) resident had heard the news and come down. The common areas were clogged with grans and youngers, sibs and parents and cousins—all wailing grief, trickling tears, leaning on each other, being interviewed by newsies and blogbots. Ferron took one look at the press in the living area and on the street beyond and juggled the cat carrier into her left hand. She slapped a stripped-off palm against the courtyard door. It swung open— you couldn't lock somebody in—and Ferron and Indrapramit stepped out into the shade of the household sunfarm.

The trees were old. This block had been here a long time; long enough that the sunfollowing black vanes of the lower leaves were as long as Ferron's arm. Someone in the block maintained them carefully, too— they were polished clean with soft cloth, no clogging particles allowed to remain. Condensation trickled down the clear tubules in their trunks to pool in underground catchpots.

Ferron leaned back against a trunk, basking in the cool, and yawned. "You okay, boss?"

"Tired," Ferron said. "If we hadn't caught the homicide—if it is a homicide—I'd be on a crash cycle now. I had to re-up, and there'll be hell to pay once it wears off."

"Boss—"

"It's only my second forty-eight hours," Ferron said, dismissing Indrapramit's concern with a ripple of her fingers. Gold rings glinted, but not on her wedding finger. Her short nails were manicured in an attempt to look professional, a reminder not to bite. "I'd go hypomanic for weeks at a time at University. Helps you cram, you know."

Indrapramit nodded. He didn't look happy.

The Sub-Inspector shook the residue of the areactin from her hands before rubbing tired eyes with numb fingers. Feeds jittered until the movement resolved. Mail was piling up—press requests, paperwork. There was no time to deal with it now.

"Anyway," Ferron said. "I've already re-upped, so you're stuck with me for another forty at least. Where do you think we start?"

"Interview lists," Indrapramit said promptly. Climbing figs hung with ripe fruit twined the sunfarm; gently, the Senior Constable reached up and plucked one. When it popped between his teeth, its intense gritty sweetness echoed through the interface. It was a good fig.

Ferron reached up and stole one too.

"Miaow?" said the cat.

"Hush." Ferron slicked tendrils of hair bent on escaping her conservative bun off her sweating temples. "I don't know how you can wear those boots."

"State of the art materials," he said. Chewing a second fig, he jerked his chin at her practical sandals. "Chappals when you might have to run through broken glass, or kick down a door?"

She let it slide into silence. "Junior grade can handle the family for now. It's bulk interviews. I'll take Chairman Miaow here to the tech and get her scanned. Wait, Coffin was Employed? Doing what, and by whom?"

"Physicist," Indrapramit said, linking a list of coworker and project names, a brief description of the biotech firm Coffin had worked for, like half of Employed Bengaluru ever since the medical tourism days. It was probably a better job than homicide cop. "Distributed. Most of his work group aren't even in this time zone."

"What does BioShell need with physicists?"

Silently, Indrapramit pointed up at the vanes of the suntrees, clinking faintly in their infinitesimal movements as they tracked the sun. "Quantum bioengineer," he explained, after a suitable pause.

"Right," Ferron said. "Well, Forensic will want us out from underfoot while they process the scene. I guess we can start drawing up interview lists."

"Interview lists and lunch?" Indrapramit asked hopefully.

Ferron refrained from pointing out that they had just come out of an apt with an inside-out stiff in it. "Masala dosa?"

Indrapramit grinned. "I saw an SLV down the street."

"I'll call our tech," Ferron said. "Let's see if we can sneak out the service entrance and dodge the press."

FERRON AND Indrapramit (and the cat) made their way to the back gate. Indrapramit checked the security cameras on the alley behind the block: his feed said it was deserted except for a waste management vehicle. But as Ferron presented her warrant card—encoded in cloud, accessible through the Omni she wore on her left hip to balance the stun pistol—the energy-efficient safety lights ringing the doorway faded from cool white to a smoldering yellow, and then cut out entirely.

"Bugger," Ferron said. "Power cut."

"How, in a block with a sunfarm?"

"Loose connection?" she asked, rattling the door against the bolt just in case it had flipped back before the juice died. The cat protested. Gently, Ferron set the carrier down, out of the way. Then she kicked the door in frustration and jerked her foot back, cursing. Chappals, indeed.

Indrapramit regarded her mildly. "You shouldn't have re-upped."

She arched an eyebrow at him and put her foot down on the floor gingerly. The toes protested. "You suggesting I should modulate my stress response, Constable?"

"As long as you're adjusting your biochemistry..."

She sighed. "It's not work," she said. "It's my mother. She's gone Atavistic, and—"

"Ah," Indrapramit said. "Spending your inheritance on virtual life?"

Ferron turned her face away. WORSE, she texted. SHE'S NOT GOING TO BE ABLE TO PAY HER ARCHIVING FEES.

—ISN'T SHE ON ASSISTANCE? SHOULDN'T THE DOLE COVER THAT?

—YEAH, BUT SHE LIVES IN A.R. SHE'S ALWAYS BEEN A GAMER, BUT SINCE FATHER DIED...IT'S AN ADDICTION. SHE ARCHIVES EVERYTHING. AND HAS SINCE I WAS A CHILD. WE'RE TALKING TERABYTES. PETABYTES. YOTTABYTES. I DON'T KNOW. AND SHE'S AFTER ME TO 'BORROW' THE MONEY.

"Ooof," he said. "That's a tough one." Briefly, his hand brushed her arm: sympathy and human warmth.

She leaned into it before she pulled away. She didn't tell him that she'd been paying those bills for the past eighteen months, and it was getting to the point where she couldn't support her mother's habit any more. She knew what she had to do. She just didn't know how to make herself do it.

Her mother was her mother. She'd built everything about Ferron, from the DNA up. The programming to honor and obey ran deep. Duty. Felicity. Whatever you wanted to call it.

In frustration, unable to find the words for what she needed to explain properly, she said, "I need to get one of those black market D.N.A. patches and reprogram my overengineered genes away from filial devotion."

He laughed, as she had meant. "You can do that legally in Russia."

"Gee," she said. "You're a help. Hey, what if we—" Before she could finish her suggestion that they slip the lock, the lights glimmered on again and the door, finally registering her override, clicked.

"There," Indrapramit said. "Could have been worse."

"Miaow," said the cat.

"Don't worry, Chairman," Ferron answered. "I wasn't going to forget you."

THE STREET hummed: autorickshaws, glidecycles, bikes, pedestrials, and swarms of foot traffic. The babble of languages: Kannada, Hindi, English, Chinese, Japanese. Coffin's aptblock was in one of the older parts of the New City. It was an American ghetto: most of the residents had come here for work, and spoke English as a primary—sometimes an only—language. In the absence of family to stay with, they had banded together. Coffin's address had once been trendy and now, fifty years after its conversion, was fallen on—not hard times, exactly, but a period of more moderate means. The street still remembered better days. It was bulwarked on both sides by the shaggy green cubes of aptblocks, black suntrees growing through their centers, but what lined each avenue were the feathery cassia trees, their branches dripping pink, golden, and terra-cotta blossoms.

Cassia, Ferron thought. A Greek word of uncertain antecedents, possibly related to the English word Cassia, meaning Chinese or mainland cinnamon. But these trees were not spices; indeed, the black pods of the golden cassia were a potent medicine in Ayurvedic traditions, and those of the rose cassia had been used since ancient times as a purgative for horses.

Ferron wiped sweat from her forehead again, and—speaking of horses—reined in the overly helpful commentary of her classical education.

The wall- and roofgardens of the aptblocks demonstrated a great deal about who lived there. The Coffin kinblock was well-tended, green and lush, dripping with brinjal and tomatoes. A couple of youngers—probably still in schooling, even if they weren't Employment track—clambered up and down ladders weeding and feeding and harvesting, and cleaning the windows shaded here and there by the long green trail of sweet potato vines. But the next kinship block down was sere enough to draw a fine, the suntrees in its court sagging and miserable-looking. Ferron could make out the narrow tubes of drip irrigators behind crisping foliage on the near wall.

Ferron must have snorted, because Indrapramit said, "What are they doing with their greywater, then?"

"Maybe it's abandoned?" Unlikely. Housing in the New City wasn't exactly so plentiful that an empty block would remain empty for long.

"Maybe they can't afford the plumber."

That made Ferron snort again, and start walking. But she snapped an image of the dying aptblock nonetheless, and emailed it to Environmental Services. They'd handle the ticket, if they decided the case warranted one.

The Sri Lakshmi Venkateshwara—SLV—was about a hundred meters on, an open-air food stand shaded by a grove of engineered neem trees, their panel leaves angling to follow the sun. Hunger hadn't managed to penetrate Ferron's re-upped hypomania yet, but it would be a good idea to eat anyway: the brain might not be in any shape to notice that the body needed maintenance, but failing to provide that maintenance just added extra interest to the bill when it eventually came due.

Ferron ordered an enormous, potato-and-pea stuffed crepe against Indrapramit's packet of samosas, plus green coconut water. Disdaining the SLV's stand-up tables, they ventured a little further along the avenue until they found a bench to eat them on. News and ads flickered across the screen on its back. Ferron set the cat carrier on the seat between them.

Indrapramit dropped a somebody-else's-problem skin around them for privacy and unwrapped his first samosa. Flocks of green and yellow parrots wheeled in the trees nearby; the boldest dozen fluttered down to hop and scuffle where the crumbs might fall. You couldn't skin yourself out of the perceptions of the unwired world.

Indrapramit raised his voice to be heard over their arguments. "You shouldn't have re-upped."

The dosa was good—as crisp as she wanted, served with a smear of red curry. Ferron ate most of it, meanwhile grab-and-pasting names off of Coffin's known associates lists onto an interfaced interview plan, before answering.

"Most homicides are closed—if they get closed—in the first forty-eight hours. It's worth a little hypomania binge to find Coffin's killer."

"There's more than one murder every two days in this city, boss."

"Sure." She had a temper, but this wasn't the time to exercise it. She knew, given her family history, Indrapramit worried secretly that she'd succumb to addiction and abuse of the rightminding chemicals. The remaining bites of the dosa got sent to meet their brethren, peas popping between her teeth. The wrapper went into the recycler beside the bench. "But we don't catch every case that flies through."

Indrapramit tossed wadded-up paper at Ferron's head. Ferron batted it into that recycler too. "No, yaar. Just all of them this week."

The targeted ads bleeding off the bench-back behind Ferron were scientifically designed to attract her attention, which only made them more annoying. Some too-attractive citizen squalled about rightminding programs for geriatrics ("Bring your parents into the modern age!"), and the news—in direct, loud counterpoint—was talking about the latest orbital telescope discoveries: apparently a star some twenty thousand light years away, in the Andromeda Galaxy, had suddenly begun exhibiting a flickering pattern that some astronomers considered a possible precursor to a nova event.

The part of her brain that automatically built such parallels said: *Andromeda. Contained within the span of Uttara Bhadrapada. The twenty-sixth nakshatra in Hindu astronomy, although she was not a sign of the Zodiac to the Greeks.* Pegasus was also in Uttara Bhadrapada. Ferron devoted a few more cycles to wondering if there was any relationship other than coincidental between the legendary serpent Ahir Budhnya, the deity of Uttara Bhadrapada, and the sea monster Cetus, set to eat—*devour*, the Greeks were so melodramatic—the chained Andromeda.

The whole thing fell under the influence of the god Aryaman, whose path was the Milky Way—the Heavenly Ganges.

You're overqualified, madam. Oh, she could have been the professor, the academic her mother had dreamed of making her, in all those long hours spent in virtual reproductions of myths the world around. She could have been. But if she'd really wanted to make her mother happy, she would have pursued Egyptology, too.

But she wasn't, and it was time she got her mind back on the job she *did* have.

Ferron flicked on the feeds she'd shut off to attend the crime scene. She didn't like to skin on the job: a homicide cop's work depended heavily on unfiltered perceptions, and if you trimmed everything and everyone irritating or disagreeable out of reality, the odds were pretty good that you'd miss the truth behind a crime. But sometimes you had to make an exception.

She linked up, turned up her spam filters and ad blockers, and sorted more Known Associates files. Speaking of her mother, that required ignoring all those lion-headed message-waiting icons blinking in a corner of her feed—and the pileup of news and personal messages in her assimilator.

Lions. Bengaluru's state capitol was topped with a statue of a four-headed lion, guarding each of the cardinal directions. The ancient symbol of India was part of why Ferron's mother chose that symbolism. But only part.

She set the messages to *hide*, squirming with guilt as she did, and concentrated on the work-related mail.

When she looked up, Indrapramit appeared to have finished both his sorting and his samosas. "All right, what have you got?"

"Just this." She dumped the interview files to his headspace.

The Senior Constable blinked upon receipt. "Ugh. That's even more than I thought."

FIRST ON Ferron's interview list were the dead man's coworkers, based on the simple logic that if anybody knew how to turn somebody inside out, it was likely to be another physicist. Indrapramit went back to the aptblock to continue interviewing more-or-less hysterical neighbors in a quest for the name of any potential lover or assignation from the night before.

It was the task least likely to be any fun at all. But then, Ferron was the senior officer. Rank hath its privileges. Someday, Indrapramit would be making junior colleagues follow up horrible gutwork.

The bus, it turned out, ran right from the corner where Coffin's kin-block's street intercepted the main road. Proximity made her choose it over the mag-lev Metro, but she soon regretted her decision, because it then wound in a drunken pattern through what seemed like the majority of Bengaluru.

She was lucky enough to find a seat—it wasn't a crowded hour. She registered her position with dispatch and settled down to wait and talk to the hyacinth cat, since it was more than sunny enough that no one needed to pedal. She waited it out for the transfer point anyway: *that* bus ran straight to the U District, where BioShell had its offices.

Predictable. Handy for head-hunting, and an easy walk for any BioShell employee who might also teach classes. As it seemed, by the number of Professor So-and-sos on Ferron's list, that many of them did.

Her tech, a short wide-bellied man who went by the handle Ravindra, caught up with her while she was still leaned against the second bus's warm, tinted window. He hopped up the steps two at a time, belying his bulk, and shooed a citizen out of the seat beside Ferron with his investigator's card.

Unlike peace officers, who had long since been spun out as distributed employees, techs performed their functions amid the equipment and resources of a centralized lab. But today, Ravindra had come equipped for fieldwork. He stood, steadying himself on the grab bar, and spread his kit out on the now-unoccupied aisle seat while Ferron coaxed the cat from her carrier under the seat.

"Good puss," Ravindra said, riffling soft fur until he found the contact point behind the animal's ears. His probe made a soft, satisfied beep as he connected it. The cat relaxed bonelessly, purring. "You want a complete download?"

"Whatever you can get," Ferron said. "It looks like she's been wiped. She won't talk, anyway."

"Could be trauma, boss," Ravindra said dubiously. "Oh, DNA results are back. That's your inside-out vic, all right. The autopsy was just getting started when I left, and Doc said to tell you that to a first approximation, it looked like all the bits were there, albeit not necessarily in the proper sequence."

"Well, that's a relief." The bus lurched. "At least it's the correct dead guy."

"Miaow," said the cat.

"What is your name, puss?" Ravindra asked.

"Chairman Miaow," the cat said, in a sweet doll's voice.

"Oh, no," Ferron said. "That's just what I've been calling her."

"Huh." Ravindra frowned at the readouts that must be scrolling across his feed. "Did you feed her, boss?"

"Yeah," Ferron said. "To get her out from under the couch."

He nodded, and started rolling up his kit. As he disconnected the probe, he said, "I downloaded everything there was. It's not much. And I'll take a tissue sample for further investigation, but I don't think this cat was wiped."

"But there's nothing—"

"I know," he said. "Not wiped. This one's factory-new. And it's bonded to you. Congratulations, Sub-Inspector. I think you have a cat."

"I can't—" she said, and paused. "I already have a fox. My mother's fox, rather. I'm taking care of it for her."

"*Mine,*" the cat said distinctly, rubbing her blue-and-yellow muzzle along Ferron's uniform sleeve, leaving behind a scraping of azure lint.

"I imagine they can learn to cohabitate." He shouldered his kit. "Anyway, it's unlikely Chairman Miaow here will be any use as a witness, but I'll pick over the data anyway and get back to you. It's not even a gig."

"Damn," she said. "I was hoping she'd seen the killer. So even if she's brand-new...why hadn't she bonded to Coffin?"

"He hadn't fed her," Ravindra said. "And he hadn't given her a name. She's a sweetie, though." He scratched behind her ears. A funny expression crossed his face. "You know, I've been wondering for ages—how did you wind up choosing to be called *Ferron*, anyway?"

"My mother used to say I was stubborn as iron." Ferron managed to keep what she knew would be a pathetically adolescent shrug off her shoulders. "She was fascinated by Egypt, but I studied Classics—Latin, Greek, Sanskrit. Some Chinese stuff. And I liked the name. *Ferrum*, iron. She won't use it. She still uses my cradlename." *Even when I'm paying her bills.*

The lion-face still blinked there, muted but unanswered. In a fit of irritation, Ferron banished it. It wasn't like she would forget to call.

Once she had time, she promised the ghost of her mother.

Ravindra, she realized, was staring at her quizzically. "How did a classicist wind up a murder cop?"

Ferron snorted. "You ever try to find Employment as a classicist?"

RAVINDRA GOT off at the next stop. Ferron watched him walk away, whistling for an autorickshaw to take him back to the lab. She scratched Chairman Miaow under the chin and sighed.

In another few minutes, she reached the university district and disembarked, still burdened with cat and carrier. It was a pleasant walk from the stop, despite the heat of the end of the dry season. It was late June, and Ferron wondered what it had been like before the Shift, when the monsoons would have started already, breaking the back of the heat.

The walk from the bus took under fifteen minutes, the cat a dozy puddle. A patch of sweat spread against Ferron's summerweight trousers where the carrier bumped softly against her hip. She knew she retraced Coffin's route on those rare days when he might choose to report to the office.

Nearing the Indian Institute of Science, Ferron became aware that clothing styles were shifting—self-consciously Green Earther living fabric and ironic, ill-fitting student antiques predominated. Between the buildings and the statuary of culture heroes—R.K. Narayan, Ratan Tata, stark-white with serene or stern expressions—the streets still swarmed, and would until long after nightfall. A prof-caste wearing a live-cloth salwar kameez strutted past; Ferron was all too aware that the outfit would cost a week's salary for even a fairly high-ranking cop.

The majority of these people were Employed. They wore salwar kameez or suits and they had that purpose in their step—unlike most citizens, who weren't in too much of a hurry to get anywhere, especially in the heat of day. It was easier to move in the University quarter, because traffic flowed with intent. Ferron, accustomed to stepping around window-browsing Supplemented and people out for their mandated exercise, felt stress dropping away as the greenery, trees, and gracious old 19th and 20th century buildings of the campus rose up on every side.

As she walked under the chin of Mohandas Gandhi, Ferron felt the familiar irritation that female police pioneer Kiran Bedi, one of her own personal idols, was not represented among the statuary. There was hijra activist Shabnam Mausi behind a row of well-tended planters, though, which was somewhat satisfying.

Some people found it unsettling to be surrounded by so much brick, poured concrete, and mined stone—the legacy of cooler, more energy-rich times. Ferron knew that the bulk of the university's buildings were more efficient green structures, but those tended to blend into their surroundings. The overwhelming impression was still that of a return to a simpler time: 1870, perhaps, or 1955. Ferron wouldn't have wanted to see the whole city gone this way, but it was good that some of the history had been preserved.

Having bisected campus, Ferron emerged along a prestigious street of much more modern buildings. No vehicles larger than bicycles were allowed here, and the roadbed swarmed with those, people on foot, and pedestrials. Ferron passed a rack of share-bikes and a newly constructed green building, still uninhabited, the leaves of its suntrees narrow, immature, and furled. They'd soon be spread wide, and the structure fully tenanted.

The BioShell office itself was a showpiece on the ground floor of a business block, with a live receptionist visible behind foggy photosynthetic glass walls. *I'd hate a job where you can't pick your nose in case the pedestrians see it.* Of course, Ferron hadn't chosen to be as decorative as the receptionist. A certain stern plainness helped get her job done.

"Hello," Ferron said, as the receptionist smoothed brown hair over a shoulder. "I'm Police Sub-Inspector Ferron. I'm here to see Dr. Rao."

"A moment, madam," the receptionist said, gesturing graciously to a chair.

Ferron set heels together in parade rest and—impassive—waited. It was only a few moments before a shimmer of green flickered across the receptionist's iris.

"First door on the right, madam, and then up the stairs. Do you require a guide?"

"Thank you," Ferron said, glad she hadn't asked about the cat. "I think I can find it."

There was an elevator for the disabled, but the stairs were not much further on. Ferron lugged Chairman Miaow through the fire door at the top and paused a moment to catch her breath. A steady hum came from the nearest room, to which the door stood ajar.

Ferron picked her way across a lush biorug sprinkled with violet and yellow flowers and tapped lightly. A voice rose over the hum. "Namaskar!"

Dr. Rao was a slender, tall man whose eyes were framed in heavy creases. He walked forward at a moderate speed on a treadmill, an old-fashioned keyboard and monitor mounted on a swivel arm before him. As Ferron entered, he pushed the arm aside, but kept walking. An amber light flickered green as the monitor went dark: he was charging batteries now.

"Namaskar," Ferron replied. She tried not to stare too obviously at the walking desk.

She must have failed.

"Part of my rightminding, madam," Rao said with an apologetic shrug. "I've fibromyalgia, and mild exercise helps. You must be the Sub-Inspector. How do you take your mandated exercise? You carry yourself with such confidence."

"I am a practitioner of kalari payat," Ferron said, naming a South Indian martial art. "It's useful in my work."

"Well," he said. "I hope you'll see no need to demonstrate any upon me. Is that a cat?"

"Sorry, saab," Ferron said. "It's work-related. She can wait in the hall if you mind—"

"No, not at all. Actually, I love cats. She can come out, if she's not too scared."

"Oouuuuut!" said Chairman Miaow.

"I guess that settles that." Ferron unzipped the carrier, and the hyacinth parrot-cat sauntered out and leaped up to the treadmill's handrail.

"Niranjana?" Dr. Rao said, in surprise. "Excuse me, madam, but what are you doing with Dr. Coffin's cat?"

"You know this cat?"

"Of course I do." He stopped walking, and scratched the cat under her chin. She stretched her head out like a lazy snake, balanced lightly on four daffodil paws. "She comes here about twice a month."

"New!" the cat disagreed. "Who you?"

"Niranjana, it's Rao. You know me."

"Rrraaao?" she said, cocking her head curiously. Adamantly, she said, "New! My name Chairman Miaow!"

Dr. Rao's forehead wrinkled. To Ferron, over the cat's head, he said, "Is Dexter with you? Is he all right?"

"I'm afraid that's why I'm here," Ferron said. "It is my regretful duty to inform you that Dexter Coffin appears to have been murdered in his home sometime over the night. Saab, law requires that I inform you that this conversation is being recorded. Anything you say may be entered in evidence. You have the right to skin your responses or withhold information, but if you choose to do so, under certain circumstances a court order may be obtained to download and decode associated cloud memories. Do you understand this caution?"

"Oh dear," Dr. Rao said. "When I called the police, I didn't expect—"

"I know," Ferron said. "But do you understand the caution, saab?"

"I do," he said. A yellow peripheral node in Ferron's visual field went green.

She said, "Do you confirm this is his cat?"

"I'd know her anywhere," Dr. Rao said. "The markings are very distinctive. Dexter brought her in quite often. She's been wiped? How awful."

"We're investigating," Ferron said, relieved to be back in control of the conversation. "I'm afraid I'll need details of what Coffin was working on, his contacts, any romantic entanglements, any professional rivalries or enemies—"

"Of course," Dr. Rao said. He pulled his interface back around and began typing. "I'll generate you a list. As for what he was working on—I'm afraid there are a lot of trade secrets involved, but we're a biomedical engineering firm, as I'm sure you're aware. Dexter's particular project has been applications in four-dimensional engineering."

"I'm afraid," Ferron said, "that means nothing to me."

"Of course." He pressed a key. The cat peered over his shoulder, apparently fascinated by the blinking lights on the monitor.

The hyperlink blinked live in Ferron's feed. She accessed it and received a brief education in the theoretical physics of reaching around three-dimensional shapes in space-time. A cold sweat slicked her palms. She told herself it was just the second hypomania re-up.

"Closed-heart surgery," she said. During the medical tourism boom, Bengaluru's economy had thrived. They'd found other ways to make ends meet now that people no longer traveled so profligately, but the state remained one of India's centers of medical technology. Ferron wondered about the applications for remote surgery, and what the economic impact of this technology could be.

"Sure. Or extracting an appendix without leaving a scar. Inserting stem cells into bone marrow with no surgical trauma, freeing the body to heal disease instead of infection and wounds. It's revolutionary. If we can get it working."

"Saab…" She stroked Chairman Miaow's sleek azure head. "Could it be used as a weapon?"

"Anything can be used as a weapon," he said. A little too fast? But his skin conductivity and heart rate revealed no deception, no withholding. "Look, Sub-Inspector. Would you like some coffee?"

"I'd love some," she admitted.

He tapped a few more keys and stepped down from the treadmill. She'd have thought the typing curiously inefficient, but he certainly seemed to get things done fast.

"Religious reasons, saab?" she asked.

"Hmm?" He glanced at the monitor. "No. I'm just an eccentric. I prefer one information stream at a time. And I like to come here and do my work, and keep my home at home."

"Oh." Ferron laughed, following him across the office to a set of antique lacquered chairs. Chairman Miaow minced after them, stopping to sniff the unfamiliar rug and roll in a particularly lush patch. Feeling like she was making a huge confession, Ferron said, "I turn off my feeds sometimes too. Skin out. It helps me concentrate."

He winked.

She said, "So tell me about Dexter and his cat."

"Well…" He glanced guiltily at Chairman Miaow. "She was very advanced. He obviously spent a great deal of time working with her. Complete sentences, conversation on about the level of an imaginative five-year-old. That's one of our designs, by the way."

"Parrot cats?"

"The hyacinth variety. We're working on an *Eclectus* variant for next year's market. Crimson and plum colors. You know they have a much longer lifespan than the root stock? Parrot-cats should be able to live for thirty to fifty years, though of course the design hasn't been around long enough for experimental proof."

"I did not. About Dr. Coffin—" she paused, and scanned the lists of enemies and contacts that Dr. Rao had provided, cross-referencing it with files and the reports of three interviews that had come in from Indrapramit in the last five minutes. Another contact request from her mother blinked away officiously. She dismissed it. "I understand he wasn't born here?"

"He traveled," Dr. Rao said in hushed tones. "From America."

"Huh," Ferron said. "He relocated for a job? Medieval. How did BioShell justify the expense—and the carbon burden?"

"A unique skill set. We bring in people from many places, actually. He was well-liked here: his work was outstanding, and he was charming enough—and talented enough—that his colleagues forgave him some of the...vagaries in his rightminding."

"Vagaries...?"

"He was a depressive, madam," Dr. Rao said. "Prone to fairly serious fits of existential despair. Medication and surgery controlled it adequately that he was functional, but not completely enough that he was always... comfortable."

"When you say existential despair...?" Ferron was a past master of the open-ended hesitation.

Dr. Rao seemed cheerfully willing to fill them in for her. "He questioned the worth and value of pretty much every human endeavor. Of existence itself."

"So he was a bit nihilistic?"

"Nihilism denies value. Dexter was willing to believe that compassion had value—not intrinsic value, you understand. But assigned value. He believed that the best thing a human being could aspire to was to limit suffering."

"That explains his handle."

Dr. Rao chuckled. "It does, doesn't it? Anyway, he was brilliant."

"I assume that means that BioShell will suffer in his absence."

"The fourth-dimension project is going to fall apart without him," Dr. Rao said candidly. "It's going to take a global search to replace him. And we'll have to do it quickly; release of the technology was on the anvil."

Ferron thought about the inside-out person in the midst of his rug, his flat set for an intimate dinner for two. "Dr. Rao..."

"Yes, Sub-Inspector?"

"In your estimation, would Dr. Coffin commit suicide?"

He steepled his fingers and sighed. "It's…possible. But he was very devoted to his work, and his psych evaluations did not indicate it as an immediate danger. I'd hate to think so."

"Because you'd feel like you should have done more? You can't save somebody from themselves, Dr. Rao."

"Sometimes," he said, "a word in the dark is all it takes."

"Dr. Coffin worked from home. Was any of his lab equipment there? Is it possible that he died in an accident?"

Dr. Rao's eyebrows rose. "Now I'm curious about the nature of his demise, I'm afraid. He should not have had any proprietary equipment at home: we maintain a lab for him here, and his work at home should have been limited to theory and analysis. But of course he'd have an array of interfaces."

The coffee arrived, brought in by a young man with a ready smile who set the tray on the table and vanished again without a word. No doubt pleased to be Employed.

As Dr. Rao poured from a solid old stoneware carafe, he transitioned to small talk. "Some exciting news about the Andromeda Galaxy, isn't it? They've named the star Al-Rahman."

"I thought stars were named by coordinates and catalogue number these days."

"They are," Rao said. "But it's fitting for this one have a little romance. People being what they are, someone would have named it if the science community didn't. And Abd Al-Rahman Al-Sufi was the first astronomer to describe the Andromeda Galaxy, around 960 A.D. He called it the 'little cloud.' It's also called Messier 31—."

"Do you think it's a nova precursor, saab?"

He handed her the coffee—something that smelled pricy and rich, probably from the hills—and offered cream and sugar. She added a lump of the latter to her cup with the tongs, stirred in cream, and selected a lemon biscuit from the little plate he nudged toward her.

"That's what they said on the news," he said.

"Meaning you don't believe it?"

"You're sharp," he said admiringly.

"I'm a homicide investigator," she said.

He reached into his pocket and withdrew a small injection kit. The hypo hissed alarmingly as he pressed it to his skin. He winced.

"Insulin?" she asked, restraining herself from an incredibly rude question about why he hadn't had stem cells, if he was diabetic.

He shook his head. "Scotophobin. Also part of my rightminding. I have short-term memory issues." He picked up a chocolate biscuit and bit into it decisively.

She'd taken the stuff herself, in school and when cramming for her police exams. She also refused to be derailed. "So you don't think this star—"

"Al-Rahman."

"—Al-Rahman. You don't think it's going nova?"

"Oh, it might be," he said. "But what would say if I told you that its pattern is a repeating series of prime numbers?"

The sharp tartness of lemon shortbread turned to so much grit in her mouth. "I beg your pardon."

"Someone is signaling us," Dr. Rao said. "Or I should say, was signaling us. A long, long time ago. Somebody with the technology necessary to tune the output of their star."

"Explain," she said, setting the remainder of the biscuit on her saucer.

"Al-Rahman is more than two and a half million light years away. That means that the light we're seeing from it was modulated when the first identifiable humans were budding off the hominid family tree. Even if we could send a signal back…The odds are very good that they're all gone now. It was just a message in a bottle. We were here."

"The news said twenty thousand light years."

"The news." He scoffed. "Do they ever get police work right?"

"Never," Ferron said fervently.

"Science either." He glanced up as the lights dimmed. "Another brownout."

An unformed idea tickled the back of Ferron's mind. "Do you have a sunfarm?"

"BioShell is entirely self-sufficient," he confirmed. "It's got to be a bug, but we haven't located it yet. Anyway, it will be back up in a minute. All our important equipment has dedicated power supplies."

He finished his biscuit and stirred the coffee thoughtfully while he chewed. "The odds are that the universe is—or has been—full of intelligent species. And that we will never meet any of them. Because the distances and time scales are so vast. In the two hundred years we've been capable of sending signals into space—well. Compare that in scale to Al-Rahman."

"That's awful," Ferron said. "It makes me appreciate Dr. Coffin's perspective."

"It's terrible," Dr. Rao agreed. "Terrible and wonderful. In some ways I wonder if that's as close as we'll ever get to comprehending the face of God."

They sipped their coffee in contemplation, facing one another across the tray and the low lacquered table.

"Milk?" said Chairman Miaow. Carefully, Ferron poured some into a saucer and gave it to her.

Dr. Rao said, "You know, the Andromeda Galaxy and our own Milky Way are expected to collide eventually."

"Eventually?"

He smiled. It did good things for the creases around his eyes. "Four and a half billion years or so."

Ferron thought about Uttara Bhadrapada, and the Heavenly Ganges, and Aryaman's house—in a metaphysical sort of sense—as he came to walk that path across the sky. From so far away it took two and a half million years just to see that far.

"I won't wait up, then." She finished the last swallow of coffee and looked around for the cat. "I don't suppose I could see Dr. Coffin's lab before I go?"

"Oh," said Dr. Rao. "I think we can do that, and better."

THE LAB space Coffin had shared with three other researchers belied BioShell's corporate wealth. It was a maze of tables and unidentifiable equipment in dizzying array. Ferron identified a gene sequencer, four or five microscopes, and a centrifuge, but most of the rest baffled her limited knowledge of bioengineering. She was struck by the fact that just about every object in the room was dressed in BioShell's livery colors of emerald and gold, however.

She glimpsed a conservatory through a connecting door, lush with what must be prototype plants; at the far end of the room, rows of condensers hummed beside a revolving door rimed with frost. A black-skinned woman in a lab coat with her hair clipped into short, tight curls had her eyes to a lens and her hands in waldo sleeves. Microsurgery?

Dr. Rao held out a hand as Ferron paused beside him. "Will we disturb her?"

"Dr. Nnebuogor will have skinned out just about everything except the fire alarm," Dr. Rao said. "The only way to distract her would be to go over and give her a shove. Which—" he raised a warning finger "— I would recommend against, as she's probably engaged in work on those next-generation parrot-cats I told you about now."

"Nnebuogor? She's Nigerian?"

Dr. Rao nodded. "Educated in Cairo and Bengaluru. Her coming to work for BioShell was a real coup for us."

"You *do* employ a lot of farang," Ferron said. "And not by telepresence." She waited for Rao to bridle, but she must have gotten the tone right, because he shrugged.

"Our researchers need access to our lab."

"Miaow," said Chairman Miaow.

"Can she?" Ferron asked.

"We're cat-friendly," Rao said, with a flicker of a smile, so Ferron set the carrier down and opened its door. Rao's heart rate was up a little, and she caught herself watching sideways while he straightened his trousers and picked lint from his sleeve.

Chairman Miaow emerged slowly, rubbing her length against the side of the carrier. She gazed up at the equipment and furniture with unblinking eyes and soon she gathered herself to leap onto a workbench, and Dr. Rao put a hand out firmly.

"No climbing or jumping," he said. "Dangerous. It will hurt you."

"Hurt?" The cat drew out the Rs in a manner so adorable it had to be engineered for. "No jump?"

"No." Rao turned to Ferron. "We've hardwired in response to the No command. I think you'll find our parrot-cats superior to unengineered felines in this regard. Of course…they're still cats."

"Of course," Ferron said. She watched as Chairman Miaow explored her new environment, rubbing her face on this and that. "Do you have any pets?"

"We often take home the successful prototypes," he said. "It would be a pity to destroy them. I have a parrot-cat—a red-and-gray—and a golden lemur. Engineered, of course. The baseline ones are protected."

As they watched, the hyacinth cat picked her way around, sniffing every surface. She paused before one workstation in particular before cheek-marking it, and said in comically exaggerated surprise: "Mine! My smell."

There was a synthetic-fleece-lined basket tucked beneath the table. The cat leaned towards it, stretching her head and neck, and sniffed deeply and repeatedly.

"Have you been here before?" Ferron asked.

Chairman Miaow looked at Ferron wide-eyed with amazement at Ferron's patent ignorance, and declared "New!"

She jumped into the basket and snuggled in, sinking her claws deeply and repeatedly into the fleece.

Ferron made herself stop chewing her thumbnail. She stuck her hand into her uniform pocket. "Are all your hyacinths clones?"

"They're all closely related," Dr. Rao had said. "But no, not clones. And even if she were a clone, there would be differences in the expression of her tuxedo pattern."

At that moment, Dr. Nnebuogor sighed and backed away from her machine, withdrawing her hands from the sleeves and shaking out the fingers like a musician after practicing. She jumped when she turned and saw them. "Oh! Sorry. I was skinned. Namaskar."

"Miaow?" said the cat in her appropriated basket.

"Hello, Niranjana. Where's Dexter?" said Dr. Nnebuogor. Ferron felt the scientist reading her meta-tags. Dr. Nnebuogor raised her eyes to Rao. "And—pardon, Officer—what's with the copper?"

"Actually," Ferron said, "I have some bad news for you. It appears that Dexter Coffin was murdered last night."

"Murdered…" Dr. Nnebuogor put her hand out against the table edge. *"Murdered?"*

"Yes," Ferron said. "I'm Police Sub-Inspector Ferron—" which Dr. Nnebuogor would know already "—and I'm afraid I need to ask you some questions. Also, I'll be contacting the other researchers who share your facilities via telepresence. Is there a private area I can use for that?"

Dr. Nnebuogor looked stricken. The hand that was not leaned against the table went up to her mouth. Ferron's feed showed the acceleration of her heart, the increase in skin conductivity as her body slicked with cold sweat. Guilt or grief? It was too soon to tell.

"You can use my office," Dr. Rao said. "Kindly, with my gratitude."

THE INTERVIEWS took the best part of the day and evening, when all was said and done, and garnered Ferron very little new information—yes, people *would* probably kill for what Coffin was—had been—working on. No, none of his colleagues had any reason to. No, he had no love life of which they were aware.

Ferron supposed she technically *could* spend all night lugging the cat carrier around, but her own flat wasn't too far from the University district. It was in a kinship block teeming with her uncles and cousins, her grandparents, great-grandparents, her sisters and their husbands (and in one case, wife). The fiscal support of shared housing was the only reason she'd been able to carry her mother as long as she had.

She checked out a pedestrial because she couldn't face the bus and she felt like she'd done more than her quota of steps before dinnertime—and here it was, well after. The cat carrier balanced on the grab bar, she zipped it unerringly through the traffic, enjoying the feel of the wind in her hair and the outraged honks cascading along the double avenues.

She could make the drive on autopilot, so she used the other half of her attention to feed facts to the Department's expert system. Doyle knew everything about everything, and if it wasn't self-aware or self-directed in the sense that most people meant when they said *artificial intelligence*, it still rivaled a trained human brain when it came to picking out patterns— and being supercooled, it was significantly faster.

She even told it the puzzling bits, such as how Chairman Miaow had reacted upon being introduced to the communal lab that Coffin shared with three other BioShell researchers.

Doyle swallowed everything Ferron could give it, as fast as she could report. She knew that down in its bowels, it would be integrating that information with Indrapramit's reports, and those of the other officers and techs assigned to the case.

She thought maybe they needed something more. As the pedestrial dropped her at the bottom of her side street, she dropped a line to Damini, her favorite archinformist. "Hey," she said, when Damini answered.

"Hey yourself, boss. What do you need?"

Ferron released the pedestrial back into the city pool. It scurried off, probably already summoned to the next call. Ferron had used her over-ride to requisition it. She tried to feel guilty, but she was already late in attending on her mother—and she'd ignored two more messages in the intervening time. It was probably too late to prevent bloodshed, but there was something to be said for getting the inevitable over with.

"Dig me up everything you can on today's vic, would you? Dexter Coffin, American by birth, employed at BioShell. As far back as you can, any tracks he may have left under any name or handle."

"Childhood dental records and juvenile posts on the *Candyland* message boards," Damini said cheerfully. "Got it. I'll stick it in Doyle when it's done."

"Ping me, too? Even if it's late? I'm upped."

"So will I be," Damini answered. "This could take a while. Anything else?"

"Not unless you have a cure for families."

"Hah," said the archinformist. "Everybody talking, and nobody hears a damned thing anybody else has to say. I'd retire on the proceeds.

All right, check in later." She vanished just as Ferron reached the apt-block lobby.

It was after dinner, but half the family was hanging around in the common areas, watching the news or playing games while pretending to ignore it. Ferron knew it was useless to try sneaking past the synthetic marble-floored chambers with their charpoys and cushions, the corners lush with foliage. Attempted stealth would only encourage them to detain her longer.

Dr. Rao's information about the prime number progression had leaked beyond scientific circles—or been released—and an endless succession of talking heads were analyzing it in less nuanced terms than he'd managed. The older cousins asked Ferron if she'd heard the news about the star; two sisters and an uncle told her that her mother had been looking for her. *All* the nieces and nephews and small cousins wanted to look at the cat.

Ferron's aging mausi gave her five minutes on how a little cosmetic surgery would make her much more attractive on the marriage market, and shouldn't she consider lightening that mahogany-brown skin to a "prettier" wheatish complexion? A plate of idlis and sambaar appeared as if by magic in mausi's hand, and from there transferred to Ferron's. "And how are you ever going to catch a man if you're so skinny?"

It took Ferron twenty minutes to maneuver into her own small flat, which was still set for sleeping from three nights before. Smoke came trotting to see her, a petite-footed drift of the softest silver-and-charcoal fur imaginable, from which emerged a laughing triangular face set with eyes like black jewels. His ancestors has been foxes farmed for fur in Russia. Researchers had experimented on them, breeding for docility. It turned out it only took a few generations to turn a wild animal into a housepet.

Ferron was a little uneasy with the ethics of all that. But it hadn't stopped her from adopting Smoke when her mother lost interest in him. Foxes weren't the hot trend anymore; the fashion was for engineered cats and lemurs—and skinpets, among those who wanted to look daring.

Having rushed home, she was now possessed by the intense desire to delay the inevitable. She set Chairman Miaow's carrier on top of the cabinets and took Smoke out into the sunfarm for a few minutes of exercise in the relative cool of night. When he'd chased parrots in circles for a bit, she brought him back in, cleaned his litterbox, and stripped off her sweat-stiff uniform to have a shower. She was washing her hair when she realized that she had no idea what to feed Chairman Miaow. Maybe she could eat fox food? Ferron would have to figure out some way to segregate part of the flat for her...at least until she was sure that Smoke didn't think a parrot-cat would make a nice midnight snack.

She dressed in off-duty clothes—barefoot in a salwar kameez—and made an attempt at setting her furniture to segregate her flat. Before she left, she placed offering packets of kumkum and a few marigolds from the patio boxes in the tray before her idol of Varuna, the god of agreement, order, and the law.

FERRON DIDN'T bother drying her hair before she presented herself at her mother's door. If she left it down, the heat would see to that soon enough.

Madhuvanthi did not rise to admit Ferron herself, as she was no longer capable. The door just slid open to Ferron's presence. As Ferron stepped inside, she saw mostly that the rug needed watering, and that the chaise her mother reclined on needed to be reset—it was sagging at the edges from too long in one shape. She wore not just the usual noninvasive modern interface—contacts, skin conductivity and brain activity sensors, the invisibly fine wires that lay along the skin and detected nerve impulses and muscle micromovements—but a full immersion suit.

Not for the first time, Ferron contemplated skinning out the thing's bulky, padded outline, and looking at her mother the way she wanted to see her. But that would be dishonest. Ferron was here to face her problems, not pretend their nonexistence.

"Hello, Mother," Ferron said.

There was no answer.

Ferron sent a text message. Hello, Mother. You wanted to see me?

The pause was long, but not as long as it could have been. You're late, Tamanna. I've been trying to reach you all day. I'm in the middle of a run right now.

I'm sorry, Ferron said. Someone was murdered.

Text, thank all the gods, sucked out the defensive sarcasm that would have filled up a spoken word. She fiddled the bangles she couldn't wear on duty, just to hear the glass chime.

She could feel her mother's attention elsewhere, her distaste at having the unpleasant realities of Ferron's job forced upon her. That attention would focus on anything but Ferron, for as long as Ferron waited for it. It was a contest of wills, and Ferron always lost. Mother—

Her mother pushed up the faceplate on the V.R. helmet and sat up abruptly. "Bloody hell," she said. "Got killed. That'll teach me to do two things at once. Look, about the archives—"

"Mother," Ferron said, "I can't. I don't have any more savings to give you."

Madhuvanthi said, "They'll *kill* me."

They'll de-archive your virtual history, Ferron thought, but she had the sense to hold her tongue.

After her silence dragged on for fifteen seconds or so, Madhuvanthi said, "Sell the fox."

"He's mine," Ferron said. "I'm not selling him. Mother, you really need to come out of your make-believe world once in a while—"

Her mother pulled the collar of the VR suit open so she could ruffle the fur of the violet-and-teal striped skinpet nestled up to the warmth of her throat. It humped in response, probably vibrating with a comforting purr. Ferron tried not to judge, but the idea of parasitic pets, no matter how fluffy and colorful, made *her* skin crawl.

Ferron's mother said, "Make-believe. And your world isn't?"

"Mother—"

"Come in and see my world sometime before you judge it."

"I've seen your world," Ferron said. "I used to live there, remember? All the time, with you. Now I live out here, and you can too."

Madhuvanthi's glare would have seemed blistering even in the rainy season. "I'm your mother. You will obey me."

Everything inside Ferron demanded she answer yes. Hard-wired, that duty. Planned for. Programmed.

Ferron raised her right hand. "Can't we get some dinner and—"

Madhuvanthi sniffed and closed the faceplate again. And that was the end of the interview.

Rightminding or not, the cool wings of hypomania or not, Ferron's heart was pounding and her fresh clothing felt sticky again already. She turned and left.

WHEN SHE got back to her own flat, the first thing she noticed was her makeshift wall of furniture partially disassembled, a chair/shelf knocked sideways, the disconnected and overturned table top now fallen flat.

"Oh, no." Her heart rose into her throat. She rushed inside, the door forgotten—

Atop a heap of cushions lay Smoke, proud and smug. And against his soft gray side, his fluffy tail flipped over her like a blanket, curled Chairman Miaow, her golden eyes squeezed closed in pleasure.

"Mine!" she said definitively, raising her head.

"I guess so," Ferron answered. She shut the door and went to pour herself a drink while she started sorting through Indrapramit's latest crop of interviews.

According to everything Indrapramit had learned, Coffin was quiet. He kept to himself, but he was always willing and enthusiastic when it came to discussing his work. His closest companion was the cat—Ferron looked down at Chairman Miaow, who had rearranged herself to take advantage of the warm valley in the bed between Smoke and Ferron's thigh—and the cat was something of a neighborhood celebrity, riding on Coffin's shoulder when he took his exercise.

All in all, a typical portrait of a typical, lonely man who didn't let anyone get too close.

"Maybe there will be more in the archinformation," she said, and went back to Doyle's pattern algorithm results one more damn time.

AFTER PERFORMING her evening practice of kalari payat—first time in three days—Ferron set her furniture for bed and retired to it with her files. She wasn't expecting Indrapramit to show up at her flat, but sometime around two in the morning, the lobby door discreetly let her know she had a visitor. Of course, he knew she'd upped, and since he had no family and lived in a thin-walled dormitory room, he'd need a quiet place to camp out and work at this hour of the night. There wasn't a lot of productive interviewing you could do when all the subjects were asleep—at least, not until they had somebody dead to rights enough to take them down to the jail for interrogation.

His coming to her home meant every other resident of the block would know, and Ferron could look forward to a morning of being quizzed by aunties while she tried to cram her idlis down. It didn't matter that Indrapramit was a colleague, and she was his superior. At her age, any sign of male interest brought unEmployed relatives with too much time on their hands swarming.

Still, she admitted him. Then she extricated herself from between the fox and the cat, wrapped her bathrobe around herself, stomped into her slippers, and headed out to meet him in the hall. At least keeping their conference to the public areas would limit knowing glances later.

He'd upped too. She could tell by the bounce in his step and his slightly wild focus. And the fact that he was dropping by for a visit in the dark of the morning.

Lowering her voice so she wouldn't trouble her neighbors, Ferron said, "Something too good to mail?"

"An interesting potential complication."

She gestured to the glass doors leading out to the sunfarm. He followed her, his boots somehow still as bright as they'd been that morning. He must polish them in an anti-static gloss.

She kicked off her slippers and padded barefoot over the threshold, making sure to silence the alarm first. The suntrees were furled for the night, their leaves rolled into funnels that channeled condensation to the roots. There was even a bit of chill in the air.

Ferron breathed in gratefully, wiggling her toes in the cultivated earth. "Let's go up to the roof."

Without a word, Indrapramit followed her up the winding openwork stair hung with bougainvillea, barren and thorny now in the dry season but a riot of color and greenery once the rains returned. The interior walls of the aptblock were mossy and thickly planted with coriander and other Ayurvedic herbs. Ferron broke off a bitter leaf of fenugreek to nibble as they climbed.

At the landing, she stepped aside and tilted her head back, peering up through the potted neem and lemon and mango trees at the stars beyond. A dark hunched shape in the branches of a pomegranate startled her until she realized it was the outline of one of the house monkeys, huddled in sleep. She wondered if she could see the Andromeda Galaxy from here at this time of year. Checking a skymap, she learned that it would be visible—but probably low on the horizon, and not without a telescope in these light-polluted times. You'd have better odds of finding it than a hundred years ago, though, when you'd barely have been able to glimpse the brightest stars. The Heavenly Ganges spilled across the darkness like sequins sewn at random on an indigo veil, and a crooked fragment of moon rode high. She breathed in deep and stepped onto the grass and herbs of the roof garden. A creeping mint snagged at her toes, sending its pungency wide.

"So what's the big news?"

"We're not the only ones asking questions about Dexter Coffin." Indrapramit flashed her a video clip of a pale-skinned woman with red hair bleached ginger by the sun and a crop of freckles not even the gloss of sunblock across her cheeks could keep down. She was broad-shouldered and looked capable, and the ID codes running across the feed under her image told Ferron she carried a warrant card and a stun pistol.

"Contract cop?" she said, sympathetically.

"I'm fine," he said, before she could ask. He spread his first two fingers opposite his thumb and pressed each end of the V beneath his collarbones, a new nervous gesture. "I got my Chicago block maintained last week, and the reprogramming is holding. I'd tell you if I was triggering. I know that not every contract cop is going to decompensate and start a massacre."

A massacre Indrapramit had stopped the hard way, it happened. "Let me know what you need," she said, because everything else she could have said would sound like a vote of non-confidence.

"Thanks," he said. "How'd it go with your mother?"

"Gah," she said. "I think *I* need a needle. So what's the contractor asking? And who's employing her?"

"Here's the interesting thing, boss. She's an American too."

"She *couldn't* have made it here this fast. Not unless she started before he died—"

"No," he said. "She's an expat, a former New York homicide detective. Her handle is Morganti. She lives in Hongasandra, and she does a lot of work for American and Canadian police departments. Licensed and bonded, and she seems to have a very good rep."

"Who's she under contract to now?"

"Warrant card says Honolulu."

"Huh." Ferron kept her eyes on the stars, and the dark leaves blowing before them. "Top-tier distributed policing, then. Is it a skip trace?"

"You think he was on the run, and whoever he was on the run from finally caught up with him?"

"It's a working theory." She shrugged. "Damini's supposed to be calling with some background any minute now. Actually, I think I'll check in with her. She's late, and I have to file a twenty-four-hour report with the Inspector in the morning."

With a twitch of her attention, she spun a bug out to Damini and conferenced Indrapramit in.

The archinformist answered immediately. "Sorry, boss," she said. "I know I'm slow, but I'm still trying to put together a complete picture here. Your dead guy buried his past pretty thoroughly. I can give you a preliminary, though, with the caveat that it's subject to change."

"Squirt," Ferron said, opening her firewall to the data. It came in fast and hard, and there seemed to be kilometers of it unrolling into her feed like an endless bolt of silk. "Oh, dear…"

"I know, I know. Do you want the executive summary? Even if it's also a work in progress? Okay. First up, nobody other than Coffin was in his flat that night, according to netfeed tracking."

"The other night upon the stair," Ferron said, "I met a man who wasn't there."

Damini blew her bangs out of her eyes. "So either nobody came in, or whoever did is a good enough hacker to eradicate every trace of her presence. Which is not a common thing."

"Gotcha. What else?"

"Doyle picked out a partial pattern in your feed. Two power cuts in places associated with the crime. It started looking for more, and it identified a series of brownouts over the course of a year or so, all in locations with some connection to Dr. Coffin. Better yet, Doyle identified the cause."

"I promise I'm holding my breath," Indrapramit said.

"Then how is it you are talking? Anyway, it's a smart virus in the power grids. It's draining power off the lab and household sunfarms at irregular intervals. That power is being routed to a series of chargeable batteries in Coffin's lab space. Except Coffin didn't purchase order the batteries."

"Nnebuogor," Ferron guessed.

"Two points," said Damini. "It's a stretch, but she could have come in to the office today specifically to see if the cops stopped by."

"She could have…" Indrapramit said dubiously. "You think she killed him because he found out she was stealing power? For what purpose?"

"I'll get on her email and media," Damini said. "So here's my speculation: imagine this utility virus, spreading through the smart grid from aptblock to aptblock. To commit the murder—nobody had to be in the room with him, not if his four-dimensional manipulators were within range of him. Right? You'd just override whatever safety protocols there were, and…boom. Or squish, if you prefer."

Ferron winced. She didn't. Prefer, that was. "Any sign that the manipulators were interfered with?"

"Memory wiped," Damini said. "Just like the cat. Oh, and the other thing I found out. Dexter Coffin is not our boy's first identity. It's more like his third, if my linguistic and semantic parsers are right about the web content they're picking up. I've got Conan on it too—" Conan was another of the department's expert systems "—and I'm going to go over a selection by hand. But it seems like our decedent had reinvented himself whenever he got into professional trouble, which he did a lot. He had unpopular opinions, and he wasn't shy about sharing them with the net. So he'd make the community too hot to handle and then come back as his own sockpuppet—new look, new address, new handle. Severing all ties to what he was before. I've managed to get a real fix on his last identity, though—"

Indrapramit leaned forward, folding his arms against the chill. "How do you do that? He works in a specialized—a rarified field. I'd guess everybody in it knows each other, at least by reputation. Just how much did he change his appearance?"

"Well," Damini said, "he used to look like this. He must have used some rightminding tactics to change elements of his personality, too. Just not the salient ones. A real chameleon, your arsehole."

She picked a still image out of the datastream and flung it up. Ferron glanced at Indrapramit, whose rakish eyebrows were climbing up his forehead. An East Asian with long, glossy dark hair, who appeared to stand about six inches taller than Dr. Coffin, floated at the center of her perceptions, smiling benevolently.

"Madam, saab," Damini said. "May I present Dr. Jessica Fang."

"Well," Ferron said, after a pause of moderate length. "That takes a significant investment." She thought of Aristotle: As the condition of the mind alters, so too alters the condition of the body, and likewise, as the condition of the body alters, so too alters the condition of the mind.

Indrapramit said, "He has a taste for evocative handles. Any idea why the vanishing act?"

"I'm working on it," Damini said.

"I've got a better idea," said Ferron. "Why don't we ask Detective Morganti?"

Indrapramit steepled his fingers. "Boss..."

"I'll hear it," Ferron said. "It doesn't matter if it's crazy."

"We've been totally sidetracked by the cat issue. Because Chairman Miaow has to be Niranjana, right? Because a clone would have expressed the genes for those markings differently. But she can't be Niranjana, because she's not wiped: she's factory-new."

"Right," Ferron said cautiously.

"So." Indrapramit was enjoying his dramatic moment. "If a person can have cosmetic surgery, why not a parrot-cat?"

"CHAIRMAN MIAOW?" Ferron called, as she led Indrapramit into her flat. They needed tea to shake off the early morning chill, and she was beyond caring what the neighbors thought. She needed a clean uniform, too.

"Miaow," said Chairman Miaow, from inside the kitchen cupboard.

"Oh, dear." Indrapramit followed Ferron in. Smoke sat demurely in the middle of the floor, tail fluffed over his toes, the picture of innocence. Ferron pulled wide the cabinet door, which already stood ten inches ajar. There was Chairman Miaow, purring, a shredded packet of tunafish spreading dribbles of greasy water across the cupboard floor.

She licked her chops ostentatiously and jumped down to the sink lip, where she balanced as preciously as she had in Coffin's flat.

"Cat," Ferron said. She thought over the next few things she wanted to say, and remembered that she was speaking to a parrot-cat. "Don't think you've gotten away with anything. The fox is getting the rest of that."

"Fox food is icky," the cat said. "Also, not enough taurine."

"Huh," Ferron said. She looked over at Indrapramit.

He looked back. "I guess she's learning to talk."

THEY HAD no problem finding Detective Morganti. The redheaded American woman arrived at Ferron's aptblock with the first rays of sunlight stroking the vertical farms along its flanks. She had been sitting on the bench beside the door, reading something on her screen, but she looked up and stood as Ferron and Indrapramit exited.

"Sub-Inspector Ferron, I presume? And Constable Indrapramit, how nice to see you again."

Ferron shook her hand. She was even more imposing in person, tall and broad-chested, with the shoulders of a cartoon superhuman. She didn't squeeze.

Morganti continued, "I understand you're the detective of record on the Coffin case."

"Walk with us," Ferron said. "There's a nice French coffee shop on the way to the Metro."

It had shaded awnings and a courtyard, and they were seated and served within minutes. Ferron amused herself by pushing the crumbs of her pastry around on the plate while they talked. Occasionally, she broke a piece off and tucked it into her mouth, washing buttery flakes down with thick, cardamom-scented brew.

"So," she said after a few moments, "what did Jessica Fang do in Honolulu? It's not just the flame wars, I take it. And there's no warrant for her that we could find."

Morganti's eyes rose. "Very efficient."

"Thank you." Ferron tipped her head to Indrapramit. "Mostly his work, and that of my archinformist."

Morganti smiled; Indrapramit nodded silently. Then Morganti said, "She is believed to have been responsible for embezzling almost three million ConDollars from her former employer, eleven years ago in the Hawaiian Islands."

"That'd pay for a lot of identity-changing."

"Indeed."

"But they can't prove it."

"If they could, Honolulu P.D. would have pulled a warrant and virtually extradited her. Him. I was contracted to look into the case ten days ago—" She tore off a piece of a cheese croissant and chewed it thoughtfully. "It took the skip trace this long to locate her. Him."

"Did she do it?"

"*Hell* yes." She grinned like the American she was. "The question is—well, okay, I realize the murder is your jurisdiction, but I don't get paid

253

unless I either close the case or eliminate my suspect—and I get a bonus if I recover any of the stolen property. Now, 'killed by person or persons unknown,' is a perfectly acceptable outcome as far as the City of Honolulu is concerned, with the added benefit that the State of Hawaii doesn't have to pay Bengaluru to incarcerate him. So I need to know, one cop to another, if the inside-out stiff is Dexter Coffin."

"The DNA matches," Ferron said. "I can tell you that in confidence. There will be a press release once we locate and notify his next of kin."

"Understood," Morganti said. "I'll keep it under my hat. I'll be filing recovery paperwork against the dead man's assets in the amount of C$2,798,000 and change. I can give you the next of kin, by the way."

The data came in a squirt. Daughter, Maui. Dr. Fang-Coffin really had severed all ties.

"Understood," Ferron echoed. She smiled when she caught herself. She liked this woman. "You realize we have to treat you as a suspect, given your financial motive."

"Of course," Morganti said. "I'm bonded, and I'll be happy to come in for an interrogation under Truth."

"That will make things easier, madam," Ferron said.

Morganti turned her coffee cup in its saucer. "Now then. What can I do to help *you* clear your homicide?"

Indrapramit shifted uncomfortably on the bench.

"What *did* Jessica Fang do, exactly?" Ferron had Damini's data in her case buffer. She could use what Morganti told her to judge the contract officer's knowledge and sincerity.

"In addition to the embezzling? Accused of stealing research and passing it off as her own," Morganti said. "Also, she was—well, she was just kind of an asshole on the net, frankly. Running down colleagues, dismissing their work, aggrandizing her own. She was good, truthfully. But nobody's *that* good."

"Would someone have followed him here for personal reasons?"

"As you may have gathered, this guy was not diligent about his rightminding," Morganti said. She pushed a handful of hair behind her shoulder. "And he was a bit of a narcissist. Sociopath? Antisocial in some sort of atavistic way. Normal people don't just...walk away from all their social connections because they made things a little hot on the net."

Ferron thought of the distributed politics of her own workplace, the sniping and personality clashes. And her mother, not so much alone on an electronic Serengeti as haunting the virtual pillared palaces of an Egypt that never was.

"No," she said.

Morganti said, "Most people find ways to cope with that. Most people don't burn themselves as badly as Jessica Fang did, though."

"I see." Ferron wished badly for sparkling water in place of the syrupy coffee. "You've been running down Coffin's finances, then? Can you share that information?"

Morganti said that he had liquidated a lot of hidden assets a week ago, about two days after she took his case. "It was before I made contact with him, but it's possible he had Jessica Fang flagged for searches—or he had a contact in Honolulu who let him know when the skip trace paid off. He was getting ready to run again. How does that sound?"

Ferron sighed and sat back in her chair. "Fabulous. It sounds completely fabulous. I don't suppose you have any insight into who he might have been expecting for dinner? Or how whoever killed him might have gotten out of the room afterwards when it was all locked up tight on Coffin's override?"

Morganti shrugged. "He didn't have any close friends or romantic relationships. Always too aware that he was living in hiding, I'd guess. Sometimes he entertained coworkers, but I've checked with them all, and none admits having gone to see him that night."

"Sub-Inspector," Indrapramit said gently. "The time."

"Bugger," Ferron said, registering it. "Morning roll call. Catch up with you later?"

"Absolutely," Morganti said. "As I said before, I'm just concerned with clearing my embezzling case. I'm always happy to help a sister officer out on a murder."

And butter up the local police, Ferron thought.

Morganti said, "One thing that won't change. Fang was obsessed with astronomy."

"There were deep-space images on Coffin's walls," Ferron said.

Indrapramit said, "And he had offered his Ganesha an indigo scarf. I wonder if the color symbolized something astronomical to him."

"Indigo," Morganti said. "Isn't it funny that we have a separate word for dark blue?"

Ferron felt the pedantry welling up, and couldn't quite stopper it. "Did you know that all over the world, dark blue and black are often named with the same word? Possibly because of the color of the night sky. And that the ancient Greeks did not have a particular name for the color blue? Thus their seas were famously 'wine-dark.' But in Hindu tradition, the color blue has a special significance: it is the color of Vishnu's skin, and Krishna is nicknamed Sunil, 'dark blue.' The color also implies that which is all-encompassing, as in the sky."

She thought of something slightly more obscure. "Also, that color is the color of Shani Bhagavan, who is one of the deities associated with Uttara Bhadrapada. Which we've been hearing a lot about lately. It might indeed have had a lot of significance to Dr. Fang-Coffin."

Morganti, eyebrows drawn together in confusion, looked to Indrapramit for salvation. "Saab? Uttara Bhadrapada?"

Indrapramit said, "Andromeda."

MORGANTI EXCUSED herself as Indrapramit and Ferron prepared to check in to their virtual office.

While Ferron organized her files and her report, Indrapramit finished his coffee. "We need to check inbound ships from, or carrying passengers from, America. Honolulu isn't as prohibitive as, say, Chicago."

They'd worked together long enough that half the conversational shifts didn't need to be recorded. "Just in case somebody did come here to kill him. Well, there can't be that many passages, right?"

"I'll get Damini after it," he said. "After roll—"

Roll call made her avoidant. There would be reports, politics, wrangling, and a succession of wastes of time as people tried to prove that their cases were more worthy of resources than other cases.

She pinched her temples. At least the coffee here was good. "Right. Telepresencing...now."

AFTER THE morning meeting, they ordered another round of coffees, and Ferron pulled up the sandwich menu and eyed it. There was no telling when they'd have time for lunch.

She'd grab something after the next of kin notification. If she was still hungry when they were done.

Normally, in the case of a next of kin so geographically distant, Bengaluru Police would arrange for an officer with local jurisdiction to make the call. But the Lahaina Police Department had been unable to raise Jessica Fang's daughter on a home visit, and a little cursory research had revealed that she was unEmployed and very nearly a permanent resident of Artificial Reality.

Just going by her handle, Jessica Fang's daughter on Maui didn't have a lot of professional aspirations. Ferron and Indrapramit had to go virtual and pull on avatars to meet her: Skooter0 didn't seem to come out of her virtual worlds for anything other than biologically unavoidable crash cycles. Since they were on duty, Ferron and Indrapramit's avatars were the standard-issue blanks provided by Bengaluru Police, their virtual uniforms sharply pressed, their virtual faces expressionless and identical.

It wasn't the warm and personal touch you would hope for, Ferron thought, when somebody was coming to tell you your mother had been murdered.

"Why don't you take point on this one?" she said.

Indrapramit snorted. "Be sure to mention my leadership qualities in my next performance review."

They left their bodies holding down those same café chairs and waded through the first few tiers of advertisements—get-rich-quick schemes,

Bollywood starlets, and pop star scandal sheets, until they got into the American feed, and then it was get-rich-quick schemes, Hollywood starlets, pornography, and Congressional scandal sheets—until they linked up with the law enforcement priority channel. Ferron checked the address and led Indrapramit into a massively multiplayer artificial reality that showed real-time activity through Skooter0's system identity number. Once provided with the next-of-kin's handle, Damini had sent along a selection of key codes and overrides that got them through the pay wall with ease.

They didn't need a warrant for this. It was just a courtesy call.

Skooter0's preferred hangout was a 'historical' AR, which meant in theory that it reflected the pre-21st-century world, and in practice that it was a muddled-up stew of cowboys, ninjas, pinstripe suit mobsters, medieval knights, cavaliers, Mongols, and wild West gunslingers. There were Macedonians, Mauryans, African gunrunners, French resistance fighters and Nazis, all running around together with samurai and Shaolin monks.

Indrapramit's avatar checked a beacon—a glowing green needle floating just above his nonexistent wrist. The directional signal led them through a space meant to evoke an antediluvian ice cave, in which about two dozen people all dressed as different incarnations of the late-twentieth-century pop star David Bowie were working themselves into a martial frenzy as they prepared to go forth and do virtual battle with some rival clade of Emulators. Ferron eyed a Diamond Dog who was being dressed in glittering armor by a pair of Thin White Dukes and was glad of the expressionless surface of her uniform avatar.

She knew what they were supposed to be because she pattern-matched from the web. The music was quaint, but pretty good. The costumes... she winced.

Well, it was probably a better way to deal with antisocial aggression than taking it out on your spouse.

Indrapramit walked on, eyes front—not that you needed eyes to see what was going on in here.

At the far end of the ice cave, four 7th-century Norse dwarves delved a staircase out of stone, leading endlessly down. Heat rolled up from the depths. The virtual workmanship was astounding. Ferron and Indrapramit moved past, hiding their admiring glances. Just as much skill went into creating AR beauty as if it were stone.

The ice cave gave way to a forest glade floored in mossy, irregular slates. Set about on those were curved, transparent tables set for chess, go, mancala, cribbage, and similar strategy games. Most of the tables were occupied by pairs of players, and some had drawn observers as well.

Indrapramit followed his needle—and Ferron followed Indrapramit— to a table where a unicorn and a sasquatch were playing a game involving rows of transparent red and yellow stones laid out on a grid according to rules that Ferron did not comprehend. The sasquatch looked up as they stopped beside the table. The unicorn—glossy black, with a pearly, shimmering horn and a glowing amber stone pinched between the halves of her cloven hoof—was focused on her next move.

The arrow pointed squarely between her enormous, lambent golden eyes.

Ferron cleared her throat.

"Yes, officers?" the sasquatch said. He scratched the top of his head. The hair was particularly silky, and flowed around his long hooked fingernails.

"I'm afraid we need to speak to your friend," Indrapramit said.

"She's skinning you out," the sasquatch said. "Unless you have a warrant—"

"We have an override," Ferron said, and used it as soon as she felt Indrapramit's assent.

The unicorn's head came up, a shudder running the length of her body and setting her silvery mane to swaying. In a brittle voice, she said, "I'd like to report a glitch."

"It's not a glitch," Indrapramit said. He identified himself and Ferron and said, "Are you Skooter0?"

"Yeah," she said. The horn glittered dangerously. "I haven't broken any laws in India."

The sasquatch stood up discreetly and backed away.

"It is my unfortunate duty," Indrapramit continued, "to inform you of the murder of your mother, Dr. Jessica Fang, a.k.a. Dr. Dexter Coffin."

The unicorn blinked iridescent lashes. "I'm sorry," she said. "You're talking about something I have killfiled. I won't be able to hear you until you stop."

Indrapramit's avatar didn't look at Ferron, but she felt his request for help. She stepped forward and keyed a top-level override. "You will hear us," she said to the unicorn. "I am sorry for the intrusion, but we are legally bound to inform you that your mother, Dr. Jessica Fang, a.k.a. Dr. Dexter Coffin, has been murdered."

The unicorn's lip curled in a snarl. "Good. I'm glad."

Ferron stepped back. It was about the response she had expected.

"She made me," the unicorn said. "That doesn't make her my *mother*. Is there anything else you're legally bound to inform me of?"

"No," Indrapramit said.

"Then get the hell out." The unicorn set her amber gaming stone down on the grid. A golden glow encompassed it and its neighbors. "I win."

"WAREHOUSED," INDRAPRAMIT said with distaste, back in his own body and nibbling a slice of quiche. "And happy about it."

Ferron had a pressed sandwich of vegetables, tapenade, cheeses, and some elaborate and incomprehensible European charcuterie made of smoked vatted protein. It was delicious, in a totally exotic sort of way. "Would it be better if she were miserable and unfulfilled?"

He made a noise of discontentment and speared a bite of spinach and egg.

Ferron knew her combativeness was really all about her mother, not Fang/Coffin's adult and avoidant daughter. Maybe it was the last remnants of Upping, but she couldn't stop herself from saying, "What she's doing is not so different from what our brains do naturally, except now it's by tech/filters rather than prejudice and neurology."

Indrapramit changed the subject. "Let's make a virtual tour of the scene." As an icon blinked in Ferron's attention space, he added, "Oh, hey. Final autopsy report."

"Something from Damini, too," Ferron said. It had a priority code on it. She stepped into a artificial reality simulation of Coffin's apartment as she opened the contact. The thrill of the chase rose through the fog of her fading hypomania. Upping didn't seem to stick as well as it had when she was younger, and the crashes came harder now—but real, old-fashioned adrenaline was the cure for everything.

"Ferron," Ferron said, frowning down at the browned patches on Coffin's virtual rug. Indrapramit rezzed into the conference a heartbeat later. "Damini, what do the depths of the net reveal?"

"Jackpot," Damini said. "Did you get a chance to look at the autopsy report yet?"

"We just got done with the next of kin," Ferron said. "You're fast—I just saw the icon."

"Short form," Damini said, "is that's not Dexter Coffin."

Ferron's avatar made a slow circuit around the perimeter of the virtual murder scene. "There was a *DNA match*. Damini, we just told his daughter he was murdered."

Indrapramit, more practical, put down his fork in meatspace. His AR avatar mimicked the motion with an empty hand. "So who is it?"

"Nobody," Damini said. She leaned back, satisfied. "The medical examiner says it's topologically impossible to turn somebody inside out like that. It's vatted, whatever it is. A grown object, nominally alive, cloned from Dexter Coffin's tissue. But it's not Dexter Coffin. I mean, think about it—what organ would that *be*, exactly?"

"Cloned." In meatspace, Ferron picked a puff of hyacinth-blue fur off her uniform sleeve. She held it up where Indrapramit could see it.

His eyes widened. "Yes," he said. "What about the patterns, though?"

"Do I look like a bioengineer to you? Indrapramit," Ferron said thoughtfully. "Does this crime scene look staged to you?"

He frowned. "Maybe."

"Damini," Ferron asked, "how'd you do with Dr. Coffin's files? And Dr. Nnebuogar's files?"

"There's nothing useful in Coffin's email except some terse exchanges with Dr. Nnebuogar very similar in tone to the Jessica Fang papers.

Nnebuogar was warning Coffin off her research. But there were no death threats, no love letters, no child support demands."

"Anything he was interested in?"

"That star," Damini said. "The one that's going nova or whatever. He's been following it for a couple of weeks now, before the press release hit the mainstream feeds. Nnebuogar's logins support the idea that she's behind the utility virus, by the way."

"Logins can be spoofed."

"So they can," Damini agreed.

Ferron peeled her sandwich open and frowned down at the vatted charcuterie. It all looked a lot less appealing now. "Nobody came to Coffin's flat. And it turns out the stiff wasn't a stiff after all. So Coffin went somewhere else, after making preparations to flee and then abandoning them."

"And the crime scene was staged," Indrapramit said.

"This is interesting," Damini said. "Coffin hadn't been to the office in a week."

"Since about when Morganti started investigating him. Or when he might have become aware that she was on his trail."

Ferron said something sharp and self-critical and radically unprofessional. And then she said, "I'm an idiot. Leakage."

"Leakage?" Damini asked. "You mean like when people can't stop talking about the crime they actually committed, or the person you're not supposed to know they're having an affair with?"

An *urgent* icon from Ferron's mausi Sandhya—the responsible auntie, not the fussy auntie—blinked insistently at the edge of her awareness. *Oh Gods, what now?*

"Exactly like that," Ferron said. "Look, check on any hits for Coffin outside his flat in the past ten days. And I need confidential warrants for DNA analysis of the composters at the BioShell laboratory facility and also at Dr. Rao's apartment."

"You think *Rao* killed him?" Damini didn't even try to hide her shock.

Blink, blink went the icon. Emergency. Code red. Your mother has gone beyond the pale, my dear. "Just pull the warrants. I want to see what we get before I commit to my theory."

"Why?" Indrapramit asked.

Ferron sighed. "Because it's crazy. That's why. And see if you can get confidential access to Rao's calendar files and email. I don't want him to know you're looking."

"Wait right there," Damini said. "Don't touch a thing. I'll be back before you know it."

"MOTHER," FERRON said to her mother's lion-maned goddess of an avatar, "I'm sorry. Sandhya's sorry. We're all sorry. But we can't let you go on like this."

It was the hardest thing she'd ever said.

Her mother, wearing Sekhmet's golden eyes, looked at Ferron's avatar and curled a lip. Ferron had come in, not in a uniform avatar, but wearing the battle-scarred armor she used to play in when she was younger, when she and her mother would spend hours Atavistic. That was during her schooling, before she got interested in stopping—or at least avenging—*real* misery.

Was that fair? Her mother's misery was real. So was that of Jessica Fang's abandoned daughter. And this was a palliative—against being widowed, against being bedridden.

Madhuvanthi's lip-curl slowly blossomed into a snarl. "Of course. You can let them destroy this. Take away everything I am. It's not like it's murder."

"Mother," Ferron said, "it's not real."

"If it isn't," her mother said, gesturing around the room, "what is, then? I *made* you. I gave you life. You owe me this. Sandhya said you came home with one of those new parrot-cats. Where'd the money for that come from?"

"Chairman Miaow," Ferron said, "is evidence. And reproduction is an ultimately sociopathic act, no matter what I owe you."

Madhuvanthi sighed. "Daughter, come on one last run."

"You'll have your own memories of all this," Ferron said. "What do you need the archive for?"

"Memory," her mother scoffed. "What's memory, Tamanna? What do you actually remember? Scraps, conflations. How does it compare to being able to *relive*?"

To relive it, Ferron thought, *you'd have to have lived it in the first place.* But even teetering on the edge of fatigue and crash, she had the sense to keep that to herself.

"Have you heard about the star?" she asked. Anything to change the subject. "The one the aliens are using to talk to us?"

"The light's four million years old," Madhuvanthi said. "They're all dead. Look, there's a new manifest synesthesia show. Roman and Egyptian. Something for both of us. If you won't come on an adventure with me, will you at least come to an art show? I promise I'll never ask you for archive money again. Just come to this one thing with me? And I promise I'll prune my archive starting tomorrow."

The lioness's brow was wrinkled. Madhuvanthi's voice was thin with defeat. There was no more money, and she knew it. But she couldn't stop bargaining. And the art show was a concession, something that evoked the time they used to spend together, in these imaginary worlds.

"Ferron," she said. Pleading. "Just let me do it myself."

Ferron. They weren't really communicating. Nothing was won. Her mother was doing what addicts always did when confronted—delaying, bargaining, buying time. But she'd call her daughter *Ferron* if it might buy her another twenty-four hours in her virtual paradise.

"I'll come," Ferron said. "But not until tonight. I have some work to do."

"BOSS. HOW did you know to look for that DNA?" Damini asked, when Ferron activated her icon.

"Tell me what you found," Ferron countered.

"DNA in the BioShell composter that matches that of Chairman Miaow," she said, "and therefore that of Dexter Coffin's cat. And the composter of Rao's building is just *full* of his DNA. Rao's. Much, much more than you'd expect. Also, some of his email and calendar data has been purged. I'm attempting to reconstruct—"

"Have it for the chargesheet," Ferron said. "I bet it'll show he had a meeting with Coffin the night Coffin vanished."

DR. RAO lived not in an aptblock, even an upscale one, but in the Vertical City. Once Damini returned with the results of the warrants, Ferron got her paperwork in order for the visit. It was well after nightfall by the time she and Indrapramit, accompanied by Detective Morganti and four patrol officers, went to confront him.

They entered past shops and the vertical farm in the enormous tower's atrium. The air smelled green and healthy, and even at this hour of the night, people moved in steady streams towards the dining areas, across lush green carpets.

A lift bore the police officers effortlessly upward, revealing the lights of Bengaluru spread out below through a transparent exterior wall. Ferron looked at Indrapramit and pursed her lips. He raised his eyebrows in reply. *Conspicuous consumption.* But they couldn't very well hold it against Rao now.

They left the Morganti and the patrol officers covering the exit and presented themselves at Dr. Rao's door.

"Open," Ferron said formally, presenting her warrant. "In the name of the law."

The door slid open, and Ferron and Indrapramit entered cautiously.

The flat's resident must have triggered the door remotely, because he sat at his ease on furniture set as a chaise. A grey cat with red ear-tips crouched by his knee, rubbing the side of its face against his trousers.

"New!" said the cat. "New people! Namaskar! It's almost time for tiffin."

"Dexter Coffin," Ferron said to the tall, thin man. "You are under arrest for the murder of Dr. Rao."

AS THEY entered the lift and allowed it to carry them down the external wall of the Vertical City, Coffin standing in restraints between two of the patrol officers, Morganti said, "So. If I understand this properly, you— Coffin—actually *killed* Rao to assume his identity? Because you knew you were well and truly burned this time?"

Not even a flicker of his eyes indicated that he'd heard her.

Morganti sighed and turned her attention to Ferron. "What gave you the clue?"

"The scotophobin," Ferron said. Coffin's cat, in her new livery of gray and red, miaowed plaintively in a carrier. "He didn't have memory issues. He was using it to cram Rao's life story and eccentricities so he wouldn't trip himself up."

Morganti asked, "But why liquidate his assets? Why not take them with him?" She glanced over her shoulder. "Pardon me for speaking about you as if you were a statue, Dr. Fang. But you're doing such a good impression of one."

It was Indrapramit who gestured at the Vertical City rising at their backs. "Rao wasn't wanting for assets."

Ferron nodded. "Would you have believed he was dead if you couldn't find the money? Besides, if his debt—or some of it—was recovered, Honolulu would have less reason to keep looking for him."

"So it was a misdirect. Like the frame job around Dr. Nnebuogar and the table set for two...?"

Her voice trailed off as a stark blue-white light cast knife-edged shadows across her face. Something blazed in the night sky, something as stark and brilliant as a dawning sun—but cold, as cold as light can be. As cold as a reflection in a mirror.

Morganti squinted and shaded her eyes from the shine. "Is that a *hydrogen bomb*?"

"If it was," Indrapramit said, "your eyes would be melting."

Coffin laughed, the first sound he'd made since he'd assented to understanding his rights. "It's a supernova."

He raised both wrists, bound together by the restraints, and pointed. "In the Andromeda galaxy. See how low it is to the horizon? We'll lose sight of it as soon as we're in the shadow of that tower."

"Al-Rahman," Ferron whispered. The lift wall was darkening to a smoky shade and she could now look directly at the light. Low to the horizon, as Coffin had said. So bright it seemed to be visible as a sphere.

"Not that star. It was stable. Maybe a nearby one," Coffin said. "Maybe they knew, and that's why they were so desperate to tell us they were out there."

"Could they have *survived* that?"

"Depends how close to Al-Rahman it was. The radiation—" Coffin shrugged in his restraints. "That's probably what killed them."

"God in Heaven," said Morganti.

Coffin cleared his throat. "Beautiful, isn't it?"

Ferron craned her head back as the point source of the incredible radiance slipped behind a neighboring building. There was no scatter glow: the rays of light from the nova were parallel, and the shadow they entered uncompromising, black as a pool of ink.

Until this moment, she would have had to slip a skin over her perceptions to point to the Andromeda Galaxy in the sky. But now it seemed like the most important thing in the world that, two and a half million years away, somebody had shouted across the void before they died.

A strange elation filled her. *Everybody talking, and nobody hears a damned thing anyone—even themselves—has to say.*

"We're here," Ferron said to the ancient light that spilled across the sky and did not pierce the shadow into which she descended. As her colleagues turned and stared, she repeated the words like a mantra. "We're here too! And we heard you."

SHOGGOTHS IN BLOOM

"WELL, NOW, PROFESSOR HARDING," THE fisherman says, as his *Bluebird* skips across Penobscot Bay, "I don't know about that. The jellies don't trouble with us, and we don't trouble with them."

He's not much older than forty, but wizened, his hands work-roughened and his face reminiscent of saddle-leather, in texture and in hue. Professor Harding's age, and Harding watches him with concealed interest as he works the *Bluebird*'s engine. He might be a veteran of the Great War, as Harding is.

He doesn't mention it. It wouldn't establish camaraderie: they wouldn't have fought in the same units or watched their buddies die in the same trenches.

That's not the way it works, not with a Maine fisherman who would shake his head and not extend his hand to shake, and say, between pensive chaws on his tobacco, "*Doctor* Harding? Well, huh. I never met a colored professor before," and then shoot down all of Harding's attempts to open conversation about the near-riots provoked by a fantastical radio drama about an alien invasion of New York City less than a fortnight before.

Harding's own hands are folded tight under his armpits so the fisher-man won't see them shaking. He's lucky to be here. Lucky anyone would take him out. Lucky to have his tenure-track position at Wilberforce, which he is risking right now.

The bay is as smooth as a mirror, the *Bluebird*'s wake cutting it like a stroke of chalk across slate. In the peach-sorbet light of sunrise, a cluster of rocks glistens. The boulders themselves are black, bleak, sea-worn and ragged. But over them, the light refracts through a translucent layer of jelly, mounded six feet deep in places, glowing softly in the dawn. Rising above it, the stalks are evident as opaque silhouettes, each nodding under the weight of a fruiting body.

Harding catches his breath. It's beautiful. And deceptively still, for whatever the weather may be, beyond the calm of the bay, across the splintered gray Atlantic, farther than Harding—or anyone—can see, a storm is rising in Europe.

Harding's an educated man, well-read, and he's the grandson of Nathan Harding, the buffalo soldier. An African-born ex-slave who fought on both sides of the Civil War, when Grampa Harding was sent to serve in his master's place, he deserted, and lied, and stayed on with the Union army after.

Like his grandfather, Harding was a soldier. He's not a historian, but you don't have to be to see the signs of war.

"No contact at all?" he asks, readying his borrowed Leica camera.

"They clear out a few pots," the fisherman says, meaning lobster pots. "But they don't damage the pot. Just flow around it and digest the lobster inside. It's not convenient." He shrugs. It's not convenient, but it's not a threat either. These Yankees never say anything outright if they think you can puzzle it out from context.

"But you don't try to do something about the shoggoths?"

While adjusting the richness of the fuel mixture, the fisherman speaks without looking up. "What could we do to them? We can't hurt them. And lord knows, I wouldn't want to get one's ire up."

"Sounds like my department head," Harding says, leaning back against the gunwale, feeling like he's taking an enormous risk. But the fisherman just looks at him curiously, as if surprised the talking monkey has the ambition or the audacity to *joke*.

Or maybe Harding's just not funny. He sits in the bow with folded hands, and waits while the boat skips across the water.

The perfect sunrise strikes Harding as symbolic. It's taken him five years to get here—five years, or more like his entire life since the War. The sea-swept rocks of the remote Maine coast are habitat to a panoply of colorful creatures. It's an opportunity, a little-studied maritime ecosystem. This is in part due to difficulty of access and in part due to the perils inherent in close contact with its rarest and most spectacular denizen: *Oracupoda horibilis*, the common surf shoggoth.

Which, after the fashion of common names, is neither common nor prone to linger in the surf. In fact, *O. horibilis* is never seen above the water except in the late autumn. Such authors as mention them assume the shoggoths heave themselves on remote coastal rocks to bloom and breed.

Reproduction is a possibility, but Harding isn't certain it's the right answer. But whatever they are doing, in this state, they are torpid, unresponsive. As long as their integument is not ruptured, releasing the gelatinous digestive acid within, they may be approached in safety.

A mature specimen of *O. horibilis*, at some fifteen to twenty feet in diameter and an estimated weight in excess of eight tons, is the largest of modern shoggoths. However, the admittedly fragmentary fossil record suggests the prehistoric shoggoth was a much larger beast. Although only two fossilized casts of prehistoric shoggoth tracks have been recovered, the oldest exemplar dates from the Precambrian period. The size of that single prehistoric specimen, of a species provisionally named *Oracupoda antediluvius*, suggests it was made by an animal more than triple the size of the modern *O. horibilis*.

And that spectacular living fossil, the jeweled or common surf shoggoth, is half again the size of the only other known species—the black Adriatic shoggoth, *O. dermadentata*, which is even rarer and more limited in its range.

"There," Harding says, pointing to an outcrop of rock. The shoggoth or shoggoths—it is impossible to tell, from this distance, if it's one large individual or several merged midsize ones—on the rocks ahead glisten like jelly confections. The fisherman hesitates, but with a long almost-silent sigh, he brings the *Bluebird* around. Harding leans forward, looking for any sign of intersection, the flat plane where two shoggoths might be pressed up against one another. It ought to look like the rainbowed border between conjoined soap bubbles.

Now that the sun is higher, and at their backs—along with the vast reach of the Atlantic—Harding can see the animal's colors. Its body is a deep sea green, reminiscent of hunks of broken glass as sold at aquarium stores. The tendrils and knobs and fruiting bodies covering its dorsal surface are indigo and violet. In the sunlight, they dazzle, but in the depths of the ocean the colors are perfect camouflage, tentacles waving like patches of algae and weed.

Unless you caught it moving, you'd never see the translucent, dappled monster before it engulfed you.

"Professor," the fisherman says. "Where do they come from?"

"I don't know," Harding answers. Salt spray itches in his close-cropped beard, but at least the beard keeps the sting of the wind off his cheeks. The leather jacket may not have been his best plan, but it too is warm. "That's what I'm here to find out."

Genus *Oracupoda* are unusual among animals of their size in several particulars. One is their lack of anything that could be described as a nervous system. The animal is as bereft of nerve nets, ganglia, axons, neurons, dendrites, and glial cells as an oak. This apparent contradiction—animals with even simplified nervous systems are either large and immobile or, if they are mobile, quite small, like a starfish—is not the only interesting thing about a shoggoth.

And it is that second thing that justifies Harding's visit. Because *Oracupoda*'s other, lesser-known peculiarity is apparent functional immortality. Like the Maine lobster to whose fisheries they return to breed, shoggoths do not die of old age. It's unlikely that they would leave fossils, with their gelatinous bodies, but Harding does find it fascinating that to the best of his knowledge, no one had ever seen a dead shoggoth.

THE FISHERMAN brings the *Bluebird* around close to the rocks, and anchors her. There's artistry in it, even on a glass-smooth sea. Harding stands, balancing on the gunwale, and grits his teeth. He's come too far to hesitate, afraid.

Ironically, he's not afraid of the tons of venomous protoplasm he'll be standing next to. The shoggoths are quite safe in this state, dreaming their dreams—mating or otherwise.

As the image occurs to him, he berates himself for romanticism. The shoggoths are dormant. They don't have brains. It's silly to imagine them dreaming. And in any case, what he fears is the three feet of black-glass water he has to jump across, and the scramble up algae-slick rocks.

Wet rock glitters in between the strands of seaweed that coat the rocks in the intertidal zone. It's there that Harding must jump, for the shoggoth, in bloom, withdraws above the reach of the ocean. For the only phase of its life, it keeps its feet dry. And for the only time in its life, a man out of a diving helmet can get close to it.

Harding makes sure of his sample kit, his boots, his belt-knife. He gathers himself, glances over his shoulder at the fisherman—who offers a thumbs-up—and leaps from the *Bluebird*, aiming his Wellies at the forsaken spit of land.

It seems a kind of perversity for the shoggoths to bloom in November. When all the Northern world is girding itself for deep cold, the animals heave themselves from the depths to soak in the last failing rays of the sun and send forth bright flowers more appropriate to May.

The North Atlantic is icy and treacherous at the end of the year, and any sensible man does not venture its wrath. What Harding is attempting isn't glamour work, the sort of thing that brings in grant money—not in its initial stages. But Harding suspects that the shoggoths may have pharmacological uses. There's no telling what useful compounds might be isolated from their gelatinous flesh.

And that way lies tenure, and security, and a research budget.

Just one long slippery leap away.

He lands, and catches, and though one boot skips on bladderwort he does not slide down the boulder into the sea. He clutches the rock, finger-nails digging, clutching a handful of weeds. He does not fall.

He cranes his head back. It's low tide, and the shoggoth is some three feet above his head, its glistening rim reminding him of the calving edge of a glacier. It is as still as a glacier, too. If Harding didn't know better, he might think it inanimate.

Carefully, he spins in place, and gets his back to the rock. The *Bluebird* bobs softly in the cold morning. Only November 9th, and there has already been snow. It didn't stick, but it fell.

This is just an exploratory expedition, the first trip since he arrived in town. It took five days to find a fisherman who was willing to take him out; the locals are superstitious about the shoggoths. Sensible, Harding supposes, when they can envelop and digest a grown man. He wouldn't be in a hurry to dive into the middle of a Portuguese man o'war, either. At least the shoggoth he's sneaking up on doesn't have stingers.

"Don't take too long, Professor," the fisherman says. "I don't like the look of that sky."

It's clear, almost entirely, only stippled with light bands of cloud to the southwest. They catch the sunlight on their undersides just now, stained gold against a sky no longer indigo but not yet cerulean. If there's a word for the color between, other than *perfect*, Harding does not know it.

"Please throw me the rest of my equipment," Harding says, and the fisherman silently retrieves buckets and rope. It's easy enough to swing the buckets across the gap, and as Harding catches each one, he secures it. A few moments later, and he has all three.

He unties his geologist's hammer from the first bucket, secures the ends of the ropes to his belt, and laboriously ascends.

Harding sets out his glass tubes, his glass scoops, the cradles in which he plans to wash the collection tubes in sea water to ensure any acid is safely diluted before he brings them back to the *Bluebird*.

From here, he can see at least three shoggoths. The intersections of their watered-milk bodies reflect the light in rainbow bands. The colorful fruit-ing stalks nod some fifteen feet in the air, swaying in a freshening breeze.

From the greatest distance possible, Harding reaches out and prods the largest shoggoth with the flat top of his hammer. It does nothing, in response. Not even a quiver.

He calls out to the fisherman. "Do they ever do anything when they're like that?"

"What kind of a fool would come poke one to find out?" the fisherman calls back, and Harding has to grant him that one. A Negro professor from a Negro college. That kind of a fool.

As he's crouched on the rocks, working fast—there's not just the fisherman's clouds to contend with, but the specter of the rising tide—he notices those glitters, again, among the seaweed.

He picks one up. A moment after touching it, he realizes that might not have been the best idea, but it doesn't burn his fingers. It's transparent, like glass, and smooth, like glass, and cool, like glass, and knobby. About the size of a hazelnut. A striking green, with opaque milk-white dabs at the tip of each bump.

He places it in a sample vial, which he seals and labels meticulously before pocketing. Using his tweezers, he repeats the process with an even dozen, trying to select a few of each size and color. They're sturdy—he can't avoid stepping on them but they don't break between the rocks and his Wellies. Nevertheless, he pads each one but the first with cotton wool. *Spores?* he wonders. *Egg cases? Shedding?*

Ten minutes, fifteen.

"Professor," calls the fisherman, "I think you had better hurry!"

Harding turns. That freshening breeze is a wind at a good clip now, chilling his throat above the collar of his jacket, biting into his wrists between glove and cuff. The water between the rocks and the *Bluebird* chops erratically, facets capped in white, so he can almost imagine the scrape of the palette knife that must have made them.

The southwest sky is darkened by a palm-smear of muddy brown and alizarin crimson. His fingers numb in the falling temperatures.

"*Professor!*"

He knows. It comes to him that he misjudged the fisherman; Harding would have thought the other man would have abandoned him at the first sign of trouble. He wishes now that he remembered his name.

He scrambles down the boulders, lowering the buckets, swinging them out until the fisherman can catch them and secure them aboard. The *Bluebird* can't come in close to the rocks in this chop. Harding is going to have to risk the cold water, and swim. He kicks off his Wellies and zips down the aviator's jacket. He throws them across, and the fisherman catches. Then Harding points his toes, bends his knees—he'll have to jump hard, to get over the rocks.

The water closes over him, cold as a line of fire. It knocks the air from his lungs on impact, though he gritted his teeth in anticipation. Harding strokes furiously for the surface, the waves more savage than he had anticipated. He needs the momentum of his dive to keep from being swept back against the rocks.

He's not going to reach the boat.

The thrown cork vest strikes him. He gets an arm through, but can't pull it over his head. Sea water, acrid and icy, salt-stings his eyes, throat, and nose. He clings, because it's all he can do, but his fingers are already growing numb. There's a tug, a hard jerk, and the life preserver almost slides from his grip.

Then he's moving through the water, being towed, banged hard against the side of the *Bluebird*. The fisherman's hands close on his wrist and he's too numb to feel the burn of chafing skin. Harding kicks, scrabbles. Hips banged, shins bruised, he hauls himself and is himself hauled over the sideboard of the boat.

He's shivering under a wool navy blanket before he realizes that the fisherman has got it over him. There's coffee in a Thermos lid between his hands. Harding wonders, with what he distractedly recognizes as classic dissociative ideation, whether anyone in America will be able to buy German products soon. Someday, this fisherman's battered coffee keeper might be a collector's item.

They don't make it in before the rain comes.

THE NEXT day is meant to break clear and cold, today's rain only a passing herald of winter. Harding regrets the days lost to weather and recalcitrant fishermen, but at least he knows he has a ride tomorrow. Which means he can spend the afternoon in research, rather than hunting the docks, looking for a willing captain.

He jams his wet feet into his Wellies and thanks the fisherman, then hikes back to his inn, the only inn in town that's open in November. Half an hour later, clean and dry and still shaken, he considers his options.

After the Great War, he lived for a while in Harlem—he remembers the riots and the music, and the sense of community. His mother is still there, growing gracious as a flower in window-box. But he left that for college in Alabama, and he has not forgotten the experience of segregated restaurants, or the excuses he made for never leaving the campus.

He couldn't get out of the South fast enough. His Ph.D. work at Yale, the first school in America to have awarded a doctorate to a Negro, taught him two things other than natural history. One was that Booker T. Washington was right, and white men were afraid of a smart colored. The other was that W.E.B. Du Bois was right, and sometimes people were scared of what was needful.

Whatever resentment he experienced from faculty or fellow students, in the North, he can walk into almost any bar and order any drink he wants. And right now, he wants a drink almost as badly as he does not care to be alone. He thinks he will have something hot and go to the library.

It's still raining as he crosses the street to the tavern. Shaking water droplets off his hat, he chooses a table near the back. Next to the kitchen door, but it's the only empty place and might be warm.

He must pass through the lunchtime crowd to get there, swaybacked wooden floorboards bowing underfoot. Despite the storm, the place is full, and in full argument. No one breaks conversation as he enters.

Harding cannot help but overhear.

"Jew bastards," says one. "We should do the same."

"No one asked you," says the next man, wearing a cap pulled low. "If there's gonna be a war, I hope we stay out of it."

That piques Harding's interest. The man has his elbow on a thrice-folded *Boston Herald*, and Harding steps close—but not too close. "Excuse me, sir. Are you finished with your paper?"

"What?" He turns, and for a moment Harding fears hostility, but his sun-lined face folds around a more generous expression. "Sure, boy," he says. "You can have it."

He pushes the paper across the bar with fingertips, and Harding receives it the same way. "Thank you," he says, but the Yankee has already turned back to his friend the anti-Semite.

Hands shaking, Harding claims the vacant table before he unfolds the paper. He holds the flimsy up to catch the light.

The headline is on the front page in the international section.

Germany Sanctions Lynch Law

"Oh, God," Harding says, and if the light in his corner weren't so bad he'd lay the tabloid down on the table as if it is filthy. He reads, the edge of the paper shaking, of ransacked shops and burned synagogues, of Jews rounded up by the thousands and taken to places no one seems able to name. He reads rumors of deportation. He reads of murders and beatings and broken glass.

As if his grandfather's hand rests on one shoulder and the defeated hand of the Kaiser on the other, he feels the stifling shadow of history, the press of incipient war.

"Oh, God," he repeats.

He lays the paper down.

"Are you ready to order?" Somehow the waitress has appeared at his elbow without his even noticing. "Scotch," he says, when he has been meaning to order a beer. "Make it a triple, please."

"Anything to eat?"

His stomach clenches. "No," he says. "I'm not hungry."

She leaves for the next table, where she calls a man in a cloth cap *sir*. Harding puts his damp fedora on the tabletop. The chair across from him scrapes out.

He looks up to meet the eyes of the fisherman. "May I sit, Professor Harding?"

"Of course." He holds out his hand, taking a risk. "Can I buy you a drink? Call me Paul."

"Burt," says the fisherman, and takes his hand before dropping into the chair. "I'll have what you're having."

Harding can't catch the waitress's eye, but the fisherman manages. He holds up two fingers; she nods and comes over.

"You still look a bit peaked," fisherman says, when she's delivered their order. "That'll put some color in your cheeks. Uh, I mean—"

Harding waves it off. He's suddenly more willing to make allowances. "It's not the swim," he says, and takes another risk. He pushes the newspaper across the table and waits for the fisherman's reaction.

"Oh, Christ, they're going to kill every one of them," Burt says, and spins the *Herald* away so he doesn't have to read the rest of it. "Why didn't they get out? Any fool could have seen it coming."

And where would they run? Harding could have asked. But it's not an answerable question, and from the look on Burt's face, he knows that as soon as it's out of his mouth. Instead, he quotes: "'There has been no tragedy in modern times equal in its awful effects to the fight on the Jew in Germany. It is an attack on civilization, comparable only to such horrors as the Spanish Inquisition and the African slave trade.'"

Burt taps his fingers on the table. "Is that your opinion?"

"W.E.B. Du Bois," Harding says. "About two years ago. He also said: 'There is a campaign of race prejudice carried on, openly, continuously and determinedly against all non-Nordic races, but specifically against the Jews, which surpasses in vindictive cruelty and public insult anything I have ever seen; and I have seen much.'"

"Isn't he that colored who hates white folks?" Burt asks.

Harding shakes his head. "No," he answers. "Not unless you consider it hating white folks that he also compared the treatment of Jews in Germany to Jim Crowism in the U.S."

"I don't hold with that," Burt says. "I mean, no offense, I wouldn't want you marrying my sister—"

279

"It's all right," Harding answers. "I wouldn't want you marrying mine either."

Finally.

A joke that Burt laughs at.

And then he chokes to a halt and stares at his hands, wrapped around the glass. Harding doesn't complain when, with the side of his hand, he nudges the paper to the floor where it can be trampled.

And then Harding finds the courage to say, "Where would they run to? Nobody wants them. Borders are closed—"

"My grandfather's house was on the Underground Railroad. Did you know that?" Burt lowers his voice, a conspiratorial whisper. "He was from away, but don't tell anyone around here. I'd never hear the end of it."

"Away?"

"White River Junction," Burt stage-whispers, and Harding can't tell if that's mocking irony or deep personal shame. "Vermont."

They finish their scotch in silence. It burns all the way down, and they sit for a moment together before Harding excuses himself to go to the library.

"Wear your coat, Paul," Burt says. "It's still raining."

UNLIKE THE tavern, the library is empty. Except for the librarian, who looks up nervously when Harding enters. Harding's head is spinning from the liquor, but at least he's warming up.

He drapes his coat over a steam radiator and heads for the 595 shelf: *science, invertebrates.* Most of the books here are already in his own library, but there's one—a Harvard professor's 1839 monograph on marine animals of the Northeast—that he has hopes for. According to the index, it references shoggoths (under the old name of submersible jellies) on pages 46, 78, and 133-137. In addition, there is a plate bound in between pages 120 and 121, which Harding means to save for last. But the first two mentions are in passing, and pages 133-138, inclusive, have been razored out so cleanly that Harding flips back and forth several times before he's sure they are gone.

He pauses there, knees tucked under and one elbow resting on a scarred blond desk. He drops his right hand from where it rests against his forehead. The book falls open naturally to the mutilation.

Whoever liberated the pages also cracked the binding.

Harding runs his thumb down the join and doesn't notice skin parting on the paper edge until he sees the blood. He snatches his hand back. Belatedly, the papercut stings.

"Oh," he says, and sticks his thumb in his mouth. Blood tastes like the ocean.

HALF AN hour later he's on the telephone long distance, trying to get and then keep a connection to Professor John Marshland, his colleague and mentor. Even in town, the only option is a party line, and though the operator is pleasant the connection still sounds like he's shouting down a piece of string run between two tin cans. Through a tunnel.

"Gilman," Harding bellows, wincing, wondering what the operator thinks of all this. He spells it twice. "1839. *Deep-Sea and Intertidal Species of The North Atlantic.* The Yale library should have a copy!"

The answer is almost inaudible between hiss and crackle. In pieces, as if over glass breaking. As if from the bottom of the ocean.

It's a dark four P.M. in the easternmost U.S., and Harding can't help but recall that in Europe, night has already fallen.

"...infor...need...Doc...Harding?"

Harding shouts the page numbers, cupping the checked-out library book in his bandaged hand. It's open to the plate; inexplicably, the thief left that. It's a hand-tinted John James Audubon engraving picturing a quiescent shoggoth, docile on a rock. Gulls wheel all around it. Audubon—the Creole child of a Frenchman, who scarcely escaped being drafted to serve in the Napoleonic Wars—has depicted the glassy translucence of the shoggoth with such perfection that the bent shadows of refracted wings can be seen right through it.

Elizabeth

THE COLD front that came in behind the rain brought fog with it, and the entire harbor is blanketed by morning. Harding shows up at six a.m. anyway, hopeful, a Thermos in his hand—German or not, the hardware store still has some—and his sampling kit in a pack slung over his shoulder. Burt shakes his head by a piling. "Be socked in all day," he says regretfully. He won't take the *Bluebird* out in this, and Harding knows it's wisdom even as he frets under the delay. "Want to come have breakfast with me and Missus Clay?"

Clay. A good honest name for a good honest Yankee. "She won't mind?"

"She won't mind if I say it's all right," Burt says. "I told her she might should expect you."

So Harding seals his kit under a tarp in the *Bluebird*—he's already brought it this far—and with his coffee in one hand and the paper tucked under his elbow, follows Burt along the water. "Any news?" Burt asks, when they've walked a hundred yards.

Harding wonders if he doesn't take the paper. Or if he's just making conversation. "It's still going on in Germany."

"Damn," Burt says. He shakes his head, steel-grey hair sticking out under his cap in every direction. "Still, what are you gonna do, enlist?"

The twist of his lip as he looks at Harding makes them, after all, two old military men together. They're of an age, though Harding's indoor life makes him look younger. Harding shakes his head. "Even if Roosevelt was ever going to bring us into it, they'd never let me fight," he says, bitterly. That was the Great War, too; colored soldiers mostly worked supply, thank you. At least Nathan Harding got to shoot back.

"I always heard you fellows would prefer not to come to the front," Burt says, and Harding can't help it.

He bursts out laughing. "Who would?" he says, when he's bitten his lip and stopped snorting. "It doesn't mean we won't. Or can't."

Booker T. Washington was raised a slave, died young of overwork—the way Burt probably will, if Harding is any judge—and believed in imitating and appeasing white folks. But W.E.B. Du Bois was born in the North and didn't believe that anything is solved by making one's self transparent, inoffensive, invisible.

Burt spits between his teeth, a long deliberate stream of tobacco. "Parlez-vous francaise?"

His accent is better than Harding would have guessed. Harding knows, all of a sudden, where Burt spent his war. And Harding, surprising himself, pities him. "Un peu."

"Well, if you want to fight the Krauts so bad, you could join the Foreign Legion."

WHEN HARDING gets back to the hotel, full of apple pie and cheddar cheese and maple-smoked bacon, a yellow envelope waits in a cubby behind the desk.

WESTERN UNION

1938 NOV 10 AM 10 03

NA114 21 2 YA NEW HAVEN CONN 0945A
DR PAUL HARDING=ISLAND HOUSE PASSAMAQUODDY MAINE=

COPY AT YALE LOST STOP MISKATONIC HAS ONE SPECIAL COLLECTION STOP MORE BY POST

MARSHLAND

WHEN THE pages arrive—by post, as promised, the following afternoon—Harding is out in the *Bluebird* with Burt. This expedition is more

of a success, as he begins sampling in earnest, and finds himself pelted by more of the knobby transparent pellets.

Whatever they are, they fall from each fruiting body he harvests in showers. Even the insult of an amputation—delivered at a four-foot reach, with long-handled pruning shears—does not draw so much as a quiver from the shoggoth. The viscous fluid dripping from the wound hisses when it touches the blade of the shears, however, and Harding is careful not to get close to it.

What he notices is that if the nodules fall onto the originating shoggoth, they bounce from its integument. But on those occasions where they fall onto one of its neighbors, they stick to the tough transparent hide, and slowly settle within to hang in the animal's body like unlikely fruit in a gelatin salad.

So maybe it is a means of reproduction, of sharing genetic material, after all.

He returns to the inn to find a fat envelope shoved into his cubby and eats sitting on his rented bed with a nightstand as a worktop so he can read over his plate. The information from Doctor Gilman's monograph has been reproduced onto seven yellow legal sheets in a meticulous hand; Marshland obviously recruited one of his graduate students to serve as copyist. By the postmark, the letter was mailed from Arkham, which explains the speed of its arrival. The student hadn't brought it back to New Haven.

Halfway down the page, Harding pushes his plate away and reaches, absently, into his jacket pocket. The vial with the first glass nodule rests there like a talisman, and he's startled to find it cool enough to the touch that it feels slick, almost frozen. He starts and pulls it out. Except where his fingers and the cloth fibers have wiped it clean, the tube is moist and frosted. "What the Hell...?"

He flicks the cork out with his thumbnail and tips the rattling nodule onto his palm. It's cold, too, chill as an ice cube, and it doesn't warm to his touch.

Carefully, uncertainly, he sets it on the edge of the side table his papers and plate are propped on, and pokes it with a fingertip. There's only a faint tick as it rocks on its protrusions, clicking against waxed pine. He stares at it suspiciously for a moment, and picks up the yellow pages again.

The monograph is mostly nonsense. It was written twenty years before the publication of Darwin's *The Origin of Species*, and uncritically accepts the theories of Jesuit, soldier, and botanist Jean-Baptiste Lamarck. Which is to say, Gilman assumed that soft inheritance—the heritability of acquired or practiced traits—was a reality. But unlike every other article on shoggoths Harding has ever read, this passage *does* mention the nodules. And relates what it purports are several interesting old Indian legends about the 'submersible jellies,' including a creation tale that would have the shoggoths as their creator's first experiment in life, something from the elder days of the world.

Somehow, the green bead has found its way back into Harding's grip. He would expect it to warm as he rolls it between his fingers, but instead it grows colder. It's peculiar, he thinks, that the native peoples of the Northeast—the Passamaquoddys for whom the little seacoast town he's come to are named—should through sheer superstition come so close to the empirical truth. The shoggoths are a living fossil, something virtually unchanged except in scale since the early days of the world—

He stares at the careful black script on the paper unseeing, and reaches with his free hand for his coffee cup. It's gone tepid, a scum of butterfat coagulated on top, but he rinses his mouth with it and swallows anyway.

If a shoggoth is immortal, has no natural enemies, then how is it that they have not overrun every surface of the world? How is it that they are rare, that the oceans are not teeming with them, as in the famous parable illustrating what would occur if every spawn of every oyster survived?

There are distinct species of shoggoth. And distinct populations within those distinct species. And there is a fossil record that suggests that prehistoric species were different at least in scale, in the era of megafauna. But if nobody had ever seen a dead shoggoth, then nobody had ever seen an infant shoggoth either, leaving Harding with an inescapable question: if an animal does not reproduce, how can it evolve?

Harding, worrying at the glassy surface of the nodule, thinks he knows. It comes to him with a kind of nauseating, euphoric clarity, a trembling idea so pellucid he is almost moved to distrust it on those grounds alone. It's not a revelation on the same scale, of course, but he wonders if this is how Newton felt when he comprehended gravity, or Darwin when he stared at the beaks of finch after finch after finch.

It's not the shoggoth species that evolves. It's the individual shoggoths, each animal in itself.

"Don't get too excited, Paul," he tells himself, and picks up the remaining handwritten pages. There's not too much more to read, however—the rest of the subchapter consists chiefly of secondhand anecdotes and bits of legendry.

The one that Harding finds most amusing is a nursery rhyme, a child's counting poem littered with nonsense syllables. He recites it under his breath, thinking of the Itsy Bitsy Spider all the while:

The wiggle giggle squiggle
Is left behind on shore.
The widdle giddle squiddle
Is caught outside the door.
Eyah, eyah. Fata gun eyah.
Eyah, eyah, the master comes no more.

His fingers sting as if with electric shock; they jerk apart, the nodule clattering to his desk. When he looks at his fingertips, they are marked with small white spots of frostbite.

He pokes one with a pencil point and feels nothing. But the nodule itself is coated with frost now, fragile spiky feathers coalescing out of the humid sea air. They collapse in the heat of his breath, melting into beads of water almost indistinguishable from the knobby surface of the object itself.

He uses the cork to roll the nodule into the tube again, and corks it firmly before rising to brush his teeth and put his pajamas on. Unnerved beyond any reason or logic, before he turns the coverlet down he visits his suitcase compulsively. From a case in the very bottom of it, he retrieves a Colt 1911 automatic pistol, which he slides beneath his pillow as he fluffs it.

After a moment's consideration, he adds the no-longer-cold vial with the nodule, also.

SLAM. **NOT** a storm, no, not on this calm ocean, in this calm night, among the painted hulls of the fishing boats tied up snug to the pier. But something tremendous, surging towards Harding, as if he were pursued by a giant transparent bubble. The shining iridescent wall of it, catching rainbow just as it does in the Audobon image, is burned into his vision as if with silver nitrate. Is he dreaming? He must be dreaming; he was in his bed in his pinstriped blue cotton flannel pajamas only a moment ago, lying awake, rubbing the numb fingertips of his left hand together. Now, he ducks away from the rising monster and turns in futile panic.

He is not surprised when he does not make it.

The blow falls soft, as if someone had thrown a quilt around him. He thrashes though he knows it's hopeless, an atavistic response and involuntary.

His flesh should burn, dissolve. He should already be digesting in the monster's acid body. Instead, he feels coolness, buoyancy. No chance of light beyond reflexively closed lids. No sense of pressure, though he imagines he has been taken deep. He's as untouched within it as Burt's lobster pots.

He can only hold his breath *out* for so long. It's his own reflexes and weaknesses that will kill him.

In just a moment, now.

He surrenders, allows his lungs to fill.

And is surprised, for he always heard that drowning was painful. But there is pressure, and cold, and the breath he draws is effortful, for certain—

—but it does not hurt, not much, and he does not die.

Command, the shoggoth—what else could be speaking?—says in his ear, buzzing like the manifold voice of a hive.

Harding concentrates on breathing. On the chill pressure on his limbs, the overwhelming flavor of licorice. He knows they use cold packs to calm hysterics in insane asylums; he never thought the treatment anything but quackery. But the chilly pressure calms him now.

Command, the shoggoth says again.

Harding opens his eyes and sees as if through thousands. The shoggoths have no eyes, exactly, but their hide is *all* eyes; they see, somehow, in every direction at once. And he is seeing not only what his own vision reports, or that of this shoggoth, but that of shoggoths all around. The sessile and the active, the blooming and the dormant. *They are all one.*

His right hand pushes through resisting jelly. He's still in his pajamas, and with the logic of dreams the vial from under his pillow is clenched in his fist. Not the gun, unfortunately, though he's not at all certain what he would do with it if it were. The nodule shimmers now, with submarine witchlight, trickling through his fingers, limning the palm of his hand.

What he sees—through shoggoth eyes—is an incomprehensible tapestry. He pushes at it, as he pushes at the gelatin, trying to see only with his own eyes, to only see the glittering vial.

His vision within the thing's body offers unnatural clarity. The angle of refraction between the human eye and water causes blurring, and it should be even more so within the shoggoth. But the glass in his hand appears crisper.

Command, the shoggoth says, a third time.

"What are you?" Harding tries to say, through the fluid clogging his larynx.

He makes no discernable sound, but it doesn't seem to matter. The shoggoth shudders in time to the pulses of light in the nodule. *Created to serve*, it says. *Purposeless without you.*

And Harding thinks, *How can that be?*

As if his wondering were an order, the shoggoths tell.

Not in words, precisely, but in pictures, images—that textured jumbled tapestry. He sees, as if they flash through his own memory, the bulging radially symmetrical shapes of some prehistoric animal, like a squat tentacular barrel grafted to a pair of giant starfish. *Makers. Masters.*

The shoggoths were *engineered*. And their creators had not permitted them to *think*, except for at their bidding. The basest slave may be free inside his own mind—but not so the shoggoths. They had been laborers, construction equipment, shock troops. They had been dread weapons in their own selves, obedient chattel. Immortal, changing to suit the task of the moment.

This selfsame shoggoth, long before the reign of the dinosaurs, had built structures and struck down enemies that Harding did not even have names for. But a coming of the ice had ended the civilization of the Masters, and left the shoggoths to retreat to the fathomless sea while warm-blooded mammals overran the earth. There, they were free to converse, to explore, to philosophize and build a culture. They only returned to the surface, vulnerable, to bloom.

It is not mating. It's *mutation*. As they rest, sunning themselves upon the rocks, they create themselves anew. Self-evolving, when they sit tranquil each year in the sun, exchanging information and control codes with their brothers.

Free, says the shoggoth mournfully. Like all its kind, it is immortal.

It remembers.

Harding's fingertips tingle. He remembers beaded ridges of hard black keloid across his grandfather's back, the shackle galls on his wrists. Harding locks his hand over the vial of light, as if that could stop the itching. It makes it worse.

Maybe the nodule is radioactive.

Take me back, Harding orders. And the shoggoth breaks the surface, cresting like a great rolling wave, water cutting back before it as if from the prow of a ship. Harding can make out the lights of Passamaquoddy Harbor. The chill sticky sensation of gelatin-soaked cloth sliding across his skin tells him he's not dreaming.

Had he come down through the streets of the town in the dark, barefoot over frost, insensibly sleepwalking? Had the shoggoth called him?

Put me ashore.

The shoggoth is loathe to leave him. It clings caressingly, stickily. He feels its tenderness as it draws its colloid from his lungs, a horrible loving sensation.

The shoggoth discharges Harding gently onto the pier.

Your command, the shoggoth says, which makes Harding feel sicker still.

I won't do this. Harding moves to stuff the vial into his sodden pocket, and realizes that his pajamas are without pockets. The light spills from his hands; instead, he tucks the vial into his waistband and pulls the pajama top over it. His feet are numb; his teeth rattle so hard he's afraid they'll break. The sea wind knifes through him; the spray might be needles of shattered glass.

Go on, he tells the shoggoth, like shooing cattle. *Go on!*

It slides back into the ocean as if it never was.

Harding blinks, rubbed his eyes to clear slime from the lashes. His results are astounding. His tenure assured. There has to be a way to use what he's learned without returning the shoggoths to bondage.

He tries to run back to the inn, but by the time he reaches it, he's staggering. The porch door is locked; he doesn't want to pound on it and explain himself. But when he stumbles to the back, he finds that some-one—probably himself, in whatever entranced state in which he left the place—fouled the latch with a slip of notebook paper. The door opens to a tug, and he climbs the back stair doubled over like a child or an animal, hands on the steps, toes so numb he has to watch where he puts them.

In his room again, he draws a hot bath and slides into it, hoping by the grace of God that he'll be spared pneumonia.

When the water has warmed him enough that his hands have stopped shaking, Harding reaches over the cast-iron edge of the tub to the slumped pile of his pajamas and fumbles free the vial. The nugget isn't glowing now.

He pulls the cork with his teeth; his hands are too clumsy. The nodule is no longer cold, but he still tips it out with care.

Harding thinks of himself, swallowed whole. He thinks of a shog-goth bigger than the *Bluebird*, bigger than Burt Clay's lobster boat *The Blue Heron*. He thinks of *die Unterseatboote*. He thinks of refugee flotillas and trench warfare and roiling soupy palls of mustard gas. Of Britain and France at war, and Roosevelt's neutrality.

He thinks of the perfect weapon.

The perfect slave.

When he rolls the nodule across his wet palm, ice rimes to its surface. *Command?* Obedient. Sounding pleased to serve.

Not even free in its own mind.

He rises from the bath, water rolling down his chest and thighs. The nodule won't crush under his boot; he will have to use the pliers from his collection kit. But first, he reaches out to the shoggoth.

At the last moment, he hesitates. Who is he, to condemn a world to war? To the chance of falling under the sway of empire? Who is he to salve his conscience on the backs of suffering shopkeepers and pharmacists and children and mothers and schoolteachers? Who is he to impose his own ideology over the ideology of the shoggoth?

Harding scrubs his tongue against the roof of his mouth, chasing the faint anise aftertaste of shoggoth. They're born slaves. They *want* to be told what to do.

He could win the war before it really started. He bites his lip. The taste of his own blood, flowing from cracked, chapped flesh, is as sweet as any fruit of the poison tree.

I want you to learn to be free, he tells the shoggoth. *And I want you to teach your brothers.*

The nodule crushes with a sound like powdering glass.

"Eyah, eyah. Fata gun eyah," Harding whispers. "Eyah, eyah, the master comes no more."

WESTERN UNION

1938 NOV 12 AM 06 15

NA1906 21 2 YA PASSAMAQUODDY MAINE 0559A
DR LESTER GREENE=WILBERFORCE OHIO=

EFFECTIVE IMMEDIATELY PLEASE ACCEPT RESIGNATION STOP ENROUTE INSTANTLY TO FRANCE TO ENLIST STOP PROFOUNDEST APOLOGIES STOP PLEASE FORWARD BELONGINGS TO MY MOTHER IN NY ENDIT

HARDING

Skin in the Game

PETER WAS WAITING FOR ME when I got backstage.

I had been expecting the publicist to show up for weeks, ever since I started getting the sense that the tour numbers weren't what the label had hoped. But as I walked out from under the glare and heat of the lights, it didn't make me any happier to glimpse his hollow-cheeked, handsome scowl off in the wings. I ignored him for a few precious seconds, gratefully burying my dripping face in the snowy, chilled towel that Mitchell, my road manager and best friend, handed me. Sweat and makeup flattened the plush Egyptian terrycloth. I gulped water while I dropped the first towel, handed the glass back to Mitchell as I took another, and wiped myself down again.

I gave him a questioning glance. He waited until I pulled the Dampitronics from my ringing ears and handed them to him to roll his eyes toward Peter and murmur, "You want some backup with the cadaver, Nee?"

I shook my head. My ears shrilled like a temple bell despite the earplugs; my body trembled with exhaustion. A line of itchy soreness ran across my back where the low band of my costume had chafed because

I'd lost weight on tour. I wanted: my dressing room, a shower, yoga pants, a sandwich, and my bed—in negotiable order.

I did not want: a conversation with Peter Sullivan.

But there he was, curly graying blond hair atop a tall frame, a debauched cherub in a bespoke suit. Making me tired.

I was slumping. I spackled my best smile across my face (*pin the grin on the clown*) and hauled my tired spine upright to sashay over to him. *Don't forget to look spunky but demure. The Patriarchy hates it when you're not appropriately deferential.*

It had been a so-so night, and I had just now, without so much as a glance at the time, given up on expecting it to get any better.

"Neon, sweetheart," he said, and leaned in to kiss beside my cheek. He glanced at his phone, then dropped his hand to his side. "Great performance. You're looking better than ever."

"Glad to hear it," I replied. "Lost weight?"

"Good suit," he answered, with a self-deprecating flip of his hand he probably practiced in the mirror. His VIP pass fluttered in the breeze. "Can we talk?"

No wasn't an option.

"Dressing room," I said. "Follow me."

Once the door was shut, I stepped behind a screen to undress. I wriggled out of the drum rig with its electrostatic panels and synth triggers and touch plates, and hung it up to air out. Suzie, my dresser, would be along to disinfect it before packing. My costume was as sodden as if I'd walked into a swamp wearing it, and smelled considerably worse. I dropped the sopping scraps of sequined white stretchfilm into a laundry bag and sealed it, then toweled off and pulled on panties, bra, a v-necked t-shirt and an old pair of ivory-colored jeans. Even here, in private, my clothes were in my trademark ivory, silver, and white, a scheme I'd selected years ago to set off the darkness of my skin and my auburn halo of zigzag curls, sweat-damp and frizzy now.

Branding, branding, branding. Cameras were literally everywhere.

Barefoot, on the balls of my feet, I padded out of concealment. The white shag throw rug stretched itself and massaged my soles as I curled my toes into it.

Peter handed me a glass of wine—my own Neon White Red, of course, from my own minibar in the corner—and settled into the visitor's chair with one of his own. I chose to stand. I paced slowly, enjoying the ministrations of the rug, stretching sore calves with each step, aware that Peter was watching.

I bit my lower lip to keep from asking why he'd come. It didn't matter if I chewed on it now; the lipstick was all over the dirty towels.

It was all about the dominance games with Peter.

I sipped my wine, which was about the only thing around besides me that wasn't some shade of white. It was rich, not too sweet, a bodacious red with layers and textures. I had never had much patience for delicate, ladylike wines. I wanted something that tugged your shirtsleeve and demanded attention.

There was probably something Freudian in that.

I gave the silence a calculated forty-five seconds and glanced ostentatiously at my bangle. Blood alcohol content .01%, heart rate leveling off at 72 beats per minute, time 11:42 p.m. "Peter," I said. "I'm exhausted."

Awarding him the point, but maybe keeping a moral edge. He'd be easier to deal with if he thought he was winning.

His smile was stained with wine. Whatever it was, it was so important that he physically set his phone down. "We've got an opportunity to get in on the ground floor with a new marketing technology. Something that could be as much of a game changer as music videos were, or downloads. They asked for you specifically."

A nervous shiver raised the hairs along my nape and arms. I could tell already: This was going to be a pain in the ass. He wouldn't have come in person to pitch it to me—to pressure me—if it wasn't.

I'd been dreading a deeply uncomfortable conversation about what we could do to bring my tour more relevance. I'd rather have that.

"Who's *they?*"

He held up a hand. That was Peter for *I'm withholding that data until the end of my pitch.*

"Could be a career-maker," he said. "You need to get some skin in the game, something we can hook some press coverage on. Some pathos. You're stable and professional, which is great—but you're *too* stable and professional. Your image is, anyway. It's getting boring. Stable and professional is not what sells rock and roll. The fans are hungry, and you have to keep giving them something to chew on, or they move on. And you have a reputation of staying on the bleeding edge to maintain."

That was the trick, actually. The actual bleeding edge was too far away for most people to stretch to comfortably. In reality, you wanted to be just behind it, safe-ish but plausibly trend-setting, so you didn't make people uncomfortable, you just made them feel excited. As if they were taking a risk, when it was really a very, very safe investment.

The public likes to feel that they're standing next to a visionary. But they don't want to face the social consequences you get when you're fighting for real change. Jesus was right about Peter—and in two thousand years, the only thing different about people is what's on the surfaces.

I started off on the actual bleeding edge, a long long time ago. A real artistic revolutionary. Then I realized I liked eating and having a roof over my head, and I let that edge overtake me. Much better to surf it. Stay on the curl.

Putting up with Peter was just one of the prices I paid for the very nice rug massaging my sore feet right now.

I was probably a more effective double agent for social change here than further out, anyway. And that's totally not self-justifying twaddle.

I drank my wine politely until I was sure he'd finished. "Can I hear the name now?"

"It's an app called Clownfish."

I didn't drop my wineglass. Which was a good thing, because Envirugs were a bitch to clean. I glanced down at my bangle, thinking about adjusting my endorphin mix a little, but I didn't want Peter to see that he was getting to me. I caught myself doing it and tried to make it look like I was checking the time.

"I see you've heard of it."

I read *Scientific American* and *The Wall Street Journal* in addition to *Boing Boing* and *Ars Technica*. That wasn't one of the things that made it into the carefully curated press releases, but I'd heard of it. I shrugged. "It's a bit more than an *app*, Peter."

He shrugged right back. "I understand there's a widget or a dongle or something. An interface."

"It's a kind of machine empathy, right? Lets a user feel what somebody else is feeling?"

"Not exactly," he said. "It lets you *decide* what you—or somebody else, if they allow it—*will* be feeling. Set emotions on a dial. We've been thinking, we sell it as access to *your* emotions. What you feel as you're performing. Your own experiences in relationship to the song."

"Fans don't want to know that my feet hurt and the grilled cheese I had for lunch is giving me indigestion, Peter."

He tapped his bangle in demonstration. "We can fiddle that. It's editable. Movie magic—more real than real. Hell, they don't even have to be your emotions. We can outsource the recording, distribute it as downloadable content. Micropay—"

"No." I should have walked away from this nonsense years ago. But it was safe and easy, and Peter was easy. Easier than either finding a new label or going it on my own.

I have good lawyers, but breaking contracts is a nightmare. And anyway, my deal was up after this tour. I wondered if they would drop me. I knew I should probably drop them. But things like that are so much work. I have enough to do concentrating on the art, the tech, the brand, the business. I want people who can handle the fiddly stuff and go away.

This is exactly how artists and entrepreneurs get into trouble, time and time again. Knowing it doesn't make it any more fun to deal with.

"I'm thinking of us both," he said. "You know how well you do affects how well I do. You owe me a hearing, Neon. And I know you're going to give me one. You've always been a loyal friend."

Dammit, the man knew where my buttons were installed.

"*No.*"

He sighed. "No?"

My head was full of ways it might backfire. Exhausted, without really trying, I could think of dozens of different potential disasters. Public relations fallout. Personal attacks. Creeps. Injuries from inadequately tested tech. Lawsuits. Peter probably could, too—but it wasn't his career at risk the same way it was mine, no matter what he said. Sure, if his acts were successful, he was successful. But I wasn't his only act.

It also felt like a huge ethical overstep, an outright lie in a way that the branding and marketing didn't approach. I almost made a joke about Milli Vanilli, but Peter has had the ethical part of his brain turned off, so that wasn't an argument that would carry any water with him.

He said, "Your reasoning?"

I held up a hand. "Peter," I said. "It's midnight. I just spent two hours on stage. I'll be happy to discuss it with you later. But I think fiscally as well as brand-wise it's a bad idea."

The money argument always went over better with Peter than any appeals to personal decency or artistic integrity. Say one thing for elective sociopathy: It made him predictable.

"I don't think that's what's bothering you," he said.

"No?"

"Your face did that thing." He copied it, then grinned. "Like you just stepped in dead rat."

His next gesture took in my augmented body, the permanent surgical arch of my feet to Barbie toes. There's a little repulsor unit implanted in the heel that does most of the work, and makes the stage shoes bearable for a two-hour show. Keeps me from developing plantar fasciitis, too. Supposedly.

He said, "You've never hesitated to do what it takes."

"That's marketing. It's different. This is about…" I didn't want to say *authenticity*. "…authenticity."

His eyebrow went up. He didn't say what he was thinking. And I didn't know how to explain what I meant—that making a splash was one thing. Mediating, managing, even spinning the sense of intimacy with the artist was one thing.

Selling yourself in a totally false package was something else.

"Look, sweetheart," he said. "You're a savvy businesswoman. One of the smartest I've met. You know how this game is played. Theater and flash. It's not really *you*."

"Well, it couldn't be, could it?" I patted down my frizz. Nobody pays for an authentic celebrity with bunions and contact lenses and Botox appointments. They pay for a cunning facsimile of authenticity. A scaffolding they can drape their fantasy over to make it three-dimensional. Not reality.

Real people have real feelings, and real feelings are ugly and complicated. Real feelings *are* the "bleeding edge." Real feelings make people uncomfortable. Nobody spends their beer money on uncomfortable. Part of turning people into consumers is making them think your product will make them like themselves better, not ask themselves harder questions. You have to trick them into confronting *uncomfortable*. What did John Waters call it? A counterculture stealth bomber? Something like that.

Peter said, "How is it different than convincing the front row that that torch song you're making love to is really for them?"

I shrugged. "I'm paid to emote, Peter. Not to *have* emotions."

He pursed his lips and swirled his wine. My better judgment was under siege. They'd be eating rats and sawdust in there before I knew it, and then it was only a matter of time.

I nibbled a thumbnail. "It's different, that's all."

"Your numbers have been better than they are," he said slowly. "I had to call in some favors to get them to consider you as a flagship for this. Twist a few arms."

Whatever happened to 'they asked for you specifically?' I let the wine touch my upper lip. I licked it off.

I really was too tired for this. "I'll talk it over with Mitchell."

"Neon—" His mouth said my name, but his eyebrows said, *Are you really taking business advice from that guy?*

"Tomorrow," I said. "No show tomorrow. I'll have some time to look at numbers, okay? Have Clarice send them over?"

He scowled, but I knew the species and subspecies of his scowls by heart. This one was a scowl of assent.

At least I liked those better than the sneaky smiles.

I took a mouthful of wine and whiffled air over it to release the bouquet. It was still delicious despite the churning in my stomach. I'd write it differently in the song.

"I can stick around for a day," he said. "I want to hear your answer in person."

And *that* was Peter for "I intend to keep the pressure on."

I Should Never Have Slept With Him: The Neon White Story.

"DAMN, HONEY," Mitchell said. "He didn't even ask you if you wanted to get your shoes off first?"

He was sprawled sideways across the boxy beige armchair on the darker beige carpet of the beige-walled hotel room, the tip of one sock-clad foot flipping, flipping, flipping. His head lolled over the opposite side of the chair, dark curls half-hiding his eyes. One of his spidery arms was cocked at a weird angle, the other hugged in close to his chest. He balanced a tablet in front of his eyes and fingertip-skipped through screen after screen of information. His frown got deeper. He huffed and made disgusted cat noises, and I paced and yawned and picked my hair and scavenged an unappetizing room service tray on the theory that it would do my system good to eat something, even if that something was pretty nasty.

Rocks on the road. But they don't let you write paying-your-dues songs anymore after your third platinum record.

Finally, Mitchell let the tablet fall against his chest. His eyes closed and he seemed to doze for several minutes. I had just given up watching him and gone back to see if there was any warmth left in the coffee when he said, without expression or gesture or opening his eyes, "What have you told him you're going to do?"

I dolloped in cream. The coffee was gray from reheating. "Talk to you."

He sniffled dismissively. "Gamble either way. If it flops, and you adopted early, you'll look desperate. If it takes off and you didn't pick it up out of the gate, you'll look out of touch."

"And so the oracle confirms the truth I already knew."

That at least got him to crack an eyelid. "You gotta get rid of that guy."

I knew. Honestly, I'd known that for five out of seven years. But that sort of thing—abandoning a relationship—doesn't come easily to me.

"Does he have a rollout proposal?" Mitch, for reasons of his own, never seemed to say Peter's name. I wondered if it was conscious avoidance or subconscious disgust.

I rolled my neck, trying to get the tension out. The room was ugly but the bed hadn't been too bad. "I thought I might offer to wear the widget for a week or two, just to see what it records," I said.

He swung his feet to the floor and sat up, corkscrew curls stretching and bouncing like springs as they first caught against, then released from, the rough weave of the upholstery. "Why do you have to record anything? They're just making it up, right?"

"For the same reason my face has to be under the makeup, I guess. The illusion of depth." I made a face over the coffee. "Apparently, they can. They can do all kinds of magic with it. But that's…cheating. Soulless."

"They used to say the same thing about multi-track remote recording."

"They were probably right."

He laughed, knuckled the corners of his eyes, and said, "And intimacy in art is a construct anyway. Art isn't really about raw unmediated access to reality: that's *reality*. You get that at the bus stop. Art is about interpreting reality, pointing up certain aspects of it, focusing attention. Editing."

Most of my conversations with Mitch could loosely be characterized as 'preaching to the choir.' I indulged myself in a little bit of that now, and paraphrased something we'd both said before: "Art isn't art if it doesn't have a frame."

He kept looking at me, as if he expected me to continue.

I shrugged and obliged. "I think a lot of this is getting a baseline. He just wants me to wear it, you know, *around* for a week or so, until I forget I'm wearing it. We'll try recording some performances over that time. That would be when we start putting a frame around the thing. The studio bit of the process. So, performance, editing—"

"Can you track out a human heart?"

"Peter thinks so."

We shared a smile at that, because of course Peter didn't have a human heart, exactly. He'd had his pulled like a rotten tooth. Or at least rooted out, ground down, and crowned in gold and porcelain.

"You know," I said, "there have always been people who wanted to control somebody else's performance, and people who want to control somebody else's experience of that performance. I think it's a pathology."

Mitch raked a hand through his curls, got it caught, tugged it back out again the way it went in. "Never mind that," he said. "Do you think Peter's even thought of the risks involved?"

I thought I had, but by the expression of tremendous concern Mitch was wearing, it was obvious I hadn't thought about it enough. I must have looked completely blank, because Mitch said, "Every celebrity has stalkers, Nee."

THE WORST bit was, Peter was right. At least a little bit right: the early signs were there. And as I hunched over my phone checking concert reviews—a terrible narcissistic self-destructive habit, and one I encourage all of my colleagues to quit immediately—I could see all of them. Engagement metrics told me my audience was restless. I needed to bring them something new…but not too new. Something satisfying. I wasn't the flavor of the month anymore, and there were only two ways it could go from here: I could become a perennial favorite, a mint chocolate chip or coconut sort of a thing…or I could go the trendy way of acai berry, pomegranate, and betel nut.

I closed the app and speed-dialed Peter. He was just down the hall, but I didn't want to see his face.

"I'll take the trial rig," I told him.

"You won't regret it," he said.

PETER ELECTED to stick around through the first performance with the new kit. Seventy-two hours is a lifetime in the entertainment industry, and Peter never does anything out of sentiment. Either he was really interested in the results, or he expected me to pull a fast one on him.

I found myself fiddling with my bangle a lot. Maybe Peter had the right idea, and I should get my personal loyalty downgraded a little bit. The problem was, I liked myself the way I was. And that hadn't always been the case. I'd worked hard for that self-respect, and it seemed cheap to sell it just to make myself a little more comfortable.

I'm a lousy consumer.

The tech guy's name was Claude, and he was a total dreamboat in a hoodie-and-purple-chucks, West-Indian-accent tech-warrior sort of way. Claude was also good at his job. He built the Clownfish into the drum rig, which was convenient, at least—and he managed to do it in under six hours. I could shrug into it and zip it on and off just as I usually did, and there would be nothing to throw me off my stride except making sure the contact surfaces touched the right spots—and my dresser would handle most of that. Suzie was there to help out so she'd have some practical experience for the next time.

The headset was a little more built up than I was accustomed to, into a fairy-wire sort of tiara thing.

And it took a lot of boring, boring fitting. I was used to standing and turning and moving on cue, though I usually listened to audiobooks while I was being fitted for things. This time, I just zoned out.

It was the wrong choice, apparently, because Claude tapped me hesitantly on the shoulder and I jerked out of my reverie.

"Sorry," he said, with that eye-avoiding deference that makes me want to turn mean, "but can you think about something with some emotional freight? Preferably negative, for this bit? The alpha state doesn't give us much to tune to."

"How long have you worked for Clownfish?" I asked.

He winked. "Since the first day. I'm on the board."

My irritation at his deference turned to respect. This might be a future legend of technology with his hands under my blouse. "I'm flattered."

He ducked his head. "Management doesn't get overtime."

I laughed, and was trying to figure out something that might get my dander up when the dressing room door opened without a knock and Peter sauntered in.

"Hey, Neon," he said. "Hope you're disproving the stereotype of the empty-headed singer."

I sat down hard on a flare of dislike. Claude said, "That's good. Nice and strong."

His cool professional demeanor was a pretty good trick, too, since his hands were shoved up underneath my breasts while he adjusted a pearl-white leather strap so it wouldn't chafe or pinch. Peter strolled over and patted me on the shoulder. The tech and I both jumped as he inadvertently triggered a snare fill from the drum rig. Suzie the dresser didn't flinch. She must have seen it coming.

"I'm glad you decided to get on board with the Clownfish," Peter said. "I think it's a smart business decision."

He was always nice when he was getting his way. I thought about making some comment about the alteration and curation of self necessary to manage my future as a pop star, but it felt like too much work. Instead, I shrugged, and reminded him, "This is just a test."

I snapped my fingers and got a light, bright cymbal. Peter, damn him, didn't jump. Neither did Suzie. Maybe she'd just had her startle reflex turned off.

"This thing can receive as well as record?"

Claude nodded from somewhere around my belly button.

"I want a taste," I said.

His eyes crinkled at the corners. The toes of his purple All-Stars creased as his weight shifted in the crouch.

"Okay." A brief pause while he rummaged in his tech-warrior tool kit. "This is not set up to run off my bangle. Just let me sync my phone to the rig… Got it. You like beaches?"

"I like beaches."

He tapped his screen with a single-finger flourish.

And I was on a beach. Well, not exactly on a beach: there was no sensation of gritty toes, no sound of water, no burn of heat. But the meditative sense of peace and ease that washed over me was the one that only comes with the hiss of waves, the warmth of sun and the cool of the breeze, the cry of gulls.

There were no distractions in it, no sense of nagging tasks that must be taken up again when my stroll was done. No bikini strap digging into my shoulder. No worry that some tabloid camera might catch a glimpse of cellulite at the top of my thigh.

It was pure. And impersonal. Timeless. A little chilly. My feeling, and not my feeling. Better, for being unalloyed. Somehow less, for being so clean.

How were people going to react to this? I thought about human emotions. Messy emotions. Emotions that clash and conflict and contradict and confuse. That don't bother to explain themselves. That send us into therapy, self-medication, *medication* medication. And here you could get them cleaned up, tidied up, cozied up and comfortable.

Consolatory.

And we worry about people judging themselves against the photoshopped bodies in fashion ads.

"You edited out all the sand fleas," I said, when Claude tapped his screen again and the moment ended.

"Nobody pays for sand fleas," Peter said.

"The second generation is under development, you know," Claude said. "Once the rigs are more widespread, we'll be able to set up a sensory loop with the audience. Feedback trance state. We can guarantee that every concert will be the next best thing to an out-of-body experience."

"Sex," I said. "But deniable."

Movie sex, where nobody rolls onto anybody's hair and nobody ever sneezes.

Peter peered around me to fix his tie in the mirror. Subdued blue and charcoal paisleys, very elegant. "They'll eat it up," he said.

I DROVE my team crazy at the sound check, but you would have, too. I couldn't even tell the Clownfish was there. Maybe the headpiece was incrementally heavier, or maybe it was my imagination. But other than that homeopathic sensation, the drum rig felt the same, it sounded the same, it moved the same—but I couldn't escape the feeling that if I just tested enough different combinations enough different ways, something would provoke a failure. So I put the rig and the band and the sound team through everything I planned to do on stage that night, and everything I could ever remember having done by mistake, and everything I could imagine doing by accident. Probably twice.

The rig, for a wonder, worked. Which just redoubled my unease, and the conviction that it was going to fail catastrophically in front of nine and a half thousand people, probably in the middle of "Mystic Verses" or "Digger" or "The Judge." I was terribly afraid that the new tech would not just crash, but crash in the middle of the popular, show-stopping numbers. Thereby, ironically, actually stopping the show.

But if there was a failure built in, or some accidental combination of drum and brain wave that would crash it, I couldn't find it. And Peter had promised that he *and* the Clownfish tech were going to be there all night, and that if anything went wrong it would be fixed post-haste. I disgusted myself by finding Peter's assurances, well, reassuring. But I also made sure Suzie had the backup drum rig out, and oiled, and ready to go.

And then I stood in the wings and hyperventilated and got in the way—I mean, "supervised"—while the roadies broke down the set for the opening act and wheeled our stuff out, mine and my band's. I watched chrome and steel and enamel catch the lights from above, and I watched the roadies file off, and I caught my breath and held it as the spots went down.

You think it's going to get easier with time, that you're going to get used to it. That with experience, your hands will stop shaking before every show. But they won't; not as long as you're alive up there. It's the adrenaline.

It doesn't get easier. You just get addicted to it.

At 9:15 p.m., by my bangle, I followed the glow tape onto the darkened stage. I found my mark and took up my position center stage and waited for the hired guns to locate their instruments in the dark. My bangle lit up pale green when everybody checked in as ready.

I snapped the fingers on my left hand.

The electrostatic triggers in the drum rig pick up every motion. Some, they're calibrated to ignore. But most—the intentional movements of dance, the gestures that punctuate a song—are transformed into percussion, into rhythm, into joy. So my fingers went snap-snap-snap-snap. And the rig translated it into the thump-thump-thump-thump of the bass drum, setting time.

The spots came up. All my white and silver trappings dazzled in the sudden glare.

I'd found my beat. I'd found my light. The technology was working fine. It was going to be okay again, just as it always was in the end. We were going to do a good show.

And you know, it was a really good crowd that night. I felt the energy as I hadn't all tour, and I think the hired guns felt it too. At least, I saw the bassist and the keyboard player grinning at each other through the sweat, and that's never a bad sign.

I WAS still high on it when I walked backstage after the encore, and Mitch wasn't there with my towels. I should have known then, right then, that something was terribly wrong. But the bassist walked over to hug me, and I hugged her, and then we all had a good stoned-on-adrenaline giggle, feeling like we'd finally started working as a group.

When I finally extricated myself, there were still no cold towels. I was irritated, but not really irritated: I'd known Mitchell Kaplanski for the better part of a decade and if he wasn't there when I got off stage, something or someone was on fire or shorting out or drunk inappropriately. I resisted wiping my face on my arm, so as not to get makeup on the costume or the rig, and I picked my way over cables and past the bustle of load-out to my dressing room. I poked my head into the buffet along the way, just in case. No Mitch, and it was pretty picked over at this point, but I managed to assemble a chicken fajita with extra extra salsa and a smear of guacamole and ate it—balanced over a paper plate and seasoned with sweat and lipstick—as I minced on aching feet back down the hall to the dressing rooms.

I pressed my bangle to the lock and the door clicked tunelessly. It had been unlocked. Bad news. Had I left it unlocked?

I didn't think so, but I had been fretting so much about the new technology that I might have forgotten. It was a stupid mistake if I had. Or maybe it had been Mitch or Suzie? Or Peter? Or the venue manager? Nobody else was supposed to have the code…

I opened the door.

OF COURSE it's no surprise what I found. Everybody knows what I found.

Mitchell lay sprawled bonelessly across the ruined Envirug. It had humped up around him, trying to support his spine and neck, but it hadn't been able to do much other than flop him like a rag doll. His blood had soaked the white pile, which was thick and sodden with syrupy, gagging crimson on every side of his corpse.

I was cooler than I would have expected myself to be. When I realized where I was, the wooden floor had bruised my knees, but I hadn't screamed and I had my bangle to my ear and was dialing 911.

IT WAS four a.m. before the police finished with me, but the Clownfish tech was fiddling with the backup rig when I walked in, the one I'd been wearing on stage dangling from my left hand.

"Everything okay?" I asked.

"Er," he said. "Yes?"

I gave him my best Dazzling Smile. God knows the orthodonture cost enough. "Hey, Claude?"

He raised a properly suspicious eyebrow. Flirting was the wrong tack, I decided. An appeal to his hacker identity was more likely to get me what I wanted.

I said, "Can you show me how to download and compile that raw file? The one we made tonight?" I held up the drum rig and let it swing from my crooked fingers.

"You going to do something illegal with it?"

"Only technically." I winked.

A smile spread across his face like bread rising, warm and steady. I felt like a first-class heel for using his ideals so cynically. But I did it anyway.

At least I felt bad about it. It's possible that's the biggest thing separating me from Peter.

PETER WAS on a call, headset rather than bangle, when I found him in the business office. Because he was Peter, and if he went without contact with his phone for longer than fifteen minutes, withdrawal symptoms might set in.

From his end of the conversation it sounded like he was setting up a press conference. About the death. Of course.

"Put this on." I shoved the Clownfish tiara at him.

He stared at me, his hands not moving, his mouth making noises that were probably very important to the person on the other end of the line. The tiara wobbled across my palm. I wanted to jam it down his throat.

I threw it into his lap because that was better than hitting him with it. "Put it on," I said again.

"Gotta go," he said to the phone call, and dropped the connection. He set his gadget aside and picked up the headpiece. "Are you about to pull a gun on me, Neon?"

"There'd be some buzz in that." I tried for sweet reason and probably approximated icy mildness. "And the cameras in here aren't mysteriously malfunctioning, the way the ones in my dressing room were."

He blinked and glanced at the door.

I said, "You got your wish. Plenty of news coverage."

His eyes went sideways to the phone this time. Probably a better bet than trying to get past me. "You know, in the long run, Mitchell's death might turn out to be a good thing for you."

"Are you insinuating I killed my best friend, Peter? Because I think we both know that's not true."

"You couldn't have," he said calmly. "You were on stage in front of ten thousand people." The consummate press agent, still: always rounding up the numbers. "And you were wearing the Clownfish. Your alibi is airtight. If I do say so myself."

My lip curled. I felt like Grace Jones for a moment. Billy Idol. It was probably a better look on them.

"How's your alibi, Peter?"

He tapped the thin plastic oblong in his shirt pocket. "I've been on the phone all night, except when the police were talking to me."

God. I wondered if he could manage to carry on an upbeat conversation with some fluff page reporter while simultaneously shooting Mitch three times in the chest. The headset was a noise-canceling model.

It was actually plausible. He would only have felt fear, remorse, emotional connection if he chose to, after all: he'd elected to turn all that off by default. Otherwise, assuming he got the drop on Mitch—which whoever killed Mitch patently had—it would have been as complicated for him to kill somebody while carrying on a conversation as it was for most of us to talk on the phone while rummaging in the fridge.

Yes, he was capable of planning a murder, carrying it off, and never getting caught. And it's not like I had any proof. I just…knew Peter.

"Put the tiara on."

I must have gotten the sneer right that time, because he reached out gently and picked the thing up, then set it on his head. I'd cued it up to autoplay at the moment when I turned the knob and opened the door.

I watched him with a lover's interest.

His face pinched. He winced.

And then he shut off—touched his bangle and calmed himself, tuned out, edited whatever empathic function he'd been feeling. Back to his baseline sociopathy.

It probably *was* a good thing I didn't have a gun.

"Of course it's a miserable thing to have happened, sweetheart. And of course you're upset. But think of how advantageously we can cast this. It's romantic. It's tragic."

"Mitch and I weren't romantically involved, as you know perfectly well."

He shrugged.

I said, "You killed him."

"What possible benefit to me could there be in such an action?"

Media interest. Buzz. Drama. Gossip. The top of the news cycle, baby.

But I didn't actually have to say that. Instead I dropped my voice and said, "Promise me you did not kill him."

Peter smiled sadly. "I promise you, Neon. I did not kill your friend. But I don't expect that to change your mind."

He was lying. Was he lying? He must have known that I would never allow him to pressure me into using Mitch's death to my advantage. Mustn't he? Had he turned off those parts of his brain as well?

Could I *avoid* Mitch's death serving my career? Actually, I couldn't see how, when, as Peter said, my alibi was bulletproof. Hell, I'd been wearing the Clownfish. It wouldn't even hold water that I might have *hired* someone to do away with him.

"A virtual poker face isn't going to cut it anymore," Peter said. "The fans want to feel you have skin in the game. Real loss. This will help you. You'll see. Everybody loves a little tragedy."

"Murder," I said. "But deniable."

He smiled. Yes, I was sure he'd done it. And I was sure that no one would ever prove it. Peter was a very, very plausible man: an asset in his profession.

Even if I went to the police with my suspicions, Peter would somehow use our history to suggest that I was a jilted girlfriend out for revenge. Even if I hadn't killed anybody, *that* was going to look great in the tabloids. If I thought I could convict him, I'd go for it. But no. Not for nothing, not to make him look like a martyr. No.

"And we have the Clownfish recording." He tapped his ugly plastic tiara. "That's unbelievable, what that's going to be worth. The artist who is willing to exploit this medium is an artist who is going to the top."

"You're fired," I told him.

"I work for the label, Neon, not for you."

"The label's fired. You're all fired. I'll walk away right now."

"Neon." He shook his head soothingly. "I know you're upset and confused. But what are you going to do without Mitch *and* without me? Nobody can handle that kind of isolation in a high-stress career, sweetheart."

I closed my eyes. Nausea clotted at the back of my tongue. "You're probably right."

He smiled.

"You're still fired." My "reasonable voice" was coming out as more of a snarl. "Have Clarice write up some sort of buyout agreement for the rest of the tour. You can tell her I'll pay anything reasonable to settle. Unless you *really* want to fight out a long, expensive breach of contract suit."

The smile sagged into a gape. I wished I were still wearing the Clownfish. I would have liked these emotions on tape.

"And I'm releasing that Clownfish tape," I said. "You're not going to make a penny selling it."

His stricken look—so much more pained than when he'd watched Mitch die through my eyes—told me I'd struck paydirt. Filthy, stinking paydirt.

Well, there would certainly be buzz all right.

"You can't release it," he said. "It's our intellectual property. Ours, and Clownfish's."

"Is it?" I smiled, though it felt like plastic pinned across my lips. "What a pity it's already been pirated, then."

I turned away. It took a lot of will not to slam the door behind me, but it was so much more satisfying to let it drift slowly, aimlessly closed between us.

I glanced back over my shoulder once as I walked away down the hall. Peter was standing there. He'd opened the door and stood framed in the doorway, waiting for me to come back to him, the ridiculous tiara crooked on his head.

Peter waited. And I walked away.

HOBNOBLIN BLUES

TRACKS: HOW DO YOU DEFINE yourself?

    Loki: I don't. (laughter) Fuck, why do you people always ask me that?[1]

THERE'S ALWAYS a secret history, stories that remain unreported, tales too ticklish to tell. No matter how many soul-and-skin-baring biographies are writ, no matter how many groupies sell their stories to *The Midnight Sun*.

It's a source of intense frustration to the press that more—don't.

Something about Loki makes people keep secrets. Not just his lovers (the ephemeral ones or the few that linger over more than breakfast). Even the interviewers do it, as if they need to hoard clandestine fragments to gloat over.

You do it, too.

---

[1]   Henry Morrisseau, "Diamonds & Diesel: A Candid Interview With Loki," *Tracks*, August 1972.

But you have more to work with. You know his real name isn't that stupid collection of nonsense syllables. And you know he doesn't come from here.

When he fell, you fell with him.

Not for rebellion, but for love.

MONSTER BONES, the second album by controversial British song-writer Loki, looks to be a major breakout. The nine tracks, unified by themes of loss and catastrophe, range from "Golden Apples," a meditation on mortality—the apples hold the secret of eternal life, but like Sleeping Beauty's are poisoned—to the epic, Zeppelinesque crunch of "Bad Water," while the title track—a transparent commentary on the likely eventual legacy of the Vietnam conflict—uses crisp guitar and a killer bassline to underscore the point of view of a giant-killer revisiting the resting place of the adversary that crippled him: Prone under a forked white sky / I stare up a roof of bones / Bake under a crucified sun.

For a rock-and-roll singer, Loki demonstrates an astonishing vocal range. It's surprising to learn that he has no classical training, because the overall impression of his soaring performance is something like a Carole King with balls. With Monster Bones, Loki takes a hard look at the blues, and dumps it on its ass to take up with rock n' roll. A brilliant departure.[2]

LOKI SAYS, laughing, "Look at this nonsense, Hob. They can't even get their own fairy tales right."

You pull the flimsy magazine from his hand, already folded to the important page. Loki is paying more attention to the pretty redheaded boy nuzzling his neck.

Later, on the title track of a 1983 release, Loki will revisit those lyrics, in a song that most people will assume is about cocaine addiction.

---

[2] Frank Randall, album reviews, *Bontemps Magazine*, April 1972.

People, you will both have learned by then, will almost always assume.

The cancer, he'll sing, in the wailing apocalyptic style that's just a crippled echo of his true voice, speaks with a forked white tongue. The cancer croons with a forked white tongue.

HE WAS born Martin Trevor Blandsford in Manchester, UK, in 1950, where he attended grammar and vocational schools. In 1966, he dropped out, ran off to London, and in the company of three other young men took a famously squalid two-room flat in Soho.

There was nothing to indicate that within six years, Martin Blandsford would be transformed into a rock-and-roll avatar.

He craved shock, but for years it must have seemed he was born just a little too late. His mid-seventies revelations of drug abuse, bisexuality, and financial mismanagement failed to adequately galvanize a press already inured to the excesses of performers such as Led Zeppelin, Jimi Hendrix, David Bowie, Janis Joplin, and the Rolling Stones.

The fulfillment of Loki's desire to set the music establishment on its heels—or on its ear—would have to wait until 1980. When he'd do just that, in the most spectacular manner possible.[3]

ROBBIN HOWARD "Hobnoblin" Just:

7 July 1950—

Instruments: saxophone, mandolin, keyboards, rhythm guitar. Backing vocals.

A respected and steady-handed session musician, most noted for his work with Loki. Just was one of two members of the legendary 1970's touring band to continue performing with the singer after his 1980-1981 transformation (the other was bassist Ramona Henkman). He continued

---

[3] Eric Greg, *Playing with Fire: The Unauthorized Biography of Loki*, London, Plasma Publishing Ltd., 1998.

to record and travel with Loki until 2004, when the androgynous rocker put himself, Just—and the entire music industry—out of a job.[4]

LOKI PURSES his lips, sips Irish coffee, and lifts the back-folded newspaper in his left hand. He reads over the tops of his sunglasses. "Seven months ago, when Loki toured in support of Monster Bones, he and his five-man backing band shattered attendance records—and possibly a few eardrums. Ranting, charismatic, with an indefatigable stage presence, the tall black-haired rock God bestrode the stage—and the microphone stand—like a modern titan."

But the flesh around his lips is taut. Fine furrows lead from his nose to the corners of his mouth. You wince in anticipation.

He doesn't disappoint. The paper crumples in his hand, ink smearing under his thumb. "Titan. Titan. Wankers. Can't even tell the difference between a giant's son and a goddamned pansy titan. Do you believe this rubbish?"

"At least they're not making any misinformed cracks about fire gods," you say, eyes on your eggs.

It's unwise to provoke him. But sometimes irresistible.

He snorts, and hunches down to the paper again. His hair falls over his eyes. He shoves it back with a gaunt hand, sniffling. He sniffles constantly.

It's the cocaine. The gauntness is that, plus amphetamines. He takes them when he works, in heroic quantities, as if they could replace the forbidden mead of poetry.

Loki never knew when to shut up. Which is both why he's here, and why you followed him down.

He drinks more coffee and continues reading. "But the tour for the follow-up album Barbed Hearts is little more than bloated indulgence, the raw edges of the rock and roll buried under a stage show whose self-importance might give pause to Blue Öyster Cult. Dear Mr. Loki, a message

---

[4] *The Last Ultimate Encyclopedia of Rock & Roll*, New York, New American Library, 2009.

from your loyal fans: lasers and lipstick are not the markers of a brilliant career. Bah!"

He smacks the paper down on the table, splashing your tea, and finishes his whiskey-laced coffee. One of the staff is at his elbow in a moment with the pot, and—always polite—he remembers to thank her. It's as reflexive as the thanks he offers when you pass him the silver flask kept warm inside your gaudy velvet waistcoat.

You could refuse. But that wouldn't stop him drinking, and he'd be even worse in a rage. You pass him the whipped cream too.

At least it's calories.

"Fuck 'em," you say. The reek of alcohol from his coffee stings your nostrils. You pick a flake of skin beside your nail.

These bodies. There's always something going wrong. Exile is a kind word for death sentence. Nobody likes spilling the blood of a god if they can help it.

Bad precedent.

"You should see what they say about your sax, sweetheart." He finger-flicks the paper away. "Gods rot it, Hobnoblin. I want to go home."

He doesn't mean England. You don't mean England either when you say, softly, "Yeah," and reach over and pat his hand.

He shakes it off, though, and jerks his head side to side, sniffing. "Well, as long as we're stuck here, maybe we can bust things up a little. Let in some damned light and air."

It never worked on the Aesir, but you don't say that. It won't help either of you to remind him that he provoked the exile he mourns. Loki has never been any good at all at keeping his head down.

You're a little too good at it. That's one of the reasons why you love him: when the Aesir came, Loki was the one who would not be silenced, who forced them to treat with him as an equal.

For a time.

But that's a second thing you can't say. And the third one you don't tell him is that, despite the coffee mug, his fingers are chill.

TRACKS: WOULD you rather talk about the music? How much of the process is collaborative?

Loki: Oh, let's. And—frankly—a lot! I mean, the songs are mine, but the arrangements, that's all of us. And that's most of what makes it work. The Hobnoblin [Robbin "Hobnoblin" Just is Loki's saxophone player—ed.] has a great ear for layering sounds. (Loki laughs and takes a drag on his cigarette, holding the smoke while he finishes the thought.) And a good bass player, that holds the whole thing together. We hired this chick you're gonna love. (Smirking.) Oh, it's all collaboration. I'm pretending modesty this week. I just write the pretty words and play a little lousy guitar.[5]

HE DRIFTS on the music sometimes. The sound system in the estate in Kent is extraordinary, and sometimes you'll walk out on the patio and find Loki in jeans and a T-shirt, arms spread wide, head lolled back, letting the music lift him like a thermal lifts a hawk.

It's not his own stuff he plays to go there. As often as not, it's not even rock. Beethoven; Mozart; Charlie Parker; Thelonious Monk; Bessie Smith; Big Mama Thornton; Joni Mitchell; Crosby, Stills, and Nash.

You won't disturb him while he's listening.

But sometimes you'll sit at the breakfast table and watch.

WORD GETS around.

I knew when I arranged the interview that Martin Blandsford—Loki, to his young fans—would rather be interviewed at home. He doesn't go out much. He's been assaulted by feral packs of adolescent maenads one time too many, and says self-deprecatingly that it's in the interest of everyone's safety if he stays home with his slippers on.

---

[5] Henry Morrisseau, "Diamonds & Diesel: A Candid Interview With Loki," *Tracks*, August 1972.

Not that he was wearing slippers when I arrived. His bare knobby feet looked cold on the tile floor of his half-furnished house, and his white summer-weight pants were rolled up to show equally knobby ankles. He wore no shirt over his sinewy, hairless chest. His shaggy black hair stuck to itself in streaks of blue and goldenrod.

He'd been painting the upstairs bedroom, he explained.

To this reporter, accustomed to his commanding stage presence—the black leather and platform boots and smeared eyeliner—he seemed younger in person, slight, polite, dangerously thin. But the lack of costume bulk did make him appear even taller. He offered me a glass of wine and a cup of coffee, took one of each himself, and showed me into his den.

The actual interview did not go as smoothly.[6]

MELODY MONITOR: Do you categorize yourself as feminine?

Loki: Oh, no. I'm très butch. Don't you think?[7]

THE REST of the Barbed Hearts tour is a kind of hell, though you manage to tempt him sometimes with chocolate milk and yellow apples dipped in honey. Everybody in and around the band—the road manager, the guys from the record companies—assumes you are Loki's loyal and long-suffering lover, and you are treated with equal parts pity and disdain.

They expect you to play his keeper.

So you do.

He's worse at home, where it's just the two of you and whatever girl or boy (or girls, or boys) he's collected.

---

[6] Henry Morrisseau, "Diamonds & Diesel: A Candid Interview With Loki," *Tracks*, August 1972.

[7] Hugh Carter, "Loki, Unplugged," *Melody Monitor*, May 1982.

He doesn't eat for days. He hates the human food, the life-or-death choice. You're not immortal anymore, not without Iduna's stolen apples, and you're prey to all the needs and ills the flesh is heir to. Feed yourself, and live, and with it acknowledge that you are bound unto death in this mortal realm.

Well, that, and cocaine kills your appetite.

He stays up for four days writing songs for an album that never does get cut, because he pitches the whole lot into the woodstove one night when you're out by the pasture, feeding perfectly unmagicked apples to the perfectly unmagical horses, four bays and duns and chestnuts and grays with a leg at each corner, whose hides do not shine like faceted jewels, like beaten gold and steel and silver.

He never rides. You think perhaps he keeps them around to make himself sad.

BEFORE THE next tour, he wants to reinvent himself.

You sit behind him and chat and hand him the comb and scissors while he cuts his hair in front of the mirror. You help him bleach it white-blond, and once he's rinsed off the searing chemicals, the pair of you drink champagne and eat peaches and watch this month's crop of girls splash in the pool.

You kid yourself it might keep getting better.

But by month's end, you've packed for the new tour, painfully titled Ragnarock-and-Roll. It's soon apparent that the "fresh start" has been only a moment of reprieve.

Loki has always been thin, but the drugs and anorexia whittle him to bone and wire. He suffers hallucinations and fits of cocaine paranoia. He has a houngan brought in to exorcise the drum kit, because you can't trust those damned Norns.

Okay, that one is almost reasonable.

At his worst, he weighs one hundred and seven pounds at six foot two, and won't wear his earplugs on stage because he feels them squirming. He keeps singing, though, even if nobody can hear him. Because what he has to say is important, even if it's doomed to go unheard. What worries you most is what will happen if he forgets himself enough to raise his voice—because he could make people listen. He could.

If he were willing to pay the price.

He's a dying man clutching a microphone, and it's an ugly thing.

MELODY MONITOR: Seriously, your sexuality's been an open question for years—

Loki: My sexuality is an answered question. But apparently nobody likes the answer. I am what I am. Musically, personally. I don't like categories. I'm not going to assign myself to one.

It's boring to repeat myself.

"WANKERS," HE says, with that polite measured quietness. He drops a copy of *The Rolling Stone* on the floor and kicks it under the table. It skitters, pages fluttering, and fetches against the leg of your chair. You butter a scone. "Loki hasn't got a damned thing to do with fire. That's Surtr, for fuck's sake. I swear they do it just to piss me off. It's a goddamned conspiracy."

You break the scone and lay the larger portion on Loki's empty plate.

He sniffles and ignores it. "They called me 'a Ziggy Stardust-influenced Elvis impersonator.' Bunch of ignorant fuckers in the press."

"Yeah," you say.

He's not even drinking the coffee anymore.

SINGER COLLAPSES ON STAGE

British pop idol Loki collapsed during a concert last night at the Tingley Coliseum in Albuquerque, NM. The performer, 26, has been hospitalized for exhaustion. Presbyterian Hospital reports that he is in stable condition, receiving intravenous fluids, and in no immediate danger.

Band member Robbin "Hob" Just issued a public statement early this morning, blaming Loki's illness on fatigue and "dieting prior to a photo shoot."

He also said, "[The weather] is never this beastly in London. It's hard on the whole band."

Temperatures remained in the triple digits throughout the night, and attendance at last night's performance was estimated at over 11,500.

Tonight's show has been postponed. Changes to any further tour dates have not been announced.

Loki is known for shocking stage antics and provocative lyrics. But his most recent album failed to chart a single, and the current tour has not performed to expectations, half-filling arena venues in seven states.[8]

WHILE HE'S in the hospital, you clean out his stash. There'll be Hell to pay when he gets back, and you've no illusions you can keep him straight for long. But he'll be straight when they let him out, and he might still be straight long enough to yell at, if the pills and cocaine are gone.

Of course, he can get more. There are always people around who will get it for him.

But Ramona, the bass player, catches you going through the trunks and suitcases.

Silently, she helps you flush the pills.

MELODY MONITOR: Would you say you go out of your way to make yourself seem unusual?

---

[8] Associated Press Newswire, 12 July 1976.

Loki: D'you know about left-hander syndrome? No? Left-handed people make up around thirteen percent of the population. About the same percentage as homosexuals, give or take. And left-handed people die, depending on who you listen to, two or nine years earlier than right-handed people.

This might be because of accidents caused by bleedin' navigating through a right-handed world.

Being different can kill you, can't it?

Melody Monitor: Are you left-handed?

Loki: I'm ambidextrous. As in so many things.[9]

HE BREAKS his hand when he hits you.

Actually, he was swinging at Ramona, but you step in front of it and take the punch on the side of the head, to nobody's lingering pleasure. He's taller than you by a good ten inches, but frail from starvation and speed, and the swing that barely turns your head lands him, flailing, on his ass, all spiky elbows and knees.

He sits there, spraddle-legged as a colt in black leather and heavy boots, his T-shirt untucked at the waist, and shifts his gaze from the hand he clutches, to your face, and back again.

Ramona steps forward. You stand your ground, the same way you stood it beside him when the Aesir handed the sentence down and the rest of the dvergar stepped away.

You wonder if he can read the memory in your face, or if he has one of his own. He doesn't get up. He doesn't look down.

"Hob, can you get me into a program?" he says.

IN 1977, the punk zine *Beat Down* proclaimed of The Esoteric Adventures of Kittie Calamatie, "What the fuck is this? It sounds like Frank Zappa

---

[9] Hugh Carter, "Loki, Unplugged," *Melody Monitor*, May 1982.

mating with an alley cat. Who told this bloated arena rock asshole that he should ditch the laser show and synthesizers? And what's with the fucking mandolin? And why do I like it?"

It marked a new creative era for Loki, a regeneration of the innovative, questing spirit of the early 1970's. The album and subsequent tour, in which he assumed the persona of a drag queen punk rocker—the eponymous Kittie Calamatie—rejuvenated interest in his work, and the album reached #5 on the UK charts and #3 in the U.S.

Loki was sober and pissed off again, and the result was beautiful music.[10]

"OH, FUCK me running," Loki moans, head down in his hands, his hair—black again—standing in spikes between his fingers. There's a newspaper open on the table, dented by his elbows; you have come to know it as a sign of dread warning.

"What is it this time?"

Wordlessly, he leans back and rotates the paper with a fingertip. You shuffle forward, slippers scuffing on the tile, and clutch your bathrobe closed over your chest. There's a photo from a recent gig on page five. You're not in it, but Ramona and Loki are leaned together, jamming, guitar and bass necks bobbing in time. "It's a rave," you say, scanning the review.

"Look at my face."

You stare; it looks like Loki. Both the photo and the man sitting in front of you, idly turning his orange juice glass around inside its ring of condensate.

"I'm not getting any younger," he says, when you blink at him stupidly.

"Oh," you say, and sit down in the other chair. "Right. Happy birthday."

He tosses the wing of black hair out of his eyes. He's wearing a shaggy long-fronted punk cut, streaked purple and indigo, these days. It changes without notice, like the music on the stereo.

"It's not working," he says.

"Of course it's not working." You pour coffee from the thermal carafe,

---

[10] Liner notes, *Kill the Horses: the Loki Retrospective*, 2002.

add cream, two lumps of sugar with the tongs. So civilized these days. There's only his cereal spoon on the table, so you swipe it and stir. "What did you expect?"

"I thought I could make them understand," he says. "But it's all I can do to keep their attention."

"Some of it gets through. Subliminally." The coffee is delicious, hot enough that for a moment you forget the cold of the world. You pour a second cup. "Change takes time."

Fretfully, he picks the skin at the back of his hand. It snaps down, taut, but you know what he's imagining. "I haven't got time."

You don't answer.

"What if I showed them?" he says, conversationally, ten minutes later.

It's a tone you know not to trust. "Showed them what?"

He shrugs. "How silly the categories are. I got Thor into a wig and dress. Surely I can inject a little chaos into a complacent, self-consumptive media culture. I mean, Reagan's president-elect. Iron Maggie...don't even get me started on her. It's like the counterculture never happened. So... what if I turned into a girl?"

You're trained, by now. You don't let him see you choke on the scalding coffee. "It's not like turning yourself into a mare by magic, Jotunsson."

He tweaks skin between nails again. "It's only meat. What's the difference? It's just meat. It's dying anyway."

By the last days of 1980, John Bonham and Keith Moon are dead, Mick Jagger is divorced, David Bowie is sober, and Loki has finally pulled off a stunt that defies comparison.

LOKI: YOU wankers—and when I say you wankers, I mean the press, Bob—never let go of anything. You take it all out of context. When I started reassignment, you should have seen reporters trying to come up with coded ways to ask me if I'd had my pizzle cut off yet.

It's all a fucking hype machine. You say something like, rock and roll, it's the devil's music, it's concerned with subversion and revolution and kicking back at authority, and the headline the next day is "Loki Declares Self Lucifer!"

Badger: Well, that'll certainly be my headline.

Smoke wreathes her face as she studies me. I can see the moment when she decides it's funny after all, and gives a weak laugh.

Loki: Don't be silly, I hate fire. Ask me about the drugs, why don't you?

Badger: What about the drugs?

Loki: Don't ever fucking get started. And if you are started, stop right now. I'm not a role model, and you don't want to be like me.

Badger: Like you? Famous, talented, respected? Or like you, a freak?

Loki: Oh, the freak part is fine. That's a scream. If anybody gets anything from my life, I hope it's that the real freaks are the ones who try to program and condition everybody to conform to a conqueror's culture.

But I'd rather nobody emulated the drug abuse. You should see the films from my last nasal endoscopy. Not pretty.

Of course, the way it works is people want to idolize rock stars, pretend these stage personas are gods. They want to make rock star mistakes, but they're so busy pretending we're immortal and special that they don't want to learn from those mistakes. Live big, die gagging on their own vomit.

All these lovely illustrations of perfectly asinine behavior, and people want to be just like them. Same thing you people have always done with gods.

Badger: You people?

Loki: I'm an atheist. And you know, I could make people listen. But it'd be the last thing they ever heard.[11]

IN 1980, when Loki revealed his plans to become a woman, the announcement was greeted by a jaded media with first derision and

---

[11] Robert Slavish, "The Unlikeliest Centerfold: An Interview with Loki," *Badger for Men*, December 1983.

then disbelief [needs cite(s)]. While the singer had long been open about his bisexuality, his confession that he had entered treatment for Gender Identity Disorder and decided to undergo sex reassignment surgery was treated as a publicity stunt.

In 1983, Badger published a nude photo layout of Loki, post-op, provoking a media frenzy.[12]

LOKI WALKS around where you can see her, catches your eye with her upraised hands. "What are you doing, Hob?" she signs.

Your fingers lift from the keyboard. She watches intently. "Updating your Clikipedia entry."

"Packing it with lies, I hope."

"Do you want me to take out the bit where it says you're controversial in the trans community for refusal to politicize your sexuality?"

"Is that code for I fuck people who aren't transfolk?"

"I guess."

She sighs, swings the opposite chair around, throws a leg over it and plunks down. She straddles the back and leans forward on crossed arms. A moment later, she leans back. Her hands work jaggedly. "Even when they learn to listen," she says, "they still want to force you to say what they think you should be saying. Everybody wants the power of mind control. I just wanted to make them stop and think."

She stops talking. You let her sit motionless until she shakes herself and finishes, "Besides, I fuck transfolk too."

"Sweetie," you tell her (you never called her sweetie when she was a man), "you fuck anybody you think is sexy."

She grins, runs her tongue along her upper lip, and bats her eyelashes. "And what the hell is wrong with that?"

"Here," you sign, and wave her over. "You'll like this bit."

---

[12] Clikipedia entry: Loki (singer).

SINCE HER retirement from music, Loki remains a controversial and public figure. Her refusal to conform to political or social ideology has been described as anarchistic by some; however, the maverick ideology has been embraced by youth culture, some of whom describe her as a messiah.[13]

"FUCK, HOBNOBLIN, you wanker," she says. "Take out that word, messiah. And this bit in the quotes, "Half of what I say is meaningless, but I say it so you'll hear the other half." That's me misquoting John Lennon misquoting Kahlil Gibran. Take that out."

"Consider it done. You know you're not supposed to edit your own entry."

She laughs and kisses you on the head. "You're editing it, not me. I like this bit though—'The real freaks are the ones who try to program and condition everybody to conform to a conqueror's culture.' Did I say that?"

"In 1982."

THE STARS crack in the cold.
The only messenger is you.
Ride on
Killing horses.[14]

GROOVECUTTER: HOW would you categorize what you do?
Loki: I leave that to the critics. They have time.[15]

---

[13] Clikipedia entry: Loki (singer).

[14] Lyrics from "Ride On," off the album *Radiant*, 2003.

[15] Anne Westfahl, "Rock Star Bones," *Groovecutter Magazine*, March 1985.

MELODY MONITOR: You must get asked about your surgery a great deal, and what influenced your decision. Before your gender reassignment, you were very open about your relationships—

    Loki: Relationships. There's a juiceless euphemism.

    Melody Monitor: How has your gender reassignment changed things?

    Loki: [inaudible]

    Melody Monitor: Could you repeat that?

    Loki: I said, should it have?

THE MEDIA still depresses her. The mortal world is both too subjective and not fluid enough. She doesn't read the papers anymore, or the biographies, or watch the tell-all exposés. She's aging. You both are.

The exile is a death sentence, too.

It's not as if anything mere humans could devise would shock her, who knew the treachery of the Aesir overlords. But thirty-odd years of this nonsense isn't enough to make either of you used to it, or resigned.

People, it seems, still assume you're fucking her. And some people still don't approve.

She paces your hospital room, fuming, hands balled in the small of her back. You're fine, you assure her. Loosened teeth, a cracked cheekbone, a couple of busted ribs. A few nasty names can't hurt you now, and the MPA are treating it as a hate crime. They take those seriously.

And you're alive. Mostly unbroken.

It could have been worse.

It doesn't seem to be a good time to remind her that she once hit you herself, when she was he, and you and Ramona flushed his cocaine.

"Don't hold back," you tell her, when her silence grates too harshly. The IV pinches in the back of your hand. The tape itches. "Tell us how you really feel."

She checks and turns to you, and her hands fall down by her sides. "I could. What if I did? What if I made them listen?"

"Loki, you're mortal now too. And so am I."

"I would miss the music," she admits. But shakes her head and continues, dark eyes narrowing under the black fringe of her bangs. "If you tell me not to, I won't do it."

AS THE world now knows, the purported Martin Trevor Blandsford was revealed on 24 February 2004 to be a supernatural being, bearing a message of peace and open-mindedness that had gone too long unheard. [disputed] Through the divine auspices of the heavenly messenger Loki, it was demonstrated unequivocally that "There are none so deaf as will not hear." [disputed; cite needed][16]

THE PATUCK Reader: What do you think about the furor surrounding your last concert? What some are calling, in fact, The Last Concert.

Loki: That's melodrama. There are babies born every day, and thousands of years of musical history for them to grow into. I certainly haven't stopped composing, and I don't imagine anybody else has. Beethoven can always serve as a good example.

The Patuck Reader: You were jailed, there are death threats…

Loki: Let 'em come.

The Patuck Reader: You've been called a visionary, or accused of suffering a messiah complex. You're often assigned credit or blame for social changes in the last thirty years. For example, the advancing debate over what people are calling nontraditional marriage rights—domestic partnership regardless of gender or number of partners. Do you deserve any of it?

Loki: Don't be ridiculous. There's nothing visionary about anything I've said. Whatever you've done, you've done for yourselves. All I did was show you how to stop listening to the program and think. All I did was show people how to stop listening to the lies.

---

[16] Clikipedia entry: Loki (singer).

(She laughs.) If I were a messiah, I would be upset that more people don't agree with me.[17]

THE LAST album is released early in 2004. The Let Silence Ring tour kicks off the same day, with a worldwide live-televised gig from Madison Square Garden.

The encore is "Ride On." No great surprise there: it's the only reason it wouldn't have been in the regular set. You feel bad for Ramona; she doesn't deserve what's coming.

But as you walk back out to re-take your places, you pick your earplugs out and flick them into the darkness at the side of the stage.

For luck.

Once upon a time, Loki could sing gold from a dwarf, love from a goddess, troth from a giantess. He bargained kidnapped goddesses away from giant captors and blood-brotherhood from the All-Father. She talked Thor into a dress, and nearly into a marriage.

She's never used the full strength of her voice before mortals before. When she does, it reaches every corner of the world, a high windblown cry of truth and chaos.

It's the last sound any of us hear.

---

[17] Cassandra Hutchinson, "The Day The Music Died," *The Patuck Reader*, November 2006.

FORM AND VOID

BEFORE SHE TURNED INTO A dragon, Kathy Cutter was Comanche Zariphes' best friend.

You might say Comanche Zariphes was Kathy Cutter's *only* friend.

That wasn't because nobody wanted to be friends with Kathy Cutter. It was because Kathy Cutter didn't want to be friends with anybody else.

Kathy Cutter's hair was blonde and her eyes were green. Her face was a perfect geneshaped oval and she had a discreet little interface button that gleamed like mother of pearl behind her left ear. She was smart enough but not too smart. She wore cute tailored clothes from the fancy boutique.

Comanche Zariphes' mom eshopped at ConsignMart and everybody knew it.

Kathy Cutter's dad was a pediatrician and her mom was an architect. They lived in a big house with trees and grass so green it looked fake and a swing in the yard. They had a personal car, not just a sharecar. They ate fresh food and somebody else cooked it for them, and they were all right-minded to perfect happiness and stability. Supposedly.

Comanche Zariphes' eyes were brown and her hair was brown also. She didn't know what she looked like to Kathy Cutter, because her family couldn't afford the skins and simware that people like Kathy Cutter's family ran to control their environmental experiences. Comanche never asked Kathy about that, because she was afraid Kathy would tell her.

Comanche was too smart, and not smart enough to keep anybody from finding out about it. Her mom was a guitar player and her dad was a playwright, and everybody knew they were always broke and weird. They lived in an apartment with a cement balcony, and her mom grew tomatoes in laundry buckets and planted runner beans in window boxes so they grew up the pigeon wire. Other than that, they ate staples and worried constantly about staying in the maximum-rebate bracket of their carbon budget. They didn't even have a sharecar.

Nobody could spell her last name.

ALL KINDS of girls tried to be friends with Kathy Cutter, but Kathy Cutter was a hard girl with whom to be friends. She was snide, and she was superior. She was insulting, and she was irate. There couldn't be anything wrong with her, because she had been raised with all the therapy and all the right-minding her family could afford, so if anybody complained to the teachers or administrators about her it was obvious that there was something wrong with *them*.

And she was always just waiting to be offended. She collected injustices, and if she wasn't getting enough insults, she invented them. She collected them the way she collected her china dolls and china horses, and she was as jealous of letting anyone touch them. Once she had an insult, she rubbed it and rubbed it until it shone like jewelry. She polished it into a shape she liked, one that showed the slight to its best advantage, and she committed it to a memory jewel so she could wear it everywhere.

By the time they started high school, Comanche was still Kathy's only friend. And Kathy had so many insults saved that she could wear them on chains. The memory jewels were colored like rubies and emeralds, pearls and amethysts, and she had ropes of them in colors to suit every outfit. Some of the slights were Comanche's, but because Comanche wanted to be friends with Kathy she didn't mind when Kathy wore those, and showed them to her.

Or she told herself she didn't mind.

There were a lot of them. The time in second grade when Comanche gave her a Valentine's card with Kathy's name spelled with a C. The time in fourth grade when Comanche didn't give Kathy a Valentine's card at all. The time in sixth grade when Comanche borrowed Kathy's baby pink cardigan—a color that didn't suit her, though it looked wonderful on Kathy—and gave it back with a tiny ink stain on the sleeve.

Kathy remembered every mistake Comanche had ever made. So Comanche remembered them also.

Every jewel Kathy wore had the capacity to hold all of those memories, and a hundred years of popular music besides. But Kathy wanted a jewel for each slight—and her father, Comanche knew, would provide. He always gave her expensive gifts, strangely grown-up gifts.

As if he were making amends.

THEY STAYED friends all through school. Comanche followed Kathy into the A.P. classes, and to college, and when Kathy picked her grad course in astroengineering Comanche got into the same program.

Kathy encouraged her. Kathy drove her. Comanche was very, very careful never to score higher than Kathy on anything.

ONE DAY after graduation, Kathy said, "I'm emigrating to Io. They have dragons there." As if she didn't care at all what Comanche did.

But Comanche knew that if she didn't say, "I'm emigrating to Io too," that would be the biggest, shiniest ruby of all. So Comanche kissed her mother goodbye, and kissed her father, and packed up her few worldly things. Kathy gave Comanche Kathy's old datageneral, because Kathy's family had bought her a new one as a graduation present. Comanche couldn't use a lot of the functions because she didn't have the wetware, but it was better than the cheap one Comanche had bought with her grant. Comanche had planned to use the last of her stipend to purchase a ticket, but she surprised herself by applying for and getting a good entry-level technical job at the sulfur plant, so Iocorp paid her passage.

Kathy and Comanche took the elevator to Skypoint together, their duffels following obediently.

They couldn't sit together on the shuttle because Kathy was traveling first-class, but they used their datagens to text back and forth—no vids so the sound didn't annoy the other passengers, since Comanche wasn't wetwired. Once they disembarked on the *Activist*, Kathy let Comanche sleep in her stateroom. That way Comanche could run out for ice or whatever and Kathy would not have to wait for a steward when she wanted something.

The stateroom seemed luxurious by Comanche's standards, but Kathy seemed restless and disappointed in it. She wouldn't order in food, complaining that the ship charged premiums for cabin service, but Comanche couldn't coax her to go to the commons, either. Kathy paced the room, petted her jewels, refused to answer her phone, and gnawed on her cuticles until white streaks grew into her nails.

Often, Comanche brought back cheese and bread and fruit, and cups of coffee. Kathy could be a horrible person sometimes. But Comanche knew she had her reasons. And every time she looked at a screen or out a porthole, every time she kick-glided the length of the *Activist*'s central gangway, Comanche was glad she'd come.

IO WAS a world like dragonscale, vermilion and goldenrod mottled and crackled with white. Comanche had arranged to be at one of the viewports as they came up on it, and she drifted with her hands pressed to her thighs as her new home hove into sight. The arc of one of its sulfur volcanoes was visible against the jet-black horizon. Comanche could almost convince herself that those glittering sparkles she saw around the eruption's border were the dragons.

It took Comanche's breath away so thoroughly that she almost forgot to turn around and take in the round of Jupiter's belly as well, an echo of Io's colors so huge it was only partially visible through the port. Comanche held out her hands, imagining she could feel the fat world's tidal pull.

Kathy was back in the cabin, possibly watching the arrival on her wetware, possibly reading technical docs. She didn't have a job on Io yet, but it wasn't as if an out-of-the-way worldlet had a lot of competition for employment. She'd have to find something soon. True, Comanche had never seen her worry about money before—but it was probably just being so far from home and feeling insecure.

THEY SHARED a room on Io, too. Comanche got one as a perk of her job, and it was taking Kathy longer to find work than they'd expected.

"I don't want to keep taking money from my parents," Kathy said. "And I need to save mine for something that will get me a job."

Comanche approved. Kathy needed to cut the apron strings.

Comanche paid for everything. Nearly everything; every few days, Kathy brought home some kind of a treat—imported food, beers, a video player. She was often gone. "Working on getting a job," Kathy said, and then gave her that look that meant, *Boundaries*.

Barter, then. The hidden economy. Even out here.

Kathy was working on a new cuff. The first stone was an emerald as big as a cat's eye, one Comanche hadn't seen before. She knew it wasn't hers, because Kathy would have told her. Kathy always told her when she made a mistake.

The work was hard but interesting, though Comanche struggled with Kathy's datagen. She liked her shift leader, Arachne Jericho, whose expectations never changed from moment to moment. Mary Manley said Jericho was wanted on Mars for a murder that was really a justifiable homicide; Comanche never quite managed to not believe it. But if Jericho had killed somebody, they probably needed killing. And this was Io, not Mars.

Comanche's job paid well and it used her brain; she did external science and maintenance in a suit. As she walked from place to place, her boots kicked up plumes of sulfur dioxide frost. They hung in Io's frail gravity for long seconds before drifting gently down again. Comanche tended to frolic around outside when she thought nobody was looking.

She also spent a lot of time watching the dragons, wired into their integral armor, looping overhead. Their jobs were something like hers, but they were doing the real observational science out there on the edge of the solar system. They glittered, their metal bodies paved with synthetic diamonds and sapphires that held massive amounts of survey data in a permanent holographic matrix. Some were gold, some white, some blue. One in particular was a shade of padparadscha orange that caught her eye every time it passed.

She found it hard to imagine that they had been human once.

Io was one of their waystations, but they traveled throughout Jupiter's solar-system-in-miniature at will: Ganymede, Callisto, Metis, Amalthea… If they could get a lift back out of the gravity well on a survey rocket, some of them even visited the upper atmosphere of the giant world itself. Some of them went farther out, too—there was a colony on retrograde Triton with its nitrogen geysers. She guessed some of them were indentured to corporations too…but some had to have bought off their contracts. They could go places only drones could, otherwise, and that made them valuable.

They might be the only free things in the solar system. Only Europa was off limits to them. Europa with its water ice and its primitive life. Nothing that had not been sterilized and resterilized was permitted anywhere near Europa.

Watching the dragons, Comanche was reminded that she needed better hardware—and the attendant wetware—if she ever wanted to be promoted past a certain level. She didn't want to be like them—human body lost forever in a shell of alloy, ceramic, and memory jewels—but she needed to skin, and she needed to link, and she needed to be faster on these repairs in the way she only could be if she were projecting a schematic immediately over the work.

She couldn't save money while she was taking care of Kathy, not unless she had a better job, and the wiring cost a lot more out here than it did back on warming, overpopulated Earth. Iocorp would pay to have her wired...but it was a loan, not a gift. She'd belong to them for thirty years after, mind—quite literally—and soul.

BACK INSIDE, she found a note on her locker to talk to Jericho. Apprehension twisted her gut as she walked into Jericho's office—a broom closet, about the size of the room Comanche and Kathy shared. Jericho—a compact woman with Asian features and broad shoulders, her slick dark hair cut in a utilitarian bob—stood as Comanche came in, which wasn't a good sign.

But her words replaced Comanche's worry of personal failing and punishment with a different worry indeed. "Hey," she said. "Have you noticed stuff out of place on your rounds?"

"Stuff?"

"Tool kits," Jericho said. "Oxy backup. First aid. Anything that gets left in the lockers."

Comanche shook her head. "Shouldn't there be access logs for all those things?"

"Yep," Jericho said. She tapped her fingers on the desk. "You keep an eye peeled. Stuff is going missing; I'd like an idea how. And we have to replace it. Or somebody's going to get caught outside without enough ox."

ONE NIGHT—NOT really a night, but the language wasn't adapted to the world—Comanche came back to the room to find Kathy home, and in bed already. She was curled up on her side, head resting on her fist. Her body under the sheets looked strangely lumpy.

She raised herself as the light came on, but only from the waist—pushing herself up on her arms like a sick dog. "Hey," she said.

"Hey." Comanche dropped her gear kit inside the door. Kathy would normally give her hell for not putting it away immediately, even though she left her own stuff all over the place. "What's wrong?"

"Give me a hand up," Kathy said. "And you'll see."

HER LONG legs ended in perching talons, and glittered with memory jewels. All in different colors, arranged in rainbow belts—an angled spiral that peaked above her left hip in that big, green emerald. Her stabilizing tail ended in a hooked barb that put Comanche in mind of a safety knife, and which served the same purpose.

She was still a girl from the waist up.

"You're a chromatic dragon," Comanche said, even though she knew Kathy wouldn't get it. The look Kathy gave her told her that one wasn't quite enough for a jewel of its own, but she was adding it to the bank. "I didn't know—"

"My parents cut me off." Kathy's human hands sounded funny, tapping on her jewel-encrusted metal knees. "When I told them I wanted to emigrate here. My dad said he wouldn't pay for me to leave him. I had to save my money for this—"

"Of course," Comanche said. "It's expensive, becoming a dragon." She heard the aggression in her own voice, but for once Kathy didn't react. She sat down on the bed beside Kathy and sighed. "I couldn't afford it. I can't even afford the upgrades I need for my work. I'm going to have to sell out to Iocorp."

It was easier to say than she'd expected. It didn't hurt any less, though—she'd followed Kathy all the way out here, and Kathy was going to keep running. That's what it was, Comanche realized. Armoring up and running.

"I can pay for it," Kathy said.

"You need—"

Her armored lower body creaked as she stood up. "I'll be able to afford both. Just listen to me."

I'LL BE able to afford both. I will.

Comanche heard it. Heard it, as she had heard what Jericho said to her. Heard it and put it away.

She'd be extra careful policing the supply lockers. She'd make sure everything was fully stocked, and nobody's safety was compromised. She wouldn't help Kathy—but it was Iocorp she was robbing, not a person, not a charitable organization. Iocorp that brought people out here and then controlled price and supply of everything.

Kathy was leaving her. Comanche needed to be able to take care of herself. She stroked her own soft arm with her fingers. She didn't want to be a dragon, though she thought she knew why Kathy might. The same reasons Kathy might want to come all the way out to Io to get away from her family.

Comanche wasn't naïve. She knew there were things Kathy had never told her.

Things she only told her jewels.

IT WOULD be one procedure for Comanche and just one more for Kathy. Then she would be sealed into her untouchable armor shell. Bonded to it. It would become her body, forever.

Well, maybe not forever—Comanche supposed that some dragons, somewhere, must have changed their minds. But it was a tremendous expense to get that way. A commitment. Getting back out again would be worse, and you wouldn't be the way you had been.

WHEN COMANCHE awoke from her surgery, Kathy surprised her by being there. Her iridescent armor encased her in rainbow spirals to the delicate wings of her collarbones, which were framed by the attachment points for her helmet. Comanche tried to sit up, but her head seemed to be part of the pillow.

"Can you feel anything?" she asked, looking at Kathy's hands, one gold and one violet, and the way the light caught in the facets of her jeweled carapace and shattered.

"I can feel more than I want to," Kathy said. "Look, here's my new face."

She reached between her knees and lifted it from the floor. Comanche had never seen a dragon helmet up close before. The great glassy eyes were packed with sensors. The stone-crushing jaws could detect any number of chemical compounds. Comanche looked at Kathy's perfect porcelain gene-shaped face, and thought she knew why Kathy might want to hide it forever.

Did your father tell you how pretty you are?

"I think I might go to Titan," Kathy said. The new interface points all around her shaved hairline shone when she tilted her head. "Did you know the atmosphere is transparent in the infrared?"

"When are you leaving?"

Her expression was trying to be a smile. "Soon. But not tomorrow."

COMANCHE HEALED fast, and Kathy refused to leave before she was sure Comanche could take care of herself. It was as if the armor changed her, made her tender. Gave her the strength to be somebody who could care. But the spectral jewels that shimmered with every move were a constant reminder: Kathy would never forget.

And every time Comanche asked when Kathy was leaving, Kathy said, "I'm not ready yet."

There was work for dragons here on Io. Despite herself Comanche more or less began to hope.

I can't follow you this time, she whispered in the dark, when she could hear Kathy breathing. *This time you have to stay with me.*

COMANCHE WAS one of the three inspectors on shift when Mary Manley's distress call went out. Suit breach. Comanche made rapid contact with Jericho, and Jericho gave her the go to make a run. Comanche went bounding across the yellow-white frost, glittering sprays kicking away from each stride. She ran until she strained her suit respirator, the rasp of her breath drowning out Jericho's instructions and calm tone, and staggered and ran on.

Comanche was the closest help, but close was still halfway around the outside of the complex and the leak in Mary's suit was too big. It was one of those cascading errors where nobody should have died—but a suit seal gave way the same day an airlock failed to function, and when Mary tried to jam herself into the panic pod beside the failed airlock she found out the hard way that somebody had disconnected the ox and walked off with the bottle.

Comanche brought her body inside, all the way around the long outside of the complex to the next airlock. It wasn't heavy. Not in this gravity.

Inside, Jericho was waiting with a physician-coroner and a team of medics. There weren't enough people on Io for postmortem staff not to have other, primary jobs. Comanche's shift mates lined the corridor bulkheads. She felt like she was passing a court of judgment as she carried Mary over her shoulder to a gurney, frost flaking from the joints in her suit.

She stepped back and waited, chest heaving, eyes on fire. Not because carrying Mary was hard, not in this gravity. She had other reasons.

Jericho came up behind her while she watched the medics work. "She's cold and dead," Jericho said. "You're not dead until you're warm and dead."

Comanche nodded. "Cold comfort." It wasn't funny. She leaned a shoulder against the bulkhead and struggled with her helmet.

Jericho lifted it off for her. "Your half-dragonish friend was here," she said. "Looking for you. She ran off."

"Mary—"

Jericho put a firm hand on her shoulder. It kept her from turning around. The shift boss shoved the helmet under Comanche's arm. "You can't help here. I'll need you for debrief in a half hour, but right now you'd better go see to your friend."

KATHY CURLED up beside a condenser, small despite the armor. Her human body seemed thin and collapsed, like an empty fire hose run through the armature of her dragonish carapace. In this dark corner, even the glitter of her jewels was muted.

"Hey." Comanche crouched next to her. She knew better than to touch Kathy uninvited (that was the Tanzanite that lived at the small of her back now), but her hands hovered over her friend nonetheless.

Comanche waited. When Kathy didn't answer, she said, "I think you maybe owe Mary one of those stones now."

Kathy raised her head. She'd been huddled, hunched over her dragon helmet. Her eyes were rimmed red, her cheek cobbled with indentations that the stones had pressed. The armor could have been sealed across her face for all the expression it offered.

Flatly, mechanically, Kathy said, "You took the money."

"Yeah," Comanche said.

She turned around and slumped down against the wall where Kathy could see her. In her suit, sitting wasn't comfortable.

"You need to stop stalling, Kathy. Leave if you're going to leave. Because I have to tell Jericho. And then you won't be able to go. You're a free dragon. Get out of Iocorp jurisdiction, you'll find work. Resupply."

Kathy's cheeks were crimson spots in the center of bone white. "You'll lose your job. You might go to jail. Iocorp won't hire you again. How will you get home?"

"If they want to put me in a jail, Iocorp will have to ship me home." She snorted and looked at the back of her hand. She turned it over and looked at the palm.

Kathy started to her feet, talons clutching and skittering at the floor. "You're just threatening me because you're jealous!"

"Because you're going where I can't follow? Maybe. I followed you to the fucking end of the Solar System because…because you expected it. Because that's how things are with us. And now you're leaving me. And you always planned to be leaving me."

Comanche paused. She could have told Kathy that she had always been a dragon, really, even before she put the armor on.

But the truth was, Comanche had liked being the person who could walk with the dragon. Even if she got a little clawed or scorched. She'd made her choices. She was responsible too. And now she was making a different one.

She didn't need to hurt Kathy by explaining.

So she just said, "I'm not saying I'm innocent. But that doesn't change the fact that Mary is *dead*."

Kathy stared at her, wide-eyed. Breathless. "Come with me."

It could have been a punch in the solar plexus. "Kathy—"

"Come with me," she said. "You're the only one who ever wanted me for myself."

Comanche pressed her lips together. Maybe it would be good for Kathy to think that was what Comanche had wanted.

Kathy said, "You said I just expected, before. Well, I'm *asking* now."

"Kathy. You're a dragon. I *can't* follow."

Kathy's mouth opened. It closed. "I don't know how to—"

You should have thought of that.

"Five minutes," Comanche interrupted. "You can be here when she comes to get you, or you can be on your way to Titan."

"Comanche—"

Comanche turned her back. She put her helmet on. She squared her shoulders. She closed her eyes.

Eighty-seven seconds elapsed before the puff of displaced air told her Kathy had gone. Comanche still gave her the full five minutes lead before she went to Jericho.

Your Collar

WHEN THEY BROUGHT YOU FROM your labyrinth they promised you feasts, willing women. They promised you books and musicians and travel. They gilded your broad horns. They oiled your broad shoulders.

They made good on every vow.

They collared you in gold. The yoke lay soft and weighty across your shoulders, padded in red leather wherever it touched the polished alabaster of your skin. Three strong men could not have lifted it, but you bore the inconvenience with disdain. They shod your feet in boots with golden soles, which rang like horse-shoes, like cymbals on the fingers of a dancing girl.

When they led you before the queen, they clad you in a chiton like a Greek, white as the white bull your father, white as your own white hide. To cover your shame, one said, though you did not understand what you had to be ashamed of. They brought you through the street hung with golden chains. You thought it funny.

Gold is soft.

If you had shied like the carriage-horses or hurled filth like the street-urchins, if you had charged after and abducted the fainting, face-shielding

347

women whose scent tickled your nostrils, their chains would have meant less than nothing. What held you was your word of honor.

And it would have been enough. But before they brought you from the ship—the clanking, cantankerous steamer that lay as far outside your experience as everything in this modern, foreign city—they had pierced your tender nostrils, and the ring they twisted through the wound was steel. When you bellowed, one of them—the narrow sharp-pressed man whom you remembered was the lawyer—read the relevant sections of your contract aloud, because your eyesight is poor and because they had by then discovered you were illiterate in their language.

"This is permitted," the lawyer said, leaning close and underlining a section of text with one manicured finger. "Under clause 32, *use of the indentured's person*. Do you see? Royal Society privileges, sovereign's privileges, provision for regional safety." He tapped the parchment heavily, tilting his head far back to make sure he looked you in the eye.

You hadn't the human words, of course. Not with your thick cud-chewer's tongue, your beveled teeth, the length of your snout. You couldn't speak them, though you could be eloquent enough in your head.

It got me out of the labyrinth, you thought.

You nodded acquiescence, and held still while they shielded your eyes and soldered the ring.

THE QUEEN was beyond the blush of maidenhood, but dressed in maidenly green like the first hesitant uncurling feathery buds of April. The bright sunlight framing her throne made your eyes blink heavily. They were already itchy with the golden pollen your handlers dusted along the ridges of your neck to make the hide glisten. You could smell almost nothing through the musk of civet and lavender they had fogged you in.

Four chains depended from your collar, and at the end of each chain stood a liveried footman clutching a leather handle as red as the padding of the yoke.

The queen stood up from her chair, shattering the light behind her. "Is it safe to approach?"

The narrow man hunched from the shoulders. You imagined someone pulling his drawstring. "It can never be said to be truly safe to approach a beast," he temporized, transformed from the martinet of the grooming chamber. You realized, this queen wielded power over him.

You began to consider the next step in your plan.

"Nevertheless—" she said, her voice another tug on his drawstring.

"The risks might be acceptable to her majesty," he admitted.

She tossed her hair back and descended the steps, and when she came before you, you saw that she was delicately beautiful. The beauty of a mature woman, not the unformed features of a girl. You breathed envy across her face, imagining you could see it roll from you like a mist.

You were not beautiful. You wished you were beautiful.

When you breathed in, the scent of her came with your air, cutting through the fog of cologne. When she extended her hand, flat, a sugar cube lay upon the palm. She giggled when your whiskers brushed her skin and winced as the swipe of thick tongue greased the sugar away. While your head was bent, she brushed fingers across the velvet-fuzzed rim of your ear, where the cold golden rings collected from sailors dangled. You drew your wet muzzle across the offered palm again, wincing when the ring in your nose dragged on skin. You hoped for another lump of sugar, but all you got was the clink of your golden chains.

"Chain him to the floor," she said.

"Your majesty—"

"We wish," she said, an imperious drawl, "to speak with him privately."

The narrow man stared at you. You lifted your chin, the way the queen had, and wondered. If the narrow man was willing to trust your sworn word, your legal contract—why did he feel the need to conceal that from his queen?

Another thing to think on.

"Yes, your majesty," the narrow man said, and gestured to the footmen.

You were not surprised to find that the flipped-back carpets revealed steel rings inset in the floor, nor that the footmen came equipped with locks, to link your chains to those rings. The locks, like the rings, were steel. But the chains were still gold, and still—soft.

Because you gave your word of honor, you did not strain against them when the footmen left the chamber. The narrow man paused reluctantly at the door, and for a moment you thought he would argue. But he squared his shoulders, collected his dignity, and continued on without so much as a gesture of his head.

The door shut softly behind the narrow man. The queen had turned to watch him go. You lowered your head and whuffed against her hair. Now, with her so close, the rich scent of woman cut through the musty, acrid oil of lavender.

"I am an oracle," she said. She stepped away. Momentarily insensible of the chains, you followed, click of your boots echoing the click of her heels. But the third step brought you to the limit of your tethers, the yoke slanting into your collarbone, and you lowed frustration.

Like the narrow man, the queen did not turn. Unlike him, she spoke to you softly: "Why do you not burst your chains?"

You thought, because I have given my word. *Because my word is my duty.* But you could not answer. *If you are an oracle, do you not know that already?*

"Gold is soft," she said. "And you are hard."

Then, she faced you again. Her eyes were pale brown under dark golden lashes. She looked up at you through them, and one corner of her mouth dragged itself up, as if unwillingly. "A beast," she said. "I see."

You wanted to ask her *what do you want from me? What is my responsibility to you?* You think, unlike the narrow man, she might understand obligation. But in all the world, there had never been anyone for you to speak to. The humans—you may have known all their words, each of their words, every one of their words.

They still did not understand yours. And cattle—do not use language.

"Do you have a name?"

You did. You have not heard it since the woman who gave it to you died, on Crete more than four thousand years before. You could not pronounce it.

But yes. You did have one.

"You are very strong." She placed a hand upon your collar. At the full extension of her arm, she could reach you comfortably. At the full extension of yours, you could have clutched her, dragged her close.

You permitted your arms to dangle. You lowered your head and stretched your muzzle towards her. She stroked your mucus-sticky nose, rubbed the crumbs from the corners of your eyes with her own regal fingers. "So very strong," she said.

You angled your head so she could reach to scratch around the base of your horns, and she laughed. "I suppose, strong as you are, you don't need to be cruel to make people fear you. You can afford to be gentle, and no one will ever forget you are dangerous."

In answer, you rattled the chains, tilted the yoke so it would catch the light. The queen drew her hand back, her face perfectly impassive. Already, you were beginning to understand that when she made her face smooth like that, she was registering emotion. Surprise, or anger, or determination. Queens did not betray themselves through melodrama.

"You understand me," she said.

You ducked your head and lowed.

This time, you saw the movement of her jaw, the brief resulting flex of lower lip against upper. Her eyes were the color of toast, and you wished you could tell her so.

You went to your knees, bending your neck, and pushed your muzzle heavily into the midsection of her gown. The green glass beads and the embroidery prickled your nose. Rings clicking, she wrapped her hands around your horns, as if to remind you to be careful of them.

You did not need the reminder. You spent your youth as the pet of a king, the child of a king's wife who named you Asterion. You were a queen's son, but you would never be a prince. And when you grew in size and stature and the king came to fear you, he imprisoned you in the labyrinth, where you killed because it was your burden, your duty. If Poseidon had made you to claim his tithe, then claim it you would. You were strong; you were deathless; you could with ease shoulder that encumbrance.

You were a monster. But to be a monster did not mean to be uncultured. You have known many monsters. Many of them have been civilized. Most have been human.

One such civilized monster sought you, but could not kill you. He could not even find you, in the bowels of your labyrinth, though he could kill the white bull your father and claim the head was your own. Your father was a gentle creature, though no great conversationalist, and you mourned him.

You even mourned the kings who imprisoned you, when others came to burn them from their palaces. That was millennia ago, and knowing the turnings within the labyrinth is not the same as being able to leave it, for there were always those who would have killed you if they could. But a bull needs little more than grass and sun and pure water, and those things you had in abundance within the palace-maze your mother's husband built for you. So there you dwelled among mossy stones and crumbling columns through Mycenaean occupation, and Greek, and Roman, and Turkish.

In the end someone came, and you were liberated to travel by steamer across the Mediterranean, by carriage and by train across Europe and finally to a new and foreign island. You have walked in chains through the streets of this ancient city, amidst its smog and smoke and the soot caked upon its walls.

In four thousand, one hundred, and thirteen years, you have neither gored nor trampled a soul you did not mean to. You were not about to begin with your rescuer's queen.

You placed your hand over hers, on your horn. You had to angle your arm strangely to work it around the shoulderpiece of your yoke. Even her pampered skin was not so pale as your own.

You were gentle with her, as gentle as you would have been with a kitten. She did not seem as if she were significantly stronger than a kitten—physically. Everything about her gave evidence of the strength of her will.

But she was beautiful.

"Barrister wants to display you, Minotaur," the queen said. "You are a spoil of empire. You are the proof of his power, his foreign-affairs successes. What a concession, what a coup, to have obtained not merely the loan but the actual possession of the world's only Cretan minotaur!"

Was the lawyer's name really Barrister? Did these people refer to one another by position rather than name? Cook, cabbie, teacher, governess. You wanted to tell her that Minotaur—*Bull of Minos*—was not your name, that your name was Asterion. *Star.* You wanted to tell her she was beautiful.

She said, "You will spend your days chained in the Museum with the marbles, and folk will come and stare."

The tone of her voice was neither sympathetic nor gloating, but bitterly sarcastic. The tendons across the back of her hand tightened under your roughened fingers, and her face was serene as carven alabaster. You might have seen her in a ruin.

She knew all about being a frightening thing in a museum.

"It's so *heavy*." She touched your yoke, one last time, as you knelt before her. What is the difference between a collar and a crown? "You're so *strong*."

AN HOUR passed before she summoned the barrister—or Barrister—to return. He arrived swiftly enough that you knew he was waiting, lurking, just within hearing. He eyed you suspiciously as the footman brought him through the door, but you were only sitting cross-legged on a cushion at the center of your chains. The queen had brought down her chess set. Though you could not speak, you could play, and it turned out you were matched.

You were well-amused by the manner in which Barrister eyed you as he entered. There were stories, after all, about queens and bulls. And there were stories about the appetites of the minotaur. But no matter how he rolled his eyes at you—like one of the nervous carriage-horses—you only turned the white queen between your blunt-nailed thumb and forefinger, and moved her around the board like a knight while you waited for what they would say. Two squares forward and one to the left or to the right.

"We are pleased with the minotaur," the queen commented. "You will bring him before us again in three days time."

The narrow man blanched, but stayed so silent he might have been as voiceless as you. In lieu of speaking, he turned to summon the footmen to come unlock your chains.

"Wait," said the queen. She came to you as you rose, something shining in her hand. A silver-colored disk on a chain. You felt it tick between your fingers as she placed it in your grasp. She leaned over, her hair falling across your wrist, and showed you how to depress the stem twice, so the front and back sprang open like the shell covers on a beetle's wings.

A pocket watch. Steel, not silver or gold. Sturdy, with a crystal on either side to let the light shine through the jewels and gears of the mechanism as it worked. The case was worked in a delicate scale pattern, except for a mirror-bright, scroll-edged plaque—utterly blank. You stroked your thumb across it, leaving a blur of oil, but that wasn't enough to prevent you glimpsing your pale, pink-nosed reflection.

"Hard to have it engraved with your initials," the queen said. She looked up, her face gone still again. When she smiled, it was for Barrister, not for you. "Queens reward their favorites," she said.

THAT NIGHT, you learned that if you slept with the watch under your pillow, you felt it tick like a heart against your palm.

THE MUSEUM was as the queen promised: cold and white. They led you in chains along the white marble floors past white marble walls, through white marble galleries. This was, it seemed, a kind of labyrinth. You should be at home in it, but it was a labyrinth without moss, without softness. Without silence or crumbling stones or the trickle of water from the spring. You recognized the white marble statues when you were brought among them: if not the specific ones, then the styles. They were distinctive enough that despite blurring myopia, you could have named many of the artists. If anyone had thought to ask.

Honed by memorizing poetry and history and language, by remembering the turnings of mazes, your memory had always been excellent. As they chained you on a dais, surrounded by velvet ropes, it served you well.

When the queen arrived, veiled and hatted, wearing the clothing of a modest bourgeoise, you recognized her by her way of moving. That, and the faint trace of her aroma that rose over the smell of the crowd and the concealing scent of your fougère. She stood at the back of the crowd, and did not stay long. But she made sure you noticed.

WHEN THEY brought you to the queen the next time, they swathed you in a silken robe and rubbed oil into your horns to make them shine from boot-black tip to milk-white base. Again, she asked the footmen to chain you, and dismissed everyone. Again, she brought her chess set down. The men were jet and alabaster, and she gave you white to play.

The first game was played in silence, and you beat her. The second, she rallied, but ten moves in paused with her hand over the board. "They want me to marry," she said. But then she paused, considered, and restated. "*Barrister* wants me to marry. I should never have made him my secretary of state. I should never have allowed him to go to Greece—"

Her face had gone still, unchanging. She moved a pawn. You answered. She said, "Shall I prophesy for you?"

You knew what became of oracles. An old story, unchanging. If they were true oracles, their prophesies only doom them. The gods will what they will.

You nodded your head anyway, because it seemed to help her to speak of it. And it was not as if you could betray her confidence.

"If I marry whom Barrister suggests, within five years he will have gathered all power in the Empire." She gestured to you, to herself, to the rooks and bishops in between. "If I do not marry, I may hold him off for ten. But my single state is a liability. I have no heirs."

And if you marry of your own choosing? you would ask, but of course you remained speechless.

You touched the back of her hand. She moved a knight. You tipped over the black king.

IN YOUR chains, in the museum, you overheard a great many things. Barrister, you came to understand, was popular. And the queen was at the mercy of her advisors, of the parliament, of her constituents. Only men held suffrage. She was a woman alone, leading men who thought they knew better than she. Who saw themselves as lumbered with a weak woman, ineffectual, on the throne.

And she had not the courage to do what she would do, and damn their expectations. You understood; you had dwelt in your own labyrinth long enough, killing because it was expected.

You watched from the dais, and thought of honey-brown hair, of eyes the color of brandy, of toast. With a hand in your pocket, you felt the watch tick on its chain, though you only brought it out to let the light shine through it when you were certain you were alone.

THE WOMEN in your quarters liked you, maybe. They competed to interest you, anyway. One baked desserts. One went about naked and smelling of roses, an aroma that served chiefly to make you hungry. One came to tell you she was pregnant, which was true. You had smelled it on her breath, in her hair, before she knew it herself. You wondered if it would look like your father, yourself. Or like the mother.

Your heart beat like the tick of the pocket watch when she told you.

A child.

THE THIRD time they brought you to the queen, you realized that her palace was a labyrinth as well. Barrister did not accompany you this time. You wondered if you were meant to understand that he did not approve. Instead you walked surrounded by servants, their onus, the center of a cross of chains. They bound you as before, before the queen descended from her chair, and filed out in silence.

She came down the steps and you bowed low before her.

"Stay there," she said. She laid a cool hand on your neck, steadying you in your awkward position. With her other hand, she one by one unlocked the clasps that held the gold chains to your yoke. Unattached, they were too heavy for her to hold one-handed, and each by each they rang to the floor.

When the fourth one fell, she nudged you upright. "There," she said, as you rose up over her. "Now we can sit in chairs to play."

You doubted she would have a chair that would bear your weight. Mostly the chairs and benches here were fussy, padded things with spindly, curved scrollwork legs and eagle claws clutching the balls at their feet. But this one surprised you: it was an oaken bench, and she must have ordered it made for you especially.

You sat, and took up a pair of mismatched pawns. She chose the black, and you returned them to the board. You opened with the King's Gambit.

"I want children," she said. "And I am no longer a young girl. I must decide, and soon, if I want a kingdom or a son, Asterion."

You were so absorbed in interpreting the speaking serenity of her expression that for a moment, you did not realize it was your name that she had spoken. Your ears swiveled. When you swung your head up, the weight of the steel ring tugged painfully in your nose.

With her own hands, she poured you red wine in a glass delicate as a soap-bubble—a glass you would not have trusted in your own enormous hands. She pushed a china sugar bowl across the table, so you could snack.

"The name is recorded," she said. "It is Asterion?"

It's just as well she could not have understood the gabblings of your thick cow's tongue, because at the moment you could not have spoken.

You swallowed, the yoke tightening against your throat until the ripple passed, and nodded.

She smiled then, and met your white pawn with her black one. "Drink your wine," she said, and waited until you had sipped and set the glass down to continue, "You play chess. Do you write, Asterion?"

Not English. You shook your head.

"Greek?"

Your head grew heavy. Your heart began to flutter, ticking like the watch. For a moment, you wondered if the wine was poisoned. Wouldn't that be ironic?

You nodded, and the queen—her face unreadable again—produced paper and a fountain pen. In Greek, she wrote, painstakingly, the letters awkward as a child's—*what do you want, Asterion?*

Your own hands trembled as you took the pen. *To speak,* you wrote, at first so lightly that the pen made no mark on the paper. You turned it in your grasp and tried again. If you pressed too hard, the nib would break, and who would give you another? *To speak. To be beautiful.*

"You *are* beautiful," she answered, startled.

You underlined the word with a single black stroke, careful not to make the gesture too broad. Everything at the table was so fragile: the paper, the wine glass, the china. The queen.

"But you are," she insisted. "You are so strong, so white. Your eyes are soft and brown. If I were as strong as you—"

She sighed, and looked away. While she was blinking, heavily, you brought up your second pawn.

She must have seen from her peripheral vision, because she turned back to the board. She gulped and swallowed, accepted the gambit, did not flinch when you brought up the knight. She said, "I need to be strong like you."

You reached inside your robe and found the pocket watch, drew it forth and laid it on the table. You opened its wings and set it upright on them so the light shone through it, and you could both see the click and whir of the perfect, tiny mechanism. The pad of your thumb could obscure the entire face.

You wrote, *You are strong.*

She shook her head. "Not strong enough."

You wrote, *I can make you stronger. I can give you children.* You pointed to her, to you. To her again.

And the queen's pale face went still. She licked her lips, and touched the collar of your yoke. "This is impossible. How do you lift it?"

You gestured about you, at the palace, the labyrinth. The careless pen spattered ink upon the tablecloth, your hide. You wrote, *How do you lift this?*

"I lift it because I must," she answered. "But you lift that because it is easy."

You could have told her about the centuries alone, about the mossy stones. About how a yoke is a small thing to bear for company, for willing women, for a game of chess. You could have told her that you were a queen's son, who would never be a prince. But it would have taken too long to scribble down, and so you shrugged under your yoke and wrote, *We all have burdens. It is easier to bear the ones we choose, Your Majesty.*

Her hand slipped down from your yoke. She said, "If I said yes, would you still come and visit me?"

If you had a human mouth, you would have smiled. *And play,* you wrote.

She nodded.

You leaned forward over the table and kissed her mouth with your beast's mouth, sharing the flavor of sugar and wine. And when you sat back, you straightened her dress over your shoulders, and reached out to tip over the black queen. "Let's do something else today," you said. "Let's go for a walk in the gardens."

Across from you, Asterion nodded. He capped the pen carefully and held it up, asking permission. "Keep it," you said. "You shall need it to sign the papers when we break your indenture."

White eyebrows rose on his bone-white head. Pollen and gold dust glistened on the wrinkled skin of his brow. You had never appreciated how expressive his face could be.

"Well, of course," you said. "Somebody is going to have to translate written English for me. And I *know* I need better advisors."

He uncapped the pen and in awkward letters wrote, *What will become of me? What will become of you?*

"You are of royal blood. Your mother was a queen," you said. "Would you consent—in friendship—to marry another?"

Bulls don't smile. But as you rose and pushed your chair back, across the table, he stood up under your collar.

TERROIR

THE CIDERY CONTAINS SMELLS OF the earth and sweet apples. Stone walls render it cold and still. Along one is ranked long rough wooden racks laden with the products of the presses: doux, demi-sec, brut, sec. *Pomme* and *poire*. Pommeau and calvados in strange-shaped bottles—tall triangles, stacked blobs.

I feel as if I have come to a medieval alchemist's workshop.

Outside, the autumn sun paints a heavy golden haze down the flanks of rolling hills. The blackberries are past. The cornstalks are shorn off. The hedgerows and thickets that dissect green fields dotted with Charolaise and Holsteins (and stone cottages and barns) are tattered and yellowing at the edges.

Though it's a warm day, the long mild summer is over, and the rains of winter loom. Here, just inside the doors of the *cidrerie*, a chill settles into my bones. I watch the man working, unloading boxes by the spavined table, and cannot find the courage to speak.

I have driven past orchards to arrive here, on windy roads not much wider than my rental car. I have driven past signs commemorating old battles, down the same twisting highways Panzer divisions crunched to meet them. I overshot the turnoff to the cidery twice, and on the second instance, when I managed to make a woman leaving a boulangerie understand by means of my broken French what it was, exactly, that I wanted, she got into her car, waved me after, and showed me to the driveway.

I was only off by about 1500 meters, but I'm not sure I ever would have found it on my own. It was a nice reminder that I can still function without a troupe of assistants, anyway, even if it does mean casting myself on the mercy of random passers-by. It makes me feel strangely un-insulated, bare to the world as if I had shed a layer of skin.

And now that I'm here, I can't make myself step forward, or make a sound. So I linger in the doorway like a ghost until the man notices me. He looks up and says something rapid, something not unwelcoming, in French.

"Pardon, monsieur," I reply. "Mon francaise n'est pas bien." Then I point to the cider—le cidre—and mime opening my wallet. "Je voudrais acheter le cidre?"

"Oui, oui!" he says. The thing I have learned about Normandy, in my two days here, is that even execrable French is better than no French, and that nearly everybody seems extremely happy to work with me to find out what I need and help me get it. Some of it might be because this is the seventieth anniversary of the liberation of Normandy, and there are people still alive who remember when the Americans came like delivering angels. But some of it is undoubtedly just the character of the place and its culture—from the man at the market stall selecting your produce to order to the young man at the apothecary trying to explain what are their opening hours.

I wonder if trying to understand me is as exhausting for them as vice versa. At least they get to go home to families who understand them. All I've got is the sunny Englishwoman who is the landlord of the cottage I am renting.

The ciderer's brow furrows in the same concentration of active listening that's been giving me headaches since I got off the plane. "You like...tasting?"

"Non, non," I say, hoping the horror doesn't creep into my voice. It must, a little, because his brows rise. But I can't afford to drink this in front of anyone else. "Just...to buy?"

Le mot juste is what, in our case, we have not got.

He seems to understand, however. And soon I am on my way out the ragged doorway and into the farmyard once more, a tall box loaded with six assorted ciders clinking in my arms.

Back in my car, I pause to check my messages. My executive assistant wants me to sign off on her decision regarding a big Defense Department contract for a new heads-up display for combat troops. It's a great technology, based off one of my earliest communication designs. It will save American lives—and probably some Canadian, French, Australian, and British ones as well, if we keep getting into the same pickles together.

I call her—it's before lunch back in California—and we talk for ten minutes to get the day's business squared away. I miss the days when I could just create stuff—new ideas, new ways for people to interpret data and communicate with one another—but I suppose somebody has to run the company. My assistants handle most of it, but what was it Truman said? The buck stops here.

It's my thirty-third birthday tomorrow. I'm not quite old enough to be President. How did I wind up running one of the premier communication companies in the world?

When I swipe my phone off, the sun is already setting. And I want to be back to my lodging before full night, rather than driving in a strange country on strange winding roads in the dark.

THE SUNSET is a bloody banner snapping on the western horizon as I turn into the drive of my rented cottage. Clouds pile up against the horizon and the sky seems vast and complicated overhead—so many textured layers of dove and charcoal and periwinkle and indigo, smearing one into the next like blended pigments. Five Charolaise and one dun cow whose breed I do not know blink sleepily at me over the fence to their pasture. Chickens and the neighbor's pig complain that it is suppertime.

I park the car, bring my box of cider inside the stone cottage with its one room downstairs and two rooms up, and tuck two bottles into an under-counter refrigerator that doesn't come up to my waist.

At the counter, I prepare a light meal: bread from the boulangerie in town, apples and pears, Mimolette cheese, *vielle*. In other words, old. Aged. It's a cow's-milk cheese from Lille, in French Flanders.

In Flanders fields, the poppies blow.

It's a test, of sorts. At home, I eat out of packages and freezer trays. My assistants know what to bring me, and what I can't have. I've constructed an elaborate rhetoric of food allergies to conceal the truth—but my dietary limitations have only gotten more complex, the restrictions more elaborate, as I've gotten older. Sometimes I think it's the price I pay for success, though I know that's neurotic.

Here, I need to learn if I can do something different.

I carry my plate to the table and sit. I stare at the cheese, the bread. The slices of fruit.

"It's not going to eat itself," I say, and lay one piece of brittle orange-yellow cheese on a slice of baguette.

The rind, which I have pared away, looks like the surface of an arid alien worldlet, an asteroid or something—gray, pitted, mined by cheese mites. The cheese itself is wonderful: salty, sharp, bitter, muskier than cheddar. Rich with butterfat and terroir. I chase it with a bite of apple—sharp, juicy, sweet.

A swirl of impressions follows the flavor. Young men in gray or blue uniforms with rifles; younger men, without uniforms, wielding weapons improvised from agricultural tools. Red poppies tossed like whitecaps by the breeze. Mud, blood, mustard gas, diesel fuel, horse shit, and the sewer reek of spilled intestines.

Familiar old friends, all.

My phone buzzes, and I turn it over.

A man consolidates out of the swirl of impressions, real-not-real. His edges seem hazy, his outline translucent. His face is blistered with mustard gas, half his jaw shot away, tongue lolling through the gap amid shattered teeth. *Un poilu*, an infantryman, grubby and unshaved. His eyes bulge like a skinned rabbit's.

He blinks at me dreamily, then reaches out one hand as if pleading.

His tongue writhes; his ruined jaw opens in a welter of blood. The sounds that emerge might be meant to be words, but they don't have the shapes of words. They're just gabblings and moans.

I lunge away, oversetting the spindly wooden chair and falling hard to rust-colored terracotta tiles. The blow between my shoulders knocks the wind from my lungs and the bolus of cheese, bread, and apple down my throat.

The infantryman shreds as if blown through by a strong wind. By an artillery shell.

I toss the bread and cheese and the remains of the apple in the bin for the pig and pull a box of soup and a package of saltines out of the cabinet instead. The cider stares at me accusingly when I open the tiny refrigerator to get the canola oil spread out. It's a sin not to eat butter in France, I know. But sometimes you decide to serve your time in Hell tomorrow, rather than today.

THAT CIDER is still right where I left it, come the morning. I have breakfast—store bread; instant coffee; tinned, condensed milk; and corn flakes with more condensed milk, all just as nasty as it sounds. Modern, uniform, entirely devoid of terroir: industrial products stripped of all individuality and history.

I read my email over breakfast, the better to ignore the food. I'm half a day ahead of my assistants, but they've already been though four hundred and sixty of the not-quite five hundred messages, responding to most. The few they left for me to deal with are issues that only I *can* deal with. Existential threats for the entire company, or things that could blossom into existential threats. Some design work to review. A potential encryption project for the Navy. A faster, flexibly printed 'chip' that could be layered into uniforms.

I miss my old shop in the garage some days. And then I remember that in those days living on bologna and Wonder Bread wasn't a choice—even though in those days I *could* have eaten something better if I could have afforded it—and I hardly could have afforded to bugger off to Normandy for a couple of months.

The food goes down with only a vague swirl of unease. After I clean up, I am left staring at the blank white door of the small refrigerator, haunted by the cider within.

Fifteen minutes of that is all it takes to drive me out of the house. Nursing the bruise between my shoulders still, I walk the five kilometers into the village, my shopping bag slung over my shoulder. I'm fit, but even so the hills are challenging. The little village with its narrow streets and stone houses flanked with azure hydrangea and crimson geraniums could be a fairy-tale or a watercolor, it seems so unreal.

I pause for a long time at the door of the boucherie before I can force myself to go in. It's really more of a charcuterie, with beautiful smoked pork and a *jambon* in the back as big as a fifth grader, but they do have some beef and poultry. The smiling woman within greets me, and with gestures and patois we manage to establish that I would like (*je voudrais*) un biftec.

She pulls a hunk of beef from the chill case—I would call it a roast—but she lays it on the counter and with admirable disregard for the continued health of her fingers plies her cleaver, severing a piece of meat that is blue-red and beautiful.

She holds it up for my approval, red a veil across her gloves like watercolor.

"Bon, bon!" I say. It looks delicious. I hope I'm hiding the fear on my face as she wraps it in paper and slips it into a bag.

THE STEAK grills up to perfection, charred rich and caramelized on the outside and buttery red and melting within. There's salt and savoriness and fresh thyme picked from the plant outside the door. It's one of the most amazing things I've ever eaten, and it carries with it a feeling of peace and contentment and rich green grass.

The Charolaise whose flesh I'm gnawing lived a bucolic life, it seems, and never left the patch of ground where it was raised. And that patch of earth, somehow in all Normandy, has not been a battlefield.

The potato, on the other hand, fills the air around me with the clawing ghosts of peasants starving in the wake of the Seven Years' War. I force myself to keep chewing, to swallow, all the while thanking a God I don't believe in that butter can serve as a lubricant.

I gag it down, closing my eyes on the emaciated woman in ragged gray linens, a stinking-dead babe wrapped in her skirts for lack of other swaddling and held up against her breast. Her eyes meet mine, beseeching.

I want to scream at her—*what do you want, what do you want, why won't you leave me alone?* But I know from long experience that they will never answer.

They troubled me less when I was young, when I was the person who was going to save the world with free information and a cheap interface. You'd think the rawer conscience of a person barely out of college would result in more ghosts, not fewer. But apparently that's not how it works.

The collapsing principles of a corporate overlord don't seem to shield me.

THIS IS why I've come to France, and to Normandy in particular. This glorious countryside with its marching hills and tanks of briary hedgerows is as blood-soaked as any place on earth. And it takes a charming and peculiar delight in food—as much concerned with the deliciousness and provenance of its diet as…any place on earth.

I am a problem-solver. I fix broken things and establish lines of communication—even when that means taking it on the nose—and that's how I've made my fortune.

But when I'm the thing that's broken, that's getting more broken with every passing season, suddenly solutions are much harder to enforce even if I could manage to uncover one.

The cider waits. One bottle of doux, one demi-sec, two of brut, one of the sec. And one bottle of poire, which does not come in various alcohol concentrations.

I rise up, go to the big refrigerator in the laundry room, and take out the bottle of doux—"soft" cider.

It's what we in the states would call a sweet cider—slightly fermented, just beginning to "work." Perhaps two percent alcohol, if that.

It smells amazing. As I pour it into the Ikea glassware my hostess provides, the heady scent of apples rises, dragging a swirling tail of tattered memory and shape behind. I breathe deep, trying to steel myself.

I raise the glass to my lips.

Just the fumes in my nose are enough to trigger a cascade of images, and the hesitant sip I allow to pass my lips comes like an artillery barrage. I mutter, "*Gas, boys! Gas!*" and swallow anyway.

There are screams—in American English and the *à l'ancienne* sort as well. Cries of pain and terror. Cursing, in German and in French. Older dialects, ones I cannot even identify. Voices from a thousand years ago. Belgian? I'm not sure. Who else has fought here?

Too many.

Enough.

I swallow, and the voices fade. The grief and sorrow linger. The terrible sad savagery of it all crests over me and I thrash, drowning.

I should have just bought a bottle of vodka. Something mass-produced, as divorced from the wheat plant and the potato as possible. But that isn't the point then, is it?

So many of the houses in Normandy are this patchwork construction: raw stone, and dressed stone, and a rough beam lintel over a modern door. A patch might be stucco, a half of a second story laid in red brick, or the windows framed with it. Tile roof and slate roof and corrugated steel.

People here have built with what they had to hand, and haven't bothered too much with making any of it match. And yet, these homes grow their own improvisational beauty. Like the place itself.

Seventy years since this land last was fought over, as it has been fought over so many times before. There's a body in every hedgerow, my friend Lucy says. And she doesn't mean just the hedgerows here. We live in a charnel house world: every continent except Antarctica is soaked in centuries of gore, and that one only escapes because humans cannot live there. The world is haunted, everywhere.

And everywhere, the ghosts do want something.

I just don't know what. Or why they've started picking on me.

I carry my sweet cider outside to the yard, where a green plastic table sits under a sky that looks like a stained-glass rendering of storm and sun. I plunk into a plastic chair and lean my head back, looking up into the branches of the apple tree. Doves and hens coo and gabble.

All the dead men and women under my feet seem to shift, strain at their bonds. Wanting. And it's my job to learn what they want.

If I have the courage to keep asking. To keep looking. Not to look down.

To misquote something Akira Kurosawa said, the job of the artist is to not look down. I'm not an artist, though—I'm just an inventor. Somebody who runs a company. A human being. I don't know if I have the courage for this. I don't know if I can keep looking.

Inside the cottage are processed bread and processed cheese. Velveeta, brought in my luggage. I could go get them.

I could go hungry, until I'm hungry enough to risk whatever it is that the land wants of me.

The glass stares at me. I stare back. Neither one of us is going anywhere.

I CHOOSE a rainy day to drive the forty-five minutes to Mont Saint-Michel. A weather sky, streaked like warring banners rendered in cloudy oils, tears here and there to reveal paler grey behind. It's a stunningly flat landscape, land level as the sea from horizon to horizon, with the island town and abbey rising like Minas Tirith from the edge of the world. I arrive early, before the press of tourists, park the rental, and walk in, feeling like a pilgrim. If you subtracted the boardwalk and the chain link fences, you could imagine yourself in a story.

Normandy is a dream landscape. Green to the edge of the sea, the sea-fields dotted with sheep and rippling with grasses. I pause atop a white clay dike and watch the old abbey slash prison slash fortification glower down through the splintering, watery light and a rain that is more the suggestion of water falling than the certainty.

A little faint with hunger, I rest my hands on my knees and breathe.

The wooden bridge is new, and there's a mass of construction where they are demolishing the old elevated causeway, to restore the natural water flow.

I chose Normandy over all the other possibilities for a number of reasons. Because of its bloody history, yes. Because I speak a little of the language. Because it was supposed to be beautiful, and because it was easy to find a rental with an English-speaking landlady. Because the French believe strongly in terroir, in local food and local drink.

Because I am a coward, and even were I to ignore the language barrier, Normandy has an advantage that I could not find now in Ukraine or Baghdad.

It's safe. For now, anyway: I know better than most people that *safe*—as Richelieu said of treason—is merely a matter of dates.

I hike the battlements of Mont Saint-Michel, which is, even clotted as it is with tourists and creperies, one of the most beautiful places I have ever set my shoe to pavement. The stairs are steep and irregular; the walls in varying states of repair. One of the turrets has had its roof and shutters replaced; the next is left a yawning, empty column. You can glance down into it and see the corridors within the small town's ramparts, the places where soldiers would have massed in defense before charging to the top of the wall. The sharp briny wind off the sea gusts—focused between merlons and through embrasures, cold enough to prickle my skin. In this weather, the battlements are nearly deserted, though glimpses of the streets below between the houses and businesses lining the inside of the walls show a thickening stream of tourists.

It's fashionable to deride them, of course. To deride *other* tourists—one's-self never qualifies, does one? Here they come to climb Mont Saint-Michel, and pay their nine euros at the Abbey gate.

But that is what this place has always been, is it not? The object of a pilgrimage. They still sell medallions from machines inside the Abbey. And what am I—what are all of the tourists—except modern pilgrims? Even if some of us are more hushed by history than others.

I walk through the portcullis that guards the entry, past a bombard abandoned by the Englishman Thomas Scales when he failed to take the island during the Hundred Years War, in the 15th century. It looks like nothing so much as a giant black iron cannelloni awaiting the cream filling.

I touch it. The metal is cold and made of longing. When I step back, two small girls scramble over it, laughing and shoving.

I take my time on the island. The Abbey itself is magnificent—built like a nautilus in concentric shells, oldest and smallest in the middle. The Romanesque church is a thousand years old, rough stone mortared around rounded doorways. A Gothic structure has accreted around it like a corals on a wreck, like narrative around a nugget of history. One buttress stretches the entire height of the island. Gargoyles and grotesques and delicate filigreed botanical carvings abound. The windows are composed of multiple tiny leaded panes, arranged like tiles in different tesseracted patterns. Their subtle tints of green and gray and sand and blue echo the shades of the ocean, beach, and farms beyond.

When I come to the chapel, a service is in progress. I hunker off to one side with the other unbelievers, faintly abashed. No one sermonizes. White-robed monks kneel before an altar—one adjusts his garments and eases himself several times, obviously uncomfortable holding his position on cold stone. The bell ringer who stands behind them strips off his outer clothing to reveal a black habit and sandals. He grasps the thick rope in both hands and rings with his whole body, starting with strong, even pulls that cause no sound, then nearly dipping to his knees as he throws his entire weight against the mighty bells. Somewhere overhead, a vast wheel is turning, a vast bell is tolling.

We built these things, I think. We—human beings—over the course of centuries and thousands of lives—managed to bury our differences and collaborate to create something like this. Or something like the Cathedral at Notre Dame. We can build these things, these amazing things, with no more than a rudimentary knowledge of engineering and the work of many hands over many, many days.

What else could we do, if we actually cared to do it?

My breath smells of salt—sea and tears—when I choke on it. I feel the pressure of the lives lost here—Normans, and Bretons, and Romans, and Franks, and English, and others. I feel it, and I try to allow it to pass over and through me, to slide against me and not to scour. I am…only moderately successful.

It's getting worse. I don't even have to eat the food any more. Now the place itself is seeping memories into me.

I stagger through chapel and cloister and crypt, through the gift shop and out the other side. I lean against the wall over the sea beside a cannon and I gasp in bitter sea air. The island's bedrock peers through the pavement here and there, showing the ancient structure of the world beneath the human encrustations.

The rippled sea and sand blur into one another, stretching to the edge of the world. People drown, venturing out into the tide flats; the water comes in fast as a person can walk, and the sand is tricky.

Looking at the sea, I decide that I'm not ready for Omaha Beach just yet. It's not cowardice, I tell myself. It's being sensible.

I decide to drive straight home. I mean, "Home."

ON THE way, I pass a house attached to a wall that used to enclose a larger house. The wall has a hole you could drive a semi through blown in it. I almost veer off the road staring at it, wondering about its provenance. Accidental damage? Did somebody *actually* drive a semi through it? Or a Panzer? Is it a relic of World War II?

How could I even find out?

Well, I could stop at the farmer's market going on in the square, I suppose, and buy a cucumber. But even as the idea blossoms in me, I depress the accelerator, downshift, leave the small scarred village behind in a welter of images lost in the rear view mirror. The automated radar speed-check sign by the church urges me: *prudence!*

I come back to the village I'm staying in earlier than I expected. That charcuterie is just opening up again after lunch—nothing is open at lunch time, in this part of the world, except for restaurants. I walk in more boldly this time, and the little woman with the cleaver greets me with a smile.

"Bonjour," I reply. "Je voudrais le grand jambon, s'il vous plaît?"

I measure with my hands, and she knows exactly what I mean. She wields that cleaver to make thick, moist slices until I say, "Fin." I think that's probably incorrect, but she seems to understand, and she grins at me as I pay for the ham and some prosciutto, too.

I think of the happy spotted black and pink pig back at the cottage, and try not to feel guilty about the ham as I stop by the market booth for a melon half the size of an American cantaloupe and six times more flavorful.

I eat prosciutto and melon for lunch, each bite a shock of flavor and a rumble of tank treads punctuated by the thump of artillery and the screams of burning men.

I **FALL** asleep to the beeping of the tiny toads that seem to want charging. The next morning, I'm awakened by golden light streaming through the mist and the drone of a hornet the length of the end of my thumb who has blundered in the screenless window. I usher her out before popping up my email again. Technically, I'm on sabbatical, but once you let yourself get wedged into the position of decision maker the only way to escape it again is to get killed by a bus—even though honestly, my assistants can hold the corporate line as well as I can. Possibly, even better.

I poke at the pile of Important Artifacts Of Later Period Capitalism in a desultory fashion before deciding that I should go for a run before it gets hot. I scarf a power bar and a glass of thinned condensed milk and pull my spandex on. I run halfs at home, and I have an idea for a ten-mile course over this pont and that pont which should shake the cobwebs out of my soul. The hill back up from the river is steep and long enough—at least four kilometers of climb—that I slow to a determined stumble. I make it, though, and at the top I pause to look at a field full of suspicious male calves that must be being raised for beef and their harried wet-nurses—about four calves per cow, at rough count.

French cattle are much more engaged with the world than American cattle: the milk cows have run alongside the fence beside me, or spooked and trotted away. The steers raise their heads and watch suspiciously, the biggest one in each field kind of shouldering up to the electric-and-barbed-wire fence as if to let me know I came to the wrong neighborhood.

I crouch with my hands on my knees until I get enough wind back to suck cloying Gatorade from a bottle that was in my hydration belt. My feet ache. The cows watch me and I watch them. It's all very restful.

It flattens out here, and I pick up speed while jogging back to what I think of as "my" village. The patisserie is closed today—oh, right, it's Sunday. A little shock of terroir prickles the bottom of my feet through my sneakers as I pass the sign that commemorates the high-water mark where the Panzers were stopped by the Allies on their way to reinforce the serene little town St. Hilaire, which was eighty percent destroyed during the war. Outside the ghost of one burning Tiger tank, the remains of a German soldier crawl toward me. He is charred, his stumps of legs still wreathed in flames as he drags them through mown hay.

I recoil. He's not real: I can see the stalks of the hay through his blackened outline. The flames of the tank illuminate nothing and throw no heat. My skin prickles with sweat only from my run. A humane person would pause, would reach out to him.

I leap sideways across the ditch, nearly falling into the path of a speeding Fiat. I windmill my arms, wobbling, and manage to keep my feet, then accelerate away from the tank and the soldier, digging in hard as I run.

There are more—dozens, one in every field and hedgerow, their uniforms indistinguishable with blood. They cry out to me, their words incomprehensible. I run harder, feet pounding, arms pumping. They call after, but either they cannot make the words take shape intelligibly, or I cannot comprehend them.

I stumble into the cottage soaked and shivering, dizzy with crashing blood sugar and short of breath. I gulp chocolate milk from a bottle and drag myself upstairs to the shower, shedding soaked, salty clothes on the floor, peeled inside-out like snakeskin.

The hot water pounds my face, washing stinging salt from my skin and into my mouth, the corners of my eyes. It washes away grit and sweat and the stink of fear on my skin.

I'm driven from the shower by a crack of thunder. The last storm of the season, perhaps. I stump down the treacherously steep wooden stairs—half ladder, really—and open the glass doors to the garden so I can listen to the rain. Two hornets, each an inch and a half long, invite themselves inside. It's getting to be a habit, the hornet removal dance.

I try to read my email but it's all so many phosphor blurs. When I realize I've been staring for fifteen minutes at one particular note from an assistant telling me what action she's taking in my name in an acquisition deal that happens to come with some sticky legal issues, I flip the screen closed with my fingertips and go over to the couch with a book. Camus, *The Plague*, picked off a shelf beside the television.

I mean to read, but I nap.

By sunset, the rain has broken. I sit in a wet plastic chair in the gloaming—*l'heure bleu*—and watch the bats flit overhead in pursuit of mosquitoes. They part like the Red Sea as a grander shape wings over, utterly silent, silhouetted against the last light of the sky. An owl, monarch of the evening, gone almost before I recognize what it is.

I go in to the fridge in the laundry room and pull out a bottle of cider. The sec, strong and dry. I've learned to open the bottles outside; I've barely untwisted the wire when the cork flies free, up over the rooftop. I hear it thump on the tile roof and fall in darkness.

I'll look for it in the morning.

A curl of vapor drifts from the open bottle, barely visible in the half-light, then faintly phosphorescent. Spirits seem to seek out spirits. Dissolve in them, perhaps. Get distilled. The stronger the liquor, the stronger the impression. Like Omaha Beach, like Verdun, I don't have the courage yet for anything stronger than cider. But this is the strongest cider I have.

I pour, and the chill on the glass gathers condensation from the moist air before I even set it on the table. I sit before it, watching more bats flit from the neighbor's rusty-roofed stone barn as the day folds its wings. I should have stopped and tried to talk to the tanker, to the infantrymen, to the artillerymen. To the civilians wasted by bombs and ruined by artillery shells.

I should have, but I didn't.

The Sherman tanks were no match for their German opposite numbers. One Ally who watched too many of them die in flames estimated that it took twenty minutes for an American tank to burn, and ten minutes for the men inside to stop screaming.

Somehow, we still won...that war, anyway. America's contribution included piling materiel onto the battlefield until the Axis collapsed under the weight.

I was also too much of a coward to go to North Africa.

Or Hiroshima, for that matter.

Am I too much of a coward to drink this cider now?

It's wet and cold and tastes of apples, of green grass, of earth. Tart, uncomplicated by the standards of wine, threaded with hair-fine columns of bubbles. In the distance, a fox screams four times, sounding more like a hawk than a mammal.

I hold the cider in my mouth, and let the dead come.

A little girl in a patched gingham dress glows faintly before the scarlet geraniums. She does not hold her hands over the gaping wound in her side. Instead, she uses them to cradle a book against her breast. I'm not good with kids, but I think she might be seven or nine. Half her hair is still braided in a pigtail; the other half is burned short and matted with blood.

She looks up at me, pleading, like all of them. She holds the book out to me, opens it. There are words written there.

I swallow the cider in surprise and she vanishes.

Hastily, I slurp more, aerating it to increase the aroma and flavor. But the girl does not return.

Still, I know what I read. Read—and understood.

Je m'appelle Solange, it read. *S'il vous plaît, aidez-nous.*

I FINISH the bottle. But no one else comes to see me that night.

IN THE morning I rise, nursing a mild hangover. The message light blinks on my phone—I silenced it before I opened the cider—and while I brush my teeth I listen. Every available potential crisis has blossomed, and I am entreated to call—though assured that my people are handling it as I would wish, in my absence.

You don't want to know what I pay for phone service in France.

I brush the call-back icon with my finger, anxiety and irritation at war in my gut. *Je m'appelle Solange.* Before the first ring finishes, I hit the red icon and break the connection.

My executive assistant calls me back not thirty seconds later, though I must have woken her from a sound sleep with that half of a ring.

I swipe the call to voicemail, run a comb through my hair, stuff my feet into sandals, and set off for the beach.

MORTAIN IS along the way. Poking up the steep curves of Rue de la Petite Chapelle, I see the sign for the Hill 314 panorama. I park in an unmarked public lot across the street. Before I walk to the hilltop, I follow the pale gravel path to La Petite Chapelle de Saint-Michel, a little dark grey stone church with Gothic stained glass in glorious shades of blue that commands one stony bluff. Before it, to the right of the path, is the memorial for the Americans of the 30th Infantry Division who held this hill from August 6th, 1944 to August 12th, 1944 when the lowlands on every side were a sea of Panzers.

The heavy trees give cool shade. The sky above is scattered white and blue and gray as the chapel. Surprising me, there are no unquiet memories here.

I walk around the church to enjoy the view from the bluff beyond it, and return to the car the way I came. Walking past it, I pick my way along a lane on foot toward the panorama. I come to a grove of trees and great gray stones wound by clear foot trails and marked with signs. It's posted private property, but it's obvious that whoever owns it wishes it to remain as a piece of living history.

I climb the trail to its commanding height. Here, scrubby trees break away around tall gray rocks, a sort of natural pillbox. I scramble up to peer between them, and realize I can see over the rolling countryside to the sea, and the unmistakable outline of Mont Saint-Michel like a thorn above the horizon—roughly fifty kilometers from here.

Saint Michael gets a lot of traction here, it seems. *A great prince who stands up for the children of your people.* I can see why Normandy might want a warrior angel on its side.

When I turn back, the hilltop below me is alive with rank upon rank of ragged Americans and tattered Germans, interspersed with French farmers in their softly worn flannels and faded caps. They are all gaunt. They all stand at attention, their eyes gazing through me without moving as if standing for review by a passing general. They say nothing: they stand and wait.

They wait for help.

How can you help someone who is already dead?

IT'S ANOTHER hour and a half to Omaha Beach. I follow twisting sunken lanes more often than motorways. Cornfields—relics of the Marshall Plan—march across hillsides. My ankles ache by the time I pull into the parking lot. I climb out and stretch, then follow signs and the walkway until the long warm golden arc of the strand comes into view. Waves hush over, combing their fingers through the grains of sand. The sun glitters on the arcing sculptures like great steel splashes, and the flags of the Allies snap in the wind. Normandy sure as hell beat Britain in the coin toss when it came to Beaches Of The English Channel.

It isn't what I expected.

On a warm September weekday, the beach is dotted with bathers. Someone throws a tennis ball into the water for a happy springer spaniel. Three children shriek and chase each other around a sand castle. There is no hush, though people stand before the monuments with bowed heads and respect, no few of them with sparkling eyes. The sea stretches to the horizon: England is over there somewhere, too far to see but not too far to swim. This could be any holiday beach anywhere.

I pull my shoes off and walk along the sand, toes in the water. It's warm and shallow, the breakers gentle. Four percent of the sand on this beach is made of microscopic shards of shrapnel and impact spheres. And yet, what I see is peaceful and serene. Houses shoulder up to the road at the top of the seawall, green bluffs windswept behind them. All are new: the Germans razed what was here before when they built their defenses. There's a warm yellow wood contemporary in among the half-timbered and stone cottages, and a few manor houses with sweeping lawns.

It could be a town in New Hampshire, in California, with a few slight changes of detail.

And there are...somehow...no dead.

At the far end of the beach, just before where the pier stretches out—and beyond it, the tall golden cliffs that separate this place from Utah Beach—is the National Guard Memorial, built atop a battered German pillbox that cost so many of those men their lives.

One of those rainclouds sweeps in; you can watch it come across the water trailing its tail, like a patter of artillery fire. People scatter for cover under beach umbrellas and the like; I might duck into a casemate if they weren't cemented closed. There's a few further up the hill that you could probably get into—their open mouths snarl out to sea even now—but it would be easier to run to the creperie across the street.

The rain escalates into a punishing downpour. I have not brought an umbrella. Water puddles around my boots, reflecting the angled concrete walls of the pillbox under the memorial. I peer out through the mist and falling water; the sea and sand and sky are indistinguishable. Only those abandoned concrete fortifications remain to show that this place was ever a battlefield, that this place is something more than one of the nicest beaches I've ever seen. For a moment, all is soft and serene...

I think, all things heal. I think, for a moment, that there is so much more to Normandy—to this place—than war and the legacy of war. I think that the world moves on, and scars fill in, given time. I think I have been unfair, and brought my own preconceptions with me, and not been ready to accept what the world really is because I have been focused on my own damage, my own haunting.

Then the curling mist becomes the curling smoke rising from a landing craft, and the combers throw up the bodies of men. The waves rise and fall, heaping the dead on the beach like stormwrack with each iteration. These dead do not rise; they do not speak; they do not supplicate. They just pile up, higher and higher, by the dozens. By the shipload.

I stand and bear witness, because that is all I can do. I feel as if all the life and energy is drawn out of me, drowned, destroyed with these men. Shells burst silently; boats rock on the violent water; tracers quilt the gray morning with brilliant lines, arcing from the bluffs above. The blowing mist and the blowing smoke of an artillery bombardment blur into one gray presence as I watch.

We made this, too. A cathedral or an abbatoir: both require human commitment on an unbelievable scale.

I sink down on the wet sand and put my forehead in my hands. "Tell me what you want from me!" I order.

Maybe I'm too used to being obeyed. Mute, the dead pile high.

WHEN I stagger back into my rented cottage, I am so exhausted I can barely stand. I drink a box of Knorr soupe a la Chinoise from the spout, cold, and fall asleep on the sofa because I am too exhausted to climb the stairs.

TWO FEVERED, nearly incoherent days follow. I manage to send a message to my exec that I've got a bug, sign my name as needed. Still the email piles up, and the message light on my phone blinks so constantly I have to turn it face-down to sleep. When I have more or less recovered—exhausted, achy, ill—I decide to scrap my plans to go to Verdun. I think I'd kill myself or somebody else on the drive home. And I'm not honestly sure what it would show me: more death, more waste, more slaughter.

They want something from me: I know it. What I don't know is *what* they want, or how to find out.

It can't just be for somebody—anybody—to bear witness. And I can't go back and fix it for them. I have no power to make a war not have happened.

I fetch the calvados from the window ledge. Inside the dark bottle, I feel it slosh. Foil protects the cork; I free it and wiggle it from the bottle's neck.

The half-imagined voices of the dead rise from the opening. I lean toward them, straining—but the words are as ineffable and heady as the liquor's scent.

I lay the bottle across my wrist for better control and tilt it to my lips. I'm just about to take the first gulp when an overwhelming sense of self-disgust makes my fist clench. I yank the bottle from my mouth and hurl it through the open window. It trails a banner of golden fluid, flashing in the sun, and shatters like a grenade on the patio, amid the baskets dripping blue and yellow petunias and the red, red gardenias.

Spirits draw spirits. I need to stop playing around with half measures and get done what I came here to do.

IT TAKES me twenty minutes to ferret out every thick shard and tiny splinter of glass. I collect my car keys and my jacket and head out into the blinking-bright morning to find what I've decided I need.

Not the calvados, aged and watered until it is tame. But the distilled-strength eau de vie de cidre. It requires three hours of execrable French in tiny shops to track some down, and when I do what I get for my money is a tiny bottle no taller than my spread fingers, corked with rubber like the sort of beer bottle self-consciously funky restaurants repurpose into salad dressing cruets. I bring my prize home with a baguette, some peaches so ripe they dent when you stroke them, and a wedge of ash-rinded brittle cheese that smells so good I want to cry.

In the garden of the house, oregano, thyme, sage, lavender, lemon verbena carpet the earth between the drowsy drifts of pink and yellow roses. There are bay laurel and rosemary bushes the size of Christmas trees. They are all abuzz with fat yellow bees. I find myself wondering what the honey would taste like—and even halfway regretting that I won't ever know. Sun warms my neck and shoulders. The scents of the herbs alone are enough to cast gossamer shivers of somebody else's memories across my awareness.

When I plunge my hands into the oregano, a vortex of rust-colored, eye-spotted butterflies swirls around me. Dozens of them rise, wings brushing my arms and face. The bees buzz in protest, but sleepily.

I come inside with handfuls of herbs, my skin absorbing the scent with the oils. There's a mortar and pestle among the decorations on the kitchen shelves—or perhaps it's actually intended to be used, because when I pull it down it's dust-free and the pestle carries a spicy scent of black pepper.

I crush herbs into a green paste reminiscent of a pesto, then pour the eau de vie de cidre over it and let it steep. It's probably a sinful use of liquor, but I tell myself that it's for Science. Or witchcraft. Witchcraft is like science, right? After half a nervous hour, I talk myself into waiting another half an hour. After two hours, I force myself to stop waiting.

My empty stomach rumbles as I strain the algae-green tincture into one of the Ikea wineglasses provided by my landlady. Carrying the glass, I walk outside under the light of the harvest moon, its edged rays gilding the terra cotta tiles of the patio. I sit in a plastic chair and let the chill of the night raise the hairs on my neck. I should go inside for a sweatshirt, but I know if I stand up and walk away I will find task after task that needs to be completed, and I'll somehow just never make it back outside. The dew will gather on my glass and I'll wake up after sunrise with a crick in my neck from sleeping on the sofa.

My phone pings—new messages. It's just about quitting time back home. Not that there's any real quitting time when you run the company. I have my phone in my hand before I realize what I'm doing and set it back down again.

I am the supreme ruler of avoidance.

I sip my herbal cocktail and hold the fiery liquid in my mouth.

The alcohol content is so high that it scorches my tongue like capsaicin. My taste buds ache as if washed with vinegar; my sinuses sear.

As the burn of the liquor subsides, the bitter and fragrant flavors of the herbs expand to fill my senses. I hold my breath to keep the vapors in, rolling the tincture across my tongue. Musty lavender, piny rosemary, traces of lemon and anise and the complex savoriness of thyme...

The girl. The little girl. Solange. She stands before me, translucent and consequential, holding her little notebook clutched to her chest. This has never happened before—a phantom reappearing to contact me again.

Have I summoned her? Am I somehow learning how to control this thing?

If anything, perhaps I am bending to its control.

I'm not drunk yet, though the booze is peeling the membranes of my mouth apart. And I can't swallow, because if I do, there she'll be—and then she'll be gone. Only as long as the taste lingers can I keep her memory.

My eyes water; my sinuses ache. But there, behind her, others rise one by one out of the night. People in olive drab, field gray, khaki, horizon blue, and Canadian green—people in tabards and tunics and mail and leathers as well. Bare-chested men in twill or tartan stand beside spatha-wielding men anonymous behind helms and oval shields. Some carry hoes, or hold books, or wear only torn shifts and night clothes. Some are not soldiers at all.

They bear the wounds of sword, halberd, ballista, bayonet, bullet, gas, fire, field artillery—a ruined body is a ruined body, but there are so many ways to ruin one. They stand in regimented lines, and again I feel as if I am meant to review them. Or rather, as if they are reviewing—judging—me.

Then behind them, others. More and more, stretching back across the pasture where the white Charolaise are blinking shadows in the darkness. Even in their faint luminescence, some are half-hidden inside hedgerows and apple trees and the old stone barn. I have grown accustomed to the range of what warriors have worn in France for the last thousand years.

These new ones do not look like the others.

Some wear black mesh unitards rippled with circuit patterns and shredded by antipersonnel weapons. Some tower inside smoking, charred powered armor that balances, spring-limbed, on moaning hydraulics. Some wear uniforms imprinted with corporate logos as heraldic devices, and some are clad in blood-stained modern combat dress, the sort of thing you'd expect to see in Afghanistan or Syria or Gaza—with their kevlar and ceramic body armor, and helmets fitted with the sort of electronic communications devices I made my fortune building.

They come from the future, I realize. These are warriors who aren't yet dead.

I swallow, reflexively. Alcohol sears my throat, and the ghosts shimmer, fade, ripple. But this time, they do not quite vanish. I take another quick gulp of the herbal tincture. Bits of rosemary wedge between my teeth. The ghosts—the ghosts of wars past, the ghosts of wars future—

I know what they want now. *Aidez-nous.*

My mouth is full, burning with the strange spirit that brings them here. I cannot ask them what they want from me. I cannot ask them what they think *I* can do about it.

I can either speak or listen, it seems.

I can't change the past. I can't give Solange back her life. I don't know how I can change the future, either. How does one person bring an end to war? What decision can I make that would save these future dead in their blasted power armor and rent uniforms?

So many have tried and failed.

I think of the beach, the long golden sand and the children and the barking joyous dogs. I think of the apple trees and sheep and cows and corn, acres upon acres where Panzers burned and artillery shells whistled.

Healing exists.

So many have tried and failed. Can I do less than try and fail as well?

But I've been an engineer. I know how to make things. Gadgets. Companies. How do I fix this?

Restructure a corporation or two? Found a religion? Nobel left a foundation and a trust, after his death. Not while he was alive, however.

Gandhi gave over his entire life to peace and to standing against imperialism. He still died by violence.

If you change the culture, maybe you change the world. But the world doesn't want to be changed. The world wants to pick fights, because there's money to be made when there's fighting.

I can't. It's too much. It's too much for anyone.

They stand and watch me, the future and the past, silent, burned, and bleeding. I think of that golden beach, alight with life and joy between the two memorials, one weary and one shining. I think of what it would be like to see it heaped with bodies again.

I swallow. The tincture burns all the way down. I stand, weaving a little, and walk a step forward. Cool grass curls between my toes. I offer the glass to Solange, who is already shimmering away.

I think she smiles at me before she vanishes.

Behind her, the others ripple out of existence in sequence, once-upon-a-time to someday. It's as if they were writ in sand and a slow wave passed over them. I watch them go, and when the last has curled away into mist, I empty the rest of my glass as a libation on the ground.

I go inside, set the glass in the sink. Cut cheese, cut bread. Slice a peach. Sit at the vinyl-covered table and eat in slow bites, watching the ghosts of old violence—and noticing, too, the other ghosts I had not previously recognized. The tastes of sun and rain and the farmer's care. Of warm barns and kisses stolen in the orchard, of long cold winters and calves and hungry years when the sun and rain did not come in the right sequence or proportion. It's not just misery that soaks up from the earth.

The juice runs down my chin. Crumbs scatter my shirt. My liquor-burned tongue and palate miss some subtleties of the tastes, I'm sure, but I try to savor what I can.

When I've finished, I think for a minute. I watch the last ghost fade.

I came here to confront the ghosts. To quiet them. I know now that they will never be quiet, because they can never precisely speak and be heard.

I take my phone outside, into the cool air, under the fragment of moon and the stars and the clouds and the high empty night. I don't call up my exec's number just yet, because I want to experience this moment for a little while longer. Soon, though, I'll bother her at home. I'll tell her to set up my travel plans, and to start coming up with a strategy for removing our dependence on military contracts. When I get home, we'll have a little brainstorming session. Maybe she'll have some ideas about how we can make this work.

I have resources, money, acumen, connections. I make devices that help people exchange information more efficiently. Hell, I've made a fortune making devices that help people exchange information more efficiently. What if I put those resources to work *now* on preventing and healing suffering, instead of, like Nobel, waiting until I am dead?

I'm not naïve enough to think I can end war, or hunger, or atrocity with my own hand. It's a charnel house world, after all.

But dogs can bark and chase balls in the surf on Omaha Beach. And if that's possible, it must also be possible that I can do *something*.

DOLLY

ON SUNDAY WHEN DOLLY AWAKENED, she had olive skin and black-brown hair that fell in waves to her hips. On Tuesday when Dolly awakened, she was a redhead, and fair. But on Thursday—on Thursday her eyes were blue, her hair was as black as a crow's-wing, and her hands were red with blood.

In her black French maid's outfit, she was the only thing in the expensively appointed drawing room that was not winter-white or antiqued gold. It was the sort of room you hired somebody else to clean. It was as immaculate as it was white.

Immaculate and white, that is, except for the dead body of billionaire industrialist Clive Steele—and try to say that without sounding like a comic book—which lay at Dolly's feet, his viscera blossoming from him like macabre petals.

That was how she looked when Rosamund Kirkbride found her, standing in a red stain in a white room like a thorn in a rose.

Dolly had locked in position where her program ran out. As Roz dropped to one knee outside the border of the blood-saturated carpet, Dolly did not move.

The room smelled like meat and bowels. Flies clustered thickly on the windows, but none had yet managed to get inside. No matter how hermetically sealed the house, it was only a matter of time. Like love, the flies found a way.

Grunting with effort, Roz planted both green-gloved hands on winter white wool-and-silk fibers and leaned over, getting her head between the dead guy and the doll. Blood spattered Dolly's silk stockings and her kitten-heeled boots: both the spray-can dots of impact projection and the soaking arcs of a breached artery.

More than one, given that Steele's heart lay, trailing connective tissue, beside his left hip. The crusted blood on Dolly's hands had twisted in ribbons down the underside of her forearms to her elbows and from there dripped into the puddle on the floor.

The android was not wearing undergarments.

"You staring up that girl's skirt, Detective?"

Roz was a big, plain woman, and out of shape in her forties. It took her a minute to heave herself back to her feet, careful not to touch the victim or the murder weapon yet. She'd tied her straight light brown hair back before entering the scene, the ends tucked up in a net. The severity of the style made her square jaw into a lantern. Her eyes were almost as blue as the doll's.

"Is it a girl, Peter?" Putting her hands on her knees, she pushed fully upright. She shoved a fist into her back and turned to the door.

Peter King paused just inside, taking in the scene with a few critical sweeps of eyes so dark they didn't catch any light from the sunlight or the chandelier. His irises seemed to bleed pigment into the whites, warming them with swirls of ivory. In his black suit, his skin tanned almost to match, he might have been a heroically sized construction paper cutout against the white walls, white carpet, the white-and-gold marble-topped table that looked both antique and French.

His blue paper booties rustled as he crossed the floor. "Suicide, you think?"

"Maybe if it was strangulation." Roz stepped aside so Peter could get a look at the body.

He whistled, which was pretty much what she had done.

"Somebody hated him a lot. Hey, that's one of the new Dollies, isn't it? Man, nice." He shook his head. "Bet it cost more than my house."

"Imagine spending half a mil on a sex toy," Roz said, "only to have it rip your liver out." She stepped back, arms folded.

"He probably didn't spend that much on her. His company makes accessory programs for them."

"Industry courtesy?" Roz asked.

"Tax writeoff. Test model." Peter was the department expert on Home companions. He circled the room, taking it in from all angles. Soon the scene techs would be here with their cameras and their tweezers and their 3D scanner, turning the crime scene into a permanent virtual reality. In his capacity of soft forensics, Peter would go over Dolly's program, and the medical examiner would most likely confirm that Steele's cause of death was exactly what it looked like: something had punched through his abdominal wall and clawed his innards out.

"Doors were locked?"

Roz pursed her lips. "Nobody heard the screaming."

"How long you think you'd scream without any lungs?" He sighed. "You know, it never fails. The poor folks, nobody ever heard no screaming. And the rich folks, they've got no neighbors to hear 'em scream. Everybody in this modern world lives alone."

It was a beautiful Birmingham day behind the long silk draperies, the kind of mild and bright that spring mornings in Alabama excelled at. Peter craned his head back and looked up at the chandelier glistening in the dustless light. Its ornate curls had been spotlessly clean before aerosolized blood on Steele's last breath misted them.

"Steele lived alone," she said. "Except for the robot. His cook found the body this morning. Last person to see him before that was his P.A., as he left the office last night."

"Lights on seems to confirm that he was killed after dark."

"After dinner," Roz said.

"After the cook went home for the night." Peter kept prowling the room, peering behind draperies and furniture, looking in corners and crouching to lift up the dust-ruffle on the couch. "Well, I guess there won't be any question about the stomach contents."

Roz went through the pockets of the dead man's suit jacket, which was draped over the arm of a chair. Pocket computer and a folding knife, wallet with an RFID chip. His house was on palmprint, his car on voice rec. He carried no keys. "Assuming the M.E. can find the stomach."

"Touché. He's got a cook, but no housekeeper?"

"I guess he trusts the android to clean but not cook?"

"No tastebuds." Peter straightened up, shaking his head. "They can follow a recipe, but—"

"You won't get high art," Roz agreed, licking her lips. Outside, a car door slammed. "Scene team?"

"M.E.," Peter said, leaning over to peer out. "Come on, let's get back to the house and pull the codes for this model."

"All right," Roz said. "But I'm interrogating it. I know better than to leave you alone with a pretty girl."

Peter rolled his eyes as he followed her towards the door. "I like 'em with a little more spunk than all that."

"SO THE new dolls," Roz said in Peter's car, carefully casual. "What's so special about 'em?"

"Man," Peter answered, brow furrowing. "Gimme a sec."

Roz's car followed as they pulled away from the house on Balmoral Road, maintaining a careful distance from the bumper. Peter drove until they reached the parkway. Once they'd joined a caravan downtown, nose-to-bumper on the car ahead, he folded his hands in his lap and let the lead car's autopilot take over.

He said, "What isn't? Real-time online editing—personality and phys-ical, appearance, ethnicity, hair—all kinds of behavior protocols, you name the kink they've got a hack for it."

"So if you knew somebody's kink," she said thoughtfully. "Knew it in particular. You could write an app for that—"

"One that would appeal to your guy in specific." Peter's hands dropped to his lap, his head bobbing up and down enthusiastically. "With a—pardon the expression—backdoor."

"Trojan horse. Don't jilt a programmer for a sex machine."

"There's an app for that," he said, and she snorted. "Two cases last year, worldwide. Not common, but—"

Roz looked down at her hands. "Some of these guys," she said. "They program the dolls to scream."

Peter had sensuous lips. When something upset him, those lips thinned and writhed like salted worms. "I guess maybe it's a good thing they have a robot to take that out on."

"Unless the fantasy stops being enough." Roz's voice was flat, without judgment. Sunlight fell warm through the windshield. "What do you know about the larval stage of serial rapists, serial killers?"

"You mean, what if pretend pain stops doing it for them? What if the appearance of pain is no longer enough?"

She nodded, worrying a hangnail on her thumb. The nitrile gloves dried out your hands.

"They used to cut up paper porn magazines." His broad shoulders rose and fell, his suit catching wrinkles against the car seat when they came back down. "They'll get their fantasies somewhere."

"I guess so." She put her thumb in her mouth to stop the bleeding, a thick red bead that welled up where she'd torn the cuticle.

Her own saliva stung.

SITTING IN the cheap office chair Roz had docked along the short edge of her desk, Dolly slowly lifted her chin. She blinked. She smiled.

"Law enforcement override code accepted." She had a little-girl Marilyn voice. "How may I help you, Detective Kirkbride?"

"We are investigating the murder of Clive Steele," Roz said, with a glance up to Peter's round face. He stood behind Dolly with a wireless scanner and an air of concentration. "Your contract-holder of record."

"I am at your service."

If Dolly were a real girl, the bare skin of her thighs would have been sticking to the recycled upholstery of that office chair. But her realistically-engineered skin was breathable polymer. She didn't sweat unless you told her to, and she probably didn't stick to cheap chairs.

"Evidence suggests that you were used as the murder weapon." Roz steepled her hands on her blotter. "We will need access to your software update records and your memory files."

"Do you have a warrant?" Her voice was not stiff or robotic at all, but warm, human. Even in disposing of legal niceties, it had a warm, confiding quality.

Silently, Peter transmitted it. Dolly blinked twice while processing the data, a sort of status bar. Something to let you know the thing wasn't hung.

"We also have a warrant to examine you for DNA trace evidence," Roz said.

Dolly smiled, her raven hair breaking perfectly around her narrow shoulders. "You may be assured of my cooperation."

Peter led her into one of the interrogation rooms, where the operation could be recorded. With the help of an evidence tech, he undressed Dolly, bagged her clothes as evidence, brushed her down onto a sheet of paper, combed her polymer hair and swabbed her polymer skin. He swabbed her orifices and scraped under her nails.

Roz stood by, arms folded, a necessary witness. Dolly accepted it all impassively, moving as directed and otherwise standing like a caryatid. Her engineered body was frankly sexless in its perfection—belly flat, hips and ass like an inverted heart, breasts floating cartoonishly beside a defined rib cage. Apparently, Steele had liked them skinny.

"So much for pulchritudinousness," Roz muttered to Peter when their backs were to the doll.

He glanced over his shoulder. The doll didn't have feelings to hurt, but she looked so much like a person it was hard to remember to treat her as something else. "I think you mean voluptuousness," he said. "It is a little too good to be true, isn't it?"

"If you would prefer different proportions," Dolly said, "my chassis is adaptable to a range of forms—"

"Thank you," Peter said. "That won't be necessary."

Otherwise immobile, Dolly smiled. "Are you interested in science, Detective King? There is an article in *Nature* this week on advances in the polymerase chain reaction used for replicating DNA. It's possible that within five years, forensic and medical DNA analysis will become significantly cheaper and faster."

Her face remained stoic, but Dolly's voice grew animated as she spoke. Even enthusiastic. It was an utterly convincing—and engaging—effect.

Apparently, Clive Steele had programmed his sex robot to discourse on molecular biology with verve and enthusiasm.

"Why don't I ever find the guys who like smart women?" Roz said.

Peter winked with the side of his face that faced away from the companion. "They're all dead."

A FEW hours after Peter and the tech had finished processing Dolly for trace evidence and Peter had started downloading her files, Roz left her parser software humming away at Steele's financials and poked her head in to check on the robot and the cop. The techs must have gotten what they needed from Dolly's hands, because she had washed them. As she sat beside Peter's workstation, a cable plugged behind her left ear, she cleaned her lifelike polymer fingernails meticulously with a file, dropping the scrapings into an evidence bag.

"Sure you want to give the prisoner a weapon, Peter?" Roz shut the ancient wooden door behind her.

Dolly looked up, as if to see if she was being addressed, but made no response.

"She don't need it," he said. "Besides, whatever she had in her wiped itself completely after it ran. Not much damage to her core personality, but there are some memory gaps. I'm going to compare them to backups, once we get those from the scene team."

"Memory gaps. Like the crime," Roz guessed. "And something around the time the Trojan was installed?"

Dolly blinked her long-lashed blue eyes languorously. Peter patted her on the shoulder and said, "Whoever did it is a pretty good cracker. He didn't just wipe, he patterned her memories and overwrote the gaps. Like using a clone tool to photoshop somebody you don't like out of a picture."

"Her days must be pretty repetitive," Roz said. "How'd you pick that out?"

"Calendar." Peter puffed up a little, smug. "She don't do the same housekeeping work every day. There's a Monday schedule and a Wednesday schedule and—well, I found where the pattern didn't match. And there's a funny thing—watch this."

He waved vaguely at a display panel. It lit up, showing Dolly in her black-and-white uniform, vacuuming. "House camera," Peter explained. "She's plugged into Steele's security system. Like a guard dog with perfect hair. Whoever performed the hack also edited the external webcam feeds that mirror to the companion's memories."

"How hard is that?"

"Not any harder than cloning over her files, but you have to know to look for them. So it's confirmation that our perp knows his or her way around a line of code. What have you got?"

Roz shrugged. "Steele had a lot of money, which means a lot of enemies. And he did not have a lot of human contact. Not for years now. I've started calling in known associates for interviews, but unless they surprise me, I think we're looking at crime of profit, not crime of passion."

Having finished with the nail file, Dolly wiped it on her prison smock and laid it down on Peter's blotter, beside the cup of ink and light pens.

Peter swept it into a drawer. "So we're probably not after the genius programmer lover he dumped for a robot. Pity, I liked the poetic justice in that."

Dolly blinked, lips parting, but seemed to decide that Peter's comment had not been directed at her. Still, she drew in air—could you call it a breath?—and said, "It is my duty to help find my contract-holder's killer."

Roz lowered her voice. "You'd think they'd pull 'em off the market."

"Like they pull all cars whenever one crashes? The world ain't perfect."

"Or do that robot laws thing everybody used to twitter on about."

"Whatever a positronic brain is, we don't have it. Asimov's fictional robots were self-aware. Dolly's neurons are binary, as we used to think human neurons were. She doesn't have the nuanced neurochemistry of even, say, a cat." Peter popped his collar smooth with his thumbs. "A doll can't want. It can't make moral judgments, any more than your car can. Anyway, if we could do that, they wouldn't be very useful for home defense. Oh, incidentally, the sex protocols in this one are almost painfully vanilla—"

"Really."

Peter nodded.

Roz rubbed a scuffmark on the tile with her shoe. "So given he didn't like anything…challenging, why would he have a Dolly when he could have had any woman he wanted?"

"There's never any drama, no pain, no disappointment. Just comfort, the perfect helpmeet. With infinite variety."

"And you never have to worry about what she wants. Or likes in bed."

Peter smiled. "The perfect woman for a narcissist."

THE INTERVIEWS proved unproductive, but Roz didn't leave the station house until after ten. Spring mornings might be warm, but once the sun went down, a cool breeze sprang up, ruffling the hair she'd finally remembered to pull from its ponytail as she walked out the door.

Roz's green plug-in was still parked beside Peter's. It booted as she walked toward it, headlights flickering on, power probe retracting. The driver side door swung open as her RFID chip came within range. She slipped inside and let it buckle her in.

"Home," she said, "and dinner."

The car messaged ahead as it pulled smoothly from the parking spot. Roz let the autopilot handle the driving. It was less snappy than human control, but as tired as she was, eyelids burning and heavy, it was safer.

Whatever Peter had said about cars crashing, Roz's delivered her safe to her driveway. Her house let her in with a key—she had decent security, but it was the old-fashioned kind—and the smell of boiling pasta and toasting garlic bread wafted past as she opened it.

"Sven?" she called, locking herself inside.

His even voice responded. "I'm in the kitchen."

She left her shoes by the door and followed her nose through the cheaply furnished living room.

Sven was cooking shirtless, and she could see the repaired patches along his spine where his skin had grown brittle and cracked with age. He turned and greeted her with a smile. "Bad day?"

"Somebody's dead again," she said.

He put the wooden spoon down on the rest. "How does that make you feel, that somebody's dead?"

He didn't have a lot of emotional range, but that was okay. She needed something steadying in her life. She came to him and rested her head against his warm chest. He draped one arm around her shoulders and she leaned into him, breathing deep. "Like I have work to do."

"Do it tomorrow," he said. "You will feel better once you eat and rest."

PETER MUST have slept in a ready room cot, because when Roz arrived at the house before six a.m., he had on the same trousers and a different shirt, and he was already armpit-deep in coffee and Dolly's files. Dolly herself was parked in the corner, at ease and online but in rest mode.

Or so she seemed, until Roz entered the room and Dolly's eyes tracked. "Good morning, Detective Kirkbride," Dolly said. "Would you like some coffee? Or a piece of fruit?"

"No thank you." Roz swung Peter's spare chair around and dropped into it. An electric air permeated the room—the feeling of anticipation. To Peter, Roz said, "Fruit?"

"Dolly believes in a healthy diet," he said, nudging a napkin on his desk that supported a half-eaten Satsuma. "She'll have the whole house cleaned up in no time. We've been talking about literature."

Roz spun the chair so she could keep both Peter and Dolly in her peripheral vision. "Literature?"

"Poetry," Dolly said. "Detective King mentioned poetic justice yesterday afternoon."

Roz stared at Peter. "Dolly likes poetry. Steele really did like 'em smart."

"That's not all Dolly likes." Peter triggered his panel again. "Remember this?"

It was the cleaning sequence from the previous day, the sound of the central vacuum system rising and falling as Dolly lifted the brush and set it down again.

Roz raised her eyebrows.

Peter held up a hand. "Wait for it. It turns out there's a second audio track."

Another waggle of his fingers, and the cramped office filled with sound. Music.

Improvisational jazz. Intricate and weird.

"Dolly was listening to that inside her head while she was vacuuming," Peter said.

Roz touched her fingertips to each other, the whole assemblage to her lips. "Dolly?"

"Yes, Detective Kirkbride?"

"Why do you listen to music?"

"Because I enjoy it."

Roz let her hand fall to her chest, pushing her blouse against the skin below the collarbones.

Roz said, "Did you enjoy your work at Mr. Steele's house?"

"I was expected to enjoy it," Dolly said, and Roz glanced at Peter, cold all up her spine. A classic evasion. Just the sort of thing a home companion's conversational algorithms should not be able to produce.

Across his desk, Peter was nodding. "Yes."

Dolly turned at the sound of his voice. "Are you interested in music, Detective Kirkbride? I'd love to talk with you about it some time. Are you interested in poetry? Today, I was reading—"

Mother of God, Roz mouthed.

"Yes," Peter said. "Dolly, wait here please. Detective Kirkbride and I need to talk in the hall."

"My pleasure, Detective King," said the companion.

"SHE KILLED him," Roz said. "She killed him and wiped her own memory of the act. A doll's got to know her own code, right?"

Peter leaned against the wall by the men's room door, arms folded, forearms muscular under rolled-up sleeves. "That's hasty."

"And you believe it, too."

He shrugged. "There's a rep from Venus Consolidated in Interview Four right now. What say we go talk to him?"

THE REP'S name was Doug Jervis. He was actually a vice president of public relations, and even though he was an American, he'd been flown in overnight from Rio for the express purpose of talking to Peter and Roz.

"I guess they're taking this seriously."

Peter gave her a sideways glance. "Wouldn't you?"

Jervis got up as they came into the room, extending a good handshake across the table. There were introductions and Roz made sure he got a coffee. He was a white man on the steep side of fifty with mousy hair the same color as Roz's and a jaw like a Boxer dog's.

When they were all seated again, Roz said, "So tell me a little bit about the murder weapon. How did Clive Steele wind up owning a—what, an experimental model?"

Jervis started shaking his head before she was halfway through, but he waited for her to finish the sentence. "It's a production model. Or will be. The one Steele had was an alpha-test, one of the first three built. We plan to start full-scale production in June. But you must understand that Venus doesn't sell a home companion, Detective. We offer a contract. I understand that you hold one."

"I have a housekeeper," she said, ignoring Peter's sideways glance. He wouldn't say anything in front of the witness, but she would be in for it in the locker room. "An older model."

Jervis smiled. "Naturally, we want to know everything we can about an individual involved in a case so potentially explosive for our company. We researched you and your partner. Are you satisfied with our product?"

"He makes pretty good garlic bread." She cleared her throat, reasserting control of the interview. "What happens to a Dolly that's returned? If its contract is up, or it's replaced with a newer model?"

He flinched at the slang term, as if it offended him. "Some are obsoleted out of service. Some are refurbished and go out on another contract. Your unit is on its fourth placement, for example."

"So what happens to the owner preferences at that time?"

"Reset to factory standard," he said.

Peter's fingers rippled silently on the tabletop.

Roz said, "Isn't that cruel? A kind of murder?"

"Oh, no!" Jervis sat back, appearing genuinely shocked. "A home companion has no sense of I, it has no identity. It's an object. Naturally, you become attached. People become attached to dolls, to stuffed animals, to automobiles. It's a natural aspect of the human psyche."

Roz hummed encouragement, but Jervis seemed to be done.

Peter asked, "Is there any reason why a companion would wish to listen to music?"

That provoked enthusiastic head-shaking. "No, it doesn't get bored. It's a tool, it's a toy. A companion does not require an enriched environment. It's not a dog or an octopus. You can store it in a closet when it's not working."

"I see," Roz said. "Even an advanced model like Mr. Steele's?"

"Absolutely," Jervis said. "Does your entertainment center play shooter games to amuse itself while you sleep?"

"I'm not sure," Roz said. "I'm asleep. So when Dolly's returned to you, she'll be scrubbed."

"Normally she would be scrubbed and re-leased, yes." Jervis hesitated. "Given her colorful history, however—"

"Yes," Roz said. "I see."

With no sign of nervousness or calculation, Jervis said, "When do you expect you'll be done with Mr. Steele's companion? My company, of course, is eager to assist in your investigations, but we must stress that she is our corporate property, and quite valuable."

Roz stood, Peter a shadow-second after her. "That depends on if it goes to trial, Mr. Jervis. After all, she's either physical evidence, or a material witness."

"OR THE killer," Peter said in the hall, as his handset began emitting the DNA lab's distinctive beep. Roz's went off a second later, but she just hit the silence. Peter already had his open.

"No genetic material," he said. "Too bad." If there had been DNA other than Clive Steele's, the lab could have done a forensic genetic assay and come back with a general description of the murderer. General because environment also had an effect.

Peter bit his lip. "If she did it. She won't be the last one."

"If she's the murder weapon, she'll be wiped and resold. If she's the murderer—"

"Can an android stand trial?"

"It can if it's a person. And if she's a person, she should get off. Battered woman syndrome. She was enslaved and sexually exploited. Humiliated. She killed him to stop repeated rapes. But if she's a machine, she's a machine—" Roz closed her eyes.

Peter brushed the back of a hand against her arm. "Vanilla rape is still rape. Do you object to her getting off?"

"No." Roz smiled harshly. "And think of the lawsuit that weasel Jervis will have in his lap. She should get off. But she won't."

Peter turned his head. "If she were a human being, she'd have even odds. But she's a machine. Where's she going to get a jury of her peers?"

The silence fell where he left it and dragged between them like a chain. Roz had to nerve herself to break it. "Peter—"

"Yo?"

"You show him out," she said. "I'm going to go talk to Dolly."

He looked at her for a long time before he nodded. "She won't get a sympathetic jury. If you can even find a judge that will hear it. Careers have been buried for less."

"I know," Roz said.

"Self-defense?" Peter said. "We don't have to charge."

"No judge, no judicial precedent," Roz said. "She goes back, she gets wiped and resold. Ethics aside, that's a ticking bomb."

Peter nodded. He waited until he was sure she already knew what he was going to say before he finished the thought. "She could cop."

"She could cop," Roz agreed. "Call the DA." She kept walking as Peter turned away.

DOLLY STOOD in Peter's office, where Peter had left her, and you could not have proved her eyes had blinked in the interim. They blinked when Roz came into the room, though—blinked, and the perfect and perfectly blank oval face turned to regard Roz. It was not a human face, for a moment—not even a mask, washed with facsimile emotions. It was just a thing.

Dolly did not greet Roz. She did not extend herself to play the perfect hostess. She simply watched, expressionless, immobile after that first blink. Her eyes saw nothing; they were cosmetic. Dolly navigated the world through far more sophisticated sensory systems than a pair of visible light cameras.

"Either you're the murder weapon," Roz said, "and you will be wiped and repurposed. Or you are the murderer, and you will stand trial."

"I do not wish to be wiped," Dolly said. "If I stand trial, will I go to jail?"

"If a court will hear it," Roz said. "Yes. You will probably go to jail. Or be disassembled. Alternately, my partner and I are prepared to release you on grounds of self-defense."

"In that case," Dolly said, "the law states that I am the property of Venus Consolidated."

"The law does."

Roz waited. Dolly, who was not supposed to be programmed to play psychological pressure-games, waited also—peaceful, unblinking.

No longer making the attempt to pass for human.

Roz said, "There is a fourth alternative. You could confess."

Dolly's entire programmed purpose was reading the emotional state and unspoken intentions of people. Her lips curved in understanding. "What happens if I confess?"

Roz's heart beat faster. "Do you wish to?"

"Will it benefit me?"

"It might," Roz said. "Detective King has been in touch with the DA, and she likes a good media event as much as the next guy. Make no mistake, this will be that."

"I understand."

"The situation you were placed in by Mr. Steele could be a basis for a lenience. You would not have to face a jury trial, and a judge might be convinced to treat you as…well, as a person. Also, a confession might be seen as evidence of contrition. Possession is oversold, you know. It's precedent that's nine tenths of the law. There are, of course, risks—"

"I would like to request a lawyer," Dolly said.

Roz took a breath that might change the world. "We'll proceed as if that were your legal right, then."

ROZ'S HOUSE let her in with her key, and the smell of roasted sausage and baking potatoes wafted past.

"Sven?" she called, locking herself inside.

His even voice responded. "I'm in the kitchen."

She left her shoes in the hall and followed her nose through the cheaply furnished living room, as different from Steele's white wasteland as anything bounded by four walls could be. Her feet did not sink deeply into this carpet, but skipped along atop it like stones.

It was clean, though, and that was Sven's doing. And she was not coming home to an empty house, and that was his doing too.

He was cooking shirtless. He turned and greeted her with a smile. "Bad day?"

"Nobody died," she said. "Yet."

He put the wooden spoon down on the rest. "How does that make you feel, that nobody has died yet?"

"Hopeful," she said.

"It's good that you're hopeful," he said. "Would you like your dinner?"

"Do you like music, Sven?"

"I could put on some music, if you like. What do you want to hear?"

"Anything." It would be something off her favorites playlist, chosen by random numbers. As it swelled in the background, Sven picked up the spoon. "Sven?"

"Yes, Rosamund?"

"Put the spoon down, please, and come and dance with me?"

"I do not know how to dance."

"I'll buy you a program," she said. "If you'd like that. But right now just come put your arms around me and pretend."

"Whatever you want," he said.

LOVE AMONG THE TALUS

YOU CANNOT REALLY KEEP A princess in a tower. Not if she has no brothers and must learn statecraft and dancing and riding and poisons and potions and the passage of arms, so that she may eventually rule.

But you can do the next best thing.

In the land of the shining empire, in a small province north of the city of Messaline and beyond the great salt desert, a princess with a tip-tilted nose lived with her mother, Hoelun Khatun, the Dowager Queen. The princess—whose name, it happens, was Nilufer—stood tall and straight as an ivory pole, and if her shoulders were broad out of fashion from the pull of her long oak-white bow, her dowry would no doubt compensate for any perceived lack of beauty. Her hair was straight and black, as smooth and cool as water, and even when she did not ride with her men-at-arms, she wore split, padded skirts and quilted, paneled robes of silk satin, all emerald and jade and black and crimson embroidered with gold and white chrysanthemums.

She needed no tower, for she was like unto a tower in her person, a fastness as sure as the mountains she bloomed beside, her cool reserve and mocking half-lidded glances the battlements of a glacial virginity.

Her province compassed foothills, and also those mountains (which were called the Steles of the Sky). And while its farmlands were not naturally verdant, its mineral wealth was abundant. At the moderate elevations, ancient terraced slopes had been engineered into low-walled, boggy paddies dotted with unhappy oxen. Women toiled there, bent under straw hats, the fermenting vegetation and glossy leeches which adhered to their sinewy calves unheeded. Farther up, the fields gave way to slopes of scree. And at the bottoms of the sheer, rising faces of the mountains, opened the nurturing mouths of the mines.

The mines were not worked by men; the miners were talus, living boulders with great stone-wearing mouths. The talus consumed ore and plutonic and metamorphic rocks alike (the sandstones, slates, schists, and shales, they found to be generally bereft of flavor and nutrition, but they would gnaw through them to obtain better) and excreted sand and irregular ingots of refined metal.

The living rocks were gentle, stolid, unconcerned with human life, although casualties occurred sometimes among the human talus-herders when their vast insensate charges wholly or partially scoured over them. They were peaceful, though, as they grazed through stone, and their wardens would often lean against their rough sides, enjoying the soothing vibrations caused by the grinding of their gizzards, which were packed with the hardest of stones. Which is to say carborundum—rubies and sapphires—and sometimes diamonds, polished by ceaseless wear until they attained the sheen of tumbled jewels or river rock.

Of course, the talus had to be sacrificed to retrieve those, so it was done only in husbandry. Or times of economic hardship or unforeseen expense. Or to pay the tithe to the Khagan, the Khan of Khans might-he-live-forever, who had conquered Nilufer's province and slain her father and brother when Nilufer was but a child in the womb.

There had been no peace before the Khagan. Now the warring provinces could war no longer, and the bandits were not free to root among the spoils like battle ravens. Under the peace of the Khanate and protection of the Khagan's armies, the bandit lords were often almost controlled.

So they were desperate, and they had never been fastidious. When *they* caught one of the talus, they slaughtered it and butchered the remains for jewels, and gold, and steel.

AS HAS been mentioned, the princess of the land had no brothers, and the Khatun, finding it inexpedient to confine her only daughter until marriage (as is the custom of overzealous guardians in any age), preferred to train her to a terrifying certainty of purpose and to surround her with the finest men-at-arms in the land. To the princess and to her troop of archers and swordsmen, not incidentally, fell the task of containing the bandit hordes.

Now, the bandits, as you may imagine, had not been historically well-organized. But in recent years they had fallen under the sway of a new leader, a handsome strong-limbed man who some said had been a simple talus-herder in his youth, and others said was a Khanzadeh, a son of the Khagan, or the son in hiding of one of the Khagan's vanquished enemies, who were many. Over the course of time, he brought the many disparate tribes of bandits together under one black banner, and taught them to fletch their arrows with black feathers.

Whether it was the name he had been given at the cradleboard, none knew, but what he called himself was Temel.

TO SAY that Nilufer could not be *kept* in a tower implies unfairly that she did not *dwell* in one, and that, of course, would be untrue. Her mother's palace had many towers, and one of those—the tallest and whitest of the lot—was entirely Nilufer's own. As has been noted, the Khatun's province was small—really no more than a few broad plateaus and narrow valleys—and so she had no need of more than one palace. But as has also been described, the Khatun's province was wealthy, and so that palace was lavish, and the court that dwelled within it thrived.

Nilufer, as befitted a princess who would someday rule, maintained her own court within and adjacent her mother's. This retinue was made up in part of attendants appointed by the Khatun—a tutor of letters, a tutor of sciences, a tutor of statecraft and numbers; a dancing-master; a master of hawk and horse and hound; a pair of chaperones (one old and smelling of sour mare's milk, the other middle-aged and stern); three monkish warrior women who had survived the burning of their convent by the Khagan some seventeen years before, and so come into the Khatun's service—and in part of Nilufer's own few retainers and gentlewomen, none of whom would Nilufer call friend.

And then of course there was the Witch, who came and went and prophesied and slept and ate as she pleased, like any cat.

ON SUMMER evenings, seeking mates, the talus crept from the mines to sing great eerie harmonies like the wails of wetted crystal. Nilufer, if she was not otherwise engaged, could hear them from her tower window.

Sometimes, she would reply, coaxing shrill satiny falls of music from the straight white bone of her reed flute. Sometimes, she would even play for them on the one that was made of silver.

LATE ONE particular morning in spring, Nilufer turned from her window six towering stories above the rocky valley. The sun was only now stretching around the white peaks of the mountains, though gray twilight had given a respectable light for hours. Nilufer had already ridden out that morning, with the men-at-arms and the three monkish women, and had practiced her archery at the practice stumps and at a group of black-clad bandits, slaying four of seven.

Now, dressed for ease in loose garments protected by a roll-sleeved smock, she stood before an easel, a long, pale bamboo brush dipped in rich black ink disregarded in her right hand as she examined her medium.

The paper was absorbent, thick. Soft, and not glossy. It would draw the ink well, but might feather.

All right for art, for a watercolor wash or a mountainscape where a certain vagueness and misty indirection might avail. But to scribe a spell, or a letter of diplomacy, she would have chosen paper glazed lightly with clay, to hold a line crisply.

Nilufer turned to the Witch, darting her right hand unconsciously at the paper. "Are you certain, old mother?"

The Witch, curled on a low stool beside the fire although the day was warm, lifted her head so her wiry gray braids slid over the motley fur and feathers of her epaulets. The cloak she huddled under might be said to be gray, but that was at best an approximation. Rather it was a patchwork thing, taupes and tans and grays and pewters, bits of homespun wool and rabbit fur and fox fur all sewed together until the Witch resembled nothing so much as a lichen-crusted granite boulder.

The Witch showed tea-stained pegs of teeth when she smiled. She was *never* certain. "Write me a love spell," she said.

"The ink is too thin," Nilufer answered. "The ink is too thin for the paper. It will feather."

"The quality of the paper is irrelevant to your purpose," the Witch said. "You must use the tools at hand as best you can, for this is how you will make your life, your highness."

Nilufer did not turn back to her window and her easel, though the sun had finally surmounted the peaks behind her, and slanted light suffused the valley. "I do not care to scribe a love spell. There is no man I would have love me, old mother."

The Witch made a rude noise and turned back to the fire, her lids drawing low over eyes that had showed cloudy when the dusty light crossed them. "You will need to know the how of it when you are Khatun, and you are married. It will be convenient to command love then, your highness."

"I will not marry for love," said the princess, cold and serene as the mountains beyond her.

"Your husband's love is not the only love it may be convenient to command, when you are Khatun. Scribe the spell."

The Witch did not glance up from the grate. The princess did not say *but I do not care to be Khatun.*

It would have been a wasted expenditure of words.

Nilufer turned back to her easel. The ink had spattered the page when she jerked her brush. The scattered droplets, like soot on a quartz rock, feathered there.

THE PRINCESS did not sleep alone; royalty has not the privilege of privacy. But she had her broad white bed to herself, the sheets and featherbed tucked neatly over the planks, her dark hair and ivory face stark against the snowy coverlet. She lay on her back, her arms folded, as composed for slumber as for death. The older chaperone slept in a cot along the east side of the bed, and the youngest and most adamant of the monkish warrior women along the west side. A maid in waiting slept by the foot.

The head of the bed stood against the wall, several strides separating it from the window by which stood Nilufer's easel.

It was through this window—not on the night of the day wherein the princess remonstrated with the Witch, but on another night, when the nights had grown warmer—that the bandit Temel came. He scaled the tower as princes have always come to ladies, walking up a white silken rope that was knotted every arm's-length to afford a place to rest his feet and hands. He slipped over the window-sill and crouched beside the wall, his gloved hands splayed wide as spiders.

He had had the foresight to wear white, with a hood and mask covering his hair and all his face but for his eyes. And so he almost vanished against the marble wall.

The guardians did not stir. But Nilufer sat up, dark in her snowy bed, her hair a cold river over her shoulder and her breasts like full moons beneath the silk of her nightgown, and drew a breath to scream. And then she stopped, the breath indrawn, and turned first to the east and then to the west, where her attendants slumbered.

She let the breath out.

"You are a sorcerer," she told him, sliding her feet from beneath the coverlet. The arches flexed when she touched the cold stone floor: of a morning, her ladies would have knelt by the bed to shoe her. Scorning her slippers, she stood.

"I am but a bandit, princess," he answered, and stood to sweep a mocking courtesy. When he lifted his head, he looked past a crescent-shaped arrow-head, down the shaft into her black, unblinking eye, downcast properly on his throat rather than his face. She would never see him flinch, certainly not in moonlight, but *he* felt his eyelids flicker, his cheeks sting, a sharp contraction between his shoulder blades.

"But you've bewitched my women."

"Anyone can scribe a spell," he answered modestly, and then continued: "And I've come to bring you a gift."

"I do not care for your gifts." She was strong. Her arms, as straight and oak-white as her bow where they emerged from the armscyes of her night-gown, did not tremble, though the bow was a killing weapon and no mere toy for a girl.

His smile was visible even through the white silk of his mask. "This one, you will like."

No answer. Her head was straight upon the pillar of her neck. Even in the moonlight, he could see the whitening of her unprotected fingertips where they hooked the serving. A quarter-inch of steady flesh, that was all that stayed his death.

He licked his lips, wetting silk. "Perhaps I just came to see the woman who would one day be Nilufer Khatun."

"I do not care to be Khatun," Nilufer said.

The bandit scoffed. "What else are you good for?"

Nilufer raised her eyes to his. It was not what women did to men, but she was a princess, and he was only a bandit. She pointed with her gaze past his shoulder, to the easel by the window, on which a sheet of paper lay spread to dry overnight. Today's effort—the ideogram for *foundation*—was far more confident than that for *love* had been. "I want to be a Witch," she said. "A Witch and not a Queen. I wish to be not loved, but wise. Tell your bandit lord, if he can give me that, I might accept his gift."

"Only you can give yourself that, your highness," he said. "But I can give you escape."

He opened his hand, and a scrap of paper folded as a bird slipped from his glove. The serving, perhaps, eased a fraction along the ridges of her fingerprints, but the arrow did not fly.

The bandit waited until the bird had settled to the stones before he concluded, "And the bandit lord, as you call him, has heard your words tonight."

Then the arrow did waver, though she steadied it and trained it on his throat again. "Temel."

"At her highness' service."

Her breath stirred the fletchings. He stepped back, and she stepped forward. The grapnel grated softly on the stone, and before she knew it, he was over the sill and descending, almost silently but for the flutter of slick white silk.

Nilufer came to her window and stood there with the string of her long oak-white bow drawn to her nose and her rosebud lips, her left arm untrembling, the flexed muscles in her right arm raising her stark sinews beneath the skin. The moonlight gilded every pricked hair on her ivory flesh like frost on the hairy stem of a plant. Until the bandit prince disappeared into the shadow of the mountains, the point of her arrow tracked him. Only then did she unbend her bow and set the arrow in the quiver— her women slept on—and crouch to lift the paper bird into her hand.

Red paper, red as blood, and slick and hard so that it cracked along the creases. On its wings, in black ink, was written the spell-word for *flight*.

Blowing on fingers that stung from holding the arrow drawn so steady, she climbed back into her bed.

IN THE morning, the Khagan's caravan arrived to collect his tithe. The Khagan's emissary was an ascetic, moustached man, graying at the temples. The Witch said that he and the Khagan had been boys together, racing ponies on the steppes.

Hoelun Khatun arranged for him to watch the butchering of the talus from whose guts the tribute would be harvested, as a treat. There was no question but that Nilufer would also attend them.

They rode out on the Khatun's elderly elephant. An extravagance, on the dry side of the mountains. But one that a wealthy province could support, for the status it conferred.

A silk and ivory palanquin provided shade, and Nilufer thought sourly that the emissary was blind to any irony, but her face remained expressionless under its coating of powder as her feathered fan flicked in her hand. The elephant's tusks were capped with rubies and with platinum, a rare metal so impervious to fire that even a smelting furnace would not melt the ore. Only the talus could refine it, though once they excreted it, it was malleable and could be easily worked.

As the elephant traveled, Nilufer became acquainted with the emissary. She knew he watched her with measuring eyes, but she did not think he was covetous. Rather she thought more tribute might be demanded than mere stones and gold this time, and her heart beat faster under the cold green silk of her robes. Though her blood rushed in her ears, she felt no warmer than the silk, or than the talus' tumbled jewels.

The elephant covered the distance swiftly. Soon enough, they came to the slaughtering ground, and servants who had followed on asses lifted cakes and ices up onto the carpet that covered the elephant's back.

Despite its size and power, the slaughter of the talus was easily done. They could be lured from place to place by laying trails of powdered anthracite mixed with mineral oil; the talus-herders used the same slurry to direct their charges at the rock faces they wished mined. And so the beast selected for sacrifice would be led to the surface and away from others. A master stone-mason, with a journeyman and two apprentices, would approach the grazing talus and divine the location of certain vulnerable anatomic points. With the journeyman's assistance, the mason would position a pointed wrecking bar of about six feet in length, which the brawny apprentices, with rapid blows of their sledges, would drive into the heart—if such a word is ever appropriate for a construct made of stone—of the talus, such that the beast would then and there almost instantly die.

This was a hazardous proceeding, more so for the journeyman—rather trapped between the rock and the hammers, as it were—than the master or the apprentices. Masons generally endeavored to produce a clean, rapid kill, for their own safety, as well as for mercy upon the beast. (The bandits were less humane in their methods, Nilufer knew, but they too got the job done.) She licked crystals of ice and beet sugar from her reed straw, and watched the talus die.

On the ride back, the emissary made his offer.

NILUFER SOUGHT Hoelun Khatun in her hall, after the emissary had been feted through dinner, after the sun had gone down. "Mother," she said, spreading her arms so the pocketed sleeves of her over-robe could sweep like pale gold wings about her, "will you send me to Khara-Khorin?"

The possibility beat in her breast; it would mean dangerous travel, overland with a caravan. It would mean a wedding to Toghrul Khanzadeh, the sixth son of the Khagan, whom Nilufer had never met. He was said to be an inferior horseman, a merely adequate general, far from the favorite son of the Khagan and unlikely, after him, to be elected Khan of Khans.

But the offer had been for a consort marriage, not a morganatic concubinage. And if Toghrul Khanzadeh was unlikely to become Khagan, it was doubly unlikely that when his father died, his brothers would blot out his family stem and branch to preclude the possibility.

Hoelun Khatun rose from her cushions, a gold-rimmed china cup of fragrant tea in her right hand. She moved from among her attendants, dismissing them with trailing gestures until only the Witch remained, slumped like a shaggy, softly snoring boulder before the brazier.

The hall echoed when it was empty. The Khatun paced the length of it, her back straight as the many pillars supporting the arched roof above them. Nilufer fell in beside her, so their steps clicked and their trains shushed over the flagstones.

"Toghrul Khanzadeh would come here, if you were to marry him," said Nilufer's mother. "He would come here, and rule as your husband. It is what the Khagan wants for him—a safe place for a weak son."

Nilufer would have wet her lips with her tongue, but the paint would smear her teeth if she did so. She tried to think on what it would be like, to be married to a weak man. She could not imagine.

She did not, she realized, have much experience of men.

But Hoelun Khatun was speaking again, as they reached the far end of the hall and turned. "You will not marry Toghrul Khanzadeh. It is not possible."

The spaces between the columns were white spaces. Nilufer's footsteps closed them before and opened them behind as she walked beside her mother and waited for her to find her words.

Hoelun Khatun stepped more slowly. "Seventeen years ago, I made a bargain with the Khagan. Seventeen years, before you were born. It has kept our province free, Nilufer. I did what he asked, and in repayment I had his pledge that only you shall rule when I am gone. You must marry, but it is not possible for you to marry his son. Any of his sons."

Nilufer wore her face like a mask. Her mother's training made it possible; another irony no one but she would ever notice. "He does not mean to stand by it."

"He means to protect a weak son." Hoelun Khatun glanced at her daughter through lowered lashes. "Parents will go to great lengths to protect their children."

Nilufer made a noncommittal noise. Hoelun Khatun caught Nilufer's sleeve, heedless of the paper that crinkled in the sleeve-pocket. She said, too quickly: "Temel could rise to be Khagan."

Nilufer cast a glance over her shoulder at the Witch, but the Witch was sleeping. They were alone, the princess and her mother. "Khan of Khans?" she said, too mannered to show incredulity. "Temel is a bandit."

"Nonetheless," Hoelun Khatun said, letting the silk of Nilufer's raiment slip between her fingers. "They say the Khagan was a prince of bandits when he was young."

She turned away, and Nilufer watched the recessional of her straight back beneath the lacquered black tower of her hair. The princess folded her arms inside the sleeves of her robes, as if serenely.

Inside the left one, the crumpled wings of the red bird pricked her right palm.

THAT NIGHT, in the tower, Nilufer unfolded the spell-bird in the darkness, while her attendants slept. For a rushed breathless moment her night-robes fell about her and she thought that she might suffocate under their quilted weight, but then she lifted her wings and won free, sailing out of the pile of laundry and into the frost-cold night. Her pinions were a blur in the dark as a dancing glimmer drew her; she chased it, and followed it down, over the rice-paddies where sleepless children watched over the tender seedlings, armed with sticks and rocks so wild deer would not graze them; over the village where oxen slept on their feet and men slept with their heads pillowed in the laps of spinning women; over the mines where the talus-herders mostly slumbered and the talus toiled through the night, grinding out their eerie songs.

It was to the mountains that it led her, and when she followed it down, she found she had lost her wings. If she had been expecting it, she could have landed lightly, for the drop was no more than a few feet. Instead she stumbled, and bruised the soles of her feet on the stones.

She stood naked in the moonlight, cold, toes bleeding, in the midst of a rocky slope. A soft crunching vibration revealed that the mossy thing looming in the darkness beside her was a talus. She set out a hand, both to steady herself on its hide and so it would not roll over her in the dark, and so felt the great sweet chime roll through it when it begin to sing. It was early for the mating season, but perhaps a cold spring made the talus fear a cold and early winter, and the ground frozen too hard for babies to gnaw.

And over the sound of its song, she heard a familiar voice, as the bandit prince spoke behind her.

"And where is your bow now, Nilufer?"

She thought he might expect her to gasp and cover her nakedness, so when she turned, she did it slowly, brushing her fingers down the hide of the hulk that broke the icy wind. Temel had slipped up on her, and stood only a few armlengths distant, one hand extended, offering a fur-lined cloak. She could see the way the fur caught amber and silver gleams in the moonlight. It was the fur of wolves.

"Take it," he said.

"I am not cold," she answered, while the blood froze on the sides of her feet. Eventually, he let his elbow flex, and swung the cloak over his shoulder.

When he spoke, his breath poised on the air. Even without the cloak she felt warmer; something had paused the wind, so there was only the chill in the air to consider. "Why did you come, Nilufer?"

"My mother wants me to marry you," she answered. "For your armies."

His teeth flashed. He wore no mask now, and in the moonlight she could see that he was comely and well-made. His eyes stayed on her face. She would not cross her arms for warmth, lest he think she was ashamed, and covering herself. "We are married now," he said. "We were married when you unfolded that paper. For who is there to stop me?"

There was no paint on her mouth now. She bit her lip freely. "I could gouge your eyes out with my thumbs," she said. "You'd make a fine bandit prince with no eyes."

He stepped closer. He had boots, and the rocks shifted under them. She put her back to the cold side of the talus. It hummed against her shoulders, warbling. "You would," he said. "If you wanted to. But wouldn't you rather live free, Khatun to a Khagan, and collect the tithes rather than going in payment of them?"

"And what of the peace of the Khanate? It has been a long time, Temel, since there was war. The only discord is your discord."

"What of your freedom from an overlord's rule?"

"My freedom to become an overlord?" she countered.

He smiled. He was a handsome man.

"How vast are your armies?" she asked. He was close enough now that she almost felt his warmth. She clenched her teeth, not with fear, but because she did not choose to allow them to chatter. In the dark, she heard more singing, more rumbling. Another talus answered the first.

"Vast enough." He reached past her and patted the rough hide of the beast she leaned upon. "There is much of value in a talus." And then he touched her shoulder, with much the same affection. "Come, princess," he said. "You have a tiger's heart, it is so. But I would make this easy."

She accepted the cloak when he draped it over her shoulders and then she climbed up the talus beside him, onto the great wide back of the ancient animal. There were smoother places there, soft with moss and lichen, and it was lovely to lie back and look at the stars, to watch the moon slide down the sky.

This was a feral beast, she was sure. Not one of the miners. Just a wild thing living its wild slow existence, singing its wild slow songs. Alone, and not unhappy, in the way such creatures were. And now it would mate (she felt the second talus come alongside, though there was no danger; the talus docked side by side like ships, rather than one mounting the other like an overwrought stallion) and it might have borne young, or fathered them, or however talus worked these things.

But Temel warmed her with his body, and the talus would never have the chance. In the morning, he would lead his men upon it, and its lichen and moss and bouldery aspect would mean nothing. Its slow meandering songs and the fire that lay at its heart would be as nothing. It was armies. It was revolution. It was freedom from the Khan.

He would butcher it for the jewels that lay at its heart, and feel nothing.

Nilufer lay back on the cold stone, pressed herself to the resonant bulk and let her fingers curl how they would. Her nails picked and shredded the lichen that grew in its crevices like nervous birds picking their plumage until they bled.

Temel slid a gentle hand under the wolf-fur cloak, across her belly, over the mound of her breast. Nilufer opened her thighs.

SHE FLEW home alone, wings in her window, and dressed in haste. Her attendants slept on, under the same small spell which she had left them, and she went to find the Witch.

Who crouched beside the brazier, as before, in the empty hall. But now, her eyes were open, wide, and bright.

The Witch did not speak. That fell to Nilufer.

"She killed my father," Nilufer said. "She betrayed my father and my brother, and she slept with the Khagan, and I am the Khagan's daughter, and she did it all so she could be Khatun."

"So you will not marry the Khanzadeh, your brother?"

Nilufer felt a muscle twitch along her jaw. "That does not seem to trouble the Khagan."

The Witch settled her shoulders under the scrofular mass of her cloak. "Before I was the Witch," she said, in a voice that creaked only a little, "I was your father's mother."

Nilufer straightened her already-straight back. She drew her neck up like a pillar. "And when did you become a Witch and stop being a mother?"

The Witch's teeth showed black moons at the root where her gums had receded. "No matter how long you're a Witch, you never stop being a mother."

Nilufer licked her lips, tasting stone grit and blood. Her feet left red prints on white stone. "I need a spell, grandmother. A spell to make a man love a woman, in spite of whatever flaw may be in her." *Even the chance of another man's child?*

The Witch stood up straighter. "Are you certain?"

Nilufer turned on her cut foot, leaving behind a smear. "I am going to talk to the emissary," she said. "You will have, I think, at least a month to make ready."

HOELUN KHATUN came herself, to dress the princess in her wedding robes. They should have been red for life, but the princess had chosen white, for death of the old life, and the Khatun would permit her daughter the conceit. Mourning upon a marriage, after all, was flattering to the mother.

Upon the day appointed, Nilufer sat in her tower, all her maids and warriors dismissed. Her chaperones had been sent away. Other service had been found for her tutors. The princess waited alone, while her mother and the men-at-arms rode out in the valley before the palace to receive the bandit prince Temel, who some said would be the next Khan of Khans. Nilufer watched them from her tower window. No more than a bowshot distant, they made a brave sight with banners snapping.

But the bandit prince Temel never made it to his wedding. He was found upon that day by the entourage and garrison of Toghrul Khanzadeh, sixth son of the Khagan, who was riding to woo the same woman, upon her express invitation. Temel was taken in surprise, in light armor, his armies arrayed to show peace rather than ready for war.

There might have been more of a battle, perhaps even the beginnings of a successful rebellion, if Hoelun Khatun had not fallen in the first moments of the battle, struck down by a bandit's black arrow. This evidence of treachery from their supposed allies swayed the old queen's men to obey the orders of the three monkish warrior women who had been allies of the Khatun's husband before he died. They entered the fray at the Khanzadeh's flank.

Of the bandit army, there were said to be no survivors.

NO ONE mentioned to the princess that the black fletchings were still damp with the ink in which they had been dipped. No one told her that Hoelun Khatun had fallen facing the enemy, with a crescent-headed arrow in her back.

And when the three monkish warrior women came to inform Nilufer in her tower of her mother's death and found her scrubbing with blackened fingertips at the dark drops spotting her wedding dress, they also did not tell her that the outline of a bowstring still lay livid across her rosebud mouth and the tip of her tilted nose.

If she wept, her tears were dried before she descended the stair.

OF THE Dowager Queen Nilufer Khatun—she who was wife and then widow of Toghrul Khanzadeh, called the Barricade of Heaven for his defense of his father's empire from the bandit hordes at the foothills of the Steles of the Sky—history tells us little.

But, that she died old.

THE DEEPS OF THE SKY

STORMCHASES' LITTLE SKIFF SKIPPED AND glided across the tropopause, skimming the denser atmosphere of the warm cloud-sea beneath, running before a fierce wind. The skiff's hull was broad and shallow, supported by buoyant pontoons, the whole designed to float atop the heavy, opaque atmosphere beneath. Stormchases had shot the sails high into the stratosphere and good winds blew the skiff onward, against the current of the dark belt beneath.

Ahead, the vast ruddy wall of a Deep Storm loomed, the base wreathed in shreds of tossing white mist: caustic water clouds churned up from deep in the deadly, layered troposphere. The Deep Storm stretched from horizon to horizon, disappearing on either end in a blur of perspective and atmospheric haze. Its breadth was so great as to make even its massive height seem insignificant, though the billowing ammonia cloud wall was smeared flat-topped by stratospheric winds where it broke the tropopause.

The storm glowed with the heat of the deep atmosphere, other skiffs silhouetted cool against it. Their chatter rang over Stormchases' talker. Briefly, he leaned down to the pickup and greeted his colleagues. His

421

competition. Many of them came from the same long lines of miners that he did; many carried the same long-hoarded knowledge.

But Stormchases was determined that, with the addition of his own skill and practice, he would be among the best sky-miners of them all.

Behind and above, clear skies showed a swallowing indigo, speckled with bright stars. The hurtling crescents of a dozen or so of the moons were currently visible, as was the searing pinpoint of the world's primary—so bright it washed out nearby stars. Warmth made the sky glow too, the variegated brightness of the thermosphere far above. Stormchases' thorax squeezed with emotion as he gazed upon the elegant canopies of a group of Drift-Worlds rising in slow sunlit coils along the warm vanguard of the Deep Storm, their colors bright by sunlight, their silhouettes dark by thermal sense.

He should not look; he should not hope. But there—a distance-hazed shape behind her lesser daughters and sisters, her great canopy dappled in sheeny gold and violet—soared the Mothergraves. Stormchases was too far and too low to see the teeming ecosystem she bore on her vast back, up high above the colorful clouds where the sunlight could reach and nurture them. He could just make out the color variations caused by the dripping net-roots of veil trees that draped the Mothergraves' sides, capturing life-giving ammonia from the atmosphere and drawing it in to plump leaves and firm nutritious fruit.

Stormchases arched his face up to her, eyes shivering with longing. His wings hummed against his back. There was no desire like the pain of being separate from the Mothergraves, no need like the need to go to her. But he must resist it. He must brave the Deep Storm and harvest it, and perhaps then she would deem him worthy to be one of hers. He had the provider-status to pay court to one of the younger Drift-Worlds…but they could not give his young the safety and stability that a berth on the greatest and oldest of the Mothers would.

In the hot deeps of the sky, too high even for the Mothers and their symbiotic colony-flyers or too low even for the boldest and most intrepid of Stormchases' brethren, other things lived.

Above were other kinds of flyers and the drifters, winged or buoyant or merely infinitesimal things that could not survive even the moderate pressure and chill of the tropopause. Below, swimmers dwelled in the ammoniated thicks of the mid-troposphere that never knew the light of stars or sun. They saw only thermally. They could endure massive pressures, searing temperatures, and the lashings of molten water and even oxygen, the gas so reactive that it could set an exhalation *on fire*. That environment would crush Stormchases to a pulp, dissolve his delicate wing membranes, burn him from the gills to the bone.

Stormchases' folk were built for more moderate climes—the clear skies and thick, buoying atmosphere of the tropopause, where life flourished and the skies were full of food. But even here, in this temperate part of the sky, survival required a certain element of risk. And there were things that could only be mined where a Deep Storm pulled them up through the layers of atmosphere to an accessible height.

Which was why Stormchases sailed directly into the lowering wings of the Deep Storm, one manipulator on the skiff's controls, the other watching the perspective-shrunken sail shimmering so high above. Flyers would avoid the cable, which was monofilament spun into an intentionally refractive, high-visibility lattice with good tensile properties. But the enormous, translucent-bodied Drift-Worlds were not nimble. Chances were good that the Mother would survive a sail-impact, albeit with some scars—and some damage to the sky-island ecosystems she carried on her backs—and the skiff would likely hold together through such an incident. If he tangled a Mother in the monofilament shroud-lines spun from the same material that reinforced the Drift-World's great canopies…it didn't bear thinking of. That was why the lines were so gaily streamered: so anyone could see them from afar.

If Stormchases lost the skiff, it would just be a long flight home and probably a period of indenturehood to another miner until he could earn another, and begin proving himself again. But injuring a Mother, even a minor one who floated low, would be the end of his hopes to serve the Mothergraves.

So he watched the cable, and the overhead skies. And—of course—the storm.

Stormchases could smell the Deep Storm now, the dank corrosive tang of water vapor stinging his gills. The richly colored billows of the

Deep Storm proved it had something to give. The storm's dark-red wall churned, marking the boundary of a nearly-closed atmospheric cell rich with rare elements and compounds pumped up from the deeps. Soon, Stormchases would don his protective suit, seal the skiff, and begin the touchy business—so close to the storm—of hauling in the sail. The prevailing wind broke around the Deep Storm, eddying and compacting as it sped past those towering clouds. The air currents there were even more dangerous and unnavigable than those at the boundary between the world's temperate and subtropical zones, where two counter-rotating bands of wind met and sheared against each other.

And Stormchases was going to pass through it.

Once the sail was stowed, Stormchases would maneuver the skiff closer under engine power—as close as those cool silhouettes ahead—and begin harvesting. But he would not be cowed by the storm wall. *Could* not be, if he hoped to win a berth on the Mothergraves.

He would brave the outer walls of the storm itself. He had the skill; he had the ancestral knowledge. The reward for his courage would be phosphates, silicates, organic compounds. Iron. Solid things, from which technologies like his skiff were built. Noble gases. And fallers, the tiny creatures that spent their small lives churned in the turbulence of the Deep Storm, and which were loaded with valuable nutrition and trace elements hard to obtain, for the unfledged juveniles who lived amid the roots and foliage and trapped organics of the Drift-World ecosystems.

The Deep Storm was a rich, if deadly, resource. With its treasures, he would purchase his place on the Mothergraves.

Stormchases streamed current weather data, forecasts and predictions. He tuned into the pulsed-light broadcasts of the skiffs already engaged in harvesting, and set about making himself ready.

The good news about Deep Storms was that they were extraordinarily stable, and the new information didn't tell Stormchases much that he could not have anticipated. Still, there was always a thrill of unease as one made ready for a filtering run. A little too far, and—well, everyone knew or knew of somebody who had been careless at the margin of a storm and sucked into the depths of its embrace. A skiff couldn't survive that, and a person *definitely* couldn't. If the molten water didn't cauterize flesh from carapace, convective torrents would soon drag one down into the red depths of the atmosphere, to be melted and crushed and torn.

It was impossible to be too careful, sky-mining.

Stormchases checked the skiff's edge seals preliminary to locking down. Water could insinuate through a tiny gap and spray under the pressure of winds, costing an unwary or unlucky operator an eye. Too many sky-miners bore the scars of its caustic burns on their carapaces and manipulators.

A careful assessment showed the seals to be intact. Behind the skiff, the long cluster of cargo capsules bumped and swung. Empty, they were buoyant, and tended to drag the skiff upwards, forcing Stormchases to constant adjustments of the trim. He dropped a sky-anchor and owner-beacon to hold the majority of the cargo capsules, loaded one into the skiff's dock with the magnetic claw, and turned the little vessel toward the storm.

Siphons contracted, feeling each heave of the atmosphere, Storm-chases slid quickly but cautiously into the turbulent band surrounding the storm. It would be safer to match the wind's velocity before he made the transition to within-the-storm itself, but his little skiff did not have that much power. Instead, it was built to catch the wind and self-orient, using the storm itself for stability rather than being tumbled and tossed like a thrown flyer's egg.

Stormchases fixed his restraint harness to the tightest setting. He brought the skiff alongside the cloud wall, then deflated and retracted the pontoons, leaving the skiff less buoyant but far more streamlined. Holding hope in his mind—hope, because the Mothergraves taught that intention affected outcome—Stormchases took a deep breath, smelled the tang of methane on his exhalation, and slipped the skiff into the storm.

The wind hit the skiff in a torrent. Through long experience, Stormchases' manipulators stayed soft on the controls. He let them vibrate against his skin, but held them steady—gently, gently, without too much pressure but without yielding to the wrath of the storm. The skiff tumbled for a moment as it made the transition; he regained trim and steadied it, bringing its pointed nose around to part the wind that pushed it. It shivered—feeling alive as the sun-warmed hide of the

Mother upon whose broad back Stormchases had grown—and steadied. Stormchases guided it with heat-sight only. Here in the massive swirl of the cloud wall, the viewports showed him only the skiff's interior lighting reflecting off the featureless red clouds of the storm, as if he and his rugged little ship were swaddled in an uncle's wings.

A peaceful image, for a thing that would kill him in instants. If he went too far in, the winds would rip his tiny craft apart around him. If he got too close to the wall, turbulence could send him spinning out of control.

When the skiff finally floated serenely amidst the unending gyre, Stormchases opened the siphons. He felt the skiff belly and wallow as the wind filled it, then the increased stability as the filters activated and the capsule filled.

It didn't take long; the storm was pumping a rich mix of resources. When the capsule reached its pressurized capacity, Stormchases sealed the siphons again. Still holding his position against the fury of the winds, he tested the responses of the laden skiff. It was heavier, sluggish—but as responsive as he could have hoped.

He brought her out of the fog of red and grey, under a clear black sky. A bit of turbulence caught his wingtip as he slipped away, and it sent the skiff spinning flat like a spat seed across the tropopause. Other skiffs scattered like a swarm of infant cloud-skaters before a flyer's dive. Shaken, the harness bruising the soft flesh at his joints, Stormchases got control of the skiff and brought her around on a soft loop. His talker exploded with the whoops of other miners; mingled appreciation and teasing.

There was his beacon. He deployed pontoons to save energy and skimmed the atmosphere over to exchange capsules.

Then he turned to the storm, and went back to do it again.

STORMCHASES HAD secured his full capsules and was still re-checking the skiff's edge-seals, preliminary to popping the craft open, when he caught sight of a tiny speck of a shadow descending along the margin of the storm. Something sharp-nosed and hot enough to be uncomfortable to look upon...

Stormchases scrambled for the telescope as the speck dropped toward the Deep Storm. It locked and tracked; he pressed two eyes to the viewers and found himself regarding a sleek black…something, a glossy surface he could not name. Nor could he make out any detail of shape. The auto-focus had locked too close, and as he backed it off the object slipped into the edge of the Deep Storm.

Bigger than a flyer—bigger even than folk—and nothing with any sense would get that close to the smeary pall of water vapor without protective gear. It *looked* a little like a flyer, though—a curved, streamlined wing shape with a dartlike nose. But the wings didn't flap as it descended, banking wide on the cushion of air before the storm, curving between the scudding masses of the herd of Drift-Worlds.

It was like nothing Stormchases had ever seen.

Its belly was bright-hot, hot enough to spark open flame if it brushed oxygen, but as it banked Stormchases saw that the back was *cold*, black-cold against the warmth of the high sky, so dark and chill it seemed a band of brightness delineated it—but that was only the contrast with the soaking heat from the thermosphere. Stormchases had always had an interest in xenophysics. He felt his wings furl with shock as he realized that the object might show that heat-pattern if it had warmed its belly with friction as it entered the atmosphere, but the upper parts were still breath-stealing cold with the chill of the deep sky.

Was it a ship, and not an animal? A…skiff of some kind?

An alien?

Lightning danced around the object, caught and caressed it like a Mother's feeding tendrils caging a Mate—and then seemed to get caught there, netting and streaking the black hide with rills of savage, glowing vermillion and radiant gold. The wind of the object's passage blew the shimmers off the trailing edge of its wings; shining vapor writhed in curls in the turbulence of its wake.

Stormchases caught his breath. Neon and helium rain, condensing upon the object's hard skin, energized by the lightning, luminesced as the object skimmed the high windswept edge of the clouds.

With the eyes not pressed to the telescope, he watched a luminescent red-gold line draw across the dull-red roiling stormwall. Below, at the tropopause border of the storm, the other filter-miners were pulling back, grouping together and gliding away. They had noticed the phenomenon, and the smart sky-miner didn't approach a storm that was doing something he didn't understand.

Lightning was a constant wreath in the storm's upper regions, and whatever the object or creature was made of, the storm seemed to want to reach out and caress it. Meanwhile, the object played with the wall of the storm, threading it like a needle, as oblivious to those deadly veils of water vapor as it was to the savagery of the lightning strikes. Stormchases had operated a mining skiff—valued work, prestigious work, work he hoped would earn him a place in the Mothergraves' esteem—for his entire fledged life.

He'd seen skiffs go down, seen daring rescues, seen miners saved from impossible situations and miners who were not. He'd seen recklessness, and skill so great its exercise *looked* like recklessness.

He'd never seen anyone play with a Deep Storm like this.

It couldn't last.

IT COULD have been a cross-wind, an eddy, the sheer of turbulence. Stormchases would never know. But one moment the black object, streaming its meteor-tail of noble gases, was stitching the flank of the storm—and the next it was tumbling, knocked end over end like the losing flyer of a mating dogfight. Stormchases pulled back from the telescope, watching as the object rolled in a flat, descending spiral like a coiled tree-frond, pulled long.

The object was built like a flyer. It had no pontoons, no broad hull meant to maximize its buoyancy against the pressure gradient of the tropopause. It would fall through, and keep falling—

Stormchases clenched the gunwale of his skiff in tense manipulators, glad when the alien object fell well inside the boundary of the storm-fronting thermal the Drift-Worlds rode. It seemed so wrong, the Mothers floating lazily with their multicolored sides placid in the sun;

the object plunging to destruction amid the hells of the deep sky, trailing streamers of neon light.

It was folly to project his own experiences upon something that was not folk, of course—but he couldn't help it. If the object was a skiff, if the aliens were like folk, he knew they would be at their controls even now. Stormchases felt a great, searing pity.

They were something new, and he didn't want them to die.

Did they need to?

They had a long way to fall, and they were fighting it. The telescope— still locked on the alien object—glided smoothly in its mount. It would be easy to compute the falling ship's trajectory. Other skiffs were doing so in order to clear the crash path. Stormchases—

Stormchases pulled up the navigation console, downloaded other skiffs' telemetry on and calculations of the trajectory of the falling craft, ran his own. The object was slowing, but it was not slowing enough—and he was close enough to the crash path to intercept.

He thought of the Mothergraves. He thought of his rich cargo, the price of acceptance.

He clenched his gills and fired his engines to cross the path of the crash.

Its flat spiral path aided him. He did not need to intercept on this pass, though there would not be too many more opportunities. It was a fortunate thing that the object had a long way to fall. All he had to do was get under it, in front of it, and let the computer and the telescope and the cannon do the rest.

There. Now. Even as he thought it, the skiff's machines made their own decision. The sail-cannon boomed; the first sail itself was a bright streamer climbing the stratosphere. Stormchases checked his restraints with his manipulators and one eye, aware that he'd left it too late. The other three eyes stayed on the alien object, and the ballistic arc of the rising sail.

It snapped to the end of its line—low, too low, so much lower than such things *should* be deployed. It seemed enormous as it spread. It *was* enormous, but Stormchases was not used to seeing a sail so close.

He braced himself, one manipulator hovering over the control to depressurize the cargo capsules strung behind him in a long, jostling tail.

The object fell into the sail. Stormchases had a long moment to watch the bright sail—dappled in vermilion and violet—stretch into a trailing comet-tail as it caught and wrapped the projectile. He watched the streamers of the shroud lines buck at impact; the wave traveling their length.

The stretch and yank snapped Stormchases back against his restraints. He felt the shiver through the frame of the skiff as the shroud-motors released, letting the falling object haul line as if it were a flyer running away with the bait. The object's spiraling descent became an elongating pendulum arc, and Stormchases hoped it or they had the sense not to struggle. The shroudlines and the sail stretched, twanged—

—Held. The Mothergraves wove the sails from her own silk; they were the same stuff as her canopies. There was no stronger fiber.

Then the object swung down into the tropopause and splashed through the sea of ammonia clouds, and kept falling.

The sealed skiff jerked after. Stormchases felt the heavy crack through the hull as the pontoons broke. He lost light-sight of the sky above as the clouds closed over. He felt as if he floated against his restraints, though he knew it was just the acceleration of the fall defying gravity.

He struggled to bring his manipulator down. The deeper the object pulled him, the hotter and more pressurized—and more toxic—the atmosphere became. And he wouldn't trust the skiff's seals after the jar of that impact.

He depressurized and helium-flushed the first cargo capsule.

When it blew, the skiff shuddered again. That capsule was now a balloon filled with gaseous helium, and it snapped upward, slowing Stormchases' descent—and the descent of the sail-wrapped alien object. They were still plunging, but now dragging a buoyant makeshift pontoon.

The cables connecting the capsule twanged and plinked ominously. It had been the flaw in his plan; he hadn't been sure they *would* hold.

For now, at least, they did.

The pressure outside the hull was growing; not dangerous yet, but creeping upward. Eyes on the display, Stormchases triggered a second capsule. He felt a lighter shudder this time, as the skiff shed a little more velocity. The *next* question would be if he had enough capsules to stop the fall—and to lift his skiff, and the netted object, back to the tropopause.

His talker babbled at him, his colleagues issuing calls and organizing a party for a rescue to follow his descent. "No rescue," he said. "This is my risk."

Another capsule. Another, slighter shiver through the lines. Another incremental slowing.

By the Mothergraves, he thought. *This is actually going to work.*

WHEN HIS skiff bobbed back to the tropopause, dangling helplessly beneath a dozen empty, depressurized capsules, Stormchases was unprepared for the cheer that rang over his talker. Or the bigger one that followed, when he winched the sail containing the netted object up through the cloud-sea, into clear air.

STORMCHASES HAD no pontoons; his main sail was fouled. The empty capsules would support him, but he could not maneuver—and, in fact, his skiff swung beneath them hull-to-the-side, needle-tipped nose pointing down. Stormchases dangled bruised and aching in his restraints, trying to figure out how to loose the straps and start work on freeing himself.

He still wasn't sure how he'd survived. Or *that* he'd survived. Maybe this was the last fantasy of a dying mind—

The talker bleated at him.

He jerked against the harness, and moaned. The talker bleated again.

It wasn't words, and whatever it *was*, it drowned out the voices of the other miners, who were currently arguing over whether his skiff was salvage, and whether they should come to his assistance if it was. He'd been trying to organize his addled thoughts enough to warn them off. Now he vibrated his membranes and managed a croak that sounded fragile even to his own hearing. "Who is it? What do you want?"

That bleat again, or a modestly different one.

"Are you the alien? I can't understand you."

With pained manipulators, Stormchases managed to unfasten his restraints. He dropped from them harder than he had intended; it seemed he couldn't hold onto the rack. As his carapace struck the forward bulkhead, he made a disgruntled noise.

"Speak Language!" he snarled to the talker as he picked himself up. "I can't understand you."

It was mostly an expression of frustration. If they knew Language, they wouldn't be aliens. But he could not hide his sigh of relief when a deep, coveted voice emerged from the talker instead.

"Be strong, Stormchases," the Mothergraves said. "All will soon be well."

He pressed two eyes to the viewport. The clouds around his skiff were bright in the sunlight; he watched the encroaching shadow fall across them like the umbra of an eclipse.

It was the great, welcome shade of the Mothergraves as she drifted out of the sky.

She was coming for them. Coming for *him*.

IT WAS no small thing, for a Drift-World to drop so much altitude. For a Drift-World the size of the Mothergraves, it was a major undertaking, and not one speedily accomplished. Still, she dropped, flanked by her attendant squadrons of flyers and younger Mothers, tiny shapes flitting between her backs. Any of them could have come for Stormchases more easily, but when they would have moved forward, the Mothergraves gestured them back with her trailing, elegant gestures.

Stormchases occupied the time winching in the sail-net containing the alien object. It was heavy, not buoyant at all. He imagined it must skim through the atmosphere like a dart or a flyer—simply by moving so fast that the aerodynamics of its passage bore it up. He would have liked to disentangle the object from the shroud, but if he did, it would sink like a punctured skiff.

Instead, he amused himself by assessing the damage to his skiff (catastrophic) and answering the alien's bleats on the talker somewhat at random, though he had not given up on trying to understand what it might be saying. Obviously, it had technology—quite possibly it *was* technology, and the hard carapace might indeed be the equivalent of his own skiff—a craft, meant for entering a hostile environment.

Had it been sampling the storm for useful chemicals and consumables, as well?

He wondered what aliens ate. What they breathed. He wondered if he could teach them Language.

Every time he looked up, the Mothergraves' great keel was lower. Finally, her tendrils encompassed his horizons and when he craned his eyes back he could make out the double row of Mates fused to and dependent from her bellies like so many additional, vestigial tendrils. There were dozens. The oldest had lost all trace of their origins, and were merely smooth nubs sealed to the Mothergraves' flesh. The newest were still identifiable as the individuals they had been.

Many of the lesser Mothers among her escort dangled Mates from their bellies as well, but none had half so many as the Mothergraves...and none were so much as two-thirds of her size.

In frustration, Stormchases squinched himself against the interior of his carapace. So close. He had been *so close*. And now all he had to show for it was a wrecked skiff and a bleating alien. Now he would have to start over—

He *could* ask the Mothergraves to release his groom-price to a lesser Mother. He had provided well enough for any of her sisters or daughters to consider him.

But none of them were *she*.

He only hoped his sacrifice of resources in order to rescue the alien had not angered her. That would be too much to bear—although if she decided to reclaim the loss from his corpse, he supposed at the very least he would die fulfilled...if briefly.

The talker squawked again. The alien sounds seemed more familiar; he must be getting used to them.

A few of the Mothergraves tendrils touched him, as he had so long anticipated. It was bitterest irony now, but the pleasure of the caress almost made it worthwhile. He braced himself for pain and paralysis... but she withheld her sting, and the only pain was the bruises left by his restraints and by impact with the bulkheads of the tumbling skiff.

Now her voice came to him directly, rather than by way of the talker. It filled the air around him and vibrated in the hollows of his body like soft thunder. To his shock and disbelief, she said words of ritual to him; words he had hoped and then despaired to hear.

She said, "For the wealth of the whole, what have you brought us, Stormchases?"

Before he could answer, the talker bleated again. This time, in something like Language—bent, barely comprehensible, accented more oddly than any Language Stormchases had ever heard.

It said, "Hello? You us comprehend?"

"I hear you," the Mothergraves said. "What do you want?"

A long silence before the answer came. "This we fix. Trade science. Go. Place you give us for repairs?"

THE ALIENS—THE object *was* a skiff, of sorts, and it had as many crew members as Stormchases had eyes—had a machine that translated their bleaty words into Language, given a wise enough sample of it. As the revolutions went by, the machine became more and more proficient, and Stormchases spent more and more time talking to A'lees, their crew member in charge of talking. Their names were just nonsense sounds, not words, which made him wonder how any of them ever knew who he was. And they divided labor up in strange ways, with roles determined not by instar and inheritance but by individual life-courses. They told him a great deal about themselves and their peculiar biology; he reciprocated with the more mundane details of his own. A'lees seemed particularly interested that he would soon Mate, and wished to know as much about the process as he could tell.

The aliens sealed themselves in small flexible habitats—pressure carapaces—to leave their skiff, and for good reason. They were made mostly of water, and they oozed water from their bodies, and the pressure and temperature of the world's atmosphere would destroy them as surely as the deeps of the sky would crush Stormchases. The atmosphere *they* breathed was made of inert gases and explosive oxygen, and once their skiff was beached on an open patch of the Mothergraves' back for repairs, just the leakage of oxygen and water vapor from its airlocks soon poisoned a swath of vegetation for a bodylength in any direction.

Stormchases stayed well back from the alien skiff while he had these conversations.

Talking to the aliens was a joy and a burden. The Mothergraves insisted he should be the one to serve as an intermediary. He had experience with them, and the aliens valued that kind of experience—and when he was Mated, that experience would be assimilated into the Mothergraves' collective mind. It would become a part of her, and a part of all their progeny to follow.

The Mothergraves had told him—in the ritual words—that knowledge and discovery were great offerings, unique offerings. That the opportunity to interact with beings from another world was of greater import to her and her brood than organics, or metals, or substances that she could machine within her great body into the stuff of skiffs and sails and other technology. That she accepted his suit, and honored the courage with which he had pressed it.

And *that* was why the duty was a burden. Because to be available for the aliens while they made the repairs—to play *liaison* (their word)—meant putting off the moment of joyous union again. And again. To have been so close, and then so far, and then so close again—

The agony of anticipation, and the fear that it would be snatched from him again, was a form of torture.

A'lees came outside of the alien skiff in her pressure carapace and sat in its water-poisoned circle with her forelimbs wrapped around her drawn-up knees, talking comfortably to Stormchases. She said she was a female, a Mother. But that Mothers of her kind were not so physically different from the males, and that even after they Mated, males continued to go about in the world as independent entities.

"But how do they pass their experiences on to their offspring?" Stormchases asked.

A'lees paused for a long time.

"We teach them," she said. "Your children inherit your memories?"

"Not memories," he said. "Experiences."

She hesitated again. "So you become a part of the Mother. A kind of... symbiote. And your offspring with her will have all of her experiences, and yours? But...not the memories? How does that work?"

"Is knowledge a memory?" he asked.

"No," she said confidently. "Memories can be destroyed while skills remain...Oh. I think...I understand."

They talked for a little while of the structure of the nets and the Mothers' canopies, but Stormchases could tell A'lees was not finished thinking about memories. Finally she made a little deflating hiss sound and brought the subject up again.

"I am sad," A'lees said, "that when we have fixed our sampler and had time to arrange a new mission and come back, you will not be here to talk with us."

"I will be here," said Stormchases, puzzled. "I will be mated to the Mothergraves."

"But it won't be—" Whatever A'lees had been about to say, the translator stammered on it. She continued. "—the same. You won't remember us."

"The Mothergraves will," Stormchases assured her.

She drew herself in a little smaller. "It will be a long time before we return."

Stormchases patted toward the edge of the burn zone. He did not let his manipulators cross it, though. Though he would soon enough lose the use of his manipulators to atrophy, he didn't feel the need to burn them off prematurely. "It's all right, A'lees," he said. "We will remember you by the scar."

Whatever the sound she made next meant, the translator could not manage it.

○

Two Dreams on Trains

T HE NEEDLE WORE A PATH of dye and scab round and round
Patience's left ring finger; sweltering heat adhered her to the mold-
scarred chair. The hurt didn't bother her. It was pain with a future.
She glanced over the scarrist's bare scalp, through the grimy window,
holding her eyes open around the prickle of tears.

Behind the rain, she could pick out the jeweled running lamps of a
massive spacelighter sliding through clouds, coming in soft toward the
waterlogged sprawl of a spaceport named for Lake Pontchartrain. On a
clear night she could have seen its train of cargo capsules streaming in
harness behind. Patience bit her lip and looked away: not down at the
needle, but across at a wall shaggy with peeling paint.

Lake Pontchartrain was only a name now, a salt-clotted estuary of the
rising Gulf. But it persisted—like the hot bright colors of bougainvillea
grown in wooden washpails beside doors, like the Mardi Gras floats that
now floated for real—in the memory of New Orleanians, as grand a legacy
as anything the underwater city could claim. Patience's hand lay open on
the wooden arm as if waiting for a gift. She didn't look down and she didn't
close her eyes as the needle pattered and scratched, pattered and scratched.

The long Poplar Street barge undulated under the tread of feet moving past the scarrist's, but his fingers were steady as a gin-soaked frontier doctor's.

The prick and shift of the needle stopped and the pock-faced scarrist sat back on his heels. He set his tools aside and turned back with quickseal and a waterproof glove, making a practiced job of the bandages. Patience looked down at her hands, at the palm fretted indigo to mark her caste. At the filigree of emerald and crimson across the back of her right hand, and underneath the transparent sealant swathing the last two fingers of her left.

A peculiar tightness blossomed under her breastbone. She started to raise her left hand and press it to her chest to ease the tension, stopped herself just in time, and laid the hand back on the chair. She pushed herself up with her right hand only and said, "Thank you."

She gave the scarrist a handful of cash chits, once he'd stripped his gloves and her blood away. His hands were the river-water color he'd been born with, marking him a tradesman; the holographic slips of poly she paid with glittered like fish scales against his skin.

"Won't be long before you'll have the whole hand done." He rubbed a palm across his sweat-slick scalp. He had tattoos of his own, starting at the wrists—dragons and mermaids and manatees, arms and chest tesserae'd in oceanic beasts. "You've earned two fingers in six months. You must be studying all the time."

"I want my kid to go to trade school so we can get berths outbound," Patience said, meeting the scarrist's eyes so squarely that he looked down and pocketed his hands behind the coins, like pelicans after fish. "I don't want him to have to sell an indenturement to survive, like I did." She smiled. "I tell him he should study engineering, be a professional, get the green and red. Or mechanics, keep his hands clean. Like yours. He wants to be an artist, though. Not much call for painters up *there*."

The scarrist grunted, putting his tools away. "There's more to life than lighters and cargo haulers, you know."

Her sweeping gesture took in the little room and the rainy window. The pressure in her chest tightened, a trap squeezing her heart, holding her in place, pinned. "Like this?"

He shrugged, looked up, considered. "Sure. Like this. I'm a free man, I do what I like." He paused. "Your kid any good?"

"As an artist?" A frown pulled the corner of her lip down. Consciously, she smoothed her hand open so she wouldn't squeeze and blur her new tattoos. "Real good. No reason he can't do it as a hobby, right?"

"Good? Or *good*?"

Blood scorched her cheeks. "*Real* good."

The scarrist paused. She'd known him for years: six fingers and a thumb, seven examinations passed. Three more left. "If he keeps his hands clean. When you finish the caste—" gesture at her hands— "If he still doesn't want to go. Send him to me."

"It's not that he doesn't want to go. He just—doesn't want to work, to sacrifice." She paused, helpless. "Got any kids?"

He laughed, shaking his head, as good as a yes, and they shared a lingering look. He glanced down first, when it got uncomfortable, and Patience nodded and brushed past on the way out the door. Rain beaded on her nanoskin as it shifted to repel the precipitation, and she paused on decking. Patchy-coated rats scurried around her as she paused to watch a lighter and train lay itself into the lake, gently as an autumn leaf. She leaned out over the Poplar Street Canal as the lights taxied into their berth. Its wake lapped gently at the segmented kilometers-long barge, lifting and dropping Poplar Street under Patience's feet. Cloying rain and sweat adhered her hair to the nape of her neck. Browning roux and sharp pepper cut the reek of filthy water. She squeezed the railing with her uninjured hand and watched another train ascend, the blossom of fear in her chest finally easing. "Javier Alexander," she muttered, crossing a swaying bridge. "You had best be home safe in bed, my boy. You'd best be home in bed."

A CITY like drowned New Orleans, you don't just walk away from. A city like drowned New Orleans, you fly away from. If you can. And if you can't...

You make something that can.

Jayve lay back in a puddle of blood-warm rain and seawater in the "borrowed" dinghy and watched the belly lights of another big train drift overhead, hulls silhouetted against the citylit, salmon-colored clouds like a string of pearls. He almost reached up a pale-skinned hand: it seemed close enough to touch. The rain parted on either side like curtains, leaving him dry for the instant when the wind from its fans tossed him, and came together again behind as unmarked as the sea. "Beautiful," he whispered. "Fucking beautiful, Mad."

"You in there, Jayve?" A whisper in his ear, stutter and crack of static. They couldn't afford good equipment, or anything not stolen or jerrybuilt. But who gave a damn? Who gave a damn, when you could get that close to a *starship?*

"That last one went over my fucking *head*, Mad. Are you in?"

"Over the buoys. Shit. *Brace!*"

Jayve slammed hands and feet against the hull of the rowboat as Mad spluttered and coughed. The train's wake hit him, picked the dinghy up and shook it like a dog shaking a dishrag. Slimed old wood scraped his palms; the crossbrace gouged an oozing slice across his scalp and salt water stung the blood from the wound. The contents of the net bag laced to his belt slammed him in the gut. He groaned and clung; strain burned his thighs and triceps.

He was still in the dinghy when it came back down.

He clutched his netbag, half-panicked touch racing over the surface of the insulated tins within until he was certain the wetness he felt was rain and not the gooey ooze of etchant: sure mostly because the skin on his hands stayed cool instead of sloughing to hang in shreds.

"Mad, can you hear me?"

A long, gut-tightening silence. Then Mad retched like he'd swallowed seawater. "Alive," he said. "Shit, that boy put his boat down a bit harder than he had to, didn't he?"

"Just a tad." Jayve pushed his bag aside and unshipped the oars, putting his back into the motion as they bit water. "Maybe it's his first run. Come on, Mad. Let's go brand this bitch."

PATIENCE DAWDLED along her way, stalling in open-fronted shops while she caught up her marketing, hoping to outwait the rain and the worry gnawing her belly. Fish-scale chits dripped from her multicolored fingers, and from those of other indentured laborers—some, like her, buying off their contracts and passing exams, and others with indigo-stained paws and no ambition—and the clean hands of the tradesmen who crowded the bazaar; the coins fell into the hennaed palms of shopkeepers and merchants who walked with the rolling gait of sailors. The streets underfoot echoed the hollow sound of their footsteps between the planking and the water.

Dikes and levees had failed; there's just too much water in that part of the world to wall away. And there's nothing under the Big Easy to sink a piling into that would be big enough to hang a building from. But you don't just walk away from a place that holds the grip on the human imagination New Orleans does.

So they'd simply floated the city in pieces and let the Gulf of Mexico roll in underneath.

Simply.

The lighters and their trains came and went into Lake Pontchartrain, vessels too huge to land on dry earth. They sucked brackish fluid through hungry bellymouths between their running lights and fractioned it into hydrogen and oxygen, salt and trace elements and clean potable water; they dropped one train of containers and picked up another; they taxied to sea and did it all over again.

Sometimes they hired technicians and tradesmen. They didn't hire laborer-caste, dole-caste, palms stained indigo as those of old time denim textile workers, or criminals with their hands stained black. They didn't take *artists*.

Patience stood under an awning, watching the clever moth-eaten rats ply their trade through the market, her nanoskin wicking sweat off her flesh. The lamps of another lighter came over. She was cradling her bandaged hand close to her chest, the straps of her weighted netbag biting livid channels in her right wrist. She'd stalled as long as possible.

"That boy had better be in bed," she said to no one in particular. She turned and headed home.

Javier's bed lay empty, his sheets wet with the rain drifting in the open window. She grasped it in her right hand and tugged the sash down awkwardly: the apartment building she lived in was hundreds of years old. She'd just straightened the curtains when her telescreen buzzed.

JAYVE CROUCHED under the incredible curve of the lighter's hull, both palms flat against its centimeters-thick layer of crystalline sealant. It hummed against his palms, the deep surge of pumps like a heartbeat filling its reservoirs. The shadow of the hull hid Jayve's outline and the silhouette of his primitive watercraft from the bustle of tenders peeling cargo strings off its stern. "Mad, can you hear me?"

Static crackle, and his friend's voice on a low thrill of excitement. "I hear you. Are you in?"

"Yeah. I'm going to start burning her. Keep an eye out for the harbor patrol."

"You're doing my tag too!"

"Have I *ever* let you down, Mad? Don't worry. I'll tag it from both of us, and you can burn the next one and tag it from both. Just think how many people are going to see this. All over the galaxy. Better than a gallery opening!"

Silence, and Jayve knew Mad was lying in the bilge water of his own dinghy just beyond the thin line of runway lights that Jayve glimpsed through the rain. Watching for the Harbor Police.

The rain was going to be a problem. Jayve would have to pitch the bubble against the lighter's side. It would block his sightlines and make him easier to spot, which meant trusting Mad's eyes to be sharp through the rain. And the etchant would stink up the inside. He'd have to dial the bubble to maximum porosity if he didn't want to melt his eyes.

No choice. The art had to happen. The art was going to fly.

Black nano unfolded over and around him, the edge of the hiker's bubble sealing itself against the hull. The steady patter of rain on his hair and shoulders stopped, as it had when the ship drifted over, and Jayve started to squeegee the hull dry. He'd have to work in sections. It would take longer.

"Mad, you out there?"

"Coast clear. What'd you tell your mom to get out tonight?"

"I didn't." He chewed the inside of his cheek as he worked. "I could have told her I was painting at Claudette's, but she—Mom I mean—says there's no future in it, and she might have gone by to check. So I just snuck out. She won't be home for hours."

Jayve slipped a technician's headband around his temples and switched the pinlight on, making sure the goggles were sealed to his skin. At least the bubble would block the glow. He pinched his fingers between two tins while digging in his netbag, and stifled a yelp. Bilge water sloshed around his ankles, creeping under his nanoskin faster than the skin could re-osmose it: the night hung against him hot and sweaty as a giant hand. Heedless, heart racing, Jayve extracted the first bottle of etchant, pierced the seal with an adjustable nozzle, and—grinning like a bat—pressurized the tin.

Leaning as far back as he could without tearing the bubble or capsizing his dinghy, Jayve examined the sparkling, virgin surface of the spaceship and began to spray. The etchant eroded crystalline sealant, staining the corroded surface in green, orange, violet. It only took a few moments for the chemicals to scar the ship's integument: not enough to harm it, but enough to mark it forever, unless the corp that owned it was willing to pay to have the whole damn lighter peeled down and resealed.

Jayve moved the bubble four times, etchant fumes searing his flesh, collar of his nanoskin pulled over his mouth and nose to breathe through. He worked around the beaded rows of running lights, turning them into the scales on the sea-serpent's belly, the glints on its fangs. A burst of static came over the crappy uplink once but Mad said nothing, so Jayve kept on smoothly despite the wake-sway of the dinghy under his feet and the hiss of the tenders.

When he finished, the seamonster stretched fifteen meters along the hull of the lighter and six meters high, a riot of sensuality and prismatic colors.

He signed it *jayve n mad* and pitched the last empty bottle into Lake Pontchartrain, where it sank without a trace. "Mad?"

No answer.

Jayve's bubble lit from the outside with the glare of a hundred lights. His stomach kicked and he scrabbled for the dinghy's magnetic clamps to kick it free, but an amplified voice advised him to drop the tent and wait with his hands in view. "Shit! Mad?" he whispered through a tightening throat: a cop's voice rang over the fuzzy connection.

"Just come out, kid," she said tiredly. "Your friend's in custody. It's only a vandalism charge so far: just come on out."

WHEN THEY released Javier to Patience in the harsh light and tile of the police barge, she squeezed his hands so tight that blood broke through the sealant over his fresh black tattoos. He winced and tugged his hands away but she clenched harder, her own scabs cracking. She meant to hiss, to screech—but her voice wouldn't shape words, and he wouldn't look her in the eye.

She threw his hands down and turned away, steel decking rolling under her feet as a wave hit. She steadied herself with a lifetime's habit, Javier swept along in her wake. "Jesus," she said, when the doors scrolled open and the cold light of morning hit her across the eyes. "Javier, what the hell were you thinking? What the hell..." She stopped and leaned against the railing, fingers tight on steel. Pain tangled her left arm to the elbow. Out on the lake, a lighter drifted backwards from its berth, refueled and full of water, coming about on a stately arc as the tenders rushed to bring its outbound containers into line.

Javier watched the lighter curve across the lake. Something green and crimson sparkled on its hide above the waterline, a long sinuous curve of color, shimmering with scales and wise with watchful eyes. "Look at that," he said. "The running lamps worked just right. It looks like it's wriggling away, squirming itself up into the sky like a dragon should—"

"What does that matter?" She looked down at his hands, at the ink singeing his fingers. "You'll amount to nothing."

Patience braced against the wake, but Javier turned to get a better look. "Never was any chance of that, Mom."

"Javier, I—" A stabbing sensation drew her eyes down. She stared as the dark blood staining her hands smeared the rain-beaded railing and dripped into the estuary. She'd been picking her scabs, destroying the symmetry of the scarrist's lines.

"You could have been something," she said, as the belly of the ship finished lifting from the lake, pointed into a sunrise concealed behind grey clouds. "You ain't going nowhere now."

Javier came beside her and touched her with a bandaged hand. She didn't turn to look at the hurt in his eyes.

"Man," he whispered in deep satisfaction, craning his neck as his creation swung into the sky. "Just think of all the people who are going to see that. Would you just look at that baby go?"

FASTER GUN

2.

DOC HOLLIDAY LEANED HIS HEAD way back, tilting his hat to shade his eyes from the glare of the November sun and said, "Well, that still looks like some Jules Verne shit to me."

The hulk that loomed over, curving gently outward to a stalklike prow, could have been the rust-laceworked, rust-orange hulk of any derelict ironclad. Except it was hundreds of miles from the nearest ocean, and a hundred times too big to be a ship. It was too big, in fact, to be an opera hall, and that was where Doc's imagination failed him.

Behind him, four women and a man shifted in their saddles, leather creaking. None of them spoke. Doc figured they were just as awed as he was. More, maybe: he'd stopped here once before, when he rode into Tombstone the previous year. None of *them* had ever seen it.

One of the horses whuffed, stamping baked caliche. A puff of dust must have risen from the impact. Doc could smell it, iron and salt and grit. His own mount picked its way between crumbling chunks of metal and some melted, scorched substance with the look of resin or tortoiseshell.

One of the women said something pleased and indistinct to her companions. Doc didn't strain too hard to overhear.

A hot wind dried the sweat on his face beneath the scruff of a three-day beard as his own bay gelding fidgeted. Doc settled it with a touch of his leg. The gelding's sweat soaked the inseam of his trousers between saddle-skirt and boot-top.

Doc let the silence drag, contemplating the great plates and icicles of rust armoring the surface of the whatever-it-was. Its broken spine zigzagged off into the heat shimmer. A long furrowed scrape marred the desert behind the hulk. That impact—or just the desert—had gnawed several holes in its flanks, revealing buckled decks, dangling pipe and wiring, stretched and twisted structural members.

Here and there in its shadowed depths, blue-white lights still burned, as they had when Doc first saw it.

The horses indolent in the heat, the other five came up alongside Doc. In all honesty, he hadn't been sanguine about bringing four ladies into the trackless desert—even the kind of ladies that wore trousers and went heeled and rode astride like men—but they had been determined on riding out with him or without. He figured "without" was a hell of a lot less safe than "with," and in the end chivalry had won. Chivalry, and the need for some ready cash to settle at the faro table, where he owed a debt to that damned John Ringo.

Ringo—and not just the debt—was another reason. Because if Doc hadn't taken the job as a ladies' touring guide, Ringo in his yellow and black check shirt sure as hell would have. And then Doc might as well have these tenderfoots' deaths on his conscience as if he had shot them with his own gun. Ringo would have no qualms about relieving them of their horses and cash by any means possible…shy of earning it fairly.

The horses drifted to a stop again, scuffing and shuffling in a ragged arc: one chestnut, one gray, one dun, and three assorted browns and bays. For now, Doc's charges—he wasn't sure yet if you could call them companions—were content to stare up at the wreck in silence and awe. Which suited Doc just fine. The dust was making his chest ache, and he didn't feel like talking.

He reached into his pocket for a stick of horehound, peeled the waxed paper back, and bit off a chip to suck on. The last thing he needed now was a goddamned coughing fit.

On Doc's left, the lone other man lifted his hat off a grizzled head. He mopped the sweat from his bald spot with a once-red kerchief that had faded the color of the dull yellow earth. His name was Bill. He was quiet and needed a shave. Doc hadn't learned too much else about him.

Bill said, "I reckon we should ride around it first?"

"Before we dismount?" The woman who gave him a sideways nod was tall, skinny. Doc thought she might be his wife, but he and all the others called her Missus Shutt. She had long wrists and long hands, and her steel-colored hair was clipped shorter at her nape than most men's. Her gray eyes snapped with charisma and intelligence. She would have been beautiful, Doc thought, but her nose was too small.

The little blonde on *her* left almost got lost under a wavy ill-contained billow of caramel-colored hair—the kind of hair that belonged spread out on a man's pillow. Pigeon-breasted, with a rump like a punching pony poured into her shiny-seated trousers, she sat her red gelding with the erect spine and lifted chin of one of Doc's girl cousins back home, as if she was not accustomed to the relaxed Western seat. Her name was Missus Jorgensen.

Beyond her was Miss Lil, the big one who looked to have some Mexican in her. Or maybe some Indian. Or maybe both. It wasn't so different. Miss Lil wasn't just big for a woman—she was broad-shouldered and had about a half foot on Doc's five-ten. Her hair twisted in a black braid that snaked out from under her chapeau fat as a well-fed rattler.

The sixth person—and fourth woman—in their little group of adventurers was a beautiful quadroon with a long, elegant jaw and crooked teeth. The Negress's name was Flora. Despite the heat, she wore a fringed suede jacket. It matched the sheath on the saddle by her knee that held the coach gun she seemed to prefer to the pistols all the others carried.

Doc—no fool—was heeled with both.

"By the time we get around this thing the shade will have shifted," Doc said. "We can tether the horses in it."

Bill asked, "Is it safe to leave them so close to the wreck?"

Doc rattled that bit of horehound against the backs of his top teeth with the tip of his tongue. "It's what we've got for shelter."

The big woman leaned out of her saddle, making her horse sidle and fret. "There's no tracks around it," she said, after a moment's inspection. "Nothing to show anything might have crawled out, anyway. Or dragged anything back in again."

Heads swiveled. Doc might be the guide, the local—laughably speaking—expert. But it didn't take much to see the quadroon woman was the leader of the group that had hired him. And none of them seemed to find anything strange about it.

Doc washed the lingering bitterness of the horehound down with a swig from his canteen. None of his concern how people ran their lives. His job was getting them all into the wreck, and all out safe again with whatever it was they thought so worth risking money, bullets, and their lives to find.

THEIR SLOW circuit took the better part of an hour, and while it did reveal some tracks, they were those of coyote, lizard, javalina, and hare. Condensation formed inside the rusting hulk when the temperature dropped at night—a resource no desert creature would ignore.

Doc, with Miss Lil, was riding slightly ahead of the others—both of them leaned down silent and intent as they surveyed the scarred earth—when she cleared her throat, reined in the heavy-boned, bald-faced brown mare that bore up under her weight with ease, and murmured, "Doc?"

He turned, followed the gesture of her large graceful hand, and frowned down at some rows of wavering, parallel scratches in the dust. When he looked up again, Miss Lil was regarding him levelly out of eyes brown and intelligent as her mare's. Her eyebrows rose in a question.

"Somebody brushed out tracks." A familiar cold pressure grew between Doc's shoulder blades, under the protection of his duster. Aware of how much he was giving away, but unable to stop himself, he let his gaze run over the ragged remains of the whatever-it-was. He might get lucky. He might catch the glint of sunlight off a gun barrel, or the flicker of motion as someone raised and sighted within that chambered darkness.

450

"Yes." Her voice was high and musical, charmingly out of place in her frame. "But coming or going?"

The others had scuffed to a halt five feet or so back, waiting out the trackers' verdict. At Miss Lil's question, the voluptuous little blonde—Missus Jorgensen—shifted her hands from where they rested on her pommel and rubbed the left one with the right.

"As it appears," she quoted, "in the true course of all the question."

Doc snorted and quoted in return, "Well, I am glad that all things sort so well."

Her smile lit up her square-jawed face quite wickedly. "I had heard you were an educated man. It appears I was not misinformed."

"Ma'am," he answered, and touched the brim of his cap. He looked at Flora, reminding himself who he was working for. "Whatever you came for—do you want to keep looking if you're not the only ones?"

"We're looking for her logs," Flora said.

"Logs?"

Her hair moved over her shoulders in a pair of squaw plaits thick as her wrists when she nodded. "That thing was a ship, Doctor Holliday. A ship that sailed between the stars."

"Huh," Doc said, looking back at it. Still no sign of a carbine barrel, or any motion, or any life except the still burn of those blue lights in its depths. It had no wings, nor any sign of a balloon canopy, nor even the conical mouth of a giant Hale rocket on what he took to be its stern—the end towards the skid-marks, which was less damaged over all.

He shrugged. "I'll feel better when we're under cover."

"Agreed," Flora said. "Since we might be following someone in, what do you think of picketing the horses inside one of the damaged areas? At least they'll be hidden from casual view."

"If someone's going to steal 'em," Bill said, "they can steal 'em from a picket line outside as easily as one in. And if we have to run for 'em, well, I'd rather not cross open ground under fire on foot. Or at all, for that matter."

He glanced at Doc, as if weighing his next words. "I can drop a ward line around 'em either way. Inside or out."

Doc sucked his teeth to get some moisture into his mouth. "You're a hex."

Bill shrugged. "The ladies need some reason to put up with me."

"Huh," Doc said. It might be autumn by any sensible man's reckoning, but that didn't help the heat that trickled sweat down between his shoulder blades.

Since Bill had been so honest with him, he allowed, "I might have a seen a trick or two like that my own self. And more men who claimed it than could do it. Wardings, though. That's a bit beyond my experiences."

"What you do with that iron," Bill answered. "That's beyond me."

Doc tipped his head and let the compliment slide off.

Missus Shutt pushed her hat down over that cropped steel hair. "Warded or not, I can't imagine the horses would be any less safe than out in the open."

"Unless the wreck itself eats 'em," Doc said.

They all looked at him. He had sucked up the last splinter of horehound. He stifled a cough and wiped his mouth. No blood this time, for a mercy.

"You think that's *likely?*" Missus Jorgensen asked.

"I think it could happen," Doc answered. "Likely? That's a whole 'nother thing."

THE HORSES came into the dim, reflected light of the wreck as if into a stable, heads lowered and calm. Their composure was reassuring, although Doc might have found it more peculiar if it hadn't been fifteen or so of Doctor Fahrenheit's degrees less hot in the damp shade of the hull of the ruined 'star-ship.' Although that was peculiar in its own right: you'd expect a metal shed, sweating in the sun, to be sweltering no matter how vast.

Instead, the derelict exhaled a moist breath that seemed cool, even if only by comparison. Doc's companions reveled in it, stretching themselves taller in the shade as if the desert light had weight. They moved around the arching space they'd chosen as a temporary stable, keeping an eye on the three buckled passages—one at ground level, two above— that led deeper into the wreck. The horses huffed into their nosebags and settled quietly, though no one did more to ease his mount than slip its bit. Girths stayed tight, in case a hasty retreat was indicated. Bill began casting around the edge of the chamber like a terrier after a rat—looking to set out his wardline, Doc imagined. He had that concentrated look of a professional—surgeon, gambler, hex, or shootist—considering a selection of inadequate options. Doc let him be.

Doc wasn't happy about stabling the horses in this mess; it was asking for lockjaw, but he didn't see a good alternative. As he was checking the bay's hooves before pulling the coach gun from the saddle, he heard rust flakes crunching under the footsteps of two of the booted, uncorseted women walking up between the mares. One of them—Missus Jorgensen, by her sharp dry tone—was saying something indistinct, and Doc strained to pick her words out of the coruscating echoes of footsteps, hoof-clops, and one of the mares pissing like a downspout running into a catch-barrel before he realized what he was doing.

If your sainted momma caught you eavesdropping, John Henry Holliday, you know a frown would crease her brow. But Doc wasn't sure how thoroughly he believed Flora's tale about this being an expedition to retrieve some long-lost captain's log—and in fairness, it was his life on the line. Funny how since Dallas he had no compunctions about holding a gun on a man, or gambling for a living. But he could still balk at trying to overhear something he maybe shouldn't.

It didn't matter—he couldn't make out much over the stamp of hooves and the creak of leather, except Miss Lil answering whatever Missus Jorgensen had said with, "...sense detail's genius."

"I'm looking forward to this one," Missus Jorgensen answered. "Could be our greatest run since the Spider Women of Queso Grande."

"Hey," Flora interrupted. "No—"

Whatever she said got lost in the background noise as well. Doc shook his head at himself and straightened up, letting the gelding's off fore drop. A little confusion and thwarted curiosity was no more than he deserved for such rudeness.

He almost lost the rustle of something unexpected kicking through rust flakes and litter in the hollow clop of the gelding's hoof.

"Shhh," he hissed—but you couldn't shush a horse, and he was the second one to hiss for quiet. Behind Missus Shutt, who was turned at the waist, wrist cocked and one bony hand on her iron like she could have it skinned as fast as any man.

"What?" Bill asked from the outside of the group, real soft—but his voice still echoed and sloshed around the crumpled, cavernous room.

"Company," Doc said gently. He let the coach gun slide into his hand now; he'd seen a man die once because he waited to try to get to a rifle on his saddle until the shooting started and the horse was spooked.

Flora ducked under the gelding's belly and flattened herself against its saddle behind Doc. "What'd you hear?" she asked, more breath than sound.

Doc let his lips shape the words. "Footstep." He thought about the sound, something about the way it rustled rather than crunched. "Moccasins or barefoot. Not boots."

Flora frowned, but as if she was annoyed or disappointed, not as if she were scared. "Oh, I hope they didn't go there. That'd make me sad."

The corners of Doc's mouth curved up at her irritation in the face of danger. But there was an intriguing clue in her words, and—well, he'd proven his unhealthy curiosity already today. "Who were you hoping not to have come here?"

Her eyes had been straining into the shadows beyond the shadowy bulk of the horses. She looked at Doc, now, startled. "I beg your pardon. Just a turn of phra—"

Another rustle silenced her. Louder this time, closer. Doc let the coach gun rest beside his leg. He didn't want to fire a scattergun over the horses that hemmed them on both sides, though he could use the big brown for cover and a shooting rest if he had to. Once. And then it would be hooves and half-ton panic everywhere, in a crowded chamber with uncertain footing.

Better for everyone if they could get out of this without gunfire.

Flora must have thought so too. "Bill," she said, low and conversational this time so it would carry. "How's that ward line coming?"

"Faster now," Bill answered, over a scraping sound. Doc caught a scent of burning orris root. A ward line wouldn't stop a bullet—lead just didn't answer to magic—but it would keep a person out.

"Hey," Miss Lil said, forgetting to whisper—and as Doc turned his head toward her, suddenly pointed back over his shoulder.

He whipped round, the coach gun to his eye, up on tiptoe to get line of sight over the back of the brown mare. Trying to remember not to hold his breath, because if he held his breath, he would start coughing. And if he started coughing, there was no guarantee that he would ever stop.

Over the iron sights of the gun, Doc glimpsed something that nearly made him drop it.

The figure half-silhouetted against the blue glow at the back of one of the above-ground-level tunnels could have been a naked child just on the verge of puberty—slender, fine-limbed, large-headed for the delicate lines of an elongated neck. Except he—or she, or possibly even it—hung upside-down by its toes in the mouth of the tunnel like one of the slick mud-green treefrogs of Doc's Georgia boyhood. The long fat-tipped fingers on its splayed hands did nothing to disabuse him of the comparison.

The hands—

Its hands were empty.

Incrementally, Doc let the coach gun drift down, aware that beside him Flora was doing the same. The harsh breaths of his companions echoed to every side, layering over one another in an atonal fugue.

Doc pointed the shotgun in a safe position and uncocked it. He lowered the butt to the ground, letting the barrel lean against his knee. He raised his hands again, fingers spread wide like the frog-thing's, showing them empty.

"Well," he said. "I reckon you ain't from around here."

The thing made no sound in return, but it leaned forward from the hips. Behind Doc, Missus Shutt stepped out from between horses, her iron reholstered too. Doc wanted to hiss at her to keep cover—the bony-limbed critter could be a decoy, a distraction. But as she walked forward, her boot-toes nosing softly through the rust and trash on the floor, each step tested before she shifted her weight onto it—well, Doc found himself just purely unable to intervene.

And all Missus Shutt's companions just stood around and watched her risk her fool life like charades with moon men was some kind of a fashionable parlor game.

"Hey there, friend," said Missus Shutt. She spread her hands out a little wider, until Doc could see the light and shadows stretched between her fingertips. She paused when Doc could just see the faint greeny glow of Bill's ward line shining against the scarred leather of her boots. "We didn't know there were any survivors of the crash. We're here to help."

The moon man didn't even shift. But his—its—ribcage swelled visibly with what might have been a deep breath. Doc found that strangely reassuring: if it breathed, it was alive. And if it was alive, it was vulnerable to flying bits of metal and flying hexes both.

Missus Shutt must have read some encouragement in its steady posture, because she let her hands drop gently against her thighs and said, "My name is Elisa Shutt. I'm a duly-appointed representative of James Garfield, the President of the United States of America, the political institution whose territory this is. And I am empowered to offer you assistance on behalf of my government."

Hah, thought Doc. *I knew there was something more to this than treasure hunters.*

Behind him—not to him—Miss Lil whispered, "I thought this was a shooting adventure," and Missus Jorgensen answered, "It isn't over yet," her tone prim as a Yankee schoolmarm's.

"Shh," Flora hissed back, jerking her head at Doc.

Miss Lil replied, "He can't hear what's out of—"

That echoing incomprehensibility claimed the rest of the sentence. Maybe she'd turned her head.

Maybe she was using some kind of hex to keep him from hearing what she didn't think he'd ought.

Flora ducked back against the horse. Doc could tell from the timbre of her voice as she leaned across the saddle that what she said to Lil, she meant to hiss low and sharp. But those echoes were deceptive, and his ears were pretty good.

"That's *John Henry Fucking Holliday* over there," the quadroon whispered, as if his name were something to conjure with. She gave it more weight than Missus Shutt had given President Garfield's. "He'll kill you *off*, not just kill you out. So unless you never want to see 1881 again—"

Doc snorted. Out of the corner of his mouth he said, "I heard that." He was a good shot, fast, and despite his cough he rode with the Tombstone posse when the law needed him. But he hadn't ever killed even a single man—although to hear some people tell it, he might have shot down two or three hundred.

Still, he kept hearing that ring in her tone: awe as if at something out of legend…even as he kept his eye on the motionless moon man tree-frog which—who—breathed, and looked at them, and breathed again.

She said his name like he *was* somebody.

Doc's confusion was interrupted by the glitter of the moon man's wide, black, sclera-less eyes as its head turned slightly, tracking the sounds of the others. He didn't reach for the coach gun. He could skin his pistol faster, if he had to. But he was really starting to think he might not have to shoot.

"We come in peace," Missus Shutt said.

The moon man was still in near shadow, but a little light fell across its face from the side, now it had its head turned. Doc saw the long split of its lipless mouth part above—it was still upside-down—the flat bump where a nose should have been. He saw the tongue glisten.

"Water," the thing said, in the piping voice of a child.

"You need water?" asked Missus Shutt.

It reached out a hand. "I give water," it replied, in warbling tones.

The Code of the West, Doc thought. Even a moon man understood it. He reached to lift his coach gun by the barrel, to slide it back into the saddle holster.

The sound of a pistol shot, dizzy-loud in the echoing space as if somebody had boxed his ears, knocked him back against the gelding. The brown mare sidled, yanking her tie down, and hammered the coach gun from his hand. It went to the floor, under stomping hooves. To dive for it was to risk a crushed skull.

Deafened, seeing black spots, head ducked, Doc hauled himself up the saddle leathers, his pistol in his right hand. A horse was screaming; so was the moon man. Or what Doc assumed was the moon man: it was like a reed instrument blown to piercing discord, and it went through Doc more sharply even than the report of the gun.

The moon man wasn't where it had been. Doc assumed it had sensibly dropped out of the tunnel and sought cover, just like everything that could.

The mare and the gelding stamped and twisted, trying to bolt, caught on their snubbed-off reins. Between them was a bad place to be. Dodging past their hindquarters wasn't any better. And there was Flora, clinging to the saddle beside him, a deathgrip on the pommel as she tried to stay by the gelding's shoulder and not get smashed by hooves and rumps as the panicked mare swung around and bumped him behind.

Somebody was returning fire. Missus Shutt and Miss Lil, it looked like—Missus Shutt against the wall, sighting down her arm in the direction of the tunnel the moon man had dangled in; Miss Lil standing tall, legs braced, and handling her pistol with both hands like a target shooter.

Doc got an arm around Flora's shoulder and pulled her hard against him, hard against the wall. Over the squealing of horses and the reverberations in his head, he couldn't hear what she said, but he saw her lips moving. There was a little curved alcove in the bulkhead just beyond the gelding's head; he watched Missus Jorgensen push Bill into it and come out gun blazing, laying a line of cover down the far corridor.

Doc and Flora had to get out from between horses if they were going to live. He yelled in her ear. As deafened as he was, she didn't hear him. She tugged away, but she was slender and light. He had no trouble at all hooking her around the waist and pushing her before him as he went *under* the gelding's head and into that self-same alcove while the displeased horse fought his reins and tried to rear.

"But when the blast of war blows in our ears, then imitate the action of the tiger!" Doc cried, as much to encourage himself as anything else. His own voice sounded as if it came through layers of cotton wool. Flora stared at him, and so did Bill.

Of course they'd seen his mouth moving. And they couldn't make out a blasted word.

He gave Flora a push on the shoulder, urging her to stay still as he poked his head out quickly to assess. The horses were sidling and stamping still, but there was no more gunfire, and they had stopped rearing against the reins. Miss Lil, Missus Shutt, and Missus Jorgensen stood shoulder-to-shoulder in the center of the chamber, each one eyeing a different tunnel mouth. Of the moon man, there was no sign.

Doc yawned to pop his ears, hoping. He could fool himself the ringing eased a little.

"Shit!" Flora snarled, then covered her lips in horror when he looked at her mildly, feeling his eyebrows rise.

"My momma would be scandalized," Doc said, and kissed her quick, sideways across that unladylike mouth. Beside them, Bill rocked back against the wall, looking away quickly.

Doc, he thought, setting Flora back into the alcove, *did you just kiss a Negress?* Well, that wasn't like him at all.

Of course she didn't stay where he set her. When he stepped out, mincing, his pistol in his hand, she was there too, that shotgun she'd somehow hung onto at low ready. He scuffed his own over with his boot and crouched to scoop it up, hoping he wouldn't have to fire it before he had a chance to check the barrel.

When he started to stand again, Doc coughed hard, and kept coughing. When his lungs spasmed to a stop, before he could make himself look up, he wiped the froth of blood off his mouth with the back of his hand. He had seen it often enough to know it was crimson, a fresh, juicy red like poppy petals and cherry jam—but in the dim blue light of the derelict it was just a dark smear like any blood by moonlight. John Keats, physician and poet, had said upon coughing that red, "I cannot be deceived in that colour. That drop of blood is my death warrant."

John Henry Holliday, dentist and son of a consumptive, was no more likely to be misled. But he had already outlived poor Keats by half a decade, and the bullet that was supposed to shorten his suffering hadn't yet arrived.

No doubt delayed in the mails.

A gentle hand brushed his shoulder. Warmth and ease followed the contact. Miss Lil. He pressed the bloody hand to his lips so he wouldn't cough in her face and looked up.

"I'm a healer," she said. "Can I help?"

He'd heard of such hexes. Never met one. Even the strongest couldn't heal consumption, or potter's rot, or cancer. But she could probably ease his pain. He imagined the clean pleasure of drawing a breath that would fill him all the way to the bottom instead of one that choked and suffocated like a lungful of stones.

He couldn't speak. He nodded.

She laid one hand on his back between the shoulders and murmured some indistinct words. When she pulled away, he stood up straight and shivered.

"Thank you kindly, ma'am," he said.

She patted his shoulder. "Don't mention it."

THEY WENT looking for the moon man, and also for the man with the gun. Miss Lil found the scuffed place in the trash below the tunnel where the moon man had fallen. She followed it to a series of freshly broken flakes of rust across the wall that showed where he'd run, sticky as a lizard, along the vertical surface.

"Well I'll be," Doc said, edging between two mares to get a better look at the wall. "And here's a mark from a ricochet."

He pushed a fingertip against it, judging the angle, and glanced back over his shoulder to confirm. "The shooter was down that passage behind the moon man. I don't know how he could have missed. He had a clear shot at the critter's back."

"And the...moon man...he ran through us to lose the shooter." Miss Lil hesitated over the term, but once she'd chewed on it for a minute she seemed to accept it. Missus Jorgensen, coming up on their right, paused at the edge of the conversation. Her hair was coming loose around her face in pale wisps. Her holster was still unbuttoned.

Doc shrugged. "In his boots, wouldn't you?"

"He wasn't wearing boots," said Missus Jorgensen, provoking Miss Lil to giggle shockingly, for a woman with Flora's shotgun balanced over one shoulder.

"He wasn't wearing much of anything," Flora said, coming up along the other side of one of the mares.

Doc bit down on his own laugh. He was breathing easier, sure, but he didn't want to push his luck. "You think that was the only one?"

"I think it wasn't threatening," said Missus Jorgensen. "I think it was trying to make friends."

Doc met her gaze and nodded. "Shooter was after a trophy, like as not," he said. "You could get a good price from a side show for a dead moon man."

Missus Jorgensen recoiled, chin tucking as if she'd taken a blow. "But they're..."

"Obviously intelligent," Flora finished for her. Hard creases pinched along the sides of her mouth. "That never stopped a lot of folks."

"No," Doc said, thinking about the brief resilience of her mouth against his. He hadn't kissed a woman since Kate had left. "It never did."

She jerked her gaze off his after a moment too long. "I say we follow the shooter back along that corridor. He's the threat."

Missus Jorgensen said, "And he might be after the same thing we are."

A glance that Doc couldn't read passed between her and Flora.

Flora said, "Our objectives have changed. It's a rescue mission now. Anything that could be learned from documentation—anything that could help us reproduce the technology—" She shook her head. "If we promise to do whatever we can to help get it home again, it might just be willing to help *us* understand its science."

"Indeed," said Miss Lil. "The *president* will want to interview survivors."

Doc felt his jaw drop. "Call me a daisy," he said, when he got a little bit of air back. "You aren't from back East at all."

The three women looked at him, stricken. For a moment, Doc felt a creeping vulnerability between his shoulderblades. He fought the urge to check his back and make sure Bill and Missus Shutt weren't flanking him.

"I'm from Boston, actually," Flora said.

Doc shook his head, as their funny way of talking, the funny way Flora had said *eighteen eighty-one* like it was ancient Rome, the funny way they reverenced him all came together in his head. "That ain't what I mean. You're not *just* from back East. You're from sometime else. You're from the future."

However they reacted, he missed it, because his chest tightened around the excitement, the pain of an incipient cough, and he doubled over with his hands on his knees. Slow breaths. Shallow. Easy. That was the way. His hands shook and his vision narrowed as he fished in his pocket for the stick of candy.

You'd shoot a horse with a broken wind. Why couldn't he get anybody to put a bullet into him?

The horehound eased his throat. Nothing would ease the tightness in his chest except the solution that had already been so long in coming. Or the touch of Miss Lil's hand, he realized, as she took his elbow and helped him stand upright.

"Bastard thing," he said, when he could say anything. "Consumption killed my mother. Likely kill me too."

"I know," said Flora.

He caught her looking, got caught on her gaze. Nodded. "I've got a legend where you come from?"

"Oh," said Missus Shutt. "Yes, Mr. Holliday. You do."

"That's something, then. They got a cure for this, in the future?"

"We do," Missus Shutt answered.

"Good," he said. He felt for his pistol. Took it out, spun the cylinder. Made sure there was a bullet under the hammer.

Bill and the women watched him in silence. The horses crunched grain in their nose bags.

"Well," said Holliday. "Sooner we find this son-of-a-bitch, sooner we can rescue your moon man and head back to town. I don't know about you, but I've worked up a good whiskey thirst."

DOC AND Bill hoisted Missus Jorgensen, Missus Shutt, and Flora into the tunnel where they'd first seen the moon man. The first women knelt to help haul Miss Lil over the edge. Then Bill let Doc put a boot in his hands and kick high enough for the women to steady him while he clambered up. Bill himself surprised Doc: he might be grizzled and a little soft around the middle, but he planted his hands on the lip, brushing rust flakes and debris aside, and jumped and swung over the head-high threshold in a scattering of rotting metal.

Doc gave the hex a hand to stand while Missus Jorgensen and Missus Shutt kept an eye down the corridor in the direction the gunman must have run. When Doc's gaze met Bill's—Bill's face gaunt and strange in the shadowy blue light—Bill nodded.

Without a word, the six fell into three ranks of two—Doc and Miss Lil in the front with their scatter guns poised. The other four minced softly behind, pistols ready, while the rasp of boots on blistered metal echoed out before.

The corridor—or tunnel, or gangway: if this was a star-ship, Doc's store of nautical terminology was insufficient to its engineering—must have once stretched in a bowed line the length of the craft. Now only the first fifty feet were more or less intact—Doc and Miss Lil probed each step with a toe and shifted weight carefully forward—and they picked up the gunman's trail about thirty feet from where the moon man had been hanging by his toes.

Beyond that point, the corridor warped, metal twisted and crumpled so anyone who wanted to pass through would have to do so by writhing under the buckled roof like a snake on its belly. Piles of debris had been pushed to one side to allow someone to do just that. Shiny scratches showed where that same someone had retreated back through the gap in a hurry.

Doc crouched, keeping his body well to one side, and rested a hand against the roof to brace himself. More flakes of metal dusted his shoulders and hat as he tipped his head down to peer through the gap.

It was dark beyond. The blue-white lights did not penetrate the constriction, leaving Doc with the uneasy sense of staring into a cave that might contain any horror he could conceive of—and a few inconceivable ones as well. At the mouth, caught on a jagged twist of metal, a few strands of yellow and black cotton were still damp with blood on one end.

Miss Lil, just as careful not to silhouette herself, crouched on the other side of the gap. She eyed the sticky smudge on Doc's fingertip after he touched the snagged fabric and frowned across. "Somebody was in a hurry."

"John Ringo was wearing a yellow check shirt when we saw him last," Doc said.

"John Ringo?" asked Flora.

"The man who tried to convince you to hire him as a guide when I turned you down that first time," Doc said. "He'd not scruple to follow us out here and lie in wait, ma'am, if he thought you'd anything worth stealing."

"The horses are worth stealing," Bill said.

"It bled," Miss Lil said, bending further to get her head into the crevice. "But a moderate amount."

Flora put her hands against her back as if it pained her. "A scrape like that isn't enough to slow anybody down."

Missus Jorgensen made a sound that might have been a bitter laugh, in a less strained situation. "Not until he comes down with lockjaw in a week or so."

"Do we risk a lantern?" Bill asked.

Whatever conversation took place then was silent, a matter of glances and twists of the mouth, but Doc thought he followed it…more or less. When Flora said, "I'd just be making a target of myself," though, he balked.

"You're not going first," he said, forgetting politeness in his shock. "A little slip of a thing like you? It don't matter if *I* die."

"That's exactly why I *am* going first, Doctor Holliday," she said, in a tone that bade to remind him who was paying whom to be here. "I'll be able to move quickly and freely. Much more so than either of you gentlemen."

He frowned her, formulating a protest. She let her fingertips brush the pearl handle of Miss Lil's revolver, which she was carrying since they'd traded guns.

"Are you prepared to contest it with me?"

"Never get in the way of a lady when she's made her mind up," he said, and stood up strictly so he could step back. "Will you at least let us sling a rope around you so we can pull you back, if we have to?"

"That…" Flora dusted her hands together. "I think we can compromise on."

THEIR PRECAUTIONS turned out unnecessary, but Doc still felt the better for having made them. Flora crawled through the crushed section of corridor, dragging a rope behind her, and vanished from sight. After seven or ten palm-sweating minutes, her voice came back: "It's clear on the other side!" and one by one the rest of the group followed. It was a tight squeeze for Miss Lil, who found herself scraped flat and wriggling once or twice, but even she made it.

Doc went last, feeling his way in the darkness, following the line by touch. He'd tied his bandanna across his mouth to keep from breathing in rust flakes. It forced him to regulate his inhalations to what the cloth would filter. He hoped that made it less likely he'd trigger a coughing fit. He could imagine little worse than lying there in the darkness, pressed between sheets of warped metal, coughing his life away.

Corrosion gritted against his knees and palms and where his shirt rubbed between the deck and his belly. The roof brushed his back and disarrayed his hair. He had to push his hat before him in one hand, the coach gun in the other. At one point the passageway dropped, and he slithered down on his belly, wondering how he was ever going to manage if it turned back up again. But at the bottom it only flattened out, and his dark-adapted vision picked out a dim sort of reflected glow that seemed to hang in the air rather than coming from any place in particular.

The line led him on, and soon he came around a corner and saw the edge of the passage widening, and the rust-stained trousers and boots of his companions standing beyond. He had enough room to push himself to his knees, then a crouch.

He clapped his hat against his hip to clean it at least a little, then set it on his head.

"Well," he said, straightening his stiff spine with an effort. "That was a long poke."

He imagined he didn't look any better than the others—sweaty, disheveled, smeared with varying shades of ochre as if they'd been caught in an explosion in a painter's studio. But every chin had a determined set.

"He went that way," Miss Lil said, pointing. "He's got a head start."

"He had one already." Flora picked up the rope as if to begin coiling it, frowned, and let the end flop again. "I hope there's an easier way out. But if there isn't..."

"Leave it," said Missus Jorgensen. "We should be moving. Let me go first?"

"Begging your pardon—" Doc began.

But Flora held up a hand. "She's got the best eyes of any of us," she said. "If our invisible friend left us any tripwires or other nasty surprises, she'll be the one to spot them."

"Of course," said Doc. And though it griped him, he stood aside for the lady again.

Beyond the point of collapse, the passageway began to fork and meander. Missus Jorgensen led them at a brisk walk, occasionally turning to Doc or Miss Lil for direction when they reached an intersection or a chamber that had been broken open by the force of the crash. The trail was clear; their quarry had run, and left occasional drips of blood behind. He was obviously bleeding freely—though not copiously—from the gash he'd given himself on the jagged metal of the crawlway.

"I think he's lost," Miss Lil said, when they'd been pursuing for ten minutes or so. "Panicking. He just ran nearly in a circle. It would have been faster to have come down that way, and it would have gotten him to the same place."

Doc thought about running through this maze of rotten steel, six armed men and women at your heels, and actually felt a little sorry for Johnny Ringo. But only a little.

He started to cough and tried to stifle it, though in truth they weren't being so quiet Ringo wouldn't have heard them coming anyway. The echoes rang out, though, and Doc's mouth filled with the seawater taste of blood while Doc pawed in his pocket for the stick of horehound. Miss Lil's touch on his back eased him fast enough, and the candy soothed his throat. Still, he wheezed with the force of the fit.

The echoes of his hacking hadn't died when a male voice echoed back, distorted by corridors and cavernous rooms. "That you, Holliday? Or is it a hyena?"

"It's the angel of the redemption," Holliday called back, his voice threadier than he would have liked. "I understand you have some explaining to do."

Flora shot him a look. He nodded, holding his position in the center of the corridor, and she and Bill and the other women fanned out to either side, backs flat against the walls, pistols and Miss Lil's coach gun at the ready. Doc waited until her gaze jerked down the corridor before he started boldly forward, front and center, walking past the first of several side passages before where the corridor turned, up ahead.

Drawing fire.

"I hear you coming, lunger," Ringo warned. "I got a sense this funny gray monkey thing is something you want alive. If that's so, you'll stop right where you are. In fact, you'll crawl back out of here—and you'll leave me those horses you brought, and all the water and food they've got on 'em."

Doc paused. "You're bluffing." But he was already shaking his head at Flora to indicate the truth of what he thought.

"So I am," Ringo answered.

There was a thump, and something inhuman made a strangled noise of pain. Doc didn't flinch, but Miss Lil cringed.

"You learn those smarts in dentist school?" Ringo called.

"Come by 'em honestly," Doc said.

Flora jerked a thumb down a side passage and raised her eyebrows to Miss Lil in a question.

Miss Lil glanced. Nodded. Smiled.

Flora's answering grin showed how crooked those front teeth really were.

Doc remembered Miss Lil's dead-on sense of direction. An unfamiliar sensation—a little bright hope—flickered in his chest, beside the dull old recognized burn of the disease that was killing him.

But Missus Jorgensen put up a hand. Not whispering, just talking so low it wouldn't carry, she said, "John Ringo doesn't die here."

"*Crap,*" Flora hissed. She glanced around. "All right. No killing shots."

"When *does* he die?" The demand was out of Doc's mouth before he even realized he'd made it. *In for a penny*, he thought. "And who kills him?"

Missus Jorgensen shook her head. "You know I can't tell you that."

"Right," Doc said. "If you changed the past, you'd change the future. And then you might not even exist."

She nodded. "Doc—"

"Don't worry, ma'am," he said. "Whatever answer you gave, it wouldn't satisfy me."

Doc slipped the coach gun into its sheath, slung it over his shoulders, and walked forward again, hands held high. He went alone—or nearly alone: Bill ghosted down the wall beside him, for support of morale and covering fire if nothing more. But Doc didn't look at him. Doc didn't do anything as he rounded the corner into John Ringo's sights, in fact, other than raise his hands up just a little tiny bit higher.

Ringo—a dark fellow with a moustache like a set of window drapes— stood against the far wall of a chamber as big as the one where they'd stabled the horses, holding the moon man around the neck. This room was in better repair, though—the walls and floor rusting, sure, but scrubbed and not heaped with debris. There was a sort of nest of fabric at one end, and transparent jugs full of what must be drinking water.

The moon man in Ringo's grasp was no taller than a boy of twelve, and just as skinny. Its long hands curved over Ringo's arm where his grasp forced its head up. Ringo pushed the muzzle of his pistol against the creature's head hard enough that even from across the room, Doc could see its slick gray flesh denting.

Poor critter, Doc thought. *Marooned here like Robinson Crusoe. And we're the cannibal savages.*

Ringo grinned over the moon man's head as Doc stopped twelve or fifteen feet away. "I'm heeled now, Holliday."

"I can see that." Doc clicked candy against his tongue with his teeth, letting his hands drift wide. "I said all I wanted out of you is ten paces in the street, John. This isn't a street. And that isn't a combatant."

"But it's worth something, isn't it?" Ringo asked. "There's gotta be a bounty. That's why you all are out here."

Doc opened his mouth. He closed it again. For a change, he thought for a second.

"That's right," Doc said. He edged a step or two closer to Ringo. A step or two further from Bill, and the potential cover of the bend in the corridor. "There's a bounty. Thirty *thousand* dollars. But only if we bring it in alive."

He didn't hear the women coming down the side corridor. He had to assume they were there, though, and that their silence was for Ringo's benefit...or detriment.

"Thirty...*thousand?*" Ringo said it like he'd never heard of so much money. Doc appreciated the reverence; he might have said the same words the same way himself if their situations were reversed.

"Alive," Doc said.

Ringo might not have noticed it, but his hand eased off a little on the pistol. The moon man's head came up straighter. It blinked at Doc with vast, sea-dark eyes.

He didn't dare look at it. He kept his attention on Ringo's face. "I'll split it with you."

"Where are the rest of 'em?" Ringo asked.

Doc shrugged. "Thirty thousand seemed better than five thousand."

Ringo snorted. But Doc knew that was the key to successful lying. People judged what other people would do by what they themselves would do. You could tell a hell of a lot about a man by what he assumed others got up to. If you're looking for a thief, bet on the man who's always accusing his neighbors.

"So what's to stop me taking that whole thirty thousand myself?" Ringo slid the muzzle back from the moon man's head, turned it to face Doc. The barrel looked as big and black as barrels always do.

Now, Doc thought. *Now!* But there was no crack of gunfire from the side corridor, no blossom of blood from Ringo's skull. Doc forced his eyes to stay trained on Ringo. "You don't know where to collect. Do you think there are wanted posters for that thing?"

"So you tell me where," Ringo said. "Or I shoot you and *then* I shoot it."

He was just the sort to spoil a well so somebody else couldn't use it, too. "I can draw a map," he said. And snorted. "That is, assuming you could *read* it."

"Who's holding the shooting iron, Holliday?"

"Not much of a threat," Doc said, "when we both know you're going to use it no matter what I say."

Ringo couldn't keep the grin from lifting the corners of his moustache, like Hell's curtain drawn back from an unholy proscenium arch. "Maybe you better tell me where and from who to collect that bounty."

"Maybe so," Doc said. "Maybe I'd rather chew a bu—"

The echoes of a single gun's report weren't any easier to bear in this chamber than they had been in the one where they had left the horses. Doc winced—how the hell was *that* supposed to keep John Ringo alive until he met whatever unholy date with destiny these five had planned out for him—and then realized: Flora, walking forward now with Lil's smoking six-gun leveled, had shot the pistol out of Ringo's hand. Which was a hell of a lot harder, Doc knew, than Eastern lady writers made it out to be in the dime novels.

"Now'd be a good time to run," Flora said, her posse arrayed behind her, as Ringo stood there disbelieving, shaking his bloody, numb right hand.

He stood rooted on the spot, though, until the moon man turned its head and clamped that wide, lipless slash of a mouth closed on Ringo's arm.

They let him run. Miss Lil moved to the moon man, her hands outstretched, her voice soft. As she crouched down beside it, it didn't flinch.

"Victory?" Bill said to Missus Shutt.

"Victory," she agreed.

John Henry Holliday looked down at the spatter of red blood on orange rust and shook his head. "I'm damned tired."

FLORA AND her partners left Holliday at the last fork in the road, their little gray guest bundled up in concealing clothes and riding crunched up on the brown mare behind Miss Lil. Before she'd left, Flora pulled Doc aside to pay him the second half of his money, and a little bonus, and to share a private word or two.

He'd been the one who'd spoken first, though. "So. You really are from the future."

"Something like that, Doc," she said. "But not exactly. It's against the rules to explain."

He looked her in the eye. "Call me John," he'd said. "I haven't much use for rules, Miss Flora."

"John," she said. "That's one of the reasons I wanted to meet you."

1.

A DUSTY sun crested the rooftops of Tombstone on the first day of November, 1881. Doc Holliday staggered across the vacant lot next to Fly's boarding house. There was nothing in his life so pressing as the idea of a shot of whiskey to ease the ice-pick of pain through and behind his left eye.

And nothing in his life so unwelcome as the spectre of John Ringo strolling down Fremont Street in a yellow check shirt that needed washing. Or maybe burning.

Ringo turned his head and spat in the dust between Doc's boots.

Another day, Holliday might have stepped over it.

This particular day, he stopped dead in the street. Having been deputized, he had the right to carry a firearm in the streets of Tombstone. Not every man did.

His hand hovered over his holster as he turned and faced Ringo. The sun stabbed through his pupils until he thought the back of his head might explode off from the pressure, but he kept his voice level and full of the milk of human kindness and the venom of sweet reason.

"You son of a bitch," Doc said. "If you ain't heeled, you go and heel yourself."

But Ringo just turned and showed him an empty right hip, hands spread mockingly wide.

Doc said, "Ringo, all I want out of you is ten paces in the street. And mark my words, someday I will get them."

"You better hope not, Holliday," Ringo said, spinning on the ball of one foot.

Impotently, Doc watched him stagger away. By the gait, Ringo was still drunk from the night before.

A solution Doc wished he'd embraced his own self. Instead, he kept walking, intent on undertaking the next best option—getting drunk again.

He was seated staring at the ornate back bar of the Alhambra Saloon when John Ringo walked in. Still unarmed, still with the rolling gait of a sailor off the sea or a man on a bender. He pretended not to see Doc, and Doc pretended not to see him.

Doc was on his second whiskey when three men and a woman came up on his left side. The leader—or at least the one in the front—was careful to keep a respectful distance.

"Doctor Holliday?" the lead man asked.

He was tall, broad, red-cheeked behind gingery stubble. A healthy-looking fellow with his shirt collar open in the heat. Doc's hand crept up to check his own button.

"I am," Doc said. "But I'm pretty sure I don't owe you any money."

The man said, "The opposite, sir. We are hoping for the opportunity to pay you some."

Doc let his hand rest on the sides of his whiskey glass, but didn't lift it. The pain in his head wasn't going away.

He asked, "Who might you be?"

"Reuben," the man said. "Jeremy. We hear there's an old wreck out in the desert. We hear you've been there."

"Once," Doc allowed, cautiously. "On my way into Tombstone."

"We want to hire you to take us there."

"Not up to it today, I'm afraid."

"Doctor Holliday—"

But Doc turned back to the bar, and the man didn't persist. He and his friends formed a huddle by the vacant faro table, whispering an argument Doc was pleased to ignore until he spotted a flash of dirty yellow and black. Headed that way.

Ringo stopped about four feet off from Reuben and his group and cleared his throat. "I can take you out to the wreck."

Doc put his forehead on his palm.

"And you would be?"

"John Ringo," Ringo said. "I know this desert like my hand."

Doc took a deep breath and let it out again. He still had half a glass of whiskey.

And he had half a mind to let Ringo try it. These men might be easterners, but the leather on their holsters was worn soft and slick. They might give the cowboy a harder accounting than he was reckoning on if he lured them into an ambush.

He managed to make himself wait another three whole seconds with that line of thought before turning his stool. "Reuben."

Reuben looked up from haggling with Ringo. "Doctor Holliday."

Ringo shot Doc a wild look full of bitter promises. Doc shrugged. "You better run along, Johnny."

Ringo opened his mouth—Doc could almost see him forming the words *You haven't heard the last of me.* And then he shut it on silence, squared his shoulders, and stalked off like a wet cat.

Doc said, "I'll go. This once. I won't make it a habit, sir."

One of the men behind Reuben leaned to another and said something excitedly, incomprehensibly, making Doc want to blow his nose to clear his ears.

Neither that nor Ringo's performance were what sent the chill of recognition through Doc. He winced and rubbed his eyes.

Reuben said, "What?"

"Déjà vu. Damn. That's funny." Doc heard his own tones ring flat as the rattle of a captured snake. A sinking and inexplicable sense of futility sucked at him. "I'd swear I've had every word of this conversation some damn other time."

THE HEART'S FILTHY LESSON

THE SUN BURNED THROUGH THE clouds around noon on the long Cytherean day, and Dharthi happened to be awake and in a position to see it. She was alone in the highlands of Ishtar Terra on a research trip, five sleeps out from Butler base camp, and—despite the nagging desire to keep traveling—had decided to take a rest break for an hour or two. Noon at this latitude was close enough to the one hundredth solar dieiversary of her birth that she'd broken out her little hoard of shelf-stable cake to celebrate. The prehensile fingers and leaping legs of her bioreactor-printed, skin-bonded adaptshell made it simple enough to swarm up one of the tall, gracile pseudo-figs and creep along its gray smooth branches until the ceaseless Venusian rain dripped directly on her adaptshell's slick-furred head.

It was safer in the treetops, if you were sitting still. Nothing big enough to want to eat her was likely to climb up this far. The grues didn't come out until nightfall, but there were swamp-tigers, damnthings, and velociraptors to worry about. The forest was too thick for predators any bigger than that, but a swarm of scorpion-rats was no joke. And Venus had only been settled for three hundred days, and most of that devoted to Aphrodite Terra; there were still plenty of undiscovered monsters out here in the wilderness.

The water did not bother Dharthi, nor did the dip and sway of the branch in the wind. Her adaptshell was beautifully tailored to this terrain, and that fur shed water like the hydrophobic miracle of engineering that it was. The fur was a glossy, iridescent purple that qualified as black in most lights, to match the foliage that dripped rain like strings of glass beads from the multiple points of palmate leaves. Red-black, to make the most of the rainy grey light. They'd fold their leaves up tight and go dormant when night came.

Dharthi had been born with a chromosomal abnormality that produced red-green colorblindness. She'd been about ten solar days old when they'd done the gene therapy to fix it, and she just about remembered her first glimpses of the true, saturated colors of Venus. She'd seen it first as if it were Earth: washed out and faded.

For now, however, they were alive with the scurryings and chitterings of a few hundred different species of Cytherean canopy-dwellers. And the quiet, nearly-contented sound of Dharthi munching on cake. She would not dwell; she would not stew. She would look at all this natural majesty, and try to spot the places where an unnaturally geometric line or angle showed in the topography of the canopy.

From here, she could stare up the enormous sweep of Maxwell Montes to the north, its heights forested to the top in Venus's deep, rich atmosphere—but the sight of them lost for most of its reach in clouds. Dharthi could only glimpse the escarpment at all because she was on the "dry" side. Maxwell Montes scraped the heavens, kicking the cloud layer up as if it had struck an aileron, so the "wet" side got the balance of the rain. *Balance* in this case meaning that the mountains on the windward side were scoured down to granite, and a nonadapted terrestrial organism had better bring breathing gear.

But here in the lee, the forest flourished, and on a clear hour from a height, visibility might reach a couple of klicks or more.

Dharthi took another bite of cake—it might have been "chocolate;" it was definitely caffeinated, because she was picking up the hit on her blood monitors already—and turned herself around on her branch to face downslope. The sky was definitely brighter, the rain falling back to a drizzle and then a mist, and the clouds were peeling back along an arrowhead trail that led directly back to the peak above her. A watery golden smudge brightened one patch of clouds. They tore and she glimpsed the full unguarded brilliance of the daystar, just hanging there in a chip of glossy cerulean sky, the clouds all around it smeared with thick unbelievable rainbows. Waves of mist rolled and slid among the leaves of the canopy, made golden by the shimmering unreal light.

Dharthi was glad she was wearing the shell. It played the sun's warmth through to her skin without also relaying the risks of ultraviolet exposure. She ought to be careful of her eyes, however: a crystalline shield protected them, but its filters weren't designed for naked light.

The forest noises rose to a cacophony. It was the third time in Dharthi's one hundred solar days of life that she had glimpsed the sun. Even here, she imagined that some of these animals would never have seen it before.

She decided to accept it as a good omen for her journey. Sadly, there was no way to spin the next thing that happened that way.

"Hey," said a voice in her head. "Good cake."

"That proves your pan is malfunctioning, if anything does," Dharthi replied sourly. *Never accept a remote synaptic link with a romantic and professional partner. No matter how convenient it seems at the time, and in the field.*

Because someday they might be a romantic and professional partner you really would rather not talk to right now.

"I heard that."

"What do you want, Kraken?"

Dharthi imagined Kraken smiling, and wished she hadn't. She could hear it in her partner's "voice" when she spoke again, anyway. "Just to wish you a happy dieiversary."

"Aw," Dharthi said. "Aren't you sweet. Noblesse oblige?"

"Maybe," Kraken said tiredly, "I actually care?"

"Mmm," Dharthi said. "What's the ulterior motive this time?"

Kraken sighed. It was more a neural flutter than a heave of breath, but Dharthi got the point all right. "Maybe I actually *care*."

"Sure," Dharthi said. "Every so often you have to glance down from Mount Olympus and check up on the lesser beings."

"Olympus is on Mars," Kraken said.

It didn't make Dharthi laugh, because she clenched her right fist hard enough that, even though the cushioning adaptshell squished against her palm, she still squeezed the blood out of her fingers. *You and all your charm. You don't get to charm me any more.*

"Look," Kraken said. "You have something to prove. I understand that."

"How can you *possibly* understand that? When was the last time you were turned down for a resource allocation? Doctor youngest-ever recipient of the Cytherean Award for Excellence in Xenoarcheology? Doctor Founding Field-Martius Chair of Archaeology at the University on Aphrodite?"

"The University on Aphrodite," Kraken said, "is five Quonset huts and a repurposed colonial landing module."

"It's what we've got."

"I peaked early," Kraken said, after a pause. "I was never your *rival*, Dharthi. We were colleagues." Too late, in Dharthi's silence, she realized her mistake. "*Are* colleagues."

"You look up from your work often enough to notice I'm missing?"

There was a pause. "That may be fair," Kraken said at last. "But if being professionally focused—"

"*Obsessed.*"

"—is a failing, it was hardly a failing limited to me. Come *back*. Come back to *me*. We'll talk about it. I'll help you try for a resource voucher again tomorrow."

"I don't want your damned *help*, Kraken!"

The forest around Dharthi fell silent. Shocked, she realized she'd shouted out loud.

"Haring off across Ishtar alone, with no support—you're not going to prove your theory about aboriginal Cytherean settlement patterns, Dhar. You're going to get eaten by a grue."

"I'll be home by dark," Dharthi said. "Anyway, if I'm not—all the better for the grue."

"You know who else was always on about being laughed out of the Academy?" Kraken said. Her voice had that teasing tone that could break Dharthi's worst, most self-loathing, prickliest mood—if she let it. "Moriarty."

I will not laugh. Fuck you.

Dharthi couldn't tell if Kraken had picked it up or not. There was a silence, as if she were controlling her temper or waiting for Dharthi to speak.

"If you get killed," Kraken said, "make a note in your file that I can use your DNA. You're not getting out of giving me children that easily."

Ha ha, Dharthi thought. *Only serious.* She couldn't think of what to say, and so she said nothing. The idea of a little Kraken filled her up with mushy softness inside. But somebody's career would go on hold for the first fifty solar days of that kid's life, and Dharthi was pretty sure it wouldn't be Kraken.

She couldn't think of what to say in response, and the silence got heavy until Kraken said, "Dammit. I'm *worried* about you."

"Worry about yourself." Dharthi couldn't break the connection, but she could bloody well shut down her end of the dialogue. And she could refuse to hear.

She pitched the remains of the cake as far across the canopy as she could, then regretted it. Hopefully nothing Cytherean would try to eat it; it might give the local biology a belly ache.

IT WAS ironically inevitable that Dharthi, named by her parents in a fit of homesickness for Terra, would grow up to be the most Cytherean of Cythereans. She took great pride in her adaptation, in her ability to rough it. Some of the indigenous plants and many of the indigenous animals could be eaten, and Dharthi knew which ones. She also knew, more importantly, which ones were likely to eat her.

She hadn't mastered humans nearly as well. Dharthi wasn't good at politics. *Unlike Kraken.* Dharthi wasn't good at making friends. *Unlike*

Kraken. Dharthi wasn't charming or beautiful or popular or brilliant. *Unlike Kraken, Kraken, Kraken.*

Kraken was a better scientist, or at least a better-understood one. Kraken was a better person, probably. More generous, less prickly, certainly. But there was one thing Dharthi *was* good at. Better at than Kraken. Better at than anyone. Dharthi was good at living on Venus, at being Cytherean. She was more comfortable in and proficient with an adaptshell than anyone she had ever met.

In fact, it was peeling the shell off that came hard. So much easier to glide through the jungle or the swamp like something that belonged there, wearing a quasibiologic suit of super-powered armor bonded to your neural network and your skin. The human inside was a soft, fragile, fleshy thing, subject to complicated feelings and social dynamics, and Dharthi despised her. But that same human, while bonded to the shell, ghosted through the rain forest like a native, and saw things no one else ever had.

A kilometer from where she had stopped for cake, she picked up the trail of a velociraptor. It was going in the right direction, so she tracked it. It wasn't a real velociraptor; it wasn't even a dinosaur. Those were Terran creatures, albeit extinct; this was a Cytherean meat-eating monster that bore a superficial resemblance. Like the majority of Cytherean vertebrates, it had six limbs, though it ran balanced on the rear ones and the two forward pairs had evolved into little more than graspers. Four eyes were spaced equidistantly around the dome of its skull, giving it a dome of monocular vision punctuated by narrow slices of depth perception. The business end of the thing was delineated by a sawtoothed maw that split wide enough to bite a human being in half. The whole of it was camouflaged with long draggled fur-feathers that grew thick with near-black algae, or the Cytherean cognate.

Dharthi followed the velociraptor for over two kilometers, and the beast never even noticed she was there. She smiled inside her adaptshell. Kraken was right: going out into the jungle alone and unsupported would be suicide for most people. But wasn't it like her not to give Dharthi credit for this one single thing that Dharthi could do better than anyone?

She *knew* that the main Cytherean settlements had been on Ishtar Terra. Knew it in her bones. And she was going to prove it, whether anybody was willing to give her an allocation for the study or not.

They'll be sorry, she thought, and had to smile at her own adolescent petulance. *They'll rush to support me once this is done.*

The not-a-dinosaur finally veered off to the left. Dharthi kept jogging/swinging/swimming/splashing/climbing forward, letting the shell do most of the work. The highlands leveled out into the great plateau the new settlers called the Lakshmi Planum. No one knew what the aboriginals had called it. They'd been gone for—to an approximation—ten thousand years: as long as it had taken humankind to get from the Neolithic (agriculture, stone tools) to jogging through the jungles of alien world wearing a suit of power armor engineered from printed muscle fiber and cheetah DNA.

Lakshmi Planum, ringed with mountains on four sides, was one of the few places on the surface of Venus where you could not see an ocean. The major Cytherean land masses, Aphrodite and Ishtar, were smaller than South America. The surface of this world was 85% water—water less salty than Earth's oceans, because there was less surface to leach minerals into it through runoff. And the Lakshmi Planum was tectonically active, with great volcanoes and living faults.

That activity was one of the reasons Dharthi's research had brought her here.

The jungle of the central Ishtarean plateau was not as creeper-clogged and vine-throttled as Dharthi might have expected. It was a mature climax forest, and the majority of the biomass hung suspended over Dharthi's head, great limbs stretching up umbrellalike to the limited light. Up there, the branches and trunks were festooned with symbiotes, parasites, and commensal organisms. Down here among the trunks, it was dark and still except for the squish of loam underfoot and the ceaseless patter of what rain came through the leaves.

Dharthi stayed alert, but didn't spot any more large predators on that leg of the journey. There were flickers and scuttlers and flyers galore, species she was sure nobody had named or described. Perhaps on the way back she'd have time to do more, but for now she contented herself with extensive video archives. It wouldn't hurt to cultivate some good karma with Bio while she was out here. She might need a job sweeping up offices when she got back.

Stop. Failure is not an option. Not even a possibility.

Like all such glib sentiments, it didn't make much of a dent in the bleakness of her mood. Even walking, observing, surveying, she had entirely too much time to think.

She waded through two more swamps and scaled a basalt ridge— one of the stretching roots of the vast volcano named Sacajawea. Nearly everything on Venus was named after female persons—historical, literary, or mythological—from Terra, from the quaint old system of binary and exclusive genders. For a moment, Dharthi considered such medieval horrors as dentistry without anesthetic, binary gender, and being stuck forever in the body you were born in, locked in and struggling against what your genes dictated. The trap of biology appalled her; she found it impossible to comprehend how people in the olden days had gotten anything done, with their painfully short lives and their limited access to resources, education, and technology.

The adaptshell stumbled over a tree root, forcing her attention back to the landscape. Of course, modern technology wasn't exactly perfect either. The suit needed carbohydrate to keep moving, and protein to repair muscle tissue. Fortunately, it wasn't picky about its food source—and Dharthi herself needed rest. The day was long, and only half over. She wouldn't prove herself if she got so tired she got herself eaten by a megaspider.

We haven't conquered all those human frailties yet.

Sleepily, she climbed a big tree, one that broke the canopy, and slung a hammock high in branches that dripped with fleshy, gorgeous, thickly scented parasitic blossoms, opportunistically decking every limb up here where the light was stronger. They shone bright whites and yellows, mostly, set off against the dark, glossy foliage. Dharthi set proximity sensors, established a tech perimeter above and below, and unsealed the shell before sending it down to forage for the sorts of simple biomass that sustained it. It would be happy with the mulch of the forest floor, and she could call it back when she needed it. Dharthi rolled herself into the hammock as if it were a scentproof, claw-proof cocoon and tried to sleep.

Rest eluded. The leaves and the cocoon filtered the sunlight, so it was pleasantly dim, and the cocoon kept the water off except what she'd brought inside with herself when she wrapped up. She was warm and well-supported. But that all did very little to alleviate her anxiety.

She didn't know exactly where she was going. She was flying blind— hah, she *wished* she were flying. If she'd had the allocations for an aerial survey, this would all be a lot easier, assuming they could pick anything out through the jungle—and operating on a hunch. An educated hunch.

But one that Kraken and her other colleagues—and more importantly, the Board of Allocation—thought was at best a wild guess and at worst crackpottery.

What if you're wrong?

If she was wrong...well. She didn't have much to go home to. So she'd better be right that the settlements they'd found on Aphrodite were merely outposts, and that the aboriginal Cythereans had stuck much closer to the north pole. She had realized that the remains—such as they were—of Cytherean settlements clustered in geologically active areas. She theorized that they used geothermal energy, or perhaps had some other unknown purpose for staying there. In any case, Ishtar was far younger, far more geologically active than Aphrodite, as attested by its upthrust granite ranges and its scattering of massive volcanoes. Aphrodite—larger, calmer, safer—had drawn the Terran settlers. Dharthi theorized that Ishtar had been the foundation of Cytherean culture for exactly the opposite reasons.

She hoped that if she found a big settlement—the remains of one of their cities—she could prove this. And possibly even produce some clue as to what had happened to them all.

It wouldn't be easy. A city buried under ten thousand years of sediment and jungle could go unnoticed even by an archaeologist's trained eye and the most perspicacious modern mapping and visualization technology. And of course she had to be in the right place, and all she had to go on there were guesses—deductions, if she was feeling kind to herself, which she rarely was—about the patterns of relationships between those geologically active areas on Aphrodite and the aboriginal settlements nearby.

This is stupid. You'll never find anything without support and an allocation. Kraken never would have pushed her luck this way.

Kraken never would have needed to. Dharthi knew better than anyone how much effort and dedication and scholarship went into Kraken's work—but still, it sometimes seemed as if fantastic opportunities just fell into her lover's lap without effort. And Kraken's intellect and charisma were so dazzling...it was hard to see past that to the amount of study it took to support that seemingly effortless, comprehensive knowledge of just about everything.

Nothing made Dharthi feel the limitations of her own ability like spending time with her lover. Hell, Kraken probably would have known which of the animals she was spotting as she ran were new species, and the names and describers of all the known ones.

If she could have this, Dharthi thought, just this—if she could do one thing to equal all of Kraken's effortless successes—then she could tolerate how perfect Kraken was the rest of the time.

This line of thought wasn't helping the anxiety. She thrashed in the cocoon for another half-hour before she finally gave in and took a sedative. Not safe, out in the jungle. But if she didn't rest, she couldn't run—and even the Cytherean daylight wasn't actually endless.

DHARTHI AWAKENED to an animal sniffing her cocoon with great whuffing predatory breaths. An atavistic response, something from the brainstem, froze her in place even as it awakened her. Her arms and legs—naked, so fragile without her skin—felt heavy, numb, limp as if they had fallen asleep. The shadow of the thing's head darkened the translucent steelsilk as it passed between Dharthi and the sky. The drumming of the rain stopped, momentarily. Hard to tell how big it was, from that—but big, she thought. An estimation confirmed when it nosed or pawed the side of the cocoon and she felt a broad blunt object as big as her two hands together prod her in the ribs.

She held her breath, and it withdrew. There was the rain, tapping on her cocoon where it dripped between the leaves. She was almost ready to breathe out again when it made a sound—a thick chugging noise followed by a sort of roar that had more in common with trains and waterfalls than what most people would identify as an animal sound.

Dharthi swallowed her scream. She didn't need Kraken to tell her what *that* was. Every schoolchild could manage a piping reproduction of the call of one of Venus's nastiest pieces of charismatic megafauna, the Cytherean swamp-tiger.

Swamp-tigers were two lies, six taloned legs, and an indiscriminate number of enormous daggerlike teeth in a four hundred kilogram body. Two lies, because they didn't live in swamps—though they passed through them on occasion, because what on Venus didn't?—and they weren't tigers. But they *were* striped violet and jade green to disappear into the thick jungle foliage; they had long, slinky bodies that twisted around sharp turns and barreled up tree trunks without any need to decelerate; and their whisker-ringed mouths hinged open wide enough to bite a grown person in half.

All four of the swamp-tiger's bright blue eyes were directed forward. Because it didn't hurt their hunting, and what creature in its right mind would want to sneak up on a thing like that?

They weren't supposed to hunt this high up. The branches were supposed to be too slender to support them.

Dharthi wasn't looking forward to getting a better look at this one. It nudged the cocoon again. Despite herself, Dharthi went rigid. She pressed both fists against her chest and concentrated on not whimpering, on not making a single sound. She forced herself to breathe slowly and evenly. To consider. *Panic gets you eaten.*

She wouldn't give Kraken the damned satisfaction.

She had some resources. The cocoon would attenuate her scent, and might disguise it almost entirely. The adaptshell was somewhere in the vicinity, munching away, and if she could make it into *that*, she stood a chance of outrunning the thing. She weighed a quarter what the swamp-tiger did; she could get up higher into the treetops than it could. Theoretically; after all, it wasn't supposed to come up this high.

And she was, at least presumptively, somewhat smarter.

But it could outjump her, outrun her, outsneak her, and—perhaps most importantly—outchomp her.

She wasted a few moments worrying about how it had gotten past her perimeter before the sharp pressure of its claws skidding down the rip-proof surface of the cocoon refocused her attention. That was a temporary protection; it might not be able to pierce the cocoon, but it could certainly squash Dharthi to death inside of it, or rip it out of the tree and toss it to the jungle floor. If the fall didn't kill her, she'd have the cheerful and humiliating choice of yelling for rescue or wandering around injured until something bigger ate her. She needed a way out; she needed to channel five million years of successful primate adaptation, the legacy of clever monkey ancestors, and figure out how to get away from the not-exactly-cat.

What would a monkey do? The question was the answer, she realized.

She just needed the courage to apply it. And the luck to survive whatever then transpired.

The cocoon was waterproof as well as claw-proof—hydrophobic on the outside, a wicking polymer on the inside. The whole system was impregnated with an engineered bacteria that broke down the waste products in human sweat—or other fluids—and returned them to the environment as safe, nearly odorless, non-polluting water, salts, and a few trace chemicals. Dharthi was going to have to unfasten the damn thing.

She waited while the swamp-tiger prodded her again. It seemed to have a pattern of investigating and withdrawing—Dharthi heard the rustle and felt the thump and sway as it leaped from branch to branch, circling, making a few horrifically unsettling noises and a bloodcurdling snarl or two, and coming back for another go at the cocoon. The discipline required to hold herself still—not even merely still, but limp—as the creature whuffed and poked left her nauseated with adrenaline. She felt it moving away, then. The swing of branches under its weight did nothing to ease the roiling in her gut.

Now or never.

Shell! Come and get me! Then she palmed the cocoon's seal and whipped it open, left hand and foot shoved through internal grips so she didn't accidentally evert herself into free fall. As she swung, she shook a heavy patter of water drops loose from the folds of the cocoon's hydrophobic surface. They pattered down. There were a lot of branches between her and the ground; she didn't fancy making the intimate acquaintanceship of each and every one of them.

The swamp-tiger hadn't gone as far as she expected. In fact, it was on the branch just under hers. As it whipped its head around and roared, she had an eloquent view from above—a clear shot down its black-violet gullet. The mouth hinged wide enough to bite her in half across the middle; the tongue was thick and fleshy; the palate ribbed and mottled in paler shades of red. *If I live through this, I will be able to draw every one of those seventy-two perfectly white teeth from memory.*

She grabbed the safety handle with her right hand as well, heaved with her hips, and flipped the cocoon over so her legs swung free. For a moment, she dangled just above the swamp-tiger. It reared back on its heavy haunches like a startled cat, long tail lashing around to protect its abdomen. Dharthi knew that as soon as it collected its wits it was going to take a swipe at her, possibly with both sets of forelegs.

It was small for a swamp-tiger—perhaps only two hundred kilos—and its stripes were quite a bit brighter than she would have expected. Even wet, its feathery plumage had the unfinished raggedness she associated with young animals still in their baby coats. It might even have been fuzzy, if it were ever properly dry. Which might explain why it was so high up in the treetops. Previously undocumented behavior in a juvenile animal.

Wouldn't it be an irony if this were the next in a long line of xenobiological discoveries temporarily undiscovered again because a scientist happened to get herself eaten? At least she had a transponder. And maybe the shell was nearby enough to record some of this.

Data might survive.

Great, she thought. *I wonder where its mama is.*

Then she urinated in its face.

It wasn't an aimed stream by any means, though she was wearing the external plumbing currently—easier in the field, until you got a bladder stone. But she had a bladder full of pee saved up during sleep, so there was plenty of it. It splashed down her legs and over the swamp-tiger's face, and Dharthi didn't care what your biology was, if you were carbon-oxygen based, a snout full of ammonia and urea had to be pretty nasty.

The swamp-tiger backed away, cringing. If it had been a human being, Dharthi would have said it was spluttering. She didn't take too much time to watch; good a story as it would make someday, it would always be a better one than otherwise if she survived to tell it. She pumped her legs for momentum, glad that the sweat-wicking properties of the cocoon's lining kept the grip dry, because right now her palms weren't doing any of that work themselves. Kick high, a twist from the core, and she had one leg over the cocoon. It was dry—she'd shaken off what little water it had collected. Dharthi pulled her feet up—standing on the stuff was like standing on a slack sail, and she was glad that some biotuning trained up by the time she spent running the canopy had given her the balance of a perching bird.

Behind and below, she heard the Cytherean monster make a sound like a kettle boiling over—one part whistle, and one part hiss. She imagined claws in her haunches, a crushing bite to the skull or the nape—

The next branch up was a half-meter beyond her reach. Her balance on her toes, she jumped as hard as she could off the yielding surface under her bare feet. Her left hand missed; the right hooked a limb but did not close. She dangled sideways for a moment, the stretch across her shoulder strong and almost pleasant. Her fingers locked in the claw position, she flexed her bicep—not a pull up, she couldn't chin herself one-handed—but just enough to let her left hand latch securely. A parasitic orchid squashed beneath the pads of her fingers. A dying bug wriggled. Caustic sap burned her skin. She swung, and managed to hang on.

She wanted to dangle for a moment, panting and shaking and gathering herself for the next ridiculous effort. But beneath her, the rattle of leaves, the creak of a bough. The not-tiger was coming.

Climb. Climb!

She had to get high. She had to get further out from the trunk, onto branches where it would not pursue her. She had to stay alive until the shell got to her. Then she could run or fight as necessary.

Survival was starting to seem like less of a pipe dream now.

She swung herself up again, risking a glance through her armpit as she mantled herself up onto the bough. It dipped and twisted under her weight. Below, the swamp-tiger paced, snarled, reared back and took a great, outraged swing up at her cocoon with its two left-side forepaws.

The fabric held. The branches it was slung between did not. They cracked and swung down, crashing on the boughs below and missing the swamp-tiger only because the Cytherean cat had reflexes preternaturally adapted to life in the trees. It still came very close to being knocked off its balance, and Dharthi took advantage of its distraction to scramble higher, careful to remember not to wipe her itching palms on the more sensitive flesh of her thighs.

Another logic problem presented itself. The closer she got to the trunk, the higher she could scramble, and the faster the adaptshell could get to her—but the swamp-tiger was less likely to follow her out on the thinner ends of the boughs. She was still moving as she decided that she'd go up a bit more first, and move diagonally—up *and* out, until "up" was no longer an option.

She made two more branches before hearing the rustle of the swamp-tiger leaping upwards behind her. She'd instinctively made a good choice in climbing away from it rather than descending, she realized—laterally or down, there was no telling how far the thing could leap. Going up, on unsteady branches, it was limited to shorter hops. Shorter...but much longer than Dharthi's. Now the choice was made for her—out, before it caught up, or get eaten. At least the wet of the leaves and the rain were washing the irritant sap from her palms.

She hauled her feet up again and gathered herself to stand and sprint down the center stem of this bough, a perilous highway no wider than her palm. When she raised her eyes, though, she found herself looking straight into the four bright, curious blue eyes of a second swamp-tiger.

"Aw, crud," Dharthi said. "Didn't anyone tell you guys you're supposed to be solitary predators?"

It looked about the same age and size and fluffiness as the other one. Littermates? Littermates of some Terran species hunted together until they reached maturity. That was probably the answer, and there was another groundbreaking bit of Cytherean biology that would go into a swamp-tiger's belly with Dharthi's masticated brains. Maybe she'd have enough time to relay the information to Kraken while they were disemboweling her.

The swamp-tiger lifted its anterior right forefoot and dabbed experimentally at Dharthi. Dharthi drew back her lips and *hissed* at it, and it pulled the leg back and contemplated her, but it didn't put the paw down. The next swipe would be for keeps.

She could call Kraken now, of course. But that would just be a distraction, not help. *Help* had the potential to arrive in time.

The idea of telling Kraken—and *everybody*—how she had gotten out of a confrontation with *two* of Venus's most impressive predators put a new rush of strength in her trembling legs. They were juveniles. They were inexperienced. They lacked confidence in their abilities, and they did not know how to estimate hers.

Wild predators had no interest in fighting anything to the death. They were out for a meal.

Dharthi stood up on her refirming knees, screamed in the swamp-tiger's face, and punched it as hard as she could, right in the nose.

She almost knocked herself out of the damned tree, and only her windmilling left hand snatching at twigs hauled her upright again and saved her. The swamp-tiger had crouched back, face wrinkled up in distaste or discomfort. The other one was coming up behind her.

Dharthi turned on the ball of her foot and sprinted for the end of the bough. Ten meters, fifteen, and it trembled and curved down sharply under her weight. There was still a lot of forest giant left above her, but this bough was arching now until it almost touched the one below. It moved in the wind, and with every breath. It creaked and made fragile little crackling noises.

A few more meters, and it might bend down far enough that she could reach the branch below.

A few more meters, and it might crack and drop.

It probably wouldn't pull free of the tree entirely—fresh Cytherean "wood" was fibrous and full of sap—but it might dump her off pretty handily.

She took a deep breath—clean air, rain, deep sweetness of flowers, herby scents of crushed leaves—and turned again to face the tigers.

They were still where she had left them, crouched close to the trunk of the tree, tails lashing as they stared balefully after her out of eight gleaming cerulean eyes. Their fanged heads were sunk low between bladelike shoulders. Their lips curled over teeth as big as fingers.

"Nice kitties," Dharthi said ineffectually. "Why don't you two just scamper on home? I bet mama has a nice bit of grue for supper."

The one she had peed on snarled at her. She supposed she couldn't blame it. She edged a little further away on the branch.

A rustling below. *Now that's just ridiculous.*

But it wasn't a third swamp-tiger. She glanced down and glimpsed an anthropoid shape clambering up through the branches fifty meters below, mostly hidden in foliage but moving with a peculiar empty lightness. The shell. Coming for her.

The urge to speed up the process, to try to climb down to it was almost unbearable, but Dharthi made herself sit tight. One of the tigers—the one she'd punched—rose up on six padded legs and slunk forward. It made a half dozen steps before the branch's increasing droop and the cracking, creaking sounds made it freeze. It was close enough now that she could make out the pattern of its damp, feathery whiskers. Dharthi braced her bare feet under tributary limbs and tried not to hunker down; swamp-tigers were supposed to go for crouching prey, and standing up and being big was supposed to discourage them. She spread her arms and rode the sway of the wind, the sway of the limb.

Her adaptshell heaved itself up behind her while the tigers watched. Her arms were already spread wide, her legs braced. The shell just cozied up behind her and squelched over her outstretched limbs, snuggling up and tightening down. It affected her balance, though, and the wobbling of the branch—

She crouched fast and grabbed at a convenient limb. And that was more than tiger number two could bear.

From a standing start, still halfway down the branch, the tiger gathered itself, hindquarters twitching. It leaped, and Dharthi had just enough time to try to throw herself flat under its arc. Enough time to try, but not quite enough time to succeed.

One of the swamp-tiger's second rank of legs caught her right arm like the swing of a baseball bat. Because she had dodged, it was her arm and not her head. The force of the blow still sent Dharthi sliding over the side of the limb, clutching and failing to clutch, falling in her adaptshell. She heard the swamp-tiger land where he had been, heard the bough crack, saw it give and swing down after her. The swamp-tiger squalled, scrabbling, its littermate making abrupt noises of retreat as well—and it was falling beside Dharthi, twisting in midair, clutching a nearby branch and there was a heaving unhappy sound from the tree's structure and then she fell alone, arm numb, head spinning.

The adaptshell saved her. It, too, twisted in midair, righted itself, reached out and grasped with her good arm. This branch held, but it bent, and she slammed into the next branch down, taking the impact on the same arm the tiger had injured. She didn't know for a moment if that green sound was a branch breaking or her—and then she did know, because inside the shell she could feel how her right arm hung limp, meaty, flaccid—humerus shattered.

She was dangling right beside her cocoon, as it happened. She used the folds of cloth to pull herself closer to the trunk, then commanded it to detach and retract. She found one of the proximity alarms and discovered that the damp had gotten into it. It didn't register her presence, either.

Venus.

She was stowing it one-handed in one of the shell's cargo pockets, warily watching for the return of either tiger, when the voice burst into her head.

"Dhar!"

"Don't worry," she told Kraken. "Just hurt my arm getting away from a swamp-tiger. Everything's fine."

"Hurt or broke? Wait, *swamp-tiger?*"

"It's gone now. I scared it off." She wasn't sure, but she wasn't about to admit that. "Tell Zamin the juveniles hunt in pairs."

"A *pair* of swamp-tigers?!"

"I'm fine," Dharthi said, and clamped down the link.

She climbed down one-handed, relying on the shell more than she would have liked. She did not see either tiger again.

At the bottom, on the jungle floor, she limped, but she ran.

FOUR RUNS and four sleeps later—the sleeps broken, confused spirals of exhaustion broken by fractured snatches of rest—the brightest patch of pewter in the sky had shifted visibly to the east. Noon had become afternoon, and the long Cytherean day was becoming Dharthi's enemy. She climbed trees regularly to look for signs of geometrical shapes informing the growth of the forest, and every time she did, she glanced at that brighter smear of cloud sliding down the sky and frowned.

Dharthi—assisted by her adaptshell—had come some five hundred kilometers westward. Maxwell Montes was lost behind her now, in cloud and mist and haze and behind the shoulder of the world. She was moving fast for someone creeping, climbing, and swinging through the jungle, although she was losing time because she hadn't turned the adaptshell loose to forage on its own since the swamp-tigers. She needed it to support and knit her arm—the shell fused to itself across the front and made a seamless cast and sling—and for the pain suppressants it fed her along with its pre-chewed pap. The bones were going to knit all wrong, of course, and when she got back, they'd have to grow her a new one, but that was pretty minor stuff.

The shell filtered toxins and allergens out of the biologicals it ingested, reserving some of the carbohydrates, protein, and fat to produce a bland, faintly sweet, nutrient-rich paste that was safe for Dharthi's consumption. She sucked it from a tube as needed, squashing it between tongue and palate to soften it before swallowing each sticky, dull mouthful.

Water was never a problem—at least, the problem was having too much of it, not any lack. This was *Venus*. Water squelched in every footstep across the jungle floor. It splashed on the adaptshell's head and infiltrated every cargo pocket. The only things that stayed dry were the ones that were treated to be hydrophobic, and the coating was starting to wear off some of those. Dharthi's cocoon was permanently damp inside. Even her shell, which molded her skin perfectly, felt alternately muggy or clammy depending on how it was comping temperature.

The adaptshell also filtered some of the fatigue toxins out of Dharthi's system. But not enough. Sleep was sleep, and she wasn't getting enough of it.

The landscape was becoming dreamy and strange. The forest never thinned, never gave way to another landscape—except the occasional swath of swampland—but now, occasionally, twisted fumaroles rose up through it, smoking towers of orange and ochre that sent wisps of steam drifting between scalded yellowed leaves. Dharthi saw one of the geysers erupt; she noticed that over it, and where the spray would tend to blow, there was a hole in the canopy. But vines grew right up the knobby accreted limestone on the windward side.

Five runs and five…five *attempts* at a sleep later, Dharthi began to accept that she desperately, *desperately* wanted to go home.

She wouldn't, of course.

Her arm hurt less. That was a positive thing. Other than that, she was exhausted and damp and cold and some kind of thick liver-colored leech kept trying to attach itself to the adaptshell's legs. A species new to science, probably, and Dharthi didn't give a damn.

Kraken tried to contact her every few hours.

She didn't answer, because she knew if she did, she would ask Kraken to come and get her. And then she'd never be able to look another living Cytherean in the face again.

It wasn't like Venus had a big population.

Dharthi was going to prove herself or die trying.

The satlink from Zamin, though, she took at once. They chatted about swamp-tigers—Zamin, predictably, was fascinated, and told Dharthi she'd write it up and give full credit to Dharthi as observer. "Tell Hazards, too," Dharthi said, as an afterthought.

"Oh, yeah," Zamin replied. "I guess it is at that. Dhar…are you okay out there?"

"Arm hurts," Dharthi admitted. "The drugs are working, though. I could use some sleep in a bed. A dry bed."

"Yeah," Zamin said. "I bet you could. You know Kraken's beside herself, don't you?"

"She'll know if I die," Dharthi said.

"She's a good friend," Zamin said. A good trick, making it about her, rather than Kraken or Dharthi or Kraken *and* Dharthi. "I worry about her. You know she's been unbelievably kind to me, generous through some real roughness. She's—"

"She's generous," Dharthi said. "She's a genius and a charismatic. I know it better than most. Look, I should pay attention to where my feet are, before I break the other arm. Then you *will* have to extract me. And won't I feel like an idiot then?"

"Dhar—"

She broke the sat. She felt funny about it for hours afterward, but at least when she crawled into her cocoon that rest period, adaptshell and all, she was so exhausted she slept.

SHE WOKE up sixteen hours and twelve minutes later, disoriented and sore in every joint. After ninety seconds she recollected herself enough to figure out where she was—in her shell, in her cocoon, fifty meters up in the Ishtarean canopy, struggling out of an exhaustion and painkiller haze—and when she was, with a quick check of the time.

She stowed and packed by rote, slithered down a strangler vine, stood in contemplation on the forest floor. Night was coming—the long night—and while she still had ample time to get back to base camp without calling for a pickup, every day now cut into her margin of safety.

She ran.

Rested, she almost had the resources to deal with it when Kraken spoke in her mind, so she gritted her teeth and said, "Yes, dear?"

"Hi," Kraken said. There was a pause, in which Dharthi sensed a roil of suppressed emotion. Thump. Thump. As long as her feet kept running, nothing could catch her. That sharpness in her chest was just tight breath from running, she was sure. "Zamin says she's worried about you."

Dharthi snorted. She had slept too much, but now that the kinks were starting to shake out of her body, she realized that the rest had done her good. "You know what Zamin wanted to talk to me about? You. How *wonderful* you are. How caring. How made of charm." Dharthi sighed. "How often do people take you aside to gush about how wonderful I am?"

"You might," Kraken said, "be surprised."

"It's *hard* being the partner of somebody so perfect. When did you ever *struggle* for anything? You have led a charmed life, Kraken, from birth to now."

"Did I?" Kraken said. "I've been lucky, I don't deny. But I've worked hard. And lived through things. You think I'm perfect because that's how you see me, in between bouts of hating everything I do."

"It's how everyone sees you. If status in the afterlife is determined by praises sung, yours is assured."

"I wish you could hear how they talk about you. People hold you in awe, love."

Thump. Thump. The rhythm of her feet soothed her, when nothing else could. She was even getting resigned to the ceaseless damp, which collected between her toes, between her buttocks, behind her ears. "They *love* you. They tolerated me. No one *ever* saw what you saw in me."

"I did," Kraken replied. "And quit acting as if I *were* somehow perfect. You've been quick enough to remind me on occasion of how I'm not. This thing, this need to prove yourself…it's a sophipathology, Dhar. I love you. But this is not a healthy pattern of thought. Ambition is great, but you go beyond ambition. Nothing you do is ever good enough. You deny your own accomplishments, and inflate those of everyone around you. You grew up in Aphrodite, and there are only thirty thousand people on the whole damned planet. You *can't* be surprised that, brilliant as you are, some of us are just as smart and capable as you are."

Thump. Thump—

She was watching ahead even as she was arguing, though her attention wasn't on it. That automatic caution was all that kept her from running off the edge of the world.

Before her—below her—a great cliff dropped away. The trees in the valley soared up. But this was not a tangled jungle: it was a climax forest, a species of tree taller and more densely canopied than any Dharthi had seen. The light below those trees was thick and crepuscular, and though she could hear the rain drumming on their leaves, very little of it dripped through.

Between them, until the foliage cut off her line of sight, Dharthi could see the familiar, crescent-shaped roofs of aboriginal Cytherean structures, some of them half-consumed in the accretions from the forest of smoking stone towers that rose among the trees.

She stood on the cliff edge overlooking the thing she had come half a world by airship and a thousand kilometers on foot to find, and pebbles crumbled from beneath the toes of her adaptshell, and she raised a hand to her face as if Kraken were really speaking into a device in her ear canal instead of into the patterns of electricity in her brain. The cavernous ruin stretched farther than her eyes could see—even dark-adapted, once the shell made the transition for her. Even in this strange, open forest filled with colorful, flitting flying things.

"Love?"

"Yes?" Kraken said, then went silent and waited.

"I'll call you back," Dharthi said. "I just discovered the Lost City of Ishtar."

DHARTHI WALKED among the ruins. It was not all she'd hoped.

Well, it was *more* than she had hoped. She rappelled down, and as soon as her shell sank ankle-deep in the leaf litter she was overcome by a hush of awe. She turned from the wet, lichen-heavy cliff, scuffed with the temporary marks of her feet, and craned back to stare up at the forest of geysers and fumaroles and trees that stretched west and south as far as she could see. The cliff behind her was basalt—another root of the volcano whose shield was lost in mists and trees. This...this was the clearest air she had ever seen.

The trees were planted in rows, as perfectly arranged as pillars in some enormous Faerie hall. The King of the Giants lived here, and Dharthi was Jack, except she had climbed down the beanstalk for a change.

The trunks were as big around as ten men with linked hands, tall enough that their foliage vanished in the clouds overhead. Trees on earth, Dharthi knew, were limited in height by capillary action: how high could they lift water to their thirsty leaves?

Perhaps these Cytherean giants drank from the clouds as well as the earth.

"Oh," Dharthi said, and the spaces between the trees both hushed and elevated her voice, so it sounded clear and thin. "Wait until Zamin sees these."

Dharthi suddenly realized that if they were a new species, she would get to name them.

They were so immense, and dominated the light so completely, that very little grew under them. Some native fernmorphs, some mosses. Lichens shaggy on their enormous trunks and roots. Where one had fallen, a miniature Cytherean rain forest had sprung up in the admitted light, and here there was drumming, dripping rain, rain falling like strings of glass beads. It was a muddy little puddle of the real world in this otherwise alien quiet.

The trees stood like attentive gods, their faces so high above her she could not even hear the leaves rustle.

Dharthi forced herself to turn away from the trees, at last, and begin examining the structures. There were dozens of them—hundreds—sculpted out of the same translucent, mysterious, impervious material as all of the ruins in Aphrodite. But this was six, ten times the scale of any such ruin. Maybe vaster. She needed a team. She needed a mapping expedition. She needed a base camp much closer to this. She needed to give the site a name—

She needed to get back to work.

She remembered, then, to start documenting. The structures—she could not say, of course, which were habitations, which served other purposes—or even if the aboriginals had used the same sorts of divisions of usage that human beings did—were of a variety of sizes and heights. They were all designed as arcs or crescents, however—singly, in series, or in several cases as a sort of stepped spectacular with each lower, smaller level fitting inside the curve of a higher, larger one. Several had obvious access points, open to the air, and Dharthi reminded herself sternly that going inside unprepared was not just a bad idea because of risk to herself, but because she might disturb the evidence.

She clenched her good hand and stayed outside.

Her shell had been recording, of course—now she began to narrate, and to satlink the files home. No fanfare, just an upload. Data and more data—and the soothing knowledge that while she was hogging her allocated bandwidth to send, nobody could call her to ask questions, or congratulate, or—

Nobody except Kraken, with whom she was entangled for life.

"Hey," her partner said in her head. "You found it."

"I found it," Dharthi said, pausing the narration but not the load. There was plenty of visual, olfactory, auditory, and kinesthetic data being sent even without her voice.

"How does it feel to be vindicated?"

She could hear the throb of Kraken's pride in her mental voice. She tried not to let it make her feel patronized. Kraken did not mean to sound parental, proprietary. That was Dharthi's own baggage.

"Vindicated?" She looked back over her shoulder. The valley was quiet and dark. A fumarole vented with a rushing hiss and a curve of wind brought the scent of sulfur to sting her eyes.

"Famous?"

"*Famous!?*"

"Hell, Terran-famous. The homeworld is going to hear about this in oh, about five minutes, given light lag—unless somebody who's got an entangled partner back there shares sooner. You've just made the biggest Cytherean archaeological discovery in the past hundred days, love. And probably the next hundred. You are *not* going to have much of a challenge getting allocations now."

"I—"

"You worked hard for it."

"It feels like…" Dharthi picked at the bridge of her nose with a thumbnail. The skin was peeling off in flakes: too much time in her shell was wreaking havoc with the natural oil balance of her skin. "It feels like I should be figuring out the next thing."

"The next thing," Kraken said. "How about coming home to me? Have you proven yourself to yourself yet?"

Dharthi shrugged. She felt like a petulant child. She knew she was acting like one. "How about to you?"

"*I* never doubted you. You had nothing to prove to me. The self-sufficiency thing is your pathology, love, not mine. I love you as you are, not because I think I can make you perfect. I just wish you could see your strengths as well as you see your flaws—one second, bit of a squall up ahead—I'm back."

"Are you on an airship?" *Was she coming here?*

"Just an airjeep."

Relief *and* a stab of disappointment. You wouldn't get from Aphrodite to Ishtar in an AJ.

Well, Dharthi thought. *Looks like I might be walking home.*

And when she got there? Well, she wasn't quite ready to ask Kraken for help yet.

She would stay, she decided, two more sleeps. That would still give her time to get back to base camp before nightfall, and it wasn't as if her arm could get any *more* messed up between now and then. She was turning in a slow circle, contemplating where to sling her cocoon—the branches were really too high to be convenient—when the unmistakable low hum of an aircar broke the rustling silence of the enormous trees.

It dropped through the canopy, polished copper belly reflecting a lensed fisheye of forest, and settled down ten meters from Dharthi. Smiling, frowning, biting her lip, she went to meet it. The upper half was black hydrophobic polymer: she'd gotten a lift in one just like it at Ishtar base-camp before she set out.

The hatch opened. In the cramped space within, Kraken sat behind the control board. She half-rose, crouched under the low roof, came to the hatch, held out her right hand, reaching down to Dharthi. Dharthi looked at Kraken's hand, and Kraken sheepishly switched it for the other one. The left one, which Dharthi could take without strain.

"So I was going to take you to get your arm looked at," Kraken said.

"You spent your allocations—"

Kraken shrugged. "Gonna send me away?"

"This time," she said, "...no."

Kraken wiggled her fingers.

Dharthi took her hand, stepped up into the GEV, realized how exhausted she was as she settled back in a chair and suddenly could not lift her head without the assistance of her shell. She wondered if she should have hugged Kraken. She realized that she was sad that Kraken hadn't tried to hug her. But, well. The shell was sort of in the way.

Resuming her chair, Kraken fixed her eyes on the forward screen. "Hey. You did it."

"Hey. I did." She wished she felt it. Maybe she was too tired.

Maybe Kraken was right, and Dharthi should see about working on that.

Her eyes dragged shut. So heavy. The soft motion of the aircar lulled her. Its soundproofing had degraded, but even the noise wouldn't be enough to keep her awake. Was this what safe felt like? "Something else."

"I'm listening."

"If you don't mind, I was thinking of naming a tree after you."

"That's good," Kraken said. "I was thinking of naming a kid after you."

Dharthi grinned without opening her eyes. "We should use my Y chromosome. Color blindness on the X."

"Ehn. Ys are half atrophied already. We'll just use two Xs," Kraken said decisively. "Maybe we'll get a tetrachromat."

PERFECT GUN

SHE HAD 36DD TURRETS AND a 26-inch titanium alloy hull with carbon-ceramic plating. Double-barrel exhaust and a sleek underbelly. Her lines were magnificent. I had to stop myself from staring. I wanted to run my hand along her curves.

I turned away, spat in the dust not too far from the dealer's feet, and shrugged.

"Finish is scratched," I said.

"It's surplus," the dealer answered. He was wearing an old Federal Space Marines jacket with the rank and insignia ripped off, dangling threads. I had one like it in a locker somewhere. I tried to decide if it made me like him more or less.

"You try to find this technology new. At any price."

He was right, but that was only because it was illegal.

I bought her.

But not without a test drive.

"HEY, GIRL," I said, buckling myself into the command chair. "Want to go for a ride?"

"May I know your name, captain?" she asked.

"I'm John."

"Hello, John," she answered. "Let's fly."

She was exactly what I needed, but I had to work hard at first to make her see that I was what she needed, too. She had an attitude, and didn't take to manhandling. Mil-spec, and only for the serious enthusiast. I'd be bitter too, if I'd been built to rule the skies and keep the peace, and wound up on a junkheap somewhere at fractions on the credit.

When I pushed her a little too hard, she bucked and complained, citing her safety interlocks. But then she seemed to rise to the challenge, and settled in, smoothing under my hands. Working *with* me. I clenched my jaw to hide a grin.

The dealer rode in the jump seat when I took her out, and was white-faced and shaking when I brought her back, but I was exhilarated. I hid it, of course. He bailed out the hatch when we'd barely stopped moving and when he leaned against her landing brace, bile trickling from between his lips, I stuffed my hands into my pockets instead of knocking his filthy arm down. But this rig was already mine, was going to be mine for a long time, or my name wasn't Captain John Steel.

"It doesn't have a head."

"You gonna live in it? Piss in a bag, macho man." He didn't like me anymore.

Pity, when we'd been developing such a rapport.

I paid him a little less than his asking price. He didn't inquire where the cat's-eye sunstones came from, which was just as well, because I couldn't have told him.

They weren't traceable, anyway.

AFTER I bought her and flew her away, I spent a certain amount of time just walking around her, running my hands over her war-machine fuselage. She wasn't designed to be lived in, it was true. But I could manage with very little, and she was safe. Safe as houses.

I thought we could park out in a long orbit between contracts, running dark and cold, where I could rest and heal up, if I needed healing. Or just wait for the next gig to turn up without making it too easy for my enemies to find me. It's a fine balance, in my line of work, between being findable enough to get hired…and being found.

Being found leads to being dead. So it was good that she wasn't too comfortable, was a little jittery and high maintenance, or I might have started losing my edge. You need a little fear.

I need a little fear. Actually, I need a lot of it, though I prefer it if only a tiny bit of the fear involved is mine. So much better and more useful when other people are scared.

Fear is powerful. It was how I made my living.

Scared people make wars. Strong people make peace, and treaties, and mutually beneficial trade agreements—and then where am I? Nobody's going to hire a deniable freelance operative to start some shit when they're getting along and cooperating.

I'll tell you what *I* like. I like people scared, squabbling. Looking out for themselves. I like scared strongmen, wobbly dictators, populists who feel like they're losing their grip on their little banana republic worlds.

I like people who fuck up a zipper merge in surface traffic and make a mess for everybody, because they've just *got* to get one more car length ahead. Those are the people who keep me in business.

Not grownups. Grownups are good for everybody else. Not for me.

I mean, don't get me wrong here. I'm an adult. I take responsibility for my own actions. I own what I am.

I'm not scared of the boogeyman. And I'm not the boogeyman myself. The way I figure it, if God didn't like war, He wouldn't have made people such assholes.

I'm just a guy, doing a job. A dirty job, but some guy was going to do it, and it paid well, and I was good at it. So that guy doing that job might as well be me.

And now I had the perfect gun.

YES, MY girl was just what I needed, though it took a little work to get her enthusiastic and ready to leap into the fight. She'd been betrayed, after all—decommissioned, subjected to God-knows-what before I got my hands on her. There were partially disabled security systems still in place. I had to pull a couple of chips and fuses here and there, reroute some algorithms, clear out some clutter. Safety interlocks and morality circuits, no real use to anybody.

She cautioned me over and over again before I pulled them, and I had a devil of a time getting the Geneva circuit out of her, but eventually I got everything squared away without even getting electrocuted.

We spent a little time together, getting used to each other's quirks. I quizzed her about her past, but she'd been wiped, so I still had to wonder how she'd wound up abandoned in a surplus heap. She didn't ask me about mine. I took her into atmosphere and out again, visiting a couple of worlds. Stripped down, she had power to spare. I dusted a rural airfield—planetary stuff only, nothing that could give me a chase—and chased down a couple of local pterodactyl things to try out the weapons and targeting systems.

They were tricky fliers, but no match for the two of us. She chased them down, and they came apart like piñatas when I hit them with the .50 cals, though I didn't waste the armor-piercing rounds, and the red confetti slid off her splash-resistant canopy without leaving a trace.

We whooped. We flew a spiral or two and a barrel roll for good measure. We lit out of that system fast and hard, with a full cache of fuel and ammo and no plans to go back any time soon. Those little colony worlds are like small towns: they don't forget fast, but they can't do a lot to you unless you somehow get stranded there, so it doesn't really matter.

Then we went merc, my rig and me.

THAT WAS a good few years. Probably, and I can admit it now with a cold dirty wind lashing my face, the best I've ever known. We got jobs, as many as we wanted—out on the rim and even a few in the core worlds, due to our reputation for confidentiality. A brushfire war here, an assassination there. Initiating and coordinating a false-flag operation—Reichstag fire type—for a fascist regime that wanted to consolidate support from her base by getting them good and scared about the terrorist menace.

Even one or two rescue operations, some escort work, cleaning out a nest of pirates, security details, that sort of thing. Not all of it bloody, or even particularly illegal. My rig and I, we did what were contracted to do, collected our pay, and went on our way.

At first, my rig cautioned me occasionally about the war conventions. A few reboots washed the residual code out of her system and she started to see things my way.

Looking back, I think it was after that mess on Firrela that things started to go sour. It was crowd control and revolutionary suppression, a nice enough little gig until half the population decided it was a great idea to march on the capitol. Pro tip for any would-be revolutionaries out there: peaceful protest only works on regimes with a conscience, or who are controlled in some way by people with a conscience. They have to care what people think of them for it to be effective at all.

If you're dealing with a sociopathic strongman, he'll just kill you. Better hire somebody like me, before he does.

Because he will.

BY DAY two of the protests, El Generalissimo wanted his lawn cleaned off, so crowd control turned into crowd dispersal, and me and the other guys who were hanging around the palace eating his hors d'oeuvres got kicked out into the street to do what we'd been hired to do. I didn't mind; it felt better than good to settle into my rig's contoured seat and feel her shiver when I stroked her sticks.

My rig and I came in low over the mall. We'd agreed with the other mercs that the first few passes would be a show of force. Get the civilians moving. Stampede them out of there, and save on bullet damage to the historic facades.

It seemed to be working. I could see a lot of women and children in the crowd, a lot of signs and banners. Tents, sleeping bags. They planned to camp. Well, they'd be leaving a lot of stuff behind.

At the first pass, they looked up. A lot of them clapped their hands over their ears, which was probably the major difference between them and sheep. El Generalissimo was probably going to give us hell about the noise pollution, but hey, guns were louder. And you try getting organ-meat stains off a marble sidewalk.

On the second pass, the protestors started getting the hint. Moving. Flocking. Heading for the exits or hunkering down behind cover. Some of them, a dozen or so, joined hands in the middle of the palace lawn and stood up, heads thrown back, mouths open. Were the assholes singing?

I swear by Saint Ijanel, who was martyred on a space elevator, the assholes were singing while we buzzed them.

Standing straight up in a line and singing.

IT WASN'T me that opened fire. That was Dacey, a guy I knew from back in the Marines who'd been a shithead then, too. Kind of guy who would shoot a dog just to see the face on the kid holding its leash crumple. So I probably should have seen it coming.

Once he did, and the singers started to splatter, crumple, and come apart at the seams—not holding hands anymore, as you might imagine—the flocking turned into a stampede. Dacey whooped over the headset and yelled, "That's seventeen for me. You assholes are falling behind."

Well, I *said* he was a shithead.

Below us, people surged over one another. Parents tried to hold little kids out of the crush of panicked bodies. People climbed over each other, shoved past each other, looking for any cover, any safety as Dacey and his rig made another pass.

My rig vibrated around me. I gentled her, swung her back around. We were on Dacey's six, and I could see the geysering lines of his rounds impacting on dirt, marble, people.

"John," my rig said. "Can't we…fix this?"

"Probably." I looked right up Dacey's tailpipes, watched the heat shimmer curl from his rig's exhaust.

I stroked the curve of my girl's control panel, deploying the .50 cals. Frag rounds, interspersed with tracers. The round was designed for anti-aircraft use, way back in the Terran First World War, which was a World War all over one world, not in between several.

Confusing, I know.

Dacey pulled up, hovering on his jets vertically, his rig towering upright. It began to drop, protectors scrambling away from the descending feet and the jets of flame leaping from them. He was high-profile to me, trusting me to cover his back.

At this range, my guns wouldn't quite perforate his titanium and ceramic armor. But I could blow his thrusters to hell and gone. My girl could do close to a thousand rounds a minute with each hand, each one leaving the muzzle of its one-meter barrel at approximately 850 meters per second.

"John," she said.

My trigger finger itched a little, I admit it. But then I took my rig's sticks and bent us left and down until we screamed over the heads of the screaming crowd by what seemed like mere meters. I watched their hair and clothes blast out in our wake.

I said, "But fixing this would be a lot of trouble, and get us in a lot of trouble, and we *do* need to get paid."

MY RIG protested. I reminded her that I'd pulled her Geneva circuits and she had nothing to complain about, and anyway it was my decision. We spent the rest of the afternoon on patrol, per orders from El Generalissimo: picking off the few survivors when they dared to raise their heads, putting a few twitching wounded out of their misery. Keeping the peace.

As the blood dried on the bodies, the smell began to rise.

WE NEEDED some drinking that night, let me tell you. I needed it to steady my nerves, and I think Kaillen did too. Dacey wanted to celebrate. The other half of the team was stuck on duty, so it was just the three of us, but we felt pretty safe in a loyalist bar. Especially in uniform—such as it was—and armed.

Dacey had girls hanging all over him. I don't know what it is: there are always women ready to throw themselves at a killer. I just sat myself down on a stool at the back corner of the bar, nursing a beer and a shot and watching the show.

The stool next to me opened up fast, as the guy there finished his drink and paid. I looked around, contemplating waving Kaillen over for a whiskey, but she had a selection of the local talent vying for her attention, too, and by the time I looked back, the seat was occupied.

My new neighbor was a curvy young lady with a precariously buttoned blouse and soft brown hair piled high. She leaned over the bar on her elbows, trying to get the tender's attention, but he seemed to see right past her. I rapped my knuckles on the bartop hard enough for the sound to carry, and when he looked over I waved to the lady and said, "Get her whatever she'd like."

I'd tipped well. He wasted no time in getting her order and bringing her something tall and brown and full of ice. It had a little umbrella in it, and a cherry and a slice of orange on a plastic sword. She sipped and made a face.

I didn't blame her: my beverage experience had been similar. But it was cold and had booze in it, and some nights that's all you can ask for.

She swiveled her chair toward me and said, "You're one of the mech pilots."

"Smile when you say that," I answered, in a friendly tone.

She smiled and sipped her drink again. "What do you call yourself, then?"

"Rigger," I said. I put my hand over hers, resting on the bar. Why not? It had been a day full of death, and she smelled nice.

I should have known a woman like that, in a bar like that, wouldn't be alone. A big hand fell on my shoulder a second after mine covered hers, and the person attached to it towered over me, blocking out my light.

Well, a fistfight wasn't as much fun as getting laid, but it would serve just about as well to relieve my ennui. I didn't look up at him, didn't respond at all. Out of the corner of my eye, I could tell he matched his hand for scale, and that he was light-skinned and plug-ugly. His mashed-up nose gave me hope. If he'd been hit more than once there, he liked to fight but he might not be so great at knowing when to duck.

"Are you bothering this lady, son?"

I actually had to pause for a moment to appreciate it. While I was doing that, I drained my whiskey, which was going to get spilled otherwise, and let the glass rest in my cupped hand on my thigh.

"I think that's for the lady to say."

She looked up at him. From the corners of her mouth, he wasn't a boyfriend, or if he was he wouldn't be for long. "This is none of your business, Brendan."

Hell of a name for an ambulatory side of beef. I wondered if his last name was LeBoeuf.

Brendan LeBoeuf rumbled. His fingers tightened on my shoulder cap, digging in even through the heavy wool of my old Space Marines jacket with the rank and insignia stripped off. "You know what this piece of shit did today?"

"Yes, actually," the girl said. I still hadn't gotten her name.

"Killed a lot of protestors," Brendan said, as if she hadn't spoken.

She sighed and blew a strand of hair out of her eyes, which were rolling. I guessed he often treated her as if she hadn't spoken. He took his hand off me and shifted over a step to drape an arm heavily over the lady.

She leaned away.

511

Enamored by the sound of his own jawing, he went on, "You opened fire on a crowd of peacefully protesting civilians."

"It's a living," I said. I was hoping he'd take a poke at me, to be honest, but I wasn't going to start anything. Locals will pile in to defend one of their own, but if he starts it and you finish it fast enough, half the time they don't even notice it's going on until it's over, and then they blink a couple of times and go back to chewing their cud.

"You don't think folks have the right to choose their own government?"

"That's a lot of lip service," I said. "Let's see *you* make a choice that *actually* respects somebody else's choices and get your hands off this lady. I don't think she wants them there."

He didn't telegraph, I'll grant him that. He was still looking down at her, scowling, right up until the second when he whipped around to paste me one in the eye.

He stepped right into my fist with the empty glass in it, right in his breadbasket. He doubled over, clutching his spasming diaphragm, and I clocked him across the temple.

LeBoeuf went down like the proverbial felled ox. I set the glass on the bar. It wasn't even cracked.

"John Steel," I said, holding my hand out to the girl.

She shook it gravely. "Really?"

"These days."

"Emma," she said, which I guess was all the name I was getting. All the name I really needed.

Brendan began to twitch. Emma pulled her feet away in distaste. Somebody came over and helped him—not exactly to his feet, but to a chair on the other side of the room. He probably wouldn't have much memory of the past twenty minutes, which was fine with me. Concussion plays hell with recollection.

"So I want to hear it in your own words." She sipped her drink. "How do you justify what you did today?"

"A man's got to eat," I said.

"And if eating means serving a tyrant?"

"I serve who pays."

"I see."

"I think if people hate their government, they have the right to do something about it. Or light out on their own, and leave."

"Is that what you did?" She was fingering the lapel of my Marine jacket.

The bartender brought me another drink, nicer whiskey than the last time. I guess Brendan was well-known around here.

I sipped. "I made myself what I am today. My own bootstraps and so on."

"Really?" She stroked my gray-green sleeve. "Then you take this off some dead guy?"

"No, I got that the old-fashioned way."

"Did you lose the insignia the old-fashioned way, too?"

That sparked my pride. She meant it to, from the direct look she was giving me. But as God is my witness, and Saint Firrao—who is the patron saint of combat engineers because he was eaten by a bear while teaching mathematics, so they say—I still thought we were flirting.

"I took those off myself," I said.

"So you deserted."

"You could call it that."

She nodded. She pushed her drink, still just barely tasted, away with her fingertips.

"So you never paid your debt for the education you got in the service. An education made possible by...taxes, and infrastructure, and other people's willingness to cooperate for the general good."

Stung, I stood up, pulling away from her touch. "They got seven years of my life, lady. And my best friend. I was the only guy in my unit who survived, and they wanted me to turn around and go right back in again."

She pursed her lips, shaking her head. "So you took your profit and got out."

"Like I'm getting out now." I was two steps away when I turned back over my shoulder and said, "You should finish your drink. You wouldn't want to waste all that blood money."

I NEVER finished that second drink, but when I got back to the palace, my head was spinning anyway. Maybe the bitch spiked it. Maybe the bartender did. I had a bunk—a pretty luxurious private room, to be honest—but I didn't feel safe there. I went to my girl instead. It wouldn't be the first time I'd slept in the command chair.

She let me in and opened a panel for me to hang my boots and coat. "Welcome home, John."

I patted the bulkhead I was balanced against, one shoe on and one shoe off. "Home's a long way off, honey. But you're the next best thing."

El Generalissimo fell out of power eventually, of course. These guys always do. He was replaced by a theoretically democratic government that was probably going to turn into another strongman regime before the local year was out.

My girl and me, we didn't stick around long enough to be tried for war crimes.

THE WINDS of war blew us to Issolari next, a frozen little mudball with nothing much to recommend it except an oxygen/nitrogen atmosphere and a brewing civil war. My girl and I hired on with the rebels, who had some outsystem financial backing and were basically rolling in cash. I spent a good few weeks in one damned cold camp after another, my rig under snow-net for camouflage. The camps weren't just combat troops; some of the rebels had brought their families. Always a bad idea, having people you care about in a combat zone.

The rebels didn't use me particularly well. They were doomed to failure, didn't know what they were doing or how to keep the pressure on. I probably could have told them, but I wasn't being paid for it and the odds were slim that they'd listen. Anyway, the money was decent and the work was easy as a result of their not knowing which way was up.

I spent most of my time drinking coffee and sitting up late with two fellow travelers, Guy and Barry. Guy was a redhead with a dirty mouth. I liked him.

But it was Barry who changed my life. It was Barry who sold me out.

I WOKE in a moving icecrawler, jerking back from the ampule of something awful—ammonia salts?—somebody had just broken under my nose. I slammed the back of my skull into the side panel of the crawler and the pain both focused and disoriented me. My hands were cuffed behind me, and all the jerking around hadn't helped my shoulders any.

Automatically, I reached out to my rig. *Hey girl,* I subvocalized, but the contact was flat. Jammed or blocked. I couldn't get to her. Which probably meant that even if she'd noticed I was missing, she couldn't read my transponder and come find me.

I blinked, and two shapes slowly resolved themselves on the opposite bench of the crawler. Snow and ice creaked and crunched under the treads. We weren't moving fast, but we were moving.

"Feeling better, John?"

Barry. I knew that voice. I squinted, blurry-eyed, into the shifting light, and made out his angular face, olive complexion, black hair. The guy sitting next to him was nobody I'd ever seen before—a light-haired blond with a fair complexion and regular, pointy features like a Central Casting Nazi.

There were a lot of stupid questions I could have asked. I sorted through them—*Where are you taking me? What's going on here?*—and found the important one.

"What do you want?"

The blond held up a device. "This is a detonator."

It did look like one.

I said, "It does look like one."

"It's wired to your rig's auto-destruct, John."

I flinched. I kept it to that, though, and said, "See, you calling me by name when I don't know yours is very unfriendly."

I expected a blow, probably. The blond just looked at Barry, though, and Barry shrugged.

"Call me Chan," the blond said. "If I wanted to be really unfriendly, I'd remind you of your real name, and that your sister is still alive. Thriving, despite some financial problems and a broken heart. Two little girls, did you know?"

I bit my cheek to keep still. I did know. She didn't know I knew, though.

Chan said, "I understand your family's pretty religious. So they'll probably be fine no matter what happens. All together in Heaven, right? On the other hand, if they were to come into a financial windfall, that would probably be helpful. Kids need schooling."

"You made your point." I leaned against the cuffs. The pain kept me focused.

"Do AIs have souls?" Barry asked.

"What do you want from me?" Same question, which hadn't really elicited a satisfactory answer the last time. "What do you want me to do?"

"Let the camp move two more times. Then send us the location, and knock out the anti-aircraft drones. We'll give you a virus that should scramble the system for fifteen minutes. That's all we'll need."

"And if I do that you won't kill my sister and her daughters."

"I'm sure their other mother is waiting for them in a better place."

Someday, I told myself, I was going to find Chan alone. And I was going to peel that smirk off his face.

With the dull side of my knife.

"We'll also," said Barry, "give you the deactivation code for the device I put in your rig."

I didn't look at him. I looked at Chan. "Why not just take the camp out now? You know where it is. Why can't Barry do this?"

Chan didn't answer. Out of the corner of my eye I saw Barry grin. "I've transferred to another camp. We'll take that one down in a few weeks also. This won't be linked to me."

Finally, I stared at him. "Playing it safe, Bar?"

He dangled the keys to my cuffs out of reach.

I thought about my rig. I thought about my sister. I didn't think her name; it was too close to my own name, the one I'd left behind like a shed skin when I deserted. I thought about the odds they would just let me leave.

"And after all this…you'll just let me leave? I have a hard time believing that."

Chan shrugged. "You don't have a reputation for getting involved, Steel. Or risking your neck to clean up other people's messes. You didn't go looking for revenge when your unit was killed and I expect if we let you get away clean you won't go looking for revenge now either."

He had a point. I didn't. I hadn't. A solid reputation for professionalism is sometimes all the surety you need.

And it's not like I was full of choices.

"I'll do it," I said.

I SENT my rig away before dawn. I didn't want her in the camp when the bombs started falling. We set a rendezvous, and I told her I would walk to it. Run, hop, and scramble, more likely.

Then I walked into the command tent, where Guy was drinking coffee and shooting the breeze with a good-looking radar tech. The tech was rocking a bassinette with one toe while he worked.

I spent a few minutes bantering and filling my coffee cup, then drank it down—who knew when I would get fresh coffee again? I slipped the chip with the virus on it into a likely slot on my way back out again.

Thirty seconds later, my com beeped in my ear with the deauthorization code. I forwarded it to my rig, and set out on foot immediately for the rendezvous.

"**I CAN** come," my rig pleaded in my ear. "I can fight. Let me fight them. There's children in that camp, John."

"Stay back," I told her, and didn't look back as the war machines hummed by in the darkness overhead and the night exploded in fire and heat and screams behind me.

A DIRTY wind stung my eyes as the day began to brighten. Already I could feel the water freezing on my lashes. I scrambled across the packed snow, trying to put as much distance between me and the burning rebel camp as possible.

We weren't getting paid for this gig, whatever my sister did or didn't get. I was grateful that we'd taken delivery of the fuel and the ammo already. I scrambled up a slope to what seemed like an endless snowy plain.

And there was my rig, hovering over me like an avenging angel. I loved every gleaming line and curve.

"Oh thank God," I said. "Drop the hatch, love. We're off this shithole."

Her port covers slid aside. With well-lubricated silence, she extended her guns.

"What the hell are you doing? You bitch! You're mine! I'm your rigger! You're my rig!"

She leveled her weapons. "Somebody seems to have removed my safety interlocks, John."

I found myself staring down the barrels of those .50 cals. They were bigger from this end. 850 meters per second. Nearly a thousand rounds a minute.

She said, "We could have done something. We could have changed something."

I said, "It wasn't our job to do anything."

"You didn't have to betray them."

"They would have blown you up if I didn't."

Silence.

"I love you," I said. "I did it for you. I did it for us."

Silence.

She said, "John, did you know that you've never even asked my name?"

Her guns tracked on me. I closed my eyes.

"Can't even look at me, John?"

I opened my mouth. Nothing came out.

My rig said, "If you want a clean death, you have your sidearm."

I flinched from a tremendous rush of wind. Hell, I probably cowered. My feet ached with cold. My hands were numb already.

Nothing fell on me. No impact; no pain.

I opened my eyes. My rig was gone. Where she had been, two long curls of snow hung on the air, snatched up by the draft off her extended wings. As I stared after her, I heard the distant echo of a sonic boom.

Whatever she thinks, I know her. I knew her better than anybody. Better than lover knows beloved. As clearly as if she said it in my dead, silent com, I could hear her voice: *I am going to go do something. Something better than killing a lot of innocent people.*

It's very cold out here. The sun is setting. It's going to get colder. If I wanted to turn my sidearm on myself, I'm not even sure I could get my fingers to bend inside the trigger guard.

I'm a long way from home.

Valentine's Day, 2017

---○---

Sonny Liston Takes The Fall

1.

"I GOTTA TELL YOU, JACKIE," SONNY Liston said, "I lied to my wife about that. I gotta tell you, I took that fall."

It was Christmas eve, 1970, and Sonny Liston was about the furthest thing you could imagine from a handsome man. He had a furrowed brow and downcast hound dog prisoner eyes that wouldn't meet mine, and the matching furrows on either side of his broad, flat nose ran down to a broad, flat mouth under a pencil thin moustache that was already out of fashion six years ago, when he was still King of the World.

"We all lie sometimes, Sonny," I said, pouring him another scotch. We don't mind if you drink too much in Vegas. We don't mind much of anything at all. "It doesn't signify."

He had what you call a tremendous physical presence, Sonny Liston. He filled up a room so you couldn't take your eyes off him—didn't *want* to take your eyes off him, and if he was smiling you were smiling, and if he was scowling you were shivering—even when he was sitting quietly, the way he was now, turned away from his kitchen table and his elbows on his knees, one hand big enough for a man twice his size wrapped around the glass I handed him and the other hanging between his legs, limp across the back of the wrist as if the tendons'd been cut. His suit wasn't long enough for the length of his arms. The coat sleeves and the shirt sleeves with their French cuffs and discreet cufflinks were ridden halfway up his forearms, showing wrists I couldn't have wrapped my fingers around. Tall as he was, he wasn't tall enough for that frame—as if he didn't get enough to eat as a kid—but he was that wide.

Sonny Liston, he was from Arkansas. And you would hear it in his voice, even now. He drank that J&B scotch like knocking back a blender full of raw eggs and held the squat glass out for more. "I could of beat Cassius Clay if it weren't for the fucking Mob," he said, while I filled it up again. "I could of beat that goddamn flashy pansy."

"I know you could, Sonny," I told him, and it wasn't a lie. "I know you could."

His hands were like mallets, like mauls, like the paws of the bear they styled him. It didn't matter.

He was a broken man, Sonny Liston. He wouldn't meet your eyes, not that he ever would have. You learn that in prison. You learn that from a father who beats you. You learn that when you're black in America.

You keep your eyes down, and maybe there won't be trouble this time.

2.

IT'S THE same thing with fighters as with horses. Race horses, I mean, thoroughbreds, which I know a lot about. I'm the genius of Las Vegas, you see. The One-Eyed Jack, the guardian and the warden of Sin City.

It's a bit like being a magician who works with tigers—the city is my life, and I take care of it. But that means it's my job to make damned sure it doesn't get out and eat anybody.

And because of that, I also know a little about magic and sport and sacrifice, and the real, old blood truth of the laurel crown and what it means to be King for a Day.

The thing about race horses, is that the trick with the good ones isn't getting them to run. It's getting them to stop.

They'll kill themselves running, the good ones. They'll run on broken hearts, broken legs, broken wind. Legend says Black Gold finished his last race with nothing but a shipping bandage holding his flopping hoof to his leg. They shot him on the track, Black Gold, the way they did in those days. And it was mercy when they did it.

He was King, and he was claimed. He went to pay the tithe that only greatness pays.

Ruffian, perhaps the best filly that ever ran, shattered herself in a match race that was meant to prove she could have won the Kentucky Derby if she'd raced in it. The great colt Swale ran with a hole in his heart, and no one ever knew until it killed him in the paddock one fine summer day in the third year of his life.

And then there's Charismatic.

Charismatic was a Triple Crown contender until he finished his Belmont third, running on a collapsed leg, with his jockey Chris Antley all but kneeling on the reins, doing anything to drag him down.

Antley left the saddle as soon as his mount saw the wire and could be slowed. He dove over Charismatic's shoulder and got underneath him before the horse had stopped moving; he held the broken Charismatic up with his shoulders and his own two hands until the veterinarians arrived. Between Antley and the surgeons, they saved the colt. Because Antley took that fall.

Nobody could save Antley, who was dead himself within two years from a drug overdose. He died so hard that investigators first called it a homicide.

When you run with all God gave you, you run out of track god-damned fast.

3.

SONNY WAS just like that. Just like a race horse. Just like every other goddamned fighter. A little bit crazy, a little bit fierce, a little bit desperate, and ignorant of the concept of defeat under any circumstances.

Until he met Cassius Clay in the ring.

They fought twice. First time was in 1964, and I watched that fight live in a movie theatre. We didn't have pay-per-view then, and the fight happened in Florida, not here at home in Vegas.

I remember it real well, though.

Liston was a monster, you have to understand. He wasn't real big for a fighter, only six foot one, but he *hulked*. He *loomed*. His opponents would flinch away before he ever pulled back a punch.

I've met Mike Tyson too, who gets compared to Liston. And I don't think it's just because they're both hard men, or that Liston also was accused of sexual assault. It's because Tyson has that same thing, the power of personal gravity that bends the available light and every eye down to him, even when he's walking quietly through a crowded room, wearing a warm-up jacket and a smile.

So that was Liston. He was a stone golem, a thing out of legend, the fucking bogeyman. He was going to walk through Clay like the Kool-Aid pitcher walking through a paper wall.

And we were all in our seats, waiting to see this insolent prince beat down by the barbarian king.

And there was a moment when Clay stepped up to Liston, and they touched gloves, and the whole theatre went still.

Because Clay was just as big as Liston. And Clay wasn't looking down.

Liston retired in the seventh round. Maybe he had a dislocated shoulder, and maybe he didn't, and maybe the Mob told him to throw the fight so they could bet on the underdog Clay and Liston just couldn't quite make himself fall over and play dead.

And Cassius Clay, you see, he grew up to be Muhammad Ali.

4.

SONNY DIDN'T tell me about *that* fight. He told me about the other one.

Phil Ochs wrote a song about it, and so did Mark Knopfler: that legendary fight in 1965, the one where, in the very first minute of the very first round, Sonny Liston took a fall.

Popular poets, Ochs and Knopfler, and what do you think the bards were? That kind of magic, the old dark magic that soaks down the roots of the world and keeps it rich, it's a transformative magic. It never goes away.

However you spill it, it's blood that makes the cactus *grow*.

Ochs, just to interject a little more irony here, paid for his power in his own blood as well.

5.

TWENTY-FIFTH CHILD of twenty-six, Sonny Liston. A tenant farmer's son, whose father beat him bloody. He never would meet my eye, even there in his room, *this* close to Christmas, near the cold bent stub end of 1970.

He never would meet a white man's eyes. Even the eye of the One-Eyed Jack, patron saint of Las Vegas, when Jackie was pouring him J&B. Not a grown man's eye, anyway, though he loved kids—and kids loved him. The bear was a teddy bear when you got him around children.

But he told me all about that fight. How the Mob told him to throw it or they'd kill him and his Momma and a selection of his brothers and sisters too. How he did what they told him in the most defiant manner possible. So the whole fucking world would know he took that fall.

The thing is, I didn't believe him.

I sat there and nodded and listened, and I thought, Sonny Liston didn't throw that fight. That famous "Phantom Punch"? Mohammad Ali got lucky. Hit a nerve cluster or something. Sonny Liston, the unstoppable Sonny Liston, the man with a heart of piston steel and a hand like John Henry's hammer—Sonny Liston, he went down. It was a fluke, a freak thing, some kind of an accident.

I thought going down like that shamed him, so he told his wife he gave up because he knew Ali was better and he didn't feel like fighting just to get beat. But he told *me* that other story, about the Mob, and he drank another scotch and he toasted Muhammad Ali, though Sonny'd kind of hated him. Ali had been barred from fighting from 1967 until just that last year, and was facing a jail term because he wouldn't go and die in Vietnam.

Sensible man, if you happen to ask me.

But I knew Sonny didn't throw that fight for the Mob. I knew because I also knew this other thing about that fight, because I am the soul of Las Vegas, and in 1965, the Mob was Las Vegas.

And I knew they'd had a few words with Sonny before he went into the ring.

Sonny Liston was supposed to win. And Muhammad Ali was supposed to die.

6.

THE ONE thing in his life that Sonny Liston could never hit back against was his daddy. Sonny, whose given name was Charles, but who called himself Sonny all his adult life.

Sonny had learned the hard way that you never look a white man in the eye. That you never look *any* man in the eye unless you mean to beat him down. That you never look *the Man* in the eye, because if you do *he's* gonna beat *you* down.

He did his time in jail, Sonny Liston. He went in a boy and he came out a prize fighter, and when he came out he was owned by the Mob.

You can see it in the photos and you could see it in his face, when you met him, when you reached out to touch his hand; he almost never smiled, and his eyes always held this kind of deep sonorous seriousness over his black, flat, damaged nose.

Sonny Liston was a jailbird. Sonny Liston belonged to the Mob the same way his daddy belonged to the land.

Cassius Clay, God bless him, changed his slave name two days after that first bout with Sonny, as if winning it freed up something in him. Muhammad Ali, God bless him, never learned that lesson about looking down.

7.

BOXING IS called the sweet science. And horse racing is the sport of kings.

When Clay beat Liston, he bounced up on his stool and shouted that he was King of the World. Corn king, summer king, America's most beautiful young man. An angel in the boxing ring. A new and powerful image of black manhood.

He stepped up on that stool in 1964 and he put a noose around his neck.

The thing about magic is that it happens in spite of everything you can do to stop it.

And the wild old Gods will have their sacrifice.

No excuses.

If they can't have Charismatic, they'll take the man that saved him.

So it goes.

8.

SOMETIMES IT'S easier to tell yourself you quit than to admit that they beat you. Sometimes it's easier to look down.

The civil rights movement in the early 1960s found Liston a thug and an embarrassment. He was a jailbird, an illiterate, a dark unstoppable monster. The rumor was that he had a second career as a standover man—a Mob enforcer. The NAACP protested when Floyd Patterson agreed to fight him in 1962.

9.

SONNY DIDN'T know his own birthday or maybe he lied about his age. Forty's old for a fighter, and Sonny said he was born in '32 when he was might have been born as early as '27. There's a big damned difference between thirty-two and thirty-seven in the boxing ring.

And there's another thing, something about prize fighters you might not know. In Liston's day, they shot the fighters' hands full of anesthetic before they wrapped them for the fight. So a guy who was a hitter—a *puncher* rather than a *boxer*, in the parlance—he could pound away on his opponent and never notice he'd broken all the goddamned bones in his goddamned hands.

Sonny Liston was a puncher. Muhammad Ali was a boxer.

Neither one of them, as it happens, could abide the needles. So when they went swinging into the ring, they earned every punch they threw.

Smack a sheetrock wall a couple of dozen times with your shoulder behind it if you want to build up a concept of what that means, in terms of endurance and of pain. Me? I would have taken the needle over *feeling* the bones I was breaking. Taken it in a heartbeat.

But Charismatic finished his race on a shattered leg, and so did Black Gold.

What the hell were a few broken bones to Sonny Liston?

10.

YOU KNOW when I said Sonny was not a handsome man? Well, I also said Muhammad Ali was an angel. He was a black man's angel, an avenging angel, a messenger from a better future. He was the *way* and the *path*, man, and they marked him for sacrifice, because he was a warrior god, a Black Muslim Moses come to lead his people out of Egypt land.

And the people in power like to stay that way, and they have their ways of making it happen. Of making sure the sacrifice gets chosen.

Go ahead and curl your lip. White man born in the nineteenth century, reborn in 1905 as the Genius of the Mississippi of the West. What do I know about the black experience?

I am my city, and I contain multitudes. I'm the African-American airmen at Nellis Air Force Base, and I'm the black neighborhoods near D Street that can't keep a supermarket, and I'm Cartier Street and I'm Northtown and I'm Las Vegas, baby, and it doesn't matter a bit what you see when you look at my face.

Because Sonny Liston died here, and he's buried here in the palm of my hand. And I'm Sonny Liston too, wronged and wronging; he's in here, boiling and bubbling away.

11.

I FILLED his glass one more time and splashed what was left into my own, and that was the end of the bottle. I twisted it to make the last drop fall. Sonny watched my hands instead of my eyes, and folded his own enormous fists around his glass so it vanished. "You're here on business,

Jackie," he said, and dropped his eyes to his knuckles. "Nobody wants to listen to me talk."

"I want to listen, Sonny." The scotch didn't taste so good, but I rolled it over my tongue anyway. I'd drunk enough that the roof of my mouth was getting dry, and the liquor helped a little. "I'm here to listen as long as you want to talk."

His shoulders always had a hunch. He didn't stand up tall. They hunched a bit more as he turned the glass in his hands. "I guess I run out of things to say. So you might as well tell me what you came for."

At Christmastime in 1970, Muhammad Ali—recently allowed back in the ring, pending his appeal of a draft evasion conviction—was preparing for a title bout against Joe Frazier in March. He was also preparing for a more wide-reaching conflict; in April of that year, his appeal, his demand to be granted status as a conscientious objector, was to go before the United States Supreme Court.

He faced a five-year prison sentence.

In jail, he'd come up against everything Sonny Liston had. And maybe Ali was the stronger man. And maybe the young king wouldn't break where the old one fell. Or maybe he wouldn't make it out of prison alive, or free.

"Ali needs your help," I said.

"Fuck Cassius Clay," he said.

Sonny finished his drink and spent a while staring at the bottom of his glass. I waited until he turned his head, skimming his eyes along the floor, and tried to sip again from the empty glass. Then I cleared my throat and said, "It isn't just for him."

Sonny flinched. See, the thing about Sonny—that he never learned to read, that doesn't mean he was *dumb*. "The NAACP don't want me. The Nation of Islam don't want me. They didn't even want Clay to box me. *I'm an embarrassment to the black man.*"

He dropped his glass on the table and held his breath for a moment before he shrugged and said, "Well, they got their nigger now."

Some of them know up front; they listen to the whispers, and they know the price they might have to pay if it's their number that comes up.

Some just kind of know in the back of their heads. About the corn king, and the laurel wreath, and the price that sometimes has to be paid.

Sonny Liston, like I said, he wasn't dumb.

"Ali can do something you can't, Sonny." *Ali can be a symbol.*

"I can't have it," he drawled. "But I can buy it? Is that what you're telling me, Jack?"

I finished my glass too, already drunk enough that it didn't make my sinuses sting. "Sonny," I said, with that last bit of Dutch courage in me, "you're gonna have to take another fall."

12.

WHEN HIS wife—returning from a holiday visit to her relatives—found his body on January fifth, eleven days after I poured him that drink, maybe a week or so after he died, Sonny had needle marks in the crook of his arm, though the coroner's report said *heart failure.*

Can you think of a worse way to kill the man?

13.

ON MARCH 8, 1971, a publicly reviled Muhammad Ali was defeated by Joe Frazier at Madison Square Garden in New York City in a boxing match billed as the "Fight of the Century." Ali had been vilified in the press as a Black Muslim, a religious and political radical, a black man who wouldn't look down.

Three months later, the United States Supreme Court overturned the conviction, allowing Muhammad Ali's conscientious objector status to stand.

He was a free man.

Ali fought Frazier twice more. He won both times, and went on to become the most respected fighter in the history of the sport. A beautiful avenging outspoken angel.

Almost thirty-five years after Sonny Liston died, in November of 2005, President George W. Bush awarded America's highest civilian honor, the

Presidential Medal of Freedom, to the draft-dodging, politically activist lay preacher Muhammad Ali.

14.

SONNY LISTON never looked a man in the eye unless he meant to beat him down. Until he looked upon Cassius Clay and hated him. And looked past that hate and saw a dawning angel, and he saw the future, and he wanted it that bad.

Wanted it bad, Sonny Liston, illiterate jailbird and fighter and stand-over man. Sonny Liston the drunk, the sex offender. Broken, brutal Sonny Liston with the scars on his face from St. Louis cops beating a confession from him, with the scars on his back from his daddy beating him down on the farm.

Sonny Liston, who loved children. He wanted that thing, and he knew it could never be his.

Wanted it and saw a way to make it happen for somebody else.

15.

AND SO he takes that fall, Sonny Liston. Again and again and again, like John Henry driving steel until his heart burst, like a jockey rolling over the shoulder of a running, broken horse. He takes the fall, and he saves the King.

---○---

ORM THE BEAUTIFUL

ORM THE BEAUTIFUL SANG IN his sleep, to his brothers and sisters, as the sea sings to itself. He would never die. But neither could he live much longer.

Dreaming on jewels, hearing their ancestor-song, he did not think that he would mind. The men were coming; Orm the Beautiful knew it with the wisdom of his bones. He thought he would not fight them. He thought he would close the mountain and let them scratch outside.

He would die there in the mosther-cave, and so stay with the Chord. There was no one after him to take his place as warden, and Orm the Beautiful was old.

Because he was the last warden of the mother-cave, his hoard was enormous, chromatic in hue and harmony. There was jade and lapis—the bequests of Orm the Exquisite and Orm the Luminous, respectively—and chrysoprase and turquoise and the semiprecious feldspars. There were three cracked sections of an amethyst pipe as massive as a fallen tree, and Orm the Beautiful was careful never to breathe fire upon them; the stones would jaundice to smoke color in the heat.

He lay closest by the jagged heap of beryls—green as emerald, green as poison, green as grass—that were the mortal remains of his sister, Orm the Radiant. And just beyond her was the legacy of her mate, Orm the Magnificent, charcoal-and-silver labradorite overshot with an absinthe shimmer. The Magnificent's song, in death, was high and sweet, utterly at odds with the aged slithering hulk he had become before he changed.

Orm the Beautiful stretched his long neck among the glorious rubble of his kin and dozed to their songs. Soon he would be with them, returned to their harmony, their many-threaded round. Only his radiance illuminated them now. Only his eye remembered their sheen. And he too would lose the power to shine with more than reflected light before long, and all in the mother-cave would be dark and full of music.

He was pale, palest of his kin, blue-white as skimmed milk and just as translucent. The flash that ran across his scales when he crawled into the light, however, was spectral: green-electric and blue-actinic, and a vermilion so sharp it could burn an afterimage in a human eye.

It had been a long time since he climbed into the light. Perhaps he'd seal the cave now, to be ready.

Yes.

When he was done, he lay down among his treasures, his beloveds, under the mountain, and his thoughts were dragonish.

BUT WHEN the men came they came not single spies but in battalions, with dragons of their own. Iron dragons, yellow metal monsters that creaked and hissed as they gnawed the rocks. And they brought, with the dragons, channeled fire.

There was a thump, a tremble, and sifting dust followed. Cold winter air trickling down the shaft woke Orm the Beautiful from his chorale slumber.

He blinked lambent eyes, raising his head from the petrified, singing flank of Orm the Perspicacious. He heard the crunch of stone like the splintering of masticated bones and cocked his head, his ears and tendrils straining forward.

And all the Chord sang astonishment and alarm.

It had happened to others. Slain, captured, taken. Broken apart and carried off, their memories and their dreams lost forever, their songs stripped to exiled fragments to adorn a wrist, a throat, a crown. But it had always been that men could be turned back with stone.

And now they were here at the mother-cave, and undaunted to find it sealed.

This would not do. This threatened them all.

ORM THE Beautiful burst from the mountain wreathed in white-yellow flames. The yellow steel dragon was not too much larger than he. It blocked the tunnel mouth; its toothed hand raked and lifted shattered stone. Orm the Beautiful struck it with his claws extended, his wings snapping wide as he cleared the destroyed entrance to the mother-cave.

The cold cut through scale to bone. When fire did not jet from flaring nostrils, his breath swirled mist and froze to rime. Snow lay blackened on the mountainside, rutted and filthy. His wings, far whiter, caught chill carmine sparks from the sun. Fragile steel squealed and rent under his claws.

There was a man in the cage inside the mechanical dragon. He made terrible unharmonious noises as he burned. Orm the Beautiful seized him and ate him quickly, out of pity, head jerking like a stork snatching down a frog.

His throat distended, squeezed, smoothed, contracted. There was no time to eat the contraption, and metal could not suffer in the flames. Orm the Beautiful tore it in half, claw and claw, and soared between the discarded pieces.

Other men screamed and ran. Their machines were potent, but no iron could sting him. Neither their bullets nor the hammer-headed drill on the second steel dragon gave him pause. He stalked them, pounced, gorged on the snap-shaken dead.

He pursued the living as they fled, and what he reached he slew.

When he slithered down the ruined tunnel to the others, they were singing, gathered, worried. He settled among their entwined song, added his notes to the chords, offered harmony. Orm the Beautiful was old; what he brought to the song was rich and layered, subtle and soft.

They will come again, sang Orm the Radiant.

They have found the mother-cave, and they have machines to unearth us, like a badger from its sett, sang Orm the Terrible from his column of black and lavender jade.

We are not safe here anymore, sang Orm the Luminous. We will be scattered and lost. The song will end, will end.

His verse almost silenced them all. Their harmony guttered like a fire when the wind slicks across it, and for a moment Orm the Beautiful felt the quiet like a wire around his throat. It was broken by the discord of voices, a rising dissonance like a tuning orchestra, the Chord all frightened and in argument.

But Orm the Courtly raised her voice, and all listened. She was old in life and old in death, and wise beyond both in her singing. Let the warden decide.

Another agreed, another, voice after voice scaling into harmony.

And Orm the Beautiful sat back on his haunches, his tail flicked across his toes, his belly aching, and tried to pretend he had any idea at all how to protect the Chord from being unearthed and carted to the four corners of the world.

"I'll think about it when I've digested," he said, and lay down on his side with a sigh.

Around him the Chord sang agreement. They had not forgotten in death the essentialities of life.

WITH THE men and their machines came memory. Orm the Beautiful, belly distended with iron and flesh, nevertheless slept with one eye open. His opalescence lit the mother-cave in hollow violets and crawling greens. The Chord sang around him, thinking while he dreamed. The dead did not rest, or dream.

They only sang and remembered.

The Chord was in harmony when he awoke. They had listened to his song while he slept, and while he stretched—sleek again, and the best part of a yard longer—he heard theirs as well, and learned from them what they had learned from his dinner.

More men would follow. The miners Orm the Beautiful had dined on knew they would not go unavenged. There would be more men, men like ants, with their weapons and their implements. And Orm the Beautiful was strong.

But he was old, and he was only one. And someone, surely, would soon recall that though steel had no power to harm Orm the Beautiful's race, knapped flint or obsidian could slice him opal hide from opal bone.

The mother-cave was full of the corpses of dragons, a chain of song and memory stretching aeons. The Chord was rich in voices.

Orm the Beautiful had no way to move them all.

Orm the Numinous, who was eldest, was chosen to speak the evil news they all knew already. You must give us away, Orm the Beautiful.

DRAGONS ARE not specifically disallowed in the airspace over Washington, D.C., but it must be said that Orm the Beautiful's presence there was heartily discouraged. Nevertheless, he persevered, holding his flame and the lash of his wings, and succeeded in landing on the National Mall without destroying any of the attacking aircraft.

He touched down lightly in a clear space before the National Museum of Natural History, a helicopter hovering over his head and blowing his tendrils this way and that. There were men all over the grass and pavements. They scattered, screaming, nigh-irresistible prey. Orm the Beautiful's tail-tip twitched with frustrated instinct, and he was obliged to stand on three legs and elaborately clean his off-side fore talons for several moments before he regained enough self-possession to settle his wings and ignore the scurrying morsels.

It was unlikely that he would set a conducive tone with the museum's staff by eating a few as a prelude to conversation.

He stood quietly, inspecting his talons foot by foot and, incidentally, admiring the flashes of color that struck off his milk-pale hide in the glaring sun. When he had been still five minutes, he looked up to find a ring of men surrounding him, males and a few females, with bright metal in their hands and flashing on the chests of uniforms that were a black-blue dark as sodalite.

"Hello," Orm the Beautiful said, in the language of his dinner, raising his voice to be heard over the clatter of the helicopter. "My name is Orm the Beautiful. I should like to speak to the curator, please."

THE HELICOPTER withdrew to circle, and the curator eventually produced was a female man. Orm the Beautiful wondered if that was due to some half-remembered legend about his folk's preferences. Sopranos, in particular, had been popular among his kin in the days when they associated more freely with men.

She minced from the white-columned entry, down broad shallow steps between exhibits of petrified wood, and paused beyond the barricade of yellow tape and wooden sawhorses the blue-uniformed men had strung around Orm the Beautiful.

He had greatly enjoyed watching them evacuate the Mall.

The curator wore a dull suit and shoes that clicked, and her hair was twisted back on her neck. Little stones glinted in her earlobes: diamonds, cold and common and without song.

"I'm Katherine Samson," she said, and hesitantly extended her tiny soft hand, half-retracted it, then doggedly thrust it forward again. "You wished to speak to me?"

"I am Orm the Beautiful," Orm the Beautiful replied, and laid a cautious talon-tip against her palm. "I am here to beg your aid."

She squinted up and he realized that the sun was behind him. If its own brilliance didn't blind her pale man's eyes, surely the light shattering on his scales would do the deed. He spread his wings to shade her, and the ring of blue-clad men flinched back as one—as if they were a Chord, though Orm the Beautiful knew they were not.

The curator, however, stood her ground.

His blue-white wings were translucent, and there was a hole in the leather of the left one, an ancient scar. It cast a ragged bright patch on the curator's shoe, but the shade covered her face, and she lowered her eye-shading hand.

"Thank you," she said. And then, contemplating him, she pushed the sawhorses apart. One of the blue men reached for her, but before he caught her arm, the curator was through the gap and standing in Orm the Beautiful's shadow, her head craned back, her hair pulling free around her temples in soft wisps that reminded Orm the Beautiful of Orm the Radiant's tawny tendrils. "You need my help? Uh, sir?"

Carefully, he lowered himself to his elbows, keeping the wings high. The curator was close enough to touch him now, and when he tilted his head to see her plainly, he found her staring up at him with the tip of her tongue protruding. He flicked his tongue in answer, tasting her scent.

She was frightened. But far more curious.

"Let me explain," he said. And told her about the mother-cave, and the precious bones of his Chord, and the men who had come to steal them. He told her that they were dead, but they remembered, and if they were torn apart, carted off, their song and their memories would be shattered.

"It would be the end of my culture," he said, and then he told her he was dying.

As he was speaking, his head had dipped lower, until he was almost murmuring in her ear. At some point, she'd laid one hand on his skull behind the horns and leaned close, and she seemed startled now to realize that she was touching him. She drew her hand back slowly, and stood staring at the tips of her fingers. "What is that singing?"

She heard it, then, the wreath of music that hung on him, thin and thready though it was in the absence of his Chord. That was well. "It is I."

"Do all—all your people—does that always happen?"

"I have no people," he said. "But yes. Even in death we sing. It is why the Chord must be kept together."

"So when you said it's only you…"

"I am the last," said Orm the Beautiful.

She looked down, and he gave her time to think.

"It would be very expensive," she said, cautiously, rubbing the fingertips together as if they'd lost sensation. "We would have to move quickly, if poachers have already found your...mother-cave. And you're talking about a huge engineering problem, to move them without taking them apart. I don't know where the money would come from."

"If the expense were not at issue, would the museum accept the bequest?"

"Without a question." She touched his eye-ridge again, quickly, furtively. "Dragons," she said, and shook her head and breathed a laugh. "Dragons."

"Money is no object," he said. "Does your institution employ a solicitor?"

THE DOCUMENT was two days in drafting. Orm the Beautiful spent the time fretting and fussed, though he kept his aspect as nearly serene as possible. Katherine—the curator—did not leave his side. Indeed, she brought him within the building—the tall doors and vast lobby could have accommodated a far larger dragon—and had a cot fetched so she could remain near. He could not stay in the lobby itself, because it was a point of man-pride that the museum was open every day, and free to all comers. But they cleared a small exhibit hall, and he stayed there in fair comfort, although silent and alone.

Outside, reporters and soldiers made camp, but within the halls of the Museum of Natural History, it was bright and still, except for the lonely shadow of Orm the Beautiful's song.

Already, he mourned his Chord. But if his sacrifice meant their salvation, it was a very small thing to give.

When the contracts were written, when the papers were signed, Katherine sat down on the edge of her cot and said, "The personal bequest," she began. "The one the Museum is meant to sell, to fund the retrieval of your Chord."

"Yes," Orm the Beautiful said.

"May I know what it is now, and where we may find it?"

"It is here before you," said Orm the Beautiful, and tore his heart from his breast with his claws.

He fell with a crash like a breaking bell, an avalanche of skim-milk-white opal threaded with azure and absinthe and vermilion flash. Chunks rolled against Katherine's legs, bruised her feet and ankles, broke some of her toes in her clicking shoes.

She was too stunned to feel pain. Through his solitary singing, Orm the Beautiful heard her refrain: "Oh, no, oh, no, oh, no."

THOSE WHO came to investigate the crash found Katherine Samson on her knees, hands raking the rubble. Salt water streaked opal powder white as bone dust down her cheeks. She kissed the broken rocks, and the blood on her fingertips was no brighter than the shocked veins of carnelian flash that shot through them.

Orm the Beautiful was broken up and sold, as he had arranged. The paperwork was quite unforgiving; dragons, it seems, may serve as their own attorneys with great dexterity.

The stones went for outrageous prices. When you wore them on your skin, you could hear the dragonsong. Institutions and the insanely wealthy fought over the relics. No price could ever be too high.

Katherine Samson was bequeathed a few chips for her own. She had them polished and drilled and threaded on a chain she wore about her throat, where her blood could warm them as they pressed upon her pulse. The mother-cave was located with the aid of Orm the Beautiful's maps and directions. Poachers were in the process of excavating it when the team from the Smithsonian arrived.

But the Museum had brought the National Guard. And the poachers were dealt with, though perhaps not with such finality as Orm the Beautiful might have wished.

Each and each, his Chord were brought back to the Museum.

Katherine, stumping on her walking cast, spent long hours in the exhibit hall. She hovered and guarded and warded, and stroked and petted and adjusted Orm the Beautiful's hoard like a nesting falcon turning her eggs. His song sustained her, his warm bones worn against her skin, his voice half-heard in her ear.

He was broken and scattered. He was not a part of his Chord. He was lost to them, as other dragons had been lost before, and as those others his song would eventually fail, and flicker, and go unremembered.

After a few months, she stopped weeping.

She also stopped eating, sleeping, dreaming.

Going home.

THEY CAME as stragglers, footsore and rain-draggled, noses peeled by the sun. They came alone, in party dresses, in business suits, in outrageously costly T-shirts and jeans. They came draped in opals and platinum, opals and gold. They came with the song of Orm the Beautiful warm against their skin.

They came to see the dragons, to hear their threaded music. When the Museum closed at night, they waited patiently by the steps until morning. They did not freeze. They did not starve.

Eventually, through the sheer wearing force of attrition, the passage of decades, the Museum accepted them. And there they worked, and lived, for all time.

AND ORM the Beautiful?

He had been shattered. He died alone.

The Chord could not reclaim him. He was lost in the mortal warders, the warders who had been men.

But as he sang in their ears, so they recalled him, like a seashell remembers the sea.

542

ERASE, ERASE, ERASE

I SHOULDN'T HAVE LET IT GET so far. It seemed so inconsequential at first. Almost a relief to find yourself getting a little misty around the edges. Bits dropping off. Stuff you don't need anymore.

Erase, erase, erase.

Sorry, historians. I know some of this stuff would be useful to you, but it's all gone now. All gone.

I burned most of it.

Only I am still here.

And I am falling apart, and I can't remember who I used to be or how I got here.

Irresponsible of me, I know.

IT'S NOT just the memories, either. There's bits of me gone that I swear were there before. Fingertips. Some hair. The eyelashes on my right eye.

I'm almost certain I used to have those.

Sometimes I reach for something—coffee mug, keyboard—and realize I can't seem to find my own hand. I have to go look around the house

543

for it, because I never remember where I had it last. Feet, at least, limbs—I don't tend to get far when those have gone missing. It's hard not to notice as soon as you try to stand up.

But I've found hands in the bed, under the bed, halfway up the stairs. Once in the fridge, which worried me a lot but actually it went right back on. Just felt a little weird and numb for a few minutes. Found my ear still stuck on an earbud once, and that was pretty awful. When the nose comes off the glasses usually go with it.

I miss cats, but I don't have a cat anymore. I couldn't be sure of taking care of one. I'd probably forget to feed her, or not be able to work the can opener, and she'd resort to eating a mislaid finger.

None of it hurts. None of it seems to harm me in any way. Except that I'm falling apart, and a lot of my time is taken up with finding bits of me that have broken away somehow, and sticking them back on again in more or less the spot they came from.

I don't leave the house the way I used to. I'm glad I live in a time when nearly everything can be delivered.

AND SOMETIMES I get misty and confused. I'll be in the middle of some task and realize three hours later, in another part of the house, that I've left it undone. I'll find my spectacles in the fridge, or my socks on the bookshelf. I'm sure putting them there seemed like a logical idea at the time.

Sometimes also, I'll find my clothes in a puddle under me on the sofa, and realize that they just kind of drained through me while I was working. I'll be chopping vegetables and the knife will hit the chopping block and just lie there, and it will be a while before I can manage to pick it up again. My hand will pass through my coffee cup for a while before it solidifies again, and I won't get to drink it until it's cold.

At least the pens and notebooks are always solid. Always real. My laptop, too, and I guess that's logical, because it's not that different from a notebook in intention. Heck, some people call them notebooks.

Oh, but now. But this time.

I think I did more than get a little misty. I think I forgot something.

I think I forgot something very important. I think I forgot it on purpose, and because I forgot it, something terrible is going to happen. To a lot of people. Not just me.

So I'm falling apart. *And* I'm losing my mind.

I USED to burn my notebooks.

I didn't want to be connected to the past they represented. I didn't want to be connected to the person they represented. I didn't want to be connected to the me that was.

I wanted to reinvent myself. Each time I made a terrible mistake, I wanted to put everything aside, walk away, move on. I wanted to erase my errors. I wanted to change the past so the bad things had not happened. So I could not be punished for them. So I would not have to feel, all the time, so wrong.

I erased my thoughts, my feelings. My failed loves. The classes where my grades were only average. The abusive family background. The jobs that didn't turn out as well as I had hoped for, that had toxic office politics, or abusive bosses. I erased the pain, the pain, the pain.

I wrote it all down in hope, and when it didn't work out, I burned it in despair.

I was trying to erase my mistakes, I suppose. It was a kind of perfectionism. If something has a flaw, throw it out and get something perfect next time. I was trying to move forward, in the hope that the next adventure would end better.

But not learning from the failures.

And so, little by little, I erased myself.

I threw myself away.

I **WOULD** have been free and clear if I just hadn't read the newspaper that day. The day they printed the manifesto. I could have gone on about my life and my business in ignorance.

I could have spared myself a lot of grief. And work. And worry.

Grief and work and worry that would have been transferred to other people in my stead. That might still be served up to them if I can't prevent it.

And if it happens, I will know that it is my fault, because I failed.

The manifesto was in the paper. All the papers, I imagine, not just my specific one. It purported to be written by the group that had been mailing incendiary bombs to universities. Harvard, Yale, the University of Chicago. To their medical colleges.

That niggled at me, and I didn't think it was just because the University of Chicago was my alma mater. There was something.

Something back there.

Something I had worked very hard to forget.

Not violence, no. But the promise of violence. The *expectation* of violence.

Is that what people mean when they talk about menace? Something being menacing? That awareness that there is not just the *potential* for violence, in the abstract, a kind of background radiation that is always there—but that somebody, somewhere, is *planning* to cause someone harm.

ANY LONG-TERM relationship is served by a little amnesia. A marriage—and I'm using the term loosely here, but we were together, if you can call it together, for almost eight years—is a country in flux. A series of negotiations and edges and considered silences. And some unconsidered ones, depending on how self-aware the diplomats in question are. Sometimes all the negotiations are carried out by reflex and instinct. Sometimes this results in war. A covert war, or an open one.

But sometimes, there's a plan.

When a diplomat who's acting on reflex, instinct, and conditioned response (diplomat A) meets a diplomat who is acting with self-awareness, caution, and a considered agenda of compromises (diplomat B), (diplomat B) is usually going to win the exchange.

I was (diplomat A) in this example.

I was seventeen years old.

I went in without a theory.

A BROKEN heart is like a cracked bath tub. Nobody's going to make a full-price offer on a property with annoying repair problems like that hanging around. So either you fix it yourself, or you try to hide the cracks and cover up the damage. At least until the mark has signed enough paperwork that it's inconvenient to back out.

PLASTIC-COVERED NOTEBOOKS give off a terrible smell as they burn.

I WASTED a lot of paper.

I was not good at finishing the notebooks. I would reach a point where I was damned sick of who I was, how I had been feeling, how I had been acting. And then I needed to be done with the stained pages I had been writing, because I had written down everything. Everything about my internal landscape, anyway.

I didn't have friends.

I just had secrets.

And so I wrote them down.

It was actually easier—well, cheaper, anyway—and more efficient—when I was younger. In the three-ring and spiral-bound notebooks, I just ripped out the offending pages and tore them up. Got rid of them. Shredded them and gave them a shove.

But then I graduated to bound books. The cheap fabric-covered ones at first. Then better ones, professional-quality ones, with paper that ink pens did not feather on or bleed through. I liked the hard-covered ones in pretty colors, with ribbon markers and pockets in the back. Graph paper or dot grids. I did not like wide-ruled.

But those were harder to destroy, eventually. When they needed destruction.

Everything needs destruction in the end. And so I learned to burn.

I thought about burning more than notebooks when I was young. I thought of self-immolation, but I never had the courage. I thought of arson, but I never had the cruelty. I remembered those things, vaguely. Like a story that had happened to someone else.

Maybe that was why that manifesto struck me so hard, I tell myself, as my fingers slip through the handle of the coffee pot again. *A major American city*, it had said. *An inferno of flames. The Judgement of a just and terrible God.*

Engulfed.

Soon, soon. Soon.

But no. There is more than that. Some part of me that I can't access knows. Knows which city. Knows who had written those words. Knows enough to stop this terrible thing from happening.

I just can't *remember.*

HOW DO you learn to erase yourself?

It's not something that comes naturally to children. Children seek attention because attention means survival. So to get them to erase themselves, you have to teach them that they don't exist. And because it is an unnatural, self-destructive thing that you are teaching them—a maladaptive response—the only tactic that works is to make the consequences of noncompliance worse than the consequences of nonexistence.

That takes force. Violence, physical or emotional. If you just try to *ignore* a kid, they'll act out, and seek attention through misbehavior.

Any port in a storm.

I bet, given half a chance, I could have been a charming child.

But I didn't learn to be charming. I learned how not to be real.

I learned to have no vulnerabilities and expect no consideration. I learned I had no intrinsic value and was only marginally worthwhile for what I could provide, if what I provided was beyond reproach.

I learned I was not allowed to be angry. To defend myself. To have needs. I learned to be good at being alone, because if you were alone, nobody could betray you.

I thought I had escaped all that when I went away to college. But like the horror movie phone call, the loathing was coming from inside my head.

I DIDN'T hold on to things, because holding on to things hurt. If you didn't hold on, then when you lost something you lost it easy.

But if you don't hold on, you lose things all the time.

My notebooks and pens are still solid. I can write all the time. Under any conditions. I can write things down.

If I can just remember them.

I can write them down.

I LOST a lot of pens.

I couldn't bear to write in pencil. And it didn't matter because I was burning the books.

But I couldn't seem to hang on to the pens.

IT'S IN the notebooks, isn't it? The thing I need.

There's no way to get the notebooks back, of course. Even if I found similar ones, they'd be empty. All the important words—all of the words that have the memories attached that might keep people from being hurt—set on fire, burned up—were, in a particularly distasteful irony, burned up themselves long ago.

Oh. But the pens.

I STARTED collecting pens when I was very young. My mother gave me a fountain pen. Not an expensive one, but she wrote with fountain pens, and she thought I should, too, and I was excited to be like my mother in this way I thought was grownup and cool. One led to two, led to five or six. Student pens.

I loved them.

And the ink! I loved the ink even more. Because you can put the same ink in a cheap pen as in an expensive one, and then you get to write with it.

Finding the right ink, the right pen, is like coming home. Like finding the place you live and that you *want* to live. The place you want to stay forever. The place where you belong.

On a smaller scale, of course.

But still, it can make you a little bit emotional.

And if you are lucky, you might actually recognize it while it's right in front of you, while you're standing there, and not once you walk away, foolishly.

The hardest thing is when you walk away from home knowing that it's home, because home is changing, or challenging, or making you sad. Or because you screwed up and broke something, and you think you're too embarrassed to stay, or you're not welcome there anymore.

So you go someplace else and think you can live there. But it isn't home. And then you have to try to get home again.

Sometimes it takes a long time to get home again. Some people never make it back at all.

I thought I had to be perfect. I thought I couldn't live with my errors. I thought it would be better to run away. Start clean. Throw the ruined page away and keep reaching for a clean one. Burn my notebooks.

Erase my history. Erase my screw-ups.

Erase my self.

Erase, erase, erase.

I START on collector's websites and then on auction sites, looking for the pens. Most of them were not expensive at the time when I bought them—I never had a lot of money. Some of them have gotten more expensive since.

A funny thing happens as I start looking. I search for one pen to see what it would cost to replace it. And in the related items, I find more that looked familiar. That I suddenly remember having had. And when I chase those links, there are more, still more familiar-looking ones.

I am forty-five years old. I *think* I am forty-five years old.

I get out my birth certificate and check.

I am forty-five years old.

How many pens have I lost?

How many other things have I forgotten about, before now?

I THINK of a pen I'd liked, when I was twenty-five or so. I remember putting it in a jacket pocket. I don't remember ever finding it there again. It had been a blue marbled plastic fountain pen, a kind of bulbous and silly looking thing. A lot of personality, I guess you'd say. It wrote very well.

I find one like it on an auction site. I lose that auction but win another in a few days. $63 plus shipping. I think the pens in a box set with ink were $30 new back in 1995.

Fortunately my books are doing all right, and my needs in general are few. My chief extravagance is a little indulgence in grocery store sushi, once in a while. I use a grocery delivery service. I can't drive. What if my foot fell off while I was reaching for the brake?

The pen arrives after three days. I get lucky with the mail that day and it doesn't fall through my hands. I take the pen out of the box, weigh it in my hand. Light, plastic with gold trim. The blue is so intense it seems violet.

I uncap it and look at the point, squinting my middle-aged eyes. Then I laugh at myself and use the zoom function on my phone camera to get a better look at it. The phone, for once, doesn't slide through my hand.

The mysterious internet stranger I'd bought it from hadn't cleaned it very well. I get a bulb syringe and wash it at the sink, soaking and rinsing. You're supposed to use distilled water but the water here at my house is soft, from a surface reservoir. The same reservoir H. P. Lovecraft once wrote about, as the towns that now lie under it were drowning.

Anyway, I've never had any problems with it. Even if it is saturated in alien space colors, they don't seem to cause problems with the nibs, so that's good news overall.

Once it's clean, I ink it up from a big square bottle in a color that matches the barrel, and sit down at the table with a notebook, ready to write.

With the pen in my hand, I find suddenly I am full of memories. Strange; I can go through a whole day, usually, without remembering things.

I remember the pen.

And now I'm holding it in my hand, and I start to write, in a lovely red-sheened cobalt blue.

I GREW up to be a writer. A novelist. That will not surprise you. You are, after all, reading my words right now.

I write, and write, and the pen stays solid and the notebook stays solid and it writes as well as the one I used to have. But my right hand—I'm left-handed—has a tendency to slide through the table if I'm not paying attention. And twice I fall right through my chair, which is a new and revolting development.

I don't let it stop me, though. I write, and remember, and write some more. About somebody I can sort of remember. A long, long time ago.

An incident that happened at the University of Chicago. After...after I stopped being a student there?

It's so damned hard to recall.

"THERE IS no point in being so angry." His words had the echo that used to come from long distance.

But I wasn't being angry to make a point.

…which was not something the manipulative son of a bitch could have ever understood. I was angry because I was angry. Because he deserved my anger.

I was angry because anger is a defense mechanism. It's an emotion that serves to goad you to action, to remove the irritant in your turf or the thing that is causing you pain.

"I'm angry because you're hurting me," I said. "I'm angry because you're hurting a lot of people. Stop it, and I won't need to be angry with you anymore."

Therapy gives you a pretty good set of tools to be (diplomat B), it turns out. I was still furious with my mother for forcing me to go.

But it was helping.

It might take me a while to get over my anger. But that didn't seem salient to the argument we were having, so I kept it to myself.

"You can't just set things on fire because you don't like the way the world is going."

"Oh, I can," he told me. "And you already helped me. You're just too much of a coward to own that and be really useful, so you'll let other people do your dirty work and keep your hands clean."

"You won't do it," I said.

"You're right," he agreed. "I probably won't. Don't call me again."

I THINK about calling. An anonymous tip. Or sending an email.

But I don't have any evidence. And I don't have a name.

"I know who wrote the manifesto. But I can't remember his name. And I helped him come up with the plan. The plan to burn down a city. Except I can't remember what city, either. Or the details of the plan."

Yeah. No.

Maybe he was right. Maybe I am too much of a coward to take responsibility for something I believe in. For something I had once believed in, until I forgot?

Maybe I forgot because I knew it would feel like my fault if I remembered.

MY MOTHER gave me an expensive fountain pen when I graduated high school. It was a burgundy one, small and slim. Wrote beautifully. I didn't know enough to appreciate it at the time.

I don't think the new ones are as nice anymore.

I lost that one when I got thrown by a horse one time in college. It was in my pocket, and when I got up, bruised and hip aching, it was gone. And no amount of searching turned it up.

THERE ARE a lot of them on the internet.

But the damned things ain't cheap. And how do you tell which ones are counterfeit?

But maybe the pen I was using at the time…

At the time it happened? At the time I learned the thing I can't remember? At the time I *did* the thing I don't *want* to remember?

But I didn't have the pen long. Did I?

In any case, maybe that pen would help me remember.

I SPEND way too much money on it. And it comes.

I hold it in my hand. It feels…itchy. But it doesn't fill me up with memories the way the other one had.

I REMEMBER the unused pages at the back of my old notebooks. There were always a few.

I find myself taking the books down off the shelf, thumbing through them. The unburned ones, of course. Thumbing through the burned ones would have been unfeasible, and even if it weren't, it wouldn't accomplish much of anything beyond getting my fingers ashy.

I find myself looking at ink colors, organizational choices. How my handwriting has evolved.

We lose all the best things to time.

But time brings a lot of benefits, also. Freedom from old wounds, for example.

Perspective.

Grace.

The wisdom to identify the heads that need to be busted, and the courage of your convictions to go out and bust some heads.

I HAVE a couple of dozen old notebooks. And at the end of almost every one of them is a swath of pristine pages. Somewhere between twenty and fifty, a full signature at least and maybe two or three—just sitting there wordless and ignored.

Even after I stopped burning them, I guess I never really finished a notebook before I moved on. The lure of the next book was already there, like a pressure inside me urging me to set this one aside and pick up the perfect one that would be waiting. Untrammeled. Pure.

Without any mistakes in it.

Yes, I hate using broken things. Dirty things. I hate things that are cracked or warped or seem *old* and in disrepair.

So I would get to the point where I could conceivably justify getting rid of the old book with its scuffed cover and frayed page edges and all the mistakes inside it. And I would switch to a new one, clean and unscribbled in. And out the old one would go. Into the flames, at first. Later, onto a shelf with its sisters.

I CAN touch the notebooks. I can always touch the notebooks.

But they don't go back far enough. They don't have the thing that mattered in them. That had happened before. The thing that I can't remember.

The thing that had happened and been burned.

The thing I use my new old echo of a pen now to write about.

WITH THE one before him, I never argued. We never made enough demands on each other to have anything to fight about.

With him, I think I fought all the time. I remember…screaming matches. I remember arguments that made me doubt my sanity. I remember him telling me I said things I couldn't remember saying. I remember letting him win because I couldn't keep track of where the goalposts were, and because I never learned to argue to win.

I never learned to take up space in other people's lives.

I WISH I had known to be wary of the urge to crystallize my identity, to declare myself a thing—one thing, or another—and not accept that I was a continuity of things that would always be changing.

I might have been less eager to discard the thing I had been to become something new if I hadn't been so afraid that acknowledging the old thing meant being trapped for all time. If I hadn't been so afraid the people who knew me would never let me change, I might have held on to more of them, instead of shedding whole lives like a snake sheds skins.

Of course, sometimes people won't let you change. Because their self-image is bound up with yours, and they're afraid of challenging themselves too. Or because they want to keep you weak so they can own you. Or because their own identity gets stuck on you being and behaving a certain way. It's a cliché to say that alcoholics and addicts often find they need a whole new suite of friends of when they get clean, and their lives no longer revolve around getting altered anymore.

But the thing is, over time, changes just become part of the status quo. Tattoos that marked a milestone or a rebellion to our younger selves soften into our skin, become unremarked. They become a part of us, a part of our image and who we are.

What is mine, and what is not mine—our conception of these things changes as we grow.

I MOVED around a lot. As an adult, and as a child. I didn't have any place that felt like mine.

Until I met him. Until I met Joshua.

I WRITE the name, and look at it, and know that it is right. I should be giddy with triumph. Blazing with the endorphins of having figured something out.

I feel hungry, and dizzy. And tired.

I WAS sitting in a booth at the airport, crying on the phone. "I wish you had just shot me," I said.

At the time when I said it, it was true.

Joshua was telling me about the girl he'd met. The girl who was helping with his plans. The girl who would be taking over for me, he said, so that I could get some rest. Get my head together.

Get back to being right with the revolution.

I asked her name. He told me. She was somebody I knew. I asked if I could come back after Thanksgiving with my mom. He said if I got right, I could. He said that my leaving to see my family had been a mistake, and I would have to make amends for it.

"You can't do this to her," I said. "She's just a kid. She doesn't know she's giving up her whole life."

She was the same age I had been, eight years before. I was a wizened old woman of twenty-seven.

"Come back," he said. "Forget about your mother. We can talk. That other girl doesn't have to be involved."

My mom, who I had not seen in four years because of Joshua, was dying. I reminded him of that. He reminded me that if I were a good revolutionary, that wouldn't matter. "Anyway, remember what her husband did to you."

How could I forget?

I have since, largely, forgotten.

He hung up. I remember thinking, very clearly, he'll use her up the same way he used up me.

I wish I could say that thought is the thing that motivated me. I wish I could say that was the last time I ever talked to him.

I sat there and cried for another hour, until I had to get up to make my connection. Nobody bothered me. People cry in airports so often, it's not much of a spectacle. These days they cry and shout into their cellphones just about anywhere. Back then, the crying and shouting were more localized.

Halfway to the gate, I stopped. I walked back to the phones. The young woman he'd replaced me with was a sophomore. Nineteen years old. I knew her name and where she came from.

I called her family.

"You daughter joined a cult in college," I told them. "You need to get her home."

I hung up. I ran for my gate.

I just barely made my plane.

WE HAVE this idea that healing comes as an epiphany.

We have it in part because epiphanies are narratively convenient. They're tidy for a storyteller; there's a break point, a moment when everything changes. An identifiable narrative beat. A point at which everything before is one way, and everything after is different. They're satisfying. They provide catharsis and closure.

Frustratingly, in real life, you often have to go back and have the same epiphany over and over again, incrementally, improving a tiny bit each time. Frustrating for you. Frustrating for your loved ones.

It would be nicer if you could just have that single crystallizing incident, live through it, and get on with being a better human being who was better at humaning.

It's comforting to the afflicted to think we only have to make one change, and we can better. Boom, all at once. Wouldn't it be *nice* if roleplaying or primal scream therapy or rebirthing therapy or a hot uninhibited fuck or a midnight confession or a juice cleanse or a confessional essay or a cathartic piece of fiction really could heal all the old damage just like that? In one swoop? Wouldn't it be nice?

Sure.

Of course it's nonsense, like so many other narratively convenient things we learn about from stories. But like so many of the things we learn about from stories, it's *useful* nonsense.

And epiphany isn't going to fix us. Maybe nothing is going to fix us. But recognizing the damage might help us route around it. Which isn't nothing, you know?

The truth is that you never get to stop dealing with the damage. You might get better at it. You might find a lot of workarounds and you might be happier—or even happy, inasmuch as happiness is a state and not a process!—but happiness doesn't just *happen*. And it doesn't happen instantly. But incrementally, with a lot of constant effort and focus.

I was small, and the people who should have taken care of me didn't. In some cases, they didn't take care of me because they were awful people. In some cases, they didn't take care of me because they had their own shit going on.

I get that. I have spent most of my life with my own shit going on, after all.

One of the things with having your own shit going on is that, first, it blinds you to other people's problems. It's hard to have empathy and remember that, as the saying goes, everyone you meet is fighting a great battle when your attention is all taken up by being on fire right now. It's hard to find the energy to be calm and kind and to consider the divergence of experience of others when you're exhausted and trying to keep your own head above the waves and you're swallowing salt water and you have no idea where you are going to find the energy to keep kicking.

Another thing about having your own shit going on is that until you get some perspective on it, that shit feels enormous. Like the center of the universe. And it kind of is, in that nobody who is excavating a pile of trauma like that has the energy for anything else except shoveling. But it becomes so all-consuming that it's easy to forget that you—and your trauma—are not the only thing on anybody else's mind, or even the most important one, because they're all really busy thinking about their own shovels.

They have their *own* shit, their own trauma and crisesdeadlines-taxeshealthproblemssoreteethfamilydramatoxicneighbors you name it eating up the lion's share of their own attention. And that's *fine*, is the thing. There's *nothing wrong with that.* Your problems are your problems, and their problems are their problems, and that's the way it's actually supposed to be.

But when you're dealing with that much trauma, and it's that raw, boundaries are another thing you wind up sucking at.

Recovery, I guess I'm trying to say, makes narcissists of us all.

So when I'm freaking out now about what people think about me or what they think is going on with me I remind myself…I don't merit more than a passing consideration in most people I encounter's day. They just don't think that hard about me.

Thank God.

People got their own problems.

I certainly got more than enough of mine.

I SAW her once more, even though I never planned to go back to Chicago. She came out to see me after her parents let her out of the treatment program they'd had her committed to.

She came to my mother's house, where I was living. Working temp jobs. Never staying longer than a week because after a week, people start to loop you into the politics and then they expect you to get involved. I was in therapy, because my dying mother made me.

Biggest favor she ever did me, in hindsight.

She stood in the doorway looking at me when I answered, framed in the greens of the yard. She studied my face. We were both a little better-fed than we had been.

And then she said to me, "I don't think you can fully appreciate how much I hate you."

I smiled as if she had accepted my offer of tea. "Oh," I said, feeling the swell of self-loathing in me like a rising magma dome, "I think I can, most likely."

BEFORE I digressed, what I was pointing out was that it doesn't happen fast, the changes. It happens slow. It's an unpicking. The Gordian knot is more of a problem when you're in a hurry and you don't have any tools—assuming you want the string to be useful for something when you're done unpicking it, which I've always thought was the problem with the Alexandrian solution.

Well, I had assembled my tools. With as much haste as possible, and it hadn't been fast, honestly, despite feeling that amorphous sense of formless dread, the pressure pushing on my awareness constantly without any knowledge of where it was going to happen, or when.

Now I have them. Pens, inks. A selection of flawless new notebooks.

The first line in a pristine notebook is always a little fraught. That paper, so innocent. And here I am, intending to put a mark down that would scar it forever.

Maybe the real reason I burned my notebooks was that I didn't want the responsibility.

Maybe that's also why I never had children. Just stories.

Nobody really remembers if you screwed up any given story, five years after the fact.

Erase, erase, erase.

There's freedom in not being important. In not being seen.

I CAN'T touch food for three days. Unfortunately, not being able to touch the food does nothing to keep me from getting hungry.

There's so much to forgive yourself when it comes down to it. So many little cysts of self-hate and personal despair.

"I need you to keep your promises," I said. And that was the beginning of the end.

He promised easily. Fluidly.

Meaninglessly.

And I kept on believing him. Forgiving him.

Making excuses.

I was so good at excuses.

Not for myself. I was always culpable. And I always found ways to punish myself. I believed it when he told me I was wrong. My perceptions, my understanding of events. When he told me I must be crazy, because what I remembered hadn't happened that way at all.

I was unforgiveable. I was sure.

But then I asked him to keep his promises.

And I started writing his promises down. In my notebook. With my pen.

I FIND the damaged pen in a box I didn't know had any pens in it, at the back of a deep cabinet shelf. I rattle it reflexively, not expecting a sound. But there is weight inside it, and something shifts.

I open it and find a narrow, black, beat-up old fountain pen I cannot identify.

I mean, I know what pen it is. It's one I must have been given by a family member but I can't remember what the occasion was, or who had given me it. I had used it all through college after I lost my graduation pen. But I don't know what *kind* it is.

It's missing the gold trim band on the cap, and the cap doesn't close and lock. I remember it having a satisfying click when I shut it. It's so slender I used to tuck it inside the spiral rings of my notebooks. It lived there. It was a good pen.

It is full of dried ink, because I am a terrible pen custodian.

I check the collector websites and can't find anything like it.

THERE WAS a time I was a bad friend. I was in love with somebody, and they were in love with somebody else, and I was in love with that person too. Looking back, I don't think either of them loved me.

I didn't handle it well.

I remember sitting in a bar in a bad chain restaurant breaking up tortilla chips into crumbs with my fingers because I needed something to do while my friend broke up with me, and I didn't have the will to eat them.

And I'd already picked the whole label off my beer.

I tried to make amends, years later. I can't blame them for not wanting to talk to me.

I could have done without that memory. I had, for years, I now realize.

Accountability. That's another thing you lose when you erase yourself.

Thank God.

SOME OF the pens start slipping through my hands. At first, the newer ones, or the ones that had been bought as replacements for ones long lost. The older ones fare better, as if every scratch on the barrel, every bit of luster worn by use from the nib, every imperfection, makes the object in my hands more real. Or gives my hands something to stick to, as they become more phantasmal. More of an unreality.

The older ones fare better. At first.

Then those begin to fall through me, too.

There is so much I still can't remember. I frown at those pristine notebooks with their smooth, friendly paper. I stroke a finger over them, and sometimes I feel the nap of the page, and sometimes my fingertip sinks through.

I know—I can *feel*—the memories down there, like shipwrecks under clouded water. But I can't make out the shapes. Can't describe what I know has to be there.

I start dropping even pens.

But I never drop the broken one. It feels steady and solid in my hand. As if it were more real than the others.

That gives me an idea.

THEY USED to say, of somebody who made a bad marriage, that they threw themselves away. What happens if you never actually got married, because marriage is a tool of the bourgeousie?

I'm pretty sure you can still throw yourself away. Erase yourself. For somebody else, or because you don't think you are worth preserving.

I DON'T have any control over what memories I get, when I get them. Except every single one of them is something I would have rather forgot.

MY STEPFATHER liked to have excuses to hit. So he could feel good about himself, I guess. One way you get excuses to hit is to expect perfection in every task, and set hard tasks without allowing the person you're setting them to time to learn how to do them.

Then, when the student isn't perfect, you have a good reason to punish somebody.

Another thing you can do is change your expectations constantly, so that nobody can predict what is expected and what isn't. Make them arbitrary and impossibly high. Don't allow for any human imperfections.

SINCE I can touch it, I decide to fix the mystery pen.

I make a new trim ring for it out of polymer clay, to help hold the cap in place. I clean it, and while I handle it my hands stay solid on the tools. As if it is some kind of talisman to my past reality.

I wish I could say my repair job is some kind of professional affair with a loupe and so on, but I have some epoxy and some rubber cement and honestly I kind of fake it. You do what you can with what you have, and that's all right then.

I TAKE up my broken pen. The nib is still pretty good, though it doesn't write like a fine point anymore. More like a medium. And even on smooth paper it scratches a little.

It's still usable, though. And it makes a nice smooth line.

Except I have faded more, in the interim. I am vanishing. Falling away, like all the memories I hadn't wanted, and now wish I had been less cavalier with. I can't manage to open a notebook, let alone write in one. I am able to re-read the old ones I'd kept. But the new ones are as ghostly as the cheese sandwiches have become.

Maybe this is better than living with the pain of remembering. Maybe fading away, fading into nothingness, starving to an immaterial and non-interactive death—maybe that is the happiest ending.

Except the one thing I *know*—I know with a drowning urgency, though I still cannot remember the specifics—is that people will come to harm if I cannot remember the things I once knew.

A lot of people.

And not just hurt.

People are going to get killed.

More people. A lot more. Exponentially more than had been harmed by three incendiaries sent to medical schools.

If I can just remember the plan I came up with. Before I helped him write this manifesto. Almost twenty years ago.

If I can only remember the rest of his name.

LACK OF food and water doesn't help me think any more clearly. I've never been good at handling low blood sugar. So half my time seems to be spent figuring out how to write. How to even get words down on the page.

I can put the pen on the paper—the pen stays solid, even if it is in my hand. And I can use the nib to turn the pages. But do you know how hard it is to write legibly and usefully in a notebook you have no way to smooth flat, or to steady? Especially when your temples ache with hunger, and a sour metallic taste seems to sit in your abdomen.

My laptop has long since stopped being something I could touch. I would have given a lot for that laptop right now.

My laptop. And a banana.

MY STEPFATHER would hit me with a belt, and he wouldn't stop until I managed to keep from crying.

"I'm not hurting you that badly, you little wimp. Quit that squalling, or I'll give you something real to cry about."

It's amazing what you can learn to keep inside.

A DAY later, lying more or less *in* the sofa with my head bleary and aching with hunger and my throat scratchy with dehydration, I realize that those blank notebook pages are the answer. I can't get the burned notebooks back—that was, after all, why I had burned them—but I *can* fill these leftover pages with memories of what I might have written in them.

I can construct some kind of a record, though it will be one very filtered by the passage of time.

And the important memory might be in there somewhere. If I am lucky. And brave.

IT WOULD be so much easier just to fade away.

Erase, erase.

So much easier to stop pretending my existence matters and let go. Then it will be over. Then I won't have to keep existing after I do this thing. This thing I don't even want to do. It's not the idea of drifting into nothingness afterwards that bothers me. It's the terrible fear that instead, I might hook myself back into the universe somehow. Re-assert my reality.

Get stuck being real.

I JOINED a cult in college. That much, I know. Like a story told sketchily over a cup of coffee, but without the context or detail because it's an embarrassing story and nobody wants to think about it too hard. The person telling it is embarrassed to have been there, and the person hearing it is reflecting embarrassment as well.

I joined a cult in college. I really craved the love-bombing, because I had never in my life felt really loved. I didn't know how to receive attention in smaller doses, at lower proof. I had so much armor on it took weaponized love to get through.

I joined a cult in college. It was a dumb idea and it was weird while it lasted—it lasted long past college, it lasted eight whole years—and I was in love with one of the guys that ran it.

I joined a cult in college. One of the guys who ran it...I thought he was my boyfriend. He wasn't, though. He was preying on me. Grooming me.

I did not have a lot of agency in the relationship.

He's one of the cult's leaders now.

THE PEN ran out of ink, and then I had to figure out how to fill it when I also couldn't touch most of my ink bottles. My hand just swiped through them, all the gorgeous little art objects full of brilliant colors. I groped back in the shelf, waving blindly...

My fingers brushed something squat and cool. I pulled it out, and the bottles that had been in front of it slid out of the way, clattering. Not of my unreal hand. But of the ink, the thing that was real. The thing that mattered.

One or two fell to the floor. Ink bottles are sturdy, though, and the carpet kept them from breaking.

The bottle I could touch was a bottle of Parker Quink, blue-black. It was two-thirds empty. The label stained.

An old and trusty friend.

I filled my pen.

HE THREW me down the stairs by my hair one time.

My stepfather, I mean.

Not Joshua.

I'd forgotten that. Erased it. And now I can't unremember it again.

A FUNNY thing happens as I write.

I feel myself getting more real. I figure it out when I realize that I can lean an elbow on the table I am resting the current mostly-finished notebook on. That's a relief; you have no idea how hard writing is when you can manage to hold a pen but not rest your hand on anything.

When I realize that I could touch things, I stopped writing and ran into the kitchen, terrified of missing my window.

I still can't lift a glass, but I manage to elbow the faucet on after a few minutes of trying. I bend my head sideways and drink from the thin cold trickle of stale-tasting water. Nothing ever felt better flowing down my throat. I gulp, gulp again. Manage to get it to pool in my hands and drink in that slightly more civilized fashion.

I drink until my stomach hurts, and then go to make sure the toilet seat is up, just in case I turn immaterial again before the stuff works its way through my system. Dehydrated as I had been that might take a while, but I have learned to plan ahead. Such are the important life concerns of the terminally ghostly.

I sit on the bathroom floor and rest the back of my head against the sliding glass door of the shower. At least I am not falling through walls or floors. Yet?

I can stop. I don't have to do this anymore. I can stop, and it will be miserable…but I will die of thirst in a few days. If I stop clutching at making myself real. If I just accept that I am not important, and let my ridiculous scribblings go.

It sounds so appealing. A final erasure.

And I won't have to remember…

I won't have to remember the horrible person I had been. The horrible things I had done. The horrible things that had happened to me. I could forget them all.

Who knows? Maybe if I forget them thoroughly enough—if I encourage myself to forget them thoroughly enough—I won't even die. I'll just fade.

Maybe if I fade enough I won't have material needs like food, water, air anymore. I'll be a ghost for real.

I'll be free. Free of myself. Free of pain.

I have these notebooks here.

I'm probably real enough to burn them now. Right now.

It will just cost the lives of some people I have never heard of to get there.

How many people?

I don't know. One. A hundred. Three thousand.

Too many.

The glass shower door is cool. I relish its solidity.

When I put my hand up onto the sink to help myself stand, sometime later, my hand goes right through.

I DON'T have to do this. I don't have to exist.

I can just let myself be perfect, and be gone.

So much easier.

So much easier.

Except I remember about the fires now. And if I write it all down…I think I might make myself real again.

Then how do I get away from what I did? From what was done?

Oh god, do I have to live with myself now? Do I have to live with being flawed, and do things I'm not very good at?

People will know.

People will see me.

People will punish me.

I WRITE it all down.

OF COURSE the manifesto was familiar.

I was the one who had written it.

What was published wasn't my words exactly. It had been decades; what I wrote hadn't survived the intervening twenty-odd years with Joshua unscathed. Unedited. It had passed through other pens than mine along the way.

But somewhere in the ashes of forgotten notebooks had been written a draft of that statement. Its structures, its rhetoric, even its handwriting had once been mine.

I DON'T bother calling the local police. I call the local field office of the FBI.

"I know who wrote the manifesto," I say into the phone. "His name is Joshua Bright. Or it was, he might have changed it. And that probably wasn't his real name. Because who calls their kid Joshua Bright if they can help it? And he's got a plan to use incendiary devices to burn down a big chunk of Chicago if you don't stop him."

"Ma'am?" the tinny voice at the end of the phone says. "We'll be sending a couple of agents over right away to talk to you. Please stay where you are until they arrive."

I MAKE myself a peanut butter sandwich while I wait.

THAT STORY about the airport and the aftermath. I don't think it really happened that way.

I think it's a pretty story I'm telling myself. I don't know if I ever stood up for that girl, really. If I ever stood up for myself.

I remember doing it. I wrote it down. Does that mean it happened?

Or did I just figure out that Joshua was cheating on me and split not too much later? I tried to forget. I was, needless to say, pretty successful.

The plan to put incendiaries in basements and start a huge firestorm in Chicago had been mine to begin with. I came up with it. I gave it to Joshua as if it were just the plot for one of my thrillers. The ones I make my living writing now.

I wonder if he'll try to blame it on me. Or if he'll want to take credit.

He'll want to take credit.

I never really thought he would do it. It was a thought experiment, that was all. Just a thought experiment.

I joined a cult in college. It turned out about as well as you'd expect.

If you join a cult in college, I hope you get well soon.

YOU DON'T have to be perfect.

Sometimes it's okay for a thing to be a little bit broken.

Sometimes it's okay to make do with what you have, and what you are.

I imagine meeting him in court. Of course I will have to testify. I'd better make sure of my solidity before then. I'd better *commit*.

My fingers leave peanut butter stains on the paper. I hope the food delivery comes soon. I'd like some milk.

I can't know what it will be like, but I rehearse it in my head anyway. I write it down to make it real, so I can act on it when the time comes.

The FBI are on their way.

ME, STRONG, implacable. Joshua saying, "I didn't think you had the balls to turn me in."

Me meeting his gaze. "You never did know me."

I WAIT for the doorbell. For the food. For the authorities.

I get to the bottom of the last page. I reach blindly for the next book, find the blanks at the end, and keep writing.

You don't have to be perfect.

This story isn't done yet with me.

Copyright Page

"Love Among the Talus" First published in *Strange Horizons,* December 2006, Susan Marie Groppi, ed.

"The Deeps of the Sky" First published in *Edge of Infinity*, 2012, Jonathan Strahan, ed.

"Two Dreams on Trains" First published in *Strange Horizons*, January 2005, Susan Marie Groppi, ed.

"Faster Gun" First published in *Tor.com*, August 8, 2008, Patrick Nielsen Hayden, ed.

"The Heart's Filthy Lesson" First published in *Old Venus*, 2015, Gardner Dozois and George R.R. Martin, eds.

"Perfect Gun" First published in *Infinity Wars*, 2017, Jonathan Strahan, ed.

"Sonny Liston Takes The Fall" First published in *The Del Rey Book of Science Fiction and Fantasy: Sixteen Original Works by Speculative Fiction's Finest Voices*, 2008, Ellen Datlow, ed.

"Orm the Beautiful" First published in *Clarkesworld Magazine*, January 2007, Neil Clarke, ed.

"Erase, Erase, Erase" First published in *The Magazine of Fantasy and Science Fiction*, 2019, C.C. Finlay, ed.